Compulsion

MEYER LEVIN

Introduction by James Ellroy

A DELL BOOK

Published by
Dell Publishing
a division of
Bantam Doubleday Dell Publishing Group, Inc.
666 Fifth Avenue
New York, New York 10103

The trademark Dell® is registered in the U.S. Patent and Trademark Office.

ISBN: 0-440-20876-9

Reprinted by arrangement with Arbor House Publishing Group, New York, New York

Design by Jeremiah B. Lighter

Printed in the United States of America

Published simultaneously in Canada

August 1991

10 9 8 7 6 5 4 3 2 1

RAD

In memory of my mother and father,
Goldie and Joseph Levin

Contents

Introduction

JAMES ELLROY

Chicago, May 1924: two wealthy youths named Richard Loeb and Nathan Leopold, Jr., kidnap and murder fourteen-year-old Bobby Franks. The professed motive: a desire to assert their intellectual superiority by committing a perfect crime. Leopold/Loeb: brilliant university graduates at eighteen, children of immense wealth. The crime: botched—every aspect—the youths were captured and confessed within a week. The great Clarence Darrow was retained as defense counsel; while the state of Illinois prosecuted Leopold and Loeb, he prosecuted capital punishment. He won, the judge sentenced the two to life imprisonment with stringent no-parole stipulations. "Babe" and "Dicky" were sent to the Illinois State Penitentiary at Stateville; their wealth allowed them to live in great prison luxury. Loeb was killed in 1936 while attempting to rape a fellow prisoner; Leopold was paroled in 1958. He moved to Puerto Rico, performed medical research, and died in 1971.

Those are the briefly stated facts surrounding the "Crime of the Century," as the case was known during its time. Since then, the Leopold/Loeb murder has been eclipsed repeatedly —the twentieth century has proven to be quite barbaric. The 1920s spawned the Hall/Mills and Snyder/Gray murder cases —sensational stories, sensationally publicized. But Leopold/Loeb stands above them: The perpetrators attracted a wealth of psychiatric attention; Clarence Darrow put their twisted personalities on trial. He wanted to buttress his mercy plea with psychological evaluations of why they killed. Darrow, the prosecution, the fledgling science of psychiatry—different motives, one drive: a determination to chart the cause and effect that resulted in Bobby Franks's death.

In *Compulsion,* Meyer Levin's scrupulously factual account of the case, he attempts the same thing and succeeds, through fiction, to a much greater degree. *Compulsion* was first published in 1956—psychiatry had grown as a science to fad dimensions. Working with an intimate knowledge of the facts—Levin was a University of Chicago contemporary of Leopold and Loeb's—he reconstructed the time, the place, the events. The result is spellbinding. *Compulsion* reverberates with 1920s Chicago, densely packed with details that only true knowledge and obsession, not plain research, can achieve.

And he tells us why. Not conclusively—no writer of his skills would be that arrogant. Instead, he places his Leopold and Loeb within the context of their time and shows how too much money/the boom twenties/too much education too soon/contributed to their acts. He takes two complex characters, gives us access to their thoughts, makes us pity them as much as loathe them. He exposits psychology through incident on a nearly unequaled level; he gives us Nathan Leopold, Jr., Richard Loeb, and the far-reaching tempest they created etched with astonishing power.

The key: stream of consciousness seamlessly linked to action linked to sociological backdrop.

Item:

Artie Straus (Richard Loeb) is a campus "Sheik"; he reads Havelock Ellis with a 175 IQ and copies the Kessler (Franks) ransom letter verbatim from *True Detective.* His compulsive "flapperizing" is a defense against his homosexual liaison with Judd Steiner (Nathan Leopold); he and Judd seduce girls on nearby blankets in a city park; the heterosexual act is explicitly homosexual. The girls leave bewildered, talking in colloquialisms quintessentially twenties:—naive, nihilistic, fake-sophisticated.

Item:

Judd Steiner almost rapes a young woman; his thought processes are delineated philosophically with rich incidental perspective. Never said, hugely powerful in ellipses: he is seeking to escape his bond with Artie Straus.

Item:

Much was made of the Leopold and Loeb "Philosophy," i.e., Nietzsche/*Übermensch,* "Explore All Limits," "Seek the Extremes of Experience," "Break the Laws Designed for Peons." A great deal of the book is given over to philosophical discussion and Steiner and Straus are stripped defenseless every time they open their mouths, because every time they do they betray their own brutal/pathetic psychopathology and the fact that they are just articulate victims of the 1920s—the time when "anything goes" and nothing did.

Item:

Perhaps more than any psychological crime novel, *Compulsion* gives us the symbolism of one single isolated death. No serial-killer book published subsequently has topped the horror of why Judd Steiner shoved that boy down that culvert.

The final truth in the unraveling of factual events is fiction, if we can willingly believe. Only fiction allows us access to catastrophic *and* intimate occurrences concurrent with the thoughts of the people living them. Some books let you believe —an author's skill and audacity can prove quite seductive. With *Compulsion,* you relinquish your skepticism early—you know this is real.

Compulsion is a masterpiece.

It is a brilliant psychological novel; one of the twentieth century's few great crime novels.

JAMES ELLROY

December 1990

Foreword

S ome may ask, *Why call up anew this gruesome crime of more than thirty years ago? Let time cover it, let it be forgotten.*

Surely I would not recall it for the sake of sensation. I write of it in the hope of applying to it the increase of understanding of such crimes that has come, during these years, and in the hope of drawing from it some further increase in our comprehension of human behavior.

In using an actual case for my story, I follow in the great tradition of Stendhal with The Red and the Black, *of Dostoevski with* Crime and Punishment, *of Dreiser with* An American Tragedy.

Certain crimes seem to epitomize the thinking of their era. Thus Crime and Punishment *had to arise out of the feverish soul-searching of the Russia of Dostoevski's period, and* An American Tragedy *had to arise from the sociological thinking of Dreiser's time in America. In our time, the psychoanalytical point of view has come to the fore.*

If I have followed an actual case, are these, then, actual persons? Here I would avoid the modern novelist's conventional disclaimer, which no one fully believes in any case. I follow known events. Some scenes are, however, total interpolations, and some of my personages have no correspondence to persons in the case in question. This will be recognized as the method of the historical novel. I suppose Compulsion *may be called a contemporary historical novel or a documentary novel, as distinct from a* roman à clef.

Though the action is taken from reality, it must be recognized that thoughts and emotions described in the characters come from within the author, as he imagines them to belong to the personages in the case he has chosen. For this reason I have *not used names of those involved in this case, even though I have at times used direct quotations as reported in the press. The longest of these is the speech of the defense attorney, and there, for the sake of literary acknowledgment, I wish to pay my respects to the real author, Clarence Darrow.*

While psychoanalysis is bringing into the light many areas heretofore shrouded, the essential mystery of human behavior still remains the concern of us all. Psychiatric testimony in this case was comprehensive, advanced, and often brilliant, yet with the passage of time a fuller explanation may be attempted. Whether my explanation is literally correct is impossible for me to know. But I hope that it is poetically valid, and that it may be of some help in widening the use of available knowledge in the aid of human failings.

I do not wholly follow the aphorism that to understand all is to forgive all. But surely we all believe in healing, more than in punishment.

M.L.

BOOK ONE
The Crime of Our Century

Nothing *ever ends. I had imagined that my part in the Paulie Kessler story was long ago ended, but now I am to go and talk to Judd Steiner, now that he has been thirty years in prison. I imagined that my involvement with Judd Steiner had ended when the trial was over and when he and Artie Straus were sentenced to life imprisonment plus additional terms longer than ordinary human life—ninety-nine years—as if in the wisdom of the law, too, there was this understanding that nothing ever ends, that it is a risk to suppose even that a prison sentence may end with the end of a life. And then as though to add more locks and barriers to exclude those two forever from human society, the judge recommended that they might permanently be barred from parole.*

Walls and locks, sentences and decrees do not keep people out of your mind, and in my mind, as in the minds of many others, Judd Steiner and Artie Straus have not only stayed on but have lived with the same kind of interaction and extension that people engender in all human existence.

For years they seemed to sit quietly in my mind, as though waiting for me someday to turn my attention to them. Yes, I must someday try to understand what it was that made them do what they did. And once, in the war, I believed I understood. Perhaps that too was only what the psychiatrists call displacement; perhaps I was only putting upon them my own impulses and inner processes. But at that moment in the war—which I shall tell about in its place—those two, from their jail in my mind, and even though one of them had long been dead, rose up to influence an action of mine.

That was the last time, and I thought I was done with them, since Artie was gone and Judd too would eventually die in prison, doomed to his century beyond life. But now a governor has made Judd Steiner actually eligible for parole. He is to receive a hearing.

Somewhere in the chain of command of our news service an editor has remembered my particular role as a reporter on this story, and he has quite naturally conceived the idea that it would be interesting for me to interview Judd Steiner and to write my impression about his suitability to return to the world of men.

Now this is a dreadfully responsible assignment. For I am virtually the only one to confront Judd Steiner from the days of his crime. Not that we are old men; both he and I have only just passed that strange assessment point—the fiftieth birthday. But it was men older than ourselves who were principally active at the time of the trial—lawyers, psychiatrists, prosecutors, the judge—all then in their full maturity. The great Jonathan Wilk was seventy. All have since died.

I am an existing link to the actual event. What I write, it seems, may seriously affect Judd Steiner's chances of release.

How can I accept such responsibility? Are any of the great questions of guilt, of free will and of compulsion, so burningly debated at the trial—are any of these questions resolved? Will they ever be resolved under human study? If I turn at all, with my scraps of knowledge and experience, to the case of the man who has been sitting in jail and in the jail of my mind, if I turn to him now in a full effort to comprehend him, will I do well or will I only add to confusion?

Much, much became known about Judd and Artie through psychiatric studies—advanced for that day—of their personalities. Intense publicity brought out every detail of their lives. And as it happened, I was, for a most personal reason, in the very center of the case. I partly identified myself with Judd, so that I sometimes felt I could see not only into the texture of events that had taken place without my presence but into his very thoughts.

Because of this identification, it sometimes becomes difficult to tell exactly where my imagination fills in what were gaps in the documents and in the personal revelations. In some instances, the question will arise: Is this true; did this actually happen? And my answer is that it needed to happen; it needed to happen in the way I tell it or in some similar way, or else nothing can be explained for me. In the last analysis I suppose it will have to be understood that what I tell is the reality for me. For particularly where emotions must be dealt with, there is no finite reality; our idea of actuality always has to come through someone, and this is the reality through me.

Nothing ever ends, and if we retrace every link in causation, it seems there is nowhere a beginning. But there was a day on which this story began to be known to the world. On that day Judd Steiner, slipping into class a moment late, took a back seat for McKinnon's lecture in the development of law. Judd sat alone in the rear row, raised a step above the others, and this elevation fitted his inward sense of being beyond all of them.

There was still, from yesterday, a quivering elation, as when you catch your balance on a pitching deck. Not that he had ever for a moment felt in danger of being out of control. No. In the highest moment, the moment of the deed itself, he had been a bit shaken. Artie had been superb.

Judd only wished Artie were here with him now, so they could share a quick wink, listening to McKinnon's platitudes. At some particularly banal remark he would touch his knee against Artie's, and Artie would turn his face and wink.

McKinnon was being what the fellows thought was brilliant. He was producing one of his sweeping summaries, casting his eye over the entire structure of the law, presenting it indeed as a construction, just as an algebraic equation is a construction built upon a first premise.

From the early and primitive Hebrew concept of an eye for an eye, McKinnon said—interjecting dryly, "Rather bloodthirsty, these Semitic tribes"—from that early concept to our law of today, was there really a great advance? Instead of an eye, it was the value of an eye, the value of a tooth, the value of a life, that was now exacted from the criminal. And in some cases the ancient primitive code remained intact, a life for a life.

Many of the fellows were making notes—especially those who were taking the Harvard Law entrance tomorrow. Directly in front of Judd, Milt Lewis was feverishly putting it all down, the hairs standing disgustingly on his fleshy, bent neck. Milt had an idea that because this was the last day before the Harvard exams, McKinnon might be giving out hints by purposely lecturing on subjects he knew would appear in the test.

As the professor talked, Judd's pen, too, became busy in his notebook. Over and over he drew a hawk. The hawk was streaking down, talons open. . . . Where was Artie? Judd had passed Artie's house, and driven past the frat, and he had looked around on campus. Surely nothing had gone wrong. Artie was purposely putting him on pins and needles. . . . Judd drew a vulture. The page filled; he turned it and drew a huge, elaborate cross, with an unfurled inscription. In Sanskrit, he wrote, "In Memoriam." At the base of the cross, in elaborate Old English capitals, he drew his initials: 𝕵. 𝕾.

Then he glanced through the mullioned window. Artie might pass. He might stroll toward Sleepy Hollow, a few silly flappers tagging onto him. In any case, Artie had better be on hand after the ten-o'clock, as they had agreed. They had everything still to do.

McKinnon had come to a pause; he had lifted up the entire structure of human law and was holding it aloft for them to admire, perhaps not so much the structure itself as his Atlas feat in lifting it. Judd could not help, now, tickling the outstretched arm.

"But granted that the law applies to the ordinary person in society," Judd said, "how would it apply in the case of the superman? The concept of an *Übermensch* in itself means that he must be above ordinary society. If he abided by ordinary laws he could never produce the actions that might in the end prove of the greatest benefit to humanity—not that even benefit to humanity should be a criterion."

McKinnon smiled patronizingly. "By a superman I suppose you mean a powerful historical personality like Napo-

leon, or others who have, so to speak, taken the law into their
own hands."

Judd was going to interrupt, to debate Napoleon, for
wasn't Napoleon's failure a proof per se that he was not a true
superman? But Milt Lewis, always eager to hitch onto someone else's idea, had filled in for McKinnon. "Didn't many of
the great American pioneers and industrialists consider themselves above the law?"

"Not exactly," said McKinnon. "Often such a powerful
figure, a conqueror or a revolutionist, considered that he was
bringing law to the lawless, or adapting old laws to newer
human ways. But always you will find such persons at pains to
justify their actions in terms of law, rather than by pretending
to be above the law." And in the grand sweep of history, he
pointed out, even these tremendous and commanding personalities were incorporated, for the general concept of right and
wrong, of crime and punishment, remained organic with the
social order, resisting individualistic innovations.

"In fact that's a case in point—*Crime and Punishment.*
The hero considered himself a kind of superman, and yet he
broke down and yielded to the law," parroted Milt Lewis,
always ready to switch sides.

"But that's no superman! That's not the conception!"
Judd cried. What was Raskolnikov after all but a weak senti-
mentalist, full of moral and religious drivel? What was his
crime but a petty attempt at theft, motivated by abysmal poverty? Where was the superman conception? Raskolnikov's
was only a crime with a motive—his need for money. All he
had done was to rationalize the murder by declaring that his
need was greater than that of the miserly old female pawnbroker's. To be above, beyond mundane conception, a crime had
to be without need, without any of the emotional human
drives of lust, hatred, greed. It had to be like some force beyond the reach of gravity itself. Then it became a pure action,
the action of an absolutely free being—a superman.

Too dense to grasp a concept, they all began gabbling:
How could there be such a person? If a person had no motive,
then he would commit no action. . . . They didn't get the
concept at all; the whole idea was beyond them. Judd almost

found himself yelling out the proof to them—"Look at Artie! Look at me!" But instead, he relished the situation inwardly. This was the true enjoyment. To see things from another area of knowledge, from a fourth dimension which none of them could enter.

"Well, it is an interesting speculation," McKinnon was saying with his tight little smile; the hour was over. "As you put it, Steiner, it is a pure concept, something in the abstract. However"—he strove for his summarizing line—"a society of supermen would undoubtedly in turn evolve its own laws."

"Superlaws!" Milt Lewis hawed.

In the corridor, Judd tried to dodge away from Lewis, who was surely going to try to set up a last cram session for tonight. He had almost got out of the Law building when he felt the thick paw on his arm. Always physically touchy, Judd over-reacted, wrenching away.

"Say, Junior, how about a little session, going over those notes?" Milton said.

"I never cram before an exam," Judd stated. "My system is to go out and dissipate."

Milton made some inane remark about geniuses.

Halfway across to Sleepy Hollow, Judd saw Artie—Artie stretched on his elbow on the grass amidst a group of coeds, who squatted with their legs folded under them. Myra was there and a stupid new little girl, Dorothea, who had a crush on Artie. . . . The ease of Artie, lying there, bantering. Judd felt a surge of envy amounting almost to hatred. Though it was urgent that they be at once on their way, though their deed was calculated precisely to the minute, Artie didn't even arise on seeing his approach. Judd raised his wrist, pointedly looking at his watch. Artie only rolled over, patting the ground for Judd to squat. This Dorothea was blond, she was literary, she was reading aloud from *Jurgen,* and all of them had on such knowing smirks, they tittered each time her pink tongue lingered on a reference to Jurgen's sturdy "staff," relishing the double meaning. Dorothea welcomed Judd with her big cow eyes—only so he wouldn't take Artie away, he was sure. And even Myra, who, he knew, couldn't endure him, offered an inviting smile.

It was one of those moments when Artie looked so golden, so perfect, stretched in his powder-blue pullover, that Judd had an urge in front of all of them to call him Dorian. But he again restrained himself, saying, "Hey, Artie, we're late."

"Late for what?" Dorothea asked vapidly, trying to make her remark sound suggestive.

"Wouldn't you like to know?" Artie said, rising to a sitting position.

Judd nearly giggled. If they knew!

"Don't forget your staff!" Dorothea remarked daringly, rolling her eyes from her *Jurgen* to a silver Eversharp that had dropped from Artie's jacket onto the grass. There was an appreciative tinkle from the other girls at Dorothea's wit.

"Thought you girls might want to use it," Artie said, sending them all into a panic, even Myra smiling. Then Artie was coming along with him to the car. But that silly Dorothea jumped up, smoothing her swishing pleats, and came hurrying after them, calling to ask which way were they going. . . . That would be a good one to take out and rape, teach her a lesson. No, she'd enjoy it too much.

"This is man stuff." Artie gave her his dazzling grin, and they left her standing there, holding her *Jurgen* to her chest.

"Some little pest!" Artie lighted a cigarette, exhaled. Judd didn't inquire how Artie felt. In a sense they were like two medical experimenters who have injected themselves with an untried drug. In himself, it had perhaps produced a slight quickening, but he was holding it well, Judd was sure. In Artie, there was not the slightest sign of an effect. But then, had not Artie secretly tried a dose once or twice before?

"Got the letters?" Artie asked in his voice of snappy action.

Judd tapped the pocket of his sports jacket. He had placed one letter on each side, to avoid any mistake. In the right-hand pocket was the letter telling the victim's father to go to Hartmann's drugstore and wait for a telephone call. In the left-hand pocket was the final letter that would tell him where to drop the ransom. Their job now was to prepare the treasure hunt, leading the father from place to place as he picked up these letters.

"You should have seen me shake your friend Milt Lewis," Judd said. "He wanted to come over tonight and study for the exam."

"That jackass would be a perfect alibi!" Artie said. "You should have let him."

"I thought we'd have something better to do." Judd glanced at Artie, and they both snickered. Then Artie told him to take Ellis Avenue and drive past.

The Kessler house was only a block out of their way. Judd would not have driven past that house; in fact, he would have gone out of his way to avoid it. But it was in just such boldness that Artie had it all over him.

As they neared the big yellow brick-and-timber residence, Artie leaned halfway out of the car to get a good look. Would it be surrounded by police cars? Would the street be blocked off? For by now their first letter, the special delivery demanding the ransom, had surely arrived.

The street looked normal. You'd never imagine anything unusual had happened to anyone in that house. Thus, the flash idea came to Judd that fourth-dimensional activities could be taking place within and through all human activity, and leaving no trace.

Even as they coasted slowly past, the Kesslers' limousine turned the corner and pulled into the driveway. "Stop! Hold it!" Artie snapped, but Judd drove on, swearing under his breath, "You gone daffy!"

Artie squirmed around on the seat so he could watch behind. Mr. Kessler got hurriedly out of the limousine—he was carrying a swelling brief case, Artie glowingly declared—and right after him came a tall man whose head angled forward. Artie recognized him—old Judge Wagner—guessed he was the Kessler family's lawyer. The two went swiftly into the house.

"He's just been to the bank and got the money!" Artie bounced around, laughing, and squeezed Judd's knee. "He's got Judge Wagner with him. Hey, I forgot to tell you, Jocko. Mums told me this morning. The two of them were tearing around the neighborhood last night looking for Paulie. They even came to our tennis court—wanted to know if the kid had been playing with Billy!" Billy was Artie's little brother, of the same age as the boy they had kidnaped. "Old man Kessler and the old Judge even dragged out Fathands Weismiller!" That was the gym teacher at the Twain School. "They had him bust into the building with them. I think Fats crawled through the window!" Artie leaned back and laughed at the image. "They thought maybe the kid got locked in taking a leak. I told Mums my theory is, Paulie's run away from home."

Judd felt slightly piqued that Artie had not come over, first thing in the morning, to share all this with him. "Mums was in a stew this morning," Artie said. "She was even worried if she should send dear little Billums off to school!"

They had by now reached Judd's house, an ornate gabled mansion on Greenwood Street. But instead of stopping, Judd drove on a block to where they had last night, after the deed, parked the rented Willys.

"Every mamma with a brat in Twain is a-twitter." Artie laughed.

But this disturbed Judd. Surely all the worried mothers would be telephoning the Kesslers. "They'll keep the phone line busy," he pointed out.

It was a detail they had only partly foreseen. For to carry out their carefully timed ransom schedule, the Kessler line had to be open for their call. Indeed, their special-delivery letter had instructed Charles Kessler to keep his line unused. But now all those anxious mothers might jam the line.

"Ishkabibble," said Artie.

It was an expression Judd hated. He had wanted this to be a perfect day between them. Sometimes—even in a big thing like this—Artie could suddenly act as if he didn't care a damn.

But as Judd pulled behind the Willys, Artie glanced up and down the street in his professional way. He was in the game again.

They approached the rented car. It stood in front of a nondescript apartment house, for this block was already outside the exclusive Hyde Park area of mansions. How anonymous, how perfectly innocent the car looked! Gratification arose in Judd at the correctness of their planning. The rented car, the fake identities, were masterful ideas. And just as this car, this shell of metal that contained their deed of yesterday, had been left a totally unaltered entity by the deed, so was the deed meaningless within themselves.

"You want to drive, Mr. Singer?" Judd used the alias, giving Artie a you-first-my-dear-Gaston bow while opening the door. But as he took hold of the door handle, Judd noticed a few small, dark blotches. No, they were surely from something else. But suppose on the wildest chance the car were discovered and under chemical analysis the spots proved . . . ? Last night, in the dark, the washing they had given the automobile, using Artie's garden hose, had been altogether hasty.

Conquering the sickening repugnance that blood always raised in him, Judd looked into the rear of the car. There were stains on the floor.

"Aw, it could be any kind of crap. Every car is dirty," Artie said.

"They're brownish." Judd felt suddenly depressed. Not that this was dangerous—they could take care of it—but simply that this had flawed the perfection of their deed.

"All right, we'll wash it out!" Artie jumped behind the wheel, heading for Judd's driveway. Judd hesitated; but it was the noon hour, and Emil would be upstairs at lunch. Anyway, what he did was none of the chauffeur's business. And Emil was used to seeing other fellows' cars around the house.

Artie pulled the Willys up to the garage entrance. Judd glanced at the house. Huge, silent, with most of the shades drawn, the way his father insisted since his mother had died, it had an unoccupied air.

Artie had seized a pail and was running water into it, full force, noisily. The maid came out of the house to ask if Cook should fix lunch for the two of them.

Judd felt spied on. "We're busy," he said, keeping his voice polite. "Thanks, but never mind. We'll pick up a sandwich downtown."

"I'll just put some cold chicken on the table." And she gave him that devoted smile of a female who knows better than men what men want.

Artie sloshed the pail of water onto the rear floorboards. Taking a rag, Judd began to rub the spots around the door handle. How could they ever have got there? The image from yesterday, the jet of blood, the whole dreadful mess, intruded for an instant, but he ruled it out from his mind. It was instantly supplanted by an image of himself as a child watching a doctor with a syringe starting to take blood from his mother's arm, and a swooning sick feeling echoed up in him. Judd ruled it all out, out from his mind. He had full control; he could master his emotions completely. He held his mind blank, like breath shut off.

Artie was swearing—the bloody crap wouldn't wash out —and at that moment Emil came down the garage stairs, still chewing on something. "Can I help you boys?" he said through his food.

"No. Never mind. We're just cleaning up a car I borrowed," Artie said, pulling his head out of the tonneau. "Boy, some party! I guess we kind of messed it up."

"What are you using, only plain water?" Emil asked, coming close and looking. "You could use some Gold Dust."

"It's wine spots. We spilled some Dago red," Artie said, laughing.

Emil turned to fetch a box of Gold Dust. "Let me do it for you."

"No, this is good enough," Judd said. "It's nothing. Don't let us interrupt your lunch."

"Oh, that's all right," said Emil. But finally the stupid Swede seemed to get the idea; he started back upstairs. Yet he paused to ask if Judd's Stutz was running all right today, if the squeak that Judd had complained about when he left it in the garage yesterday was gone. "I put a little oil on the brake," Emil said. "Not too much. Too much is bad for the brake bands."

"It's fine now—fine, thanks," Judd said. He looked at his watch. And to Artie: "Let's go."

Artie took the wheel and backed out with a roar. "Christ, you never could back a car! Watch out!" Judd complained.

They drove to Vincennes. The corner they had selected for the first message relay was a large vacant lot at 39th and Vincennes. At the curb stood one of Chicago's metal refuse boxes, about the size of a hope chest, painted dark green. On one side, stenciled in white, were the words HELP KEEP THE CITY CLEAN.

Artie stopped directly in front of the box. They got out. Judd drew the letter from his pocket. There were few people on the street, and anyone observing them might think they were only throwing some junk into the box.

Judd lifted the lid. He had brought along a small roll of gummed stationery tape, and now he tried to tape the letter to the underside of the lid. The tape didn't stick. "Hold the damn lid!" he snapped at Artie, so as to get both hands free to press on the tape.

"That junk will never hold," Artie criticized. "Jesus, I can't leave a single thing to you! Where's the adhesive, that roll of adhesive!"

It was a roll Judd had taken from the bathroom yesterday, to wind around the chisel blade, the way Artie said, so the wooden end could be used as a club. "You told me yourself to use the whole roll, to make it thick."

"You stink!"

Judd glanced at his watch. "We've got time to drive over and buy some."

"Hell with it!" Artie cried. He was watching the street nervously. Kids were coming along, getting curious. Artie let the lid drop, nearly catching Judd's hand. He snatched the envelope from Judd. "We'll leave out this stop."

"Then how'll he know where to go next?" Judd objected.

"When we phone him at home," Artie snapped, "instead of sending him to this box we send him straight to Hartmann's Drugstore for the next instruction. That's all this crappy letter tells him to do anyway."

"We can't make any last-minute changes—everything will get all balled up!" Judd felt suddenly panicky. The spots on the car had been dismaying. Now he was becoming depressed. There was something vaguely ominous in little things going wrong, in changes having to be made in the plans they had so long and carefully devised.

And besides, this Help Keep the City Clean box had seemed so right, as part of the plan. It had seemed to give the entire adventure the proper sardonic flavor, this garbage box of life. The idea had been his own contribution, too. It had come to him a few months ago during one of their sessions. How to make the ransom collection foolproof had been the problem. If any specific rendezvous were named, police could appear.

Artie, half tight, had got off the subject, telling about some asinine frat party with a new stunt, a "treasure hunt" in which kids were sent all over town to the craziest places, and in each place they picked up a clue to where they had to go next.

Suddenly Judd had seen it. An actual treasure hunt in reverse! The father chasing from one place to another for his instructions to deliver the ransom! And in the same instant, as the idea itself came to him, Judd had visualized the refuse box. First stop! A portly man, he had imagined him, because during that time they had figured Danny Richman as the victim, and Danny's father—that stuffed shirt, who never opened his mouth except to make a speech full of noble precepts, Polonius in person, even worse than Judd's own old man, if possible—Danny's father was *it!*

Artie had loved the idea. They could just see Richman *père* waddling toward the Help Keep the City Clean box, bending his carcass, pulling up the lid, putting on his pince-nez to read the instructions! At this image, they had hooted so loudly they had actually awakened Judd's old man, who had called from upstairs, "Boys, boys!"

Then they had whispered, Artie nearly rolling on the floor with stifled laughter. Artie had been wonderful that night, planning all sorts of mad surprises for the father. "Hey, how about he pulls up the lid—we have a jack-in-the-box, a great big jock that jumps up at him!"

Judd improved on it. They could rig up a spring, so that

when the box was opened it squeezed a bulb and—right in the face!—a fountain!

But even as Artie had gone on, with more and more ghoulish ideas, another image had crowded into Judd's mind. He had seen the box as the place for the body itself. He had no thought of it as something dead. He had merely visualized the shape, curled up, fitting inside snugly. Of course he had dismissed the image as impractical. In a street box like this, nothing could remain hidden for more than a few hours; someone would come along and open the lid. And afterward, Judd had thought of the real place, the perfect receptacle for the body. Nevertheless, more than once the image had returned, the curled boy in the box, an image flickering in his mind.

"C'mon!" Artie was already in the car. He was tearing up the letter that should have been in the box, letting bits of it fall to the street.

"Hey! For crissake!" Judd grabbed for his arm. Artie started the car with a jolt and let the bits of paper flutter out a few at a time from his hand, laughing goadingly.

He drove to the main I.C. station at Twelfth Street. There the other letter, containing their final instructions, had to be placed in a certain spot on a certain train.

That morning I may have passed Artie as he lolled in Sleepy Hollow with his little harem of coeds. I may even have waved to him and smiled at Myra Seligman, may have wanted to linger on the chance of getting better acquainted with her, even though I had a girl, my Ruth. But I would have rushed on, busy, busy, picking up campus news for my morning call to the *Globe*.

I see myself as I was in those days—eighteen, a sort of prodigy, my long wrists protruding from my coat sleeves, always charging across the campus with a rushing stride, as if I were afraid I'd miss something, and with my Modern Library pocket edition of Schopenhauer banging against my side as I rushed along.

I was eighteen and I was already graduating, having taken summer courses to get through ahead of time. For I had a terrible anxiety about life. I had to enter life quickly, to find out how I would make out. Already I was a part-time reporter on the *Globe;* besides covering campus news I would rush downtown afternoons and wait around the city room for an assignment.

On graduating, I would work full time on the *Globe*. I would test myself against the real world. And I would try to write, too.

That day I had a little feature story. I remember that it was about a laboratory mouse that had become a pet, too precious to kill. And when I telephoned, the city editor said, as he said only rarely, "Can you come in and write it?"

I skipped my ten o'clock class, half running the five

blocks to the I.C. station, hoping that people I knew would
see me rushing downtown with a story.

I was lucky. A train pulled in as I reached the ramp, and
I was in the office in twenty minutes. I used a typewriter at the
back of the large newsroom, near the windows from which
you could almost touch the El tracks. I carried the story up to
the desk myself, and as I hovered there for an instant, hoping
to get a reaction, the city editor, Reese, glanced up and said,
"Going back south?" And without waiting for a reply he circled a City News report on his desk. "Drowned kid. Take a
look at him." He handed me the item.

In Chicago the papers jointly used the City News Agency
to cover routine sources like neighborhood police stations. If a
City News item looked promising, the papers would send out
their own reporters for fuller stories.

This item was from the South Chicago police station. An
unidentified boy, about twelve, wearing glasses, had been
found drowned in the Hegewisch swamp at the edge of the
city.

I saw my feature piece already, a tender, human little
story about a city kid who had tried too soon in the season to
go swimming and had caught a cramp in the cold water.

"Better check with Daly," said Reese. He blinked up at
me with the ragged, sour little smile he had. "He's on a kidnaping. They say it can't be the same kid, but you better take
a look."

Tom Daly was to me a "real" reporter; he always knew
whom to call, where to go. More, Tom had a brother on the
police detective force; thus Tom Daly belonged to that inner
world I then thought of as "they"—the people who were really a part of the operation of things.

I spotted Daly in one of the phone booths that lined the
wall. He had a leg sprawled through the partly open door, and
kept tapping his toe as he worked on the difficult phone call. I
heard a man's voice, a thread of it escaping from Tom's receiver, "No, no, a drowned boy—how could it be Paulie? We
have just heard from . . . those people. We are sure our own
boy is safe."

Tom cut in. What had he heard? How had he heard?

"Please don't put anything in the paper as yet. Please, you understand? Your editor gave us his word of honor—your chief, Mr. Reese. Please allow us this opportunity. In a few hours we hope it will be all over. We will give you the full story the moment our boy is returned to our hands." The voice was not exactly pleading; it retained a reminder of authority. A rich man, a millionaire. A self-made man who could control himself and deal with a dreadful emergency. Tom promised cooperation.

"Thank you. I appreciate it in this terrible thing. But this other boy you speak of—I am sorry. A poor drowned boy. I am sorry for his parents too, but he cannot be our boy. Our boy is safe. We have a message. Besides, this boy you say has glasses. Paulie does not wear glasses."

Still trying to keep the father on the line, Tom Daly protested that although the *Globe* would cooperate, we might be of real help if we were meanwhile trusted with the fullest details. Glancing up at me, he said into the phone, "Mr. Kessler, we are sending a reporter out to look at the poor kid that was drowned out there in South Chicago, and if we could have a picture of your son to go by . . . Yes, I know you said he doesn't wear glasses, but there might always be a mistake."

He listened, foot tapping, glancing up at me again. Tom had a round, pinkish face, the kind that is typed as good-natured Irish. Now he was evading telling where he got wind of the kidnaping—"of course we have our exclusive sources of information"—and he was trying to find out how the mother was taking it. Then with a final offer of our help, he hung up. Without emerging from the booth, Tom told me all that was known. Charles Kessler was a South Side millionaire. Last night his boy, Paulie, had not come home from school. They had searched for him. About ten o'clock someone had phoned the Kesslers to say that the boy was kidnaped and that there would be instructions in the morning. This morning a special-delivery letter had come demanding ten thousand dollars. The police were being kept out of it. Only the Detective Bureau had been notified, by the family lawyer, ex-Judge Wagner.

Kessler seemed sure his boy was safe. "Still, you'd better take a look," Tom said.

"How will I know if it's he?" I asked.

Tom shrugged. I was to call him back, with a description.

*   *   *

So the story began, with a routine police-blotter report about a drowned boy in the Hegewisch swamp, and with an inside tip on a kidnaping. On the city editor's desk the two items came together, belonging to the clichés of daily head-lines—kidnaping, ransom, unidentified body.

And hurrying back to the I.C. I saw myself, a Red Grange of the press, open-running through Loop traffic. Would other reporters be there? Were some there already? I became tense with the dreadful fear of being scooped that permeated newspaper work, I think more then than now. Each time the train made a stop, I was almost pushing against the seat to get it going again.

We passed the University, came to the edge of the city where Chicago dissolved away into marshes and ponds, inter-spersed with oil tanks and steel mills.

The police station was in a section unknown to me, an area of small shops with side streets of frame houses inhabited by Polish mill workers. There was grit in the air; I could see a few licks of flame coming out of the smokestacks that rose off toward Gary—pinkish, daylight flame.

Inside the station, one glance reassured me there were no other reporters. I assumed the casual air of the knowing news-man. "Say, Sarge, I'm from the *Globe*. You got the kid they found drowned in Hegewisch?"

The policeman looked at me for a moment without an-swering.

"I'm looking for the kid——"

"Swaboda's Undertaking Parlor," he said, and gave me the address. It was nearby, an ordinary store with a large rubber plant in the window. Inside, there was the roll-top desk, the leather chair, the oleo of Christ on the wall. And not a soul.

My scoop anxiety had faded; no other paper had both-

ered to send a reporter this far out. Conversely, the feeling of
being on the verge of something big was now strong in me.

I opened the rear door. A cement-floored room, smelling
like a garage. Nobody. A zinc table, covered.

There was scarcely a bump under the cloth. A child has
little bulk.

I approached, and, with a sense of being a brazen newspaperman, drew back the cloth. For the truth is that until that
moment I had never looked at a dead human being.

A newspaperman had to take death casually. I noted,
rather with pride, that no feeling arose in me. Was this because of my role of observer, I asked myself, or was it because
life had so little value in the modern world? We had shootings
in the streets; we rather boasted of Chicago as a symbol of
violence. And I thought of the 1918 war, when I had been a
kid, and every day the headlines of the dead; the numbers had
had no meaning.

The face of the child had no expression, unless it was that
curious little look of self-satisfaction that children have in
sleep. It was a full, soft face; the brown hair was neatly cut,
and the skin showed, I thought, a texture of expensive breeding. I drew the cover farther down to find out one thing immediately. A Jewish boy. Surely Paulie Kessler?

I experienced the irrational, almost shameful sense of triumph that comes to newsmen who discover disaster. I felt an
impulse to sweep the body away with me, sequester my scoop.

"Say, you!"

I jumped. Another reporter?

There stood a paunchy man in a brown suit. Hastily I
asked, "You the undertaker? I'm from the *Globe*. The door
was open so I . . . . The cops said you had the boy here."

Mr. Swaboda advanced, frowning, but not antagonistic.
He was sucking at a tooth.

"Any other reporters been here?" I asked. "Any calls
from the newspapers?"

"Oh. You are from the newspapers."

"Did anybody identify this boy? Do you know who he
is?"

He shook his head. "Maybe you know? In the papers?"

"They sent me out to see," I said. "All we got is a report of a drowned boy."

Again Swaboda shook his head. A glint of clever know-ingness came into his eyes. "He is not drowned." He pointed to the boy's scalp, moving closer. "Even the police officer don't see this. I am the one to show them." Brushing back a lock of hair, the undertaker disclosed two small cuts above the forehead, clotted over, like sores.

The scarehead flashed into my mind—ABDUCTED, MUR-DERED. MILLIONAIRE'S SON! And this time, surely, there was a sense of exultation in me.

"Can I use your phone? I've got to phone my paper."

"Help yourself." He followed me to the roll-top desk. "You know who is this boy's family?"

He might give away my story. I should have gone outside to phone. While hesitating, I noticed a pair of glasses on the desk, tortoise-shell. I picked them up. "They said he was wearing glasses. Are these the ones?"

The undertaker took the glasses from me and smiled again. "These are not his glasses." He carried them into the back room; I followed. Swaboda placed the glasses on the boy and turned to me triumphantly. I could see that the glasses were a poor fit; the earpieces were too long. "Police put these glasses on him," he said. "I take them off."

I hurried back to the phone and got Tom Daly. "It's him!" I said.

"He's been identified?"

"No, but looking at the body, I got a hunch."

His voice dropped. "Look, kid, tell me now, just tell me what you know for sure."

"For one thing, he's a Jewish kid," I said. "Anyway, he's circumcised."

I could feel, in his instant hesitation, the stoppage people always had before things Jewish. He was weighing, then cred-iting me with somehow knowing.

"What about the kid's glasses? Kessler said his boy didn't wear any."

"They're not his. They don't fit him. Listen. They must

be the murderer's. He must have dropped them. Listen. He's got bruises on his head——"

"Wait, wait!" I heard him yelling my news to Reese. Then: "Stay there. I'll call the Kesslers to come and identify him."

*   *   *

It was even said afterward that but for my going out there just then, the murderers might never have been caught. It's not a question of credit; indeed it has always bothered me that I received a kind of notoriety, a kind of advantage out of the case. Obviously what I did that morning was only an errand, and if I hadn't gone there, the identification would have been made in some other way, perhaps a day later. True, the ransom money might in the meantime have been paid, but the money was quite an insignificant item in the overwhelming puzzle of human behavior that was to be uncovered.

In any case, the journalistic credit should have gone, not to me, but to Reese for connecting the two items on his desk. And the discovery goes back after all to the steelworker who walked across the wasteland and happened to see a flash of white in some weeds—the boy's foot.

There was much moralizing to come; providence was mentioned. I believe I have grown beyond the cynical pose of the twenties; I would not argue today that all existence is the random result of blind motion.

It did happen that Peter Wrotzlaw, a steel-mill worker who usually went to his job by another path, deviated that one morning to pick up his watch from a repairman. He cut across the Hegewisch wasteland. At 118th Street there was a marshy area, a pond, with the water draining through a culvert under a railway embankment. Wrotzlaw mounted this embankment to cross the pond, and then he noticed the flash of white at the opening of the drainpipe.

It was even said to be providential that Wrotzlaw had once lived on a farm, for in a submerged way his nature sense knew something strange was there, neither animal nor fish. He climbed down and, parting the weeds, recognized a boy's foot. Bending low, he made out the whole body, crammed into the cement pipe.

Just then, up on the tracks, a handcar appeared. Wrotzlaw shouted. The two railway workers stopped their car and came down. One spoke Polish.

"Here, look!" Wrotzlaw explained. "Just this minute, I saw something white. I found this!"

The railwaymen were wearing boots. The Polish one stepped into the water; it came just to his knees. He took hold and pulled out the body of the boy; he carried it to the water's edge and put it down, the face turned to the gray, misty morning sky. "Is drowned. Poor kiddo."

How could the boy have got into the culvert? Maybe foolish kids, trying to play a game, crawl through the pipe. And this one got stuck and drowned.

A kid of someone. A pity. "You ever seen him around here?"

The two railroad men lifted the body to carry it up to their handcar. But then they asked, Where are his clothes?

Wrotzlaw searched in the weeds. "Hey!" He picked up the pair of glasses, glinting there, and placed them on the boy. He searched farther along the downtrodden grass. "Stocking."

He held it up, a knee-pants stocking, a good one, new, not like the black cotton stockings of the neighborhood kids, with mended holes at the knees.

But no other clothing could be found. "Other kids maybe got scared, ran away, took everything." Now the railway men said Wrotzlaw should come with them, to bring the body back to their railway yard. He would be late for his job, he protested, but the other Pole insisted, "You found him, you come with us." So he climbed up. "Poor kid, he's got drowned."

By the freight platform, men gathered. The yard boss called the police. A patrol wagon removed the corpse. "Unknown boy, drowned" was marked on the blotter, and the body was sent to Swaboda's.

*   *   *

Tom Daly called Kessler. Almost before Tom could hear it ring, the phone was picked up. "Yes? Yes?"

"This is the *Globe*."

"Please. We are expecting an important message. Please don't call this number. Please leave the line clear."

"But our reporter believes he has identified your boy, Mr. Kessler."

*   *   *

Charles Kessler had been sitting with his hand ready to the phone, waiting for the call promised in the special-delivery letter. He was a small-made man, always keeping himself neat and correct looking. His chair was high backed and carved, one of the ornate throne-chairs common in those days. In his solid house with his solid furniture it seemed an impossible thing that a kidnaping should have happened to him.

He had always dealt with everyone to the penny, exact. Even when he had been a pawnbroker, long years ago, he had been proud of his reputation for honesty and exactitude, ninety-five cents on the dollar. In Chicago's wide-open days, when elaborate gambling salons had studded the downtown area, he had kept his elegant little pawn office open far into the night to accommodate the princelings of the first great Chicago meat and wheat fortunes, who would pledge their diamond studs in order to go on with a game. It was thirty years since he had gone out of the loan business into real estate, but could this crime be some long-nurtured, crazed act of revenge for a fancied wrong?

A man accustomed to dealing correctly and exactly in mortgage notes and debentures, how could he deal with a ransom letter? He wanted to deal with it precisely, not to deviate, not to take any risk. The letter lay there on the mahogany table, unfolded. It said he must keep the telephone line clear—a call would come.

The letter itself proved that the kidnaping was real and not some crazy joke, as he had hoped it might be when he had come back from searching the school building last night—he and Judge Wagner—to find his wife sitting dazed by the phone. "Someone—a man. He said, Kidnaped, instructions in the morning. He said a name. I don't know. A name . . ."

A joke? Paulie was not a boy to play such jokes. Maybe some of his schoolmates? Or should the police be called? An alarm be sent out?

Judge Wagner, a wise man, a man with connections, said, Wait. A big alarm might prove dangerous for Paulie—if it was really a kidnaping. Then all night long they had tried on the phone to reach important people—the Chief of Detectives, the Mayor, the State's Attorney.

And early in the morning, Kessler himself had run to the door to answer the bell. A special-delivery letter. A name, Harold Williams. No use trying to recall anyone with such a name; it was surely a fake. "But why me?" All morning long Charles Kessler kept asking this of his friend Judge Wagner, of his brother Jonas. "Why me? I never hurt anybody. Why me?" And: "Who would do such a thing? Who? To a decent honest man, to a poor innocent woman, the boy's mother . . ."

There lay the letter. It was typewritten.

DEAR SIR:

As you no doubt know by this time your son has been kidnaped. Allow us to assure you that he is at present well and safe. You need fear no physical harm for him provided you live up carefully to the following instructions, and such others as you will receive by future communications. Should you, however, disobey any of our instructions even slightly, his death will be the penalty.

1. For obvious reasons make absolutely no attempt to communicate with either the police authorities or any private agency. Should you already have communicated with the police, allow them to continue their investigation, but do not mention this letter.

2. Secure before noon today ten thousand dollars ($10,000). This money must be composed entirely of OLD BILLS of the following denominations:

$2,000.00 in twenty-dollar bills.

$8,000.00 in fifty-dollar bills.

The money must be old. Any attempt to include new or marked bills will render the entire venture futile.

3. The money should be placed in a large cigar box, or if this is impossible, in a *heavy* cardboard box, SECURELY

closed and wrapped in white paper. The wrapping paper should be sealed at all openings with sealing wax.

4. Have the money with you, prepared as directed above, and remain at home after one o'clock P.M. See that the telephone is not in use.

You will receive a future communication instructing you as to your future course.

As a final note of warning—this is a strictly commercial proposition, and we are prepared to put our threat into execution should we have reasonable grounds to believe that you have committed an infraction of the above instructions. However, should you carefully follow out our instructions to the letter, we can assure you that your son will be safely returned to you within six hours of our receipt of the money.

Yours truly,
HAROLD WILLIAMS

Charles Kessler had hurried to the bank the moment it opened, and he had told them to make no record of the bills; he did not want to take any chances. What was ten thousand dollars for a life, his son's life? Then there had been no sealing wax in the house, and he had almost sent his older boy Martin out to buy the wax, but caught himself in time and sent Martin and little Adele with the chauffeur to his brother Jonas's house. Perhaps they would be safer there. And he had run out himself for the wax.

One o'clock. Waiting for the call. Jonas with him, Judge Wagner with him. Poor Martha upstairs; the doctor had given her sedatives.

The cigar box, wrapped in white paper, sealed, on the table.

And now came this call from the newspaper, saying that Paulie was dead. How could it be possible that the boy was dead when the letter said he was safe and unharmed? It said Paulie would be delivered six hours after the money was paid. Safely, safely returned to you. How could it be . . .

Judge Wagner took the phone. He pleaded, "Please cooperate. Do not call. . . ."

But the newspaperman insisted there was good reason to believe the dead boy was Paulie. It seemed to be a Jewish boy.

Then the Judge said, "I see." He took the address of the mortuary. He said that Paulie's uncle, Jonas Kessler, would go there at once, but please, not to print anything as yet.

A t that moment, Judd was sitting on a bench in the waiting room of the grimy old I.C. station. A bareheaded college boy, alert-looking, with intense dark eyes, he kept one hand in his jacket pocket, on the final instruction envelope. He had just printed on it the words MR. CHARLES KESSLER, PERSONAL. Now he kept his eyes on Artie, who was at the ticket window. Artie would come toward him in a moment for the letter. And then Artie would board the Michigan City train, staying only long enough to deposit the letter in the telegraph-blank box in the last car. Then Artie would get off the train. They would phone Kessler, giving him only the address of the drugstore near the 63rd Street station. Kessler would have precisely enough time to get to the store and receive their second call, instructing him to board this train as it arrived at 63rd Street and to look in the telegraph-blank box in the last car.

The man would just have time to rush aboard, find the letter, and read its instructions to go out to the rear platform and watch for the large building on the right-hand side, with CHAMPION MANUFACTURING printed on the wall. When the train came alongside that building, near 75th Street, the father was to toss the ransom package, as hard as he could, toward the factory. By then, Judd and Artie would be waiting in the Willys near where the package must fall.

Having the package thrown from the moving train had been Artie's contribution. He had come running over with the idea, all excited, one night about a month ago. "I've got it! I've got it!" The perfect end to the relays. And the beauty of it, Artie had explained, was that even if the victim's father tipped off the cops, the two of them could be watching at 63rd Street to make sure no one but the father got on the train. And even if the cops knew what train it was, how could they, in that last moment, watch the entire length of the tracks all the way to Michigan City? The cops couldn't drive alongside, either; there was no road directly alongside! Foolproof!

All evening they had examined the plan. Great—the work of a mastermind, a superman! Judd had congratulated his friend while suppressing, in himself, the little question, Hadn't Artie got the idea out of one of his detective magazines?

Then, once this main part of the problem was solved, the foolproof system found, Artie had become impatient to set the day. "Let's do it. Let's do it." But Judd had said that it had to be done perfectly; they had to pick the right train; they had to make a test run.

Together they had come down to this station and chosen an afternoon train, so that there would not be too many passengers, and they had chosen a short-line train, going only to Michigan City, so no one would be likely to use the telegraph-blank box. And they had tested the train, sitting together—Artie by the window and he pressing against Artie—to get a good look, to select a spot for the "delivery." There were mostly women on the train, biddies on their way back to Gary or Michigan City after their downtown shopping. There they sat with their packages—as the victim would today sit with his package of ransom—and how could those biddies have known what was being whispered and laughed about by those two college boys! That was the delight of the entire adventure. On that ordinary train, among the dull little women on their everyday errands, he and Artie had been picking the spot where a ransom should be tossed to them!

Or now, sitting here in the railway station, watching Artie, with his easy smile, stooping to the ticket window, and knowing why. And only the two of them knowing! You could go through life carrying always your extraordinary deeds between you, sealed off from all the little people, and sealed together by your doing and your knowing!

And sitting with his eyes on Artie, Judd must have told himself that he felt no different than on all their previous trips to this station. Just as during the months of planning it had seemed as if the thing would never happen, so it seemed now as though it had not happened. The thought habit of those months was stronger than the occurrence of a single day. All yesterday was a void, an intrusion, for yesterday had been a part of the deed that they could not have rehearsed. And today was like a going back to before the thing was done, like another rehearsal, a repetition of the part of the deed they had so often rehearsed in this station.

The rehearsal with the dummy package, to see where it would land when thrown from the moving train . . . A few weeks ago, together on the train, watching the package land in an alley near that factory . . . And Artie crying happily, "Let's do it, Jocko! Monday!" And he had told Artie, Wait. What about picking up the package? How could they be sure the alley would be clear? How could they be sure it wasn't a spot where a flying package would attract attention?

"Christ, people are always throwing crap out of trains—pop bottles and crap."

Still, Artie had agreed to another delay, for another test. They would separate, one on the train, the other on the ground. How heavy would ten thousand dollars be? A whole evening they had spent, laughing conspiratorially as they prepared an exact dummy package. Judd had calculated the weight in ones, fives, tens, twenties, calculated the best combination to fill a cigar box, for a box would sail good and solid. He had taken one of the old man's perfecto boxes, and a magazine of the right weight to stuff inside. That awful *Literary Digest.* The next day, Artie had taken the package and boarded the train.

Judd had posted himself in the alley, behind the factory with the windowless back wall. To test everything precisely, he had left his car only two hundred feet away with the motor running. And there came the moment when he saw the train, and Artie emerging to him on the rear platform, Artie first throwing away a cigarette, and then tossing the box. It rolled down the embankment almost to his feet. In a few minutes he was in the car, and at the next station meeting Artie. Still, he had temporized, "Maybe it's not the best place. Someone could have seen me from the street."

And Artie had stormed, "It's nearly summer, you sonofabitch. We'll never do it if you keep on crapping around!"

Judd wondered, now. Had he really meant that it should never happen? That one thing or another should delay them until the day he would be going away on his trip to Europe? And Judd was a little ashamed of his own past hesitations. For everything was working fine. Here now was Artie coming from the ticket window, wearing the easy smile whose meaning was known only to the two of them. As always, Judd felt illuminated by Artie's smile. The real collegiate carelessness about Artie, the jauntiness of him in that jacket with the half-belt in back, the quality of ease that Judd himself could never acquire, no matter how he handled himself, no matter how thoughtfully for insouciance he selected his clothes. . . .

Artie scooted past him as if they didn't know each other. (Railway stations are full of detectives; best not be too conspicuous.) Judd arose, walked over to the magazine stand, and brushed against Artie, feeling as always the contact pulse through his entire body. But in that moment he had slipped Artie the letter, and now he watched Artie going through the wicket, having his ticket punched.

Judd sat down again. Now the machinery was in motion. The minute Artie, having planted the letter, slipped off the train, they would phone Kessler. Michigan 2505. Judd couldn't quite picture the man. A skinny twerp, Artie had said. Until yesterday he had been Mr. A, for Adversary. Now he had a name. That too had been wonderful, sitting and drinking the old man's liquor while playing over names of possible victims. Anyone you had a hate on for a day, you could put down as the victim. Of course it was a platitude to say that the greatest fun was in anticipation, but it had to be admitted that platitudes were grown out of experience.

Evening after evening, playing the game, picking out victims, discussing the size, the maximum weight of a victim practical to handle . . . Nobody too large—a struggle would be abhorrent. And then the long arguments—almost fights—

he had had with Artie, trying to convince him that it should be a girl. The image of it swept back on Judd: making it a girl, and raping the girl, would have been part of it. From the beginning he had seen it that way, the image of the rape always sweeping through him like a dizziness.

But Artie had eliminated the idea of a girl. He had no really valid reasons. He was simply against it. A boy, then. A small one.

After that, they had spent evenings debating the amount of the ransom. If you asked for a hundred thousand, Artie said, every cop in town would be on the job. How much would a man risk, and keep away from the police, just to get his son back?

"How much would your own old man give?"

"Hah! That depends on which son!" And, eyes snapping, Artie had begun to stutter as he did only when he was extremely excited. "Billy now! Billy, the baby, the cutie! They'd pay a hundred thousand, a million for him! Hey! Why not really kidnap Billy?"

For a moment he had been serious, Judd was sure. But then they had dismissed it as impractical. Artie would be surrounded by police all over the house. It would be too difficult to collect the ransom.

For a whole evening their game had followed that vein. Suppose they staged a kidnaping, one with the other? "My old man would give a hundred thousand simoleons and say, 'Keep the punk!' " Artie had kidded. And he had pictured where he would send his old man to pick up messages. His dignified pater. A message in a ladies' toilet! That had convulsed him.

Judd had in turn pictured how his own father would react. Oh, he'd pay; he was proud of his prodigy! The boy ornithologist! Judah Steiner, Sr., had to have his prodigy's achievements to brag about at the club. As if the old man understood the first thing about ornithology, or anything at all but bills of lading!

Then Artie had produced an even better idea: kidnaping their own old men, in person! They had fallen over each other with laughter. Artie, imitating his father—dignity outraged!

Judd could just see Randolph Straus, the richest Jew in Chicago: "Boys! What is the meaning of this!"

Even now, sitting waiting for Artie, Judd had to smile at the thought. As if the whole thing were still to be done. And then he saw it as his own father, the old man's bewilderment as they tied him up and took off their masks. "What are you doing to me?" the old man would demand in his ponderous way. Ah, there would be a crime for posterity!

But the thing was already done, Judd reminded himself. Though if they got away with this, Artie might want him to—— No. For when he returned from Europe and went to Harvard, he would be different; maybe he wouldn't feel this way about Artie anymore. . . .

Judd drew in his breath, and looked fearfully toward the wicket, as if by this disloyal thought alone he might lose Artie.

In a moment Artie would be coming out. Judd rehearsed the Kessler phone number, the address of the drugstore, and told himself he must now be sure *not* to tell the Adversary to go to the Help Keep the City Clean box. That was eliminated, and there jumped into his mind the other thing about the box, the final, macabre idea Artie had proposed, a skeleton popping up as the lid was opened, or maybe—his eyes darkening —even better than a skeleton, a severed hand!

"You'll give the guy heart failure; we'll never collect!" Judd had said. "Besides, where would you get it?"

And Artie had given him that look, as if, despite all they had done together, Judd really wasn't in on the real, the inside things. "Oh, I could get it all right." Laughing, he added, "From a medical student. From Willie."

And Judd had felt a fear, a sadness, that gripped him again even now as the scene came back to him; Artie's merely naming Willie Weiss had brought the convulsed feeling around his heart that there were things Artie did with others, maybe with Willie, activities, secrets, from which he was excluded. He had even tried to turn it, to make Willie the victim.

"Willie!" he had exclaimed, but with a fear in watching Artie's reaction. "Hey, he'd be a good one. How about him?" For a moment Artie had joined in the idea. Had it been to tease him? Picturing Willie, the astounded look on his face, Willie trying to talk his way out of it and his cleverness failing him, Willie with the gag in his mouth, then dead between them. But finally Artie had said no, because Willie's old man was a notorious tightwad. He'd never pay. Artie had got out of making it Willie. . . .

There was Artie, coming from the train, smiling, as if he were just stepping out to buy a magazine before his train left. Now was the time to make the phone call. Judd pictured Mr. A by a phone, waiting. It was again a man like his own father. Still, it was better, purer, that nothing personal had guided them in their final choice. To have left blank the address on the ransom envelope, even as they prowled the street for the victim—that had been a superb affirmation. It proved destiny was accidental. Yes, they themselves had proved it; they had made a destiny, purely at random. Wouldn't that settle forever the silly argument about any meaning in life? Concatenation of circumstances—admitted—but meaningless, meaningless . . .

Judd arose to the gladness of Artie coming toward him. Now they were continuing. Yesterday had been an intrusion. Now the game was continuing.

He had already changed a nickel for a telephone slug, as each public phone had its own token. With the slug ready in his hand, Judd waited for Artie to crowd in beside him in the booth. They heard the busy signal together. Artie yanked the receiver from Judd's hand, and slammed it back onto the hook. "Sonsabitches! They're violating our instructions!" His eyes were yellow. Judd knew these sudden rages Artie could have. But after all . . . "Maybe somebody called them, by accident," he said.

"Let's get out of here!"

They hurried from the station. Artie, with his long stride, was already starting the car when Judd caught up with him. "Let's call again from a drugstore," Judd said. The note was on the train, the train would soon be on its way.

Pulling up at the nearest drugstore, on Wabash, Artie was out of the car before it had completely stopped. He snapped his fingers at the clerk for a couple of slugs. The clerk was busy with some blobby-faced woman over shades of rouge. Stupid little things like this, Judd muttered to himself, could wreck a plan of perfection.

But Artie turned on his charm. "Excuse me," he said to the lady, "I don't want to keep my girl waiting by the phone." She broke into a fat coy smile, while the clerk changed Artie's dime.

Hurrying into the booth, Artie took the phone; Judd seized it from him. Kessler might know Artie's voice. "I was only going to get the number," Artie snapped.

The ringing began.

*   *   *

Charles Kessler seized the phone almost thankfully. "Yes, this is Charles Kessler personally. My boy is all right?" The kidnapers were keeping their word; they were calling. Surely that newspaper reporter was crazy. Paulie was safe. The transaction would be completed, and in a few hours Paulie would be home safe.

"Do you have the money ready, according to our instructions?"

"Yes, yes. Is Paulie all right?"

"Your boy is safe. A cab will shortly call at your door. Proceed in the cab to the drugstore at 1360 East 63rd Street. Wait for a call in the first phone booth from the door. Is that clear?"

Kessler tried again, about the boy. Could he talk to Paulie?

"Remember, the address is 1360 East 63rd Street. You will receive further instructions at that time." Their receiver clicked down.

"Wait! Wait——"

Judge Wagner seized the phone. "Operator! Operator——" But it was too late to trace the call. If only they had not been afraid, and had allowed the police to listen in.

"He told me a drugstore, on 63rd Street . . ." Then, despairingly, Kessler clapped his hand to his head. He couldn't remember the address of the store.

*   *   *

From the phone next to Judd's, Artie had meanwhile sent off the cab. Judd felt anew the pleasure in the whole thing, a kind of duet with Artie, the smoothness of their working together.

The woman had selected her rouge, and now she turned to them with a naughty-boy gleam. "Well, whose girl is it?" she asked coyly.

"Oh, it's a double date," Artie said, giving her his smile.

Judd looked at his watch. "Come on, we can just make it." This time he took the wheel. Artie's wild driving might get them into a smashup. Especially if he had an idea he was racing a train.

I was waiting on the sidewalk when the Pierce-Arrow drove up to the mortuary. "He's in here, Mr. Kessler." Jonas Kessler, taking off his derby hat, followed me into the rear of the shop.

"That's Paulie!" he cried instantly. And from him came a harsh, gasping wail of grief piercing through, as from archaic times.

Two policemen had come. They stood with Swaboda, their faces fixed in respect. "Oh, this is dastardly," the uncle kept saying, and I noted that people in a crisis seem to use words they have read somewhere. "Dastardly! They murdered him, and now they are trying to collect a ransom. My brother is waiting with the money in his hand for them to call." He approached the body, raised his arm to touch it, but let his arm drop. "I have to telephone. No time must be lost."

We led him to the desk, but for a moment he did not have the heart to pick up the phone. "I have children of my own. Paulie was like one of my own," he remarked. I offered to make the call. "No time must be lost," Jonas Kessler repeated, and still sat motionless. "They said the boy is safe. How can they . . . Oh, this is dastardly."

* * *

At the Kessler house, the doorbell rang. A Yellow Cab driver stood there. Kessler picked up the cigar box full of money and started toward the door. But the address, the address! A drugstore on 63rd Street?

"Did they tell you the address?" he asked the driver.

The cabby was bewildered. "Didn't you call, mister?"

"The address to go to, on 63rd Street—?"

And at that moment, the telephone rang again. Kessler hurried back into the house. Perhaps it was the kidnaper calling once more, a miracle from God.

Judge Wagner handed him the phone. "It's your brother."

"Charles, this is Jonas. I have to tell you. Charles, they were right. It is Paulie."

Kessler's face remained rigid. Automatically, tonelessly, he asked if his boy had suffered.

*   *   *

It always seemed to me a telling part of this tragedy that the victims were somehow external to it. The boy himself, since we came to know him only in death, never existed for us. The father we saw a good deal of, as he gave himself entirely to the case, and yet he was an utterly enclosed man. The mother we only glimpsed, once or twice. We never learned much about her, except that she was some fifteen years younger than her husband and that she suffered a nervous collapse. One of the sob sisters wrote that Paulie's mother would not believe the boy was dead, and for months kept imagining that he was coming home from school.

In a sense, this impersonality of the victims seemed fitting; in the world as I was to come to know it, the victims mattered very little. The Kessler murder was the first to show us how the victim can be chosen at random.

J udd made it to 63rd and Stoney Island with seven minutes to spare, before the train arrived. He drove a block farther, to a Walgreen's; he had Walgreen phone slugs ready in his pocket. Everything was working beautifully. Artie clapped him on the back as they entered the store. "He's only a block away!" Artie said. There was a curious thrill in the idea.

Judd called the number they had noted—the booth in Hartmann's Drugstore—where Kessler should by then be waiting. Artie was jittery, watching out the window, watching the I.C. tracks.

The phone was ringing. There had been ample time for the cab to bring Kessler there. Since ordering the cab, Judd himself had driven all the way from Twelfth Street, over twice as far.

Artie opened the booth door. "You sure you got the right number?"

At that moment someone answered the phone. "Hello?"

"Is that the Hartmann Drugstore?"

A Negro voice said, "Yah, who do you want, mister?"

"Will you see if a Mr. Kessler is in the store? He should be waiting for this call." If Kessler was there, why hadn't he answered, himself?

"Mr. Who?" the Negro asked.

"Isn't there a man waiting for a call? A Mr. Kessler?"

"What number do you want?"

Judd kept his voice under control. "Just ask if a Mr. Kessler, a customer——"

"Don't see any customer in the store right now."

"Are you sure?"

"Nobody here, mister." And the receiver clicked.

Artie had gone pale. He rushed out of the store, half ducking as if expecting cops to be waiting outside.

Curiously, Judd found in himself no sense of oppression, nothing of the despair he had felt when that detail had gone wrong at the Help Keep the City Clean box. Instead, he experienced a new, sharp excitement. Joining Artie outside the store, he said, "Let's drive past Hartmann's."

"Too risky." Artie flung away a just-lighted cigarette.

"We could phone and check if the Yellow went out."

Artie's restless eyes fell on a newsstand, on a *Globe* headline: UNKNOWN BOY FOUND DEAD IN SWAMP.

"The jig is up," Artie said, with his nervous way of lapsing into detective-story talk. "Come on, let's get the hell out of here!"

But in Judd the sense of ascendancy grew stronger. Artie was getting jittery, but his was a cool, cool mind. Buying the paper, he stood against the window of a men's-wear shop, reading the story. "So they found the body," he said. "They still have no clue to its identity."

"Christ, don't be a fish! Since the paper got this story, that's hours ago. The cops can put that much together—a body, and a kidnaped kid. They're not that dumb."

"Don't get scared so easy," Judd said. "One must go to the end of an experience."

Artie stared down into his eyes. Judd felt strong, the stronger. "You stupe, this is the end!" Artie hissed. "We'd better get rid of this goddam car and split up!"

Folding the newspaper, Judd started back into Walgreen's. Artie caught his sleeve. "Where are you going?"

"I'm going to try another call. We've still got a minute before the train. Maybe the cab was late, or anything. Why should we give up just because he might be stuck in the traffic?"

"You and your frigging bird-chasing!" Artie burst out. "You knew just the right place. Birdland! Nobody ever went near there. Nobody would even find the body!"

That was unfair. And something in Judd still kept denying the finding. Something in him insisted it was still the right place, the only place, the place where the body had to be put. And there could be no identification! Had they not poured the acid, to obliterate identity? But beyond that, deeper, was some kind of knowledge, some kind of insistence that the body would be impossible to identify because . . . because who was it? Deep in himself something was saying nobody could ever know.

It was a confusing, unclear thought. Judd didn't like it, because it was unclear. He canceled it. He wrenched free of Artie to go and telephone.

"Jesus, not from here. They might have traced the last call!"

They hurried to the next corner, a candy store.

*   *   *

As Artie stood watching the street, fearful every moment of sirens, of cops closing the block off, he saw a train pulling in on the I.C. viaduct. That was surely their train. Even if Judd connected with Charles Kessler now, it would be too late for the man to run and catch the train. The train would pull out, and no longer would there be the moment when the package would come sailing to them through the air.

There arose in Artie then a frantic sense of deprival, a denial. No! No! It can't have gone wrong; I want it, I want it to be! It was Judd who had screwed it up, Judd, Judd! There came an impulse to scream, to rage, to stamp his feet in a tantrum. And then he swallowed his anger; he had to be keen, cunning, the master.

In other things before, without Judd, nothing had ever gone wrong, nobody had ever found out. And Artie was engulfed by a wave of negation, a commanding need to wipe out all that had gone wrong, to wipe out Judd. As though he could will the dissolution of Judd, will him not to exist, by a pointing finger. You're dead! You're gone! That's what you get for lousing everything up! And Artie turned, staring into the store, half anticipating that Judd would have vanished out of existence by his punishing wish. But through the glass of the phonebooth door, he could see the back of his partner's sleek, small head, dark, tilted.

*   *   *

As Judd phoned, a different voice answered, not a Negro's. "Jackson 2502."

Judd felt triumphant. "Mr. Kessler?" he asked.

"Who? This is Hartmann's Pharmacy."

He got the druggist to call out, "Anybody named Kessler been asking for a message?" But: "No, nobody of that name."

"Thank you," Judd said. Then it was clear. Kessler had not taken the cab. In the last half hour, the body must have been identified.

The way Artie looked at him as he emerged was murderous. "Granted that we lost out on the ransom part of it," Judd said, still feeling his mind working concisely, clearly, in the crisis—"the fact that they may have identified the body still does not mean they can identify us."

Artie cursed and turned to the I.C. tracks. Judd, too, looked at the train, still standing there, as though waiting for Kessler to get aboard. Then the train pulled away. They turned back to their rented car. "Let's just ditch it," Artie said.

That would be the worst thing to do, Judd pointed out. The rental man would be bound to start a hunt, and by some freak, even though they had used fake names, a trail might be found leading to them. No, they had best return it at once and check out.

Now that the dead boy was known to be a millionaire's son, police cars swarmed the street in front of Swaboda's, and cab doors slammed as reporters arrived. Some looked at me with the hostility and respect owed a man for a clean beat; others disregarded me—I was just a kid who had broken this big story by some fluke. And now that the real newspapermen were here, I began to feel inadequate.

There was Mike Prager from the Hearst afternoon paper, our direct rival. He was the inside-contact type, who would immediately take aside the most important official present and indulge in whispers. And then the *Tribune*'s star crime reporter arrived, a middle-aged man, or so he appeared to me then, though I suppose he was only in his thirties. Richard Lyman, like all *Tribune* men, seemed to take charge, not so much asking questions as demanding explanations. For a few details he had to come to me, and I gave him what I had, the spelling of the names of the men who found the body, things like that.

It was then, as the plain-clothes men and reporters and police piled into the back room, that the pervert talk was heard. It seemed to arise of itself, as the natural, obvious explanation, and indeed I pretended that I too had thought of it at first glance. The men would look at the corpse saying, "Some goddam sonofabitch pervert," and look again, as though a mark were there, for those who knew.

I felt it was shamefully naïve of me not to know. And yet I wonder now how much the others really knew? All were ready to use the horror-word as a stamp to explain everything, and in the rage and disgust and fear that followed and pervaded the city for months to come, and indeed attached itself permanently to the Steiner-Straus case, there was a blanketing of homosexuality with every form of depravity, and despite all the "expertizing" that was to come into the case, there was little attempt to learn from it, to understand.

For myself the subject was vaguely covered by the word *degenerate,* which we used often enough in the paper. I had even been sent out one Saturday to interview a woman on the west side whose little four-year-old girl had been attacked. For such matters, the word *degenerate* was used, and that explained everything. Chicago still reverberated with the horrors of the Fitzgerald case—the sex fiend who had been dragged half conscious to the gallows for attacking and killing a little girl.

But with a boy, I was in my own mind perplexed. For in that time, among those of us who carried around the purple-morocco-bound volumes of Oscar Wilde, there was more knowingness than knowing. Love between men or love of boys scarcely seemed to suggest a physical act. I associated such love rather with purity, love of beauty, and high-mindedness. Lines from Keats, fantasies of an elderly philosopher, a Socrates, walking with his hand on the shoulder of a stripling youth, images of an elegant Oscar Wilde exchanging epigrams with an elegant young lord, seemed to make such love simply an avoidance of the clumsy, sometimes disgusting physical part of the act that took place with women.

For at eighteen, and already a newspaper reporter in Chicago, the wicked city, I was innocent. At the frat house, I had taken part in the smut sessions, and in the gym I had taken part in the horseplay, the towel snappings aimed at the sex organs, and I could use the bugger words as freely as the rest —so freely precisely because the words had for me no meaning in experience.

Perhaps half, perhaps more, of my classmates, I think, were as innocent as I. At the frat there were those who bragged about their prowess at the cat houses, and those who loudly acclaimed that every girl they took out "went the whole way." There were those who solemnly warned you against catching a disease, and those, like Artie Straus, who bragged about the "dose" caught at the earliest opportunity.

The fear of disease, and an idealistic notion of "being fair" to the girl you would one day marry, perhaps a kind of magical sense that by keeping yourself pure you would insure her purity, had kept many of us innocent. We had handed around smutty pictures, we had read a few dirty books, we had even looked into Krafft-Ebing, but such things had not entered our lives. Everybody called everybody a c——, yet without any actual image of perversion. And we did not even have, then, the common words that today denote the homosexual; *pansy* and *fairy* and *nance* were unknown because the whole subject was somehow legendary.

So I stood in the circle of police and reporters, and we stared at the boy's body as if it could reveal unspeakable last events and thereby show us the assailant. But there were to be seen only the few scratches that might have come from the concrete culvert, and the two small marks on the head. The face, around the mouth, had a yellowish discoloration; we did not yet know this was the only result of an attempt at obliteration with acid, and we speculated that this might have come from some chemical in the water where the body had lain all night.

But if it were a deed of perversion, what did the kidnaping and the ransom have to do with it? And we speculated even upon the mystery of the actual cause of death, for the blows were not enough to have killed the boy, and he did not seem to have drowned.

Then the coroner's physician arrived, a paunchy man with dark eye pouches that gave him a constant look of irritation. In a shrill, authoritative voice, he cried, "One side, one side!" Even while Dr. Kruger was taking off his coat, Mike Prager's huge, sequestering hulk was around him, Mike was enveloping him in whispers, and all the others were demanding, "Was it a pervert, Doc?"

In vest and shirt sleeves, the physician leaned over the body. Death had taken place some time in the evening, he said. It didn't appear to be from drowning. Probably suffocation. Look at the throat muscles, swollen.

"Was he mistreated?" the *Tribune* man insisted.

The coroner's physician turned over the body. A cop kept saying, "Imagine the kind of sonofabitch fiend."

"It certainly looks like it to me," the physician said.

A growl, almost of satisfaction, went through the room. Richard Lyman asked if it could be positively stated that there had been an act of degeneracy, and Dr. Kruger shrugged— hell, they could see as well as he, but as for proof, it would take an autopsy, and then maybe nothing would show up. The body had been in the water all night; anything would have been washed out.

I looked, with the others, feeling as though everything were being dirtied—the dead boy, too—feeling I was truly in the midst of it now, the real bottom muck of the city, of humanity. I could see no sign of what they talked about, but was sure that the others saw.

The *Tribune* man pre-empted the phone, and we all hurried out to look for nearby booths. I had only the words of Dr. Kruger to phone in, but seeing Jonas Kessler leaving, I walked quickly after him, asking if I could ride along. He gave a little nod, as if to acknowledge my feat in identifying the boy. A few of the reporters stared after me as I got into the car, and again there came the little sense of triumph, within my respectful sympathy.

The uncle said, "We have to tell them he didn't suffer, you understand? Death was instantaneous. The papers, too, ought to say it."

I promised my paper would handle it that way.

For a few blocks we were silent, though I felt burningly that I was losing an opportunity. But this sense of intrusion has always remained with me; I suppose it is a defect in a newspaperman.

Again it was Kessler who spoke. Why, why should it come on Paulie?

I tried, "Did his father have any enemies?"

He shook his head. Who would do a thing like that, even to his worst enemy? And his brother was a respectable businessman, a real-estate man, practically retired. He had no enemies.

The car swept across the Midway, past the university. "Paulie was going to go there in a few years," the uncle said.

"I go there; I'm just graduating," I remarked, and I thought of the sensation I would make about this, with my campus crowd, with Ruth. We crossed Hyde Park Boulevard. The area of red-brick apartment houses ended, and there began the enclave of tree-shaded streets, with mansions set far back on their lawns.

It was odd that I had never penetrated this section, though it was only fifteen minutes' walk from the university and a few minutes from where Ruth lived. Indeed, this was where some of my rich fraternity brothers came from. And it struck me, only just then, that none of them had asked me to visit their homes here. I recalled that the Straus mansion was supposed to be a palace.

It might even be that this was a hostility that entered into the case and caused me to become so persistent, so obsessed, when suspicion began to fall on Artie Straus and Judd Steiner. It may be that I was driven by envy, and the sense of not really belonging that I had experienced at the frat. For soon after being pledged and finding myself among the rich boys from Hyde Park and the North Shore, I had concluded that I had been let in simply because I was a sort of freak all-A prodigy, expected to bring glory to Alpha Beta.

The last year, I had moved out of the house on the pretext that my newspaper work demanded another kind of setup, my own phone and all. But whenever I appeared they would slap me on the back and demand how the hot-shot reporter was doing, so they could say an Alpha Bete was a big newspaperman.

The Pierce-Arrow halted in front of an imitation English brick-and-beam mansion. Two police cars were parked in the driveway. An officer stood inside the portico. He deferred to the Pierce-Arrow, but gave me a questioning look. I said, *"Globe,"* and the uncle said, "He's all right, officer. He's with me."

We entered a large room, with heavy dark furniture. It was filled with men, more reporters and photographers, and important-looking plain-clothes men. Tom Daly was in the midst of them all, his note-taking yellow copy paper in his hand, and the sight of him was both a disappointment and a relief to me. Let Tom take over; I didn't want to make any mistakes on such a big story.

At the same time I saw the father of the boy, getting up from the high-backed, carved chair and coming toward his brother. Everyone stayed off, to give them their moment together. The two men walked to an alcove. The father's face was like the brother's, contained, clueless; it seemed to me to grow a shade darker as they stood there talking.

Tom came over to me, putting his hand on my shoulder. "We got a clean beat!" He looked at his watch. "We're on the stands. Know any more?"

"His brother says he's got no enemies." We looked at the two men. In a peculiar way they were now our adversaries; if they wanted to keep anything of their lives private and secret, we would nevertheless have to pry and prod and find out. Impeding me was still my sense of awe before a bereaved person, and my sense of awe before a millionaire.

But even the bereaved may be suspect. Tom said, "Sure, nobody has enemies." And we wondered what secrets of the past they might be combing. For in all of us I suppose there remains a belief in retribution. If a man is struck by misfortune, surely he must have committed some sin. And thus the victim immediately becomes the accused.

"Show me a pawnbroker that hasn't got an enemy in the world," Tom went on.

I was startled. "His brother said he was a real-estate man."

"Years ago he ran a fancy hock shop," Tom informed me.

I looked around the room. Here was this imposing house, with its beamed ceilings, in this solid millionaires' neighborhood; thirty years of respectable business dealings had accumulated to cover the early days, but the sting of the pawnbroker stigma was still strong enough for the brother to have kept silent, to me, about the shop.

Vengeance, money, degeneracy, the rubber-stamp motives took their turns in the forefronts of our minds. Tom came back to the last; it was first again. "You saw the kid. Could you tell—?"

This intimate knowing, seeing, was the reward of our news jobs —this being on the inside, knowing more than might be printed. I said, "It can't be proved. But Doc Kruger thought so."

"Sonofabitch pervert," Tom muttered like the others, and he turned to a theory that it was one of the teachers. Indeed, the entire room seemed to hum with it now. Those private-school teachers were all a bunch of perverts. Besides, look at that ransom letter. It was clearly the letter of an educated man.

We went over to the table, where one of the photographers was copying the letter, carefully laid out on the desk. The buzz of conjecture was still going on around the letter—the way people will repeat to each other a few known facts, as if by the repetition itself something new will be found. The postmark was the Hyde Park station's, only a few blocks away. I knew the place, on 55th Street—I bought my stamps there. The address, printed in ink. Mailed last night. That meant after the boy was dead.

And there was the use of the word *we*. Then more than one criminal was involved.

The letter was typed, but not professionally. Here and there, a mistake had been typed over. About the way I typed, I reflected. That, too, fitted the teacher idea. Suppose it were some teacher who had been misusing the boy. And who needed money. Those teachers were paid very little, anyway. Suppose he got the idea of satisfying the two desires at one stroke—sequestering the boy, and at the same time collecting ransom. Since the boy could later expose him, he had to kill the boy. Indeed, the crime might even have started with Paulie Kessler's threatening to tell on some teacher who had been making advances.

Tom drew me aside. "Sid, why don't you take a look around the school?"

Just as I was leaving, there was a stir at the door as the chief of detectives appeared. Captain Nolan strode in, a huge man who looked as if he had been picked for size. His lieutenants gathered around him, and we all gathered on the periphery. Captain Nolan expressed his sympathy to Kessler briefly, and then, with an air of getting down to business, went over all the facts we had already shredded to bits.

Charles Kessler had mastered himself so well that one could not have recognized, offhand, that he was the father of the slain boy. All his energy was available; grief had not drained him. Throughout the case this impressed me. It was not that I felt he lacked emotion; it was simply that his remarkable control seemed in some obscure way linked to a pattern that lay beneath the entire crime, a pattern of feelings pushed down so that nothing could show. In him, and in the criminals too.

"I am racking my brain," the father kept saying to Nolan. "It had to be someone who knew Paulie, or Paulie would never have gone with him. Paulie was not a boy to go with a stranger. If they tried to take him in a car he would have put up a struggle. It had to be someone he knew."

Tom motioned me to be on my way.

I walked down the block where Paulie had walked perhaps at this same hour just the day before. The body I had seen on that zinc table had walked under these trees, past these hedges, past these fine brick walls, and somewhere along here he had been snatched from life.

I pictured the kid, idling home from his after-school ball game. A man approaches—but it must have been in a car. A boy of thirteen doesn't respond to an offer of candy. An ice-cream soda, maybe—an offer from a teacher, driving home?

And once in the car? Perhaps a suggestion to go to the teacher's house? No, that would risk being seen. Just to take a ride, then. Out through the park, and toward Hegewisch.

Somewhere, the perversion had taken place. I tried to imagine in my own body the impulse to do such a thing. I suppose this is a test that everyone makes. I tried to call up in myself such a sick lust, and to watch my own reaction. Could I comprehend such a perverted impulse? Only kid things in back alleys came to me. In today's popularized Freudian knowledge, I suppose I should say that I stopped myself from homosexual imaginings because of some fear. But at that time, walking on Ellis Avenue, I felt, rather sanctimoniously, that it wasn't in me.

As I turned the corner, there was the Mark Twain Academy, a square brick structure annexed to a former mansion. And there was the baseball lot where Paulie had played. It was partly cindered, with a screen-wire backstop at the far end. The lot was deserted.

Indeed, the street was deserted. This was ordinarily an hour when children loitered outdoors, but though the murder itself was not yet known, the disappearance of Paulie had by now filled the exclusive neighborhood with rumors. The moment school was over, mothers had appeared in cabs, or chauffeurs had appeared, or governesses had come to walk the children home. The block was now hushed, deserted.

And then the quiet was broken by a newsboy shouting, "Extra!" He came at a half run, a large boy, and he kept on yelling while I was buying my paper. "Extra, all about the kidnaping, murder!" I gulped the banner, MILLIONAIRE BOY SLAIN. And in large type the lead read, "Identified by a *Daily Globe* reporter today as Paulie Kessler, son of—"

I wanted to tell that newsboy it was I—I, the *Daily Globe* reporter. But he rushed on. Doors, windows, were opening; he was being called from every house.

I read Tom Daly's story, Tom's and mine, then folded the paper and approached the school. If the fiend who signed himself "Harold Williams" was indeed one of the teachers, he would have been careful to attend to all his normal duties today, slipping out only to make the ransom phone call mentioned in Tom's story.

There was still a small group of teachers in the entrance hallway, discussing what was to them, until that moment, only the mysterious disappearance of Paulie Kessler. They didn't look like the teachers I had had as a kid. More of them were men then in a public school, and these wore tweedy jackets and pullovers.

I tried to sense the building, the teachers, for what impulse to crime might be here. Surely a lot of pampered kids, bossy kids, and teachers having to be especially careful of the way they talked to the children, teachers resentfully watching governesses and chauffeured limousines calling to fetch the brats home.

"Reporters, already?" said one of the young lady teachers, with an air half annoyed, half intrigued, as I introduced myself. "Really, we don't know a thing. We've no idea where he can be."

"He's been found. He's dead," I said dramatically, and handed them the paper. I was watching their reactions, looking them over with the question in my mind, Is this one a pervert? A murderer?

When the exclamations had died down, I asked if any of them had had Paulie in class, and two men spoke up. The tall, athletic young man in the belted sports jacket had taught Paulie American history. He had that inordinately clean, scrubbed look that certain people achieve; I half imagined a British accent when he spoke. Could this be a degenerate?

Today, an intonation, a movement of a hand in a nightclub is enough to bring a laughing roar of recognition. But I looked for I don't know what—some indication of nervousness, I suppose.

No teacher had been absent from school that day, they told me, the first young woman taking the lead in answering, a slight asperity in her tone. As for Paulie, the usual things were said, several joining in. He was alert, a likable boy. Not at the head of his class, but a real boy, intelligent and quite popular.

Paulie's other teacher now dropped a remark of the kind newspapermen seize upon for feature touches. Why, only day before yesterday, Paulie had won a debate on capital punishment. Paulie had been on the negative side.

This teacher's name was Steger. He had soft, red cheeks, and he spoke in a somewhat breathless voice. He went on talking, it seemed to me almost defensively, mentioning how he had noticed the kids after school yesterday at their ball game as he was going home.

Indeed, several of the teachers seemed to be dropping alibis into their remarks, telling, as though accidentally, what they had done last night, whom they had been with. And they seemed to be breaking away from one another, under the uneasy, spreading suspicion. How could anyone know what was inside the mind and heart of his nearest colleague? Speech, and what was visible, could lie. Beneath all human communication there was a dark ocean, lava-like—the real human action lay there, the force we could not measure, nor check, nor even detect from the surface.

Steger mentioned a book he had been reading last night, talking so insistently that it seemed, when the police car pulled up, that he had by some compulsion drawn the whole thing upon himself. We all saw the car halting directly in front of the door. A silence fell. Two of the plainclothes men I had seen at the Kessler house now entered the school.

The sprightly young woman spoke to them. "But, officers, police were here this morning. We've all been questioned, we've told all we know."

One of the detectives looked at his notebook. "There a teacher named Wakeman here?" Wakeman had gone home. The detective went on, "Anybody named Steger?"

"That's me," said Steger softly. "Paulie was in my English class. But I've already——"

"We've got instructions to take you along, Mr. Steger."

There was a gasp again, in the group, and a half gesture from one or two of them, as to intervene, to explain. And then the falling back, the not looking at Steger.

What Steger would have to go through, in the coming weeks, I suppose can be called an inevitable by-product.

The teachers were suddenly quiet. Without talking further to me, they went their ways, in pairs, singly. I started back to the Kessler house.

L eaving Artie waiting in the Stutz, which they had picked up on their way downtown, Judd drove the rented Willys into the garage of the Driv-Ur-Self. He got out of the car and stood leaning against its door while the manager walked around the vehicle, glancing at the fenders.

Judd looked away from the car; he would not let himself think of the spots on the rear floorboard. The manager would never inspect the rear. If he did, Judd was prepared to make the remark about the spilled wine, to hint about laying a broad back there—boys will be boys, what's a car for, ha ha.

But the nausea invaded him again. It pulsed up in him like a pulsing flow of blood. Blood on the ground, blood when his fingers touched his forehead, and he was shrieking . . . wrestling on the lawn with his big brother Max, his forehead cut on a stone, and Max at first concerned and then getting sore . . . "Stop crying. Stop bawling. That's enough! Boys don't cry. What the hell are you, a girl? A girl?" And his own shrieking—"I'm not a girl! I'm not a girl!"—while Max taunted, Max laughed . . . Max laughing at him, Max making fun of him, his big brother Max, he couldn't stand it; it was worse than the pain, the bleeding. Then he had known he had to hide everything inside himself, hide from Max. Keep Max outside himself, keep everybody outside himself—they could hurt too much. A man didn't let anything hurt. And he was no girl. He was no girl to cry at blood. And his mother had come out of the house and folded his face in her skirts. A girl. A girl.

Judd shut it off. To fill the mental void came the image

from yesterday. He had not counted on the blood. In all the months of planning, he had seen the thing as perfectly clean. They had even talked of it as neat, clean, talked of using the ether. And he had taken along the ether, yesterday morning, as if for his bird collecting, taken two whole cans, enough for a thousand birds. And put the two small cans into the side pocket of this car. . . . Judd's mind leaped back to the immediate scene—the cans! Had he forgotten them there, since they hadn't been used? No, he knew for certain he had taken them out and placed them back on the shelf in his room. Late last night. Yet it was all Judd could do now to restrain himself from opening the door and checking.

At least, he noted, this sudden scare had ended his nausea. . . . And why hadn't they used the ether? To put the boy cleanly to sleep, and in his sleep to do as planned—in his deep sleep to slip the rope around his throat, Artie and he each holding an end of it—to pull, with equal force, equal participation, forever linked in that way, he and Artie. Instead, it had all happened so quickly once the kid was in the car. The car had scarcely turned the corner. It had happened while Judd had still been feeling that perhaps the whole final deed would not take place at all. . . . Could Artie have sensed this last hesitation in him, and jumped the deed the way you ought sometimes to jump a girl before she can gather her resistance?

The rental man was putting his head inside to check the mileage. So outside nothing showed. They had washed it well enough. But it was a damn stupid thing. That damn stupid Emil had to come along offering the Gold Dust. It was a damn stupid thing to have taken the car into the driveway to wash. For that, Judd blamed himself. Last night's washing should have been enough without the second going-over in the morning. Modern version of Lady Macbeth . . . out, out, damned spot!

What was the use of taking all the trouble to establish a fake identity, with hotel registrations and all that stuff, so as to rent a car and not use your own car, and then the next thing you do is let some dumb Swede chauffeur see you with it and tie you up with the strange car?

The only safety was, the question must never arise. For right now this car was being returned to anonymity; tomorrow it would be out in someone else's hands.

"Fifty-three miles, Mr. Singer," the rental man said. "Want to check it?"

Judd smiled, feeling refreshed. How natural the name sounded! This part—the carefully established false identity, the car—it was all his idea and it had worked perfectly. Artie would have to give him credit for that much. "What about the gas I bought?" Judd said. "I filled up the tank." And he wished Artie had come in with him to savor this moment, to observe his complete self-possession. It was all there, the evidence of their deed was registered in the atoms of the vehicle, this inanimate object had experienced what they had experienced—the man had it standing before him as Judd stood; yet he could tell nothing, from either.

"Did you get a slip for the gas?"

"No, I didn't bother, but you can see it's practically full." He had filled it at home from the pump in the driveway just before they had started out to find the victim; at least Emil hadn't walked in on that.

With an air of creating good will in a customer, the man agreed to allow for a couple of gallons. "Call on us again," he said, his upper lip folding back over his toothbrush mustache in a smile.

"I will," said Judd, wishing Artie could hear that one.

*   *   *

"What took you so long?" Artie demanded before Judd could climb into the roadster.

"I made him give me an allowance for the gas."

Instead of laughing, Artie snapped, "The longer you gab the better he knows you, you sucker." Judd was getting in from the driver's side, making Artie push over. And in that instant, in Artie's anger, Judd suddenly felt the failure of the entire venture. It came over him blackly, fully—a grief, an anguish, that nearly brought tears.

It was all closed now. They had turned in the car. The whole thing was a failure. The killing itself had been wasted. Even if the killing had been a necessary waste, an experiment, there remained the death of the thing itself. The whole thing had represented a plan, an entity, perhaps a poetic unity, a flower of evil, a union between Artie and himself. And it was dead.

What had killed it? What was it really that had gone wrong?

Judd pulled away from the curb, but Artie, in the midst of lighting a cigarette, made a motion for him to stop, and jumped out to a newsstand—a new headline had caught his eye: MILLIONAIRE BOY SLAIN. Artie stood there on the pavement, reading. Judd honked. Still reading, Artie got into the car.

"How did they find out who he was?" Judd asked.

"Some stupid sonofabitch reporter went out there—"

Judd parked partway up the block and leaned over to read with Artie. His eye skipped down the column, and together they saw the line about the glasses: "Desperately awaiting word from the kidnapers, the Kessler family at first refused to believe that the boy found dead in the culvert was Paulie, because the police reported that the dead boy wore glasses. Then it was learned that the glasses had been picked up in the weeds, and placed on the boy by his finders. The glasses, police now believe, were dropped by the murderer, and should prove a valuable clue."

Artie turned his face full on Judd. His cheek was twitching, high up under his eye. "You buggering sonofabitch, you had to go and spoil it."

Automatically, Judd's hand had gone to his breast pocket, though he already knew that it was so: this was the flaw. And a curious thrill went all through him, the first complete thrill of the entire experience. It was not the dark thrill he had imagined he might feel at the height of the deed itself, as at a black mass, nor was it the elative thrill he might have felt had the package been tossed from the train. It was a thrill as from some other being within himself; it was a gloating.

He told himself that it was a thrill to the challenge that now existed, the challenge to outwit pursuers, even when they possessed a clue. For there was no game unless you gave the other side a chance.

But why had the glasses been in his coat pocket at all? He speculated on causation. He had scarcely used the glasses during the past few months, not even for studying. It must have been weeks ago that he had stuck them in this coat pocket, and, hardly wearing this suit, he had forgotten they were there. Then what had made him choose this suit yesterday?

And when could the spectacles have dropped out? Judd tried to bring back the scenes of yesterday, to see into them, but only briefly, partially, only for that one item, as a man, to shield his sight from the burning sun, will cover part of a view. Had it happened when he was bending over, in the back of the car, the glasses dropping into the lap robe half wrapped around the boy? Judd saw again the boy entering the car, the quick blows, the suffocation—that part of it already done, so hastily, so irretrievably done before you could decide finally whether or not to do it. Then driving through the Midway, past the university, through the park, south to the edge of the city, then stopping at a hot-dog stand, leaving him in back there while they ate the franks, then cruising, then parking on the little side road back of a cemetery, waiting for darkness. And both climbing into the back seat, and Artie's high-pitched, "Let's see."

Like kids in a dark closet, to do the most awful imaginable forbidden things. Huddling down. Had the glasses fallen out then, onto the robe? Artie beginning to undress the body, pulling off the knee pants. And Judd in himself wondering at himself, now that the opportunity had come to test the farthest human experience, dispassionately, as in a laboratory. Remembering the untried experiences from the list in Aretino's *Dialogues*. Artie's saying, almost petulantly, "He's dead all right. Getting stiff." Then all at once, tumultuously, himself losing interest . . . Now Judd shut off the dark image. The glasses, only the glasses—were they glinting there, fallen on the robe?

Pulling out of that cemetery lane, dark enough then, and driving down Avenue F . . . the turn, the ruts onto the wasteland, the spot where he always parked and left the car, going birding. Lucky, lucky no love birds parked there this night; then the two of them removing the long bundle wrapped in the lap robe, lugging it all the way across the weed-grown wasteland . . . Artie stubbing his toe, stumbling and swearing and letting down his end, the bundle dragging on the ground. Stopping to rest, Artie complaining, "Why the hell so far? Why not an easier place?" But no, this had to be the place—and stooping to pick up the bundle again, was that the moment when the glasses had fallen out? No, they were found too near the culvert. That weird and exhilarated march, the sky rim reddish from the Gary chimneys, the clumsy bur-dened feeling of endlessness, weighed down awkwardly with the bundle on one side, and under the other arm the boots he was carrying, and the container of hydrochloric in his pocket bumping his hip . . . Why labor so? Only for something that had to be done, had to be done!

And all the time trying to quiet Artie, to shut up Artie in his high mood making his jokes, waving his flask—"We come not to bury Paulie but to baptize——"

"Shut up! There's some bastard railway switchman got a shack up the track. He'll hear you."

"Invite him! Let's give him a drink of that old acid! You sure you got the ass-it?"

"I've got it, right in my pocket."

Then coming to the edge of the pond, putting down the long bundle. And there it must have happened. . . . Judd saw himself there, sitting for a moment on the slope of the low railway embankment, bending to take off his shoes and pull on the boots—his brother Max's fishing boots, taken from Max's closet. You're in it with me, Max, you sonofabitch, big man Max. How's this for sissy stuff? Who's a sissy now! And as he bent, Judd could hear a distant train, a muffled rhythmic pounding under the earth like a heart under the earth. And before him, the dark flat water, going into the dark hole, the culvert. Then, heated from the long exertion, and knowing he had yet to lift the body and carry it into the water, Judd rose to remove his coat. He placed the coat carefully folded upon the grass, beside his shoes.

The remainder of the scene flashed through his mind now, accelerated, for he still found it distasteful to review. First, Artie unrolling the lap robe. The lower part of the body, bare except for the knee-length stockings, appearing grotesque under the low-held beam of Artie's flashlight, looking like those manikins you sometimes see half undressed in store windows . . . when you see the cold glassy surface of the middle portion . . . No! the glasses would have glinted then, under Artie's light. No! Now Judd felt sure; he could sense the glasses lying there still folded in the breast pocket of his folded coat.

"Cold stiff," Artie said. "Help me with his goddam clothes."

"Rigor mortis," Judd repeated, kneeling. They both worked to finish the undressing.

Artie joked—the punk was like some broad that goes rigid and won't let you get her clothes off. He kept up the stream of jokes the way he had in the car, kept it on a level of high deviltry, good and ginned up, handling the body so casually, the way he had in the back of the Willys. Then the nude body lay there, a pale streak on the lap robe, and Judd knew his part had come. He rose and got the can of hydrochloric. Was it then? Not then; he had not disturbed the folded jacket —the can was already out of the pocket, placed on the ground.

And Artie had moved the body off the robe, to the water's edge, and Judd stood over it, raising the can of hydrochloric, so well forethought—acid to dissolve all evidence of mortality. Then he was pouring the stream from the can—"I hereby baptize and consecrate nothing to nothing"—and with his high giggle, watching the stream, silvery, upon the face. To obliterate, all, all! A thought, an urge, a dark wing beating far back in his mind, so they never might recognize, never might identify, but it was more than that, it was all, all faces, and no face. It was as though he himself were being obliterated so he could never be caught. And then there was a sure impulse, a thing to do so no one could ever ever know who, what it was. And he turned the stream downward, giggling, giggling—he was a kid again playing in the sand, holding a can of water over a body of sand, the stream hitting the sand, dissolving away, the sand dissolving away to nothing—so now the stream upon the penis . . . dissolve, dissolve and be no more!

And Artie laughed with him, and it was right, right! There was a great lifting within him, Judd thought, because now the deed was done, the whole terrible superhuman god-devil deed was done. They had achieved! But it was a feeling that continued, even stronger, more obscure, a lifting feeling within him, as though something utterly wrong had been corrected, put back right.

Then wading in Max's boots into the water, seizing the body, feeling no longer squeamish to touch it bare, feeling it cold as the touch of the water. And the whole thing had become easy. Shoving the object into the culvert, the non-being, face and sex soon dissolving, how neatly it fitted, as he had estimated it would, fitting perfectly in the perfect place. And then retreating to get cleanly out of there. ·

Had he then picked up the coat?

And the precise image of that moment came before Judd. Artie's form, looming out of the dark, Artie breathlessly offering him his coat and shoes, the coat snatched up in a tangle any old way, the disorderly way Artie handled things, upside down.

That was how it had happened. That had been the moment. Judd could virtually sense the glasses sliding from the upside-down pocket, among the weeds.

"I'm sorry to have to contradict you," he said now to Artie, "but I believe the slip-up was yours. It was you who picked up my jacket and brought it to me. That's when the glasses must have dropped out. But I accept my share of the error in failing to notice——"

"Me!" Artie turned on him, raging. "Trying to shove it off on me! You and your buggering sure-shot hiding place! You and your buggering eyeglasses——"

"Take it easy," Judd said. He felt cool, controlled, exhilarated. He began to understand the strange electric thrill he had experienced a moment ago—the challenge.

If the whole thing had gone off without a slip-up, it would have been perfection of a kind: a deed conceived and planned and carried out, like some intricate construction—a matchstick palace with even the last piece fitting perfectly into place. There would have been a mathematical purity to it.

But the glasses were an error, an error tearing down Artie and himself from their superhuman state as beings who could achieve an act of perfection. And in some center of his self, Judd rejoiced that they were united in this error, united in their imperfect action; he rejoiced that Artie had committed his part of the flaw.

Now their action permitted a different kind of triumph, for they must try to retrieve their error and still emerge superior. And in their error they were united even more firmly than by a perfect deed. For had the adventure succeeded, they would have divided the ransom and been done. He would have gone on, in two weeks, to Europe.

Perhaps now he would never go. Even in this dread anticipation of being caught, Judd felt a subterranean satisfaction; he and Artie were entwined in what was still to come.

"By the law of probabilities," he said to Artie, "there is one chance in a million that they can trace the glasses."

"Shit on all that," said Artie.

But something perverse in Judd made him see the spectacles already traced. They had to be traced—he had to be confronted with them—for the next part of the action to occur, the infinite ordeal through which he would redeem his error, prove himself a truly superior being. The ordeal in which, by facing down all accusation, he would save Artie, too.

To Artie he said, "They're just the most ordinary reading glasses. There must be hundreds of thousands of the same prescription. The chance that their ownership can be identified is infinitesimal. But even if it should be, that still doesn't prove anything. I could have dropped my glasses any day I was out there birding. I was even out there with my class in the same spot last week; I could have dropped them at that time. A mere coincidence. In fact, I can use my bird class as witnesses!" *There* was a Machiavellian touch that Artie should appreciate.

Judd saw himself standing before some powerful man—a heavy mustache, an authority—but he remained unflustered, controlled, saying, "A mere coincidence," as he accepted the spectacles back into his hand and placed them back in this same coat pocket. For no matter who they were, the authorities would know they had to accept the word of Judah Steiner, Jr.

In fact, they would conduct their questioning with the utmost deference, and probably apologize to his old man for even calling him in. And the old man would say to him quietly, "You don't have to answer them if you don't want to. What kind of nonsense is this?" But Judd would say, "It's routine. I'm perfectly willing to answer any questions they ask. And since you are so insistent that I become a lawyer, you ought to be glad, as this will give me a little direct experience with matters of law." And all that time it would be a howl over the old man and his slow-minded righteousness! For he would be fooling the old man as well as all the inquisitors.

"I ought to kill you for making such a boner," Artie said, hurling the newspaper to the floor.

Judd put the car in gear. Starting homeward, he said, "I agree—if it were entirely my error, I would deserve death." Indeed, in a superior society, no one capable of such a stupid oversight should have a right to live. Nietzsche would certainly have condemned him, for in the end it was his own fault for having the glasses in his pocket. Thus, the pendulum in him swung to the other extreme, and Judd saw Artie enthroned, with golden wristbands, golden breastplate and greaves, judging him as he knelt abjectly. And the sentence — Artie's outstretched gold-banded arm, decreeing death. And suppose he went out now with Artie to some dark field and insisted that Artie carry through the sentence—Artie shooting him, his body crumpling—it would be his sacrifice for Artie. They would find his body; he would leave a note acknowledging the glasses as his, the crime as his. That would be part of the sentence. And Artie would be forever safe.

But aloud, Judd proposed a bold idea. To go directly to the police and claim the spectacles. "I read the story in the papers, and realized that on my last birding expedition——"

"You'll bugger it up," Artie said. "You'll bugger it up, sure as Christ." He whistled at a couple of chicks on Michigan, reaching over to pound the horn, and elbowing Judd to pipe the broads, the sun coming right through their dresses.

The girls went into a building. "Crows, anyway," Artie said, but his spirits had lifted. "Suppose you go and say they're your glasses. All right. They give you the third degree. You think you can take the third degree?" he challenged.

"I'd be glad to help you in any way I can, officer," stated Judd, looking him unflinchingly in the eye.

"Watch where you're driving, you sucker. All right, Mr. Steiner, where were you last Wednesday?" Artie's restless glance lit on another chick; he called. She turned, smiling, her tonguetip darting in and out between her lips—this part of Michigan was red light.

"The hell, you want another dose?" Judd remonstrated, then resumed, "Last Wednesday, yes, I recall distinctly, I spent the entire afternoon and evening with Artie Straus, a friend of mine."

"All right, so then they pick me up and check your story. I ought to kill you first, you crapper."

They rehearsed once more the story they had agreed upon, should they ever be questioned. Artie became suddenly attentive. "All right, we had lunch at the Windermere. That's a fact. Willie was there with us. They can even check that with Willie."

They laughed again. Judd felt pleased. They would be using Willie Weiss, and Willie wouldn't even know how he and Artie together were having a laugh at him. "Then after lunch"—Judd picked it up—"we spent several hours in Lincoln Park, at the lagoon, mostly sitting parked in my car, as I was watching for a species of warbler that arrives in this area late in May——"

"Hey, give them the scientific name," Artie said.

"Dendroica Aestiva, of the Compsothlypidae family," said Judd, and they snorted, imagining the cops handling that one!

Then Artie took over the story. "I went along with Judd Steiner and sat in the car while he did his bird scouting. I thought it would make a good effect on my mother to tell her I spent the afternoon with Judd and his bird science, so she would get the idea I was doing something real studious. But I'm afraid, sir, we had a pint of gin in the car and by supper-time I had too much gin on my breath, so I didn't think that would impress my mother very well. We stayed out for supper, had supper at the—let's see——"

"Coconut Grove," said Judd.

"Then we drove around awhile, trying to pick up a couple of girls."

"You mean, girls you didn't know?"

"Yes, sir, you know, just a couple of janes."

"Do you frequently engage in this practice?"

"Well, officer"—winking—"you know how it is. We coasted around on 63rd Street——"

"How did you make out?"

"Well, we picked up a couple, around 63rd and State. And we drove back to Jackson Park——"

Judd interrupted. "I thought we were going to say Lincoln Park."

"Shit no. The first time, the birds, is Lincoln. The second time, the twats, is Jackson. Over by the lake. . . . Only you see, officer, these girls wouldn't come across, so about ten o'clock we told them to get out and walk."

"Can you give us their names, Mr. Straus?"

"Well, mine said her name was Edna, but you know—we didn't give them our right names, either. She was a blonde, well built—" He made curves with his hands, and just then spotted a girl in a Paige, passing them. "Hey! Follow her!"

"Listen"—Judd chased the Paige—"how about if we change the story? If we say they did come across, then it's even less likely the girls would ever come forward and identify themselves."

"All right. Wait a minute. If they came across, then we'd have taken them home. So where do they live?" Judd passed the Paige, but the girl ignored Artie's waving.

"We could say they told us to let them off at the corner where we picked them up," Judd suggested. "That sounds genuine."

"Hey!" Artie eyed him cleverly. "How about giving them the story you were out with a nice girl? Let on you hosed her. Then you've got to be the gentleman protecting a nice girl's rep."

"You mean, we had a double date with nice girls?"

"No, just you." After all, no glasses of Artie's had been found.

Judd felt a quiver of grief, more than anger. A feeling of loneliness, as if Artie had actually deserted him and left him with some jane he didn't even want. But then he finessed the game on Artie. "I could say I was driving, and you had Myra in the back seat. She'd back it up for you. As you say, she'll do anything for you."

"Damn right," said Artie, still eying him in that cunning, disturbing way.

Desperately, Judd tried to recapture the mood. "How about we both take her out tonight and rape her?"

"You'd be scared to try."

"Yah? Anything you'll do I'll do."

"Yah?" Judd knew what it was now in Artie's look. It was the accusation over what had happened yesterday, at the crucial moment—when they had the kid in the car, and the sudden blows and the blood, and Judd had heard himself crying out, "Oh my God, this is terrible! This is terrible!"

"You were scared pissless," Artie said with finality. "That's why you dropped your goddam glasses."

In his tone, Judd felt everything possible. Maybe Artie would do it to him. Like things Artie must have done. Maybe Artie coming up behind him, the slug on the skull with the taped chisel, and the quick push off the end of the Jackson Park pier, his body plopping into the dark water, and his own look, upturned to Artie, accepting.

"I'll stick to the alibi for a week," Artie said. "After that, it's each man for himself."

"If a week goes by, we ought to be safe on the glasses," said Judd.

He turned on Hyde Park Boulevard. At the Kessler house, police cars lined the curb. Photographers and newspapermen were all over the lawn. Artie was about to hop out. "Stay away from there!" Judd cried.

Artie chuckled. "It's only natural I'd be interested. I live practically across the street. Why, poor little Paulie used to play on our tennis court all the time. Why, he's a chum and classmate of my little brother Billy!"

"You'll spill the beans, the way you gab. Keep off of there!"

"The hell! You going to tell me what to do?" But he remained in the car.

Silent, Judd pulled up to Artie's door. But as Artie started into the house, Judd asked, "What're you doing later?"

"I don't know. I'll give you a buzz."

Judd drove on.

*   *   *

I must have just come back to give Tom the details of the teacher's arrest when Artie and Judd drove by, for I remember seeing Artie go into his house. I remember thinking, So that's the Straus mansion. Some class.

With the rest of the press, Tom was now outside on the Kessler lawn. It was understandable: they couldn't have all of us camping in the house, and they couldn't play favorites.

Everything was up a tree, Tom said. Anyway, our last replate was gone; if something happened now, we'd read about it in the morning papers. Was there any place around here a man could get a drink?

I knew a place on 55th Street, where they had spiked beer. We took the coeds there to give them a thrill. I had meant to rush over to Ruth's, but now I went along with Tom. The place had a cigar-maker in the window, a natural lookout. This always gave me an odd feeling, for my father was a cigar-maker, though he didn't work in a store window—he worked in a small shop in Racine. Now Pop would have big things to tell about his son, the university reporter.

As we stood up to the bar, Mike Prager and a couple of other afternoon-paper reporters found the place. We began to trade theories of the crime. I felt I was a full member of the profession. I was drinking with the boys.

*   *   *

When Judd dropped him at the house, Artie ran in with the *Globe* extra, to make a sensation. His mother wasn't there. She would be at some meeting, doing good. By the time she got home, she'd know. He felt cheated. Something always cheated him, with her. *Mumsie, you know what happened to the Kessler kid!* She'd have gone white. *It could have been Billy! Why, Mumsie, Billy was right there playing with Paulie on the baseball lot. I saw them myself!* No. Maybe better not go that far.

Artie leaped up the stairs. Billy's room was empty. There, for an instant, Artie's mind stood blank, with some weird confusion. As if the room were of course empty because it had been Billy they— Then he told himself, Hell, the kid was over in that crowd at the Kesslers', soaking up all the excitement; he'd give a full report before his big brother could get in a word—a bright, cute Billy-boy report.

They should really have snatched *him,* the brat, as they had once planned. Only Judd had taken it as a joke. Artie saw it now as if they had done it, grabbing Billy, feeling the kid in his arms in a squirming struggle, like sometimes when they playfully wrestled. But *this* time—the look on the kid's face when he was bopped! And if it had been Billy, Artie wondered, would he himself have wanted to weep?

Then his imagining switched suddenly to a jail. He was behind bars, and people passed, grimacing at the monster killer; then came girls he knew, that big-eyed Dorothea, and Susan French, and that babe in Charlevoix, Betty, and then strangers, all grimacing at the monster, and he grimaced and made faces back at them, stuck out his tongue, made funny faces; Dorothea laughed, then he let his arms hang long and he pranced like an ape. Some fun!

On Billy-boy's bed was an open box of chocolates. Artie grabbed a handful and ate them. The images of the jail went on. They were giving him the third degree.

He heard a gasp. The maid was in the doorway. "Oh, it's you, Artie! I didn't hear anyone come in." She looked scared stiff. "We've all got the heebie-jeebies today. You know what happened to poor little——"

"Yah, it's in the papers. Where's Billy?" he asked with concern.

"Oh, he's safe! Your mother went with the car the minute we heard something was wrong, and took him out of school.

She wouldn't leave him there another minute. All the mothers have been calling up, all day! Your mother took Billy along with her to her meeting. It's in the papers, is it?"

"Sure." He showed her the headline.

"It must have been a fiend that did it," Clarice said. "He could be someone in that school!"

Artie wished he had been there to see that sight, all the limousines filling the street. There must have been a regular traffic jam, with all the anxious mommies hurrying to get their darling children safely home.

"It could be a fiend in the neighborhood," Clarice repeated.

"That's right, and they come back to the scene of their crime," Artie said. She was excited, moistening her lips with her tongue. If she weren't so dumpy, and her hands always damp, he might give her a shove. She was always asking for it, brushing against him. But once he made the push he'd have to go through with it, and maybe the disgust over her would hold him down so he couldn't do anything. Then he'd always have that funny feeling, having her around, knowing. The hell with her.

"I hope they catch him," she said. "No one will feel safe until they catch him. That poor little Paulie, I hope he didn't suffer. I hope the end was quick."

The delivery bell rang, and she had to go. Artie picked up Billy's bow and arrow, thrown on the floor. No Miss Nuisance to make Billikins pick up things. Mumsie herself took care of her precious little boy.

The image returned. He was in the jail. They had him. Two huge dicks with rubber truncheons. He bent over, and they delivered the blows. He took all the blows, on his shoulders, on his ass. But he kept silent. They could never prove anything on him. He was the master criminal and they knew they had him, but they could never prove it on him! What a guy! At last they had to let him go. They followed him, the stupes, as though he would lead them to his gang. He gave them the slip. He got to his headquarters, in the basement hideout, and now he would take care of that rat, Judd. A couple of his strong-arm men brought in Judd and hurled him on the floor. Leaving his goddam glasses!

Artie threw the bow and arrow on Billy's bed. He shook Billy's piggybank—the hell with it—and flung it down. From Billy's secret store of marbles he selected a couple of aggies, prize ones, milky, translucent, slipping them into his pants pocket.

With Judd lying prostrate at his feet, in the hidden cellar headquarters, Artie arose to give judgment. He stretched out his arm. The surge of power was in him. He pointed his finger downward at the quivering traitor. *It is my will that you cease to exist.* And the power passed like unseen lightning through the form of Judd, and life was gone from him.

Or else, take him with the pistol in his back to the pier, maybe late tonight. *You see, Judd, this makes everything perfect. You have to agree, this is the perfect solution and therefore I am obliged to carry it out.* That would be slick, using Judd's own crappo philosophy on him. Judd would agree—they had found his glasses, they would find his body floating in the lake, a suicide. Q.E.D.

Suddenly Artie felt the fear. The fear, the heebie-jeebies, the unbearable shrieking thing coming up in him—he'd snap! Someone—to be with someone, to keep him from— Not Judd. He tried to call Willie Weiss, but Willie wasn't home. Piling out of the house, Artie strode across the street, passed right against the Kessler place. The lawn was clear; all the reporters were gone. But police cars were still there. How would it be to ride in one of those Marmons, the siren blowing, a big cop on each side of you, while already you had the feeling of their truncheons across your naked back?

Artie forced himself away, circled back to his own house. His brother Lewis's Franklin was in the driveway. *Go screw yourself, Lewis!* Behind the wheel, Artie felt somewhat easier. He swung the car down Hyde Park Boulevard. Not to Myra's house—screw Myra . . . string bean with her long stringy fingers, she gave you the jitters. Halfway across the Ingleside intersection, he swung the car violently into a left turn, barely missing a flivver and causing a couple of old ladies who were crossing the street to squawk and scramble exactly like hens.

Artie laughed out loud, feeling better as he braked in front of Ruth's house.

She was exactly the one. He hadn't called her in a month. But she was the one, with her round face, milky and smooth as an aggie. Have Ruthie sitting here beside him as he coasted out by the lake. Tell her a big story. She swallowed everything. Like the bootlegger act. The time he shot a hole in a shirt and wore it, showing her the hole, telling how he went bootlegging for the kick of it, and had to shoot it out with some hijackers. As if to prove she never believed the story, she would always ask how his bootlegging was getting along. But she was one of those who swallowed it. He'd tell her now that it was he who had kidnaped the Kessler kid! "Oh, yes, uh-huh," she would say, with her serious eyes fixed on his, while keeping a you-can't-fool-me-again note in her voice.

Looking in, through the window of her father's drugstore, Artie could see that Ruth wasn't downstairs. Their flat was on the second floor. He sounded the horn. Three, four times. Finally her mother appeared at the window over the store. The old lady went away, and then Ruth appeared. Artie blew again.

She pulled up the window. "Artie, is that nice?" she said, not too reproachfully. "Are you too lazy to get out and ring the bell?"

"Hey, come on down," he said. "I've got something to tell you."

"Well, you may come up if you wish."

"Come on down."

People were beginning to get interested. Ruth closed the window, and a moment later came out of the hallway, with an air of pique.

She looked good enough to eat. Her round, soft face had a glow, and her reddish hair glowed, drawn back from her forehead under a green velvet band, and fluffed out behind.

"Hey, come on for a ride," Artie said.

"Artie, you're cuckoo. I can't go now."

"Sure. Come on." He gave her the boyish grin. "I feel lonesome."

"What's happened to all your girls?"

"Oh, I got sick of the whole bunch of them. I thought of you."

"Well, that's not very complimentary. The bottom of the list."

He blew the horn. "Come on."

"I can't. I'm helping Mother. Maybe tomorrow."

"Sure you can. Come on. I'll buy you a beer."

"No, really I can't just now," she said in that way girls have, when you know damn well they can. He let his face fall, moody, serious. It worked. She asked, "Is anything wrong, Artie?"

It was the shock of that thing in his block, he said, that horrible thing. Right across from his house. It could have been his own kid brother Billy!

"I know," Ruth sympathized. "It's ghastly. Such an incredible, fiendish thing." For a moment, he had her. But then she shook her head and said, "I really do have to go upstairs. But another day, if you like, Artie. Only you should give a girl more notice."

Hell with her. She was a wet rag. He slammed the car into gear and drove away, glad of the surprised, almost dismayed look on her face as he left her there on the sidewalk.

Artie pulled up at the frat, ran in, told the big news, talking a mile a minute about the crime, his brother, the ransom, then suddenly, in that way he had, shifting his attention to a bridge game.

L eaving Tom Daly, I decided to stop at the frat for supper before I went over to see Ruth; I suppose I wanted to display myself and collect glory for my scoop. A bridge game was in progress in the lounge, and Artie was pulling his usual act of jumping from one side to another, handing out advice.

I tossed the paper onto the bridge table. "Hear about the big story? Kid got murdered." And to Artie: "Say, he lived right near your house."

"They've got my whole street blocked off!" Artie cried. "You never saw so many cops! I was just telling everybody——"

"Blocked off? I was just there," I said, irked by his habit of exaggeration. "Didn't run into any street blocks."

The fellows were exclaiming over the news. "You on this story, Sid?" Milt Lewis asked with awe.

". . . identified by a *Globe reporter,*" Raphael Goetz read out loud.

I admitted I was the reporter who had identified the boy. They whistled.

"Say! Some scoop!" Artie stared at me, mouth agape. Then he flung his arm around me, patting my back. "Sonnyboy Silver, the hot-shot reporter! Fellows! We have a star reporter in our midst! The Alpha Beta is really getting there!" He seized the paper, glanced at it, waved it. "Hey! If not for Sid's identifying him, it says they were just going to pay the ransom! Boy!"

He gazed at me so intently, his expression so strange that

I clearly remembered the moment. "It was beginner's luck," I said. "I just happened to get sent out——"

Artie was avid with questions. How had the poor kid looked? Any marks on him? Any clues? Sometimes the cops made the papers hold back certain information, to trap the criminals. What was the inside story?

His excitement over the case seemed perfectly natural. Artie was a notorious detective-story addict. It was a common wonder around the house that he, who was supposed to be so brilliant, read practically nothing but pulp magazines and all that trash.

Actually, though he now developed a sudden friendship for me, Artie and I had never been more than nodding fraternity brothers. He had been on campus only during the last year, having spent the two previous years at the University of Michigan. And in Chicago, he lived at home, hanging around the frat only to play bridge. He was a shark. I didn't play much, and anyway his crowd played for money, and Artie was always pushing up the stakes.

Moreover, I had an obscure hostility toward Artie. I suppose it was because everyone tended to bracket us. We were the prodigies, both graduating at eighteen. Indeed, Artie was ahead of me—he already had his bachelor's—and was loafing along taking a few extra courses.

I resented being paired with him because Artie was, to me, a waster, a playboy. Certainly he was bright, but he used his brightness to get away with everything. He took snap courses, borrowed everybody's term papers. He bragged about his all-A's at Michigan, but I had heard differently—mostly B's and C's. I felt he was just a rich kid who had the carpet laid out for him; he was spoiling what could have been a good mind. And I suppose I was jealous that he had rubbed off the glamour of my being the youngest graduate.

Now Artie pulled me aside, conspiratorially. "Say, Sid, I'll give you a scoop! I can tell you all about that Kessler kid!" And he rattled on, about Paulie Kessler using his private tennis court, about his being in the same class with his own little brother, at the same school he, Artie, had gone to. That's where I ought to look for clues—the Twain School!

I told him I had just come from there. I mentioned the arrest of the teachers, a piece of news that was not yet in the papers. Artie became even more excited. So they had pinched that ass-pincher, Steger! He would lay ten to one they had the right guy! Did I want some inside dope about Steger? He could tell me a few things, all right! His own kid brother, Billy, had been approached by that pervert. Sure. A kid doesn't know what it's all about, but Billy had come home one day and said there was something funny about Mr. Steger, he was always putting his arm around you. Billy had even asked if it was all right to go in Mr. Steger's car. God! What a narrow escape that must have been!

There was no doubt, Artie declared—the cops were on the right trail. Steger must have been monkeying around with Paulie, and killed the boy to keep his mouth shut.

"What about the ransom?" Some of the fellows had gathered around us.

"All right, what about the ransom?" Artie said. "Why not? That's exactly what he'd do. Those poor suckers, those teachers, you know how much they get, maybe twenty-five bucks a week; they see all the kids coming to school with limousines—Christ, what a temptation!" In fact, suddenly Artie was all for the kidnaper—he should have collected from Kessler, the millionaire pawnbroker!

"After killing the kid?"

"I'll admit that was terrible. But you can see, those teachers need money; it's an obvious temptation."

One of the fellows pointed out a flaw: how could the teacher have collected the ransom money if he wasn't absent from school?

"He must have an accomplice!" Artie said. "Probably another pervert!" That school was full of them. He had gone there himself, and he knew.

"Yah, by experience!" Milt Lewis razzed.

"Nothing like Stratmore Academy," Artie retorted, referring to Milt's fashionable military prep school. "There, it's an order!" Turning back to me, he wanted to know what the cops would do to Steger. Had I ever seen the third degree? Would they get it out of him?

"They're not supposed to use it," said Harry Bass, another of our law students. "If they use the third degree, he can repudiate the confession."

"Crap," said Artie. "They've got a way that leaves no marks."

"Yah, in cheap detective stories!" Harry laughed.

Artie appealed to me as an expert, about the rubber truncheons that left no marks. Besides, he said, the cops got them in the balls.

Sure, the police had ways, I said knowingly. Could I go talk to his little brother about Steger?

His mother had the kid in hiding, Artie told me. All the mothers were scared out of their pants. But he would fix up an interview for me.

Too keyed up to sit at the dinner table, I decided to go over to Ruth's. Artie followed me to the door, telling me to be sure to meet him tomorrow. "I'll give you the benefit of my expert knowledge," he half jested. And in the same breath he snagged Milt Lewis, who was passing. "Hey, Milt, you want a sure lay? I've got a terrific number."

*   *   *

Ruth was my girl at that time. Or rather, I should say Ruth was my sweetheart, for there is no period that encompasses my feeling; whenever I think of her, and now as I write of her, the aura of that young love comes back, and I realize that what we then felt was indeed love. We were in love and afraid to know it, and nobody told us it was the true thing. Everybody, all the kids of our time, had endless doubts; we used to analyze ourselves and decide it was only sex attraction, and we didn't quite have the nerve to test that out either.

She was eighteen, a few months younger than I, and a sophomore. We had met on campus, and dated, and petted; in the long moony evenings we spent together we would stroke and excite each other and decide that this alone couldn't be love. She was bright, all A's, and we would discuss the new poetry of Amy Lowell, and we discovered Walt Whitman together, and read his poems of the body aloud to each other sometimes as we lay close side by side on the grass in Jackson

Park. We read them wholesomely, without any suspicion in those days that he could be singing of another kind of love.

And innocently reading Whitman, we used to discuss whether Ruth should give herself to me—that was how we put it—or whether we should wait. And waiting was vague; I had to go out in the world and become a great writer, or something.

Ruth's folks were better off than my family, but still something of the same kind. Her mother, like mine, was always plying you with food, putting a plate in front of you even if you said you had just eaten. I felt comfortable in her house; I called it my second home.

Pushing the bell, I took the stairs two at a time; Ruth appeared in the doorway. "You're a nice one!" she said reproachfully. And only then I remembered we had had a date for the afternoon.

"My God, look at you. Did you even shave today?" her mother demanded, from behind Ruth. "I'll bet you haven't eaten all day either."

"I haven't stopped going since morning!" I said, bursting to tell my big news, but Mrs. Goldenberg disappeared into the kitchen, immediately fetching a bowl of noodle soup, calling, "Well, you're lucky Ruth isn't gone."

"Yes," said Ruth archly. "You might have found me missing, out riding."

"Who with?"

"Oh, a swell machine, a Franklin, stopped at the door," said her mother.

"He honked enough for the whole street to hear," said Ruth.

"Millionaire's manners." Mrs. Goldenberg went back for meat and potatoes.

"In fact, it was a frat brother of yours," Ruth teased. "The sheik of the campus, no less, suddenly remembered I was alive."

"Artie? I just saw him at the house," I said. "I didn't know you go out with him."

Oh, Ruth told me, not really. Sometimes, on campus, they kidded around. So it was odd, the way he had appeared all of a sudden today, saying he was lonesome. He had seemed quite upset.

"It must have been the murder, so close to his house," I said, and pulled the paper from my pocket, spreading it on the table. I had been waiting eagerly to tell my big news.

"Oh, I know," Ruth said. "I read the extra. Isn't it terrible!"

It really was, I agreed—after all, I had really seen it. "You mean this was you? The reporter that identified the body! Oh, Sid!" Ruth's voice hovered between pride and shock.

"Horrible, a horrible crime!" her mother said, and urged me to eat. Chicago was becoming so terrible, you couldn't even let a child go out in the street. And it was I who had reported all this, on the front page? Sid was getting ahead!

"You saw the body? Poor kid." Ruth was gazing at me, as though she could virtually see the child, through me.

I told how the teachers had been arrested, and how Artie's little brother was in the same class.

"I know. Artie told me. That's why he was so upset. He tries to act blasé, but I think Artie is really softhearted," Ruth said.

"Oh yeah," I said. "You'd better watch your step with him. That's how he gets all the girls, with that winsome boyish line."

"Do you think he'll seduce me?"

"No, but he'll say he did."

Her mother disappeared. Mrs. Goldenberg always said she was broadminded and if her girl was going to do anything like petting, it was better for her to do it in her own home than out in a dark car on a dark street. So we sat on the overstuffed sofa in the sun parlor, and I kissed Ruth and put my hand over her breast. That was our limit. We fell into a kind of trance, a melancholy dreamy state of yearning love, mingled with a sense of futility, even of the horror of the world.

"It's so horrible about that little boy," she said.

I remarked that it seemed pretty certain the crime had been done by a pervert.

We were silent for a moment, and then she said in a classroom-questioning voice, "What exactly is a pervert, Sid? I guess I'm supposed to know, but I don't."

I explained, trying not to reveal that my own knowledge was limited. I said it was like Oscar Wilde.

"Oh. That was what the scandal was about him?"

"Uh-huh."

"But then," Ruth said, "aren't they suffering from a sickness?"

It was the first time in the whole day that I had remained still long enough for this thought to come through. And while I might ordinarily have expected myself to concur in this broader view, I found now that the thought made me almost angry.

"We can't forgive crime by calling it a sickness," I snapped. "It was murder, after all. It was a cold-blooded attempt to collect money from a kidnaping. And the perversion was just an added act of viciousness; maybe it was even a cunning way to disguise the rest of the crime."

Ruth had drawn her hand out of mine. I went on, "It's simply like a savage—murdering, and then mutilating his victim out of sheer savagery."

"But, Sid," she said, "why are you so angry? I was only asking, not arguing."

She looked at me so earnestly, her eyes puzzled, and I melted with love of her, and took hold of her and kissed her. In the kiss, our melancholy feeling returned, our loving seasoned with bitterness over the world I had seen that day. We sometimes said we had *Weltschmerz,* but it was more like a presentiment that everything would be vile in our time. On that day it was as though the crime had split open a small crack in the surface of the world, and we could see through into the evil that was yet to emerge.

From the other room, Ruth's mother spoke. "Children, why don't you dance? Put on the Victrola." And after giving us time, an instant for Ruth to smooth her dress, perhaps, Mrs. Goldenberg snapped on the light behind us. "You know, Ruthie," she said, "I'm thinking of bobbing my hair."

E ven though there were only the three of them at the table, Judd's father, neatly carving the roast, gave the meal almost a formal air. This was the way of the Pater. In everything always so certain of how he measured things out. So he must have been in the early days, with Grandfather in the woolen business—measuring with his yardstick, the solemn, upright young Judah Steiner. And so with his honest yardstick he had measured the growth of the woolen house as it was drawn along with the growth of Chicago's garment industry, and with his yardstick he had measured what family to marry into, and purchased woolen mills, and measured his real estate, and his honorable place in the world.

Yet tonight Judah Steiner was trying to speak in a lighter mood to his sons. There was Max's engagement party; next week his fiancée would arrive from New York. Aunt Bertha must see to it, the house should be filled with flowers; it must no longer look so gloomy, so much like a bachelor's den.

Max was sitting there quite proud of himself for the fine piece of merchandise that had been selected for him by brother Joseph in New York, a Mannheimer, no less.

Could it be, actually, that neither of them had heard of the sensational crime? That neither had seen the headlines? Judd considered bringing it up—the topic would be normal enough: the kid had been snatched from Twain, almost across the street. But now the old man was turning to him. Was Judd ready for his exam tomorrow? "A Harvard law entrance should be taken seriously, even by a genius." He chuckled, wiping his mustache. Judd could watch every move in his mind, each word reached for as though it were something in a filing cabinet.

"Huh, he'll probably spend the night chasing tramps with Artie," Max remarked. "That's how a genius prepares. Me, I had to bone."

"Even a genius can trip up sometime; look at the tortoise and the hare," said the Pater. "And how would a genius like to spend the summer preparing for Harvard instead of touring Europe?"

"Try and stop me. I've got the ticket!" Judd said, and all at once like a hand coming down on him was the thought that he really might be stopped in the two weeks before sailing. Should he try to get an earlier boat, leave immediately after tomorrow's exam? Pass the test brilliantly so the old man would . . . He'd go up and glance at his notes. He had them typed up, a complete set, from the session a few weeks ago with Milt Lewis and the fellows. The old man would have his Harvard lawyer to brag about. *Step right up, folks, and see the youngest, smartest LL.D. in the universe, Harvard* cum laude *—Judah Steiner, Jr., son of Judah Steiner, the merchant prince of Chicago!* What if a cop stepped in right now to make the arrest? *Are these your glasses?* What if the old man were told his Junior had achieved the greatest crime in the world? Could he ever understand such a conception? Could he comprehend that there was as much greatness on one side as on the other? Indeed, more. For the crime had to be created against the grain, *à rebours,* and law was with the grain. Judd felt a shivery, perverse wish that the arrest would come, and come that very instant.

His father was passing the pickles, remarking that he had stopped at the delicatessen for them himself. The staff forgot such things since Mama Dear had passed away. "Now Italy—" the old man was saying. "It might be advisable to avoid Italy in these unsettled times." Judd let him talk. The pickles were good. At least this taste they had in common.

"Oh, Italy isn't so bad since that fellow Mussolini took charge," his brother declared. "The country is under control."

"You never can trust the Italians," said his father. "The Italians are a violent and lawless people, with their Black

Hand. Even here in Chicago, all the bootleggers are Italians. With their law amongst themselves, their killings, they give the city a bad reputation."

"Sure, only the Jews are perfect," Judd found himself snapping.

"At least we Jews are law-abiding, and engaged in respectable businesses and professions," his father said.

"All the Italians gave us is Dante and Leonardo da Vinci and Michelangelo and Raphael," said Judd, "Cellini and Aretino."

"Maybe they were a fine people once, but today they are only gangsters."

Max cut in. "I hear this Mussolini is a real leader, bringing back the glory that was Rome—a kind of superman." Judd was startled by Max's use of the word. But Max wore a smile, to show he was for once trying to use his kid brother's intellectual language. "Judd, maybe you can get in to see Mussolini."

"Why, yes, I can give you letters to some important people in the shipping line in Italy. We do business with them," his father said, adding proudly, "You could speak Italian to them."

In Judd's mind, the word *superman* was echoing. The sullen, angry, god-furious figure of Artie, getting out of the car. Yes, Artie was the superior one! Yesterday he had proven it completely. Superior to all emotions. If Artie were through with him now, because of the glasses . . . If Artie turned to Willie . . . The fear came over Judd—Artie leaving him alone. Like last time, before New Year's. The trouble hadn't been his fault then either. Artie had been ready to blame him, and go off with Willie and some girls for New Year's, the one night, the most important night. He would have. Only Judd's letter had kept him. A letter saying everything, analyzing everything, explaining. Now, too, Judd would write a letter. In his mind, Judd began to form the words, showing clearly why the spectacles had to be counted as a shared mistake. Just as the entire experience was shared. For if Artie were really through with him, if Artie started chumming with Willie . . .

Christ, he couldn't! They were bound together now, like when kids take an oath in blood. . . .

Instantly, the blood image welled up, the pulsing spurt, sickening. It was himself, a child. He'd be sick. . . .

Just then the phone rang. Papa gave him a look and emitted a half growl, his usual objection to telephone interruptions during meals.

The maid came to say it was for Junior. Judd's heart bounded. It was Artie, he was sure. He hurried out of the dining room.

*   *   *

When Artie got home from the frat, he noticed quite an assembly still in the dining room, and remembered that Mumsie had wanted to show him off to one of her chums visiting from the East. He walked in, just to have a look at the biddy.

"Arthur!" There was the usual loving reproach in his mother's voice, but relief, too, that he had appeared at last. She was looking wan tonight, a bit overethereal in her greenish dress. The New York woman had bangs and horse-teeth; she was from far back, from that Catholic school of Mumsie's. The brothers were present, too—James, and even Lewis, complete with his recent bride. Full show.

"Arthur, dear, I was beginning to get frightened," his mother said after the introduction.

"Now who would kidnap me?" He laughed.

His father said, "It isn't exactly anything to joke about."

Artie dropped his lip to look contrite. "I know," he said solemnly, and even felt a touch of sorrow. "Poor Paulie. Just the other day I took him on for a game, on the court. You know, for a kid his age he was real good—real strong arm muscles, had quite a smash. He must have put up a real fight with those fiends. I even asked him about buying a racket like his for Billy. Where's Billy? Upstairs? How's he taking it?"

"I tried to keep him distracted," his mother said, drawing in her breath sharply. "But it was such an upsetting day I gave him his dinner upstairs. I'm taking Billy to Charlevoix first thing in the morning. I'm getting him away from here; there's no telling what kind of madman is loose!"

At her words, Artie felt alive, glittery. On the table, they had their dessert: fresh strawberries. Mumsie hadn't touched hers. "Hanging is too good for a fiend like that!" she was saying, her eyes fiery with indignation. "I don't believe in capital punishment, but in a case like this, if they catch him, I think he ought to be tarred and feathered and then strung from a lamppost! Oh!" She shuddered at her own words. Artie reached for her dish and helped himself. "Artie!" But her little sigh admitted her adoration for her incorrigible Artie, admitted that she had ordered the early strawberries especially for him. "At least sit down! Did you have any dinner?"

"I ate at the house. I'm sorry," he apologized to Horse-teeth. "I guess I was upset and excited about this case." He told all about his frat brother, the reporter who had identified the body.

"Poor Mrs. Kessler, she's prostrate, I read," Lewis's bride put in, her cowlike eyes on Mumsie.

Horse-teeth remarked that it was the war, the destruction that had taken place in the war. Life meant nothing anymore.

"Sure, after all that mass killing, human life becomes only an abstraction," Artie pronounced, feeling Jocko would have enjoyed this, and diving into a second dish that Clarice had set before him, without neglecting to brush her bosom close to his face.

"What do you know about mass killing?" Lewis, the war veteran, demanded of Artie. "You were just a kid." Big hero.

"That's exactly when the effect is strongest," Artie replied, glittering at the guest. Bet she'd wet her pants before he was through. "What did we play?" he demanded rhetorically. "Kill the Huns! Mow them down! We even had a scoreboard at school, how many Huns were killed! Hey! I forgot to tell you—I've got the inside news! They arrested a couple of the teachers! Steger and Wakeman! It isn't in the papers yet. Sid Silver told me." He gazed around, reaping their reactions. "I think they're on the right track. You better watch out for Billy, Mums. That school is full of perverts."

"Kiddo! Watch it," his older brother Lewis sniffed, while his father looked pained. James, however, gave him a funny, keen look. James knew too damn much.

His father reminded Artie that it was unfair to come to

hasty conclusions merely because a teacher was being questioned. It could have been any stupid brute.

"Oh, no! Take the ransom letter in the paper," Artie exclaimed. "That's no illiterate crook! That's the letter of an educated man, also of someone who can type. Say, they ought to check every typewriter in that school!"

And in that instant, Artie saw the goddam portable still sitting in Judd's room. Gobbling a last spoonful of strawberries, he leaped from the table.

"Date?" his mother asked.

"Yah. Just remembered."

"Lucky girl," Mumsie smiled. "You at least remember your engagements with her."

"That's the way it is; we've got to resign ourselves." Horse-teeth joined in a tolerant sigh over the younger generation.

"Myra?" his mother asked. "Or would it be violating the etiquette of our flaming youth for a mother to ask?"

"It's a new frail; you don't know her," he said. And on the spur of the moment added, "Ruth Goldenberg." That way she couldn't check up. "Brilliant babe—all A's, and a good dancer. Folks are nobodies."

He rushed to the phone.

*   *   *

Only to hear Artie's voice, breathless, talking in their private code, gave back to Judd a sense of life; even if there were danger, it relieved the caged feeling he had had at the table—the sense of being defenseless there, alone, open to be caught. "I saw a bargain in portable typewriters," Artie was saying, and Judd felt alert again, to match Artie, to catch the hidden meaning. "Thought you might want to pick one up with me, two blocks south of Twelfth Street." That meant two hours before twelve, Artie would be over. And portable typewriters? Judd gasped. Another error! His! And Artie had spotted it. The portable on which he'd typed the ransom letter, Artie leaning over him, suggesting phrases to make it sound real businesslike. The typewriter could give them away! If the glasses were traced to him, and the house searched, the portable found . . . They'd have to get rid of it tonight.

"Thanks," he said. "I was thinking of getting rid of my old portable at that. Two south of Twelfth. I'll go along with you."

As Judd came back into the dining room, preoccupied, Max remarked, "Your chum again?" Max never let up about him and Artie. "You two guys are like a couple of gabby dames. Spend the whole day together and the minute they get home they've got to call each other up! I never could figure out what two guys have got to call each other up about all the time. Weren't you with him all day today? And yesterday?" Max said it jovially, but there was that smutty look back of his eyes. Ever since a certain story had got out about Judd and Artie, a couple of summers before, at the Straus's summer place in Charlevoix, Max had never let up. "What were you guys doing all day long?"

"We went birding."

"I'll bet. Chickens," he said with his fat chuckle, but with an air of letting it go. After all, Judd would be off to Europe soon and that would finally separate him from Artie. Max put a big cigar in his mouth, like the old man, and the two of them resumed talking business.

Judd looked at them, his father and brother, feeling acutely the "who are you?" that he sometimes wanted to blurt out. When his mother had been alive, there had at least been someone for him, at the table, when the "men" got off on their business dealings.

Sure, that same old story about himself and Artie was why the old man had been so easy about the trip to Europe. What a joke it would have been on them if the ransom had been collected and Artie had joined him abroad! Not that Artie still couldn't do it if he wanted to—Artie certainly had the money.

"Too bad Artie isn't going with you," Max's voice banged in; it was frightening how that stupe seemed to sense his thoughts. "You two could have gone birding all over the place. I'll bet you'd have picked up some rare specimens."

Judd didn't answer; but as Max, chortling, went back to the business talk, the whole scene of yesterday flooded Judd's mind. Birding, yes, birding for a rare specimen. Parking the rented car under the tree shade where the branches hung low to give a natural cover, so that from the school entrance the kids could hardly see anyone sitting in the car. And sitting motionless, hushed, just as when birding, until you are part of the landscape itself—a bush, a tree, not hidden really, but a natural part of the environment. Sitting quietly in the car you became part of the street, and you waited for the flock to pour out of the school doors like a flock whirring up suddenly out of a thicket, when quickly you snagged your specimen.

Waiting. "All set?" Artie's eyes flicking, checking the pockets of the car. All the equipment on hand? Nothing forgotten, of the items they had planned, so many evenings, planning this.

In the pocket on Judd's side, handy, the ether cans. The length of clothesline. Artie had wanted a silken cord, but at the last moment they couldn't find one. In the other pocket, on Artie's side, the chisel and the hydrochloric.

What made this the day?

Again Judd saw the last test of the train. "Perfect! Let's set the day!" And even then he had thought of something. What about the car? If someone spotted his car? Artie had the answer—cover up the license, smear mud on it the way bootleggers did, running stuff in from Canada. Anybody'd know the Stutz, Judd objected. Then Artie wanted to make it a stolen car, but Judd said no, that would only increase the danger of apprehension. To make it a perfect crime, the car had to be unidentifiable.

There it hung. Artie became sullen. But driving down Michigan, passing the Drive-Ur-Self place, Judd suddenly had the idea. A rented car. This proved he still wanted to do it, and Artie came partly back. A shitty idea, he argued; if they trace the car, they trace who rented it. You can't just use a fake name; they check references. Okay, Judd had said, we establish a fictitious identity—with references!

That brought Artie back entirely. Shifting closer on the seat, Artie plotted an identity. A fake name. You could open up a bank account. And register in a hotel. Then the personal reference. That was easy. "You give them a number where I'll be waiting, and I'll answer. Why, I've known Jonesey for ten years. He's a fine, upright citizen!"

Great! Judd slapped Artie's knee. Another thing, Judd said. Better take the car out at least once before, so there would be no suspicion.

Artie gave him a glance. Was this more stalling?

It was a whole chain of things, then. It stretched from one week into the next; could it even have stretched till the day never came, till he sailed with the thing undone? Had he really meant to do it?

There was the going down to the Morrison Hotel, Artie throwing a suitcase into the Stutz, the one he claimed he always had ready for registering with a girl. The suitcase felt too light, and Artie threw a couple of books into it, a history from the university library, and H. G. Wells—that made it heavy enough. And what about a name? J. Poindexter Fish, Artie offered, and how about P. Aretino, Judd proposed, and that led to a great game, each outdoing the other. Jack Ripper, Mark Sade, D. Gray, and Peter Whiffle. Or how about making it someone they knew, like Morty Kornhauser, the prig, for causing all that trouble at Charlevoix? Or Milt Lewis, the ponderass? But then, settling down to it, they chose a name from a store window—Singer Sewing Machines. Artie signed *James Singer* in the register, and they went up, and laughed and laughed in the room, and had a drink and fooled around, and then Artie said, "Come on, how about renting the car?"

Leaving the suitcase, they drove up Michigan, and Judd said, "Wait, don't forget the bank account for Mr. Singer." Artie put in three hundred, signing *James Singer, Morrison Hotel* at the Corn Exchange Bank. And then, how about some mail at the hotel for Mr. Singer? They wrote a couple of letters, crazy stuff: *How about a jazz, Jimmy dear? My husband is out of town. Your devoted Cuddles.* It was getting better and better! Next, they would meet Mr. James Singer coming out of the Morrison!

Then, the reference. A name: Walter Brewster. Then, stopping at a lunch counter on the corner of 21st, Judd taking down the number in the phone booth, leaving Artie sitting at the counter, waiting. It was smooth, perfect.

Selecting a Willys at the Drive-Ur-Self. "What business, Mr. Singer?" . . . "Salesman." . . . "Any references in town, Mr. Singer? You know, we are required to have at least one business reference." . . . "Oh, that's all right, you can call—Mr. Walter Brewster." And giving him the number. Then waiting while the dope called. "We have a Mr. James Singer here, to rent a car. . . . Yes? Yes, thank you, Mr. Brewster. Any time we may be of service to you, sir." . . . And driving out with it, picking up Artie at the lunch counter —smooth as silk.

"O.K., let's set the day." Not too soon after the first car rental. So the rental guy wouldn't remember you too clearly. A week must pass, at least. That would be past the middle of May.

And the day his steamer ticket came, Judd had to show it to Artie. Artie's eyes, wise to him, until Judd had to say, "How about writing the note tonight?" That made it so close, it had to happen. The ransom letter ready—*Dear Sir*—and the blank envelope waiting for a name to be written on it. The specimen to be selected. That was it. Life and death, pure chance. The day itself a random choice, yet descended from a million determinants, from the days of testing the train, the days of establishing identity, until Artie said, "Friday?"

And Judd said, "No, I've got the lousy Harvard Law exam." And if it waited past the exam, and past the week end, it would already reach the week before his sailing. Then, Max's engagement party . . .

"All right," Artie gave him that cunning look, and pinned him, moving the date forward instead of farther away. "Wednesday."

And Judd could say nothing except, "Hey, we were supposed to have lunch with Willie."

"The nuts!" Artie said. Willie would be an alibi, ready-made. Wednesday, then. Yesterday.

After his ten-o'clock, driving down Michigan with Artie. "I had one of your cars out, once before. James Singer. Just got back into town." And then the two cars driving back south, Artie ahead of him in the Willys, pushing the speed, and himself racing the Bearcat, nose to tail, as though the cars were magnetized. Then, picking up the last things. The hydrochloric, though he wasn't entirely sure—maybe sulfuric would work faster. But hydrochloric should do it. The first drugstore didn't have it in quarts. Two drugstores, without any luck. At the third, Artie going in, otherwise too many druggists might remember the same short, dark young man with the unusual request. Artie, bringing it. And finally the chisel. A hardware store on Cottage Grove. Artie knowing the kind that was best, the kind with the steel going all the way up through the wooden head.

And then stopping to get Max's boots. And remembering —a silken cord. Artie tramping through the bedrooms. "Hey, how about this?" The cord from the old man's dressing gown. Great!

"No, he might miss it." Then, Artie: "All right, the hell, any piece of rope. Buy some clothesline. Wait, don't forget to pick up the goddam adhesive tape." In the medicine chest.

And then just time enough before lunch to stop in Jackson Park, Artie showing him how to wind the tape around the chisel, thick around the blade—tape makes a perfect grip.

Thus, all set. The lunch at the Windermere, and Willie the dope, Willie the Horrible Hebe with his oily dark face, trying to act real clever, quoting from Havelock Ellis, flashing his medical-student sex-anatomy knowledge, trying to play up to Artie, and never knowing, never having the faintest idea what was going on between his luncheon partners, never in his thick head being even capable of imagining what was in the car they had outside.

And after a long gay luncheon, it was nearly time. Coming out, they ducked Willie, so he wouldn't see the car they were using. Then, on the way to the Twain School, Judd went into his house once more. From the bottom drawer in Max's room, he took the revolver. Artie already had his own, in his pocket.

Even when they were ready on the spot, waiting, so close to the school, it still did not seem that the thing was happening and that the plan would after all be carried out. The school doors opened, and a flock emerged —first a few, then the thick mass of them, spreading over the street. Judd saw himself as he had been among them only a few years ago, the spindly-legged crazy bird, smaller, younger than anybody. "Hey! Genius!" a redheaded comedian would call—"Hey, Genius, I saw a funny bird, right on Ellis Avenue." And, falling for it, "What was it like?" "A Crazy Bird!" and the comedian would be pointing at him, and the whole gang howling. The punks, the snots! Why, even at that time he could name and identify over two hundred species! Judd saw himself, Crazy Bird, hurrying, scuttling across the street, to get away—away from everyone, away from the shrieking, flapping, shoving crowd. He saw himself, that spindly-legged, large-headed kid, and he loathed that genius kid. Yes, Crazy Bird would have been a victim easy to pick off, one kid all by himself on the street.

And maybe picking up one of these punks today would be a kind of revenge for his miserable years in this miserable school. Today's flock, or the flock around him four years ago —all crowds were the same, raucous humanity, stupes. . . .

But coolly, Judd checked himself. What he was doing today was not for revenge. He must have no feelings about those days. Even then, as a kid, he had known that he must not feel anything. That way, nothing could hurt. The stupes couldn't hurt you.

Therefore, no revenge. No emotional connection. This was an exercise in itself, a deed like a theorem, begun and carried out according to its own premise.

"Hey, ixnay." Artie gestured for him to drive on. Too many of these kids were coming toward the car. Some might know them. Artie slid down in his seat, while the car rolled around the block. By then the flock was already broken up. A few kids walked with maids who always called for them, and some lingered in small groups, girls especially, twittering, stopping, starting. Several big cars rolled past, each with a kid or two in the back seat. Then Artie nudged, pointing his chin. "Richard Weiss."

A good one. A cousin of their pal Willie, and a grandson of Nathan Weiss, the biggest investment banker in Chicago, the financier behind all their family fortunes, the Strauses, the Hellers, the Seligmans. Little Richard Weiss was turning into

49th Street; the entire block ahead of him was clear. "After him!" Artie tried to grab the wheel. It took a moment to make the U-turn, and by the time they came to 49th Street, the kid was not in sight.

"Where does he live?" Judd asked. "In this block?"

"No, on Greenwood, I think. Maybe he cut across someplace." Artie leaned forward. "Step on it. Let's double ahead of him." They cruised on Greenwood. Their prey had vanished. Cursing, Artie hopped out at a drugstore to look up the exact Weiss address.

In that momentary interval, the whole thing went down again in Judd. Perhaps losing the kid was an omen that it wouldn't really be done. But Artie came loping out, waving for him to move over from the wheel, then shooting the car three blocks down, on Greenwood. "Where could the little punk have gone?" he muttered angrily, as if the kid had double-crossed them by failing to play his part of the game. They coasted up and down. "The hell with him," Artie said. "Let's go back to the school."

If by now the school street was clear, then today's chance would have been lost, and tomorrow Judd could say he really had to get ready for his exam.

"Hey!" Judd followed Artie's glance. Across from the school, on the play lot—a whole flock of them. "Watch me!" Boldly, Artie walked across to the lot. Judd sat staring, feeling a kind of awe. This was the way of a man entirely above normal fears and rules. So bold an impulse would never have occurred in himself, Judd knew.

Artie walked casually onto the lot. Judd saw him stop and put his arm around his kid brother, Billy. Would he really bring Billy! Not with everybody watching!

He was leaving the lot alone. Judd pulled the car ahead a short distance to get out of sight of the kids. Catching up, jumping into the car, Artie said excitedly, "There's a whole bunch of good ones. Mickey Bass." His old man owned the South Shore Line. "And the Becker kid—but he's pretty husky."

"How about Billy Straus?" Judd suggested. "His old man is the richest Jew in town."

Artie grinned. His knee swung back and forth. A cinch to get that kid into the car. Then he shook his head. "How would we collect? Cops would be all over the house; I couldn't make a move." He looked back toward the lot. "I'll tell you. Let's make it the first good one that leaves the ball game."

They waited. Artie became restless. Motioning Judd to follow, he dodged around behind the play lot; from the alley they could watch the kids—birds with their random movements, stirring on the vacant lot. One runs suddenly. Others hop. They hop and run about on the flat open area, and there seems a kind of pattern, a ritual. Now they all stand attentively. One circles his arm. Another waves a stick and runs. On the field, another may run, while a few move restively on their legs, or stoop and touch the ground. Then a whole little group will converge, join together, and move toward the end of the field, while another group will run out over the field, scattering. To detach a specimen . . .

Artie dodged forward to a closer telephone pole. He was getting dangerously close. And yet not near enough to recognize one kid from another, especially those at the distant end of the field. They seemed to go on endlessly with their ball game. Wait—one kid was leaving. "I think it's Mickey Bass." No, Mickey was still on the field. "Damn it," Judd said, "you need field glasses."

"Hey! You're a genius!" Artie squeezed his arm. "Let's go!"

"What?"

"Let's get your goddam glasses!"

Fleetingly, Judd wondered, was even Artie at that moment giving the whole plan a chance to collapse? Allowing a chance for all the kids to disappear while they went back for the field glasses?

The house was quiet. Up in Judd's room, Artie went straight for the Bausch and Lomb, grabbing the case. "Take it easy!" Judd cried. "They're delicate!"

Standing by the window, Artie focused. "This is the nuts!" You could see part of the playground. "Christ, you could reach out your mitt and grab one of them!"

Judd stood close to Artie. It was one of those moments,

perhaps because of being safe together in the room, and yet in the midst of their wild game—one of those moments when he could almost groan with excitation.

Artie turned to let him use the binoculars. And from the look in Artie's eyes, that almost mocking look, Judd knew that Artie knew. "Come on!" Artie laughed, bounding for the stairs. "We'll miss them!"

Into the car again, and back beneath the tree. They took turns with the field glasses. It was so strange, watching a kid as he bent to tie his shoelace, then stood up, waiting. Like a bird, preening, lifting his head, listening.

Artie said, "One's coming!" Judd started the motor. Then Artie shook his head. "No. I dunno." They waited, the motor running. Judd felt Artie's hand on his thigh, warm, tense, ready. Anything, anything to have times like this with Artie.

A squeeze would be the signal.

On the field, the boys had formed in a knot; it was an argument. Perhaps the game was breaking up.

"The ump," Artie muttered. "I think the ump quit." Then, elatedly: "He's coming! It's the little Kessler punk. Hey! He's just right!"

"Who is he? You know him?" Judd's voice went suddenly high. "They got dough?"

"They own half the Loop. Old man used to be a pawn-broker."

Somehow, with that, the boy seemed the right one. Exactly the right one.

The squeeze came, on his thigh. Let out the clutch, slow, easy, crawling. Let the boy walk ahead a bit, lead your bird.

Artie climbed over to the back seat. They had four blocks to work in, he said; the kid's house was near his own. "Street's clear," he observed happily.

Now they were almost even with the boy. Judd waited for a truck to pass, then coasted along the curb. "Let me handle this. He knows me," Artie whispered, leaning across to the front door. "Don't honk." And as they drew abreast: "Hey, Paulie."

The kid turned. Judd slid the car still nearer to the curb. Conditions were right.

*   *   *

Judd's father's voice cut in, "Thinking about your exam?" The memory images braked, halting sharply. Judd looked up. "I guess I'll do Harvard the honor of glancing at my notes," he said, rising.

Upstairs, he even took out the typed notes. And as he went over them, entire pages of text were revived complete in his visual memory. His hand fell on the Bausch and Lomb, brought upstairs last night; Artie had neglected to put it back in its case. Even in Artie, sloppiness irritated Judd. As he arose to set the glasses away, he thought of the boy they had watched through these sights. Was the image still on the lens? Like the story about the last image on the retina of a murdered man . . .

Judd tried to bone again, and then the sexual excitement came. Always, always when he sat trying to study. He was oversexed, he was sure. Images intruded: a slave, a slave rewarded by his master.

With a little gasp, almost a groan, Judd gave himself over to the fantasy. His master was extended on a stone couch, drinking from a silver cup. His splendid muscular torso was bare, the skin golden, glistening, not oily but luminous.

The slave was no common slave, but had been purchased because of his learning. He was crouched, reading to his master, and the master laughed at the tale, a witty account of an ass, making love to a woman.

As Judd read, he looked up to his master, and saw the half smile, the beginning of excitation. The master's arm lay free, and a short whip dangled from Artie's hand. Artie caught his slavish eyes, and laughingly commanded him, "All right, you bastard, you sucker," and flicked the whip. The slave put aside his parchment and . . .

Then a tumult. An attacker plunged into the room, more, three, five, a dozen assassins. Judd leaped up, defending his master, with his bare hands wresting the sword from one of the villains, charging them, forcing them backward, plunging the sword.

Excited beyond endurance, Judd arose, circled the room, trying to keep away from the bed. It would be an hour before Artie came. Then, making sure the door was closed, he lay down.

He let himself slide completely into it, without fixing on any one image, letting the images come one upon the other: a street in Florence, and figures in capes and tight trousers, a young man, blond—Artie—rushing into a shadowed alleyway, a grinning backward, inviting glance, and then it was yesterday and the little girls scattering in twos and threes on the street, and why had Artie always been against making it a girl? Maybe that would finally have rid him of the need, but now he still had something left over that he must do. The girl . . . and there came the image of the Hun and the girl, the war poster in the hallway when he was at Twain—the young Frenchwoman with the dress half torn crouching against a wall, her arm up in defense, and the Hun with the slavering mouth coming toward her, then grabbing her by the hair and doing it to her. Then the almost naked body of the woman, the limbs all awry, broken, in a field of grass . . .

With an effort, Judd pulled himself up from the bed. The typewriter. It was standing against the wall, beneath the glass cases of his mounted birds. Picking up the portable, Judd held it undecidedly, set it on his desk, removed the lid. For this second terrible mistake, Artie would be through with him. Artie would erase all their times together, as though they had never met.

*   *   *

It had been one of the last occasions when Mother Dear had been well enough to go out. Indeed, she had probably overstrained herself, Judd imagined, in arranging the visit for his sake. He had known it was a little plot, of the kind Mother Dear and Aunt Bertha loved to arrange, in their little schemes to manage other people's lives.

For a long time he had been aware of their whispery worryings about him. Poor Judd, he ought to have more friends. He's alone with his books too much. And even when he goes out birding, he'll drive off with the chauffeur on a

Saturday afternoon and leave the car to go way out someplace all by himself.

Poor Judd, they meant, the kids all hate him. The kids all think he's conceited. But poor Judd, they said, all the boys in his class are three years older than he is, and at that age three years makes a great difference. And he's really not interested in baseball and such things. If we could only find someone . . .

And then they had cooked up the meeting with Artie. Of course Judd knew about Artie, the paragon who had skipped through Twain a year ahead of him, and was even a few months younger. He would have got to know Artie at Twain, most likely, if Artie hadn't transferred to University High in his last year, to go right into the university at fourteen.

But when people talked about Artie Straus, the brilliant prodigy, Judd always remarked that entering a university at fourteen was not necessarily a criterion of intelligence. Any parrot with a large enough medulla oblongata could absorb the kind of knowledge that was required in a classroom. Judd could easily have done it at fourteen instead of fifteen, if he had not been out of school with his terrible skin rashes and boils, for weeks at a time. And besides, Artie Straus, as everyone knew, had had special tutoring from his governess.

Yet Judd admitted to himself a certain curiosity about Artie Straus. He therefore accepted the pretense that it was just a casual afternoon bridge party at the Strauses, to which he was escorting his mother and aunt. And if there had been hushed telephone calls between the ladies, to arrange this meeting for the two brilliant boys who really ought to be great friends, he pretended not to have noticed. Judd disregarded, too, the thought that although his own family was worth several million dollars, his mother and aunt would consider it advantageous for him to become the close associate of one of the Strauses, with their ten million and their palatial new mansion with the private tennis court. Only the best, as his father always said.

There was another uneasiness about meeting Artie. While Artie was brilliant like himself, Artie was more. He was an athlete, a fellow who had fun with the crowd. Tall, a lively figure on the tennis court—instead of a bookworm.

Still, Judd was aware that on his side he was supposed to exert a steadying influence on Artie, because the moment he had got into the university, young Straus had started running wild, with collegians who were several years older than himself. And recently Artie had had a bad smashup in a car.

*   *   *

It was a warm, sweet day in May, and as they left the house Mother Dear paused to sniff the air—she could catch the scent of the lake, she said. Judd offered her his arm, and she give him her smile, the Madonna smile. The smile he had identified far back in childhood when his Irish nurse had taken him into a church with stained-glass windows. "Is this Heaven?" he had whispered, and of the glowing Lady in the window: "Is she God's wife?" Then the nursemaid had told him who the Madonna was. The Mother of God. And though as soon as he began to grow up he knew himself an atheist, the Madonna image persisted as someone in whom he believed, and as his mother; even the most empirical of scientists, he told himself, retain certain curious irrational beliefs.

That day of the bridge party, as Judd helped his mother down the cement steps to the walk, his aunt gushed about the fine-appearing pair they made. Mother Dear was in something gray, gray silk—he wished he could recall precisely—and he, nearly fifteen, was still in knickerbockers, although they were tailored wide, to look more like golf plus-fours.

"You will meet Artie Straus," Aunt Bertha insisted again. "I asked Mrs. Straus if Artie would be home. You know, Judd, dear, Artie can give you lots of pointers about the university, what teachers to take."

"Professors," he corrected her.

Aunt Bertha had come in her electric, and now gave him a chance to drive it the few blocks to the Straus mansion. Driving the Edison always gave Judd a kick, though he already could drive a regular car and was campaigning for the old man to get him his own sportster for graduation. If he came first in his class, it was a half promise.

"I hear Artie is a nice fun-loving boy, and I hope you will

become friends," his aunt kept on, not realizing how a remark like that could push a fellow in the other direction. Especially if they were working on Artie the same way.

But Artie came running out of the house as the electric drove up. With a politeness that might have had some mockery behind it, he opened doors.

At first sight, Judd felt disappointment. It was an instant feeling that Artie wasn't for him, Artie wasn't the one. His long narrow face was like tallow. And everything about him was too long—his arms, his neck, his fingers. Even before emerging from the car, Judd knew he would scarcely reach to Artie's shoulders. A shrimp in any crowd, beside Artie he would look like a midget.

And at that moment Judd found himself thinking of Rocky, his camp counselor the summer before—the bronzed and muscled Rocky, whom he had pictured, every night as he lay in his bunk, as his king of slaves. . . . Artie would never be anything to him. Judd even felt a kind of triumph that he had come along as Mother Dear and Aunt Bertha wished, but had proven immune to their plotting. He would remain his solitary and superior self.

Artie was charming to the ladies; he had those manners. Helping Mother into the house, he said he would park the electric—he loved electrics; his own aunt had one exactly like this, the same model, and he made a joke about all aunts coming equipped with Edisons. Then Judd saw Artie spin the machine around the curve of the driveway, as if it were a speedster.

It was a small bridge party of ladies, several of whom Judd had seen at his own house—Mrs. Seligman, Mrs. Kohn with a K, and Artie's mother, a thin, energetic-looking woman, with great, clear blue eyes. Judd remembered that she was not Jewish and was always held up as an example, when Hyde Park talk turned on mixed marriages, of a Catholic who fitted very graciously into the South Side Jewish circle—indeed, took the leadership.

There were three tables. Mrs. Straus warned everybody that Artie was a whiz, a shark. Oh, yes, since the two brilliant boys were going to be partners, the ladies had better watch out!

Judd wished they would settle down to the game—he couldn't stand chitchat, all the ladies clucking over him and trying their bits of French and Italian on him because they had heard he was such a genius at languages. He got aside for a moment to glance over the titles in a bookcase, but it was just the usual stuff, sets of Thackeray and Dickens. Mrs. Straus was said to be a highly intelligent woman and a great reader; indeed, she was the moving spirit of the Hyde Park Literary Circle, where famous authors like Theodore Dreiser had lectured. A copy of the new sensation, *Main Street,* lay on the table.

"Why don't you take Judd up to your room? We'll call when we're ready," Mrs. Straus suggested to Artie, who motioned—"C'mon!"—and took the stairs two at a time.

The room was as a collegian's room was supposed to look, with pennants and sports stuff on the walls—tennis rackets and even crossed fencing foils. Immediately, Artie lighted a cigarette, and offered his Caporals to Judd. "Smoke?" Judd accepted one, remarking that his own preference was for the Turkish brands.

It was too bad he was going to register at the U. of C., Artie told him at once. That was no good because you had to live at home and you couldn't fool around too much—they had their eye on you. He himself was going to switch to Michigan, to Ann Arbor, in the fall. Another thing, the girls at the U. of C. wouldn't put out. "You interested in girls?" And in the same moment, Artie opened a heavy atlas that was on his desk. "I keep them in here so the spies won't get wise." And he handed Judd a packet of postcards.

They were French cards. Judd had never seen any before, but he made it his rule always to be inwardly prepared for anything. He didn't flicker. The cards were certainly unaesthetic, particularly the females—the way their half-removed clothing dangled and dripped. In one, the man was nude. Muscular, he made Judd think of Rocky, poised for a swim. Handing back the postcards, he said, "Not bad," and Artie said he could get Judd into Alpha Beta, only they were a bunch of sissies, the whole gang—he'd bet a ten-spot half of them were still cherry. "You cherry?"

Judd grinned ambiguously. He was saved from the need to answer further by Mrs. Straus calling from downstairs, "Boys, we're beginning."

"Hey, I got an idea," Artie said. "You want to have some fun with these hens? Let's have some signals."

That was the first spark between them; the idea of defrauding these clucking women was pleasant to Judd. Artie proposed finger signals, but Judd feared even those dumb females might catch on. His own idea was word signals. Let the first letter of the first word you spoke represent the suit, say, for clubs, any word beginning with a *C*. Then the number of words in the remark would be the number of cards of that suit. His mind leaped ahead, even to word signals for the high cards, but Artie said he had a better system. He would tap Judd's toe under the table—that's what long legs were good for. Once for spades, twice for hearts, and so on. Then you tap the number held in each suit.

"What if they catch you?"

"They never catch me." Artie laughed, and his mother called again, and the boys went downstairs.

*   *   *

As the foot reached, pressing on his toes, Judd felt an odd combination of mischievousness and tense excitement. He lost count of the taps. He messed up the bidding. But Artie played with bravado and brilliance, and fished them out of the mess. Afterward they got a little better at it. Then they got so good, the women *ooed* and *aahed,* and Judd found himself giggling with the secret fun. Then Artie's mother made a remark about how nervous he was, his legs rattling all the time, and Judd got scared and drew back his feet, holding them under the chair. He gave Artie a meaningful look.

They came out winners, nearly five dollars apiece, and during the coffee and French pastries, Artie took him upstairs again and produced a hidden flask of gin. Then Artie wanted to try Judd's aunt's electric to see if it could get up any more speed than his own aunt's Edison.

In the driveway, the two electric cars were lined up. Aunt

Bertha's still had the key in it. And Artie suddenly had a thought. He tried the key in the second car. It fit. All those Edisons must have the same key!

And so it started. Artie came over for bridge one evening, Judd and Artie trimming Aunt Bertha and Mother Dear, using Judd's word system this time. Then Artie borrowed Aunt Bertha's electric, and, while he was out, had a duplicate key made. Artie was car crazy, but since his accident, his family very strictly wouldn't let him drive.

One afternoon he said, "Hey, how about some fun?" And he and Judd walked into a garage on Harper and tried the key in an Edison, driving the buggy right out. The garageman's face fell open half a yard as they passed him—what a riot! But after a few blocks he was chasing them in his repair truck. You couldn't get any speed on an electric, Artie cursed, so he slewed it against the curb and they both leaped out, lamming down an alley and dodging across a vacant lot, Artie pulling Judd quickly behind a shed. Artie held up the key he had saved, and they laughed.

It was there in the sun, laughing, pushed up close together against the wall, that Judd first saw Artie differently. His face was no longer pasty but alive, his eyes shone, and his body had suddenly a lanky grace. And that night in his imagining, when Judd waited for Rocky, the king, to come into his fantasy, it was Artie.

*   *   *

Every afternoon they were together. They swiped another electric and whizzed down Cottage Grove. Then, while they were in an ice-cream parlor, a cop looked in and asked if anybody belonged to that electric. Judd almost piped up, but Artie kicked his foot. A stolen-car alarm must already have gone out. They kept their faces in their sodas until the cop departed.

Electrics were too risky, too slow, Judd said. Anyway for graduation he would have his own car, a red Stutz Bearcat. Artie was almost more eager than Judd for that day.

There it was, sitting in the driveway when he came home from Twain's silly, juvenile graduation exercises. Red as a fire engine, and with a rumble. Artie must have been waiting around the corner, for he appeared at once, tested the horn, sprang open the rumble. "Just right for picking up gash!" he said. "Ideal for two couples."

Immediately after dinner, Artie was back at Judd's house. It was a moonless night. Max haw-hawed, and even Mother Dear joked about the two young men going out to do the town. Judd could imagine their remarks after he had left. "It's a good thing for him to have some fun; he's much too serious." Or: "Let him sow a wild oat or two," Max would declare grossly, using every cliché in the book. "Artie may not be any older," Max would say, "but he's been around. He'll show Judd a good time."

So the family stood in the doorway waving them off on their adventure, with admonitions to be home early, now, and don't do anything wild.

The first thing Artie did was to stop at a drugstore on Stony Island where he said he could get the real stuff. "Your share is three bucks," he told Judd when he came out with the pint. Judd knew that Max never paid more than three dollars a pint, so this was the entire price he was paying; but he gave Artie the money, telling himself this way he would have something on Artie, even while Artie thought he was being fooled.

Then Artie wanted to take the wheel, but Judd decided to establish firmly from the first that it was his car, and he would be the driver. Artie shrugged.

In the park they had a few swigs, then Judd said how about a fond farewell to the institution? They drove down to Twain, gazing upon the brick castle, dark and solid as a prison. "Why is it the tradition that one is supposed to look back upon one's Alma Mater with affection?" said Judd. "All I experience is relief at no longer having to have daily contact with those imbeciles."

Artie climbed out of the car. A pile of bricks was lying there, where a wall was being repaired. He picked up a few, handing one to Judd. There was a corner window, where old Mr. Forman always stood, whirling his watch fob.

"Here's to Old Foreskin!" Artie saluted. They heaved, and glass rained down. Climbing into the car, they roared off. Judd was actually laughing out loud. "Too bad he wasn't standing behind the window as usual!" He nearly doubled over the wheel, finding the image so funny.

Artie still had a brick in his hand. Judd drove to Lake Park. It was a crummy street, with few lights. A good street for gash, Artie remarked, though mostly professionals, and he didn't want to get himself another dose just yet. Of course Judd might as well get the experience, he taunted; Judd was cherry, and never even had a dose. But it wouldn't be long now. . . . There was a pair! Slow down!

And so they coasted and blew the horn, but no dice, and they went through the same routine with other pairs. Then at one moment Artie spied a perfect store window and heaved his brick; the Stutz had wonderful pickup, roaring away from the clattering, collapsing glass.

They circled, stopped a block off, and sauntered over. Two men were struggling to block up the window—it was a shoe-repair shop—and a dozen rubbernecks had already assembled, giving each other versions of what had happened.

The owner kept telling how he ran down from upstairs. "Who do this to me? Why anybody do this to me? I work hard——"

"Maybe it was the Black Hand," Artie suggested. Turning to Judd, he said, "Looks like a typical Black Hand job to me. This is just a warning."

"That's right," Judd said. "The next time they give him the works."

Police arrived and scattered the crowd. Back in the car, Artie and Judd laughed themselves silly, Artie mimicking the terrified cobbler: "Black Hand! I don't know no Black Hand!" And the most wonderful part of it, sensed for the first time there, was that they two together were a kind of secret power, like their own Black Hand—they could stand right there in the midst of the crowd, and nobody could even suspect they were the ones.

For Judd, this was a kind of proof. As a kid, parents tried to make you fear an all-watching God, and ever after that you felt a kind of fear that if you did something, people might somehow see it on you. But there was nothing! Nothing

showed! You did whatever you damn pleased. And that was
Artie's philosophy.

They drove downtown, came back up Michigan, and
passing 22nd Street, Artie said, "Hey, how about going to
Mamie's? Come on, I bet you never even had a piece. Tonight's the night."

Judd felt the blood flooding his brain. He wanted to get it
over with, and yet something in him was repulsed. "I don't
like to pay for it," he said. "I'd rather pick something up."

"Yah, you'll pick something up all right." Artie laughed,
but they tried a few streets. Garfield Boulevard he said was
good for gash hunting. They drove up and down the length of
it, a few times spotting pairs of strolling girls, and once coast-
ing slowly while Artie went through a long conversation with
two stupid gigglers. The whole time, Judd's head was pounding with scenes from *Fanny Hill*, which Artie had lent him to
read. Despite his excitement, he wanted to roar away from the
two females, with their smeared mouths. Why should a man
have to demean himself to make vapid remarks to such brain-
less creatures, merely for biological release!

He had never allowed himself to develop a crush. The
girls in his classes were all older than he. They treated him
like a flea. There was a cousin, a year younger, whom he had
taken to the prom, a wispy, fairywaist girl, but she had talked
all the time about who was in love with whom, and when he
had said it was merely a biological impulse, and had kept on
referring to girls as females, Alice had announced that she
didn't think his line was clever at all; it was simply disgusting.

But it *was* biological. And that was what dragged a man
down. From way back, from deep in childhood, Judd had the
feeling that the entire female mechanism was nauseating.
Somehow he knew about the blood, from far back with that
fleshy fat governess, Trudy. Occasionally at night the almost
suffocating sense of her came over him. More often it was the
girl in the war atrocity. In different ways—dragged out of her
bed, or huddling in a barn. And dark female blood. Over her,
the stiffnecked officer in uniform. Sometimes it was like the
military-school uniform Max wore, buttoned to the chin,
when he came home for the holidays. And lately Artie, he and

Artie running from the cops, the cops firing after them, and Artie pulling him behind the telegraph post in the alley, laughing. And there in the alley, the girl from the war poster . . . Judd would surrender himself to his excitement, at the same time cursing the terrible need that nature had forced upon an intelligent being, the tormenting, relentless sex need. . . .

That first evening in the car they didn't have any luck. But one night just before Artie and his folks were going up to Charlevoix for the summer, they connected.

The pair they picked up were on 63rd Street, just west of Cottage, where the street gets dark under the El. After the girls got into the car you could see they were a little older; they had creases in their necks. Judd's girl put her hand on his knee right away, and from behind Artie called, "She wants to know if we carry a blanket!" All four exploded with merriment. Still laughing, Judd's girl lifted his right hand from the wheel and placed it on her thigh. One-arm drivers were her favorite, she said.

He drove straight out on 63rd, beyond the new airfield there, and on the way the girl said she hoped he wouldn't get the wrong idea about her, though she and her friend loved to be taken places, and of course every girl loved to receive presents, but she hoped he wouldn't get the wrong idea. Then she tilted back her head and sang "Margie," and he was relieved, not having to make conversation.

When they parked, the girls got out on different sides of the car, as if by habit. They kept calling to each other with suppressed but shrieky laughter. It was a sultry night and there were mosquitoes on the field; Judd kept getting bitten. He felt angry at the need in himself to do this. Just as he embraced her, the girl looked into his face in a serious way and said, "You all right? I never had anything, honest; I swear." It took him an instant to realize that she meant the disease. "Sure, I'm okay," he gasped, but he was completely invaded by fear, wanting to quit, for probably she did have it, and he thought of Artie on the other side of the car—Artie not caring if he gave the girl a dose, and sure, that was the way to be—the hell with all females—and even as the girl guided him, Judd's mind was filled with images of Artie giving it, with godlike anger and vengeance, to the twat.

Judd's climax came instantly. The girl emitted a low, surprised "Hey?" and then an odd little laugh. He didn't want her to look at him. There was light enough so that he could see every particle of powder on her face; and her bangs had been brushed back, disclosing her low, sloping forehead—practically no forehead at all, apelike. He had read about the feeling of after-disgust. But he was sure that what he felt was more, much more. Utter nausea. He had done it quickly, to have the least possible contact with her, yet she was trying to hold him to her, to be playful. He couldn't find a word to say to her. Instead, all the while, he was trying to hear, to see, Artie. Laughter and squealing came from the other side of the car, and then silence, and his own girl giggled at what must be going on there. And then they heard Artie's partner. "You had too much gin, sonny." And then that girl had jumped up, shaking straight her dress, and Judd's girl stood up as at a signal.

Suddenly the girls began jabbering gaily again, and suggesting places to dine and dance, calling them "sports." It was as if the intercourse itself had been some minor preliminary. But he didn't want to go anywhere with them; he didn't even want to be in the car with them driving them back to where they had been picked up. Judd managed to conceal his distaste while returning up 63rd Street. The girl sank back into her singing, but now, over and over again, it was "Constantinople."

Judd finally remarked, "You think you can spell it now?" and she said, "Say!" Then her partner called from behind, "How about going to the show at the Tivoli? Pola Negri's playing." Artie quickly made up a big story in his bootlegger role about having to meet a certain connection in a certain spot in Little Italy. No dames.

Judd pulled up at the corner, and just as the girls were beginning to look angry, Artie slipped his a ten-spot, saying that would take them to the show and maybe the Stutz would be waiting when they came out, if he finished his deal.

Judd's girl, smiling, offered her mouth, repeating, "I

hope you won't think we're that kind." He couldn't stand to kiss her; he zoomed the car away before Artie was half settled beside him.

Artie shook his head, laughing. What a pair of bags. With a bag like that he never could get really excited.

Only then Judd understood that Artie hadn't done it. And suddenly his own nausea was gone. Artie kept on talking. It was no kick with a cheap slut, a semipro. And Judd said females were disgusting anyway; all of them were disgusting. It was a foul trick of nature to make a man need to consort with the creatures. They took a swig to get the taste out, and then Artie had an idea for some fun. Back on 63rd were some sheds, and he had an idea.

They drove west again and Artie picked out a shed at the end of a vacant lot, just an old shed—couldn't hurt anybody. He got out of the car and went to the back of the lot and found some old newspapers and cardboard. He lighted a little bonfire against the wall of the shack. They waited till it caught on, then circled the block, coming back to see the whole shed ablaze.

Artie put his arm on Judd's shoulder, watching. Judd felt cleansed. He wished he had thought of this himself. How Artie's eyes glittered! He felt the wine of full friendship in them at last.

Soon they heard the fire engines coming.

*   *   *

Lying on his bed, one ear cocked for footsteps, Judd restrained himself. He wouldn't give himself to the final exciting imaginings, for at any moment Max or his father might come upstairs. If he locked the door they might suspect, and that would be worse. At last he heard them on the stairs, talking; Max was going to drive downtown to a show, and would leave the old man for a card game at the club, picking him up after the show.

Good! They wouldn't be here when Artie came.

And the image was upon him, of the first time with Artie. On the train going up to Charlevoix to be Artie's summer guest. It was an overnight ride, and Artie had taken a compartment, and once they were in it Artie had unloaded a bottle and a deck of cards—this would be one big night. They had scouted the train looking for a couple of bims, but all the time Judd had felt sure they wouldn't really find any; it would be themselves, the two of them in the compartment.

Judd had taken along the *Perfumed Garden* in French, and he translated a few of the best parts to Artie while they played a couple of hands of casino, a nickel a point, Judd winning. And all the time they were drinking, and Artie was getting looser, the way he had of clowning so you couldn't tell exactly whether he was tight or only pretending to be tight. Artie talked of all the girls they would have in Charlevoix—he had them lined up; he knew some terrific lays on the farms around there; it would be a great summer—and all the while Judd kept feeling freer and bolder, and the pounding was in him.

He hardly knew how—perhaps he was half drunk himself, maudlin—they were patting each other. "Old pal." Maybe singing. Then they started to go to bed. Artie lost the toss for the lower, but refused to abide by the decision. He dove into Judd's bunk, and Judd started to push Artie out; and then horsing around like that, wrestling, they lay extended together to catch their breath, and when it began Artie made no sign, pretending to be half-drunkenly half asleep. Then Artie laughingly muttered a few dirty names, and let it happen as if he were too drunk to know or care.

In the morning they said nothing about it, both pretending to have been drunk. The Straus car was at the station for them, and they drove up to the place, the terrific showplace the Strauses had on the bluff over the lake, a reproduction of a castle on the Rhine.

They had adjoining bedrooms.

*   *   *

"Junior," Max called from the hallway, and Judd leaped up from the bed and went to the door, to be told about their going downtown. Then he forced himself to sit at his desk again and look at his law notes while waiting for Artie.

*   *   *

As he hung up the receiver after calling Judd, Artie experienced one of those dark surges of feeling, a wave of deathliness, as if he could have sent a wave of death through the telephone and seen Judd stricken by it, paralyzed, turned to stone. Electrocution by telephone. That would be a good mystery-story idea, and it might sometime even be possible. Himself, the master criminal. He'd call up his enemies, and then they would be found dead, telephone in hand.

He saw Judd, sitting like that. And picturing it, Artie felt a flash of comprehension: Judd wanted to be caught and executed. For if you left things around like that, the glasses, the typewriter, you wanted to get caught. Like the kind of girl that leaves hairpins all over the back seat. She wants it to be known.

So Judd was a terrible danger to him. Rage and grief shuddered through Artie. Spoiled, spoiled, why did that punk bastard have to go and spoil the whole thing! All the other things he had done, the things he had done by himself, were done without a trace. Artie himself could not prove that he had done them. The last one in winter, the ice-cold night, the upturned coat collar covering the face, the tape-wound chisel in his pocket, hard against his hand, then the body falling off the pier into the lake. Had he done it, or only pictured it to himself?

That was the sad part of doing things all by yourself, on your own. You lost them. You really needed someone else to be in a thing with you so that the deed stayed alive between you.

Then all the little things he and Judd had done together, the fires and the thing at the frat house in Ann Arbor—all those things rose up in Artie and pleaded for Judd. Pleaded for dog-eyes Jocko. But Artie wasn't sure. He would decide about Judd after they had got rid of the typewriter. Perhaps, if the feeling came over him . . . He put his automatic into his pocket.

Artie did not fail to call out good-bye to the family, flashing a charming smile at Mumsie's guest. Then, though it was the wrong direction for Judd's, he walked past the Kessler house. Only one police car was parked there now.

In that house, were they getting any clues leading to him? Ah, let them follow him now! Instead of leading them to his accomplice, he would throw them off the track! And Artie turned up Hyde Park Boulevard, toward Myra's. Let Judd sit waiting, worrying.

Suddenly Artie felt keen and light. He laughed out loud, thinking of Judd sitting under his glass cages of stuffed birds, gnawing his fingernails.

*   *   *

In the gilded lobby of the Flamingo there sat the usual two groups of little ladies in retirement, and Artie could sense the buzz among them as he passed toward the elevators: there goes the brilliant Straus boy, youngest university graduate, they were saying, and surely plotting about catching him for their nieces and granddaughters. This always gave him a kick; he loved the old biddies, ready to lay out all their girlies for him.

Myra's mother herself opened the door, welcoming him, but with an air of confusion. "Why, Artie! Hello, Artie. It's so nice to see you, but you know Myra's just going out."

Myra bubbled out from her room; she had not quite finished dressing, and was holding a sash for her beaded green frock. He and she always laughed as soon as they saw each other, a kind of surprised and even silly laugh—*Well, look at us!* And a kind of guilty conspiratorial laugh, like the times as kids when they were almost caught playing doctor. Yet despite the laughter, Myra's eyes were always melancholy, befitting a poetess, and she talked in breathless rushes of words, curiously like Artie.

Her date was a goof, she said, a football player. She had been roped in, but "When he is silent, I can imagine he is a Greek god. Oh, I want to have lots of lovers, like Edna St. Vincent Millay."

Her mother, assuming a calm knowingness, always let Myra run on, sure it was all mere talk. And while Myra rushed back to her room to find a poem she had just written, Mrs. Seligman managed to inquire conventionally about his family. How was his mother? How was his father's blood pressure?

Fine, Artie said, everyone was fine, but Mumsie was rushing to Charlevoix tomorrow morning with little Billy, because of that terrible crime—wasn't it a monstrous thing? And spying a huge box of candy, Artie poked his finger into one of the chocolates. "Aha! Liquor!" he cried, sucking the finger, and then poking it down the entire row of candies while Mrs. Seligman giggled in horror—"Really, Artie!"

"He's wacky!" Myra called. He walked into her room.

Myra thrust herself up against him and kissed him briefly, moving the tip of her tongue, and gyrating her abdomen to show she knew how to be wicked. She broke off and pulled back, looking at him intently with her huge brown eyes. "Is anything wrong, Artie?"

The girl made him impatient sometimes with her understanding looks. He said, "Nah, I just got the willies," and she said he had to hear her new sonnet. She always sent her sonnets to the Line O'Type column in the *Tribune*, signing them "The Dark Lady," and occasionally they were printed. The new one lay on her desk, over an open copy of Baudelaire, in French; Myra was trying some translations.

"My Unfaithful Lover" was the title; Artie picked it up and read out loud. "I share my lover with the wingspread sail—"

She shared her lover with the sleet, the gale. He said it was swell.

They were, of course, not lovers. And yet she was in love with Artie; she had loved him since she was a little girl. They were remote relatives, fifty-eleventh cousins they called themselves, Myra always explaining, with a bubble of laughter, that anyone whose family owned Straus stocks was a cousin. Her father had been one of the founders.

She called Artie "lover," as a kind of promise within herself that it would one day be he. She was sure she knew the Artie others didn't know; she knew an Artie who was not always shining and being smart, but who was torn. This she cherished as a love secret. Sometimes when they were out together, Artie would admit to having the blues; he would drop his air of good-time frenzy for a despondent silence, and then Myra would feel that he was hers, that she was the only one with whom he could act this way, and she would be sure Artie was much deeper than he let on.

So now he said there was nothing wrong, he just was sick of the world, had a touch of the blues, and that reminded Myra of a terrific place she had heard about, downtown, where they had a wonderful blues singer. It was in a cellar on Wabash. Why not go there tomorrow?

He agreed; maybe they would make it a double date.

Myra groaned. Not Judd.

Well, he had sort of agreed to help Judd celebrate his Harvard exams tomorrow. Why did she always have to pick on Judd?

"Maybe I'm jealous." Myra laughed without meaning anything. But she simply couldn't see why he let that dreary drip hang around.

It was not a new argument. Especially if you went in a crowd, she said, Judd was so unlikable, with his conceited ideas, and his eyes that never blinked.

Aw, Artie told her, Judd was a brilliant little sonofabitch, and the reason he was so unpopular was that people knew they were inferior to him.

"I don't care how brilliant he is, he gives me the creeps," she said, trying to pin on her sash.

Well, Artie admitted, maybe he let Judd hang around so much partly out of pity because the guy had no friends.

"So you nearly get yourself thrown out of your fraternity for his sake."

Anyway, Judd would be going abroad in a few weeks.

The bell rang; it was her date. Artie grabbed the sash from Myra, and holding it around his waist, shimmied into the other room. Her mother had just opened the door, and Artie swayed toward the young man there, announcing, "I'm your date. Myra has just been kidnaped."

"Don't mind him. He's my wacky cousin, just dropped in from Elgin," Myra said, taking the sash, and then Artie solemnly declared that he was sorry he couldn't join them on their date—he had an appointment to hijack a shipment from Canada. He seized Myra and gave her a passionate kiss in front of the young man and her mother. "Don't drink any wood alcohol," he admonished, whisking out of the apartment, laughing.

*   *   *

Why *did* he let Judd hang onto him? Her question resounded as he walked. Certainly he had been too damn softhearted in letting Judd hang on. Ever since the beginning, every piece of trouble had been on account of Judd, and now Dog Eyes had brought him to the edge of real danger.

Walking on Stony Island, purposely past the police station, Artie was now conducting the trial of Judd Steiner. All-powerful, in his hands was the life-or-death decision.

Take the second summer Judd came up to Charlevoix. They hadn't seen each other much that year, because that was the year Artie had transferred to Ann Arbor. Morty Kornhauser, from the Ann Arbor chapter of Alpha Beta, was visiting him just then, too.

Sunday morning, Judd had to walk into Artie's room through the connecting bathroom, to wake him up. They were going canoeing to an island where Artie knew a couple of girls —fishermen's daughters. As Judd started pulling him out of bed, Artie made a playful grab, and then they were wrestling and fooling around.

And Morty had to walk in. They didn't even hear him. Morty had a sneaky way of slipping around, with a look of apologizing for intruding. Who the hell knew how much he had watched, before Judd finally noticed him standing there with his mouth open like at some goddam stag show?

Artie made the best of it and said, "Want to join the fun?" But that prig Morty said, "No, I don't indulge, excuse me"—and walked out.

For a while they lay silent, except for that silly giggle Judd had. There was nothing to laugh about; Morty was the biggest tattler at the frat. Then, when they were putting on their trunks, Judd remarked, "Hey, didn't that sonofabitch say he can't swim? It might be dangerous for him in a canoe."

Their eyes caught, and Judd let out his giggle. The day before, when they had all gone down to the lake, Morty had indeed remarked that he didn't swim. With three boys in a canoe, anything could happen.

They hurried down to breakfast, so as not to give Morty

a chance to talk to anyone. Then, rather sullenly, he walked down with them to the boathouse.

When they were a good way out on the lake, Artie stood up, complaining, "For crissake, Judd, you don't know your paddle from your asshole," and Judd insulted him back and started a scuffle. Before Morty knew what was happening, they were all in the water.

They saw the bastard come up thrashing. He glared at them, and with his mouth full, sputtered, ". . . on purpose!" and then went under, thrashing. They swam away. But Judd looked back, treading water. Morty was flailing, but keeping his head up.

Artie saw it, too. The whole damn thing was Judd's fault, he swore. He'd heard the bastard wrong. "I don't swim" didn't mean "I can't swim."

Morty came ashore some distance from them, and they hurried over to him solicitously. Panting, he gasped out, "You did it on purpose. I know, you filthy degenerates!" His eyes were narrow, meaningful. He wouldn't walk back with them, but trailed, slowly, by himself.

All day, they stuck to him. When they told the story of the accidental overturning of the canoe, he was silent. And that night he discovered he had to cut his visit short and return to Lansing.

Then the bastard wrote his letters.

He sent them to their brothers. One to Max Steiner, and one to James Straus. They were neatly typed, sanctimonious letters—"unpleasant as the subject may be, I feel it is my duty" and "by chance came upon an exhibition of unmentionable character" and "not my place to give advice but perhaps you are unaware of—"

Brother James brought it up on the tennis court, just before starting to play. "Say, Artie, what was your friend so sore about when he left here, that Kornhauser kid?"

"Why? Has Morty been telling any stories?"

"Well, he wrote me a letter."

"That stinking little crapper. Sure he was sore. We took about forty bucks away from him, shooting craps, up in my room, Saturday night, so he got mad and the little bastard even tried to suggest the dice were loaded—"

James had on his knowing smile.

"Is that what he wrote about?" Artie demanded.

"Oh, it was some junk about you and Judd." In the look James gave him, everything was included. All the things James had covered up for him—the swiped things, the dose. But he wouldn't spill this either; James had to imagine himself a real guy, protecting his kid brother. "It's all a dirty lie!" Artie exclaimed. "Morty's just a dirty troublemaker!"

James said, "Listen, Artie, this is for your own good. That Judd's a freak. You know, funny. Maybe you fellows had better not be seen so much together. People make up all kinds of stories. Maybe there ought always to be somebody with you if you go with him——"

"Why, that dirty-minded lousy— Why, for crissake I know what it is he made a story out of. Why, we were just horsing around."

"You try to let Morty drown?" James asked coolly.

"Why, he fell out of the canoe. Why, that——" Their eyes met. Artie grinned. James shook his head, but could not hide the beginning of a smile as he thought of Morty flailing in the water.

It was lucky the letter hadn't been sent to Lewis, because Lewis would have insisted it was a matter for Momsie and Popsie, a matter, Christ, affecting the family reputation. But James, Artie felt he could handle. James didn't like trouble. He liked a good time himself. And he couldn't have already told anyone, or he wouldn't be bringing it up like this. Christ, if the family knew about this one, it would be worse than that time with the car accident.

Artie took it easy with James, giving him the boyish wink, and letting him win the set.

But that was a mark against Judd, Artie told himself, turning down 49th Street toward Judd's house and casting quick glances right and left. Ha, that elderly woman walking her dog might be a secret police agent. He would give her the slip. And he curled his hand around the barrel of the automatic.

Judd's fault, that time with Morty. First, being such a damn fool as to start playing around, with the door unlocked. Hell, he himself didn't get any special kick out of it, but he let Judd play around just for the hell of it. Judd was the one who started all that stuff. And then, once Morty had seen them and once they had got him out in the canoe, and when they saw he had tricked them about not being able to swim, they ought to have held the tattler's head under water. If you start something you should go through with it. If Judd hadn't been so scared, scared pissless, Morty would have been taken care of right there.

Instead, they had let him leave. So he not only had the story to tell of catching them fooling around, but, even worse, about their trying to drown him. Morty told everybody he saw that summer. Then, instead of coming back to the frat in the fall, he had to spend a year in Denver, with TB—the reason he didn't exert himself swimming.

Even with Morty Kornhauser away from the frat, Judd should never have insisted on coming to Ann Arbor. That was another mistake to charge up against Judah Steiner, Jr. First he had to go and make a whole issue of it with his brother Max, who had received the same kind of dirty letter as James. Instead of simply gabbing his way out of it, Judd had to make an issue, declaring that just for that, the family had to show they trusted him by letting him go to Ann Arbor even though Artie was there.

And then another mistake. Mr. Judd Steiner had to insist he wanted to get into the frat! Morty heard about it and wrote one of his letters from Denver: to Al Goetz, president of the chapter. "Do you want to have a real pair of perverts, right in the house?"

The president took Artie aside for a man-to-man talk. Hell, it was so bad, Artie even had to get James to come up, casually, like for a football game, but to remind Al Goetz of a thing or two. And hell, Al finally admitted everybody knew Artie was okay—why, Artie helled around in the Detroit cat houses with the rest of the boys; they knew he was regular. As James said, he'd even caught a dose at fifteen. But after James was gone, Al told Artie, Why not face the facts? The thing wasn't only because of Morty's tales. Judd simply was not well liked, so why make an issue of getting him in? "Oh, I know he's your friend. You get along with him because you're both brilliant young bastards. But let's face it, Artie, there'd be more than one blackball. Why should he want to get his feelings hurt?"

At least—a point for the defense—Judd didn't push it. He suddenly was against fraternities. He even made a Hebe question out of it. A principle.

The fact was, the Delts had taken him for a ride. For a couple of days he had the idea he was going to show up Alpha Beta by getting into a real gentile fraternity. Some Delt had made the mistake of inviting Judd over because of his being a genius prodigy and a millionaire too. But then they dropped him cold, and Judd suddenly made a principle out of it. He was against the idea of Jewish frats and non-Jewish frats. Being a Jew was simply an accident of birth. So now he was anti-fraternity. He would never join a Hebe frat either, on principle. Moreover, frat men were all a bunch of rubber stamps, Judd declared. They would come out a bunch of Babbitts. He would drop over to the house and spout this stuff, and some of the fellows would laugh, but a lot of them didn't like it. They started telling Artie to keep his friend away from the place. On account of Judd, he'd almost become unpopular.

Artie walked a little faster. He thought of an idea that suddenly made him feel bubbly, even gay. He would go in through the basement and up the back stairs. He would give Dog Eyes the scare of his life.

*   *   *

Judd was sitting erect, unable to study. He detested being at the mercy of a physical need. It seemed never to leave him. Others didn't have it so bad. Artie didn't have it so bad. Those two years at Ann Arbor, near Artie, had nearly driven him crazy.

None of the co-eds would put out. At least, not for him. The cat houses weren't enough. He had to have it all the time —oversexed, he guessed.

And that was the time when the image of Artie began to get in the way. Even when he was with a girl. Inside himself he would be saying to a drunken, laughing Artie, "You goddam whore! You goddam whore!" And he would be tearing at Artie; whoever she was, he would make her into Artie, and he would be tearing in a rage at his own bondage, at having to have it, at the flesh being stronger than the intellect.

The times he had waited, in agony like tonight, always waiting for that capricious bastard—"See you at nine"—and you'd wait, getting more and more excited, imagining what you would do to him as soon as he came in.

Then, like some damn girl, Artie would behave as if the two of you had never done it at all, as if an idea like that never entered his thoughts. The bastard didn't need it. He was like the girls who didn't really need it the way a man did.

The house was safe now. If only Artie would show up, they could be alone to themselves in the house, in this room. For two hours, even longer, without the worry of someone walking in.

Artie was already late. You could never be sure with Artie. He could be precisely on time if it was for carrying out a plan. Or else he could stand you up. But under Judd's fretful impatience there was an almost gratified feeling. Artie, superior, should acknowledge no convention of punctuality.

Judd touched the typewriter. He felt a dreadful reluctance to part with it, to destroy it. It was the one thing he had kept from all they had done together; it was like a token of their pact. Perhaps instead of getting rid of it, they could hide it somewhere? The brawls they had had over this machine! Artie, every time he came over, claiming by right it should have been his!

Judd had an impulse, tender and tragic, to write a farewell note on the machine, a lone confession, taking all the blame. He could mail the note and then disappear. They would recognize the typing. If one could vanish, vanish without an act of death and yet somehow cease to be, truly vanish, dissolving into nothingness as though never even born! Would Artie feel regret? Would Artie appreciate what he had done?

For, caught or not, Judd had a heavy presentiment that it was over now between Artie and himself. And parting with this machine would be like closing the circle.

The night they had got the typewriter was the night they had made their pact. Only last fall. Both of them were back living in Chicago. A bunch of Artie's frat brothers from his old Ann Arbor chapter had come down for the football game. And Artie had got into their pool on the Big Ten. Then after getting back to Ann Arbor they had ruled him out. He claimed he was the winner. Was he burned! He'd show those bastards! And suddenly the inspiration struck him. "Hey, Jock, we'll drive up there and clean out the whole frigging house!"

They could do it the following Saturday. Leave at midnight, three hours of travel, twenty minutes for the job, home by daylight. If anybody wondered where they had been, they'd had a big Saturday night and wound up on 22nd Street, and boys will be boys! He could even fix it at May's Place to back up their alibi!

In Artie's room, they had plotted it. A lazy November late afternoon, with Judd stretched out on Artie's bed—one of those afternoons when he felt his energy ebbed, when he didn't want to go anywhere, do anything, and Artie, for once matching his mood, hadn't even suggested driving around chasing tail. The steam hissed softly, and Artie, relaxed in his Morris chair, his face in a desk-light glow, the petulant lips full-blown in his anger at the frat—in that moment Artie was Dorian Gray.

And as though recognizing a new closeness, in his anger at the lousy bunch up there in Ann Arbor, Artie suddenly offered, "Hey, you want to see something?" Artie went to his closet. There, under a jumble of sporting goods, catcher's mask, skates, junk, which he swept aside, was a treasure trunk that Artie had from when he was a kid. Opening it, he dug beneath a cowboy suit and broken toy guns. Underneath was his loot.

Not merely from the Five and Ten. That dime-store game of Artie's wasn't much of a secret. You walked through a crowded store with Artie, and he lifted items off the counters. Or at a party Artie would whisper, "Watch this!" and lift a wallet from the pocket of some half-crocked idiot. Later, when the guy missed it, Artie would fork it up and there would be a big laugh on the stupe.

But here in the closet as they knelt down close together, Artie let Judd finger the wallets, emptied now, and some women's purses, too. Dozens. The trunk bottom was covered with loot.

To no one else, Judd felt, had Artie ever revealed this secret.

That was when Artie made the plan for cleaning out the frat house in Ann Arbor.

That day, Judd felt their intimacy sealed as never before. What his Dorian was revealing to him might be interpreted by the superficial as a mild kleptomania. But these trophies were, instead, tokens of a laughing superiority to the little rules of little men. Artie had made him catch onto something he had never realized before: an adroit theft was like a daring insult. It was wit. It would be their retort to the whole frigging frat, for everything!

And to do it was to do something real. This Saturday would be the real thing, Artie said. With real guns. Judd could take Max's. Artie knew where it was kept, in Max's desk. And Artie let Judd handle his own, an automatic.

Saturday would be a cinch, because the big game was in Ann Arbor; it would be a big night. Win or lose, the brothers would be stewed and dead to the world. Even if they heard anybody moving around the house, they'd think some guys had gone to a cat house and were pulling in late, or merely that someone was going to the can. And when they woke up in the morning—! Artie only wished he were still living in the house, so he could watch the hullabaloo and the guys accusing each other!

Whispering, kneeling in the closet, they made the plans.

On Saturday, Artie came over. While Artie stood in the hall, lighting a cigarette, Judd walked into Max's room and put Max's pistol into his pocket, feeling a little silly, and yet somewhat scared. Because he was sure Artie would go the limit if anybody tried to interfere. And Artie was right; if you were extending your sphere of experience into this kind of deed, then you did the deed in its own terms, all the way.

There came a quick vision of himself and Artie, pistols out, backing down a hallway as they held off a crowd of men, of himself holding them at bay while Artie ran to the car, himself covering for Artie, until the last instant . . .

"Let's go!" Artie snapped, and when they got into the Stutz, Artie fished in his pocket, pulled out two black silk handkerchiefs, and gave one to Judd.

On the way, the whole ride, they didn't talk much of the adventure. Instead, Judd brought up the subject of New Year's. Judd was anxious about New Year's Eve. Willie Weiss had dropped a remark that he and Artie would be double-dating, Artie dragging Myra. Judd couldn't believe it. That Artie would leave him out of New Year's. Perhaps Willie Weiss had been needling him. So now Judd proposed his own idea, for Artie and himself, just the two of them. Instead of loading themselves down with girls, they could go out on the town, crash one party after another. Artie said sure, that's what they would do. The two of them. No sense getting tied up with broads. New Year's was the best time to pick up new gash.

It was then, on that ride in the November night, that Judd experienced the sense of the two of them in their unity apart from the world. A light snow began to fall, and traffic died away until theirs was the only car on a long stretch of road, and on either side not even farmhouses, only trees and fields, with cornstacks like small Indian tepees—white shapes, deserted.

Then the thought came to Judd that at this moment no one in the whole world, only he, knew where Artie was. No one knew where they were going. The night was between them alone. If something should happen right now, an auto accident, and they should be killed together, and later found and identified, then their folks might wonder what were they doing way out here. If someone, even Myra, should want Artie right now, she wouldn't have the ghost of an idea where to look, where he might be.

He glanced at Artie, who was unusually silent, and saw that Artie had passed out, in the way he sometimes did, his mouth hanging a bit open. And a thrill of happiness went

through Judd, to be riding like this as though he were carrying Artie with him into infinity.

Their adventure would be a continuation of their separation from the world. For in the theft tonight, in the masked
silence of it, and in going through it together, they would be
even more as they were now, united in space and time, enclosed in an action that no one else might know of, no one else
might ever share.

It was as though for this length of time they indeed escaped the world and inhabited their private universe together.

A thought intruded. Judd found himself wondering
whether this was what happened between men and women
when they were in love. Was this the secret feeling of a honeymoon? Would he ever repeat some feeling of this kind with a
girl? He could not imagine it with any girl he had met.

His brother Max would soon announce his engagement,
and then be married. No, such a thing was exhibition. There
was in it something repulsive, because of the way everyone
would know what the couple would be doing.

As they drove into the outskirts of Ann Arbor, Artie
woke. The timing so far was perfect. It was exactly three
o'clock, and the streets were still; only an occasional car
passed silently on the snow. Judd drove through the familiar
streets; fraternity row was dark, hushed. He parked in an alleyway close to the Alpha Beta house.

"Come on, tie it!" Artie turned his head for Judd to knot
the black handkerchief. All alive now, alert. "Now this is
business. If we get into trouble, give it to them!" The revolvers
were against their hands, in their pockets.

They walked up the front stairs. Artie still had his key,
but the door was open. Judd followed, across the living room
and up to the second floor. They could hear snores. His eyes
were adjusted now; he could make out the walls, the door
spaces, Artie's form, his beckoning arm.

Now Artie used his trick fountain-pen flashlight, the
beam pointed to the floor. They entered Morty Kornhauser's
room first. The snitching sonofabitch was back from Denver.
He and his roommate lay on their beds, dead to the world,
Morty with the covers half twisted between his legs.

Judd's fright was almost paralyzing, but greater than his fright was a pride. He was mastering his fear.

Artie picked up Morty's pants and went through the pockets. Judd went for the other fellow's clothes, found the wallet, a watch. Artie seized them from his hands, indicating Judd was only to act as guard.

After his first shock of resentment, Judd put down the clothes. Just then, he saw the portable typewriter, in its case by Morty's bed. Artie was already moving out of the room. Judd picked up the typewriter. Teach that snitch to write letters.

In the hall, Artie muttered, "For crissake. Loading us down with junk!" Judd set the typewriter near the stairs, to be picked up later. "You keep your hand on your rod," Artie instructed. "Lemme do the cleaning."

They went through several rooms. In one, the guys were away. Home week-enders, Artie said. He prowled through their drawers at ease, finding a pair of gold cuff links, a fancy fountain-pen set, even stopping to read a love letter.

"C'mon!" Judd whispered urgently, but Artie lingered over the letter. Somewhere a door opened. Artie stepped quickly into a closet. They heard a guy shuffling to the bathroom, heard the plumbing, Judd all the while feeling murderously angry at Artie.

The guy was back in bed. "Let's get the hell out of here!" Judd said. At last they were in the corridor. What if the guy had seen the typewriter, even stumbled over it! "You frigging boob!" Artie snapped. But Judd picked up the machine.

As they got into the car, Artie let out a big laugh. They pounded each other. Success! Artie began to flip open the wallets. "Wait! Jesus, not here!" Judd pulled out and down the block. The plan had been to do another house, too, and for his turn Judd had picked the Delts.

It was nearly four o'clock—some furnace tender might begin to stir. But Artie was lit up, excited. Judd didn't want to seem a coward. Besides, he owed it to the snotty Delts. Jews and dogs not allowed!

The door was unlocked there, too. Yet it seemed somehow more dangerous; robbing from gentiles was real.

Even while they were on the stairs, they heard a light switch snap on in one of the bedrooms. Judd turned and hurried back downstairs. He tangled with something, a lamp cord; he managed to catch the lamp before it fell, but it made a noise.

"I'll kill you!" Artie snapped. They stood stock still in the hall. On the table lay some books, a camera. Artie picked up the camera. Things had become quiet upstairs. Artie started for the stairs again, but Judd held still. "You nuts?" he hissed. Towering over him, black-masked in the dim hallway, his partner gave Judd a fleeting, shuddery, delicious thrill of suffocation, of death. "Somebody's up," Judd muttered. Artie growled, "You stink, you punk," and pushed him out the door. "Christ, that's the last time I take you anywhere!"

"There was someone awake. We'd have been caught, sure," Judd objected.

Artie grabbed the wheel, and the car leaped away. "Take it easy," Judd begged. What a time for a smashup, with all the stuff on them.

Suddenly Artie let out a wonderful laugh as he toyed with his pistol. "Morty! The way he was laying there, you could have stuck a rod up his ass, he'd never wake up!"

Judd had to laugh at the picture. He reached for his flask, opened it. Artie grabbed it from his hand, took the first swig, and in that moment Judd felt young, young, crazily happy; he felt the way a guy should feel, collegiate!

Collegiate, the robbery a great joke on those imbeciles, what the hell!

Artie pulled into a side road to examine the haul. One of the wallets had a twenty-dollar bill in it. "The lying sonofabitch!" Artie complained. "He brags he always carries a fifty." Altogether, there was nearly a hundred dollars. Saturday night. They should have figured the guys would have been out spending. As for the rest of the haul, several pretty hot-looking stickpins, cuff links, a couple of good watches, along with several cheap turnips. And the typewriter, Judd reminded Artie.

"That stupid piece of junk!" Artie burst out. "If you try

to sell it, that's just the kind of swag they can trace by the numbers on it."

"Why should I sell it?" Judd said. He could use it. He'd say he'd bought it or won it on a bet, but the chances were no one at home would even notice he had it.

Keep it? That made Artie decide he had a share in it, too. Judd flared. "You never even wanted to take it!" They screamed at each other. Artie drove a hard bargain. He'd keep the best of the gold watches.

"Keep them all!" Judd cried bitterly. "If that's all it means to you."

Artie called him a stinking punk amateur. If not for his backing out, they'd have cleaned the second place, too! Hell, Judd had no right to any of the swag; the Delt house was for him and he had screwed it up. Screeching, grabbing for the stuff, they scuffled, and then suddenly Artie started laughing, and Judd too.

The atmosphere remained that way between them, swaying from playfulness to brawling. Artie was finishing the flask. Judd cried, "Save me some, you sonofabitch!"

Artie fended him off, laughing. "Screw you!"

And Judd grabbed for him. "I ought to tear your balls off!"

Artie started the car, pulled onto the road. "You bastard," he said, "if we'd have cleaned out the Delts, we'd be in clover." Suddenly Judd had fallen into silence, moody. He hadn't wanted Artie to start the car just then. And he hated to have Artie drive his car. Artie began a kind of act. "Listen, Mac, next time we go out, you do the way Charley says, or I get me another partner."

Judd took it up. "For crissake, Charley, if not for me, you'd have got us both pinched. I saved you from getting caught."

"Yeah? Mac, I pulled plenty of stuff and I never got caught. You're just so goddam green you're scared of your own shadow."

Judd seized the flask. There was still some left. He drank and said, "Screw you, Charley."

"You didn't even get a kick out of it!"—Artie was getting querulous again—"that's why you wanted to stop."

"Well, not the same kind of kick you get," Judd said. "To me, it's more of a stimulant than a gratification."

Artie might not have heard. "I think I'll get me a goddam date for New Year's Eve," he said. "You're just a wet blanket."

Judd drew in his breath. He must remain in full control of himself now; everything depended on it. Artie was teasing, that was all. Teasing. "New Year's would be a hell of a night for a haul," he observed.

Artie gave him a sidewise glance. Maybe he'd let Mac in on some more jobs; maybe they could pull some real stuff together instead of chickenshit. Only Mac had to know who was boss.

"Well," Judd said quietly, "Charley, if I do what you want, you've got to do what I want. That's equitable."

Artie turned his face to him, this time, and there was the Dorian smile. "You want to make that a deal?"

"Sure."

"Okay, we could make it a kind of a deal."

Their eyes held together, in the bargaining. Judd felt himself almost unbearably quickening.

And then, in that same instant, a blur crossed the corner of his vision, something on the road in front of them; they were going through a small town, a figure was crossing the street. Judd cried out, and jerked the wheel from Artie. The car slid around the bundled figure—some goddam drunk; the car skidded, wavered. Artie gave Judd a terrible shove with his elbow, and somehow managed to put the car under control. "You goddam stupid sonofabitch, what did you do that for?"

"You didn't see him! You'd have run him down!"

"I saw him."

Artie was dead serious, sober, cool.

"You could have killed him."

"So what? Who'd have known?"

Judd was silent. His mind worked around Artie's words. Artie could do things, say things, flashing in an instantaneous reaction understanding, that he, Judd, had to attain in several steps of thinking. It was true again—by everything his intellect accepted, Artie was right. And yet he felt as though he had made some great, shivery effort, dragging himself up to a peak, an icy peak, alongside his friend.

"How about it, Mac? You want to make the deal?" Artie said, and the teasing note was there, just an edge of it.

"If we're agreed on the terms," Judd managed, quietly.

"Yah. But Charley's the boss. What he says, you do. Life or death."

Judd nodded. Yes. In any action, one had to be the master. And the slave, a slave.

Artie accelerated. The car swayed but held on the slippery road.

But not a slave to grovel. A slave of sure reward, the golden slave, his sword protecting his master, his beloved master, of long ivory limbs.

"Only, not for kid stuff," Judd stipulated. "I don't have to obey if it's crap."

"What do you mean?"

"No initiation stuff, no dressing up in skirts and marching on Michigan Boulevard."

Artie laughed at his apprehensiveness. "No, this is for real stuff."

"Any crap, Mac has a right to refuse."

"Wait a minute, Mac. If you start refusing every time I get a hot idea, what the hell."

They defined it. Only things that might make Judd look ridiculous could be challenged. But if once he refused to go through with a serious thing, then they'd be finished. Artie would get someone else.

"But Mac has a right to question an order," Judd insisted.

"Okay. But Charley has the last word. If Charley says so, it's so."

It hung between them for a moment. "Hey, Jocko, let's make that the signal," Artie said. "When I say 'Charley says so,' that means no more questioning. 'Charley says so,' you've got to do it, no comeback."

It was like handing over his life. A fluttering elation went through Judd. "Okay, Dorian," he said. They squeezed some last drops from the flask. Judd heard something like a giggle coming out of himself, the high girlish giggle he used to have when a kid. And just then the car skidded. It whirled completely around and landed in a ditch.

Judd sat rigid for a moment, but Artie lay back, laughing. Then Judd got out and walked around the car. They had been lucky; the ditch was quite shallow. He could pull out, he felt sure.

He came around to Artie's side. The laughter had stopped. Artie's head was against the back of the seat; his eyes were closed.

"Move over. I'll drive."

Artie didn't budge. Judd opened the door and pushed at Artie. Artie swayed over, limp and warm-feeling in his raccoon coat. Judd slipped in and closed the door. The snow had stopped. It would be dark for quite a while yet. He switched off the headlights.

It was one of those times when you couldn't tell if Artie had really passed out or was only letting things happen. The deal.

*   *   *

In Michigan City, a diner was open. Artie, in high spirits, gabbed of the stunts they could pull off, now and then letting a word like "hijack" escape loud enough for the waitress to hear. There was Ned White's house in Riverside. His folks had a cellar full of the best stuff straight from Canada. Ned had once swiped a bottle, for a date. A couple of cases would be worth a couple of centuries. Maybe they could let Ned in on the job. No, Judd objected, Ned was a pet hate of his—a bore, and being a bore was the worst crime of all. Okay, Artie had a better idea: let Ned in on the job and then plug him. He was a snot anyway. Snots like that, Artie said, shouldn't be allowed to exist.

Then they started on pet hates, who shouldn't be allowed to exist. They took turns naming candidates, beginning with Morty Kornhauser. And the blackballing president of the chapter, Al Goetz—Artie said they ought to shoot his balls

off. And they named a prof or two, and William Jennings
Bryan. And how about including females, Judd said, the old
bitch who had spoiled his all-A average with her B in Medi-
eval History. Sure, Artie said, and his own bitch of a governess, Miss Nuisance, he had always wanted to kidnap and torture her. "Cut her tits off!" Judd said. And it was like
splashing, splashing, and he was tittering, and Artie said in a
solemn voice, "Kidnaping, that's the thing to do—pull off a
snatch. That would be the real trick, a snatch for a big wad.
Some real rich kid we know."

"How about Myra?" Judd suggested, seeing the German
soldiers, the French girl dragged by the hair. "And rape her
for the hell of it."

"Rape?" Artie laughed suggestively. "She'd beat you to
it." Then, serious again: "A boy is better. A kid."

*   *   *

And suddenly now in his room, as Judd sat waiting, his
blood pounding with the exciting remembered images, the
lights snapped on and a rough voice demanded, "Okay,
Steiner, where's that typewriter?"

He didn't show, he knew he hadn't shown, the leap in
him. Yet it had been a dreadful leap of fear, before he told
himself it was Artie. Artie, slipping in through the basement
and up the back stairs, had soundlessly opened the door and
switched on the overhead lights.

Judd said, "What took you so long, you sonofabitch?"

Artie said that Myra had called just as he was leaving—
she was alone, so he had to stop by and give her one. A man
had to keep his girl serviced. He was in high humor. "Boy,
you should have been at the house for dinner!" He told of his
mother discussing the big murder. "The murderer ought to be
tarred and feathered and then strung up, she said! I nearly
stood up and announced, 'Mater, I cannot tell a lie, it was
me!'"

"Why didn't you?" Judd said, his voice soft, Artie's nearness almost uncontainable to him. "They wouldn't believe you
anyway."

"Hey, how about if I try it? Confess to the cops!" Artie
bet that was what Steger was doing right now! That would be

great! If every suspect the cops picked up would confess! The third degree . . .

His words tumbled on. He'd met that punk reporter, Sid Silver. "Boy, did I fill him with crap about Steger." And Sid had told him about the third degree, the tricks the cops used so as to leave no marks.

As Artie talked, he picked up the typewriter. "Let's get rid of this goddam evidence." He began to twist at the keys. "Hey, got a pliers or something?" Judd had a pair in his desk, but the keys were springy, his fingers got nipped, and he squealed. He never could stand physical pain. Artie laughed. "My God, you're bawling!"

It was more than Judd could endure. After the way he had worked himself up with all that waiting, and then having Artie suddenly near him, but gabbing as though unaware of him. Now Artie was throwing the typewriter on the floor, jumping on it. "Cut it out! You want the goddam maid in here?"

It was odd how the machine seemed indestructible, a goddam machine. "We better throw it in the lake," Artie said. "This won't come up and float."

"Okay." Judd suddenly felt it would be better to get out of the house. He put the cover on the machine. And in that instant he remembered the robe, the bloody robe, hastily thrown into the bushes last night, after burning the kid's clothing in the furnace. The robe, the worst clue of all! How could they have been so stupid! And in that moment the first ghastly doubt of their cleverness spread through Judd. The spectacles could have been an accident. But the bloody robe lying in the open all day, with the neighborhood filled with police! Then, if they weren't really so clever, if they weren't really superior—if they were just anybodies, where was their right to do what they had done?

It was a misty night, the sky almost milky, the air awesomely silent. They drove rapidly to Artie's. Judd told himself that if the robe were still there it would be a sign that they'd get away with the whole thing.

The robe lay, a dark clod, under the bush.

They drove into the park. Along the lake the cars stood,

each with its mingled shape of lovers. Judd circled the old World's Fair building, its crumbly Grecian pillars making him think of Europe, soon, in a few weeks, but throwing an anticipatory pang of loneliness into him, too. Behind the building was a little bridge over the lagoon. They parked the car, and walked out together, Judd carrying the typewriter. Not a soul around. No lovebirds, even.

They stood on the little bridge. He could feel Artie leaning beside him. In daylight you could see the bottom through the shallow water. "Hell, it'll sink in the mud," Artie said. He took the machine from Judd and was about to drop it.

"It'll splash," Judd warned. Suppose some damn cop happened to be attracted by the sound.

"Drowning kittens, sir," Artie said. "This is where I always drown my kittens." He let the machine fall. The plop was small.

They were almost free now of every thread to the thing. There was only the robe. It might float. Best to burn it somewhere, drive out where there'd be nobody around. Maybe the dunes.

Going south, they passed the building, the marker where they should have caught the ransom only that afternoon. The building loomed vague in the mist. Artie slumped in his seat, subdued. Judd came to a turn: leftward led to the lake; right, to the Hegewisch swamp. And he felt Artie beside him blaming him, and he felt it was true, something in himself had betrayed them. Why had he insisted so on the swamp, when Artie would have chosen the lake? Why had it had to be that one place, the cistern under the tracks? Why had that seemed the safest hiding place in the world, when now it seemed so foolish a place, so easily discoverable, the wasteland constantly crisscrossed by all kinds of people—workmen, fishers in the swamp, kids going there to play? Why had he never thought of all that?

He drove on a side road the short distance to the lake. The mist had lifted a little; you could see a few stars, and the flame licks from the steel-mill furnaces.

There was a stretch of crummy beach here, littered with cinders and junk. They were in luck: the area was deserted.

Artie lugged the robe, a huge dark wad under his arm. Judd gathered some pieces of wood and tried to build a fire.

"You're a hell of a Boy Scout," Artie said, and arranged the sticks in tepee form, so they would burn. Then they put the robe into the fire. Smudge and smoke arose; the flames were almost smothered. "Hell, we should have brought some kerosene. This'll take all night," Artie said.

If the fire would only burn off the blood, they could leave the charred rag. Artie lay down on the cindery sand, limp, as though suddenly pooped of everything, the way he was sometimes, limp, passive. Momentarily Judd felt the stronger, felt better about everything.

Now at last everything was in the clear. The robe was burning, and even if found, who should ever imagine the boy's body had been held in it? To all things material, he was superior. He was a mind. Why had he wept and been scared yesterday at the moment of the blow? Judd wanted now to say something to Artie, to say he hadn't really been himself, to say he was recovered now, was beyond that kind of weakness.

"Hey, Mac," Artie murmured. "All we need is some wieners, huh, and we could have a wienie roast." Artie turned over on his stomach, relaxed.

"Yah, Charley," Judd said. He never was sure with Artie. Even after a couple of years. He lay down alongside, his face toward the fire.

Now and now was the culmination, the completion of their deed, the fulfillment of the compact. Now, now he felt released of fear. He would never be caught, for he was strength itself. The lake, the blackened sand, the stars, the long close body of his friend, the fire-tipped chimneys, and the power in himself—the dark power growing toward release, eruption, the bad stuff, the dark evil clot in him pushing like a ball of fire in the huge tall chimney, wildly flaming out.

I had two morning classes, and all through them I kept trying to think of some campus angle, some way to stay on the big story. But when I made my routine call, Reese said it himself. "See if Tom needs you over at the inquest." A reward for my work of yesterday. From the morning papers I learned the inquest would be held at two o'clock, and I started for the frat house, to lunch there. It was raining, I was half running, soaked, and just as I reached the house Tom Daly called to me, coming up the street. He'd come looking for me, anyplace to get in out of the rain. The story was up against a stone wall. He had been to the Kesslers, to the police—hell, a man couldn't even get a drink around here in the morning.

I said I could probably find him a drink in the house. We had not even shaken the rain from our hats before Artie Straus was up from a chair, holding an early *Globe.* "Anything new on the story?" he asked me. "Did you give them all that stuff about Steger? I gave you lots of stuff they haven't got in here."

I introduced him to Tom, and he became even more excited. Sure, he'd rustle up a drink. What about going out on the story with us? "Listen, I bet I can get you another scoop!" Artie said. "I've got lots of ideas!"

"Artie, the Boy Detective!" Milt Lewis kidded. "Now's your chance, Artie."

Hell, Artie said, just from the papers he could see there were lots of things that hadn't been tried. There was the drugstore on 63rd Street, where the father was supposed to go with the ransom, only he forgot the address. How about tracking down that drugstore?

"You think the killer is still standing there waiting?" Milt jeered.

"The killers would never have been there!" Artie said excitedly. "That shows how much you know. The way they'd do it, it would be a relay. The father would get another call in the store, to relay him to the next spot——"

"Well then, what use would it be to find the store?" Milt asked.

"For crissake, you never know; it could be a clue."

"Jesus, it's raining cats and dogs," Tom complained.

"Come on. I've got a car. I bet we find it!" Artie said. "All we have to do is check drugstores on 63rd Street. Ask them if anybody phoned yesterday for Mr. Kessler."

By this time it was raining heavily, but Tom and I followed him out to his car. Artie drove along 63rd, talking about the crime the whole time.

Tom asked, "You knew this kid pretty well?"

"Sure. Like my own kid brother."

"What was he like?"

"A cocky little bastard," Artie said. "Christ, if you were looking for a kid to kidnap, that's just the kind of cocky little sonofabitch you'd pick."

We were both struck dumb. Artie resumed. "I mean, why crap around, that's the straight dope. It might help you to find the murderer. This little punk could have got somebody real sore."

Tom pursued it. Who, for instance? Did Artie have any ideas? Did his little brother have any ideas? Who could be sore enough at a kid to do a thing like that!

"I'll ask Billy," Artie promised.

As 63rd Street was miles long, it seemed a crazy chase, but Artie said he bet the criminal would have chosen a store in the busiest part of the street, somewhere east of Cottage. He parked in the middle of a block; there was a drugstore on each end. "Let's divvy up," he said.

Tom and I ran for one of the stores, and Artie toward the other. We told the druggist we were from the *Globe* on the kidnaping murder, hunting for the drugstore. He kept shaking his head, at first confused, then simply to say no. As we left the store, Artie came hurrying from the other end of the block. "Nothing doing," he said. "Let's try some more."

That way we worked up the street, two, three blocks, dashing from the car in the rain. After a dozen stores, Tom said the hell with it—even if we found the store it would be meaningless. "Hell of a newspaperman you are!" Artie laughed. "Persistence is the only way in a case of this kind."

"Fine," Tom said, "that's the spirit." Artie and I could persist and he would wait in the car. We parked again, at Blackstone. There was only one store, and Artie and I made the dash. A Negro was behind the fountain. Artie headed for him while I approached the druggist. As soon as I uttered the name Kessler, the druggist's face broke into a gasp. "Why, yes, yes, I never made the connection in my mind——"

At the same moment Artie was yelling triumphantly, "It's here!"

Later on, we could ask ourselves whether it was a compulsion to bring down punishment on himself that drove Artie to reach closer and closer to the fire; for if Judd had been the one to leave a trail of clues during the crime, it was Artie who persisted in the days immediately afterward in taunting fate, thrusting himself into the center of the search, pushing in among us, the reporters, and even among the police, like some perversely teasing, transgressing child, being bad and being bad until he brings the slap of anger down upon himself.

The fountain man and Mr. Hartmann told how they had answered the calls, about ten minutes apart, each time a man asking for a Mr. Kessler. "He said look around and make sure," the Negro recalled, "so I even yelled out in the store. Then I told him there was nobody of that name."

"The nearest booth to the door," the ransom letter instructed; now Artie went and stood in the booth, as though it might contain the presence of the criminal. We all examined the booth. "He must have come in here at some time, to copy down the number of this phone," Mr. Hartmann said, the astonishment still on him.

Artie even lifted the receiver and tried on a wild chance

to trace yesterday's calls. What was the man's voice like? he
demanded of Hartmann. "Any accent? Did he use good English?"

I had to admire the way he thought of every angle.
"You'd make a better reporter than I am!" I told him.

"Aren't you going to call your paper?" he urged. "See! I
told you I'd get you a scoop!"

I said Tom should make the call, and Artie ran ahead of
me to Tom, waving his arms, yelling, "We found it!"

Our paper made much of the feat, crowing that the first
tangible scent of the criminal had been picked up by the same
Globe reporter who had identified the victim. It was a small
thing to hail as a triumph, but there was no real news. The
city seemed to stand transfixed by the murder. From the very
first instant, the case had seized the public imagination as a
crime beyond other crimes. Perhaps it was because of the
wealth of the boy's family. But perhaps, I was to think as the
story developed, because by some uncanny process people
sensed from the beginning that this crime had meanings that
would project far into our time.

We drove back to the campus. We ought to have him
stick with us on the story, Artie insisted. He'd get us scoop
after scoop!

On Woodlawn, spotting the red Stutz, he began to honk
madly. "It's Judd Steiner. You must know him," he said to
me. "Those clucks just had their Harvard Law entrance
exam." The rain had stopped, and there was a knot of collegians around the Stutz. Artie pulled alongside. "Hey, Jock! I
just got a scoop for the *Globe!* I found the kidnaper's drugstore. How'd you come out?"

Judd quietly said he came out okay, it wasn't a tough
exam at all, and while the fellows around him were groaning
at this remark, he asked, "What was that? What drugstore?"

Artie explained how he was on the trail of the Kessler
kidnapers, and in the same breath said, "Hey, Judd, you
ought to celebrate. How about going out tonight?" He and a
hot date were going to the Four Deuces, Artie said, and Judd
should come along. Then turning to me: "Hey, drag a frail,

we'll make it a real party! Bring that babe of yours, Ruthie. I'll cop her from you!"

Judd was trying to say something, but Artie called out, "I'm driving them to the inquest!" and zoomed off with us.

*   *   *

Paulie's body had been moved to an undertaking parlor on Cottage Grove, a refined place with electric candelabra spaced along the walls. "This beats Balaban and Katz," Artie whispered, yet with a proper note of commiseration under his remark. In a few moments he had crowded in among the police, among the reporters; he had gathered the arguments of the chief of detectives, who swore he would round up every known pervert in town, and he had caught the remarks of the chief of police, who maintained it was obviously a straight ransom job—there was no proof of perversion at all. "The cops don't even know which way to look," Artie commented to us.

"That's what the inquest is supposed to be for," I said; I was getting a little tired of Artie, his pitch of excitement was exhausting, and I felt relieved when his friend Judd suddenly appeared, pulling Artie aside. I supposed the Harvard Law candidate wanted to talk about the celebration plans, for presently Artie called to me, "See you tonight," and they were gone.

The inquest itself only added to the uncertainty and hysteria. First there were the identifications of the corpse by the uncle and the father, both of them controlled, unexpressive. The questions went quickly, quietly, to spare them. There was the Polish workman who had found the body; he told nothing new. Then, importantly, his lips pursed over each statement, came Dr. Kruger to give the cause of death. Not the blows on the head, he declared, but suffocation. The tongue was swollen, and the throat. No marks of strangling. Suffocation. Perhaps from a gag. Death had occurred before nine o'clock. Previously, the victim had been subjected to an attack.

The word resounded. It was official now. A degenerate!

But immediately after Dr. Kruger, walking up hurriedly as if to correct a mistake, blurting his words before the questions could be asked, came a chemist, Dr. Haroutian, who had analyzed the organs. There was no evidence of an attack, none at all, he declared.

Dr. Kruger leaped up, shouting. He had seen the body and if that wasn't an attack—!

They began arguing about sphincters and muscle tension; it was too sad, too gruesome, and yet it seemed bitterly necessary to know just how, exactly how bestially some human had behaved. Only from this would the hunting pack know which direction to take. And as the argument grew, those who believed in the perversion became violently insistent, as though to exclude the evil of degeneracy would be virtually to condone the crime.

Both opinions had finally to be left in the record. Presently the inquest was over, and all of us, the reporters, were surging around the public officials, as though some extra word could settle what had happened to that poor boy on his way to his death.

At the same time we were all watching each other, watching Richard Lyman to see if he went off with Detective Chief Nolan, watching Mike Prager to see if he got anything from Police Chief Schramm.

With Harry Dawes of the *Post*, Tom and I traded details of our drugstore scoop in exchange for his story of a kid on Ellis Avenue who claimed he had seen Paulie get into a Winton car, a gray Winton.

But after we had phoned in and were sitting at a sandwich counter, Tom said the hell with watching everybody; it was clear that nobody knew a damn thing—we had done pretty well by ourselves so far; we would go off and work on our own. He kept speculating about the place itself, Hegewisch. All the kids who went to Twain had at some time been out to that place. True, the science teachers who conducted the excursions had been cleared; they had airtight alibis. Still, by going out there we might get an idea.

*   *   *

It was a dreary nothing of an area, half swamp, half prairie, stretching from where the city left off, from streets of scattered frame cottages, out a few miles to where factory buildings began—steel mills and oil refineries. In walking over the ground, we first fully realized how far it was from where a car could park to where the body had been found. The length of a couple of blocks, it seemed. Had the boy walked? Willingly? Was it with someone he knew, who promised to show him something? Or had he been carried, already dead? Carried all this distance? And why, particularly, to be hidden in that culvert? Why there, instead of simply drowned in the pond? We stood staring at the open cement pipe.

It seemed a haphazard choice, a wild, crazed choice, and yet there arose in me the tantalizing feeling of something unresolved that one experiences sometimes in the presence of the seemingly irrational. We speculated. Could the criminal be someone from around here? Some poor local inhabitant who had picked up an acquaintance with the rich kids coming for their nature studies? Did people hang out here for anything? Fishing?

Strange how naked the area was only two days after the murder. Not even a policeman. But what would a cop be watching for, we kidded each other—the murderer's return?

We decided to go back to the local police station, maybe to ask about the neighborhood. The station was quiet; the case had already passed it by. The captain himself, named Cleary, talked to us.

Well, he said, in summer kids went swimming there, and some guys went fishing, some of the Polacks, just for bluefish, and there was even a little rabbit hunting, but these Polacks around here were hard-working mill hands. Hell, in the first place none of them could even write a letter like that ransom letter.

Tom asked if there were any other teachers, besides those from the Twain School, who brought classes out there. Cleary said he didn't know much about that; in fact, the prairie was officially outside his territory—it was state land, and the Forest Preserves had charge of it; they took care of permits for fishing and hunting and things like that.

After we left, as it turned out, Captain Cleary telephoned a Forest Preserve guardian. He only wanted to protect himself, to make sure he didn't leave any loose ends. Captain Cleary asked the Forest Preserve man if he knew of any natu-

ral-history teachers, or specimen collectors, or anything like
that, hanging around the Hegewisch wilds. And he got an
answer. There was some bunch went out there on Sundays
sometimes, Warden Gastony said; some lad brought them out
there—he had his name down because the lad had a gun permit for shooting specimens. So if anyone bothered the lad, he
had his name down to say the kid was all right. A millionaire's kid by the name of Steiner—Judah Steiner, Jr., a real
studious boy. Young Steiner would know what classes went
out there.

Captain Cleary made a note of the name.

*   *   *

Coming home from the visit to Hegewisch, I saw Artie,
driving along my street as though he had been lying in wait
for me. He hailed me, waving a *Globe,* with our scoop about
the drugstore. And he reminded me of our date.

I had really intended to forget about it; I always felt ill at
ease when going out with rich guys, always felt they might
suddenly drag the party to someplace expensive. But now
there was no getting out of it; Artie said he had run into Ruth
on campus and told her.

I took the paper upstairs. There were two full pages
about the crime. Rumors and reports of all kinds, people who
had seen mysterious cars in the night, people who had seen
mysterious strangers in the neighborhood, the gray Winton, a
woman and a tall man. There was the inquest story; there
were rumors that one of the teachers was cracking and would
confess.

Just when I was ready for the date, a call came from
Tom. He was at the Bureau. A suicide had been found, at least
a dead man, off the Oak Street Beach. And a typewritten
letter had come to the police, confessing to the crime and
saying, "When you get this I will be a dead man. I am very
sorry I did this inhuman piece of work." It was signed, "A
Sorry Man." Chief Nolan believed the note had been written
on the ransom-note typewriter, and an expert was checking it.
Tom was staying with the story at the Bureau, and if I
wanted, I could go out to the suicide's address; it was on West
Madison. Sounded like a flophouse.

I called Artie, catching him at home. Perhaps he could pick up Ruth, and I would meet them later. Artie became intensely excited over the new clue. Sure, sure, he'd pick up Ruth; in fact, Judd didn't have a date, so Judd could take care of Ruth for me. I didn't have to hurry; I could meet them at the Four Deuces any time. But wait, he had a better idea. Why not let Judd pick up the girls, and he, Artie, would drive me over to West Madison Street on my story?

But I had had enough of Artie's jittery intensity. I said he had better go fetch Ruth since she didn't know Judd. Then I called her and joked about how this was what it would be like to be married to a newspaperman.

*   *   *

It was indeed a flophouse on West Madison, one of those places that smells like a spittoon, and where everyone is suspicious of all questioners. The manager, elderly and tired of everything, said, Nah, this John Doe had flopped there for a few days—nobody knew anything about him; there were no possessions. The cops had taken a couple of rags of shirts he had had there in a bag.

It was a gruesome, depressing end of a life, the kind of thing you could not help describing as the garbage heap of the city. As for his being the kidnaper, the murderer, "Hell, how could that bum have done it?" the manager said. "He was laying here all boozed up most of the time."

I even ran out to the morgue at the county hospital and looked at the corpse, a runty, meager body, a battered, boozy face. Had he written that note?

Certainly I knew, even as a young punk reporter, that every crime drew lunatic confessions, but downtown Chief Nolan was already declaring the crime had been solved. It was a degenerate vagrant who had murdered the boy and then tried to extort money, and finally, in fright, committed suicide.

Before it was over, the case was to reach into many such pitiful corners, like a random cyclone that leaves exposed the refuse of a city's cellars.

I met Tom at the Bureau and gave him what I had. Between us we decided this was nothing at all, even though the

morning papers were giving it their banner headlines. It was
by then ten o'clock. I almost wanted to ask Tom to come
along to the speakeasy, but we might seem like kids to him, I
thought. So I said good night and went on to my date.

* * *

The place was a cellar nightclub. I ran down the stairs,
slightly apprehensive about Ruth being with those smoothies,
and I was curious, too, about Myra, whom I knew only from a
poetry class. I felt full of importance, breathless with my impressions of the morgue and of a derelict's death, while all
they knew about was college life.

The room was a dim-lit box, with a few burly men
around the doorway. Liquor was served openly there, I saw.
The brassy music, slapped down by the low ceiling, made the
whole box throb. This was a place already known among the
knowing ones, the people like Myra and Artie who always
knew ahead of the rest of the crowd.

The lighting was a subdued rose color, on walls of a kind
of yellowish stucco that was considered fancy at that time,
and there was a small square dance floor. The Negro band sat
on a strip of platform with their heads against the ceiling. I
could not have known that in years to come jazz enthusiasts
would look back reverently to this dim cellar as the birthplace
of the Chicago style.

I made out first, from the stairs, Artie and Myra dancing,
and even in that glimpse I caught something about Myra, the
way she was entirely given over, her glossy head tilted, lost. I
saw Ruth and Judd at a far table, their heads bent close together so as to hear each other under that noise. Ruth caught
sight of me, raising her face, and there came over it the glow
that was for me—but slowly, as though it had to be summoned, so absorbed had she been with Judd.

Artie broke off dancing and came rushing toward me. He
wanted to know the news. Was the suicide really the murderer? I said it didn't look like it. Breathlessly, Artie speculated, "Maybe it was a plant—the real murderer wrote the
note and found this bum and gave him some knockout drops
and pushed him in!" We reached the table. "That would be a
good move for him to get the police off the trail, wouldn't it?"

Myra shook her head over his imaginings, and Judd said why didn't he leave the case to the police? A chair had to be pulled up for me, and I sat at the corner of the table, feeling it was I who was the extra man since the party was a celebration for Judd. But didn't he have a girl of his own?

I had seen Judd around campus, but now I had my first full impression of him, and I was made uneasy by the dark glow of his eyes in their disturbing intensity. And I felt at once that those eyes, that entire personality, fascinated Ruth. She was wearing her classroom expression of earnest attentiveness.

My setup came, and Judd poured some of his liquor into it. Artie ordered me to catch up fast. Myra said she had wanted to get to know me in the modern-poetry class—wasn't this music like Vachel Lindsay's "The Congo" ? We recited it, Artie beating out the rhythm with spoons. Judd asked if he could dance with my girl. For a while I watched them; he seemed to keep on talking while they danced, and Ruth remained absorbed.

In the middle of the number, Artie excused himself and dragged Myra up. Then they were doing the Charleston in a spectacular way, but with great ease; presently half the floor was watching them. Ruth and Judd came back, and we clapped for Artie and Myra, clapped them on. The tenor sax-man stood up. The drummer rattled and jerked his head to the flash of Myra's knees.

Did I feel, already then, something heartbreakingly intense about Myra—a peak reached, yet an imprisonment, because no matter how fast, she couldn't get free? Later, we discussed love like, oh, such emancipated people. Judd insisted that sex should be quite free and apart from love, and Myra said breathlessly that's what it was like in Russia, where women at last were as free as men. But what about children? asked Ruth. Judd said the state should take care of all children, as was of course suggested in Plato's *Republic.* Didn't he believe in parental love? Ruth inquired, and Judd declared he didn't believe in emotion; emotion was illogical and weak.

He was deadly serious, his eyes burning. Ruth drew him on, so understandingly, with her way of making a man feel she understood on his own level. Judd was beyond any shyness now. Ideas poured out of him.

Put down coldly, that sort of talk sounds sophomoric, and yet it sounded bright and fresh and even important at the time. Why were children supposed to have emotional feelings for their parents? demanded Judd. Did children have any opportunity to select their parents? Or even vice versa? It was pure chance—one spermatozoon out of trillions. He, for example, certainly had very little in common with his father.

Now Judd had become vehement. Myra said, suddenly, "Let's dance," and led me onto the floor. Artie took Ruth.

Myra moved her long bare-feeling body into contact with mine, and it seemed utterly pliant, boneless. Her head fell back a little. "Oh, listen to that trumpet!" Then, with a peculiar, sudden assumption of intimacy, she asked if I were going to marry Ruth, and I said, oh, we hadn't gone that far. "But you're in love with her?" she repeated. She asked it earnestly, as though in the light of all that conversation above love she were trying to find out if there really were people who felt it.

I said, "How is one supposed to know?"

"You know, I think Judd is getting a crush on her," she remarked, and I glanced at Judd alone at the table. His eyes were following Ruth and Artie.

"What about you and Artie?" I asked, out of form.

She answered with a peculiar eagerness and sincerity. She was fond of him, Myra said, since they had been kids, but of course Artie had a million girls. "Artie's just a baby," she confided. "He's so immature. Although sometimes I do get worried for him. He has black moods—you wouldn't imagine it. He's deeper than he lets on." Then suddenly Myra thrust her belly in and belly-rubbed for an instant. She glanced knowingly at me, and let our cheeks come together. As the dance broke and we started back to the table, she said, "You know I'm just a tease. I try to prove to myself I can get every man I meet away from his date." She squeezed my hand. "Friends?"

"Sure," I said.

Ruth was flushed and so beautiful as she sat down. I looked from one girl to the other.

Myra made me talk about being a newspaperman—was it the best way to become a writer?—and I described going to the scene of the murder. We were on the favorite subject again. Artie got all excited about our interview with Captain Cleary about who hung out at the swamp. Nature lovers. Did I know that Judd was a big natural scientist? He had discovered some very rare bird—a crane or stork. That was on the dunes, Judd said.

Ruth became quite interested, drawing Judd out, and soon we were discussing Judd's question. Did birds have intelligence? He was convinced they could think. Thinking was choosing, he said, between one set of acts and another.

"Bushwah, it's all mechanical reaction," Artie declared. Every action had a mechanical cause—and from there we were soon on the question of free will. "With humans, too, it's all mechanical," Artie shouted. The place was crowded now and a kind of roughness and explosiveness had come into it. The trumpet was screaming high, but Artie outyelled it, in some passion to prove his point. "Schopenhauer!" he cried. "He proved there is no free will. We are all a bunch of slaves to our instincts!"

"If that is so," Ruth said, "then no one is responsible for anything. Even criminals and murderers are not to blame, if there is no free will. It's all cause and effect."

"Of course!" said Artie.

"If you talk like that," I said, feeling I was about to trap him, "then you might just as well believe in God."

"What?" Artie cried, falling into my trap.

"A determinist does not believe in God," Judd corrected me. "He believes in absolute cause and effect, and nothing— no God—can intervene and change anything."

"That's right." Ruth recognized the distinction and smiled to him. "People who believe in God believe God can change things, can punish them for doing wrong. So they still believe in a certain amount of free will." Then she added, "My father and his friends are always philosophizing at our house."

"There can be free will," Judd said, "but it has nothing to do with right or wrong. That's just old-fashioned moralizing."

Ruth knit her brows. "What do you mean?"

Judd suddenly began to talk like a whirlwind, with passion, explaining his ideas to Ruth. If you accepted a set of regulations about right and wrong, you might as well believe in cause and effect, for everything was exactly laid out for you, what to do and what not to do—you had no choice. But if you believed in free will, then you had to feel free to choose. You had to say there were no rules. Of course, you might for your own convenience decide to accept some of the minor rules, the minor conventions like wearing clothes. But to prove you were free, you had to know you could break the rules, too.

He went on and on. Sometimes his ideas seemed jumbled, even contradictory, but every time I tried to cut in and argue, Judd would screech me down, throwing in names, labels, Nietzsche, and the Will to Power, and the Greek Stoics, and Kant, in a crazy kind of mixture. About all I could make of it was that the multitudes weren't strong enough to make use of their free will. Only the few. *Thus Spake Zarathustra.*

Myra was saying philosophy was her worst subject, she wanted to dance, and Ruth was summarizing like an intelligent student. "Well, according to Artie's idea, there isn't any right and wrong because of fate; everything is determined forever."

"Sure," Artie said, "you are my fate!"

Ruth laughed, and went on to summarize Judd's point of view. "But you say there isn't any right and wrong, but for the opposite reason, because people do have free will and should use it to do exactly as they please."

"That's anarchy," I said.

Anarchy was merely a simple way of putting it, Judd declared, as though to push me out of the argument. Ruth's brows were knitted. Somehow she always was most appealing to me when she assumed that very serious and attentive expression.

I had no further desire to argue; I wasn't too strong on philosophy anyway. I drank, and just then a huge Negro woman pushed her way between the musicians and started shouting out snatches of blues.

Ruth had her eyes intently fixed on Judd's. The two of

them seemed to have forgotten I was there. She asked whether he was really interested in law, in going to Harvard. He was interested in everything, Judd said, in language, in science—his was a universal mind, like da Vinci's, and it would be a waste to study law.

But wasn't he interested in law too? Ruth asked. Surely it would be fascinating; there were great lawyers like Jonathan Wilk who gave their lives to justice.

He laughed his clever laugh. After all, being a lawyer meant being able to argue on either side of a case, so a lawyer really couldn't have any convictions about justice.

That part of it at least fitted with his ideas about right and wrong, Ruth said, so he ought to be interested in law after all.

It was a neat response and I saw his face quicken, for it showed she had followed him. I was beginning really to feel annoyed, and yet was too proud to break up their tête-à-tête. Then Artie and Myra were back at the table, raving about that singer, and we all drank and drank.

*   *   *

Sometime late that evening, the idea about Ruth could have come to Judd. Ruth was dancing with Artie. I saw Ruth cutting loose; the quietest girl can turn into a flashy dancer when she's with one. Judd's eyes were upon them, unwavering.

I imagine there coming to him in that moment a sensation like a double beat of the heart, a knowledge, an intention, a recognition: she is the one to whom he will do it.

Every man and every woman has a testing image, like the photographer's painted setting with an opening for the sitter's head. *How will she look every morning, across from me at the breakfast table?* Or the girl is pictured in some graceful attitude of undressing. Or in the midst of a kiss, her lips parted. Or mothering a baby.

With Judd, the test image was the fantasy scene of rape that so haunted him. Was this the one to do it to? How would she look afterward, lying overcome, her clothes in shreds? Would he feel touched? Would love spread through him?

Would he turn to her tenderly to devote a lifetime to removing the horror of his act?

The image of violence was perhaps a final assertion of his darker self, wrestling him down to keep him from a love that might alter him. And yet the violent fantasy had in it something of that very love. For below the image was a throbbing sense that therein lay release—afterward he would no longer need Artie. This would be an action entirely on his own, just as Artie had done things on his own.

It was a struggle of wish and counterwish—in the same action to make himself equal to Artie and therefore more than ever a partner, and yet to make himself free of Artie through a woman.

Hardly identified, these images swept through him as he raised his heavy lids and looked at Ruth dancing with Artie, and she sent him a smile.

*   *   *

When we reached Ruth's house, I told the others I'd walk home from there, and Artie made the expected remarks.

It wasn't extremely late, about two. We could have gone upstairs. But this hallway was fairly private; only one other family lived in the building, above the Goldenbergs.

We embraced, and I decided Ruth had only been curious about Judd. After a few long, dreamy kisses, she said, "You liked Myra, didn't you?" I laughed and teased her about Judd. We kissed a real love kiss, tenderly, without opening our lips, and then Ruth had to talk about him. I could sense her frowning a little, in the dim hall. That Judd, she said, he was really brilliant. She had never met anyone so brilliant—squeezing my hand—but there was also something disturbing about him, something sad. Then she added, a bit archly, that he had asked her to lunch tomorrow. But of course I needn't worry about competition, as he was going to Europe in two weeks.

I told her she was free to marry any millionaire she could get, and we kissed the last kiss, which was always frankly passionate. Then she would say, "Oh, Sid, I wish we really were lovers," and then we would break because it was too much to endure, and then she would hurry upstairs, though I might pull her back by her fingertips for one more such embrace. Then I would walk home, resisting the impulse to grab a cab and indulge in the traditional after-date release of a whorehouse. And anyway that wasn't really what you wanted, not the first time—and anyway, a girl couldn't, so why should you?

T he boys dropped Myra at the hotel, and then they picked up a paper. Chief Nolan still maintained that the suicide solved the crime.

"You didn't give that bum a push?" Judd said to Artie.

"Naw, not this time." Artie grinned. "We should have thought of it, though."

It would have been the perfect idea. Again, Judd had that fleeting, melancholy sense that they were not as perfect as they had thought themselves.

For a moment they considered continuing the night, but Judd felt a sudden sag of energy; he didn't want anything, not even to stay with Artie. He wanted only some absolute oblivion, perhaps not exactly death, but something cleaner, deeper than sleep, something like a permanent hibernation, crawling away somewhere, someplace close and warm, to have no thoughts.

*　　*　　*

And I see him, remaining quite late in bed, drowsing, and rubbing against the bedclothes, and indulging in fantasies. There comes the image of Ruth. Has he made his date with her in order to do it? But there is a strong counterfeeling about this girl. He feels her almost as not a girl. A person. He has a certain eager curiosity about how it will be with her at lunch. Will the pleasure, the stimulation he felt last night continue?

Then as he tries to seize and analyze the sensation, the sex thoughts grow over it.

Suppose only a short time is left to him, in freedom, even

in life. Suppose he and Artie may soon be caught and locked up? (He never sees it farther than being locked up in a cell.) But then, if he is locked up for life, what of the things he has left undone, untried? Most insistent of all is the rape. Much stronger than the pressure had been for that deed with the boy. That deed had not been in him at all; he had told himself it stood for the rape; but in the act itself, no end had come. Had it been a wasted substitute for the deed that was still there in him, clamoring?

Should he tell Artie? Do this one with Artie?

No. Alone. At least, go on a way toward doing it alone.

Judd pictures himself driving to her house to pick her up. Take the pistol along, as Artie would? The lunch date is known; her mother would know. If he did only the rape, without the killing, a girl wouldn't tell. The soldiers dragging the girls—the killing wasn't always part of it. But an absolute part of it is the girl being a virgin. He has to find out for sure at lunch. After all, she goes out with this newspaper fellow; you can never know.

*   *   *

The maid knocked.

In an odd voice, constricted, the maid said there were two police officers downstairs who wished to speak with him.

Judd told himself he was delighted to observe there was no panic in him, none whatsoever. Undoubtedly they had traced the glasses. Now everything depended on his savoir-faire. Should he phone Artie, warn him? No, they might already be watching the telephone. Would he, even if they applied torture, have the strength to avoid naming Artie?

As he dressed, without undue haste, Judd could not help noticing a subtle fleeting sense of pleasure that they had come.

He had slept late; the old man had gone downtown, and Max was out golfing. Lucky they were out. No, suppose it became serious? The maid could tell them. Judd descended the stairs.

Two policemen stood there. On their faces there was nothing to go by; or did he detect a shade of deference for the neighborhood, the house? The nearer one said Captain Cleary would like to ask him some questions. At the South Chicago station.

The easy way they talked, it couldn't be that they had anything serious. "South Chicago?" Judd repeated as though completely mystified. "Why?"

The cops exchanged glances, and now the second one said, respectfully, "He just told us to bring you in for some questions."

Should he act a little indignant? No. Only completely mystified. But obliging. "Is it for speeding or something?" He smiled. They smiled back but didn't answer. Judd shrugged, and acted indulgent though a trifle worried as anyone should be when called for by the police. If only Artie had been watching!

Feeling the two of them bulking huge behind him, Judd led the way to the door. Would there be a police wagon? No, a Marmon.

Should he ask if he were under arrest? That might show too much anxiety.

One policeman got into the back seat with him. Judd glanced hurriedly around. The street was inordinately quiet; kids were still being kept indoors. Nobody had seen, he guessed. There was sunlight on the trees. Everything appeared curiously motionless, at rest.

Judd offered his Helmars. The cop's fingers seemed almost too thick to grasp a cigarette. With a comforting snort he remarked, "It's just something routine."

But why the South Chicago station? From the way the papers had it, the case was being handled by the chiefs downtown. If the glasses had been identified, surely they would be taking him downtown and not to an outlying police station.

Then Judd recalled, on our date the night before, my talking about interviewing the captain out there. About nature students. That was certainly it. Somehow they had got his name. Because of that punk reporter. That smart-aleck reporter, Sid Silver, had to go nosing around. Rape his girl for him, would serve him right. And Judd imagined himself telling the whole thing to Artie, afterward, and Artie's laughter.

But something could go wrong. And if they kept him

under arrest, there would be no rape; in fact, Ruth would even be stood up on her lunch date.

The cops were talking about the chances of the Cubs in the coming season. It would have been useful for him now, Judd reflected, if he could discuss batting averages. Finally the car halted in front of the two-story brick station. It looked a lot like the Hyde Park station where he had been taken as a kid when some cops picked him up in Jackson Park with his .22, shooting birds. The old man had straightened that out quickly enough. Dragging a well-brought-up boy of good family into a police station! Indeed, Pater practically had the police apologizing, afraid of what he could do to them with his influence. "Why, this boy is already a recognized ornithologist!" And the old man had got him the only permit in the entire city, to use his gun in the parks. "You see?" His father had wanted him to be impressed. Judah Steiner, Sr., could handle anything, get anything he wanted, in Chicago. Well, let the old man get him out of this one! Out? If they really had him in. And there arose in Judd that curious mixture of resentment and expectancy that came when he thought of his father. This whole thing was like a final challenge between them.

He walked with the cops into the vacant-looking room, with the railing and the desk and the pale bare floor and the stale smell. He still could not be sure but that this represented the remainder of his life.

A cop in shirt sleeves stood by a window, gazing out on a vacant lot, his gun important-looking in the hip holster. Turning, he said, "The captain wants you, inside," motioning to a partition, with a door. Judd reached over the railing to undo the catch on the gate, and walked across to the private office.

The captain was writing at his desk. Giving Judd a glance, he motioned to a chair. He was middle-aged, fat, even easy-looking. "Judah Steiner, eh? Well, I'll tell you, you been around out in Hegewisch quite a lot, the game warden tells me."

"Yes, sir." It would be nothing at all, he already felt sure. He felt calm and safe, and glanced at his wrist watch; he could get back in time for the date with Ruth.

Judd spoke of his bird-watching classes, and told how he had conducted the last group out there only a week ago. With respectful curiosity, the captain inquired just what they were studying about birds, and Judd spoke of the mating habits of several species at this season. The captain became interested. Oh, and who was in the class?

Judd would be glad to supply a full list. In this particular group there were several young married women. The captain chuckled. The mating season, eh? Then, returning to business: "Ever been out there around the Pennsy tracks, there by that culvert?"

"You mean where the Kessler boy was found?" Judd said easily. "I know the precise spot quite well, as it happens."

"How does that happen?"

"Only the last time I was out there, I recall climbing over the tracks, because I slipped, coming down, and got my feet wet. It's quite swampy there." Thus, Judd felt, he had paved the way for discovering he had lost his spectacles, in case they had already been traced to him. They might have fallen out of his pocket when he slipped.

"You ever know of this Kessler kid going out there?"

"He certainly wasn't in any of my groups, but he might have gone out with a school group. It's used quite a lot, as you know. It's the nearest place to the city where you find so much wild life."

The captain had picked up a file card of some kind, and he tapped it against his desk. He swiveled and faced Judd. "You use glasses?"

Perhaps this was the moment to say it. To say, "As a matter of fact, those glasses found out there were mine. I must have lost them last week, but I didn't notice it until I read about the case in the papers, and then—I guess it's quite natural—I was rather frightened of becoming involved."

Instead, he heard himself saying, "You mean field glasses? For observing the birds?"

"No, I mean regular eyeglasses."

"Why, yes, I do—or did. For reading, at home. I had them prescribed for headaches last year, but the headaches stopped, and I haven't used my reading glasses for several months."

The captain nodded. "Any of those people with you, or anybody you know goes out there, wear eyeglasses?"

Judd gave himself time for reflection. "Well, as a matter of fact, a few of the women wear glasses, and I have an assistant, occasionally—Jerry Harris is his name. He wears glasses. He's quite nearsighted. He was with us last week. But I'm sure he would have mentioned it to me, if he had lost his glasses."

The captain took down the name and address, writing slowly, in a schoolboy hand. He didn't ask for the phone number, and it occurred to Judd to call up Jerry and warn him.

Then the captain just sat there as though trying to think of more questions. Judd didn't want to appear anxious to leave. He was indeed beginning to enjoy the situation, beginning to form an account of it in his mind, for Artie. Still, the silence became somewhat tense, and he allowed himself to glance at his watch. "As a matter of fact," he remarked, "I have a date to take a girl birding this afternoon, but I guess we won't be going to Hegewisch." The captain's flesh wobbled with his chortle. "That's a new name for it. Birding!"

Judd took a full breath.

"Okay," the captain said, pushing a sheet of paper toward him. "Tell you what, son. You write me out a little statement, all you just said, the facts you just stated, for the record."

As he opened his fountain pen, Judd felt in himself, perhaps a little more faintly but still quite recognizably, that shiver of elation he had experienced when he had first read in the papers of the glasses being found. For he had after all come under suspicion. This had been a mild third degree. He had acquitted himself. He had gone through the sieve.

"I'll have the boys drive you home, so you won't be late for your date—birding." The captain chortled again.

Judd watched himself, so as not to write too much. A paragraph. He wrote fast in a careless hand; one thing was sure, this wouldn't match his lettering on the envelope of the ransom letter. "This all right?" He passed the sheet to the captain.

The officer read it over slowly; he was a lip-reader, but concealed it by mouthing a cigar. He nodded, pushing the paper under a corner of the blotter on his desk.

"I'm afraid I haven't been of much help," Judd said, rising. A clear, mathematical conviction of superiority had come back to him. Against such people, it was a certainty he and Artie had to succeed; they could not be caught, any more than two and two could make five.

"Well"—the captain leaned back—"it's a downtown job now. But we've all got to give them all the help we can."

Judd went to the door, opened it, even enjoying a fluttery feeling that a peremptory voice could still halt him. His two escorts were sitting, idle. They arose as though they had expected him, and led him out to the car. So he was now checked off the list.

He thought of asking them to drop him at Artie's. That was how Artie would have done it—try to scare the piss out of him by pulling up in a police car. But for himself, Judd reflected, he could enjoy the thought as much as the deed. Artie was excitable; if Artie saw a police car pull up without warning, he might even shoot, or do something equally wild, and give himself away. And anyway, there was just time to keep his date with Ruth.

The two cops dropped him at the house. The maid rushed forward as though she had been waiting at the door. Judd laughed at her. "I'll bet you were scared I'd never come back."

"Oh, no."

"It was just some routine junk about my bird-watching classes," he said, so she wouldn't be spreading stories.

He went upstairs. There was an elation in him now over the way he had handled the interrogation. His victory was like a confirmation of his entire code of behavior. He was right, right, right!

I see Judd then, starting for his date with Ruth, picking up his field glasses to prove he really meant it about going bird-watching. And besides—a weapon? Does he definitely intend . . . ? Let her fate hang on chance. That will be more exciting. Let there be some omen. If he spots a warbler. That will be a sign. Do it.

* * *

When the bell rings, Ruth goes to the door, while her mother looks out the window and notices the red Stutz. "My, my! My daughter is getting popular these days," she comments. "Who is this one? Have I met him?"

"He was out with us last night," Ruth says. "Artie's friend, Judd Steiner."

"And you've got a date already? Fast work," says her mother. "The Steiners. Is that the millionaire Steiners? Poor Sid, what kind of competition are you giving him?"

"Oh, don't jump to conclusions, Mother," Ruth protests. "We just like to talk. He's very brilliant. He just passed his exam for Harvard Law School, besides being Phi Beta Kappa at seventeen."

She picks up her scarf and her handbag. "Aren't you going to ask him up to introduce him?" her mother demands.

"Another time." And Ruth runs downstairs to where Judd waits in the hallway.

* * *

Coming down, she makes a kind of illumination for the brown-walled stairhall—her reddish hair, her yellow pleated skirt, her bare forearms, the streak of her scarf, giving a passing gladness to the hall. Ruth feels friendly—curious, she would say—toward Judd. Despite his reputation among the coeds. They can't say what is wrong with him, but have listed him as n.g. Some say Judd gives them the creeps.

Ruth hasn't found him at all repellent. It's true that he shows off his brilliance a little too much, but Ruth already feels a kind of pity for this. He is somehow a stray person, and her upbringing has been in a house of warmth toward strays. Her mother and father are the kind who, some years back, attended Emma Goldman meetings and collected Yiddish poets visiting from New York, or stray anarchists, or intense-looking men with long hair who were vaguely "studying." Often a half-dozen derelicts of this kind would be discoursing around her mother's plentiful table.

So what others find odd or even disturbing in Judd rather attracts Ruth. And physically, though Judd is quite short, he is not smaller than she; they danced quite well together. He is something of a change from her gangling reporter.

There is in her, that day, the unworried adventurous confidence of a girl who has a devoted steady and yet is uncommitted, who may tease herself that perhaps there is yet something unknown, something supreme, in romance to be encountered.

With his curious perfection of manners that contains a touch of condescending irony for the custom itself, Judd opens the door of his car for her. Then he walks around to his own side.

As she settles into the fancy car, her skirt rimming her knees, Ruth smiles to Judd. "I almost expected to see you with Artie," she says. "You're practically inseparable, aren't you?"

"Oh, I have a life of my own, too," he parries. As he drives away with her, he wonders at the unusual feeling of glee that wells up in him. Is this a feeling of happiness? More likely an enjoyment of the power in himself, of his secret imaginings. Can there really be something special about this girl, about having her sitting next to him, and feeling her interest in him? Wryly, Judd permits himself to appreciate the image of the pretty girl and himself, gay youth breezing through the town in his Bearcat!

She, too, must be feeling the image, for she leans back with a delighted sigh, saying how perfect the day is for a ride. Then Judd has a suggestion: "Instead of going to a restaurant for lunch, why not pick up some hot dogs on the road?"

And Ruth says, "Oh, that sounds scrumptious."

He heads through the park and along the lake. A hackneyed refrain comes into his mind. "A pretty girl is like a melody." He drops one hand from the wheel and catches her knowing smile, but at least she doesn't make any callow remarks about one-arm driving; Ruth lets her hand lie in his, against her thigh, so warmly firm through the short pleated skirt.

She remarks that she has been wondering about his friendship with Artie, because they really are so different. Artie acts like a college sheik, while he is so quiet and even shy. Of course, as everyone says, Artie is very brilliant, and she supposes there aren't many people around who—

"—can meet my lofty requirements?" Judd says. "There is no sense in false modesty."

That's true, she agrees. The average man at the university is interested only in football and his frat. "You're not a frat man, are you?"

"No," he says.

"Sid practically dropped out," Ruth remarks. She smooths her dress, for it has crept up, leaving a little gap above her rolled stockings and showing, too, the soft dip in the flesh made by her round garters.

"Is Sid your lover?" Judd asks.

"Oh"—she gives him a candid glance, tinged with a knowing smile, over his so quickly opening the usual subject —"it's not that I believe strictly in the conventions. But I don't believe in rushing things either. I mean, if I were really certain I was in love and we wanted each other, and for some reason we couldn't get married, then I should give myself." There is something almost prim in the way she makes this announcement. It excites him.

"And you're not sure you're in love?"

"Oh," she says thoughtfully, "I sometimes feel as if it's already settled that I'm going to marry Sid. Though there's no engagement or anything. And then sometimes I feel as if some wonderful unknown thing still has to happen."

"Does he intend to marry you?"

She laughs softly. "Even after he gets out of school—a reporter doesn't earn enough to get married on. And Sid wants to write. And . . . I don't know."

"I see." They are silent for a moment. "You don't mind my being so inquisitive?"

"Don't you have to find out if the coast is clear?" Again her soft laugh.

"Is it?" He reflects how cleverly this female has put him into the role of a possible serious suitor. Now she only smiles, without answering his question. Judd finds himself saying, "Perhaps Sid will win the reward on the murder case—he's working so hard on it. And then you can get married." Why has he mentioned the case? He is getting as bad as Artie.

But it seems a normal subject to her. "Oh, is there a big reward?"

"The papers said several thousand dollars, I think."

"I don't think anybody needs a reward to try to catch them," she remarks. And after a musing silence: "I'm not really ready to get married. There are still things I want to do."

"Like what?"

"Oh, go abroad."

She recalls that he is to go in a few weeks, and she says she envies him, and Judd offers the expected persiflage about her coming along, and she says she would if she only had the money, and he finds himself saying, "Well, I've got an idea how to get the money for you! I'll confess to the murder! I'll get the reward—and that will pay for your trip!"

"There's only one thing wrong with that"—she takes up the game—"you wouldn't be able to come along!" And then: "Would you really do that for me?"

"Why not?" he says. "And it would be an experience to see if I could make them believe me."

"I'm afraid I couldn't accept such a sacrifice," she says,

but then her voice drops. "It's cruel for us to be joking about such a thing."

"Why?" he demands. "Why is it cruel to joke about death? After all, what is one creature more or less in the world?"

Her mouth opens. But then, as though catching onto his line, she says, "I think you say things just to shock people, to be different. You're not really so bad."

A tiny spasm of irritation runs through him at her words. Unaccountably, Judd thinks of his mother, of the first time he brought down a bird, a robin, with a BB gun they had given him, as a little kid. How Mother Dear softly explained to him that he really didn't want to kill the bird for no purpose. People made guns that could kill, it was true, Mother Dear had said, but they used their guns always for a reason. To protect themselves from wild beasts, or to hunt for food. Or to study animals, like the mounted birds in the museum. As she talked, Judd had felt angry, cheated. And the same shadowy feeling of resentment has come over him now at Ruth's sententious words.

With a secret pleasure, he heads for the stand where he stopped with Artie. "They've got wonderful hot dogs here," he says.

Ruth leans back. "Oh, I'm so hungry I could eat an elephant."

"With mustard and piccalilli?"

"Everything!"

She sits waiting as he goes to the stand. She looks so right, the pretty girl in the car. Judd tells himself she isn't precisely beautiful; it is rather a supremely blooming quality that gives her such appeal. It is the sex urge that is causing him to endow his reactions with aesthetic value.

He is conscious of the hot-dog man, in need of a shave, with sleeves turned up over hairy arms, a wop or Polack probably, holding out the frankfurters, grinning approvingly, showing a couple of gold teeth. And momentarily the balance wavers the other way—why can't this be just a date; why can't he simply take a nice girl out on the dunes?

*　　　*　　　*

He turns down the side road toward Miller's Beach, stopping the car at the edge of the sand. Ruth gets out; she stands for a moment, breathing full, her blouse rising with her breath. Judd takes the binoculars from the side pocket.

"Is this where you come to watch the birds?"

"This is one of the best places." He tells her it was here that he discovered the Kirtland Warbler.

"Discovered?"

The species hadn't been seen for decades, he informs her, and was assumed to be extinct. "I don't go by other people's assumptions," he says. It is this kind of remark that makes people dislike him, Ruth realizes. But can't they see that he has to do it, from some need, some weakness?

Judd tells her how he searched all last spring. Not far from here, where the beach is unusable, there's an area where hardly anyone ever intrudes. And there, one day, he recognized the warbler's call.

"But you had never heard it before?"

"When I heard it, I knew it."

"That must be such a wonderful feeling," Ruth says, "to be the discoverer, to be the first."

"I'd like to be the first with you," he remarks, with the expected double meaning. Boys feel they have to say things like that, Ruth knows, and momentarily it even gives her a sunny sensation that Judd has made a silly remark, like an ordinary boy. She feels a surge of sureness—something good is happening—and she gives him her hand so he may pull her up a steep dune. She is thinking about him. Everyone likes being "different," but with Judd it is such a terrible passion. Like the way he has to brag about the different courses he takes at school, how he is the only student in that course in Umbrian dialect. And here, his pleasure seems to have been not so much in what he discovered but in having been alone to prove others were mistaken. Even the freethinkers who used to come to her mother's table wanted to gather together with others who had freethinking views, but Judd seems to need to prove himself unique, alone.

He drops her hand and hurries ahead. There is a dip between dunes, an area of stunted bushes, forming clusters in the sand. She comes alongside him and stands still, as he is standing.

"Oh, it's so wonderful here," Ruth says. "The sand is untouched. It looks as if no one in the whole world had ever been here before."

He moves a few steps, and she moves, but then Judd makes a halting gesture with his hand, and Ruth freezes, her arm arrested gracefully. Judd listens. There are a few calls. Not the warbler. "Hear anything?" he asks.

"I was afraid to breathe," she says softly.

"You can breathe," he says.

"Doesn't it frighten them to hear people talk?"

"You can talk. Just naturally, so the voices fit in."

"I think I never listened to nature before," Ruth says. "I mean, just to the air. It's as though the sky itself had a sound, not quite a sound, but—"

"I know," Judd says. And he is startled, at a feeling as of anguish rising up in himself.

He leads her farther, over several dunes, until they are well away from where any beachgoers might wander. Then he slips down on the sand, nesting down behind some shrubs. She settles herself beside him, her legs neatly folded. "Is this where you found your bird?" she asks.

Judd draws out his wallet to show her the picture of the warbler perched on his hand, feeding. This is the same picture that his father has enlarged to keep on his desk at the office. Judd tells himself that he has not forgotten his purpose in coming, and the self-wager he made over the call of the bird.

Then they listen for calls. She sits alert, listening. "A mating call," he remarks. He focuses the field glasses, and directs her to a low distant branch, the birds flickering around it, alighting, circling, alighting. As she tries to follow his pointing, a curl of her hair moves against his cheek.

"This is what you really love, isn't it?" Ruth says.

Judd doesn't reply. He feels a choking rush of conflicting emotions; he feels invaded by her, and he turns against this a scorn for her, for her female sentimentality. And yet the same sense of anguish has returned, as though her voice had touched upon some unbearably sensitive mechanism within him. Now, on the binoculars, their fingers touch. "I mean, this seems so far from being a lawyer," Ruth says. Then she has kept that in mind from last night. She is really interested in him.

"I can always do this," he says.

He puts the glasses to her eyes. After a moment Ruth remarks, "It makes you wonder if we ourselves might be watched, like this, by superior beings."

This breaks the spell, he tells himself. And he tells her she might just as well ask if the birds are speculating about being watched by human gods.

"Why not?" she says. "Last night you were arguing that birds have intelligence and can think."

"Then perhaps we exist only in the minds of the birds," he says. He feels he is not at his best; a resentment is growing.

Ruth smiles; she seems to settle in, a little lower, to relax alongside him in the sand. "Philosophy 3," she says. "Berkeley."

"Well, why not?" he persists, irritated. "What proof is there of anything else? If God exists, it is because we created him in our minds. And if man can conceive of God, then God is less than man—he is merely a conception in man's consciousness. Isn't that right?"

"I know it's logical," she says softly, "but it seems so conceited. According to that idea, everyone is his own God."

"Why not?" he demands again. She is once more merely the female, refusing to recognize logic! Can't she see that a person, a consciousness, can be sure only of itself? Of itself alone? A flood of ideas rushes through his mind—the "God is dead" of Nietzsche—but it is no use explaining to her. Judd sees the archaic bearded gods, the Jehovah—all those gods that little men had invented to fill up their areas of fear. Even his father doesn't have the nerve to swing out alone into the universe, to admit God is dead. No. He still sends checks to the Sinai Temple.

Ruth seems somehow to have followed part of his thought. "I thought you were an atheist," she says. "Are your folks atheists, too?"

It angers him that she has touched on his folks. What

should that have to do with his beliefs? "My father still adheres to vestiges of Jewish superstition," he declares. "He still belongs to a temple."

"Do you have brothers and sisters, Judd?" she asks.

He feels even more resentful; she has diverted him from the main discussion. "I have two older brothers," he mutters. "But they're just Babbitts."

Looking up at the sky, Ruth tells him, "My folks are agnostics. I think I am too." Then, with almost an apologetic note: "Oh, Judd, sometimes the world seems so beautiful, like here, don't you feel that things have to be good?"

"Good?"

Her warm throaty laugh acknowledges that sophisticated people don't speak of such sentimental concepts. Oh, she remembers from last night. His philosophy. There is no such thing as good or evil. Things just are.

"What about the beauty in evil?" he challenges. "What about Baudelaire?"

Ruth says, "Of course, there is a deeper kind of experience, as in Dostoevski, an evil that has good in it too."

"No! There is only experience itself!" Judd insists. And he feels he is almost ready now for his intention. He feels that somehow she has revealed herself, she is really from the other side, from the enemies of his own kind. He guides the conversation now to the Medici, to Aretino, to the rare book he wants to translate, listing all the forms of perversion.

"Are you trying to excite me?" Ruth asks, but with a slight strain under the apparent lightness.

"Why not? I've got you alone here."

"Yes." She is a trifle breathy. Then she tries to return to the lighter tone, impersonal. "You men! For all we intellectualize about it, the double standard is still in force. Men want women to be pure, don't they?" And then, with a sudden burst, "Oh, darn, Judd, sometimes I think the whole question is silly, and what am I waiting for, and I just wish something would happen to me so I would get rid of the whole question. I suppose all girls feel something like that."

"It's well known," he says, "that every woman really wants to be raped."

"Oh, don't talk like a callow youth with a line," Ruth answers. "I thought you'd have a more original line than that."

"Well, you invited it," he snaps, beginning to feel the necessary anger toward her.

"It's not really like that," she says, her tone trying to recover something easy between them, a kind of girlish request for friendship. "I think what every woman dreams of is more like a dream I used to have as a little girl, that the great lover is going to climb through the window, and then something wonderful will happen."

She continues, appealingly, and it is anguish for me to imagine her saying this to Judd, for this is a fantasy Ruth once confided, so intimately, to me. "When I was a little girl, we used to live in a downstairs flat where there were bars on the windows, and I used to imagine that was why the bars were there, but that somehow my Lochinvar would come in, even through the bars. It used to give me kind of nightmares, but I knew I wanted to have those nightmares."

He moves so that the whole length of their bodies touch, as they lie side by side in the sand. She turns her face to him, like on a bed, Judd thinks. "Please don't—you know—get excited," Ruth says. "I don't want you to think I'm a tease."

"I believe in doing everything I want to do."

She looks directly into his eyes. "No. How can you, Judd? I mean, there are things people think of, impulses, not only sex—"

"If we imagine things, then those things exist in us. It's only cowardly not to do what we want."

Her voice becomes low, intimate, almost pleading. "I know, Judd. Ideas like that, Nietzsche and such ideas, they may seem very logical. We can even believe them with our minds. But we don't have to do them."

Is the fear coming up in her? he wonders. For that is what he would need to go through with it.

"But, Judd, suppose everyone believed like that," she whispers. "Then everyone would be justified in doing anything. Even murder." Her whisper is somehow schoolgirlish, and he has an impulse to laugh, yet to kiss her and tell her not to be scared.

He hears his own voice repeating his favorite ideas. There have to be people who are ready to explore all the possibilities of human experience, people like Aretino, like Sade—

"Oh," she says, as though trying desperately to keep up with him, "oh, there have been plenty of people who have done all that, found out all about evil."

But the higher the type of mind, Judd says, the more there is to be discovered.

And then she says it. Lightly. She hopes he doesn't feel, because he has such a brilliant mind, that it is his duty to taste every crime like rape and murder.

"Oh, the murder now won't be necessary," Judd remarks, almost idly. And he catches himself. But she is too confused to notice meanings within meanings. Her brows are contracted, a shadow is over her face. Yes, she is beginning to get the idea, to feel the chill.

"I mean," he says, "if I were to rape you now, I wouldn't have to murder you because it would be unlikely that you would announce that you had been possessed. You would be more likely to keep it a secret and become my mistress." She is breathing quickly. If she makes a move to get up and run away, he knows her movement will unleash him from the last restraint. His arm, his hand holding the heavy field glasses, will describe an arc . . .

But she does not move. Are tears coming into her eyes? There is such a questioning in them, such a dismay. And now the moment has come for him, for an act of will. Inwardly Judd feels tumultuously threatened; he doesn't dare examine what doubts may be rising in him, but some horrible upheaval is there, as if all, all he were ever sure of were suddenly crossed out, wrong! And it is a partner-feeling, too, to the strange sense of almost—almost— Of almost being free, almost attaining. Yes, attaining! The same feeling that he experienced the other night, beside the cistern. To reach the sense of having done, done!

With an act of will, he rolls his body upon her. Ruth's

body is rigid. Her face is so utterly close to his that Judd can no longer see it, only the eyes, still puzzled and hurt.

"Please don't," she begs. "Judd, please don't."

It can still be thought a tussle such as any boy and girl might find themselves in after letting themselves go a little too far in their petting.

He tries to insert his knee between her legs, and recalls some definition in a piece of sex literature that it is really impossible to rape a woman, that in the last moment, even against her conscious will, she physically consents.

With his free hand he tears at his clothing. She seems not so much to be resisting as to have become unliving, frozen. He feels his throbbing power. He will do this. He alone.

"Judd, Judd, I'm afraid for you!" Ruth calls, with awful anxiety, and he seems to hear the call over a distance of years in the voice of his mother as he tries to walk atop a fence. And all at once her arms are around him, holding him close, close, somehow protectively.

In that moment it isn't predominantly a fear of what might happen to herself that pervades Ruth, but a dreadful anguish for the boy, for the sick, sick eyes, for the tyrannic needs in him—not only his sex lust but something far beyond, some horror. And her intuitive gesture is to draw the sick soul into herself, not the drawing in of sex that might come to a mature woman, but the girlish impulse, the drawing in to her heart.

And then, suddenly, he is spent.

Her head turns sidewise, under him, and he rolls from her.

Now if death could come through a wish, he would will himself to cease existing. For it is not only the after-sorrow and the physical disgust of spilling; it is the whole sense of failure, incompetence to live, that invades him.

He lies motionless as she looks at him. He supposes, somehow, he will have to say he is sorry, and he tries to move his lips.

Ruth says, "Don't. I understand. I want to understand." And she makes a slight, tentative gesture, as to touch him, but withholds, knowing she must not touch him.

Presently the tension lessens. And then a thought begins to come up in Judd, like some distant memory. One way in which the experience has perhaps succeeded, or meant something. For through the entire attempt, even at the most urgent moment, the moment when it always came, there had not come the image of Artie.

Could he, then, only be like everyone else? Could it be possible that he may come really to be in love with a girl, perhaps this girl? Even marrying, raising a family? Would the whole idea of what that is all about, what ordinary life is all about, come to him, too?

But if he can be ordinary . . . He shudders in horror and fear, as of losing his very self, and at the same time he experiences a frightful sense of something wasted, the murder as a false and wasted act. He has to make an effort to confirm the murder experience as part of his own being. And then it has returned into him, with even a more terrible sense of doom and error, because if the newer self is the real one, he has in previous dark error forsworn it.

*   *   *

On the way back, they do not refer to the experience. They scarcely speak, and yet Judd does not find himself uncomfortable with her. When he leaves her at her house she asks, "Shall I see you again?"

"Do you want to?" Judd says.

"If you do."

They make a date for Monday evening.

The crime had become our total obsession. I worked with Tom, running after the police and with the police and ahead of the police from one glimmer to another, and watching the other reporters, and eluding the other reporters, and conjecturing and imagining and listening, and gathering more and more the feeling in the city that some hitherto unknown terror was among us. The child's fear of wolves prowling in the forest, wolves that will eat you up—even when the child lives in a city where there are no forests, even though he has been told that really there are no such wolves anywhere around him—this childhood fear seemed now to have leaped awake in every soul in Chicago, and the wolves were the primordial menace, some unknown beast, more savage than any beast ever encountered by man. There was a growing anxiety, a growing presage that something new and terrible and uncontrollable, some new murder-germ, was here involved.

The entire police force was at work in the search. The entire city was preoccupied with it. The threat seemed to be against the logic of life itself, for we must have sensed, beyond the touchable aspects of the mystery, that some killing factor, some element purely murderous, had broken loose. Even before the boys were arrested, there was this dreadful foreknowledge of the escape of some always present, imperfectly contained violence, and if we did not capture it, if we did not hold it and examine it and master its containment, we were all unceasingly exposed, lost.

Tom and I were only a couple of reporters caught up in this hysteria. Yet we could see how, among the police chiefs, there was a growing bewilderment. Their statements daily became more contradictory. Every hour there would be a new crop of sensational clues; by nightfall everything would have been disproven; and on the next day the chiefs would again announce that the murderer would soon be caught.

On Saturday morning, Nolan still declared, in an interview in the *Tribune:* "There is no doubt in my mind that the man who wrote the suicide letter was the same man who wrote the kidnaping letter." But by noon the poor suicide had been discounted, forgotten. And a number of other suspects —teachers, even relatives of teachers who owned Underwood portable typewriters—were suddenly being discharged. For though the first expert had stated that the ransom note had been typed on an Underwood, a new expert declared that the machine was a Corona.

The Kessler mail was flooded with tips, and with abuse. There were threats to kidnap the other Kessler children. "Those questioned are innocent. Better watch Adele—she is next!" one letter warned, and the guard was increased. Chief of Police Schramm told us that nearly all of his men were working extra shifts, with leaves canceled, for a veritable epidemic of kidnaping threats had broken out on the South Side, and along the North Shore's Gold Coast, too. It was always like that after a big crime, he said, but this was the worst.

And actually, three youngsters, sixteen-year-olds, sent messages and made a rendezvous in an elaborate plot to have Kessler bring $25,000 or risk the abduction of his other children. The plotters were caught and arrested. But the imitative fever and the released flood of evil continued unabated. All the quiet-faced people of the city, all the open-faced youngsters—were they all cunning madmen? "You dirty, stingy—! If I had you here I would strangle you to death. We will go a little farther, so watch yourself. You couldn't keep your dirty mouth closed. To hell with the police. You are crying. You made your money honest. Hah hah. But you will suffer minute by minute you low-down skunk. So low you could walk under a snake. And now every time you disobey us we will strike. Go ahead." Anonymous.

From these hate letters, police turned again to the revenge theory. But not one out of a thousand of those letters could have come from people who ever had known Charles Kessler. What weird, filthy, primordial imaginings were revealed, carried around behind unidentifiable city faces, walking around in coats and pants of ordinary men, in dresses of ordinary women! The police passed around to us a number of their scrawls, the obscene symbols, the daggers and mystic suns and moons, and the religious quotations and admonitions! Surely so ghastly a punishment, they wrote, was a visitation for some ghastly sin.

Yet each day what was known for sure seemed to be diminishing. Even the suspected teacher, Steger, had not confessed, and doubtlessly the police had used everything on him. Mike Prager came out with a story that Steger had finally admitted to an unnatural liking for young boys. But no one could find out where the teacher was being held. Even Tom Daly's brother, on the force, couldn't tell us. We kept asking Captain Nolan. We kept trying the office of State's Attorney Horn. Then suddenly, instead of merely shrugging, "I haven't got him," Horn changed his reply. "For all I know, he's home."

We rushed to the apartment building on Dorchester. Within seconds, a half-dozen cabs with other reporters pulled up. No one answered the bell, no one responded to our knocking, though neighbors kept saying knowingly, "He's in there." Through the teacher's door, Mike Prager called offers for an exclusive story. "Name your own price." We kept calling questions. "Are you going to sue for false arrest? Did you get the third degree?" And finally a tormented, imploring howl came through the closed door. "Let me alone, can't you!" The questions, the offers, increased. A sob sister, Peg Sweet, was given a chance to speak quietly while the rest of us all pretended to walk down the stairs, going away, making a big clatter with our feet. But the siege proved futile. After some time, a brother of the teacher arrived with a doctor. "Leave him alone, can't you! Be human, can't you!" they pleaded, and managed to slip inside. After more useless badgering, we finally gave up, leaving in little groups as our deadlines passed.

Even the idea we had had of the criminal as an educated

man seemed to become uncertain. For this idea had been founded on the wording of the ransom letter. Now, from New York, came a story that the letter was virtually copied from a ransom letter in the previous month's issue of *Detective Magazine*. The murderer could be anyone who could read and copy what he read. The letter was in a story called "The Kidnaping Syndicate," and the author, interviewed, declared, "The murderers will be caught because they demonstrated a total lack of inventiveness and cunning, without which escape from the law is impossible."

Yes, the murderers would be caught soon, soon, everyone declared. As fright increased in the city, the *Tribune*'s front-page cartoon showed a cowering man, huddling in a dingy hotel room, clutching a newspaper, with other papers scattered over the floor. "Closing In" was the caption.

But Artie and Judd, following the editions, as yet felt no such dismay. Only once during those days was Artie irked. A late edition of the *News* appeared without the murder in the banner headline. Instead, the headline was about some exclusive interview obtained in Rome. The new boss of Italy had given an audience to a crack foreign correspondent. "Fascism is a spiritual movement," Artie read. And he suggested to Judd, "Say, while you're over there in Italy, how about buying a couple of those black shirts? They look pretty snazzy."

Judd read the rest of the interview, becoming rather excited. "Listen, I must try to see him!" This Mussolini certainly understood the philosophy of Nietzsche. It was by the will to power, Mussolini declared, that Italy would rise again.

Artie laughed and pulled away the paper to turn to the pictures of the newest murder suspects. There were some good ones.

A picture of a young woman, a showgirl type, a gangster's moll. Yes, she really was. She had been living with a confidence man, and she herself had phoned the police. She suspected her friend was the murderer. He kept all kinds of poisons in their room, she said, and he possessed a portable typewriter. She was pointing to it, and to a row of poison bottles, in the photograph. Her friend had behaved strangely since the murder, the woman said, and a day ago he had disappeared. That was a good suspect, Chief Nolan stated.

And the police were also investigating a man who lived only a block away from Hartmann's Drugstore and who had formerly taught science at the Twain School. The man's neighbors had tipped off the police. They were suspicious of him because he owned a portable typewriter and he liked small boys.

Police were checking, too, on relatives of the school's athletic coach. Several of them had been picked up for questioning. Meanwhile, Artie read, preparations were being made to provide absolute privacy for the funeral of Paulie Kessler.

*   *   *

That night, a floral bouquet arrived at the Kessler home, with condolences from "Harold Williams." Police cars, cabs rushed to the florist shop, not ten blocks away. The shop was closed. Four of us located the owner in a nearby flat. Yes, he had sold the bouquet, but he had not noticed the name on the card. We told him—the same name as on the ransom letter. Slowly, his first fright-reaction was replaced by a sense of importance, for was he not the sole being who had actually seen the kidnaper-fiend in person? The florist concentrated on recalling the appearance of the customer. Only a few hours ago. Yes. A tall man, about thirty, wearing gray clothes. Wearing glasses? No, but he squinted slightly.

From this, a portrait of the killer was evolved; newspaper artists drew the picture, everyone was alerted to be on the lookout for a thinnish man—long face, high forehead, age about thirty—wearing a gray suit.

Moreover, he drove a Winton car! The florist was certain he had seen his customer drive away in a Winton. Thus he corroborated the story told by the little boy who had seen Paulie get into a gray Winton with a tall, thin man!

And on Sunday morning we were all pretty sure of his identity. He was a druggist named Clement Holmes, who had just tried to commit suicide. Holmes had been taken to the South Side Hospital. He was tall and thin. Police had questioned his wife and daughter, who told how strangely Holmes had been acting. He was half wild. He had been terribly worried about money matters, having recently lost his drugstore. Saturday, he had left the house. . . . Was it at the time "Harold Williams" had appeared at the florist? It proved to be during the very same hour. Later, Holmes had returned in a terribly agitated state and had chased his wife and daughter out of the apartment. When they ventured back, they had found him on the bed, an empty vial of poison in his hand.

At the hospital, Holmes had been restored to consciousness, but to all questions he gave only babbling, meaningless replies. In the morning, the florist was rushed to the hospital to identify the suspect. But Holmes had vanished! SUSPECT FLEES HOSPITAL! Would the madman turn up at the funeral?

Somehow, the funeral was held with a degree of dignity. On the plea of the bereaved millionaire and of his friend Judge Wagner, all editors were prevailed upon to restrain their coverage. A police cordon kept photographers at a distance. We agreed among ourselves not to try to interview Paulie's mother, watching respectfully from across the street as she walked, trancelike, almost carried by her husband and his brother, to the black limousine. Judge Wagner had given us the list of pallbearers, Paulie's classmates, the richest boys on the South Side. We watched from across the street as they came out, in their knickers and black stockings; each of them might have been the victim. They were solemn, and seemed grown-up in their gravity.

At the cemetery we all stood in a knot, whispering and conjecturing as to whether the murderer might appear. The police formed another small group, with re-enforcements discreetly deployed on a side street. The family procession passed into the grounds, and we followed, remaining at a respectful distance. I heard the rabbi, speaking briefly—the crime was not mentioned; he spoke only of a young life taken in purity. Then the Kaddish, recited very softly by the father. And thus was Paulie Kessler buried a second time.

*   *   *

We came away hurriedly, for there was a police tip that Clement Holmes had been seen, in a Winton, on Skokie Road.

Monday, police were checking every registered Winton owner in Chicago. One had even turned up whose name was

Harold Williams. But it seemed he had an absolutely airtight alibi.

In the afternoon there was a sudden wild alarm, and we followed police cars to an address on Harper Avenue. The sidewalk was filled with people asking one another what had happened. Police came rushing out of doorways; police were scouring the alleys. It seemed that a tall man in a gray suit, wearing a fedora hat, had come hurrying into a rooming house saying excitedly, "I want a room right away. I've got to get off the street!"

He had behaved so strangely that the landlady had whispered to a roomer to call the police. The stranger must have heard, for he had turned and run out of the house. There had been a wild chase through back yards. But the suspect had got away.

By then we were looking for a woman, too. The clue came from the glasses. A Lieutenant Cassidy had been detailed to try to trace the spectacles, and he had consulted an optician near the Bureau. The lenses were of a common prescription, as we all knew. But the frame, the optician said, was not a style that he handled. It was a tortoise-shell frame manufactured, he believed, outside of Chicago. Perhaps the murderer was from out of town. Also, the frame was quite narrow. He judged that the glasses might have been worn by a woman. Someone with a thin nose bridge and a narrow forehead. Pictures were drawn of the female accomplice of the man in the gray suit, both of them sitting in a gray Winton car.

Nearly a week had gone by without a single serious indication that the murderer might be found. We began to hear stories of pressure. The almost mythical multimillionaire founder of the Weiss-Straus enterprises had appeared in the office of State's Attorney Horn. He had come down with Judge Wagner. The magnate had asked pointedly about the progress of the investigation. For though the slain boy had been only remotely related to the Straus clan, there were among his classmates two of Weiss's favorite grandsons. Were they safe? Were any children in Chicago safe as long as this monster remained uncaught, unknown? An editorial of the same tenor appeared in our own paper and in the *Post*.

Suddenly, police raids were taking place. Flophouses were combed, derelicts were picked up. Police Chief Schramm came back into the headlines by announcing that he had dropped the ransom theory and now favored the pervert theory. ROUND UP ALL DEPRAVED, we headlined. The police were combing their files, checking on every known pervert. Petty ex-convicts, floaters, queers were brought into the stations by the score, and we went and looked at them in the sour-smelling Canal Street lockup, the restless little men with puffy faces, the whisperers, the morons, as we called them. How many were kicked around, battered, abused? Who knew? Who cared?

Then Captain Nolan, chief of detectives, recaptured the headlines from the chief of police. "Dope will be found at the bottom of it all," he announced in one of his exclusive interviews with the *Tribune.* And every dope addict in town was to be picked up and examined.

But as Nolan and Schramm failed to provide convincing suspects, our headlines were turned over more and more to State's Attorney Horn and his eager staff of investigators. "The most important clue to appear so far," we declared, had been provided by Horn, whose men had been questioning a railroad switchman oddly overlooked by the police. The switchman, who worked only a few miles from the scene of the crime, was certain that on the night of the deed he had seen the actual murderers, a woman and three men, in a sedan. In fact, he had talked to them.

In Horn's office we all listened to the switchman's story. An elderly man with the scrubbed look of the intensely sober, he was quite convincing. On Wednesday night about midnight, he said, he had been driving home to Gary, and just past Hegewisch he had come upon a car stuck on a little side road. A dark sedan. It was a Nash or a Moon, not a Winton. He had given the car a push to get it back onto the road. Those people had been carrying a bundle of some kind, like something wrapped in a tent. He had even made a remark to the woman, "This is a hell of a time to go camping." They had thanked him for the push. And one detail he remembered: their car had a broken front bumper. All garagemen were asked to notify the police if they had repaired any such bumper on any such car.

More and more rewards were offered for information leading to the capture of the murderers. And then Detective Chief Nolan issued an extraordinary statement: "I ask everybody in Chicago to look around and ask whether his neighbors, friends, or acquaintances showed signs of muddy clothes last Wednesday night, or were away from their usual haunts or callings last Wednesday afternoon or evening."

"Hey, I saw mud on your shoes last Wednesday!" became the jest of the day, but Nolan's invitation was followed by a new wave of telephone tips, letters, denunciations, arrests. Everyone was looking at his neighbor with strange eyes. An alert citizen forwarded to the police an envelope on which the address was hand lettered, as on the ransom letter. Its writer proved to be a draftsman, jobless, and the owner of a Winton! After a severe day, the man declared he would sue the police, but nothing came of his threat.

And at night, police pounced upon a group of people in a vacant lot at Cottage Grove and 44th—a few blocks from the Kessler home. There were two men and a woman. They had been acting strangely, burning something on the lot. And they carried a small bundle. It proved to be a shirt wrapped around something hard, which was nothing else than a broken typewriter! But it turned out to be an Oliver.

And near Aurora, police saw two cars stop. Their drivers got out, talked. A portable typewriter exchanged hands. The cars drove off in different directions. The police car chased one, and an officer commandeered a passing automobile to pursue the second fleeing vehicle. But the exchange proved to have taken place between a typewriter repairman and a respectable customer.

Neighbors of a mysterious redheaded woman reported that her room was filled with newspaper clippings about the murder. "I know all about the case," they had heard her say. She was arrested as she was parking her old gray car. In the car was a shoemaker's hammer, a weapon that might well have caused the death wounds on the boy's head. She turned out to be a harmless eccentric.

Then we were haunting Steger's block again. An anonymous telephone caller had informed the police that the dead boy's clothing would be found "inside that block." "We can't afford to pass up anything," Chief Schramm said, and the police combed the block. A woman was noticed acting suspiciously, running and peering under shrubs. But it was proved that she had merely lost her cat.

Meanwhile a truck filled with street laborers arrived, the block was closed off, and the men began breaking open the pavement. With the other reporters, I ran up and down the stairs that led to Steger's apartment. Front and back doors were locked; blinds were drawn. It was rumored he had been rearrested. Nobody would confirm a thing. One of the officers who was friendly to Tom, Lieutenant Cassidy, arrived on the scene, and Tom dogged him for half an hour. Cassidy swore he didn't know anything new about the schoolteacher. As for the digging operation, he only repeated our own guesses. "Maybe the sewer is stuffed up." Maybe Paulie Kessler's clothes would be found stuffed in the sewer.

The job continued into the darkness. Special lights were set up around the trench. In the crowd, the wisecracks flew, and the shocked, self-conscious giggles of flappers could be heard, as suggestions were made about what people might want to get rid of down the sewer. Among the bystanders there was a paunchy man with a low, almost monotonous voice who said he was a plumber; he was reciting to Tom in a friendly way the list of foul and bestial things he had found stuffed in various pipes—females were the worst, he said; no man could have respect for females when he knew the disgusting things that went down the drains of the city.

And in that same crowd, inevitably, Artie Straus had turned up with his satellite, Judd, hailing me, pausing to add a few horrors to the plumber's list, and swirling away among the watchers. I had a momentary impression of Artie's voice laughing above some girlish shrieks, and then the sewer was finally opened. They found only a lot of muck.

In this muck, all the activity seemed to have come to a dead end. Of the hundreds of perverts and morons arrested and grilled, a score were still being held, among them an ex-policeman. We had taken to filling out our stories about them with the views of alienists, as we called them in those days. We quoted Dr. Arthur Ball, whose own grandson had been a playmate of Paulie Kessler and who declared that the killer would be found to be a degenerate of "the same mental type as Fitzgerald," the sex maniac who had been hanged only two years before for mutilating a little girl.

After the alienists came the turn of the psychics. From Detroit, the police received a telegram signed by a Mme. Charlotte High, who declared she had had a vision of the killing and could describe the killers.

Reese had me get her on long distance. A strange voice, breathless, masculine, poured out the detailed vision. "There are two men; one has a sort of gray streak in his hair. I see him hiding, in a big place, a hotel, in the southwest part of the city. The boy's clothes are there. In my revelation I saw a car," she continued. "It is not a Winton, as the police think, but a Buick. I traced the course of the car. It started in Evanston and doubled back. A woman wrapped her skirt over the boy's mouth to gag him, and he strangled. They went to a red frame house on Wabash Avenue at the end of the line where cars turn. The police are on the right trail. In a day or two, someone will attempt to commit suicide. There will be a confession."

And indeed on the next day someone did try to commit suicide. It was again the poor deranged druggist, Clement Holmes, who had escaped from the hospital. Now the news came from Louisville, where Holmes had been found in a rooming house, again nearly dead from poison. Police were waiting at his bedside for a confession. Only a thread of life remained. Would he live long enough to confess?

The report had come late in the day. Tom and I hurried back to the Bureau, hoping for the confession. If Holmes lived, Tom was to take the sleeper down to Louisville.

As we walked across the Loop, we felt that our job together on this story was drawing to an end. Somehow it was in the air—the murderer was about to be caught. Perhaps it wasn't even that poor dying druggist. But we both felt, with our fagged-out nerves, that the thing was culminating.

We had worked together without rest all week. I had cut my classes, certain that in this assignment I was at last gaining my maturity. Already I was treated as one of the men, a regular. And with Tom I had experienced something I had never known before, a kind of partnership that I was to find rather rare even as I went on in my newspaper work. More and more as the week wore on, we had taken to keeping together, going out on the leads together instead of dividing them up. We hadn't invaded each other, yet I felt that each knew the inside of the other. I knew only the barest facts about Tom Daly's life, and he knew little more about mine. Yet we could curse each other out, call each other Hebe and Mick; each could tell when the other had reached a limit of fatigue, yet each would overcome his own fatigue to run down one more clue. And while Tom kidded me about my literary ambitions, I made in him the startling discovery that not all newspapermen intended to become writers; some thought of eventually becoming managing editors.

And so, as we entered the Bureau, it came over me that when Tom went down to Louisville, I would feel that something good was over. Tom would get the last part of the story down there, and I would go back to graduate. I'd have time to be with Ruth again.

The Bureau was tense. The case was coming to a head. We couldn't see Nolan; Cassidy was just going in. Tom caught Cassidy's sleeve as he passed. "All set for Louisville?"

"Hell, what do we want with Louisville now!" Cassidy let out excitedly as he hurried to his chief.

What could he mean? We looked at each other. "You chase over to Horn's," Tom said. "I'll see what I can get here."

I found the State's Attorney's suite strangely quiet. The large outer office was deserted. But at a desk near the door was an oldish fellow, a kind of ward heeler on a sinecure. "Everybody gone to Louisville?" I asked.

He smiled slyly. "They don't have to go that far on this case."

That was all he would tell me. Clearly, Horn and his staff

were questioning some new suspect, in secrecy. Or did all the other reporters know? Where were they all?

"Dick Lyman been here?" I asked. "Mike Prager?" He waved his hand reassuringly. "I told them boys all to go home."

I hurried back to the Bureau. I found our rivals were all on hand. In the same mysterious way that had worked with us, others, too, had felt impelled to look in on the Bureau. Word had spread to Louie's Place, and a few laggards were hurrying in now. Someone had recalled it was to the tracing of the spectacles that Cassidy had been assigned.

Finally Nolan emerged with his arm around Cassidy, and he let Cassidy tell the story. It was the rims. The horn rims had a slightly unusual hinge. Cassidy's optometrist across the street didn't handle any such rims, but from a catalogue he had found the name of the firm that made them, in Brooklyn. Cassidy had written to the Seemore Company, and discovered that only one store in Chicago handled their product.

For the time being, Nolan said, he had to withhold the store's name. We all shouted our guesses. When Almer Coe, the biggest optical shop on Michigan Avenue was mentioned, we could see from Cassidy's face that we were right.

"That special frame, on that prescription of the glasses—it cuts the prospects down," Cassidy said.

"How many?" we all wanted to know.

Chief Nolan shook his head, smiling. "Just a few, just a few." Now would we please play square with him? He had played square with us. He could not divulge that little list, and it would be no use pestering Almer Coe. Mr. Horn was checking on each and every one of those people. Nolan could not divulge to us where Mr. Horn was, with the suspects. But before the night was over, he promised, the owner of the glasses would be known.

O n Monday, Ruth was sitting in the university library. She had drawn a large volume filled with pictures of birds, and she was reading in it when Judd sat down next to her.

It was somehow an impulse that took hold of students, when a new romance was coming upon them, either to linger around Sleepy Hollow or to go and sit in the main reading room, with its cathedral windows and the soft light lying across the tables. So if anyone was interested in anyone, he would wander through the library just to see if anyone was around.

Judd had caught her nicely. Had she really become interested in bird behavior? he asked. Mostly, she replied, in what it might explain about people. And she didn't want to seem such a nitwit if he talked to her again. In a low library voice he asked whether she was angry with him about Saturday. She looked at him, her eyes fully open. She shook her head. "I suppose you couldn't help it."

In those remaining few days, were they in love? Judd was living under heightening tension. A week, he and Artie had agreed, might be enough to let them feel in the clear. The week had not quite passed. The pressure was still within him to live as if each day were his last, as if the gripping hand might fall at any moment upon his shoulder; this was indeed what he had sought—the intensification of life. And he carried it, containing in himself all the pressure, with no outward change in his manner.

But inwardly Judd seethed with a sense of being on the

verge of a whole new area of cognition. It was not only the murder that had so sharpened his awareness, he felt. It was what had happened to him with Ruth on Saturday. Would it not be unique for a person of really unusual intelligence to permit himself to enter into an ordinary experience of love, to see what would happen? He might transmute that love into something hitherto unknown, something unusual, for it had to be said that Ruth was quite intelligent, exceptionally so for a female. As to the idea of the rape, it had turned in another direction; the force of the idea had propelled him into what might prove to be a novel experiment. Was there still time for this other kind of experience? What if he began something of importance to himself with this girl and in the meantime were caught? Wouldn't he then suffer more than if he allowed no feeling to develop about loving a girl? And Judd even found himself thinking, Would it be fair to the girl?

They had their date that evening, and spent their time analyzing what they might feel for each other. The discussion started over dinner, in the Coconut Grove. Judd maintained that there was no such entity as love, that it could always be reduced to self-interest or physiological response. "In your presence," he explained, "I experience a certain ocular stimulation that causes a heightened activity in my glands." Glands were a constant topic just then, and Judd went on to explain about nerve paths and brain cells, elements combining in a whole pattern of reactions called love.

Ruth sat smilingly before him. But why, she inquired, should this stimulation be higher in the presence of certain members of the opposite sex than in that of others? And even if you explained the entire physical mechanism, she said, weren't you still left with the same question? If you felt a longing for one certain person, and just wanted to be with that person and not with anyone else, didn't you have to admit it was more than physiological?

I find it somewhat painful even today to project myself into this love scene between Ruth and Judd, for as I summon her up, I respond to the glow of her as though I were sitting opposite, at the small, round table with the menu card against the flower glass. I hear the music, "The Japanese Sandman," and see all the couples around us, the trick dancers, the cheek-to-cheek dancers, and feel Ruth's own wonder at what was happening in herself, in regard to this boy, and in regard to me. Was she going to discover that what she felt for me was only "girlish attraction" and that her fate was with this tangled and intense boy, sometimes a genius, sometimes so childish about the most obvious things?

Judd must have tried to analyze what, in particular, drew him. He had a few times before experienced sudden compelling drives to "make" some certain girl—you gave the girl a rush, but always with the feeling of hurrying back to tell Artie. Now, since that stupid spilling of Saturday, he hadn't wanted to tell Artie anything about himself and Ruth. He felt an endless need of exploration with this girl.

Was there for Judd a possible going-over? Was the time nearing for his going-over? Another day, another day, and would the emotion grow deep enough in him to hold?

So I torment myself with their little scene, with the certainty that while sophisticated words poured out, their fingers touched, and they reacted like any two kids made goofy at the contact; I imagine them dancing together, and smiling in intimate joy. I see them later in the car, sitting mooning by the lake, and Judd not even trying to pull her heavily to him, perhaps only their hands clasped on the seat between them.

And he is still talking, talking as he never before talked to a girl, or to anyone. The slight clacky accents of self-satisfaction, so often irritating when Judd speaks, fade down and vanish. He is earnest. He tells her, his tone just barely tinged with sorrow, that he has never had a true friendship with a woman and has never thought it possible, because every connection between men and women becomes falsified through sexual desire; indeed even with her, he suspects that sexual desire will ruin things. (There wings through his mind the image of his father, his mother, but how could his father ever have understood the delicacy, the fastidious quality, the purity of Mother Dear? The times when they must have copulated, since children were born, Judd banishes as gross, gross moments that didn't really count in her life.) And so he explains to Ruth that pure love, disinterested love, can be felt only between men, just as Socrates said, for only then is nature unable to intrude her ulterior motive and to make people imagine they are in love. Yet as he speaks, Judd reserves within himself the knowledge that he includes the component of physical love between men. This knowledge gives him a feeling of power over her, the power of deception, but tinged with a tender shade of protectiveness—she need not know this thing in him, and how he has always felt toward Artie.

As he talks, headlong, about pure love, abstract love, love that is not chained to the purpose of procreation, it is almost as though he were staving off some moment, exorcising the moment when he will be caught by that same dreadful purpose, by the demands of real life, that make a bond between men and women. He is still free, and perhaps in the crime he has committed with Artie he has made himself free forever, for as the toils of natural love reach toward him, the toils, also, of the punishing law may be reaching to seize him.

And thus as Judd talks, his sense of inverse pleasure increases: it is as though a self-thrust knife were already in his flesh, to cut off this prospect of love, and as he twists and turns in his emotions the heightening tension of his muscles presses exquisitely against the ready blade.

This, too, in her innocence Ruth cannot know. And Judd hints only darkly; he says he does not believe happiness ever to be obtainable for himself. And when she spoofs, "Oh, Judd, you're just having *Weltschmerz,*" he pretends perhaps she is right, but lets her feel there may indeed be something more, something dark and personal.

"But what *is* it, Judd?" Ruth begs. "Why do you have these fits of melancholy?"

"Oh, the whole world," he says. "It disgusts me. The things people do."

"I know," she says. "Sometimes you wonder how human beings can be so ugly, when they are capable of beauty, too. The meanness, and the crimes."

He plays with the idea of a sudden Dostoevskian confession. To tell her everything, the crime, and even how he intended to rape her. What would she do? Could he possibly discover in Ruth a soul so deep that it could encompass the horror of his own? Or would she jump out of the car? He feels she might burst into prolonged tears. That would finish everything.

But perhaps the black knowledge would draw her in, seal her to him, like the time, the breathless night, when Artie had let him guess about the body pushed into the lake. From that night, he had felt sealed to Artie; and the whole need to take part with Artie in another such crime was perhaps a need to put himself beyond the reach of ever squealing on Artie.

Could Ruth be up to it? In the remaining days, if only days remained, to treat all of life like some Huysmansesque Black Mass! Could she join him in a carnival of the senses?

"A penny," she says.

And with a short laugh Judd reminds himself that Ruth is nevertheless a nice girl, that this is a component part of his permitting himself to be drawn to her, as an experiment. Perhaps a girl like Myra could go into some mad final carnival, but not Ruth. So he responds to her conventional query with, "Oh, just the same old subject."

"Dat old dabbil sex," she quotes knowingly, soothingly. The sophisticated note returns to his voice and Judd makes some remark about Paris, soon—Paris, where they know how to make the most of such pleasures—and she mock-slaps his wrist, and he says well, of course, he believes in the same freedom for women as for men.

Ruth begins to say, "Would you like it if I—" but cuts it short, and Judd says, with a show of self-surprise, "You know I do believe I would feel quite furious; I would feel possessive about you," and she laughs softly. "You see, all our smart theories—" And there is a lapse, and she remarks that she heard his brother is getting engaged.

Oh, he had meant to invite her—the party is Wednesday, Judd says. But is he sure it isn't meant to be strictly a family party? Ruth asks. Perhaps she would be . . . "Oh, no!" he insists. "It's a big brawl. The whole South Side will be there, and anyway even if it were a family party"—he feels suddenly peculiarly not himself to be saying a thing like this, yet tells himself he means it—"you must come!"

And the girl, his brother's girl, Ruth asks, what is she

like? Has he met her? Max met her in New York, Judd tells her; it was one of those conventional things, a perfect match, a Mannheimer; they do business with the old man. Their oldest brother, who lives in New York—Joseph—arranged it. The girl is said to be very nice, quite pretty. She will arrive day after tomorrow for a visit, to meet Max's friends, and from then on Judd is sure the house will be unbearable. It will be filled with their engagement talk, and what he wants . . .

Suddenly he remarks that he has often thought of simply going away, leaving home on his own, bumming around, something like Harry Kemp tramping on life. She restrains herself from observing that all boys have such an impulse. And he continues, saying with a self-conscious little laugh, "Or maybe even getting married."

"Now," Ruth says, *"that* is surprising."

Yes, Judd says, he has thought how it would be to have a wife and a home, but with someone quite different from his own family.

Ruth says she understands how he may sometimes feel a stranger at home, because even in her own home—though her mother and father are angels, and her mother is very young in feeling, more like a girl friend—still, parents can't really tell you everything; you have to find out for yourself.

Then Judd is speaking of his mother. An invalid for many years, she was ethereal, he says—she was like a Botticelli madonna—and within himself he goes on to say that truly she was a madonna, a virgin, and she was like Ruth—from Ruth there is something of the same emanation of purity and goodness—and then he sees himself being held aloft by a virgin mother. Though he is an infant, he is a person fully developed, speaking and able to walk, and already complete in intelligence.

He hears himself telling Ruth deprecatingly how he was indeed a prodigy, speaking his first words at the age of four months. She laughs softly, saying it is difficult to imagine him as a baby, and he declares he never was a baby; he resents the idea of having been a helpless baby.

Ruth has become so tender toward him; now their talk drifts into silence, and they sit looking at the dark lake, and their faces turn with the same impulse, and there is a slow tender kiss, the lips touching without weight, simply as though they were of one being. A lovely melancholy fatedness rises in their hearts. And it seems to Judd that he has the power to make the whole deed with Artie turn nonexistent. It seems to him that he must somehow have drawn back that deed, erased it, erased that entire night from the schedule of time.

*   *   *

In bed that night, Judd could not summon the image of Ruth. He could not summon the madonna image of his mother. He could not summon the image of Artie. Instead there was his brother in the dark-blue uniform with the brass buttons, the uniform of the military academy. He remembered when Max came home the first time in that uniform, Max, so huge, so strong, and Judd just a shaver eying him from the hallways.

And he remembered, too, the morning he was still in bed and Max caught him doing it and said if he kept on, the thing would come off and he would be a girl. Then way, way back there was fat Trudy, his nursemaid, her huge mouth open, laughing, the irregular teeth, and suddenly her head swooping down, and his terror, her laughing sounds through it all, and her joking threat that he would be no more than a girl, and the torture, pleasure, torture, like tickling, and big Trudy making imitation devouring sounds . . . "I love my little boy, my little man!"

*   *   *

The following morning all this was absent; he awoke with only the strange tenderness in him. The sense of wanting to see Ruth persisted. And as he drove to school, a whole new drama was being enacted in his mind; the play continued during class. He might perform it tomorrow at Max's engagement party. "I have an announcement to make!" Oh, that would be a good one on brother Max, the self-satisfied groom, with the cigar always fat in his face—Max, the center of attention, suddenly fading into the background while the startled gasping crowd listened to his kid brother. Judd had to stand on a chair for his head to rise above their shoulders, to get their

attention, and he announced—was it his own engagement or
the crime? As he sat through the lecture his fountain pen was
busy: again a hawk, the talons open, sharp, long, and ready to
strike. Near it he made, over and over in different sizes, patterns of the sun, with streamers of energy flowing out. Now,
spread-winged on a cross, a great bird, an albatross. But still
he was following something the instructor was saying about
compound crimes—sometimes in compound crimes the lesser
crime took precedence! And Judd's mind was already darting
along a plan of argument. Suppose they traced the glasses. To
him. Suppose they somehow traced the letter. His. And it was
he who had rented the car. (The cleverness of Artie! Judd
smiled inwardly in appreciation.) But if he were caught by
these items, wasn't he free to make his own deal? Suppose
even now they were coming awfully close. Wouldn't it be better to confess and make a deal? Premeditated murder was
death. But if the kidnaping had been a prank, the death accidental, if he made a deal for a charge of manslaughter, there
might be only a few years in jail. He saw himself a model
prisoner, studying, reading. Ruth waiting, and coming to visit
him, and waiting . . .

What could you get, then, for kidnaping alone? Judd was
shading in the initials on the cross, class was ending, and he
managed to walk out alongside the instructor.

It wasn't difficult to steer the conversation to the Kessler
crime, as a striking current example of a compound crime.
Suppose the criminal were apprehended, Judd asked, in preparing a defense would it not be advantageous to let him stand
for the kidnaping instead of the murder?

Well, in some states, yes, that would be a distinct advantage, the instructor said. But in Illinois, kidnaping had quite
recently been made a capital offense—since that miserable
case of the abducted little girl assaulted in the coal cellar, the
Fitzgerald case. A law had been passed. So there would be no
tactical gain. "And in this crime," said the instructor, "if they
ever catch the perpetrators, I'm afraid the best legal manipulation would be of no avail. There are times when law seems
pointless—any verdict short of hanging would be corrected by

a lynch mob, I imagine." He flashed an academic smile that had in it a touch of their shared superiority to the mob.

* * *

She wasn't in Sleepy Hollow. Judd didn't see her on any path, walking with her books.

After his next class he met Artie. They strolled across the Midway, Artie hooting about the latest stupidities of the cops —checking every Winton in town. They even had the car wrong! And the two tramps and the vagabond woman who had been caught with a busted typewriter—now that was something! And that reminded him. "How'd you make out last night, Jocko? Did you get in?"

"Oh," said Judd, "it wasn't that kind of a date." Ruth was just a nice girl.

Artie horse-laughed. She'd been running around with a frat brother of his, and Sid was no chump—Sid was a newspaperman. Hell, when they had all been together on Friday, hadn't Judd been able to see that the girl was Sid's push? Did he think a newspaperman would be wasting time with a girl that didn't come across? Artie was willing to bet a ten-spot he could lay Ruth on his first date.

Judd was silent.

* * *

When he reached home, Aunt Bertha was already there, busily directing Emil in hanging summer curtains and draperies. It should have been done long ago! No woman in the house! Ah, at least this would give the house a lighter air for the big festivities tomorrow. A pity Max's bride wouldn't be living here but still, she and Max were right: a young couple should have a place of their own. And suddenly Aunt Bertha fixed her eyes on Judd, examining him, coming up to him and touching his sleeve. "And how are things with you, Judd? You're looking worried. What can a boy like you have to worry about? He passes his Harvard exam with flying colors. And in a week he's running off to sow his wild oats in Europe, and he's worried!"

He smiled. She contracted her brows. "Maybe you are in love?"

"Maybe I am," he said, to give Aunt Bertha some excitement.

"You just hate to have Max do something you can't do," she remarked, pleased at her shrewdness. And with a sigh: "If only your mother had lived for this. You see, Judd, it's the same way with sisters, too. They're jealous of each other and still they love each other."

He kept the smile fixed on his face. Jealous of Max the Mope! "I was jealous of your mother when she married first," his aunt said. Then, with a streak of asperity she added, "You know something? I was almost jealous of her for passing away first and being done with it all."

It was this in her, this cheerfully admitted pessimism, that made him every once in a while feel you could talk to Aunt Bertha. She might even understand the whole thing with Artie, the whole long game; if any of them could get a glimmer of it, Aunt Bertha would be the one. No, she would put the blame on Artie, as his mother would have done. Just as they had blamed others every time he got a childhood disease. "He was exposed, he was exposed!"

Judd remembered suddenly the one year when he had gone to public school, and his mother had admonished him, "Don't ever touch anything. You'll get germs. Don't sit on the toilets. You must absolutely wait until you get home, Judd dear, you understand? They're just common children." And it had indeed scared him, because being sick all the time with hives and boils and eruptions on his skin, he was in horror of more hurting and more ugliness of oozing and scabs. Judd recalled how he had felt all that time, with his nurse walking him to school and walking him back, and the kids jeering, but keeping their distance. And in the corridors of the school, he had always tried to walk so as not to touch or be touched, until it seemed there had always been a space around him, everyone leaving him alone. Until that one day . . .

"What is it? Something bothering you?" his aunt appealed.

"You know, I may not be going to Europe," Judd remarked. For an instant he was going to add, "I might get caught." But instead he let the story of his love affair come out, saying he was quite interested in a new girl and might not care to leave just now.

"A new girl! And you'd give up your trip for her! Well, that's really serious! Tell me! Who is she?" Aunt Bertha was beaming with curiosity, yet there was a slight anxiety in her glance.

Someone she wouldn't know, he said. Just a girl.

Not a *shikseh!* Even with her supposedly liberal philosophy, there was this automatic horror. But Aunt Bertha covered it at once, giving him her lecture about how of course if he were truly in love with a nice gentile girl of good family, it would be no tragedy—there had been some good intermarriages on the South Side. Look at Artie's mother, a Catholic. But still it was always luckier if you happened to fall in love with someone from your own background—like Max going to New York and meeting a wonderful girl at his brother's, a Mannheimer, too! But suddenly she halted, eying him with new apprehension. It wasn't some little tramp like that one he nearly got into trouble with last year, a pickup?

Judd shook his head. "This is serious, I assure you."

Then he told her about Ruth, a brilliant student. Her family were respectable little people; her father owned a drugstore.

"Russian Jews, I'll bet," she said with a sigh. Still, there could be worse tragedies. "But you're so young, Judd, a brilliant boy. Your father would be disappointed if—" If he didn't get the best, a high-class German-Jewish family, a Straus girl, a Mannheimer.

Then his aunt observed that perhaps the trip would really be the best thing. If he found himself still interested in the girl when he returned, and if she would wait until he got through Harvard Law School—

Wait. The word instantly brought an image; he was coming out of prison, his hair white at the temples, and Ruth was waiting at the gate, her dear face softened with years of faithfulness. Then a gush of grief came up in Judd, almost breaking out as tears, and at the same time he chided himself in disgust for this cheap sentimentality.

With her eyes still on his face, his aunt had caught the

passing emotion. "It'll be all right, Judd. It's youth, youth. We all have to go through it," and she patted his hand.

*   *   *

At dinner everything centered on Max. All the arrangements were reviewed again, to the last detail, for the arrival of his girl and for the engagement party. Uncle Adolph permitted himself some smutty jokes about Max's impatience, with advice about what to do during the engagement period—"put it in the icebox"—and even the old man laughed indulgently. Max carried it all off with a large air of tolerance.

There was talk of honeymoon plans. "Kid, we might even meet you in Italy." And Judd was squirming more and more at this smugness, while at the same time a choking self-pity was in him. "Never for me, never anything so ordinary and simple as happiness." Then he took an inward vow—if he weren't caught, if he got away with the thing, it would be a sign, an omen for him to marry Ruth and be conventional all his life.

They were sitting down for a little family game after dinner, and he even felt a kind of dopey pleasure in the ritual, perhaps for the last time. Then Artie burst in. Ignoring Max's invitation—"Sit, sit down. You can play if you don't start those wild stakes of yours"—Artie shouted, waving his long arms, "Jocko, you've got to see this! They're tearing up the whole street where Steger lives! The sewer is stuffed up! They think he shoved the clothes down there."

"Steger?" It took the family a moment to think back to poor Paulie Kessler. "But I understood they let that teacher go," Max said.

"They arrested him again." Artie could hardly keep the laughter out of his voice.

Judd hurried him from the house. "Like a couple of kids to a fire," he heard his aunt say as they rushed out.

*   *   *

The street was blocked off, and lights had been brought up, flaring over the small area where the crew chopped away at the trench, now waist deep. The light made bluish all the faces around, three, four rows of them, and cast shadows over groups lingering on the sidewalk, all the way to the corner.

"We should have thought of this too," Artie whispered. "Stuffing the clothes down there." Getting out of the car, Artie remarked that this was a good place to pick up some gash —easy to start a conversation. "How about those two?" Then began the game of undressing the girls with their eyes. That one's bones would go through you; that other one—look at her blotches—she's got syph, sure.

Artie pushed up against a pair and in great innocence asked what was going on, requiring a full explanation of the Kessler case. "Hey, don't you even read the newspapers?"

He gave them the bootlegger act. "We've been up to the border for a shipment." Judd tugged, getting him away. "What's wrong? They'd have put out," Artie snapped at him.

"Their teeth were bad," Judd said.

"Oh Christ, just for a lay, you examine a twat as if you're going to marry her." He started on another pair, cute ones, full blown, with knowing looks. By this time Judd felt almost uncontainably excited. The peculiar feeling of tension, of expectancy about seeing Ruth, with which he had awakened that morning, seemed to have been multiplying progressively all day until now it was a general uncontainable lust. If being in love with one girl should make you lose your want for any others, then, he told himself, he was certainly the opposite of other men, and with far greater needs. The presence of Artie had excited him even more than always; from the moment Artie came into the house, the need had been unbearable. And now it was the pressure of the bodies, Artie's among them, until all the bodies seemed Artie's, and something even more, something special in the excitement of the crowd, a crowd lust, the smutty things they were talking about. And perhaps compressed with it all, with Max's engagement and the marriage talk, there was the danger in being here within arm's reach of dozens of policemen. A cop was right in front of the girls, and Artie, instead of drawing the girls aside, started a conversation with the officer. This time Artie was an ex-pupil of Steger's, sure that the police were on the right track.

Pressed against the girls and against Artie, and tormented by the tumultuous raging need, Judd could have torn the bastard apart. "Come on," he urged Artie.

But there was no moving him. "They're just getting there!" Artie exclaimed. And someone wisecracked that the diggers had found a dead skunk. No, Artie said, it was a five-month baby! With a shocked gasp, the girls walked off. Artie pressed after them, loudly telling tales about the dreadful things women did—women were much dirtier than men, but women couldn't help it. After all, the way they were made, they had their own sewer pipe.

And in that moment Judd recalled a chart in a drugstore window, first seen in childhood, with square-angled pipes going through a cross-section of a human body, a woman's. And was there a baby curled in one part, or had he seen that in a medical book? But the picture remained in his mind, ugly, horrible. Yes, what was a female, down there, but a mess of sewer pipe! A nausea came over him; he backed out of the crowd. That nursemaid, Trudy, and even his mother, and even Ruth, the way a baby was made in there—no, it was too disgusting, too filthy in there. Females! He leaned against the car, feeling weak and ill.

*   *   *

Just then Artie spotted me in the group of reporters talking to the captain. He waved and pushed his way to me. "Anything new on the case?"

"They've got us running around in circles," I said. "They're even listening to a medium!" I told him about that crazy phone call. "She predicted a confession on Friday."

"That's only the day after tomorrow," Artie said. "Want to bet on it?"

I said I wouldn't be sorry if it happened; I hadn't had any sleep for a week.

"You'd better watch out. Judd is making time on you, he's stealing your girl," Artie said.

We all laughed, and as they pulled away Artie blew the horn.

*   *   *

Judd was annoyed by that last remark; it was a night when everything that Artie did or said rubbed him the wrong way. And yet this only heightened his need. He was sure Artie was teasing him.

They ended up in a cat house, Judd agreeing to go just to get the stuff out of his system. But when the moment came when he always imagined himself doing it to Artie, this time again it didn't happen. The act itself lasted longer, and for a time he imagined a wedding scene—Ruth in white, a shining bride, coming toward him. He would not picture himself doing it to her. There came back the scene on the beach, and then a kind of blank grief was in him, and, at his climax, a dreadful trembling, a sense of tumbling, like giants crashing in a circus act.

Going home, Artie was half potted. Judd still felt querulous; the postcoital compound of disgust and remorse was on him, and with it some dreadful unidentifiable anticipation.

Artie started to tease him about Ruth, making cracks. "Did you think of her when you threw it in? That's a test. The girl you think of is the one you love."

"Shut up," Judd said.

"Wow," said Artie. "This is getting serious."

"Aaw, cut the crap!"

He looked at Artie, and all at once his friend's face appeared to him the way he had seen it the very first time when his mother brought him over to Artie's house: he saw it as long-jawed and pasty. A tumult of revulsions and fears raced through Judd; everything, everything in the whole past of creation was wrong. In that moment he knew Artie, knew him objectively, as a being apart from himself. He was momentarily freed of longing, and it passed through Judd's mind that Artie was demonic. In the thing that they had done, they had not been doing the same thing. Artie had been doing something else, something he had done before, like the one in the lake, and the ones Artie had made dark hints about—the campus fellow who had been found shot, the taxi driver found castrated. Artie was driven by some demonic force, and in himself it was not the same. Had everything, then, been a gargantuan mistake? When he had believed himself to be participating, joining with Artie, had they really been separate, doing their separate things? If that could be so, then what—what had he been doing there? The possibility was a gasping void. Judd closed it out of his mind, and yet found it continuing into another thought: when people imagined they could be immersed together performing the act of love together, it was also like that: each was doing a separate thing.

Judd was silent the rest of the way home. Artie once or twice took gulps from the flask, then brooded. He got off at his house, saying in no obvious connection, "All right for you, you shit."

*   *   *

The tumultuous sense of some impending change, something tremendously imminent, remained in Judd through half the night. He could not analyze it, though he attached it to Ruth, Ruth. In the morning the feeling was still with him, and with it he felt a compulsion to talk. If he met Ruth, he would perhaps babble out everything.

Instead, he found himself talking about her, about being in love with her. On impulse he was visiting a young married woman, a member of his birding class. She was one of the more interested ones, or at least she pretended a serious interest—a nice-looking young matron, Mrs. Cyrilla Sloan—and his excuse for ringing her apartment bell on South Shore was the delivery of a book he had promised her.

It had come upon him, that morning, that he must leave no promise unfulfilled; it was as though he were propitiating the nonexistent gods of luck. And maybe he had always felt that Mrs. Sloan was encouraging him to make her.

Just after his ten o'clock class, he found her looking morning-fresh, neat; Ruth would be a young wife like that, a secret bird in her nice neat little package of an apartment.

Mrs. Sloan offered him coffee, drew him into conversation. He must be looking forward to going abroad and then going to Harvard. And presently Judd was talking in a rush, more easily than to Aunt Bertha, saying he was considering changing his plans—perhaps he would get married, perhaps he would get a job as a teacher instead of going to law school. Of course, this might displease his father, but—

"Don't tell me you've fallen in love, Judd!" She smiled warmly as though she now understood his sudden visit. She wanted to know all about the girl, surely a very remarkable girl, to attract a man with a brain like his!

And as he described Ruth, Judd became convinced it was really love—he wanted only to be with Ruth; all the tumult in him was the result of some complete change-over.

She kept smiling, letting him talk, telling him that she was glad he had found someone to be interested in, that she had always felt he needed someone. But he mustn't be too emotional, she said; he mustn't let his emotions run away with him. For now he was talking about getting married secretly, about going away somewhere to live. After all, the young matron said, his people hadn't even met his girl; he must not assume they would be opposed to her. Even if she was from a . . . less selective background, after all, she was a university girl.

The tumult in him was subsiding a little. Judd had no idea why he had made up all these things about family opposition, going so far with the drama. But he felt easier now, felt somehow that he was beginning to know about women—they weren't all so stupid. It was another kind of sense that they had.

It seemed to him that she held his hand lingeringly, perhaps invitingly, as he was leaving. Only by telling her he was in love he had caused her to change toward him. It was as though he had inadvertently used a password for the closed little world of ordinary people.

As he came out of the apartment building Judd felt relieved, eased as never even by intercourse. He heard himself whistling.

*   *   *

He spied Ruth with a little group in Sleepy Hollow, and lay down beside her on the grass. The crowd would begin to talk of them as a pair. It was an idyllic scene.

Someone had left a newspaper lying on the grass, and after the first glimpse of the headlines, Judd made himself avoid looking at it. They were still churning, churning over the city. But he would be safe. He was changing; he had to be safe to find out what he was going to be like.

*   *   *

The house had a different atmosphere; there were plants all around, huge green potted palms and rubber plants, and

there were vases filled with flowers. Against an entire wall of
the so-called library were the catering tables. Cases of real
stuff from Canada were stowed in readiness under the boards.
Max, hustling everywhere, showed Judd all this while telling
him what a good buy he had got on the liquor, and that
Sandra would be down in a minute; she was resting.

Then, as though she had sensed the young brother's arrival, Sandra appeared. She was a statuesque girl, and each
speech seemed to have been thought out in advance so that
every word was precise. But as he had expected, her remarks
had the utmost banality. "So this is the genius of the family,"
she said, offering her hand and pressing his for a second, with
proper sincerity. "I wonder if you know how proud your
brothers are of your accomplishments! I understand you speak
eleven languages." She stood alongside Max, who was smiling
fondly at her—the perfect picture of an engaged couple.

Max said that Sandra was interested in literature, especially the French, so they would have much in common. Judd
tried her quickly, mentioning Huysmans, Verlaine, Anatole
France. She had not read any of them—if she had even heard
of them—but she declared she would make a mental note to
look them up, and you could see her inscribing the titles on
her mind. She had made a study at college of Balzac. She had
not even read Baudelaire. The conversation hung, though in
her complete aplomb Judd had a sense that it was he who
appeared to have failed.

Max was looking at them almost desperately, wanting
everything to be right and fine, and Judd even felt a surge of
warmth toward his brother on this day. "Looks like it'll be
some party!" he remarked stupidly, and suddenly wished
nothing would go wrong. If they were going to catch him, let
Max have his dumb engagement party first, unspoiled.

*   *   *

The dinner was in grand style, the full table, all the aunts
and uncles, and the old man at his best, even genial, with
cigars like huge bullets in all his pockets, and everybody toast-
ing happiness—a real feast of the high bourgeoisie, Judd told
himself, and when he went to fetch Ruth he prepared her in
that vein.

She looked as if she belonged perfectly in the crowd, he was surprised to find—her dress, shoes, all. She was as shining as any girl at the party. He introduced her as he might an ordinary date. But Aunt Bertha gave Ruth her knowing scrutiny, then told him privately, "I don't blame you—she's charming. This time you can't be blamed." Then she added conspiratorially, "You haven't told anybody? Nobody knows?"

"I haven't told even her," he said. He felt gay, suddenly crazily elated.

The whole South Side was there, all right, the Weisses and the Strauses in force, including Artie's entire family. The moment Artie came in he began to make a noisy play for Ruth —"I saw her first!" Then Judd had a peculiar feeling, as if everything he had been building up in the last few days about himself and Ruth was an act; in Artie's presence it all fell apart.

Artie was taunting Ruth about that reporter, Sid. Did Sid know Judd was giving her the big rush? "Oh, Sid's so busy I can't even see him to tell him." She laughed, and then Artie was on the crime again, full of the latest reports, and—hey, here was an idea for her boy friend, the reporter. What about the other unsolved killings on the South Side during the last year? That university student who had been shot, and the young man who had disappeared, just a few blocks from here, in April, Perry Rosoff—maybe the same fiend was responsible for them all! She ought to tell Sid to investigate the connection.

Myra appeared just then, touched Artie's arm, and they started dancing. Judd danced with Ruth, feeling he was dancing better than ever in his life. Even Myra was behaving half decently to him tonight.

Later they were all at the punchbowl, Ruth was flushed. Judd was becoming somewhat drunk. Again, everybody was around Artie, talking about the crime. Judd signaled, trying to shut Artie up. But it was as though his excitement flashed between Artie and Ruth in an alternating current. Perversely, he did not entirely want Artie to stop. Judd heard himself laughing loudly at a monkey-gland joke about the castrated

taxi driver. He was losing control of himself. In sudden need
of escape, he went upstairs.

A moment later he realized Ruth had followed him. So
this was his room. "How strange," she said. "It isn't like a
room to be lived in at all." It was so like a museum, with all
these birds in their display cases. The collection was the work
of ten years, he told her.

"But, Judd," she said, "weren't you ever a boy?"

The word shocked him. What did she mean?

Of course it was a thing boys did, collecting insects and
birds. But the way he had done it, so seriously. "I just meant,
you never seem to have had a real childhood. Always so precocious." Her words, peculiarly, affected his lachrymal
glands, misted his eyes. Judd didn't let anything show; he
offered her a Beardsley book to look at, with risqué illustra-
tions. But scarcely glancing at them, Ruth said, "You know,
Judd, I can see you must feel all alone in your family. They're
not at all like you—your father and brother."

She understood him, she understood him truly, he told
himself; she was the first one, the only one. Then he felt a
sweep of panic. He must get out, get out with her, escape! No,
he was becoming intoxicated; he had been drinking since afternoon, mixing whisky with champagne. But Artie was certainly going to give everything away—he should stay and
watch Artie! No, it was hopeless; he should flee. "Let's get
away from this," he said. "Let's go somewhere."

Ruth would perhaps have wanted to stay longer at the
party, yet in another sense she was an outsider. It was really
an affair of the big South Side millionaire families, and from
some of the girls she had already sensed a slightly hostile
gleam. If she were to become truly close to Judd, if anything
really developed between them, then she would have to be
brought into his circle in some other way; she would not slip
in by means of a crowd.

In the car he put his arm around her and they laughed.
Being outside, away from those gasping, grinning faces, Judd
felt all right again. He tried to think of a place to go—perhaps
this was even a night for consummation; he should have

brought a suitcase just in case. The way Artie said he always did.

Judd turned west; out on the Cicero road there was a place with a dance floor and booths. Maybe even rooms upstairs.

They danced. Then they were sitting and talking intently, again about love. Judd began sardonically: "My brother and that self-satisfied girl of his—could people like that really be in love?"

Ruth brought him down neatly. Could someone as conceited as he be in love? He said "touché," and she pressed his hand and smiled, and then she said the essence of love was completely knowing each other. She hoped if she ever loved someone, they would always tell each other everything, no matter what they did, even infidelities.

Her words were banal, Judd told himself—she was after all ordinary—and yet the tug of her was more powerful than ever. He told himself that the two of them really looked like an ordinary nice college couple. Was that what he wanted so much, wanted to tears? To acquiesce in the commonplace, and to be two people who tried telling each other everything, everything?

Something far inside him was laughing. It was as though he were with Artie, laughing at the sight of Judd sitting here with this girl. Then a thought came, one of those awfully simple things you suddenly recognize, things that everyone else must always have known. To experience everything, to experience every possibility of life—why, that included not only the unusual, the bizarre, the depths of evil, but it should have included the other side too; the other range of experience should have come first. How could he, now? How could he ever experience the most everyday common feelings, love and truth, with a girl like this? How could he know whether after all this common thing might not be the most important of all? An overwhelming sense of deprivation came to him because of what he had missed, what the simplest stupe, a prosaic soul like Max, could possess and enjoy. And he had gone too far away now ever to secure it. Why had he not at least tried that ordinary experience before he went this far?

In the dim pink lamplight, Judd knuckled his eyes, as if he had a headache. Ruth suspected there were tears. But why? Why?

"Is something very wrong?"

"Yes," he said.

"Tell me."

"I can't."

And Ruth began to feel that it was more than youthful melancholy, more than the dark self-dramatizing in men, when they assume a Hamlet moodiness and seek comforting. This was something serious and real. But what evil could she know? Seeing Judd so profoundly depressed, there came to her only the dread bogeys of childhood fantasies, used to explain any threat of great sorrow. They were the primal threats of girlish imaginings. What would I do if I loved a man and there was insanity in the family? There even appeared the specter of the ghastly disease: perhaps he had caught syphilis in his running around with Artie. But she cleared all that away. There could be nothing wrong in the family since his brother was getting engaged, and another brother in New York was married. And in this modern age diseases were curable.

No, perhaps much more reasonably Judd was still disturbed about the occurrence on the beach. Being alone with her like this, that powerful male sexual desire that boys had to cope with, so much more powerful a desire than women's, must be upon him again. It was a need that made men so miserable. He was perhaps afraid it would again force him to do something that would spoil things. But ugly as the moment had been, Ruth wanted to comfort Judd, to tell him she understood. What girl had not sensed similar things? Sometimes in dancing close, men pressed their sex against you and then could not control themselves, until you felt the small convulsion in their bodies, and sensed something in their clothes, poor helpless creatures. But what could people do? These were the compelling things of nature, and especially if you loved—if you began to have a feeling for a man—you only sympathized with him for it. True, that moment on the beach had had another kind of strangeness, disturbing, for an instant even terrifying, but Judd had mastered himself for her sake, and in a sense that made Ruth feel he did respect her. If he was "different," even moodier than Sid, this was perhaps what attracted her; this was the challenge of him. Everyone knew he was brilliant, and it would take an extraordinary girl, an extraordinary woman, to be equal to a man like Judd. And he had never found one, he had been so lonesome. Now perhaps she could give him the first happy feeling of true friendship, and even love might develop.

"Judd," she said, "if it's something about me, you mustn't worry. You'd never hurt me."

He shook his head. "I know I'd hurt you. I'd make you miserable."

She touched his hand, and moved her head forward with the tender smile of a woman who has no wish to belittle a man's suffering but yet sees that other times will come. "Let's dance," she said.

*   *   *

Then later, I picture them sitting in a car in a small woods along the Desplaines River. The despondency has come over Judd again, even more darkly. Between kisses, Ruth chides him, "But, Judd, what's so terrible? You're young, bright, rich; you'll get what you want out of life."

"You don't know," he says. "I just feel—"

Gradually she begins to feel his hurt, to feel it powerfully, deeply, to know that there is something more, some unknowable sorrow stemming perhaps even from the brilliance of his mind—his mind apprehending some fated evil that ordinary people cannot see, some inescapable world sorrow. And Ruth begins to believe that anything, anything must be done to assuage such a hurt, a hurt that comes only from very life itself. If sexual release may lift away even a little of this dreadful pain in man, then the whole structure of purity becomes meaningless.

She wants, wants to help him, by some magic womanly touch to dispel his ache. Yet it is not her ignorance or even her own innocence, she feels sure, that impedes her. This trouble of his is something uncommon, as Judd is uncommon. This intensity of pain is not merely what other men feel.

She draws his head down to her bosom. "Tell me, tell me," she whispers, desperate over her own inadequacy—a girl trying to play the role of a woman. He is silent, caught in some bleak indescribable horror; it is surely the life-horror that comes over people at times.

Her dress has small buttons all down the front, and in a chaotic wish to help him, Ruth undoes the buttons and draws down the edge of her chemise. His cheek rests against her bare breast. As it touches her, Ruth feels a warm pulse through her entire body, and in her sex, and she wonders whether now, now she will become a woman. His lips touch, and she wishes that her body could draw from him all the hurt, all the grief of living. She places her hand on his head. She feels a slight shudder going through his body. Is he weeping?

Judd sees the boy. For the first time, he sees the face of the dead boy—a kid's face gazing up at him from the night-time water. And staring at him with a child's unblinking candor, the face becomes his own.

Ruth is white-faced. She sits utterly still. And she hears Judd say, "I wish I had never been born."

The words stagger Ruth; there is a strangeness in the intonation. It is not the way people usually say this.

She can only press his head tightly, feeling in herself a great distress that she cannot help this man, a great tugging to relieve his suffering, and a frightened wonder—can this be love?

*   *   *

Judd puts his hand on the gearshift. With an effort of will, he starts the car. Once the machine is in movement it is easier. He even is able to tell himself he has done a noble thing. He could have had Ruth tonight, and he refrained. Perhaps it will count, in a kind of bargain exchange with his fate. Perhaps it will help him not to get caught.

O n the next day—the day Lieutenant Cassidy secured the list of Seemore spectacle owners—Judd was telling Artie how he had made Ruth. Describing the seduction, Judd assured himself he was talking that way only to keep himself from really talking about her to Artie. So he told how he had lifted her out of the car. Artie's face wore a loose, skeptical look; no one was taking him in. That meant he was believing it. "You bastard!" Artie cried. "Why didn't you take me along? You know I always had my eye on her; I knew she was tail. Let's the two of us get her tonight—"

Judd shrugged. For one thing he wasn't interested in her anymore, he said.

"Okay, you bullshitter. I don't believe you ever laid her."

That was when the maid came in to say some gentlemen wished to see Judd.

Artie and Judd were in the library playing casino, not even for money; the debris of the engagement party was still around them, the uncovered buffet table on its horses, and the cases of empty bottles underneath. Now Artie sank far down in his chair, holding his cards in front of his face.

Two large men entered. Obviously they were not entirely at ease in this imposing house. Their hands hung stiffly.

"Who is Judah Steiner, Jr.?"

Judd arose. Let Artie see he could handle it. After all, he had been through it once; Artie hadn't. He had faced the police and got away with it. Now Artie would see him do it again.

"What can I do for you gentlemen?" Judd said.

"The state's attorney wants to talk to you, Mr. Steiner. We'll take you downtown."

"Is this about the Kessler case?" he said blandly, watching their faces. One of them reacted as though he had been handed a confession.

The other looked suspicious. "Huh?" he said.

"Well, I'd be glad to tell the state's attorney all I know about it, although I already talked to Captain Cleary out in the South Chicago station last Saturday."

"Captain Cleary?" They exchanged glances. Perhaps, mentally, the detective was already crossing him off the suspect list, and cursing at the duplicated effort.

"Yes," Judd said. "Out there where the poor kid was found. I go birding out there, and the captain asked me if I could help out, give him any ideas as to who might habitually visit the swamp out there."

The impassive look came back over their faces.

Then this was more. This time it must be the spectacles. The second detective said, "We don't know about all that. We're just supposed to—"

"—bring me in," Judd said easily, and they all chuckled. "Sure, let's go."

He glanced toward Artie. All kinds of things were on Artie's face. It was almost the way Artie looked when playing drunk, pretending he didn't quite know what was happening, and wasn't really taking part. "Artie," Judd said, "would you tell my folks, should they want to know my whereabouts?" Then he introduced the cops. "This is Artie Straus, a friend of mine, Mr. ——"

"McNamara," the first one introduced himself. The other said his name was Peterson.

A third dick was at the wheel of the car. Judd sat in the rear with McNamara. He offered cigarettes. No conversation started, so he tried the Carpentier fight as an opener. The cop thought the Frenchman would win. He hoped he could get there, but he might be busy.

"This case is keeping you on the go, I'll bet."

"You said it."

"Perhaps it will be solved by then."

The dick said nothing.

This was more serious than last Saturday, Judd felt sure. But assume they did have the glasses traced to him. Or suppose it was something that hadn't been thought of at all? Fingerprints? Anything. The telltale atoms in the universe. Each atom left its trace.

But apparently they still had nothing on Artie. Artie should stay out unless caught. There was the wish for Artie to be with him, and a sly kind of counterwish, to be alone, to suffer punishment that would make him worthy of Ruth.

No, no sentiment. It was his mistake. The glasses in his pocket where they could fall out.

He was a stoic. He knew that all in the end was fated badly. A man should combat the putridity of life to the limit. Therefore he would go through everything without changing, without breaking. He would show himself consistent in his beliefs. Even to the execution.

But not Artie. Not Artie, dead. A wave of emotion returned as from some far distance, engulfing and washing out everything Judd might have felt for Ruth, his silly puppy love of the last few days, making him ashamed of the moment a few nights ago, after the whorehouse, when he had loathed Artie's face. He saw Artie now, the laughing, easy college guy whom everyone loved—Artie standing at Judd Steiner's execution, watching, talking with clever pity about the poor Judd he had known, a deranged genius. With the old quick pleasure, Judd saw himself on a scaffold, his hands tied behind him—on the scaffold as on a platform where slaves were sold in ancient times, sold or executed. Multitudes stood below, and great, immortal words of parting came from him, his legacy to mankind.

Ruth would weep.

Crap. He would not be defeated, not by such clods as were beside him, like this beefy McNamara, a bull stuffed into a human suit of clothes. Now was the real test; now he would outwit everyone. Now was the chance to prove to himself that he was of another mental caliber, of another orbit entirely.

When the car stopped in front of the La Salle Hotel, Judd was surprised. The men escorted him through the lobby. Why a hotel? Perhaps it was all nothing. "We've got a suite here," Peterson offered. "The state's attorney don't want to expose people, you know, if the papers get hold of it."

It was a dead giveaway, then. They didn't have anything for sure. The outcome depended on him.

*   *   *

It was not only to protect innocent people from publicity that Horn had moved over to the hotel. There had been no such consideration for other suspects during the previous week. The schoolteachers, the crazy drug clerk, the unemployed architect who owned a Winton—they had all been thrown to us, as though to stop our mouths. But after that frustrating, killing week, here was at last a hard clue. And Horn was simply at nerves' end. His staff was exhausted. He didn't want any distraction while he dealt with this one good lead. Because if this one petered out, the case seemed hopeless.

It would be conventional to suggest political importance. Certainly it would look bad if the case remained unsolved. But in the midst of the work, I doubt if the state's attorney, any more than we reporters, thought predominantly of an effect on elections. All of us, including the police, were much more deeply embroiled. We were struggling with the first and lifelong problem of man—to find out how things happen.

Now, from the optometrist, Horn had three names. Only three pairs of glasses of this prescription, encased in this new, expensive brand of frame, had been sold in Chicago.

Those three names could bring only bafflement and dismay to the prosecutor. One was a middle-aged lady piano teacher, who lived on the North Side. The other was a fairly prominent accountant. The third was the son of a millionaire, living in the Kessler neighborhood.

The piano teacher was quickly eliminated. Her glasses were on her nose. The accountant had been out of town for the past three weeks. He had his glasses with him, he wired, and would be glad to show them to anyone designated by the authorities. That left Judah Steiner, Jr. A last chance. It might all blow away in a fizzle, this great clue of the spectacles. Maybe the glasses came from some other town.

In the inner room of the suite, Horn gave his instructions. With his characteristic, choppy motion of the elbows, he emphasized that this had to be it. He wouldn't have a trick remain untried even if the youth were the son of the mayor himself. Horn left the preliminaries to Joe Padua. He would hold himself in reserve.

Padua had a liquid voice and liquid eyes, a touch of Rudy Valentino in the fluid way he moved. He was a tripper, because he could go along, polite and soft-toned, and then, in the conventional manner of a stage prosecutor, suddenly turn cold and murderous, a gun.

So Judd was brought up the elevator and into the suite. Joe Padua introduced himself, and his handshake was affable. His antagonist, Judd surmised, was in his thirties and probably a graduate of John Marshall or one of those downtown diploma mills. At once, Judd told of his interview with Captain Cleary. Padua, too, he saw, had known nothing of it. Glibly, Judd repeated how he frequently took his birding classes to that very area. He was sure he felt his opponent's hostility shrinking. The glasses might have been lost out there at any time.

Nevertheless, Padua tried. "We just wanted to ask you, Mr. Steiner, you do wear glasses?"

"Well, as I told Captain Cleary—in fact, I left a statement in writing with him—I did wear glasses for a while, when I was boning." He put on a you-know-how-it-is smile. "I'm studying law, and this is quite interesting to me, my first practical contact; but as I was saying, the reading can get pretty heavy."

"Don't I know." Padua gave him back the smile.

"I was getting headaches, so I had reading glasses prescribed, but the condition disappeared a few months ago."

"You stopped boning?"

Judd chuckled. "Well, it's curious, I still read just as much, but in any case the headaches ceased, so I don't believe I've made use of the glasses in two or three months."

"I see." Padua picked up the glasses from the table, one of those hotel-room writing tables that look like vanities, and handed them to Judd. "Are these yours?"

Judd felt them against his hand, with that sense of natural contact given by a familiar possession. He put them on. "Well," he said, "I would say they were mine, if I weren't sure that mine are at home right now." He laughed shortly. "That is, unless someone swiped them, though I can't imagine why."

If it went that far he could suggest a whole flood of possibilities. He might have left his glasses at the university, or anywhere; the murderer could have picked them up. He was certainly safe if he played it right, because with this bit of evidence alone—and it was clear it was all they had—they wouldn't dare go to court. Not against a son of Judah Steiner!

"You say your glasses are at home?"

"Why, yes. As I haven't worn them for months." He turned to McNamara, who was sitting by the door. "If you'd have mentioned it at my house, I'd have produced them for you."

"Well—" Padua smiled—"it won't take long to pick them up."

McNamara arose from the chair.

Judd placed the glasses on the desk. "I believe mine are a very common prescription," he said, and then checked himself. He didn't want to seem to have been thinking about the case. Could it be possible that they had called in everyone in town with glasses of that prescription? No, that would have meant thousands. There must have been some other factor leading to him. What could it be?

He smiled at his questioner, and made an abortive gesture to shake hands on leaving. But Padua didn't stand up, didn't reach out his hand. As he left with McNamara, Judd felt that he had not exactly won the first round. A draw. He felt subdued. In any case, he decided, he ought not to talk so much. Just treat the whole thing as an understandable nuisance.

He thought over the interview. It was a little disturbing that his antagonist had been so brief. Why hadn't they asked for his alibi? Or perhaps that was on the good side. As for the glasses, perhaps Almer Coe had recognized them in some way as their product. Even so, a big firm like Almer Coe must have sold hundreds of the same prescription.

Would Artie still be in the house? Perhaps he had fled.

Artie could run up to Charlevoix, take his boat, and hide out on one of those little islands, as he had so often dreamed of doing. Perhaps they should both have beat it up there, and they would be living there together now, hermits bound together for the rest of their lives.

Max had just come home; he was dressing to take his fiancée to the theater. Judd explained curtly, annoyed with Max for being there, "These men are from the state's attorney's office. It seems the glasses found in the Kessler case are similar to mine. They've been checking all the people who have similar glasses."

Max blinked once or twice, as though uncertain whether to take an insulted attitude toward the authorities or make a gag of it. "I'm just going to get my glasses and show them," Judd said. "They're in my room."

But McNamara and Peterson followed him upstairs. On entering the room, the detective was startled. "What's this, a museum?"

Judd explained that he was an ornithologist. But he felt instantly that the room had made a point against him. He was now someone queer. Trying to recover, he made an effort to impress the detective, telling him this was the most complete collection in the Midwest, and that he had a special permit to shoot specimens, even in the city parks. The man's dumb-animal stare altered. A glint of respect had come into it.

Meanwhile Judd made a show of looking among his papers, on his desk. Then he opened a few drawers. "I haven't used them for such a long time—" At the second drawer he said, "Oh, here!" He picked up the spectacle case, then held it in his hand with a puzzled look.

McNamara took the empty case from him, as though he had expected something like this.

"I can't imagine—" Judd frowned. "They must be around here somewhere." He poked aside a pile of books.

The maid had come to the door. "Have you seen my glasses anywhere?" he asked. "I haven't used them for some time. I can't imagine where I left them last."

"Why, no," she said. "Did you look downstairs in the library?"

He never read in the library. The last one who read there had been his mother; not a book had been added since. Frowning, Judd started downstairs, to make a show of it. "There was a mob in here yesterday; we had an engagement party," he remarked. "A lot of our friends got tight and turned the house upside down."

McNamara nodded but did not at once follow him to the stairs. It swept through Judd's mind that they would search his room. In that moment he tried to visualize everything that was in his desk, every scrap of paper. The ransom letter had been typed on stationery bought outside. The envelope was not from his stock, either. No, the place was safe. And yet he felt uneasy. If they started to search, should he demand a warrant? Or would that be bad, arousing suspicion? But McNamara turned away from the desk and came downstairs. The other one, Peterson, still stood there.

Judd made a big show of searching the library, the living room, irked as they followed him from room to room. Peterson had come down, finally; he remained aloof, but McNamara seemed to want to be helpful, picking up a magazine here and there as if expecting to find the glasses underneath. Or was he a cagey brute, using this means to rub it in? Judd said, "Well, I really can't explain it. I must have lost them somewhere without realizing it."

Max, all dressed up, ready to leave, appeared in the hallway. "Look, kid, what's this all about?"

"Can't you see!" Judd snapped. "I'm looking for my glasses."

"Well, so you lost your glasses, so what?" And to the detectives Max said, "This is ridiculous." But he checked himself. "Of course, I realize you have to go through with it and make a thorough checkup. But——"

"I'll have to go downtown with them again," Judd said, "and explain."

"Say——" Max half laughed at the idea of even having to make such a statement, but he told the detectives, "anyone you want to vouch for the kid here—why, Judge Wagner is a friend of my father's. I understand, I've read in the papers, the Judge has been very helpful to the Kessler family. Now, Judge

Wagner's known Judd since he was a kid. Why don't you give him a ring?"

"Well, that would depend on them downtown," McNamara said.

"Do you want me to come along, Judd?" Max offered.

"Why, no! What for?" Judd was smiling again, but his hostility to his brother was rising in him, stronger than ever.

"Well, give Judge Wagner a buzz if there's any complication," Max repeated.

*　　　*　　　*

Now on the drive downtown the silence was ominous. Whatever he thought of saying might be interpreted the wrong way. Judd remarked only that he hoped his carelessness wasn't going to keep them working very late. It was all right, they said; they were used to it.

McNamara asked about the birds, and Judd started to talk enthusiastically. "A kind of hobby?" the policeman inquired.

"Well, it's more than that." And he gave them examples of puzzling things about migration and mating. Perhaps all this would show them he was unworried.

The hotel room looked messier. The men had had sandwiches and coffee sent up; plates and cups were scattered on desks and chairs. As they looked up toward him, Judd had a schoolboyish sense of shame, as though he had struck out. McNamara handed the empty spectacles case to Padua. "He couldn't find the glasses," he said.

Padua picked up the horn-rimmed spectacles from his desk, slipped them into the case. He made nothing special of the little action, but, gesturing with the same hand, introduced Judd to an older man.

"This is Mr. Horn, the state's attorney," Padua said.

On first sight, Horn had a way of confusing people. He was not so much ugly as odd-looking; his face was exactly half-moon in shape, with a tiny, almost caved-in nose. His torso was bulky, his legs were very short, his movement was abrupt. And his voice had a shrill, rather feminine pitch.

Horn's presence had intensity. There was never anything relaxed about him. He had an intensity, I suppose, beyond his capacity; otherwise he would have become a very important man. The drive was there.

"Do you want to admit now that these are your glasses?" he demanded in his shrill voice.

Judd retained his schoolboy smile. "I don't want to admit anything I'm not sure is so," he said.

Horn went in again. "You know this looks serious, Mr. Steiner."

"Indeed I do," Judd said. "It's quite embarrassing. They may even be my glasses. But after all, my family is quite well known. Judge Wagner is a friend of the Kesslers' and he knows me quite well——"

"Do you want to talk to Judge Wagner?" Horn said.

"Well, he could tell you something about me."

"All right." Horn tilted his head to Padua. "Let's get Judge Wagner on the line."

They all subsided into a kind of neutrality while Padua tried the Judge's home, and finally reached him at the Kesslers'. Padua handed the phone to Judd.

"Judge Wagner," he began, "this is Judah Steiner, Jr. . . . Yes, fine, thank you. I'm calling you in rather unusual circumstances, from the state's attorney's office, or rather his suite at the LaSalle Hotel. They are investigating persons whose glasses resemble those found in the Kessler case, and mine happen to fit. Well, I thought, or my brother Max thought, you might want to say a word——" Smiling, he handed the phone to Horn. The least it could do, Judd told himself, was to keep them from pulling any rough stuff. If they didn't lay hands on him, he was sure he could ride it through.

*   *   *

Charles Kessler leaned close in to Judge Wagner, listening. Their faces had the same expression, troubled, disappointed and yet persistent. Of all they had hoped for, when the glasses would be identified, only this had come.

Judge Wagner repeated that Judd was a brilliant boy, a Phi Beta Kappa at seventeen, a law student, and the son of one of the most respected men in Hyde Park. "Still, you have your investigation to make," he said. "Let justice take its course."

Sighing as he hung up, he said to Kessler, "No, this is really impossible. Some kind of accidental coincidence."

*   *   *

Horn replaced the receiver, musing. Padua turned to Judd, as with a new thought. "Tell us this, Mr. Steiner— Judah——"

"My friends call me Judd."

"Well, Judd, if I may—you say you've been out to the field there, in Hegewisch?"

"I should say a couple of hundred times. As I told Captain Cleary, I was out there quite recently, the Sunday before this awful event. I even remembered running across the mouth of the culvert there. I was trying to get a shot at a species of crane, and I tripped."

"You tripped?"

They were all staring at him. "Why yes, I recall it distinctly." He waited for one of them to make the connection, and Padua obliged.

"You could have dropped your glasses then?"

"Well, it doesn't seem probable. I don't recall bringing them along. As I said, I hadn't used them for a few months. Unless—" he reflected "—unless I had quite simply left them in the pocket of my jacket and entirely forgotten they were there."

They all looked at each other. A chubby, silent one, in a corner, taking notes, he didn't like.

"Well," Padua said, with that impersonal air of having to go on until every detail was clarified, "when you saw all this in the papers about the glasses, and you knew you had been on the spot, and even had tripped there, didn't it occur to you that these might be your glasses?"

The moment had come for a decision. "Well, no," Judd said.

"No?"

Horn put in, "Didn't you check up to see if you had your own glasses?"

"Well, even if it had occurred to me, I believe I would have avoided checking on it."

"How's that?" asked Padua.

"In a hysterical situation of this kind—" he laughed, a bit nervously "—one wouldn't have wanted to risk having to get involved. I might even have had some silly notions about the third degree."

They all chuckled. Then Horn said, "Now, Judd, you, a law student, ought to know better than that."

"There were all those stories about what was happening to that teacher."

"What stories?"

"Well, I happen to be acquainted with a newspaperman on the case, and——"

They wanted to know what newspaperman. And what had the newspaperman said. Oh, he hadn't said anything specific, but it was just one of those popular ideas.

"Well, all right. No one denies there is a lot of talk about the third degree." In Padua's smile there was almost a hint of "you'll see for yourself." But he persisted, "So even as a law student, you didn't think it your duty to check what appears to have been in back of your mind, whether they were your glasses, so you could identify them and save the state a lot of trouble if they were. And you also must have realized that in the meantime we were running down false clues, and giving the real culprit more opportunity to get away."

"There might have been a question in the back of my mind," Judd said. "But in the situation——"

Horn said, "Then you admit now that these are your glasses?"

"Why, I can't say for sure. It could be possible."

A point had been reached. There was a prodigious relaxation in the room; the note-taker put down his book; men moved around; Horn whispered something to McNamara, who went out. Everyone was smiling now.

So they had pinned that on him. But what was it? Nothing. His explanation was perfectly logical. No one could ever prove it had happened otherwise. There were half a dozen witnesses to vouch that he had been out to Hegewisch that Sunday, birding.

Horn stood up, crossed the room in the most casual way —oh what a cheap show they were putting up; wait till he imitated Horn for Artie! Horn took the glasses from the case, and put them in his breast pocket. "You carried them in your pocket like this?"

"Why, yes, that was where I would habitually carry them. I could have left them in the pocket of my jacket. I hadn't worn the suit for some weeks. But—I believe it is this suit I have on now."

Suddenly Horn performed a curious little shuffle with his feet, and half flopped over, like a vaudeville dancer in a buck-and-wing, nearly losing his balance. Startled, Padua and the others lunged to catch their chief. But Horn steadied himself, grasping the back of a chair. He straightened up. Then he touched his hand to his breast pocket. The glasses were still there, intact. "Would you like to show me, Judd, how you might have fallen, and the glasses dropped out? Especially since you have on the same suit."

"Why, it seems to me that when I did use them habitually, they were always falling out of my pockets when I bent over." Horn was holding out the spectacles. Judd slipped them into his coat pocket, smiling.

"How did they fall? Will you show us?"

"Well, I'm not much of an actor," he said, chuckling.

"Just let's see if they fall out."

"Well, the terrain isn't exactly the same, you know. I tripped, I think it was down an incline, down the overpass of the railway tracks there."

"You do know the site quite well," Padua remarked.

"Still," Horn said, "let's give it a try."

With a slight frown at being put in a situation where he had to make a fool of himself, but yet a forced, politely obliging smile, Judd made a few steps toward the center of the room, and then fell forward, landing on his palms. As he straightened himself, he had difficulty concealing an angry sense of humiliation. But he made himself chuckle. "Of course when you try it never happens."

They smiled with him.

Padua now came forward and arranged a little pile of stuff in the middle of the floor; there were a couple of telephone books, with a few smaller books on top.

"Do you want me to break my leg?" Judd said.

"I'll risk mine first." Padua reached out his hand for the spectacles, but then corrected himself, putting them aside, "Anybody got another pair? We might be needing these some day in court, who knows."

The secretarial fellow, now introduced as Czewicki, also an assistant state's attorney, handed over his shell-rims. "Be careful. You want to leave me blind?"

"Don't worry," Horn said humorlessly. "The state will buy you another pair."

Padua slipped Czewicki's glasses into his pocket, walked back a few steps, then allowed himself, with a certain elegance, to trip over the phone books. Nothing happened. He offered the substitute glasses to Judd. "Want to try?"

Judd thought of protesting at this point. Still, this nonsense could turn in his favor. "I suppose I might stand on my head," he joked. "That ought to do it." Then he let himself trip over the books, pitching forward. At least, he wished that the bastard's glasses would be smashed. But no such luck.

It became too stupid. Five, six times, he must have tried it. Horn was sitting there like a schoolteacher watching some inept pupil try an ordinary experiment. Frowning, he rose and said, "I've got an idea. Would you mind taking off your coat?"

"Why, no," said Judd, "I'm getting hot from all this exercise anyway."

The state's attorney took Judd's jacket and placed it on the floor. Then, as one absorbedly performing some abstract demonstration, he picked up the jacket by its bottom. The glasses slipped soundlessly from the pocket and lay on the carpet.

All looked at Horn as though he had performed a great feat.

"That's how it might have happened, isn't it?" said Horn, helpfully.

"Why, obviously," said Judd, "glasses can fall out that way. But I don't recall having my coat off that day." Instantly he wanted to kick himself. Why hadn't he said sure, he had taken off his coat, and let it go at that. He tried to backtrack. "But of course I might have."

Padua was shaking his head, thoughtfully. "You wouldn't pick up your coat that way."

"Why?"

"You're pretty careful about your clothes," Padua said. "I noticed it, because I'm the same way. But if you were in a hurry, or perhaps—in the dark—"

Judd stared back at the fellow, unblinkingly. Certainly, he told himself, he was superior in intelligence to this wop. He must simply be careful not to be tripped by his own overconfidence. He must not try to prove them wrong on each remark, as he had done so far. He would let this remark pass entirely.

Receiving no reply, Padua resumed, "Another point confuses me. When you spoke to Captain Cleary last Saturday, the question of the glasses did come up." So during the last hour, they must have been in touch with Cleary. They must now have the report he had written at the station.

"Yes. I told him I used to wear glasses."

"Then, surely when you got home you checked up?"

"No," Judd said. And as they stared at him: "Perhaps that was when it crossed my mind, and I decided not to. As I said, I would have hated to see my family get involved over an unhappy coincidence of that kind."

Horn nodded.

Padua took a long breath, and said, quietly, "As a matter of fact, you knew they were your glasses the whole time. You lied both to Captain Cleary and to us."

"I resent that!" Judd snapped.

Horn looked toward Padua. There might have been a hint of disapproval in his expression.

With elaborate casualness, Padua said, "You've seen this ransom letter in the papers. What did you make of it?"

"Well, I didn't study it very carefully."

"Here." Judd was handed the letter. He made himself read it over, word for word, so as not to seem familiar with it.

"Judd, what sort of man wrote that letter, do you think?"

"Well, obviously he is not uneducated. I would say at least a high-school graduate. There don't appear to be any errors in grammar or spelling. Unless—the word *kidnaped*. It is spelled here with two *p*'s."

"Isn't that correct?"

"I think it would be the British way," he said. "I believe we would use one *p*. But either could be called correct." How he had argued with Artie about it! But now, Judd felt that making this point separated him from the letter. He replaced the letter on the desk.

After a short silence, Horn said, rather formally, "Suppose you tell us where you were on the afternoon and evening of May 22."

"May 22?" Now, this would be the last round. "Oh, the day of——"

"Yes."

"Well, offhand, I suppose it was a day like any other day. I went to my classes. . . ." Should he say he had had classes in the afternoon? No, they could easily check on that. Now he was approaching the barrier. The alibi. The week that he and Artie had agreed upon for using the alibi was technically over. Today was Thursday. "May 22—that was a Wednesday, wasn't it?"

"Yes. A week ago yesterday."

"I don't recall any special activity on Wednesday."

"But surely, only one week ago—you've got a pretty good memory about almost tripping out there in Hegewisch a few days before that."

"Well, I had my Harvard exam on Friday morning, so I was pretty busy studying."

"Friday morning—you took an exam?"

"For Harvard Law," he said modestly, so as not to antagonize these cheap cram-school grads.

"How'd you make out? Was it tough?" asked Czewicki.

"Of course it was only an entrance exam, and I boned up pretty well."

"A Phi Bete would have no trouble," Padua said.

"That's a great school," Czewicki said. "You'll probably come back here and beat the pants off us."

"Oh, he'll be doing corporation work," Padua remarked.

Horn brought them back to the topic. "What time did you leave the university? On Wednesday."

"About noon."

And where had he lunched? At home?

"Well, I usually lunch with friends. Yes, Wednesday I believe I lunched at the Windermere with a few friends— Willie Weiss and Artie Straus." They wrote down the names. Artie's name. For the first time, he had brought Artie into it. "Wednesday, Wednesday—I recall driving my aunt and uncle home, in the evening."

"What time was that?"

"About ten. Perhaps a little after."

"They had been visiting?"

"Yes. For dinner." Let them assume he had been home for dinner.

"You were home for dinner?"

Too easily checked. "No. I was out. I came home to drive them." Now he would have to use the alibi. He had to tell some kind of story. Why had he and Artie chosen to put a time limit on the alibi? They should have agreed to stick to it until he sailed. He tried desperately to think of some other plausible story, but his mind seemed frozen, blank. There was only this path.

"Were you out alone?"

"With a friend."

"Girl friend?" Padua said.

"Well, yes, in a way."

Respectfully: "Can you give us her name?"

Judd hesitated.

After all, Padua kidded, the girl's honor was scarcely at stake, since he had come home by ten o'clock.

Perhaps he could still keep Artie out of it. He said he couldn't tell the girl's name because he didn't really know her name. It was a pickup.

They exchanged looks again.

"I thought you were so busy studying," said Horn.

"Well, you know how it is before an exam. You bone on the last day—at least I always do. I stay up all night before the exam, as I find that a sleepless night makes me extremely alert. So I did my intensive studying on Thursday."

"And Wednesday you were out on the town." Padua clucked his tongue.

Judd gave them the alibi, but without Artie. How he had gone birding most of the afternoon in Lincoln Park, then he hadn't returned home for dinner because—well, his dad might then have expected him to stay in and study, as his dad was a bit overanxious about that Harvard business. So he had eaten in a restaurant, and then cruised around. He had picked up this girl on 63rd Street, and taken her to the wooded island in Jackson Park, and tried to make her, but she wouldn't come across, so finally he had let her out to walk home. She had said her name was Edna.

And just where had he picked her up?

He gave the corner again.

Could he find her?

Well, possibly she hung around that neighborhood. He was pretty sure he could recognize her.

"By the feel?" Padua cracked, and they all laughed.

Padua resumed. And was there no one else to substantiate his whereabouts on that day? Judd smiled, as if to recognize that it sounded pretty fishy. But all the more reason for them to believe it. Surely a guilty person would have prepared a pat alibi.

"A lone wolf," Padua said.

They went over the whole thing again, and again and again.

Horn, sitting on the edge of a table, remarked in a toneless voice, "Look, Judd, you see where that leaves us. Now, we've talked to the judge and he vouches for you. Your family is one of the most respected in town. Now, we don't want to prolong this. If there is anyone at all who can corroborate this account of yours, that would be a great help."

For what happened at this point, Judd blamed himself. He could have tried to go through with it on his own. What made him bring Artie in, he never quite understood, unless it was a sense of fairness—he had been going through this ordeal for a couple of hours, and it was only fair for Artie to share part of it. Perhaps there was even a feeling that Artie would want to share the experience. And beyond this was a certain terror. Despite all their soft expressions, he had reached a stone wall. There was nowhere else to turn.

"Well," he said, "I wouldn't want to involve anyone."

They jumped on it. Surely it would simplify things if someone had seen him, been with him.

"Well, a friend of mine was along with me, but the fact is, his mother is a highly refined woman and it would be quite a shock to her to hear that her son participated in such—"

"—pastimes?"

He waited.

"Perhaps we could handle it in such a way as to spare her feelings," Horn said. "You notice we are over here in the hotel, so as not to attract any unnecessary attention."

Padua asked, "You had another fellow with you when you picked up this girl?"

"Who was it?" Horn demanded.

He couldn't back out of it now. "Artie Straus."

Once more, the sigh of relaxation spread through the room. Judd hated baseball, but from way back in his Twain School days, when they had tried to get him into things by making him the baseball manager, he recognized the feeling among the men: the second out.

"Straus was with you when you picked up this girl?"

"Well, we picked up a couple. The fact is, we had some drinks, in the afternoon while we were watching for the birds." Somehow that always tickled them. "And we thought we had a little too much on our breath to go home—it would show—so we went to the Coconut Grove for dinner, and then we drove around and picked up these girls."

"Straus," Horn repeated as he wrote down the name. "That the Straus Corporation?"

Judd nodded.

A low, appreciative whistle came from Czewicki.

"Can you give us his address?"

McNamara was already coming forward to take the slip of paper. "Say, that's right across from the Kessler house," he said. "Say, I know this Artie Straus—he gave us all that dope on the schoolteachers."

"He's been extremely interested in the crime," Judd said. "His little brother was in Paulie's class at Twain. And Artie is a kind of amateur detective."

As McNamara left, Horn stood up, smiling. "How about some dinner?" he suggested, in the tone of a man who has done a good day's work. "I'm starved."

"I could eat," Padua agreed.

They discussed having dinner sent up, but then, to Judd's surprise, Horn suggested they all go down to the dining room.

It was an amiable meal. Not once during that hour did they touch on the crime. Various law schools were discussed, and, as Judd had suspected, it turned out that Padua was a product of evening courses at a downtown school.

The University of Chicago's law school was outstanding, Padua said—it would certainly have been good enough for him, without going off to Harvard.

"My father insists on Harvard because Harvard is the best," Judd remarked. "That has always been his attitude. Buy the best."

He said it inadvertently. He would not have wanted to antagonize them. And indeed, none of them seemed to take it as a bragging remark.

*   *   *

During that dinner, the feeling began to grow in Padua that he would soon understand this case. No such feeling had come to him with any of the other suspects. With that poor, broken schoolteacher, Steger, he had felt only vacant. So many circumstances had seemed to fit, and he had dutifully pounded down every scrap of Steger's resistance. He had left Steger in the fishbowl to experience other tactics, and had come back to pound down farther on the jellied brain of that misbegotten, denuded suspect. But he had done it all by rote. Now, with Judd Steiner, Padua had that unmistakable glimmering, the feeling that, even aside from the material facts of the case, the crime would become comprehensible.

Why had it come just now? Had the glint in his mind come from Judd's remark about buying the best, always having the best? A pampered kid, a prodigy, a young man who had always had everything he wanted. How did that lead to the murder? And the ransom? To prove he could get something on his own?

Padua remained quiet while the conversation flowed into

other channels. Judd was discoursing on ornithology now, explaining about the stuffed birds McNamara had seen in his room, throwing in Latin names of species, and mentioning some rare specimen he had discovered.

One of the squad, a sergeant named Fleury, said bird shooting was his favorite sport; he knew a fine lake in Wisconsin.

It wasn't the shooting part, Judd broke in. He didn't particularly enjoy killing birds, but when there was a scientific reason, the killing became incidental. He went on elaborating his point, his voice becoming somewhat clacky as his self-assurance mounted.

But once more, a word, a phrase, had glimmered for Padua. ". . . the killing became incidental."

Toward the end of the meal, Judd wanted to go to the men's room. He had been drinking a great deal of water—was his thirst a sign? As he arose, Fleury made an involuntary movement to follow the suspect, but Horn shook his head.

* * *

The moment Judd was away from the table, the discussion began.

"That was a pretty fishy story about those broads," Sergeant Fleury offered, to make an impression on Horn.

Czewicki pursed his lips. "He's a smart cooky. He had a whole week to fix up a better story, if he had anything to do with it."

"I think he did it," Padua said.

They all looked to Horn. "We'll damn well find out," he said, his voice rather shrill.

* * *

When the detectives picked up Judd, Artie felt excited to the point of elation. Of course Judd would get out of it, the bugger. Or were they swatting him? Judd couldn't stand a scratch. He'd bawl. He'd confess.

Maybe the best idea would be to scram, right now. But if he beat it, the game would be up. What did the cops have so far? If they knew anything much, they'd have arrested him, too. Then, if it was only Judd, it could be the glasses. Or it might be only some more questioning about birding. That was it. The police were baffled. They were going over the same old ground, just as they had picked up Steger a second time. Judd had got through it once; he'd do it again.

Artie prowled around Judd's house. No, it might be dangerous to stay there. He decided to go home and wait for Judd to call.

Suppose he beat it up to Charlevoix? That could be natural—merely running up there ahead of the Memorial Day crowd. And then, if he heard anything bad about Judd, he could jump into a boat, hide out among the islands. Go across to Canada, up to Alaska. . . .

At home, Artie retreated to his room. Two hours had passed. Surely Judd was back from downtown. The little bastard was teasing him.

Artie phoned the Steiners. The maid answered. She told him in an anxious puzzled voice, Mr. Judd had come back with those men, but he had gone again.

"What?"

Yes, they had all come back, to look for Mr. Judd's eyeglasses. Mr. Max had been home at the time.

"Did Max go with Judd and those detectives?"

No, Mr. Max had gone out to a social engagement, she believed.

Artie hung up. Still, it couldn't be too bad, or Max would have gone along with Judd.

*   *   *

His mother was talking about the week end at Charlevoix. Did he want to invite anyone special? Artie held back the news about Judd. He made all kinds of funny suggestions about Charlevoix. How about Fatty Arbuckle? There was a good man for a party!

"Arthur! Fun is fun, but do you have to be so vulgar?"

Putting on a record, Artie snapped his fingers to the music. He seized her and danced her around for a moment. Then, all through dinner, he was subdued. Mumsie even remarked on it. He was thinking of his future, Artie said, and everyone laughed. His father remarked, "Well, in fact it's about time." But Mumsie said he was still only a baby.

After dinner he watched from an upstairs window. And

he saw the Marmon drive up. That goddam little bastard, could he have confessed! Artie rushed into his room, seized his automatic. Should he shoot it out? Should he lam the back way?

His mother approached, calling from the stairs in a puzzled voice that there were some gentlemen to see him. Artie threw the pistol into the drawer. Carrying a gun might spoil things. Coming down with Mumsie, he recognized McNamara and the other guy. "Hi!" he said. And to his mother: "It's some friends of mine from the detective force. I've been helping them on the Kessler case. There's an important new clue."

"Oh God, I hope they've found the culprit," she said.

As he went out the door with them, Artie said, "I've always wanted a ride in one of your Marmons."

"You've got it," said McNamara.

*   *   *

With a dozen other reporters, I was on watch in the state's attorney's office. We had been there for hours. Somewhere, we knew, Horn was questioning the possible owners of the glasses.

All we could do was wait. A couple of squad men were on duty, and whenever one of them left the room, several reporters jumped up and followed, hoping to be led to Horn. Most often, it would be to the toilet, and we'd all guffaw. Whenever the phone rang, to be answered by Olin Swasey, an assistant on duty, we pleaded to talk to his chief, if that was Horn on the wire. But he only smiled, shaking his head.

It was then that Artie Straus came in with McNamara. We all stirred. But Artie was not an unfamiliar figure, and it actually did not occur to us that he was brought in for questioning.

"Well for crissake! Are you on the force now?" I joked.

"The boy reporter!" he greeted me. "You seen Judd? Say, Sid, were those really his glasses?"

Before I could fully grasp the immensity of his remark, the whole crowd converged on him. Judd? Judd who? Startled, Artie turned silent. The pack wheeled on me, on McNamara. Meanwhile Swasey rushed Artie into a private office.

The morning-paper men beat angrily on the door. Why should the *Globe* get all the breaks? they complained. Since the *Globe* man knew who this Judd was, everyone had a right to know.

Swasey said he would telephone for instructions. A moment later he emerged and said all right, the glasses belonged to Judah Steiner, Jr., a law student at the University of Chicago. Artie Straus was a friend of his. That was all.

Everyone knew the Straus family. And the Steiners? The word spread that they, too, were multimillionaires. Instantly, we were all on the phones, trying to contact the two families. At the Steiners', no one was home.

I saw Mike Prager hang up his phone and go out. He was probably rushing out there to see if he could find someone.

At the Straus mansion, a brother, James, made a statement. Artie had been trying to help from the beginning, he said, and would surely do all he could to aid the police now. As for Judd Steiner and his spectacles, he was confident some reasonable explanation would be forthcoming.

*   *   *

Meanwhile Olin Swasey had begun to question Artie. The interrogation was matter-of-fact, and had Artie then given the same story as Judd, about the two girls, suspicion might have been turned away from them for a time, perhaps altogether. But the week of their alibi compact was over, and so Artie utilized their agreement that after one week it was "each man for himself." He was the master criminal making his own getaway.

Wednesday? he repeated. He'd hung around the frat, maybe played cards. He'd eaten at the frat and gone home. No, he hadn't been with Judd Steiner.

Swasey didn't press his questions. Indeed, after going over the story a few times, he left Artie sitting with McNamara, and slipped out through a side door. But as it happened, an extra man from the *Examiner,* just arriving, recognized Swasey coming out of the building and followed him across to the hotel and up to the mysterious suite. Thus, the hiding place of the state's attorney was uncovered. Soon enough we were all there.

We couldn't get to see Judd Steiner. But from Sergeant Fleury we learned that Steiner had definitely taken a bird-lore class out there to Hegewisch the Sunday before, when he must have dropped his glasses. That seemed the end of all the excitement. A false alarm again. And the best clue was eliminated.

Tom and I went into a Raklios for coffee. I started to speculate on whether it was even remotely possible that Judd could have committed such a crime. Why, I had been out with him last Friday. Ruth had been going out with him since then. And suddenly my sense of a fated personal involvement, whose meaning had not yet been disclosed, came over me again, and I believed it was possible.

Tom brushed speculation aside. The hell with the psychology, he said; that comes later. So far we knew Judd claimed to have lost the glasses on Sunday. Suppose we could find someone who had seen him wearing them between Sunday and Wednesday? "Isn't Judd the fellow we saw Artie talking to, coming out of that law exam, the day Artie helped us locate the drugstore?" Tom recalled. "Maybe some of the boys in his law class would remember when he wore his glasses the last time."

Then the whole drugstore incident stood in a new light. Artie's weird insistence on our going out with him in the rain, to search for it. And another recollection struck me. How Artie had said, about Paulie, "If you were looking for a kid to kidnap, that's just the kind of a cocky little sonofabitch you would pick. . . ."

The crime seemed to lie within reach.

We decided Tom had better stay with it downtown. I took the I.C. train, wanting, somehow, the few moments of sitting by a window on a train, instead of hurtling through the streets in a cab.

The light spilling from the windows touched up the ragged edge of the lake, and there came into my mind a scary image. It was once when I was a kid in Racine, and some other kids had taken me to the lake shore, and we had stayed after dark, and they had told me of monsters that crawled in the bottom of the waters and crawled out at night reaching to pull you under. Slimy shapeless monsters, you couldn't even imagine.

There came again to me the whole perverted side of the story, and I found myself matching Judd to it. That night at the Four Deuces, his ceaseless sex talk, his lustrous eyes. I began to visualize him with the murdered boy. And then a shuddering anger took hold of me. All week, what he might have done, going out with Ruth!

*   *   *

She was downstairs in the drugstore, taking care of the soda fountain, as she usually did when her parents went out. Ruth was wearing one of those white waitress coats that I loved to see her in. A middle-aged man was eating a sandwich. I went to the other end of the counter.

Like her mother, Ruth made you eat something right away; and it was true, I hadn't had any dinner, only coffee and sandwiches at odd hours. But I felt also that her busying herself immediately was a sign that she didn't know where she stood with me. Something had been happening in her.

Ruth drew coffee, and as she leaned to give it to me, I wanted to take her face in my two hands. She had put on a provocative smile, and was going to inquire about my big activities, but changed as she saw my own expression. "Is anything wrong, Sid?" Then: "You look so tired."

I told her quietly, "Listen, Ruth, the glasses in the Kessler case, they've found out they belong to Judd Steiner."

She kept staring at me, her pupils getting dark.

"He says he dropped them out there, the Sunday before, when he was birding." I had meant to be roundabout; perhaps I had even intended to try to find things out about Judd from her. But under her gaze I had to say it all at once, so as not to seem to be personally accusing him.

Without taking her eyes from me, Ruth came around the counter. This was an old signal; we would go to the back of the store, to the prescription cubicle. We had used to go there, and swiftly kiss. Through a slot that showed the store proper, you could see if anyone was coming.

Ruth seized both my hands. "Sid. You want to prove he did it."

"I want to find out," I said.

Her mouth had remained slightly open. Now the tears came slowly, on her cheeks. I could not know, then, about the night before at his brother's engagement party, and about the ride she had taken with Judd, and the misery in him she had felt, against her breast. I could not know about the strange time on the beach. Yet it was all conveyed, somehow. I knew something had happened in Ruth, some kind of love for him. And if I had not seen her in these last days, if I had stayed away, it had not been only because I was so busy; surely I had remained aside, with the instinct of a man who knows he must give a rival emotion a chance to prove itself, or to run itself out.

My heart hurt for her. It seems that I can still feel the ache of it, today. "You poor kid," I said. I held her close, to comfort her.

"Sid." She controlled herself enough to talk to me. "I don't know what it is. But—things happened between us. I feel he is somebody, somebody who—you can't explain." I stroked her hair.

The man at the counter had finished; there was a pharmacist on duty, who came from behind the drug counter to take his money. Still holding Ruth, I watched them as though there were some importance in the transaction. I kept saying to myself with murderous irony, Now you can get a scoop, the girl angle, Judd Steiner's girl, exclusive story. Or would I now become one of those people trying to keep a girl's name out of the papers? My own girl, who happened to have had a few dates with Judd Steiner while I was busy on the story.

And what was Ruth to me now? Was she still my girl? Hadn't something happened in her during this last week? If Judd proved really to have done the crime, and got convicted and executed, would I not always feel that but for the crime, Ruth's love for him would have developed?

"Ruth, can't you tell me?" I begged. "Not for the paper. For us."

"Oh, Sid. I don't know what I feel. Only, last night, he was so terribly, terribly unhappy about something." She gasped.

I thought that perhaps we were both being melodramatic. Judd might simply have been frightened, all this week, knowing that the glasses could be identified. His whole story could be true. He might really have lost them out there.

I tried to tell this to Ruth, sitting her on a stool by the prescription bench. She became calmer. But now we couldn't meet each other's eyes at all. We both knew the dreadful truth of her first intuitive reaction. It could be Judd. Knowing him closely now, she had admitted it was not impossible.

Presently I left. I walked past Woodlawn. I didn't go to the frat. A bitterness and a grief for Ruth kept mounting in me. I grappled with the image of Judd Steiner, someone like myself, my own age, a prodigy like myself, graduating at eighteen, in the same school, reading the same books, and attracted to the same girl.

If we were in so many ways alike, surely I would come to understand him. And yet he had done that most incomprehensible, that most horrible murder. Yes, he had done it. I knew it. Ruth had known it instantly, and now I knew it. And since I knew it, I would somehow find the means to prove it.

It was a fury that seized me then. A fury that there were so many things in Judd like those in myself. I would find what else there was in him, to prove that he was far, far different from myself.

I had walked to the Fairfax. I remembered that coming home from the Four Deuces last Friday, Artie's girl Myra had told me I must call her, at the Fairfax. And I marveled ruefully at the symmetry, the reporter's rote, that had led me from Judd's girl—for so I must now think of Ruth—to Artie's girl.

Myra was home. Her voice had that combination of surprise and knowingness that girls have for young men who they were sure would one day phone. I said I was downstairs; could I come up? Myra was heartbroken, but she was going out—why hadn't I given her more warning? I told her I was there in my working capacity and she became quite intrigued. Her date hadn't yet arrived, so would I please come up?

I entered the huge living room, overlooking the park and the lake. Myra introduced me to her mother, who then withdrew, and Myra settled me beside her on a huge custom-built sofa. I told her the news.

Her thin cigarette-stained fingers clutched my sleeve. Could anything happen to Artie? Myra's voice, in excitement, had a hoarse quality; it seized you, like her fingers.

I said I was sure Artie was only being questioned as to whether he had been with Judd on Wednesday. Judd had to be checked in every detail, because of the glasses.

"That little worm. That devil. Oh, Sid!" Her eyes glowing darkly, she became solemn. "Do you think Judd could have done it?" Myra sucked in her lower lip, like a little girl who has said something forbidden. I didn't answer.

"I always told Artie that Judd would get him into real trouble. You know, Artie likes to have fun, and he'll do wild things, but he'd never hurt anybody. But Judd——" Then she said no, this was beyond Judd. How could the police even imagine, even of someone a bit strange like Judd, how could they imagine—?

And yet she was imagining it, with me.

"Did Artie say he was with him?"

"I don't think so."

Oh, Artie had probably been out chasing girls that night. Didn't I know Artie! But he had his serious side, too, she said. All his playboy act was a cover-up. He could be extremely sensitive. Whereas Judd really gave her the creeps. She had nearly broken with Artie over his constant companion. Judd was always tagging along, like the other night when we had our double date at the Four Deuces. And did I know that Judd had been taking out my little friend, that attractive, lovely girl, Ruth? Judd had taken her last night to his brother's engagement party.

"Yes, I know. In fact——" I stopped.

Myra's huge burning-coal eyes examined me. She moved a trifle closer, and lowered her voice. It was as though we were both, in our ways, jealous of this same Judd.

"You know, Judd's never really had a girl," she said. "I mean—if there is really something serious between you and Ruth—he's probably just experimenting. He likes to experiment."

I shrugged, to show I wasn't worried about Ruth, and she hurried on, "I don't mean there's anything wrong with him; it's just he's such a conceited intellectual. He thinks women are inferior." She was babbling as though to distract herself from the real, the dreadful question. But it had been running on, underneath her babble. "You know what he sometimes called Artie? Dorian." Myra sucked in her lip again. We looked at each other.

Then I asked if she could remember about Judd's glasses. Had she seen him wearing his glasses early last week? Between Sunday and Wednesday?

She shook her head. "I'm almost ashamed to try," she began. Then, again, intimately: "Sid, you don't really think he could have—" Soon she went on: of course, this wouldn't be for the paper, I must swear. But we were friends, weren't we? Well, from what she had heard was done to that poor little boy, and Judd was obsessed with pornography, we had to be ready to face the ugliest truths in the world. Didn't I remember the other night how he kept bringing perversions into the conversation, the perversions of Aretino? Of course some boys utilized talk like that to excite girls, but with Judd it was different, she was sure; he was always bringing up such things. In fact he had translated some especially pornographic thing from Aretino, the thirty-two perversities. And he was always talking about the decadents, Oscar Wilde and Sade. "I used to think it was a pose."

I said maybe it was. Nothing had as yet been proven.

Myra clutched my arm again. "Oh God, Sid!" And then, determinedly: "I'll say I was with Artie on Wednesday." But it was with a feeble laugh, at the pathetic preposterousness of anyone like herself taking part in an alibi.

Her mother came in, and Myra said we were talking about books, and her mother asked had I read Sherwood Anderson? She liked to keep up with modern writing because of Myra, she said, and she thought Sherwood Anderson was very interesting.

Suddenly Myra jumped up. "Sid is taking me downtown," she told her mother. "Artie arranged to meet us at the Sherman."

"Oh?" her mother said, and smiled. "You youngsters all went out together last week, didn't you? That's nice, I like it better when you go in a group. Have a good time, dear, and don't stay out too late."

*   *   *

All the way downtown, Myra talked incessantly, a flood of coquetry, of sophistication, shot through with sudden worried remarks about Artie, but simply as though he were in a scrape, another of his scrapes, and quite confidentially she told me now, Artie was always in scrapes, a wild driver, for one thing—there was the time he had nearly killed someone, in Charlevoix, and nearly killed himself, too, in the accident, his car overturning, and the worst was, he had stolen out the back window to drive to a dance. She giggled. But it was only things like that he did, madcap things; Artie would never hurt anybody deliberately. And then she would suddenly be quoting from Amy Lowell, and A. E., and arguing about something I had said in class about Keats. Then some gasping questions about law, as though at moments the possible reality struck her. Then she would tell me all about Artie's girls— Artie told her everything, how far he went with each one. Of course every flapper on campus was chasing him, but for all his flamboyance, for all his clowning, she said, Artie was really very unsure of himself. Could I believe it?

We got out by the County Building, and I showed her the lighted windows on the eighth floor, where Artie was; but no, I told her, she couldn't go up, and I walked her over to the College Inn. She begged me to go and see how things were, so I left her while I hurried over and talked to Tom. I had Artie's girl at the Inn, I told him, but I didn't want to use her name, and as for Judd, she couldn't remember seeing him with his glasses.

Tom said nobody was bothering Artie much; he was just sitting in there. And Judd, across at the LaSalle Hotel, was still sticking to his alibi about their picking up the two girls. But Artie didn't confirm Judd's story.

*   *   *

Late into the night, the situation remained unchanged. Judd had no idea that Artie was failing to corroborate his tale.

Cool, in perfect control of himself, he kept repeating the details of the story, how they had picked up the girls, Edna and Mae, how they had taken them to the Coconut Grove and then to Jackson Park. He even appealed to Horn to have the newspapers request the girls to come forward. And so detailed was Judd's story, in contrast to Artie's vagaries, that Padua himself finally went over to question Artie. It seemed impossible, Padua remarked, that he couldn't recall what he had done nine days ago.

"Well, can you?" Artie challenged.

Padua tried, and after a while, managed. But Artie had had his laugh.

Then Padua asked, had Artie ever had dinner at the Coconut Grove?

"The Grove? Lots of times." He had dragged all kinds of dates there.

Had he been in one of the parks, that Wednesday? Jackson Park? Lincoln Park?

Had he ever heard of a girl named Edna? Or Mae?

So Artie surely knew, then, that Judd was using the alibi; still he did not corroborate the story. He became a little more doubtful, saying maybe he had cruised around—he must have been blotto most of that day; he couldn't remember anything for sure.

Padua left Artie and returned to Horn's suite at the LaSalle. Now the questioning of Judd became a little harder. They shoved an envelope in front of him, and had him print out Kessler's name and address. Then over again. And again.

*   *   *

Several times I stepped out of the College Inn to see if the lights were still on, up on the eighth floor. "Do you think he is getting the third degree?" Myra would ask breathlessly when I returned, and I would reassure her. But she recalled the tales Artie had told her, all week, about that schoolteacher getting the third degree. "Artie looks strong but he isn't," she said. "They could make him confess to anything!"

I reminded her that the state's attorney would be a little more careful with a Straus than with a mere schoolteacher.

Myra shuddered. "Ply me with liquor," she said, and I replenished her glass. Then we danced.

Dancing belly to belly, Myra whispered she wished she could get up the nerve to give herself to Artie. Not as a way of holding him, but because anything else was dishonest. Virginity was just a rag; a girl should have the courage of her convictions. She didn't want to be a fake—did I think she was a fake, a false alarm? "I'm a tease, I'm no good," she repeated. But then, it wasn't only sex attraction between her and Artie. She was his real friend. As far back as when he had that awful governess, Miss Nuisance—Newsome. Again, Myra sucked in her underlip. What a game it had been for years to fool Miss Nuisance, who practically never let Artie out of her sight, making a model boy out of him. The triumph was every Saturday afternoon, when Artie wanted to see the serial movies— you know, where the heroine was tied to the tracks, and the train was coming. Artie loved them, *The Perils of Pauline,* and of course Miss Nuisance would never allow him to see such things. So on Saturday afternoons he was supposed to go to the Children's Symphony, with Myra, and her mother would leave them in the concert hall while she went shopping, and then Artie would slip out to a movie on South State Street, and Myra would cover up for him. Oh, the angelic face on Artie when he told Miss Nuisance about the symphony!

I thought of the college-boy face on Artie, upstairs now answering their questions, and I thought of the easy laugh of Artie at the frat, telling us how he had got by some gullible prof with a borrowed term paper, and then I thought of that ghastly remark about the "cocky little punk." Something must have shown in my face, for suddenly Myra's fingers dug into my shoulder, frantically. "Oh, Sid, I'm saying all the wrong things. Sid, you believe he could have done it!" We stood there, the sweet music flowing around us. "You don't know him, you don't know him!" she pleaded desperately. "Artie couldn't have done it. He's just a playful kid. Judd is trying to drag him into it. Judd could have done anything!" She was limp on my arm, and I guided her back to the table.

In her hoarse, almost sepulchral voice, Myra kept begging me to say I didn't believe Artie could have done a thing like that. Instead, something in me kept pressing forward those words of Artie's; I kept wanting to tell her his remark: "the cocky little punk." But I couldn't let myself add to her fear. I began arguing it down in myself. A murderer would never have made a remark like that, a dead giveaway. I ended by reassuring her. Artie would come out all right.

We left the Inn. Up there in the County Building, the lights had gone out. "Do you think he is still there?" Myra asked. I said probably he had been taken somewhere for the night.

Where? Where would they take him? Not to jail! Oh, why didn't Artie just leave that devil Judd to his fate!

It was after three. An occasional cab moved on the quiet Loop streets. Myra couldn't bear to go home yet; she wanted to walk to the lake. As we walked, her spirits lifted. She quoted Edna St. Vincent Millay, about burning the candle at both ends, and about the ferryboat, and then I quoted Carl Sandburg about the lake and the fog coming in on little cat feet. Someday, she said, perhaps I would get to know the real Artie who was like us, who was only trying to escape the futility, the nothingness, of the world. It was nearly four when we got into a cab. She rested her head on my shoulder.

In the lobby of her hotel, there were only a few all-night lights. Out of sight of the desk, she told me good night, and then turned her whole body to mine, her mouth to be kissed. It was partly the conventional good-night kiss of a date, and yet it was voracious, with a ghastly emptiness. Her body felt utterly boneless to my hand, and her eyes were open with a kind of beady look, child-eyes watching for the result of a naughtiness.

Then in her husky voice, she begged that whatever I did, I wouldn't put her name in the paper, would I? I said of course not, as if it were sacred.

I had the driver take me back downtown to the LaSalle. Tom was just coming through the lobby. "They took them someplace to sleep," he said. "That's all for tonight." A couple of other reporters speculated with us for a moment, then drifted off.

It was no use going home. We were too keyed up. We sat

in an all-night Thompson's. We went over everything again. I described both girls, feeling myself a betrayer, but telling myself it was not for the paper; it was truly to help solve the crime that I betrayed their emotions. I told about Ruth. "She really feels Judd could have done it; I can tell. Something happened between them in the last few days—I don't know. But when I told her about the glasses—"

"That's your girl, Ruth," Tom said.

I nodded. He passed me his cigarettes. I said Myra, too, believed Judd could have done it. But not Artie.

Tom looked up with an odd smile. Nobody had really suggested it could have been Artie. He was only being held because of Judd's attempt to involve him in a phony alibi. So why had Artie's girl felt she had to deny the possibility?

Then I recognized that Myra was as afraid as Ruth.

The families, Tom said, seemed not to be worried. They had called Horn, and he had assured them the boys would be sent home as soon as certain technicalities were clarified.

And that seemed all that was known. "Listen," I said to Tom, "I promised we wouldn't use the names of the girls." He shrugged.

We went out and picked up the morning papers. The *Tribune* had dug up some campus talk about Judd: "a brilliant atheist." His friend Artie Straus, it said, had not yet confirmed Judd's alibi.

And there was one new item, exclusive. A chisel had been picked up on the night of the murder by a private night watchman who had seen it thrown from a car, on Ellis Avenue, not far from the Kessler house. The blade of the chisel was wrapped in adhesive tape. There was blood on the tape. The chisel was believed to be the murder weapon. And the car from which it had been thrown was a dark sports model. It could have been a Stutz, like the one owned by Judd Steiner.

The *Examiner* had more about the millionaire playboy suspects. Judd was a strange sinister genius who kept to himself. Artie, whom Judd was trying to involve in his alibi, was one of the most popular men on campus, especially with the girls. Myra's name was mentioned, as was Dorothea Lengel's —"girls of good family" often seen with him.

We went up to the office. At daybreak, there wasn't a soul in the *Globe* building. We walked up to the newsroom on the second floor. The desktops were clear, the wastebaskets were empty. It didn't look like a place we knew.

We went to Tom's desk, and on a sheet of paper began to enumerate the points against Judd. The glasses. An unproven alibi. Now, the chisel.

Coldly enumerated, in the calm of that huge empty room, each point in itself seemed dubious, and the whole monstrous accusation seemed a nightmare. But for me, the strongest point of all, unwritten, was Ruth's weeping. Yet with the distance of morning, this, too, seemed to have a thousand possible meanings. Perhaps she had wept in dismay that I could be trying to prove Judd a murderer, only because he had gone out with my girl.

Tom too, starting to put together our story, said we had better be careful. There was nothing really definite. The boys might even be released by the time the noon edition was out. After all, they had been questioned a whole night, without results. Boys from families like that couldn't be held much longer. Probably some big lawyer would appear the moment the courts opened, with a habeas corpus writ.

*   *   *

Instead, we heard that Horn was permitting an interview. Thus the families could be reassured that the boys were receiving no rough treatment. After the late-hour questioning, Judd had been sent to rest up, at the South Clark Street station, and Artie to Hyde Park.

I felt sure that when I saw Judd face-to-face, I would know. I would see him somehow as with Ruth's eyes, with Ruth's intuition. All that I had learned about him would help me to understand whether the Judd I now saw was capable of a perverted murder.

And when I saw him my instant reaction was one of shame, for having last night been half convinced of his guilt. A large group of us, reporters and photographers, assembled in the South Clark Street station. We were led to the rear detention cells. Judd was in one of them; the door stood open for us. He greeted us with utter calm, chatting about his "adventure," and answering, with politeness and gravity, even the silliest sob-sister questions.

Some food had just been brought in for him; there was coffee, but no spoon, and Judd eased the atmosphere at once by borrowing a pencil from Richard Lyman with which to stir his coffee. "I hope you have another one for your notes," he said. And recognizing me, he said "Hello" with a smile that admitted social acquaintance, but made it clear that this would not give me an edge in the interview.

There was a sandwich, and Peg Sweet had to know what kind, so Judd showed her that it was an egg sandwich, and offered to share it with her, and then he politely made sure no one else wanted a share. We joked a bit about his few hours in jail, and Judd declared that in Mr. Horn's place he would do the same—it was the state's attorney's duty to make an absolutely thorough investigation.

Lyman took the lead, and asked about the glasses.

"It's queer," Judd said. "All along when I read in the papers about the glasses, I had a feeling they might be mine."

"Why didn't you check on it?" Mike Prager cut in.

"Well, I suppose there are things we don't really want to find out. Wouldn't that be the psychology of it?"

The questioning got to his alibi. "I certainly hope those girls come forward," Judd declared. "I wish all of you would appeal to them in your stories. It may be a bit embarrassing, but it is more embarrassing for me if they don't."

We all laughed, and made the point about their honor being safe since they walked home. Peg Sweet said archly, "That is, if they did walk home?"

Judd smiled amiably. Somebody behind me asked, "What would you do with ten thousand dollars?"

Eagerly Judd replied, "Why on earth should anyone imagine I would kidnap someone for ransom? I get all the money I want from my father, and besides, I teach three classes in bird lore, and get paid for it." He seemed to be speaking directly to me. And in that moment I was sure he was innocent. What indeed had I been blaming him for? An interest in sixteenth-century Italian pornography? Was that any worse than guys at the frat showing you dirty postcards?

Did that make him a pervert and a murderer? Confronting him, I found the whole idea impossible to believe, and from that moment, I suppose, there had to grow for me the mistrust of human confrontation that is so deep a mark upon our time. What could you truly know of anyone by looking into his face, his eyes? How can you be certain of anything among human beings?

Tom's stock phrase—"What do you know for sure?"— reverberated in my mind as I walked from the police station. For besides Judd's story, there was Artie's. If you believed one, you couldn't believe the other. Yet both were polite, smiling, and eager to help solve the dreadful crime.

Artie had been brought back to the state's attorney's headquarters. Through the glass door to the corner office I could see him talking to Padua. Artie waved to me, and presently Padua came out.

"Listen, Sid, maybe you can help us." Padua walked me to a quiet spot near the windows. Wasn't I the one who had been with Artie that day, finding the drugstore? And wasn't I a fraternity brother of Artie's?

I nodded, but said that didn't mean an awful lot.

Still, he said, maybe I could talk to Artie. The other fellow, Judd, had at least told some kind of a story. But Artie wouldn't remember anything. "You know how it is. We don't want to keep these fellows any longer than we have to. Ask him for God's sake just to tell the truth. Maybe they were up to some kind of shenanigans—"

I didn't believe Artie would tell me anything, but I couldn't refuse to try.

"Just one thing," he said. "Don't tell him Judd's story."

I went in. "Hail the boy reporter!" Artie said. "Hey, have you got me in the papers?"

"You're famous."

"Am I a suspect? Hey, this is the nuts!"

I grinned. "Well, you know this is a hell of a case, Artie, and the glasses were all they had to go by."

"Oh, I don't blame them," he said. "But my mother is kind of upset; otherwise this would be fun. They let me call her this morning, but she's still upset." He threw away a half-smoked cigarette and almost instantly lighted another.

"Artie, look," I said. "Why don't you tell the truth, whatever it is, and get it over with? Whatever you and Judd may have been up to, it isn't worth being suspected of the crime."

"You think I was up to something with Judd?" he asked.

"Oh, hell, you're always together," I said.

"That what he said?" He smiled back at my smile. "What do the guys at the house say?"

"I haven't been out there yet."

"Yah, you've been busy making time with my girl!" he kidded. "I've got my spies in operation. Hey, what does Myra think? She think Judd could have done a thing like that?"

"Well, those glasses were pretty embarrassing," I said. "And the fact that you don't remember anything specific about Wednesday makes it look worse for him."

"It looks bad for him?"

"Oh, I wouldn't say that exactly. But I guess the question has to be cleared up."

"Listen, you don't think they're going to make him confess, or any crap like that?" he demanded. "You know Judd. If they start pushing him around . . ."

I said I didn't think there was any pushing around. "But, Artie, if you know anything, if you can help him out of it—you know him better than anybody."

"He says I was with him?"

"Well—"

"Aw, can it. Why would the cops pick me up if it wasn't to check on his story? I didn't lose any glasses anywhere."

"Well, if you were with him, no matter what you were up to," I repeated, "it can't be as bad as this. Otherwise, they can't let him go. There's nothing to prove his story."

Artie stared at me. Again he flung away his cigarette. "Okay, kid." He walked around, then perched on the desk. He cracked, "If you see Myra, don't do anything I wouldn't do." Then he said, "Stick around out there. I may give you another scoop."

Padua looked inquiringly at me as I came out. I smiled

but shrugged. He hurried back into that office. Now Artie
began to remember a few details about Wednesday. He had
been all ginned up all that day and evening, he said, but some
of it was beginning to come clear.

I suppose Artie feared that with his story uncorrobo-
rated, Judd might break down. If Judd confessed, would he
not in his bitterness involve his partner? Then the only hope
for both of them now was for him to help Judd get released.

So Artie remembered that Wednesday. He now recalled
that there had been a couple of broads involved—he could
even think of their names: his was Edna, kind of redheaded.
They had picked up the girls on 63rd Street. . . . And so,
point by point, he told the same story.

Why had he waited so long to tell it? "My mother doesn't
like me to run with these cheap broads," he said. "And if it
gets in the papers, it's very embarrassing."

Yet, even his waiting could be interpreted favorably. For
if it were simply an alibi that the boys had agreed upon,
wouldn't Artie have come out with it at once, the way Judd
had?

*   *   *

And so, that morning, the suspicion was lifting. Judd
Steiner, cheerful and candid. And Artie Straus finally cor-
roborating the story of Mae and Edna.

Probably, because of their wealth, I thought, I had been
resentfully ready to believe anything of them.

As I entered the newsroom, Reese tilted his chin, a signal
for me to step to his desk. "I think they're clean," I said.
"Artie Straus just told exactly the same story as Judd Steiner,
about the two girls."

He shoved the early edition of the *American* toward me,
with part of their lead story circled in red pencil. It was a beat
on us. A letter, a carbon found in Judd Steiner's room. "Dear
Artie," it began. I stood there, reading, trying to understand
the strange letter. It seemed to deal with some bygone incident
between Judd and Artie and Willie Weiss, and at first glance I
could not see its importance. There was some quarrel about
whether Judd had betrayed to Willie Weiss a secret that Artie
had confided to Judd. This letter was Judd's denial of be-

trayal. It had been written after a big scene between them. A passage, printed in bold type, read: "When you came to my house this afternoon I expected either to break friendship with you or attempt to kill you unless you told me why you acted yesterday as you did." This was Judd, to Artie.

The letter continued: "You did, however, tell me . . . Now, I apprehend, though here I am not quite sure, that you said that you did not think me treacherous in intent, nor ever have, but that you considered me in the wrong and expected such a statement from me. This statement I unconditionally refused to make until such time as I may become convinced of its truth. . . ."

It was a strange letter, but what did it have to do with the case? I glanced back at the date—months ago, last November. I moved away from Reese's desk, and went on reading: "The only question, then, is with you. You demand me to perform an act, namely, state that I acted wrongly. This I refuse. Now it is up to you to inflict the penalty for this refusal—at your discretion, to break friendship, inflict physical punishment, or anything else you like, or on the other hand continue as before. The decision, therefore, must rest with you. This is all of my opinion on the right and wrong of the matter."

I looked up, puzzled. Reese was watching me. I shook my head to show my mystification, and resumed reading: "Now a word of advice. I do not wish to influence your decision either way, but I do want to warn you that in case you deem it advisable to discontinue our friendship, that in both our interests extreme care must be had. The motif of 'a falling out of— —' would be sure to be popular, which is patently undesirable and forms an irksome but unavoidable bond between us. . . ."

Feeling Reese's eyes still on me, I had drifted down the aisle, and was standing near Tom. At the moment it didn't even strike me as important that the paper indicated some words omitted after "falling out." Perhaps they had been undecipherable. There was more to the letter. Judd begged Artie for his decision, yes or no, and he suggested that in any case they keep up an appearance of friendship such as "salutation on the street" and on all occasions when they might be thrown together in public.

But what did it mean? Aside from showing the intensity and violence of their relationship, what bearing could it have on the murder of Paulie Kessler?

Tom was typing rapidly, to catch us up on the story. He had a scrawled copy of the letter on his desk. That bastard Mike Prager had gone out with the squad last night when the cops had ransacked Judd Steiner's room. Mike had pocketed this letter. Only just now, after his paper was on the stands, had Mike turned the letter over to Chief Nolan.

Tom handed me up his notes, made in Nolan's office, containing the left-out words, where the dashes had been used. "The motif of 'a falling out of a pair of c----------' would be sure to be popular. . . ."

I saw again the naked body of the boy, I heard again the gruesome argument at the inquest, I saw the candid smile of Judd Steiner, whom I had just left, I saw the boyish smile of Artie Straus, whom I had just left, and I felt a sick bewilderment, an inadequacy. I was too innocent; I was unable to recognize the ugly and the bestial that lay underneath the smiling world.

They had seemed so bland. I had been equating them with myself. I had made a fool of myself just now, telling Reese, "They're clean." These diseased creatures, these perverts, they had been going out with me and with my girl. Judd had done something to Ruth, disturbed her deeply in some way. Perhaps something of this was what she had known. Through Judd's ways, she knew they had done it. They had done it to Paulie Kessler.

Then I held myself back. I tried to tell myself the word could have been used in jest, the way we commonly used it around the frat house. I tried to tell myself, even if they were perverts with each other, that still didn't prove they had done anything to Paulie. I tried to tell myself not to let my anger run away with me, at having been fooled, and at having been scooped by Mike Prager.

"What do you think of your pals now?" Tom said.

"God, this looks like they really might have done it."

"You can't prove it from this," he said.

"And Horn looked about ready to let them go." I told him of Judd, so easy in his interview; I told how Artie had finally confirmed Judd's alibi about picking up a couple of girls.

"Picking up a boy, he means," Tom said. While he typed, he handed me a few more pages, copied from Judd's letters.

First there was a document that had been attached to what was to become known as the "c - - - - - - - - letter." It was a legal-sounding document, and its purpose was explained in the letter itself: "I wanted you this afternoon, and still want you, to feel that we are on an equal footing legally, and therefore, I purposely committed the same tort of which you were guilty, the only difference being that in your case the facts would be harder to prove than in mine, should I deny them. The enclosed document should secure you against my changing my mind in admitting the facts, if the matter should ever come up, as it would prove to any court that they were true."

Then came the document: "I, Judah Steiner, Jr., being under no duress or compulsion, do hereby affirm and declare that on this, the 20th day of November, 1923, I for reasons of my own locked the door of the room in which I was with one Arthur Straus, with the intent of blocking his only feasible mode of egress, and that I further indicated my intention of applying physical force upon the person of said Arthur Straus if necessary to carry out my design, to wit, to block his only feasible mode of egress."

I stared at Tom. As he sent up his story, we tried to reconstruct what had gone on between the two boys, to bring Judd to compose the strange letter with its accompanying "document." Judd was handing Artie "evidence" that he had locked Artie in a room, saying, meanwhile, "I purposely committed the same tort of which you were guilty." So, apparently, in a bitter wrangle they had been locking each other up! First Artie locking up Judd, because he claimed Judd had betrayed a confidence, had been "treacherous." And then Judd locking up Artie.

It had a weird overwrought echo of childhood games, locking someone in a closet—"I won't let you out until you tell me the secret." But these were university graduates, prodigies of eighteen. Where on earth did Judd imagine, before what "court," would Artie presumably ever produce Judd's legal-sounding admission of a "tort"?

And there was the curious, even touching intensity of his plea for Artie to decide the whole issue. "Now, Artie, I am going to make a request to which I have perhaps no right, and yet which I dare to make also for Auld Lang Syne. Will you, if not too inconvenient, let me know your answer (before I leave tomorrow)? This, to which I have no right, would greatly help my peace of mind in the next few days when it is most necessary to me. You can if you will merely call up my home before 12 noon and leave a message saying, 'Artie says yes,' if you wish our relations to continue as before, and 'Artie says no,' if not. . . ."

I felt almost guilty, peering into so intimate a confession. Judd, at one moment pleading with Artie to judge him, to "inflict physical punishment, or anything else you like," if he had been "treacherous," and at the next moment arrogantly vowing that he had been ready to kill Artie. And again, a few paragraphs later, abjectly begging his friend to leave a message so that he could have peace of mind. For the first time, I began to understand the strange bondage, to glimpse a love relationship entirely outside my knowledge.

And what could Artie think Judd had betrayed that was important enough to have brought the boys to imprisoning each other and to threatening death?

"Something Judd knew about Artie," Tom reasoned. Again, we studied the dense wording. At bottom it was a sort of "you said he said I said" affair. It had the ring of tempestuous accusations among children and—yes—among girls. One could see them, shrilling accusations against each other, screaming their threats, locking doors.

And I tried to set this image against the two young men I had seen only an hour ago, sophisticated, self-possessed, superior to their little predicament.

Tom handed me another sheet. This was a copy of a letter Judd had written two days later, from a train; he had been making a trip to New York. It was clear that Artie had in the meantime chosen to "continue their relationship" by taking back his accusation of "treachery." And Judd was "forgiving" him.

The point in the whole controversy, Judd said in the forgiveness letter, was to determine which of them was guilty of a mistake, for a mistake was the greatest crime a person of their sort could commit! "But I am going to add a little more in an effort to explain my system of the Nietzschean philosophy in regard to you. It may not have occurred to you why a mere mistake in judgment on your part should be treated as a crime when on the part of another it should not so be considered. Here are the reasons. In formulating a superman, he is, on account of certain superior qualities inherent in him, exempted from the ordinary laws which govern ordinary men. He is not liable for anything he may do, whereas others would be, except for the one crime that it is possible for him to commit—to make a mistake.

"Now obviously any code which conferred upon an individual or upon a group extraordinary privileges without also putting on him extraordinary responsibility, would be unfair and bad. Therefore, the superman is held to have committed a crime every time he errs in judgment—a mistake excusable in others. But you may say you have previously made mistakes which I did not treat as crimes. That is true. To cite an example, the other night you expressed an opinion, and insisted, that Marcus Aurelius Antonius was practically the founder of Stoicism. In so doing you committed a crime. But it was a slight crime, and I chose to forgive it. . . ."

Tom repeated a phrase from the beginning, ". . . exempted from the ordinary laws which govern ordinary men. . . ." I read that part over: "In formulating a superman, he is, according to the superior qualities inherent in him, exempted. . . ."

"These dirty perverts think they can do any damn thing they want," Tom said.

I was trying to recall things from Nietzsche, but then I realized that it really didn't matter what Nietzsche had said or meant. What mattered was the meaning expressed here by Judd himself—he and Artie were playing some kind of game, a superman game, and these were their rules. The rules perhaps did not provide a motive for murdering Paulie Kessler. But if Judd and Artie were "exempted from the ordinary laws which govern ordinary men," then what would stop them from murder?

It was as though two dense curtains had shrouded the possibility of seeing these rich, clever boys as perpetrators of the crime. The outer curtain was the negative one, the one that excluded them from the action, a curtain of "why they would not." For all the fears of punishment, all the laws of man provided a "why not." And this curtain seemed now to be lifting. If they really believed in this idea of being superior to ordinary law, then there was no "why not" for them. The inner curtain was the "why?" and was still impenetrable, though the sexual motive provided a rent in it.

Yet their superman idea was hard to grasp because I had seen them in everyday life. It was hard to grasp that people who lived in your own milieu, who abided by the day-by-day conventions and rules of life, paying their fares, buying their tickets, standing up for ladies—people who even followed the conventional rules of breaking the minor rules when you could get away with it, like speeding at times, or cribbing in an exam—it was hard to believe that within this very appearance of living under the same rules as the rest of us, they had their own contrary rules. It was hard to take their own words and believe them, just as it was to be hard, only a decade later in our lives, to believe that an entire nation could seriously subscribe to this superman code.

And so I went out, with a sense of deep bewilderment, to the university. What I had sensed emotionally, intuitively, the night before, from Ruth, I was now trying to justify by fact and by reasoning, and the effort seemed heavy, like trying to provide a mathematical formulation for an answer you had already glimpsed.

*   *   *

In Horn's office, too, they were puzzling over the letters. Horn was no reader of Nietzsche. He tended to brush aside the superman letter as show-off kid stuff; you never could hang anybody with that.

Perhaps he was right. We were to see the philosophy for a time as an explanation—it was even offered as a kind of excuse. But could it ever have been a cause? A rationalization, yes, even diverting us from the real source of human deeds in individuals, in nations, in ourselves.

The first letter, Horn said, was only a lot of wild talk about some silly quarrel. Except for the one fact in it: the perversion business. But even that had to be taken up carefully. In a roundabout way, Padua might try to find out if these fellows had anything to do with young boys. One thing was sure after these letters: you couldn't let these two fellows go so soon.

Padua and Czewicki had a short discussion of their own. Padua had always meant to read Nietzsche, but never found the time; perhaps Nietzsche could have helped him trip these wiseacres. Czewicki wasn't so sure. He had read *Ecce Homo* in a Haldeman-Julius Little Blue Book. It didn't tell you you could go out and murder anybody. It was just philosophy.

*   *   *

But the strange letters, published in the papers, even with the key words omitted, had raised an active apprehension in one other person who was to enter the case. Edgar Feldscher was a cousin of Randolph Straus, Artie's father. A lawyer, engaged with his brother Ferdinand Feldscher in corporation work for various members of the family, Edgar Feldscher had interests outside the law. He was something of an aesthete, a bachelor in his early forties who went often to Europe; from his last trip he had brought back the very earliest edition of *Ulysses* and a few paintings by Braque. He read a great deal, and was fond of Havelock Ellis and D. H. Lawrence. He was also acquainted with the works of Freud, and when people made jokes about suppressed desires or the inferiority complex, Edgar Feldscher was apt to start lecturing on the serious meaning of the terms.

After reading over several times the newspaper quotations of Judd's letters, Edgar Feldscher telephoned Artie's father. He was a little disturbed, he said. Of course he knew the boys had been close to each other for several years. But if stuff like this was going to be dragged through the papers, it might prove harmful to them and to the families. Besides, who could tell what might turn up? It might be time, he suggested, to get Artie, at least, out of the hands of the state's attorney.

"The harm's already been done," Randolph Straus said wearily, bitterly. Every reporter in town knew what the un-printed word was in that letter. They had been calling him. In a way, he almost wished the police would give Artie a good pushing around, to teach him not to play detective and get himself into this kind of a mess. After all, what did Artie know about the Kessler murder? But he supposed Artie would soon be released, having been held just long enough to blacken the family name and give nasty publicity to the Cor-poration. To go in now and demand his release might only make things worse, give the papers a story about the family trying to use influence.

"Yes, there's something to that," Edgar Feldscher agreed. The feeling of apprehension was deepening in him, but he couldn't find it in himself to utter the real question. No, it was impossible that the boys had done it. . . . He would keep in touch with the situation, he said. Perhaps put in a call to Horn's office. Just to make sure the state's attorney didn't pull anything too raw.

*   *   *

At the university, I tried to find Willie Weiss. For it was he who had been involved in Judd's wild letter to Artie. And wasn't it Weiss who had lunched with Judd and Artie on the day of the kidnaping? Perhaps he would tell me what kind of a secret it was, of Artie's, that Judd was supposed to have be-trayed. And also, Willie Weiss might remember whether Judd was wearing his glasses during lunch that Wednesday. I couldn't find Weiss on campus. And no one answered the phone at his home. He was probably keeping out of the thing.

It was hard to find anyone that afternoon—people were going away for Memorial Day. The frat was almost empty. I thought of two fellows I had seen coming out of that law exam with Judd Steiner—Harry Bass and Milt Lewis. Bass had al-ready gone home to the North Shore, but Milt Lewis, one of the brothers said, might still be on the tennis court.

Starting for the court, I ran into our chapter president,

Raphael Goetz. God, he said, he was glad about only one thing in this mess—that Judd Steiner had never been let into the frat. It was bad enough with Artie, but if Judd had ever got into the Alpha Beta! The papers would give people the idea that all that stuff was going on at the house. They would make out we were all a bunch of perverts. Oh, he'd been getting funny questions all morning, from police, from reporters.

Well, I said, he knew he could trust me to handle anything he told me, in a way that would protect the frat as much as possible. But things were very serious, and whatever was known about the fellows would have to come out.

We took a quiet walk down the alley. Raphael was a huge fellow, a halfback on varsity, a good student, and one of those men who endow any meeting with an atmosphere of earnest good will. In later years, he was to become a big personnel man. So now, putting his arm around my shoulders, he said, "Have they really got something on them?"

I showed him the story containing Judd's letter. He already knew the omitted word. "That all happened when they were up in Michigan," he said. His cousin had been in the chapter up there and had given him the inside story. And Goetz told me about the Morty Kornhauser incident. "He caught them at it, and they tried to take him out in a canoe and drown him." We stopped. We stood facing each other, feeling gravely that the fate of others might be in our hands. "Morty even tried to get Artie thrown out of the frat." But all the fellows thought it was Judd who was to blame. "Hell, you know Artie—he'll try anything just for the hell of it. He's happy-go-lucky, but Judd, there's something that gives you the shivers about him."

We talked more. About Artie's being such a drinker, about his betting high stakes at cards, all that stuff, but you still couldn't say he was capable of murder. He was just a loose character. He'd been lectured, and given hell, he'd been voted incapable of mentoring a pledge, but what was the use —being such a prodigy, he'd been pampered since he was a kid, and with all that dough in the family, naturally the guy was spoiled. But you couldn't say he was a pervert—why, hell, Artie was playing half the girls on campus.

I said I knew.

"I'd believe anything of Judd Steiner, but if Artie is in trouble, I'll bet that little bastard dragged him into it."

We started back toward the house. Raphael's words reverberated. Artie would try anything once, and Judd was capable of anything at all, and if Artie was in trouble Judd had dragged him into it. And suddenly I saw why Artie had held back from admitting he had been with Judd on Wednesday. For if they had been together, they could have been together committing the crime! *Judd was capable of anything.* Why not even of murder? Artie's hesitation in placing himself with Judd actually tended to confirm the crime. The story about the picked-up girls was a fake they had agreed upon in advance, but then Artie had held back from telling it, trying to save himself from implication with Judd should the alibi collapse. Artie's hesitation was actually the proof!

And just then, as if the thought of their guilt in itself caused me to find the conclusive evidence, I noticed Milt Lewis. He was in his tennis clothes, hurrying into the house. I caught up with him. "Listen, Milt," I said, "the early part of last week, do you remember if Judd Steiner was wearing his glasses?"

"I refuse to answer on the grounds of possible self-incrimination," Milt cracked. "And who the hell could remember on what day some guy was wearing or not wearing his glasses? All I know is I read in the papers that Judd Steiner lost his glasses in a very inconvenient place."

We were climbing up to his room. "That's it," I said. "He claims he lost them on Sunday. But if he was seen wearing them, between Sunday and Wednesday—"

He began pulling off his sweatshirt. "Listen," Milt said, "if you're trying to hang that conceited bastard, I'm with you." He attempted little tricks of memory. Had he seen Judd reading anything in class? in the library?

"He claims the last time he actually used them was in March."

"Hell no, I'd say more recently than that. Wait a minute." Milt Lewis seemed to pick an image out of the air. "At his house, about three weeks ago. A gang of us went there to make some notes on equity. Judd put his glasses on when he opened that portable and started typing. I can just see him sitting there under all those birds, because I kidded him that he looked like one of those owls, with his horn-rimmed glasses."

A few weeks ago? That still wouldn't prove anything. But—"You say he was typing on a *portable*?"

"Yah, it was a real hot session. We had two machines going. Harry Bass was using a big machine Judd had there, and Judd opened his portable."

"Did you notice, was it a Corona?"

"How should I know?" He stared at me. "Hey listen, Hawkshaw—" Then he grinned. "All right, I've got carbons of that typing, right here, from both machines."

He began pulling out papers, folded in among his notebooks. There were indeed two kinds of typing. In itself there was nothing startling in the fact that there should be two typewriters in a millionaire's house. The second machine might have belonged to his brother. Or he might have bought a portable when he went to Ann Arbor.

I stared at the typing, feeling somehow silly to be going so far, and yet headily sure. I picked out some of the clearest sheets. "Anybody got a Corona in the house?"

Milt was excited now. We ran through a couple of rooms, located a Corona. The style of lettering seemed the same as on one set of notes. But still, there were millions of Coronas.

For real comparison, I needed a copy of the ransom letter. It had been reproduced over and over in the papers, only a few days ago, but while the house was usually littered with old newspapers, we could now find nothing.

The only sure place seemed to be downtown. I ran along the street, found a cab. The ad-taking counter at the office was just inside the main door. There was a file of papers kept for the public. I found the page, exactly a week ago, with the reproduced ransom letter. Our story, alongside, quoted typewriter experts, pointing out that there was a faulty *p*, and that the tail printed faintly on the *y*. The same faults were on

Judd's law notes! The same, the same. I tore the page from the file.

Running the few blocks to the County Building, I felt I was watched by Judd's eyes, morose, lustrous, unblinking. At the building, I checked myself. I stepped into the cigar store, and phoned Tom in the press room. He came down. We huddled in a corner, while I showed him the two samples.

"Kid, if that bird hangs, you did it!" he said, staring at the evidence. Then, to be more sure, we hurried out to find some kind of magnifying glass. A drugstore had one. We used it right there, on the counter. The similarity was unmistakable.

Could we hold this till tomorrow, for our paper? We decided it was too important. We had to inform Horn.

But upstairs, the offices were empty. They had all gone out to dinner, taking the suspects with them. Nobody knew just where.

*   *   *

This was the famous dinner at the Red Star Inn, near Lincoln Park, an old-style eating place, renowned for its huge schnitzels, apfelkuchen, and other German specialties. If there was a moment when Artie and Judd savored their adventure, I suppose it was at the time of this dinner. For the sense that they had sought to achieve, the sense of power and superiority in knowing what others did not know, was theirs, here, and together, in the presence of baffled authority itself.

This was the thrill, vibrating in the tension of their still undecided fate. They were so far the masters, and yet, like aerialists who have already completed their act but might slip before getting off the wire, they were under a delicious suspense.

Until the cars drew up in front of the old-world restaurant on Clark Street, they could not know they would be together. It was a thought of Horn's, to confront them in this way, and perhaps catch something in an unguarded moment of surprise and pleasure.

Horn's own car, with Judd, pulled up first, and Judd in a worldly manner expertized about the restaurant, remarking that his family always had a German cook at home, though they always had to teach the cooks Jewish seasoning. Just then the second car drove up, and Swasey emerged with Artie. Seeing each other, the boys saluted with hand waves, Artie calling, "Hey! When did they let you out?"

"I'm joining the staff!" Judd retorted.

For the large party, two tables were put together at the end of the main room. The boys were only a few seats apart, with Padua and Horn between them. There was beer to be had at the Red Star, real German beer it was said, none of that needled stuff, and a good deal of jesting took place about protection and payoff, as the state's attorney and his men permitted themselves to indulge.

It might, indeed, have been construed as a farewell party, a sendoff with no hard feelings. The boys had endured twenty-four hours of examination. Since Artie had confessed his drunken afternoon and the pickup ride, and since their stories jibed, what could they be held for?

But Horn, Padua, Czewicki, Swasey, and the squad of detectives might also have been exulting inwardly, with the secret power of knowing something their adversaries did not know. For newspapers had been kept from the boys. They did not know that Judd's intimate letter had become public. They did not know that they were being looked at with the peculiar contemptuous mirthfulness of bull-showy men for a pair of perverts. No one actually had said, "Watch the fun," but holding that knowledge key was like having a special pair of glasses through which you could see the punks, nude.

Only you couldn't see anything. These rich kids had smooth manners that carried them through. Judd was perhaps a bit jumpy, hardly taking his eyes off Artie, but if you didn't know about that letter, you could put it down to apprehensiveness rather than passion.

Talk started again about the Carpentier fight, and McNamara remarked that a Frenchman could never win the championship because those frogs used up their strength in other ways.

This led to jokes about the French way, and McNamara, looking directly at Judd and Artie, said that he had been over there during the war, and some of those frogs were just as expert in the French way as their women.

But the boys showed no reaction; Artie remarked that Judd was going over there pretty soon and would send back a full report on Frenchwomen. "You mean, you boys are splitting up?" remarked the usually silent Sergeant Peterson, and still there was no reaction. Artie said his family was too poor to send him to Europe and there was a big laugh.

Judd was giving his order to the waiter in German, with minute instructions about the seasoning, and all listened, admiringly. Czewicki asked how many languages was it that Judd knew, and Judd replied fourteen, although a few were really only dialects.

"You must be a superman," Padua remarked, and Judd quietly responded, that wouldn't exactly be the qualification, according to Nietzsche.

Padua had got in a few hours at the library, reading up on Nietzsche. After all, he said, wasn't the superman definable as someone with extraordinary abilities? No, Judd said, a superman had to be extraordinary in every way.

Well, how *was* a superman recognized? Did Judd know any supermen? Was Napoleon a superman?

No, Judd replied. Napoleon had been defeated, and that in itself automatically eliminated him, because a superman could never be defeated.

"You mean, he never makes mistakes?" Padua said.

Judd was apparently too eager to expound his views to catch the echoing word. A superman was really an ideal, he said—what Nietzsche meant was a man who was more than man. In fact you couldn't precisely translate the word *Übermensch*—you had to read Nietzsche in the original to understand the concept.

But, Padua persisted, couldn't a person strive to be a superman, to act like one? At least that was his understanding from Nietzsche even though he had to read him in translation unfortunately.

The rest of the men had fallen silent, watching the duel. Yes, Judd conceded, people could strive to exceed themselves, to live by a greater measure of life, the measure of the *Übermensch*.

Well, for such people, Padua probed, what happened to the laws? If the law said you could drive fifty miles an hour but you wanted to be an *Übermensch* and drive a hundred miles an hour, who was to decide? Did the ordinary laws of ordinary people apply to the superman, or were supermen exempt?

Smilingly, Artie backed up Judd's explanation. Naturally, a superman would have to live by his own laws—all the great men of the world had made their own laws. Alexander the Great, and Caligula, and Napoleon, too, had made new laws.

Judd had suddenly grown quiet; he was studying Padua.

But those people were all rulers, Padua argued. They were trying to make new sets of laws for all men to follow. But a superman who was not a ruler, just a citizen—he would still have a law unto himself that would permit him to do anything he wanted, even things that were crimes for other people. Wasn't that the idea?

"Sure," Artie began. But Judd cut in; the trap had become too obvious. The Nietzschean idea was only an abstraction, Judd said. You couldn't apply it in practice because what Nietzsche meant was really for all men to strive to free their spirits, to become greater than they were. First, there had to come naturally gifted individuals, and they might stimulate ordinary men, but eventually there would have to be a society of supermen, a whole nation to try to live by that idea.

"I guess we haven't got there yet," Horn said.

The food came then, on huge thick platters. Padua and Judd were staring at each other, smiling as at the end of a round with no one hurt. The eating began.

After a while, Padua made another try. Not really questioning the boys, for this was a social affair, of course. But he remarked about Judd and Artie having gone to the University of Michigan together. They'd really been pretty close friends for several years, then?

Sure, Artie said. He had superintended Judd's loss of virginity; and he went on to tell about whorehouse escapades in Detroit. Czewicki suddenly made a remark about Oscar Wilde. "You know he was married and had two children. I never realized you could have it both ways." He giggled.

Judd coolly informed him that among the Greeks it was quite the custom for married men to maintain their favorite boys.

Horn declared he had learned all he wanted to know about perverts going through the dragnet in this investigation. Artie brightly recalled—hadn't a member of the police force been caught up in the net, a respectable married man?

Anyway, said Swasey, it was pretty soft for a couple of college boys to have their own car, to run around chasing gash.

There was clinical talk about pick-up techniques. And then: "Now, about those girls the other night, you mean they really didn't come across?" And Peterson offered expert advice on how to make them come across.

From McNamara came a throaty gurgle. "Anyway, if they don't, you can always help each other out."

Artie laughed with the rest of the crowd. Judd, after an instant, laughed as though he had just caught on.

There was a lull in the conversation. One of the squad asked for more beer.

*   *   *

It was said that if not for our typewriter evidence, the boys might, that evening, have been released. One other bit of evidence was to come that night, but it was tenuous, and I suppose, had the boys been released, the chauffeur would never even have offered his story.

But Emil had been troubled ever since he had read Judd's alibi in the morning papers. Judd claimed to have been riding in his car all that afternoon and evening. Emil thought about the matter, driving home by himself after taking Mr. Steiner down to his office. In the kitchen, Emil found the three servants, indignant over what was in the papers, and angry because the police had pawed through the house—it shouldn't have been allowed; why, it was only a natural accident about Judd's eyeglasses.

Emil didn't say anything in front of them. But he carried

the *Examiner* upstairs to his apartment over the garage, and he discussed the story with his wife. Of course Judd couldn't have been connected with the crime, but correct is correct. Now, a week ago Wednesday—

She joined his thought at once, as though she, too, had been going back over the days to find identification marks. "That was my dentist day. Remember, I spoke to you downstairs. Judd was with you."

They remembered well, because Emil had told her a thousand times never to interrupt when he was talking to one of the Steiners. And Judd had been impatient, too.

"But I needed the dentist money."

Then Emil came out with what bothered him. Just then, young Steiner had been telling him the brakes of the Stutz needed adjustment. "He left his Stutz in the garage. He didn't have it out at all that whole day."

"Well, he went with that Artie Straus chasing girls. They must have had some other car."

"Yes, but here he told the police he was in his Stutz. And at first Artie wouldn't even admit he was with him."

"It's none of our business."

Another thing: Artie and Judd, the next day—that was Thursday, about noon—had come around the driveway with a Willys.

"See, I told you they had some other car."

They had been washing it. Now, the Willys was not one of the Straus cars, Emil was sure. He had thought it was some borrowed car and maybe they had got drunk and been sick in it. He had offered to help clean the Willys—there were some dark spots in the rear, wine spots they said—and Artie had refused his help, saying they were all through anyway.

"Well, that would explain it," she said. "They borrowed some other car."

Yet Emil kept puzzling. By nightfall he felt it was his duty to mention the matter to the police.

"You want to make a fool of yourself?" his wife argued. "These people are good to us. . . ."

*   *   *

By evening, after the boys had been held more than twenty-four hours, each family was assembled. At the Steiners, there were Judd's aunt and uncle, his brother, his father. After all, Max insisted, Judd had explained about the glasses; both boys had explained where they had been. Why were they still being held? Max was for sending down a lawyer and getting the kid out, before any more dirty stuff, like that letter, was spilled.

Judd's father was rather silent. He had a way of being present in a discussion without speaking, except to make summaries—not exactly decisions, but summaries that left only one possible decision.

But Aunt Bertha was indignant. The boy had spent the night in jail. What was he getting to eat? Had he had a chance even to change his clothes?

"We can see that he is well treated," his father said. "But when the authorities are satisfied the boys don't know anything, they will let them go."

*   *   *

At the Straus mansion, Artie's uncle Gerald was taking charge. He was older than Artie's father, and was the most decisive character among the Straus brothers—a businessman who operated in spectacular flashes. Gerald Straus was something of a dandy in attire; he had been three times married, the last time to a girl twenty years younger than himself.

Arriving with Edgar Feldscher, he demanded action. "What's Horn holding him for? Is he arrested? If not, let's get him out." Feldscher counseled going easy. Perhaps it was the time for a member of the family to go down, put in an appearance. But not to press things legally. After all, if Horn started to dig behind that letter . . . The men's voices dropped, as though a shade were drawn between them and the women.

Finally, after phoning back and forth between the two families, the Steiner men came to the Strauses. The two brothers, Max and James, went aside. It was Max who said, "We've got to look at the thing realistically. We have to consider all the possibilities, even the worst."

For an instant, their eyes admitted it to each other. They were of about the same age. To each, the brother was still "the kid," some seven years younger—a kid with whom you couldn't have much rapport. Max tried now to make a practical suggestion. Maybe the simplest thing would even be, since the boys couldn't produce those two girls they had picked up —it shouldn't be impossible to dig up a couple of girls.

James shook his head—too risky.

"I just thought we ought to be prepared for everything. Those cops will stop at nothing to get off the hook on this case."

That was why somebody ought to go downtown, James said. Just to remind them who the boys were.

And so the two fathers and Uncle Gerald Straus went downtown. Emil drove them to the County Building.

The whole press gang was still waiting around for the boys to be brought back from dinner. Only a staff assistant, Healy, was on duty to answer the phone when the three older men walked into the office.

The press crowded around them, these men of millions who had come, we felt sure, to take their sons home out of the hands of the law. And I looked at the two fathers with a dazed sense of my own power, for I held the proof of guilt in my pocket. How had they known so little of their sons! And what did my own father know of me?

Judah Steiner, Sr., looked somehow so fatherly, so decent. The other, Randolph Straus, was of a pair with his brother Gerald—both of them more polished-appearing than Steiner, and colder in their manner.

Gerald Straus was the spokesman, turning first to the reporters. "Now, boys, we have no information; you fellows know more than we do. We only came to see Mr. Horn."

Healy explained that Mr. Horn was out to dinner. Yes, he was expected back at the office.

And the boys? Were they in jail? Or where?

Now, they could be sure the boys were well treated, Healy said; in fact, they were probably having dinner with Mr. Horn. It was just a matter of getting all the information they could provide. . . .

The mention of dinner with Mr. Horn somewhat surprised and mollified the men. "Naturally, we want them to give all their information," said Gerald Straus. "We want them to give every assistance they can in this horrible thing. You say they are in Mr. Horn's personal custody?"

"Yes, he personally is responsible."

"We merely wanted to assure ourselves," Straus said. "You know, sometimes the police can get, uh, overzealous."

Healy smiled.

Straus spoke again, choosing his words carefully, noticing that we were all taking down his statement. "Both families want Mr. Horn to keep the boys until he is fully satisfied. Mr. Horn must be satisfied that they know nothing that may have a bearing on this crime."

"The minute he is satisfied," Healy repeated, "they will be sent home."

The three men looked around, uncertainly. They were big men; they clearly knew it was only a third assistant, upon whom they had made their presence felt. Still—what more could they do?

Steiner added that if the boys were going to be held any longer, perhaps it would be best to send down a change of linen, pajamas.

"Why don't you give us a ring a little later?" Healy suggested, with his bright Irish smile.

The men spoke a moment among themselves, then thanked him, and withdrew. We all followed them to the elevator. Gerald Straus was again the spokesman. "Give us a break, gentlemen. You can see how it is. We want to help, but we also are concerned for our boys and for the family reputations. Some of you fellows have run some pretty damaging stuff about a couple of innocent boys. Now I know what you're up against, too. But, gentlemen, remember we are pretty responsible families in this town."

And so they departed.

*   *   *

Fifteen minutes later, the cavalcade arrived from the restaurant. Everyone seemed animated, friendly, but Horn laughingly steered the boys straight through the press crowd. Judd went into Padua's office; Artie went along with Swasey.

"I guess the boys won't need any pajamas," Healy remarked cheerfully.

Tom had tried to stop Horn on the wing; now he strode to the corner door, knocked, and walked in. I followed. "We've got something," Tom said. I put the material on Horn's desk.

Horn's short, jabby arms fell on the papers. He gave us a startled look, appreciative, and confounded at the same time. An instant later, he buzzed for Healy, told him to fetch the original ransom note, and to keep his mouth shut. Of us, he demanded whether we could get hold of the boys who had been with Judd when he typed the law stuff? I said two of them were waiting for my call at the frat.

He nodded. "Get them down here." His hands were clenching, unclenching. As he looked up, his eyes were glazed. "That dirty pair of fairies," he muttered. "They had half my staff believing them."

Tom made our request. Could this break be kept quiet till morning, for the *Globe?*

Horn stood up, sympathetic. "Fellows, this is bigger than a scoop. You're helping me and I appreciate it. I'm going to see your paper gets credit for this."

Padua brought Judd into the room. We were waved out. As I walked past him, Judd gave me a wary, inquiring look. In my excited state of mind, I imagined that it asked if I were trying to do something against him.

* * *

Only the typewritten legal notes were in sight on Horn's desk. Judd read a page carefully, wondering how this could possibly matter. Horn asked if he remembered typing this stuff at his house in the presence of several of his classmates? Then Judd saw himself using the portable. So they had him.

But it did not seem possible. Only now, he had bested them all. He and Artie had proven they were truly of another level; they were minds moving in a fourth dimension unreachable by these mundane police. He stared at his adversaries— Horn, who could say parlez-vous, and Padua, a slick Valentino.

And he began his last struggle, squirming and twisting to

slip through their fingers. Yes, he recognized that this added bit of evidence made a link in a fantastic chain. But, he declared, it had not been his typewriter. One of the boys must have brought it along. Who? He couldn't be sure; the typing session had taken place over a month ago. Probably Harry Marks. Marks? Where could he be reached? Well, he was the son of Gordon Marks of the Marks Stores.

"Call him," Horn told Padua.

Harry Marks proved to be in Europe.

Horn's eyes, held on Judd, shone with that unfocused metallic luster. "You think you're too clever for us," he said. "Maybe you're too clever for yourself."

Then Judd was in a Marmon again, surrounded by squadmen, speeding once more toward his home, this time to search for the typewriter.

*   *   *

When they entered the house, Judd's father came toward them with a relieved smile. But Judd spoke loudly. "Now it's the ransom letter! They want to search the house to see if I've got the typewriter that typed the ransom letter!"

Judah Steiner, Sr., seemed not to comprehend. "Is everything all right? Are they treating you all right?" he asked.

"Sure. This is quite an experience," Judd called from the stairs.

Entering his room, he saw the ransacked desk and angrily began to sort his papers. McNamara seized more typewritten notes. Padua, in the doorway, asked, "Those the same batch?" They were. But no Corona was in sight.

The maid was hovering in the corridor. "Say, Miss"— Padua smiled at her—"have you seen Mr. Steiner's portable typewriter recently?"

"The portable?" Elsa said helpfully. "Well, now, last time I saw it, it was just there, by the desk as usual."

"And when was that?"

She had come halfway into the room, and now she caught Judd's eye. "Well, I don't know."

"She doesn't know what machine she's talking about," Judd snapped. But her first words couldn't be pulled back.

The men searched the room, the closet, other rooms.

"No use. I guess he got rid of it," Padua said. The group started downstairs.

"Did you find what you want, gentlemen?" Judd's father asked.

"Well, yes and no." Padua put on his glittering smile. "Does your son own a portable Corona typewriter?"

Hopefully, Judd realized that the old man might never have noticed the machine. "Why, a portable typewriter, no, I never bought him one that I recollect. He has a regular standard typewriter, I'm sure." Steiner looked questioningly from one to the other. "Are you going to need my son much longer downtown?"

"That's hard to say. We haven't got everything cleared up yet," Padua stated.

Judd showed his father an annoyed smile. The group departed.

Judah Steiner stood there for a moment. His head was moving almost imperceptibly from side to side. Then he went to the phone. He was beginning to feel outraged. But his sister-in-law counseled him to have patience a little longer. And better to send Judd down some fresh clothing.

* * *

More and more attackers were lunging at him, but he was fencing them off. He was keeping them from plunging in the last blow. If only Artie could see how he was holding them off! But once more they were separated. Once more Judd had been taken to the hotel suite, to be worked on. And there in the room stood Michael Fine, Harry Bass, Milt Lewis. They kept their eyes averted from his; they were embarrassed. But in quiet voices they formally identified the law notes, and said when and where and by whom they had been typed.

Judd confronted them. "But you fellows know I didn't have a portable! I typed on my own machine, on my desk. Don't you remember? Harry Marks must have brought along the portable."

The others shifted on their feet silently, but Milt Lewis looked right into his eyes for the first time. "That was your machine. You had it right there. You bragged about having two typewriters, one for traveling."

Horn thanked the boys, and they went out.

They stood with us in the other room. Now it was coming, we felt. Now they might knock it out of him.

We waited, as outside a hospital door, for the doctor to emerge. But still it did not happen, and after a time the three boys departed.

*   *   *

Across the street from the hotel, the Steiner chauffeur appeared in the state's attorney's offices, carrying a suitcase of clothing. As he turned it over to Healy, reporters surrounded him for a feature story. Did the suitcase contain any snazzy silk pajamas? And how were the families reacting?

Emil fled. He drove all the way back to the house. Somehow, while on the family's errand, he had not been able to bring up his own thing. But back in the garage, he could not get out of the automobile. His wife came down; she was in her nightgown. "I won't be able to sleep," Emil said.

So he drove back downtown on his own errand.

It was just then that Horn and Padua, still unable to break Judd's denials, decided to try a little stratagem.

During the evening's frantic activity about Judd's typewriter, little attention had been paid to Artie. Hour after hour, he had been sitting in the assistant's office; Swasey didn't even ask him any more questions, only waited with him there, reading.

Now Padua came in. Artie jumped up. He confronted Padua. "Hey, maybe you can give me a straight answer. Am I supposed to be under arrest, or what?"

Padua smiled.

"You're holding me, aren't you?"

"Well, you guessed it," said Padua.

"What for?" demanded Artie, with a show of petulance. "You haven't got anything on me. I said I was willing to help you. I've told you all I know."

"You said you were with Judd Steiner all that day and evening," Padua reminded him.

"Yah, sure."

"Okay. Things don't look too good for your friend. Besides the glasses, it turns out that his typewriter was the one the ransom letter was written on. Since you admit you were with him all the time, whatever we've got him for, we've got you for."

Artie's cheek was twitching. "Are you nuts!" he shouted. "I told you we just went to pick up some janes."

"Yah, I know, that's what you both said."

It was then that the chauffeur walked in. He marched past everybody—the squadmen, Healy, all of us reporters— toward the glass-doored offices. It was so unexpected that no one moved to stop him. Opening the door, Emil stood rigid, like some converted sinner intensifying his resolve to confess. "I want to talk to the state's attorney."

Startled, Padua said, "The state's attorney is very busy. What's it about?"

"I'm the chauffeur for the Steiner family."

"Yes, I know. I've seen you. Bring Judd's toothbrush?" Padua snapped.

"I have some information I must give," Emil stated almost shamefacedly.

Padua's manner changed. "I'm the state's attorney's assistant. You can tell me."

Artie, everyone, listened. "I saw in the papers that Junior said he was driving the Stutz all day, the day it happened. I have to say that is a mistake. The Stutz was in the garage; he left it for me to put oil on the brakes; they were squeaking."

Artie seemed to sway. His gaze went from Emil to Padua. Then he moved back, and folded onto a chair. Not the glasses, not even the typewriter had had this effect on him. For both those points, there had been some degree of preparation. But Emil's testimony fitted into that detective-story nightmare, the insignificant, forgotten detail. It was as though Artie had been waiting for this to strike him.

Padua was leaning over him. "All right," Artie gasped, and ran his tongue over his lips, his eyes still evading, evading. "All right. Can I have a glass of water?"

Padua hurried to the cooler, brought the water. Swasey

pushed us away from the doorway, Emil among us, and closed the door.

In the outer room, there had come a stunned unbelief. What had been awaited, what had been so wanted, was happening.

Emil swallowed, staring at the closed glass door. He had the bewildered look of a man who only gave someone a shove, a tiny push. How could he know the fellow would crumple, collapse? Healy led him into another room before we could ask him any questions.

A court stenographer had been kept in readiness. We saw him go inside.

We waited. The men from the morning papers kept calling their offices, telling them to hold open for the big story.

Presently, Czewicki came hurrying through, from the hotel. He went into the corner office. After a brief interval, he emerged, his expression hovering between a smirk and fright, his wide cheeks seeming to wobble.

We besieged him. "Is he confessing? Did they do it?"

"It's on the way," Czewicki said, officiously, happily. "It's going on right now." And he rushed back to the hotel to give his details to Horn.

There, the chief came out into the hallway to meet him, and they walked up and down, Horn's arms already making his choppy courtroom movements. Then the state's attorney returned to the room where Judd sat. "Your partner is confessing," Horn said. Judd didn't blink. A primitive trick.

"All right," Horn said. "What about the Driv-Ur-Self agency? What about registering at the Morrison Hotel?"

Judd gave him an almost abashed look. He arose, moving about in distress, murmuring, "He can't be! He would stick till hell freezes over!"

"He says it was all your idea," Horn continued in a quiet voice, not without sympathy. "And you're the one that struck the fatal blow."

If maturity can ever be traced to a single moment, perhaps this was the instant of transition for Judd Steiner. He began to shake his head, slowly. "Oh, the weakling," he said. Then, with a spurt of anger: "So Mr. Straus imagines he can blame it all on me. You can go back and inform Mr. Straus that I shall tell the truth. The account I give shall be precisely accurate and complete." Judd drew a full breath, then added, with a kind of satisfaction, as if after all the main results would be as desired, "I shall reveal the true purpose and meaning of the deed."

BOOK TWO
The Trial of the Century

We waited half through the night, with the news leaking out to us. The confessions were going well. The time was long because the state's attorney was going over each fact, nailing down the evidence so every point could be proven even if later some smart lawyers had the boys withdraw their statements.

Thus we hovered between the two confession rooms, catching bits of the story, certain it was turning out to be a sex murder, perversion, with the ransom plan tacked on to cover the act. Just as Tom and I had thought. We waited, the hours broken only by a call from Louisville informing the state's attorney that the miserable, almost forgotten drug clerk, Holmes, had died without talking.

Behind each door the story was pouring forth; each of the culprits seemed bent on getting ahead of the other. And as usual when it came right down to the end, Horn's assistants let us know, these smarties were like everyone else—they were frantically blaming each other.

Then gradually a new and curious idea came out to us. It was that there was something else to the crime, something other than a motive of lust. This different idea was being insisted upon especially by Judd, with a kind of triumphant disdain for the authorities who, even with the murderers in their hands, failed to see the real nature of the crime. Judd vowed that lust really had nothing to do with it. And as for money—would two millionaire boys risk their lives for ten thousand dollars? He had a strange explanation to offer. This was a crime for its own sake. It was a crime in a vacuum, a crime in a perfectly frozen nothingness, where the atmosphere of motive was totally absent.

And as we learned how Artie and Judd thought of their crime, the whole event again became a mystery. For was even their own notion of it the truth?

We could, in that night, only grasp their claim of an experiment, an intellectual experiment, as Judd put it, in creating a perfect crime. They would avow no other motive; their act sought to isolate the pure essence of murder.

Before, we had thought the boys could only have committed the murder under some sudden dreadful impulse. But now we learned how the deed had been marked by a long design developed in full detail. What was new to us was this entry into the dark, vast area of death as an abstraction. Much later, we were to seek the deeper cause that compelled these two individuals to commit this particular murder under the guise, even the illusion, that it was an experiment.

Just as there is no absolute vacuum, there is no absolute abstraction. But one approaches a vacuum by removing atmosphere, and so, in the pretentious excuse offered by Judd, it seemed that by removing the common atmospheres of lust, hatred, greed, one could approach the perfect essence of crime.

Thus one might come down to an isolated killing impulse in humanity. To kill, as we put it in the headlines, for a thrill! For an excitation that had no emotional base. I think the boys themselves believed this was what they had done.

At first their recital sounded much like an account of daydreams that all could recognize. They had been playing with the idea of the "perfect murder." Is not the whole of detective-story literature built on this common fantasy? True, in such stories we always supply a conventional motive. We accept that a man may kill for a legacy or for jealousy or for revenge, though inwardly we may make the reservation—that's foolish, the butler wouldn't go so far. We accept that a dictator may unleash a war out of "economic needs" or "lust for power" but inwardly we keep saying, "Why? Why? Why?"

In this case, the conventional motivation was omitted. Judd Steiner and Artie Straus were saying that they had killed the boy, a victim chosen at random, truly for the deed alone, for the fascinating experiment of committing a perfect crime. At first we hooted at their explanation because we felt it was offered with an accent of superiority, even in a kind of triumph, as in a game where the puzzler says, "You didn't guess the right answer!" They had been caught, yes, but by a fluke, and not because we had discovered the right answer.

As the details emerged, we took apart their "perfect" action; how clumsy, how imperfect it was! We saw in each step of their scheme mistakes of construction, as any scientist, any engineer, sees clumsiness in any prototype machine and is led to wonder how a universal law could have been exposed with such a blundering device.

So each related how the plan had begun, Artie vaguely saying "a few months ago," but Judd, with his passion for precision, saying "the first time we thought of a thing like this was on the twenty-eighth of November" and telling us how on that night they had robbed the fraternity house in Ann Arbor, and how they had quarreled on their weird drive homeward. Quarreling lovers must break, or bind themselves into deeper intimacy, and so their pact was made to do some great and perfect crime together. That it should be a kidnaping came out in Artie's thought—perhaps it had been waiting in him. Now it emerged as a crime whose accomplishment would be the highest test of skill, of perfection.

Then, the step of pure logic: for security, the victim must never be able to identify the kidnapers; therefore he must be killed at the earliest moment. Thus the killing was nonemotionally arrived at; it was incidental to the perfection of an idea.

How needlessly emotional people had always been about death! In the pursuit of an impersonal plan, it was nothing, as Judd was to insist; it was no more meaningful than impaling a beetle, than mounting a bird.

The truly intriguing element of the problem would follow: how to secure the ransom, without risk of contact? Though money was not the actual motivating force, still it was part of the set exercise, and as the boys were to say, ten thousand dollars is ten thousand dollars. After the feat of a perfect murder came the feat of a perfect transfer of ransom. And so came the idea of a transfer in moving space—the train, the rented car, an abstract identity.

"And so you registered at the Morrison Hotel as James Singer?"

"Yes, Artie brought an old valise. It was of no value, less than the bill—we left it there."

Instantly, McNamara was hurried over to the Morrison. The registration was found: James Singer. In the storeroom, the tagged, abandoned valise. For weight, a few books. So clever, so careless the perfect plan—books from the university library, one of them containing a library card made out to Artie Straus.

By such tangible items the whole nightmarish, incredible tale began to become real even while the recital continued, behind each door. The rented car—and putting up the side curtains so no one could see into the rear.

"And even then you still could have stopped, desisted from the whole idea?"

"Yes." And then the lunch with Willie Weiss, and then hunting the victim, and the boy coming into the car.

"And at that moment it was not too late to stop?"

Was it? You could think it was too late from the moment Judd first met Artie, from the moment when he was born so bright, born a boy though a girl was wanted. Or you could believe that even with an arm upraised, holding the taped chisel, it was not yet too late. . . . The striking arm raised as in one of those movies where the action is frozen. How many murders are halted only as a thought in our minds? *I could kill that sonofabitch!* In how many tales do we have the moment of the pointed gun, the *Go ahead and shoot,* and instead, the dropping arm? And so from buying the chisel to the act of wrapping it in tape it had seemed that the arm would never really strike. When the first chosen victim, Dickie Weiss, had disappeared on 49th Street, it had seemed the end of their adventure. And yet the arm came to be raised.

"And in that moment you were still able to distinguish between right and wrong?"

"Right and wrong in the conventional sense, yes," Judd answered.

And so the blow was struck and perhaps even directly afterward it seemed not to have happened and that the deed could still be halted. But then they were driving the body through the streets. And then came that strange burial, the vain attempt at effacement.

"Then it was our plan to pour acid on the face in order to obliterate the identity, in case of the finding of the body."

But in the actual deed, suddenly it had seemed necessary, essential to go on pouring. "And when we were doing it, we continued pouring it also on another part of the body—"

"Where?"

"The private parts."

Then wasn't it after all a sex crime? Something sickening, to be hastily covered up, and turned away from? But the questioners had to be relentless. In that closed room, Judd was asked, "What made you do that?"

"We believed—yes, we were under the impression that a person could also be identified by—" He stopped. Perhaps he was seeing the moment more clearly than during the actual deed.

"Surely, university graduates like you couldn't really have believed that."

"We were under the impression at that moment."

But why? Why had this strange idea come over him, and why had the other obliteration seemed so absolutely necessary? In that intensely charged confession room, with all the men staring at him—Horn, Czewicki, the stenographer, as though staring through his clothes, and with all the dirty meanings in their eyes—could there then have flashed through Judd's mind some image from his childhood, seemingly disconnected, undressing somewhere, naked, and fellows, maybe even his brother, making crude jokes? For myself, I recall an incident as a boy, in a shower room—one of the kids closing his legs so that only the hair showed and jumping around yelling, "I'm a girl! A girl!" And the ribald laughter. Could some such image have pressed itself forward? Could it perhaps have given Judd a shadowy hint as to the meaning of that attempted obliteration?

Thus, there was the deed, poured out, relived in that night of confession. The body dissolvingly anointed over mouth and genitalia, then pulled into the mire, pulled blood-flecked through the swamp water and pressed into the dark tube.

Then hurriedly away, dragging the bloodied robe, bits of garments trailing, up the night lane. Wait. To scoop the earth with the sharp tool, the chisel, and bury the belt buckle which never would burn. And farther on a piece, stop, wait, bury the shoes under a crust of earth. Then as far as the road, the city, returned from the swamp to the city streets and lights. And stopping at a drugstore, Judd to phone home—the dutiful son, "I'll be a little late," to drive his aunt and uncle to their house —and Artie in the meanwhile calling a girl—"I got held up, babe, detained, puss, make it tomorrow," kidding as if he were drunk and maybe out with some other babe. Then to Judd's house, and parking the Willys a few doors away while pulling out his Stutz to drive his aunt and uncle home, leaving Artie calmly playing a hand of casino with Judah Steiner, Sr. And then Judd back—"Good night, sir," as Pater retires upstairs —then both into the Willys, the robe, the clothes still inside it. (Couldn't Paulie's father, out scouring the streets that night, have looked into the car standing only a few blocks from his house?) Then to Artie's house, sneaking down to the base-ment, the clothes bundled into the furnace, but not the lap robe—"It'll make a stench. We'll stuff it behind a bush, get rid of it tomorrow. If anyone finds it, that's virgin blood—boys will be boys, ha ha." But wait—the blood in the car. Take the gardener's watering pail, wash off the worst of it—"Can't see, that's good enough," says Artie. "Park the damn Willys in front of some damn apartment house. Clear the stuff out of it." The ether can, never used. Rope. Chisel. Thrown into the Stutz. Then drive Artie home. "Wait—get rid of the frigging tool!" And driving along Ellis Avenue, Artie flinging the taped chisel out upon the stupid world . . .

*   *   *

"Premeditated—why, they planned this thing for weeks, months," Horn told us when he emerged into the hotel corridor. He was a man with a great work done, a book written ready to be published, a sculptured monument waiting to be unveiled. "I've got a hanging case, no question. I don't care how many millions their families throw in to try to save their skins." He was not vindictive, not bloodthirsty. He was a man who had carried out a most difficult task and could be satisfied that he had handled it well.

The confessions were being typed up, he said. There was only one basic difference between them, and he chuckled at the predictable. "Each says the other struck the fatal blow."

Soon we had their own words. Artie, in the room with Padua, the quick jabbing puffs of his cigarette hardly an interruption for his breathless flow of words, had pictured himself as driving. "I pulled up alongside of Paulie and said, 'Hey Paulie,' and Paulie came over and I asked, 'Want a ride?' and Paulie said no, he was only a block from his house, and then I said, 'I want to talk to you,' and the subject came to me—a tennis racket Paulie had been using when he played on our court a few days before, a lightweight racket that would be a good present for my little brother Billy, and I said, 'It's about that tennis racket you had the other day,' so Paulie said okay and I leaned across and opened the door and Paulie got in beside me. I introduced him to Judd, who was in the back seat, and I asked Paulie, 'You don't mind if I drive around the block?' and Paulie said okay, and I pulled away from the curb and as I turned the corner the blow came from behind, three or four quick blows on the head, and the hands were over Paulie's mouth before he could yell, and then he was dragged into the back seat and a cloth stuffed into his mouth."

For several minutes, Artie said in his confession, Judd had lost his nerve there, crying, "Oh this is terrible, terrible!" and Artie had had to talk fast, make wisecracks, until Judd got hold of himself.

"This is terrible, terrible," echoed to me. It was no extenuation. But what did it mean, there at that moment? That the reality broke in, for one of them at least? Tore a rent, to be patched by Artie, kidding, "You going to get remorse?"

But for himself, Artie said, he noticed his pulse racing, he felt exhilarated, his blood beating intensely, from the moment the boy got into the car.

The way Judd told it varied mainly on the question of who was driving. He had been at the wheel, Judd insisted, with Artie in the back seat; the blows had come from the tool in Artie's hand.

At the time, in the immense excitement of having the story, the dual accusation was only an ironic sidelight to the crime, and the fact that each accused the other only made them more alike in our minds. It was only later that the simple realization came that one of them must have been telling the truth. What we had accepted as a point of likeness was actually the point where we could have begun to see a difference between them.

To this day, the crime has been thought of as a deed in which they were organically joined, like Siamese twins. This may be true as to legal guilt. But understanding will never come through such an assumption. And if we see them as two beings who became wedded in the deed, then it does become momentous that one, here, had been telling the truth while the other had been lying.

*   *   *

Again Tom and I worked in the deserted office; our long sleeplessness only made us feel sharper. Tom put the story together, gloating in the lead that said that due to the typewriter evidence secured by a reporter for the *Globe,* the murderers had broken down and confessed just as they were about to go free.

I knew I had to phone Ruth. She should learn it all from me and not from the papers. Yet I could not take the phone. In some shameful way, whatever I said would sound like a personal triumph. I procrastinated, telling myself I didn't want to wake her with this news. Then when I finally called, she had already learned it, from a *Tribune* extra in the streets. I said I would come over as soon as possible. Then she asked, "Sid, will you see him?"

"Maybe."

"Sid, Sid." It was as though she were crying, "Judd, Judd."

      *   *   *

We rushed out to interview the families. They had been wakened with the news, and the Strauses let us all in, begging for us to tell them—since we were reporters, since we had been there—hadn't it been the third degree? And as none of us had been in the room when the confessions were being made, surely it *was* the third degree; as soon as the boys had rested, and had some sleep, they would repudiate the story. It was absurd, insane!

Artie's father left the room. Mrs. Straus held herself upright. "I won't believe it," she declared, "unless I hear it from Artie's own lips."

And at Judd's house, his father, in his measured voice, repeated to us only, "No, no, this is some mistake, it cannot be true." His brother Max told us, "It must be the boys' idea of a joke. They must be sore at the cops for keeping them so long."

After his confession Judd felt, if anything, rather proud, as after making an unusually comprehensive report in class. Indeed, he could see around him the same admiring astonishment that came into the face of a professor when a student exhibited an extraordinary grasp of a subject. He wished only that Artie had been there in the room—forgetting, momentarily, his rage at Artie for breaking down and talking. It would have been good for them to have shared the sensation of the constabulary trying to grasp the extraordinary nature of their crime. The crime had a certain altitude, he told himself; the action had a wholeness—the word was consistency. Now, through a trial, through an execution, he would maintain the same consistency, the same dignity of living and dying by a set of ideas. Even with the blunder, even with being caught, he and Artie had somehow achieved their aim. They had demonstrated something that was beyond the ordinary mind.

The state's attorney, to his credit, had carried out the interrogation in exactly the proper tone, with respectful curiosity. Thus when it was all over, they had even thanked each other, and Judd, signing the stenographer's notes, had been asked if he would like to rest until the statement was typed up. He stretched out on a couple of chairs, and, the tension gone, for a tumultuous second imagined himself and Artie mounting the scaffold together. Repeating to himself that he had no fear, that he was consistent, Judd presently slept.

*　　*　　*

When Judd awoke there was coffee, and Horn was back, looking newly shaven, refreshed and still gentlemanly. Then the other one, Padua, came into the room with Artie.

Judd's first look to Artie was a quick, habitual glance to make contact, to be together. But he did not connect, for Artie was wearing a hiding, self-conscious grin. The nearness of Artie had brought in Judd the automatic throb of mind and heart together, but now there came an emptiness as he recalled what Artie was doing. In trying to twist the story, Artie was deserting their togetherness, killing it.

Mr. Horn was amiable. "Now, boys, we want to read you your statements. Don't interrupt—just make a mental note of it and you'll have plenty of opportunity to give us your corrections."

Artie sat down, across the desk from Judd, the alert smirk still on his face; and Padua handed Judd a copy of Artie's statement. At once Judd saw the little mistake about when they first planned the thing, and even that small error was incomprehensible to him. How could Artie have forgotten that night ride after raiding the frat—the terrible closeness of that night when they had made their compact? He read on, until there came the part about who was driving the Willys.

A choking, dizzying sensation came upon him. This was the second moment of shattering for Judd, after having been told, the night before, that Artie was confessing. Now, Artie was breaking their union.

Judd fixed his eyes on his friend, who had been reading Judd's own confession. At that moment, Artie flushed and leaped up, talking a mile a minute, angrily. "In the first place, he says the chisel was wrapped by me. It was wrapped by him, Judd Steiner, and wrapped by him in Jackson Park. He wrapped that chisel while waiting there in Jackson Park on that little nine-hole golf course. All right."

It was clever of Artie to start with an insignificant detail. Yes. And Artie's objection was partly true. Sitting next to each other in the car, Artie had said, "I'll show you," and started the tape around the hard blade, then handing it to Judd to wrap.

"In the second place, he mentioned the idea of the thing,

well, the main thing was to get the burial place, and the means of throwing that package. The place was his, and he struck on that idea of the train. It was his idea."

That was it, then—Artie wanted step by step to put the full blame on him, his idea, his burial place, his chisel, his killing! Artie would make himself out as only an accessory. For one instant the scene of their planning, the chummy evenings in the house, came back to Judd, and he felt grief. Oh, how could Artie destroy that feeling that had been between them! But he listened on. "He doesn't mention the method of killing," Artie declared. "He had that very well conceived and planned out, as evidenced by the ether in the car, which was absolutely the notion to be followed through. The boy was to be etherized to death, and he was supposed to do that because I don't know a damn thing about it and he does. He had a number of times chloroformed birds and things like that, and he knows ornithology. I don't know a damn thing about that."

"Yes, but the ether wasn't used, was it?" Horn asked. "Who hit him with the chisel?"

Artie snapped, "He did."

"Who is *he*?"

Judd tried again to catch Artie's eye, to look him straight in the eye. Artie affirmed, "Judah Steiner, Jr. He was sitting up in the front seat—" and then he caught himself.

At Artie's terrible slip, a double impulse of pity and of exultation, like some reversible electric current, went through Judd, and as Artie floundered, trying to recover his aplomb, Judd even felt an anxiety for his partner, now at last proven the weaker.

"I mean I was sitting up in the front seat," Artie started again. "This is obviously a mistake. I am getting excited." The prosecutors scarcely concealed their smiles. "This Kessler boy got up in the front seat. Now, that was a boy that I knew. If I was sitting in the back seat, he would have got in the back seat with me. He was a boy I knew and I would have opened the door and motioned him in that way. As it was, he got in the front seat with me because I knew the boy and I opened the front door. He didn't see Judd till he was inside the car."

Artie was fully recovered now, and despite his own powerful desire to intervene and contradict, Judd felt a satisfaction that Artie was doing better. "I introduced Judd to this Kessler boy and then took him into the car, and when he got in the car I said, 'You know Judd? This is Paulie Kessler.'"

With these words Artie turned, pouring the rest out directly at Judd. "I have been made a fish of right along here. When you came down here Thursday you told a story which you had agreed not to tell. This story—all this alibi, all these women, and being drunk in the Coconut Grove and everything—we planned that definitely. It was definitely decided that that story was not to go after Wednesday noon, which was to be a week after the crime. After that we were just to say we didn't know what we were doing. And there was no evidence. We felt that you were safe with your glasses after a week had passed and that your glasses being out there would not necessitate an airtight alibi." It was as though Artie were explaining to him why he was betraying him now, explaining that it was all his own fault. "And then you came down here Thursday and told the story you had agreed not to tell!" Artie was shrieking now. "I came down to Mr. Horn, he questioned me about my actions and I denied ever being drunk, I denied being with you, Steiner, and being at the Coconut Grove; I stuck to our agreement! But when they started talking about the Grove and about being out in Lincoln Park, I put it together and knew you had told the alibi story you should not have told, so I stepped in to try to help you! And I think it is a damned sight more than you would have done for me. I tried to help you out because I thought that you at least, if the worst came to the worst, would admit what you had done and not try to drag me into it in that manner."

Artie was staring into his face. It was for Judd like the moment that comes to any man in the discovery that the woman who had glowed for him, whom he loved, is a slut, and there is a bewildering dismay in him, and he thinks to himself, *But I knew it all the time; I knew it when she was abandoned with me, when she did all those dirty things with me—they don't count for dirty only because you yourself are doing them—but I knew she would do the same with other men.* And sinkingly the man knows he may have to love her still and be alone forever in his love.

So at this moment Judd felt eternal solitude coming upon him. The dignity, the consistency, of the deed had been broken; they were no longer willful gods, but caught boys squirming to throw blame, and he wanted only to detach himself so he might at least retain his own idea of integrity. He spoke firmly. "Those are all absurd dirty lies." But despairingly he knew that to the listeners there could be no difference between his denials and Artie's. And was it after all important? Should he not withdraw into his superior self? Yet Judd persisted. "He is trying to get out of this mess. I can explain myself exactly how I opened the door to let the Kessler boy in, and then Artie got up from the back seat, leaned over and spoke to the boy from in back. I was driving the car, I am absolutely positive."

But about one thing, Artie was justified. Judd appealed, almost, to Horn, "The reason for using that alibi story was, as you remember, when you first questioned me as to my actions I was very indefinite, and I was urged to remember—" Artie was sneering at him—"I was urged quite strongly to remember what I had been doing." Then what other alibi could he have given? And even so, it was not the alibi that had caught them! That alibi had nearly saved them! It was Artie who had broken down and started to confess, even while the police were believing the alibi! Judd turned on Artie. "I am sorry that you were made a fish of and stepped into everything and broke down and all that. I am sorry, but it isn't my fault."

Horn broke in. "Now listen, boys. You have both been treated decently by me?"

Judd responded, "Absolutely."

"No brutality or roughness?"

"No."

"Every consideration shown you both?"

Let them have it in their record. "Yes, sir."

Artie was still silent. "Not one of you has a complaint to make?"

"No," Judd said.

"Have you?" Horn asked Artie.

"No," Judd heard Artie mutter.

As they were led out, Artie didn't look at him.

* * *

There was to come, then, the cavalcade over the route of the crime. With unrelenting speed and energy, Horn sought to gather in his evidence, to sew up his hanging case before lawyers could get to the boys and tell them to keep their mouths shut. Already his men were tracing that final ransom letter in the railway car, were impounding the rented Willys. But even beyond these proofs, Horn thought ahead to the defense. An insanity plea, undoubtedly. Some chance, with their brilliant school records! And Horn sent out men to secure depositions from fraternity brothers, from teachers, and from girl friends —had they ever known Judd or Artie to be anything but intelligent and self-possessed?

When we assembled again in Horn's office, as if by some prearranged signal, we found the atmosphere to hold neither horror nor sorrow; it was as though we were all engaged in something historic. The boys were brought in to us, refreshed, alert, though hostile to each other.

A new phase of the bizarre story was opening. A great legal contest would surely develop.

At once came our questions about remorse. Artie said he was sorry, but only because the adventure had not succeeded. Judd said, "I have examined my reactions and can't say that I have experienced any such sentiment as remorse."

Would he do the thing again?

No, Judd said, with deliberation, but only because he now knew that there could be no perfect crime—some error would always be made.

While Artie scarcely spoke, Judd suddenly became torrential. After all, he said, it was not entirely wrong that they had been caught. Now they could fully explain their ideas; even if they paid with their lives, it was in a sense the only way to establish the new concept that had guided them. The failure, the slip-up, was a flaw in the experiment. The magnitude of the idea remained.

He began then to explain his superman philosophy—the freedom from all codes, sentiments, superstitions, even from fear of death itself. He was to go on talking all day, as our cavalcade retraced the path of the crime.

A half-dozen limousines were lined up in the street, but they were already insufficient for all the newsmen, the sob sisters, the photographers, the out-of-town press people who were arriving in droves.

Horn was brisk, even festive. At one moment, as Tom and I were near him, he threw his arms around us, declaring he wouldn't forget the good work we had done.

Artie and Judd talked easily with their captors, with the press, but they avoided each other, and if they had to communicate, it would be through a third person: "Would you please inform Mr. Steiner . . ." "Would you suggest to Mr. Straus . . ."

Meanwhile, with Sergeant McNamara always behind him, Judd came over to where I stood with Tom. "I understand that we owe our predicament in good measure to you gentlemen," Judd said, "but I want to state that I don't regard it as anything personal. In fact, I must congratulate you on your accomplishment."

I felt embarrassed. There was something febrile and yet false about him, as though he were living up to the image of the brilliant, suave murderer. I looked at his intense dark eyes, his full mouth that had been kissing Ruth. What had drawn Ruth to him? I looked at him, trying to erase in myself the knowledge that he was a murderer. There had to be something human, something worthy, to draw a girl like Ruth—or was all love a delusion? Or was this worthier quality buried so deeply that only an occasional rare person like Ruth could sense it? And was it buried more deeply than ever now, under the hard mask of emotionless sophistication?

Should I give him Ruth's message? There were too many people around us. They were badgering him again, about remorse. "I regret having been caught, of course, but only my own errors are to blame for this."

Richard Lyman of the *Tribune* fixed his eyes on Judd and said, "You think it was merely an error? If God didn't make you drop those glasses, who did?"

Judd said, "I happen to be an atheist, so I will have to seek another explanation for that question."

We were all scribbling down notes, but Horn interrupted the session; until he had every bit of evidence sewn up, he wanted to keep the boys moving. We were herded into the cars. I managed to crowd into Artie's car with Padua, Mike Prager, and a sob sister from the *Herald,* a stringy pale blonde named Rea Knowles, who set herself to monopolize Artie.

He was now being serious and penitent. His face was absolutely bloodless, white, and the twitch of his cheek muscles was incessant. "I don't see how that cold-blooded fish can sit in that other car and laugh over this thing," Artie told us. Rea asked if he felt the meaning of what he had done, and Artie said, "The first few days I didn't feel it; it seemed to me that I could have carried this secret the rest of my life. It didn't bother me much. But now I feel it."

She immediately got after the girl story. "You went out on dates, during this last week, didn't you, Artie? Didn't it bother you when you were out with a girl?"

With his boyish candor, Artie said, "No, just a thought or two at times. I would think of that little boy, and then I would drive it from my mind. But I'm appreciative of the thing now. Every once in a while the whole thing comes up and a realization of the thing we have done comes over my mind."

He paused, as if it had come just then. Rea persisted. Did he have a particular girl? Glancing at me, with a wink, Artie said there were several girls of whom he was very fond, but of course he wouldn't drag a girl's name into this, and he hoped the papers wouldn't either. He had had a pretty hot date on Sunday, he confided, but he guessed those things were over now for quite a while, if not forever. But presently his spirits rose. "This thing will be the making of me," Artie declared. "I'll spend some years in jail, I suppose, and then I'll be released. I'll come out to a new life, I'll go to work and have a career." We all stared at him. Could it be that it hadn't really hit him yet? Or did he feel so sure his people could get him off?

Artie turned the questioning on us. Did we think any

lawyer could save his life? Inevitably, the name of Jonathan Wilk was mentioned. Artie had already been thinking of him. "But he only defends the poor," he said. "Do you believe he would take our case?"

There was a silence. Padua, sitting up front, turned his head with a curious smile, and Rea resumed her attack. If he went to jail, did he have any girl in mind who might wait for him? And Artie said remorsefully that he didn't know if any woman could ever marry him after the thing he had done. Though sometimes he felt as though it were another person who had done it—

Mike Prager leaped on this. Did Artie believe he had been dominated by Judd Steiner, in the crime?

Artie looked at us candidly, including Padua in his open gaze. "What do you think?" As one thought of the swarthy Judd, with his intense dark eyes, there could be only one answer to the boyish Artie: Judd, the mastermind. Hadn't the crime been organized from Judd's house? Wasn't it Judd who had rented the car? If each accused the other, it was surely Judd who struck the death blows. And if they had an unnatural relationship, it was surely Judd's doing.

Was it true that Judd was unpopular, that he didn't go out with girls? Rea asked Artie.

"Oh, we've been on double dates." Again Artie eyed me confidentially.

"Well, you know what I mean, Artie. Has Judd got a girl? Has he ever been in love?"

"Well, I wouldn't know anything about that," Artie said.

"Have you ever been in love?"

He smiled winningly for her. "Lots of times."

"Yes, but I mean just once. The real thing."

Artie winked. "Now, kid—" I reveled in my private knowledge, in having it all over Rea and Mike Prager.

*   *   *

The cavalcade had halted in front of the Driv-Ur-Self place. The manager, confronted with Judd, gasped, "Yes, I remember him—James Singer. Rented a Willys a couple of times. We made our usual full check——" he started to say, but Horn reassured him, "That's all right." The manager babbled earnestly, "How could I have known?" In a moment the cavalcade was on its way again.

At the next stop an incident occurred. It was the lunch counter where Artie, as the reference for Mr. Singer, had waited for a telephone call.

When the crowd started into the place, a round-faced woman behind the cash register pointed at once to Artie. "That's him!" Artie half pitched against the wall, fainting. A detective caught him, propping him up.

"The poor weakling." We all turned our eyes to Judd. His voice had had neither contempt nor pity; there was merely the effect of a statement.

Artie was revived; he made an effort to joke it off, saying he usually required a pint before he passed out. The cavalcade was resumed.

We were following the death ride. Here, Judd said, was the stand where they had stopped to eat, leaving the dead boy rolled in the rug in the car. And then came the turnoff lane to Hegewisch. Briskly Judd led the group across the prairie, indicating where the body was carried and how he had pushed it into the concrete tube. "A few inches farther and it would never have shown," he remarked, and his voice had that odd, clacky classroom tone.

Someone in the crowd asked, "Why, particularly, in this place?" And at this, Artie burst out, "This was all Mr. Steiner's idea. I'm not even familiar with this place. I couldn't even find it again!"

And vaguely, I think I felt then what Judd may have felt: the cistern, the close snug fit, as when little kids, finding a packing box or a barrel, feel impelled to crawl in and hide.

"Why here?" someone repeated, and Judd looked confused. Why? Why hadn't he realized that people passed all the time on the tracks, on the path?

He turned away. We followed the cars. Judd was walking at a quicker pace—like this, it occurred to me, he must have led his birding classes here. He was in conversation with McNamara about his chances. The big cop had become familiar. "I don't think I've got a chance before a jury, do you?" Judd said. "They'd hang us." McNamara agreed, professionally, that a jury would be a big risk. Sometimes a judge could be friendlier.

"I suppose our families will secure the best legal talent for us," Judd said. "Maybe with a smart lawyer before a judge, our lives could be saved. What do you think?" That speculation was to provide a fantastic climax to the trial.

*   *   *

Down the lane, Judd showed where the belt buckle could be dug out, and it was found, and then the shoes. We drove to the beach, where the half-cindered remnants of the lap robe were located, and finally to the lagoon in Jackson Park, where divers sought the remains of the typewriter. Thus it was all proven, exactly, exactly.

It was toward the end of the afternoon, when we came downtown again and struck Michigan Boulevard, that we encountered a parade. There was a Masonic band in red trousers, and there was a large float on a truck draped in red, white, and blue crepe paper, and Judd cried, "Oh, yes, Memorial Day!" And he added, "The annual parade for legalized murder."

Then it was dinnertime and Horn expansively ordered the entire cavalcade to proceed to Crown's, near Lincoln Park. Several huge round tables were commandeered. Judd again became discursive, like an instructor following up his laboratory demonstration with a lecture.

And it was then that he made his second irreparable remark. When someone asked if Nietzsche's superman philosophy justified murder, Judd perversely replied, "It is easy to justify such a death, as easy as to justify an entomologist impaling a butterfly on a pin."

The room became quiet. Danny Mines of the *News* said, "We all had a little Nietzsche in college, Steiner, but that doesn't mean you have to live by it."

"Why not?" Judd demanded. "A philosophy, if you are convinced it is correct, is something you live by."

"You sound like some of those characters in F. Scott Fitzgerald," said Mines.

"I hope not," Judd rejoined. "I hope I am not like his sophomoric characters, showing off after a swallow of gin.

You newspaper boys want to make me out a conceited smarty, but at least you must admit I have tried to live up to my convictions."

We all studied our menus. And as in the meal at the Red Star Inn, Judd did not fail to make one of his remarks about being Jewish. "The herring is excellent here," he announced to McNamara, "but I suppose you don't like herring—you aren't Jewish."

He went off to discourse about odd foods. Last year he had accompanied his father to Hawaii on vacation, he said, and eaten seaweed and also, he was convinced, dog meat. Throughout the meal he continued to flash his erudition, discoursing on Walter Pater, quoting from Laurence Hope, quoting Dante in Italian, and even leaning across to tell me if I wanted to become a writer I ought to study languages—to read the Bhagavad-Gita in the original was alone worth the effort of learning Sanskrit. As he mounted, mounted, in his show of erudition, Judd concentrated on me, as though to prove his superiority over the one who had done so much to catch him.

Against my will, I was being pushed by the others, set up as the antipode—for I, too, was a university graduate at eighteen. Repeatedly, Judd seemed to challenge me, with a reference to Anatole France, a reference to Voltaire. On these I could keep up with him, but I could not quote Latin or Greek, I had not read Sappho, even in translation. "The Medicis!" he cried. "We all have a time to be born in. My real error was in being born in the twentieth century. I should have lived in the time of Cellini or Aretino, don't you think? You've read Aretino, surely?"

How much Judd was a part of his own century we could not then know. I said that even in Aretino's time it was considered against the law to kill people for a whim. "But at least in those days murder was considered an art!" he countered triumphantly.

Only at the end of the meal, as we arose, Judd took an opportunity to talk quietly with me, as two who are publicly opponents but privately have much in common. "Have you seen our friend Ruth?"

"No," I said. "I haven't had a chance in the last few days, but I talked to her on the phone. She—she sent you her sympathy."

He gave me a furtive, abashed look. "Make my apologies to her, will you?"

As Horn was hustling the boys away, a reporter called a last question. Did they have any word for their parents?

"Yes," Judd snapped, "tell my father isn't it about time he got me a lawyer?"

*   *   *

As it was Saturday night and we had no Sunday edition, Tom said there was no more we could do. I went to see Ruth.

From the first moment, the date was a parting. As I climbed the stairs, raising my eyes to the door, I knew she would not come out eager and smiling. Yet this should have been my moment of triumph—a young reporter coming to his girl after trapping the most sensational murderers in all history!

Ruth's parents were busy in the store; I had slipped by unseen, for I wanted to talk only to her.

As I entered, she came toward me with a forced smile. "No, really, Sid, it was fine what you did, it was brilliant, and I want you to know—" We stood near each other, we almost leaned to kiss, but then only grasped hands, and I knew it was gone.

I had imagined that I would tell her everything in fullest detail, but now I couldn't begin to communicate with her. Finally, forcing myself, I gave her Judd's apology. She whispered, "Poor kid."

My nerves were all gone; I was exhausted. I burst out, "Why keep sympathizing with him? He's a plain monster! It was he who instigated the whole thing; he even dominated Artie in the whole affair. Artie at least has some remorse, but not Judd! He's even bragging! He throws us all this fancy Nietzsche superman philosophy as if it makes everything excusable!"

She stood listening, silent, and this provoked me to a stumbling, even patronizing, effort at reconciliation. Too bad,

I went on, that she had been attracted by Judd for a few days, fooled, but now—

Her eyes had filled with tears. I reached for her, but she drew aside. "Oh, Sid!" was all she said. Then Ruth let her tears flow, and I felt they were not only for Judd, not only for us, but for the whole sick world. Yet, as if I couldn't feel, I had to charge her, "Ruthie, what is it? For God's sake what is it?"

"I don't know. Let's not talk about it. I read it all in the papers."

But then we could find nothing to talk about. Our intimacy was gone—we were like mere half-strange schoolmates. She asked if my folks were coming up for graduation and I said yes. In the old days with her I could have gone on to say my mother was probably now bragging to all the neighbors in Racine, as if her son personally had caught the murderers in a chase in the streets. But I censored myself.

It crossed my mind that if I had a car, all this with Ruth might have been easier; this might have been one of those nights just to ride. And Ruth said, "Let's go for a walk."

As we walked to the park, I found myself suddenly talking in a streak about the case, about us. "Ruth, it was when I told you about Judd's glasses that I saw you believed he had done it. Something in you knew. That was when I went out to find more proof. They were talking their way out of it but something in you knew. God, that was only two nights ago!"

She drew her hand from mine. "Then I did it too," she said reflectively.

"What, what did you do? For God's sake, how can you blame yourself, how can you blame us for catching them?"

"Oh, no. They had to be caught. Oh, I suppose I'm a coward."

We stood in the park, as if not knowing where to go, and then, oddly, sat on a bench.

"Sid, I owe it to you—there's something I have to tell you," she said. And she told me about going out with Judd that time to the dunes.

I felt sick, sick for myself, then frightened as she talked. Alone, out there. He could have done anything.

"Nothing happened," Ruth said.

But the sickest part I couldn't ask in words. Had she felt —as with me?

She sensed that question, too, and took my hand this time. "It was something different, not like with you. Sid, something drew me to him. Perhaps because he needed someone so much and he keeps everything down deep inside himself."

How could I feel jealousy for the poor bastard? And yet I blurted, "And after that, on the dunes, you went out with him again?"

"Yes."

"Why, Ruth? Why?"

"I don't know . . . he even spoke of marrying. . . ." Her voice cried for understanding. "I—I think then I loved him. Oh, Sid, it would be wrong not to tell you. He did awaken some kind of love in me. Perhaps it was only pity. I knew he was suffering from something terrible he couldn't tell me. He hides everything in himself. Perhaps—" her voice became small, choked—"perhaps that's even what made him do it."

I didn't quite understand that remark and felt that she would not be able to explain it either, that it was one of those fleeting perceptions, a light on and off, a truth only glimpsed. Then she was calmer; Ruth even asked, it seemed to me quite impersonally, if I believed they should be executed.

I said I believed intellectually that capital punishment was pointless, merely vengeance, but when you saw a thing of this kind you simply felt that the perpetrators should be put out of this world.

She was silent, and I blundered again. I said, "Ruth, why should this make anything wrong between us? After all, I didn't murder anyone."

Then it all burst out of her, in agony, in bitterness. "No? Haven't you been working night and day, so excited, so eager, too, to be in on the kill, and don't you want to see them hang even though you're intellectually against it!" She doubled over, weeping. "Oh, I'm sorry. Beasts, beasts."

If I could have admitted, then, some feeling of shame,

instead of going on with a sense of righteousness to justify myself to myself, we might have got past that dreadful barrier. I see that now.

After a while we got up and walked, silently, until we came to the lighted street.

*   *   *

The two families could no longer deny the facts to themselves. Artie had been permitted to telephone his mother; thus she had indeed finally heard it from his own voice. "Yes, Mother, it's true, I did it. I'm sorry for what it'll do to the family. I'll do anything you want me to." It went on like that. His mother couldn't speak except to repeat his name and ask over and over again, "Why? Why? How could you, Artie?"

And afterward, dazed, she became obsessed by a single impulse—to go across to Mrs. Kessler, to say to her, "Now we are two mothers who have lost our sons."

People had been hovering all day, close to her, as if to help her keep away the truth. Her sisters, a brother, and the Straus brothers, Gerald particularly, all had kept up indignant talk about third degrees and crazy confessions, but all day long the down-drag had grown stronger on her husband and on her eldest son, Lewis, who had arrived dumfounded from Charlevoix. The unspoken "What if it's true?" had grown stronger, compelling.

Mrs. Straus was upstairs when Artie's telephone call came. She and Artie's father took the call together; though he would not speak into the phone, he sat beside her. Then he went into his study.

All were afraid for him. Randolph Straus was high-strung, sensitive; that was why he was sometimes so unapproachable. A nephew of Nathan Weiss, the founder of the great Corporation, he had come into the business as a young lawyer, when the Corporation was only taking its first full strides, when it was a business of construction materials, steel, concrete, and asphalt. Randolph Straus had worked alongside the great old man, and he had carried on when Nathan Weiss had retired. He was now the executive head of the great Corporation, and under him the strides had become giant strides,

from supply of materials to construction itself, railroads in
Chile, bridges in Africa.

Already, Straus knew he would resign. The name must
not blot the company. He would resign, for he could not face
the world.

What private guilts arose in each of the parents? Inevitably there had to come the frightened self-asking. Is this retribution? Did Artie's mother in that breaking moment ask herself if it was a punishment for unfaithfulness to her church,
for not raising her children as Catholics? Did his father partly
revert, asking himself if the ancient archaic laws could be in
force? Was this a retribution for his having married outside of
his faith, for having raised sons without faith? Was all the
good done in life to be canceled?

Then, at last, they knocked for him; his brother Gerald
knocked and walked in and said, "You have to face it. We
have to make plans."

Plans, plans—what plans were there to make? It was
done, everything was done. But he came out with Gerald, and
sat with them; his sons, his brothers, his wife's brothers, and
the Feldschers had come. There was talk in twos, in threes,
mostly hushed. But loud words would break out. "It was that
awful Judd got him into it!" Only then did Randolph Straus
speak. "Oh, no, we won't throw the blame on the other fellow!" And again, hushed words, awful visualizations—the
child's clothes burned in their own furnace, right here in this
house—and the dreaded word unuttered, then uttered at last.
It could only be insanity.

And that word sounded at last the deeper fears. Even
among themselves, these fears could not be brought out, but
were touched upon in corners, husband to wife, brother to
brother, whispered. Could it have anything to do with——?

For as in every large family, there was one who was sick
—a cousin in an asylum—and now the waves seemed to reach
for them all. Would every girl of the family feel the dread fate
in her womb? Was this what Artie had done to them?

But Randolph Straus would not accept it. He had lived a
constructive, decent life. His two sons stood here, decent
young men, rational! No one would be tainted! And he stood

up all at once and spoke for all of them to hear. "It's his own fault! That boy had everything! Everything he wanted. Money —he had only to ask my secretary. Since he was a child, he's been taking advantage, getting himself into trouble because he knew we'd have to get him out of it, taking advantage of his family situation. We've covered it up, we covered up every mess he got into—he lied, he was wild, he cheated at cards, he stole; yes, we all knew it. He drove like a wild man, not caring for anyone's life. We warned him, no one can say we didn't try with him; he's no good, he's no good, and now he has done this and he will pay for it himself! Let him take the consequences of the law."

His voice did not break but seemed barely to reach to the last word. And he would speak no other word. He sat through the remainder of the evening, through the planning, through the discussions, but he had turned his face from his son, he had renounced Artie, he had reverted to those ancient archaic laws, he would not speak Artie's name ever again, he did not want to hear of him; the sound of the name, spoken in his presence, would not enter into him.

After a moment his brother Gerald said, "But we've got to get him a defense. You can't call that interfering with the law."

"What is there to defend?"

"He was sick, crazy. What else would he be, to do a thing like that?"

The father was silent.

Lewis remarked, "Whatever we do, they'll say we're trying to buy it."

James said, "If we don't help him, it'll look worse."

The sons confronted their father. But the father remained silent. No matter what was done, Artie's life saved, or his body hanged, to him Artie was eliminated.

"Let me handle it," his brother Gerald said finally. Randolph did not nod his head, but his assent was felt.

With this point reached, cousin Ferdinand Feldscher suggested talking to Judah Steiner; the families should perhaps best act in unison.

*   *   *

At the Steiner household, the pulse was slower. Aunt
Bertha was there, and Judah's brother-in-law, and the thought
stood before them in the huge gloomy room, perhaps if Judd's
mother had lived . . .

And there, too, the thought of blight had to arise. In this
family, too, were the sick ones—two cousins in an asylum.
Max had already gone to his fiancée to offer her release, for if
it were something in the family . . .

Now Max returned; his eyes filmed as he told them Sandra was so good, so wonderful. Only when trouble came did a
man know it was true love. Her feelings for him could not
change, she had said. Then he himself had insisted, for the
sake of—in case of children, they must wait, they must make
sure.

*   *   *

When the call came from the Strauses, Judah Steiner did
not have the strength to go. "You go, Max. What needs to be
done for him, do it."

Max had seen many of them only a few days ago at his
engagement party, and they showed their thought of what all
this might do to his romance. It was in their voices as they
asked solicitously about his fiancée—had she gone back to
New York?

"She's fine, just saw her—she's taking it like one of the
family," he said.

Artie's father was no longer in the room; his Uncle Gerald had taken charge. The gloom and shame had been brushed
aside; there was work to be done, a campaign to organize.

The question had two parts, as Ferdinand Feldscher put
it: What was best for the families? And what could be best for
the boys?

Who could say in so many words what stood darkly in
every mind: best for all might be the quickest, the quietest
end. If the boys had to hang, then let it be got over with; there
was no need for a spectacular trial with the family names in
the headlines for months to come.

It was Ferdinand Feldscher who finally suggested, "Plead
guilty, then there's no jury trial, only a quick hearing. Ordi-

narily on a guilty plea you would get a deal, a life sentence, but in this case—"

Perhaps that would be the most honest thing to do, Max said. And meanwhile the families could get to the papers. After all, both families had a few connections in this town. Why should so many people be made to suffer because of a couple of unfortunate boys? They must have been crazy with cheap moonshine. Let it end quietly.

But Uncle Gerald Straus spoke up. Was it a foregone conclusion that there could be no other verdict? What about insanity?

Edgar Feldscher spread his palms. "Of course they're sick, the crime itself shows it. But if you plead insanity you automatically go before a jury, that's the law. And in a case like this, I can't imagine any jury letting them live."

Gerald said, "There is no such thing as being sure of what a jury will do." He addressed his remark to Ferdinand instead of Edgar Feldscher. Hadn't Ferdinand got off a certain embezzler, and even a certain wife-murderer? Every criminal, every gangster, tried to save himself! And finally Uncle Gerald cried, "All right! No pretenses! Let's say I want to save Artie! That's why! Is anything wrong with that? Is it wrong to feel something for the kid! Is it wrong to say, if he did what he did, and none of us saw it coming, then maybe all of us are partly to blame?"

He would get the best help there was, he said, even if it cost a million dollars! And if the case remained in the headlines, let it! The harm had already been done. At least, let the world see that their families stood by these two brainsick children!

That seemed to settle it. He had spoken what was in all their hearts. Only Ferdinand Feldscher uttered one thought on the other side. "Let's help them, sure, but it must always be made clear that the family does not condone what they did."

The younger Feldscher, the bald-domed Edgar, had been listening as though gathering up all that was valuable; his voice was soft, in contrast to Uncle Gerald's. "No, not condone," he agreed. "But we could do something more than merely defend them. We could spare nothing to try to find out, as far as modern science can, what made them do it." They all looked at him with the respect owed a man who worried over the deeper elements in things. All of them knew how close Edgar had been to the cousin who had become mentally troubled. From this had come Edgar's intense, even scholarly absorption in studies of the mind; sometimes he seemed more interested in his hobby than in the practice of law. Edgar should have been a doctor, his older brother had always thought. Now Edgar ended, rather tentatively, "Suppose we get the best men, even from Vienna. Make a full study. Perhaps it could prove of some use to humanity, too."

Uncle Gerald said that was a real point. Especially if it was going to be an insanity defense. But right now strategy was the problem. First, as to legal counsel. With no reflection on those present, for Ferdinand Feldscher was certainly one of the biggest trial lawyers in the whole country——

"No, no, you don't have to watch out for my feelings, Gerry," Ferdinand interrupted. "We need all the help we can get in this case, and we all know there is only one man to go to."

"My father always believes in getting the best," Max Steiner said.

James Straus said, "The question is, would Wilk take it? I understand he only defends the poor."

There was a short laugh from Gerald. "Wilk's got nothing against a big fee. He used to be counsel for the railroads."

"He'll take it, he'll take it," Ferdinand Feldscher said, "out of vanity if for nothing else."

Even though it was past midnight, Gerald was for going directly to Wilk's house.

*   *   *

"Go home, go home," Judah Steiner kept telling his sister-in-law and her husband, until at last she said, "You'll be all right?" and he promised her he would go right up to bed.

He did as he had promised, and he went through the motions of undressing, and then he sat for a long while in his pajamas on the edge of the bed. He drew on a robe and returned downstairs.

Unaccountably there had come into his mind the thought, Maybe it was because for the last baby they had wanted a girl.

He was uncomfortable with it. He had never let his mind go into such things, these complicated psychological things that people brought into the conversation nowadays. He had not even wanted to know, exactly, that story about the boys a couple of years ago, in Charlevoix; Max had brought him the story—well, you know, a couple of young boys horsing around. Such things, the dirty things in life, had to be shut out. Children did plenty of dirty things before they knew.

But then, he should not have permitted Judd to go up to the university in Michigan with Artie. He had never been firm enough with Judd, maybe because he was so proud of him; because the boy was so bright, maybe he had always been a little intimidated by him.

His head began to shake, no—as though he were discussing it with Mother Dear—no, all such things still could not lead to so terrible an end as this. And Max had told him many stories about Judd with girls; Judd himself had talked about different girls—there was even that trouble he had got into with a cheap girl a year ago. There was no doubt that Judd was manly. As a father he had always meant to talk to the boy, explain, but how could you? How could you? Judd was so clever, he read everything; a man would feel foolish.

Still, it came to his mind again, Judd's going to school that first time when they had lived on Michigan Avenue, and the only decent school nearby was Miss Spencer's, where they had only girls.

He was so small, so delicate, so shy. To send Junior with boys, rowdies in the public school, in the bad neighborhood, how could it be done? He was always the smallest, the baby. Besides, as he was so shy, his mother and his aunt said it would do him good to be among girls.

The unending arguments! Mother Dear, can't you see the boy is miserable, everybody teases him, a sissy with all those girls. Finally he had taken Judd out and sent him to the public school. But that had lasted only a few months. Rough boys, micks who yelled "sheenie" at him. Until that day when the stupid nurse had been late to fetch him, and Judd had come running home himself with the bloody nose.

No, no, even so, a bloody nose, every boy has to go through it, he had argued, but his wife and her sister had talked him down. This proved they were right! The boy was weak and frail even for his age. So Mother Dear insisted it was better to send him back to Miss Spencer's—at least the girls didn't beat him up and call him sheenie. Until they moved up to the new house and Junior could enter Twain.

Judah Steiner had been sitting in the dark in the large leather chair where he usually smoked. Now he leaned over and switched on the lamp, startling himself to hear the click in the silent house.

He went to the back of the library and uncovered a projector he had bought especially because of Judd's little film last summer. Taking out the film, he managed to thread it, though this was something he had usually asked Judd to do. To set up the screen, he moved almost stealthily; he did not want servants to come. Then he sat on the high-backed chair by the carved-legged library table, watching the picture.

There was the boy, crouching, alert, his eyes so bright, crouching by a bush. It was on the dunes, the high weeds, the sand. Now the camera picked out the birds, hopping on the branches of a high bush—a special lens had been used to enlarge them from that distance. A nest was there, two, three birds—they hopped, flew out, one came back. The picture wobbled, trying to follow the bird as it circled around the nest.

Now Judd came out, standing near the bush. He came out and stood there so quietly. He held out his hand, with some birdseed, or crumbs, whatever he used for them. A bird hopped close. You had to keep in mind these were birds of a very rare species. For thirty years no one had seen them in these parts. It was thought these warblers were gone altogether, migrated forever, or maybe died out, until Judd discovered them there on the dunes. For people interested in such things it was important. The State of Michigan had sent the cameraman to make a record of the discovery. An ornithology magazine had printed an article Judd wrote. Perhaps the boy was right, perhaps he should have been a scientist, although there was no future in it. An eminent lawyer, everyone could understand. Still, if Judd really wanted . . .

The tears came to his eyes.

Mistily, he saw the bird hopping up onto Judd's forearm —how steadily the boy held—and Judd was smiling now, his serious, dignified smile, people said like his father's. And then came another bird, and a third, they were on his boy's shoulder, they were eating out of his hand.

Judah Steiner's eyes were so filled with tears that he couldn't see anymore. He felt the tears roll down his face.

*   *   *

By then already a legendary figure, Jonathan Wilk devoted more time to lecturing, writing, philosophizing than to the law. Perhaps he was already then somewhat outmoded, with his agnosticism and his argufying. But Wilk had enormous if disordered erudition. He loved to debate religion; he was an old cracker-barrel philosopher, a Lincolnesque figure.

In a courtroom, he was purely and simply a great pleamaker. None like him has since arisen. Though from a technical point of view he was an amazing cross-examiner, dogged, devious, even cunning when necessary, his spectacular qualities emerged on the simplest level of pleading for human compassion. In every one of his great trials, compassion was the heart and essence of his plea. He spoke of himself as a materialist, an unbeliever, except in mechanistic causation, but I suppose what came through was the heart of a mystic, a man of great soul who sought to open the souls of other men.

He had become famous as a labor lawyer in a great railway strike. For an entire generation he had defended labor leaders accused of violence, but those were already the legendary days of the I.W.W. In a frame-up, Wilk had been completely broken and nearly disbarred; he had then regained his career in an endless series of trials, defending criminals, defending underdogs, defending Negroes, defending, defending. He had lectured against the jail system, he had preached the social and economic roots of crime; he was a reformer, sometimes an iconoclast, an awakener, and he had lived long enough to become a legend.

His wife was trying to keep him now from cases that drew forth his full energy. His body was beginning to show weariness—rheumatic spells sometimes kept him bedridden for weeks. Wilk resided in a third-floor walk-up overlooking the university and the park. The stairs were too much, but he would not abandon the apartment, with its magnificent view.

Gerald Straus led the way up the stairs. James Straus and Max Steiner had come with him; the Feldschers had thought it best to remain behind.

Mrs. Wilk herself came to the door, a compact woman, with a humorous mouth, quick eyes. They told her who they were.

"Why didn't you phone?"

"We were afraid you'd tell us not to come," said Gerald Straus with his winning candor.

Wilk had heard the bell; he was sitting up in bed. Gerald Straus said dramatically, "We've come to you as the only man who can save our boys."

As he had been secluded all day, reading, the last Wilk knew of the Kessler sensation was that two rich boys had been picked up for some silly coincidence about eyeglasses.

"But anyone can get your boys out," he said. "It's obviously only a coincidence."

"No, no, they've confessed!" Hoarsely, Gerald Straus pleaded, "You've got to take the case, Mr. Wilk. You're the only one who can get them off."

Wilk sat erect. "Get them off?"

Max quickly interjected, "Save their lives. Just so they don't hang. Let them go to jail for life, we wouldn't even ask for less."

"It will be a great case," Uncle Gerald said, recalling Feldscher's suggestion. And he added, "You can name your own fee."

Wilk seemed not to have heard the last part. He looked at his wife, whose face had become anxious. By his lifelong philosophy he was doomed to defend them, even if it killed him, and it might, it just might.

"I don't know," he said cautiously, sighing. "Where are they now?"

"State's Attorney Horn has them. He's been running them all around town; they've been talking their heads off."

Wilk's jaw moved. "By now, you won't be able to get a writ to get them out of his clutches before Monday morning. He's got all Sunday to keep them babbling. God knows what he'll get them to say." He pulled his hand along his face.

"You certainly can't do anything now in the middle of the night," his wife said. "Jonathan, at least get some sleep before you decide."

Wilk sighed again. "I don't know if I can do you much good. You've got a fine man in your own family, haven't you?" Everyone knew the Straus connections. "You've got Ferdinand Feldscher."

"He begged us to get you," Uncle Gerald said earnestly.

"Well, come in the morning." Wilk looked at his wife. "I suppose the Feldschers thought about alienists. There are only a few top men in town. Arthur Ball—you'd better try to get him."

"I'll call him right now," Gerald offered.

Wilk waved him down. "If Horn hasn't got him already, it'll keep till morning." He pursed his lips. "Come in the morning. I'll see. Bring the Feldschers."

When they were gone, his wife said, "Jonathan, it'll kill you. And everybody will say you're doing it for the money."

Wilk found the answer, the inevitable slogan, at once. "The rich have got as much right to a defense as the poor."

*   *   *

Horn had got to the alienists. Dr. Ball was already in Horn's office, early Sunday, when the boys were brought from the hotel where they had been allowed a last night of ease. Horn welcomed his charges warmly, as though they were star performers. And here was the famous psychiatrist, Dr. Arthur Ball, to talk to them.

Several of us were in the room. There was a constant coming and going of Horn's aides, of photographers, of messengers, and the phones kept ringing. Padua kept giving instructions, and Chief Nolan and Horn discussed the final bits of evidence yet to be assembled.

Dr. Ball was keen-looking, kindly, quite aged; he was a

professor emeritus of the Northwestern Medical School's department of neurology. Actually, Judd reminded him, they knew each other. One of Dr. Ball's grandchildren had been in Judd's bird-lore class. And instantly Judd began exhibiting his knowledge of psychology, talking about the mental processes of birds. When birds altered their migratory routes by selecting between various sensory stimuli, wasn't that reasoning? Just as when humans made decisions by selecting between sensory stimuli—like a man between two women. "I am a behaviorist," Judd announced, while the professor smiled and asked whether in his view a human being had no more control over his conduct than a bird.

"I take a materialist determinist position," Judd said, and just then another psychiatrist arrived. This one came rushing in as though afraid he would miss something. Congratulating Horn and Nolan, the new arrival, Dr. Stauffer, turned to the boys with zest.

Judd recognized his name. "Ah, you're an advocate of the Stanford-Binet test—you're sold on it," he challenged. "We had your book in our psych courses. I don't agree with you. I don't believe there is any test that can measure every aspect of intelligence."

He kept on, talking about reflex actions and reaction time, things I recognized from a course at the university, where the behaviorists were in full sway. He had measured reactions of a ten-thousandth of a second, Judd said.

The term "ten-thousandth" caught Horn's ear, for he now turned to the boys, asking why they had fixed on ten thousand dollars as the ransom. Judd laughed at the association and said, "See, everything has a cause."

But surely they hadn't needed the money, Horn said. What had they wanted it for?

"Why shouldn't we want it?" Artie said. "Ten thousand dollars is ten thousand dollars."

"Well, if I had ten thousand in my pocket right now would you try to lift it?" Horn said.

"It would be highly improbable that you had ten thousand dollars," Judd remarked, and everyone laughed at the jibe.

The curious mental examination continued. Dr. Ball asked the boys to tell their story, and Artie began to relate it all over again in every detail. Time went by and sandwiches arrived. There were elaborate shiftings around, Judd using a filing cabinet as a table. There were thank-yous at the water cooler. All this, we learned later at the trial, was being noted down by Dr. Stauffer—the responsiveness, the well-oriented behavior, the ability to carry on the complex recital through incessant interruptions.

When Artie had completely finished his story, Dr. Ball looked from one to the other and inquired, in a tone of unaffected curiosity, "But can you tell me why you did it?"

"I don't know why on earth I did it!" Judd blurted out.

Artie was silent.

At that moment, Judd's father entered the room.

* * *

Judah Steiner could not say why he had come downtown. He did not yet know how he felt toward his son, for his numb horror was impersonal. As much as he wanted to see Judd, he did not, out of some dread, want to look upon him. He had awakened with the feeling that he must go and see the boy, and the dread had been there, the dread felt before every childbirth, the dread that the infant might be born malformed, a monster. And then, should it live, or not live? Would a father have to decide?

That morning was the first time Judah Steiner had called for the car since the thing had happened. He had not seen Emil since the papers had said it was the chauffeur's unexpected story that had proved to be the last straw, causing Artie to break down and confess.

Emil stood holding the car door open, as always. His face was drawn, his eyes were averted. Judah Steiner stopped for a moment before getting into the car. "I don't blame you, Emil," he said. "You did what your conscience told you."

Emil gulped some words, how sorry he was. They drove downtown.

Judah Steiner went up to the same door where, a few nights before, he had appeared as a proud man to make his presence felt. Today he walked uncertainly, dazed, bewildered. All his measurements of life had proven wrong. As he entered, he heard those words of Judd's in the high clacky voice, "I don't know why on earth I did it!" and at the same moment their eyes met.

Judd said, "Hello, Dad."

Everyone in the room waited. The state's attorney was the first to break the silence, his voice respectful with commiseration. "Is there anything we can do for you, Mr. Steiner?"

"No, no, sir." Perhaps Steiner felt he had already received the answer to whatever had brought him there.

"Did you wish to speak with your son alone for a few moments? I would be glad to arrange it."

"Did you get me a lawyer?" Judd demanded, without waiting.

"Yes," his father said. "That is arranged. We have engaged the best. Mr. Jonathan Wilk will defend you."

A look of elation, indeed of triumph, came onto Judd's face. He turned involuntarily to Artie, forgetting for the moment their estrangement. Artie was grinning.

Several reporters hurried out to the press-room phones. The words "million-dollar defense" were already in the air.

The father was still looking at his son, his head beginning to shake slightly from side to side. Judd said, "I'm sorry this happened."

"Yes," Steiner said. "We are all sorry." He turned and withdrew.

From there, he had Emil drive him to the Wilk apartment. Max was there, with the rest, in the library with its overflow of books in piles on the floor. Young James Straus and his Uncle Gerald sat closest to Mr. Wilk, who rose and took Judah Steiner's hand in a long, firm clasp.

Judd's father inquired after Mr. and Mrs. Straus. How were they?

"Lewis took them to Charlevoix," Gerald said. "Doctor's orders." Randolph Straus had a bad heart. Mrs. Straus had fallen into a state of depression. "It's best for them to leave. What can they do here?" And the hounds, the stupid dirty hounds of the public had already started on them, Gerald said bitterly. Anonymous phone calls, even telegrams. The Straus name was more widely known than the Steiners'; they would get the worst of it.

Judah Steiner listened. Yes, it was better they should go. It was better his wife was not here.

Gerald Straus turned abruptly back to the discussion. The papers were already full of violent editorials. From a clipping he read, "Democracy is dead if these sons of the rich evade the gallows."

With all this hysteria, said Ferdinand Feldscher, there was only one course—to delay. To wait for things to die down.

"Horn will scream his head off if you try any delay," Wilk said. "We all know him." No, they had to get right to work on a defense. Unfortunately, Dr. Ball had already been nabbed by the state. So had Dr. Ralph Tierney. Of course there were others.

Edgar Feldscher had his intent, concentrated look. He offered his thought. "Why can't we both use them, if they're the best?"

Wilk's eyes lighted up as he caught the idea, but the others were all staring at Edgar Feldscher, uncomprehendingly. He elaborated. Why not do away with the usual practice of having rival teams of alienists to contradict each other? Why not make a truly honest, serious attempt to get the best, the latest that modern science could offer, to have a joint comprehensive study made of the boys? Wouldn't it inspire public confidence, reduce some of this hostility, if both sides agreed to use the same scientific study?

"Where would you be?" his brother asked. "You'd still have to get expert evaluation."

"And after all that," Wilk said with melancholy humor, "some totally ignorant layman on the jury will decide on their sanity according to how he likes their faces."

That brought the question right back. No jury could be trusted in this case, Ferdinand Feldscher insisted. A plea of guilty should be considered.

Max explained to his father that a plea of guilty came before a judge alone.

All looked to Wilk, the swayer of juries. He drew his hand slowly along his cheek. Just then Mrs. Wilk, with a slight groan, passed him a copy of the *Sunday Examiner,* pointing to an account of Judd's conversation with one of his guards while retracing the trail of the crime. Wilk read it aloud: "Young Steiner also discussed the possibility of a guilty plea, saying the best thing for him and for Artie might be to avoid a jury and go before a friendly judge. With their family millions——"

Ferdinand Feldscher reached angrily for the newspaper. His brother Edgar bent to read it over his shoulder.

"Well," said Wilk dryly, "if we don't get at those boys and make them stop talking, they'll hang themselves for sure, judge or jury."

"If they haven't already," Ferdinand Feldscher muttered.

Meanwhile an item in another column had caught his brother's eye. It was about an annual meeting of psychiatrists, opening in Atlantic City. The top men in the country would all be there, Edgar pointed out excitedly. Dr. McNarry, the president, had made history with his psychiatric testimony in the Thaw case.

Gerald spoke decisively. "Somebody better take the night train to Atlantic City."

*   *   *

Judah Steiner seemed scarcely to have been following the details, but as the group broke up he drew Edgar Feldscher aside. In an almost ashamed voice, he asked, "Could it be that we are doing wrong to try to defend them?" Edgar Feldscher studied him, his large serious eyes seeming to know the full meaning. "I am trying to think," Judah Steiner said, "if they were not our sons."

"If you were on a jury." The studious lawyer slowly filled his pipe.

Judah Steiner inclined his head. Again, that dreadful image came to him, of the moment before the birth of every child —waiting outside the delivery room, holding back the fear that you did not even discuss with your wife, the fear of the monster-birth. But once, after all the children were born perfect, once when Dr. Reis was visiting socially, the discussion had come up: What does a doctor think about this problem? And Abe Reis had said, confidentially, every doctor has to face it, and there are ways, without killing it, of letting such a creature die. Many, many doctors, perhaps, have sometimes let it happen, he guessed.

And now, if the monster was of a different kind, a mental monster, grown, and if it destroyed others, and was caught—perhaps you should "let it happen." Perhaps you did not have the right to defend it.

Edgar Feldscher placed his hand on the older man's shoulder. "Our conception of justice requires a defense. That's why justice holds the scales blindfolded. So as not to see the monsters."

Judah Steiner's head was beginning to shake again, in the slight, almost imperceptible movement. "You feel that anybody has to be defended, no matter what he did?" A lawyer was something like a doctor, bound to the highest ethics. Yet even for the doctor, there had come a point. . . .

"Yes," Feldscher said with his small, rather worried smile. "Everyone. That is the basis of our law. Everyone is entitled to a defense."

Steiner's head steadied. "Then you believe we are not responsible for what we do?" he asked, heavily.

"Yes. Yes, we are responsible. We are responsible for all that we do. But when our behavior becomes abnormal, there are causes, pressures from outside and from inside, and there is a border line, an area of doubt, let us say, where the individual needs help to overcome such terrible pressures. Besides, there is the whole question of the kind of punishment. Take these boys—" and the way he said it, they could be strangers. "What would be served by their execution? Judd has already shown so much creative power."

Again, the father's eyes filmed. He did not try to hide the tears from Feldscher. "If he is allowed to live, even in prison he might repay with some good—"

"Yes. That is what I thought."

Steiner sighed, immensely relieved.

Edgar Feldscher continued, "You must also have thought, who knows what is good? Were Napoleon's wars justified by the reforms he tried to introduce? Obviously, we can never measure the balance."

"But what made them do it?" the father asked.

"Who knows?" the lawyer repeated. "I look at all this as human energy we're dealing with, free energy, a natural force, which we try all our lives to control. Like electricity, which we use and control, even if we don't understand its nature. What we have in us, this energy, is a flow of force, and sometimes a part of it flashes out, like lightning." Judah Steiner was staring at him, unhappily. "I know it doesn't exactly fit, but it seems to me, and the newer psychologists try to explain it this way, we all have this psychic energy, and we have to channelize it, but sometimes, like a baby—a baby doesn't know good from bad—it lets through every impulse, what it wants it does, what it wants it seizes."

"But how can they be still like babies? They are grown, brilliant, intelligent boys."

"Some parts of us can stay ungrown; in some parts of us we are still like babies," Feldscher said. "We use it in our daily conversation—we say someone is infantile. You can't blame a baby for what it does."

Steiner's head was shaking again; he couldn't understand. "You never blame anyone?"

"Yes. Yes, I do believe there is blame. But I try not to blame right away." He held his pipe elegantly.

"I don't understand it at all." Steiner turned away. "I don't understand."

The other men were in a circle, their voices subdued, for there had come up a remaining part of the subject so disagreeable to touch that each had held off from it. Yet, as they moved to depart, it had to come out. Judah Steiner did not know, at first, what they referred to, for he had found himself unable to look at the newspapers. But he caught their words now. About other crimes. Ferdinand Feldscher was saying, "It's to be expected Horn will try to pin every unsolved crime of the last five years on them. There isn't an iota of evidence." The newspapers were asking about that horrible crime of a few months ago, the taxi driver who had been found mutilated, the "gland robbery" on the South Side. Two assailants, he had said.

"But he admitted he never got a good look at them; he could never identify his assailants," one of the others insisted.

".Well, maybe I shouldn't mention this," Max put in, his voice quite low and solemn. "But at my engagement party Artie kept talking all the time about the kidnaping, saying he bet the same criminals committed the two crimes. A lot of people heard him. Someone else is liable to remember it now."

"So what?" said Uncle Gerald. "Everybody was saying things like that all week."

James Straus said, with his hasty way of getting rid of something nasty, "In the *Examiner* they mention that student who left the house to mail a letter and was found drowned. I think Artie knew him. Perry Rosoff."

"That poor Rosoff boy was a suicide," Uncle Gerald stated.

Hesitantly, James suggested, "Wouldn't it be better if we asked the boys about all this?"

There was a silence, a fear-laden silence. Then Gerald said, "Can't we wait and deal with these matters when and if any evidence is offered?"

The group began to break up.

"If there is anything like that," Ferdinand Feldscher said to his brother Edgar, "can there still be a question of sanity?"

*   *   *

We were all, by then, puzzling over the other crimes. At first, the idea seemed too much. We did not want to have to learn any more. But Tom and I could not keep our minds from the story.

We sat in Louie's place, speculating. Tom recalled that strange stormy letter stolen from Judd's desk. About betraying Artie to a friend. Couldn't that have been about the other crimes? To have caused such a storm of denial? And the friend, Willie Weiss, was the same fellow they had lunched with on the day of the murder! Police had even wondered if it was a triumvirate.

Things had gone so quickly that none of us had talked to Weiss. True, the police had checked and dismissed him. Still, shouldn't we try to see Willie?

Tom had to go home; he explained he always had Sunday

dinner with his folks. We agreed I should try to see Willie
Weiss by myself. This time he proved not difficult to find. I
phoned his home and was told he had gone over to do some
work at the lab. It seemed almost too appropriate—the deserted medical building, permeated by its heavy, sweetish,
formaldehyde smell.

Working at the end of the long room was a round-shoul-
dered figure in a smeared lab coat, perched on a high stool.
"Weiss?" I said. He turned.

He had a long, narrow head, held a trifle cocked to one
side; his eyes were keen, but his dark skin was completely
pocked and his nose was a caricature. "The Horrible Hebe,"
we learned Judd called him, and he was ugly in the grand
manner. You could see at once that he was sensitive about it,
and covered this with a mocking expression around the
mouth. As he slipped off the stool, I saw that he was dwarfish,
the head overlarge.

Willie didn't seem hostile. Indeed, before I could ask him
any questions, he was drawing out from me in extreme detail
everything I had done on the story, getting me particularly to
tell how Artie had injected himself among the reporters, even
among the detectives, with his advice, theories, clues. I was
aware that Willie had reversed the situation on me, but even
as a cub reporter I had already learned that people like to
question newspapermen, and that a good way to get them to
talk freely is to let them question you first.

"True to form, true to form," Willie kept saying about
Artie's behavior, and then, "I would have guessed he'd be the
first one to break down and confess."

I observed to Willie that he probably knew them better
than anybody.

"You think I was a third member of the team?" He
grinned. "Sure, we had lunch regularly every Wednesday. The
three of us." Looking squarely at me to enjoy the effect, Willie
said, "I was studying them."

"Oh."

"Yes. I'm interested in their psychology. You seen them
since they confessed?"

"I just came from there," I said. "The state's attorney had a couple of alienists in the office, questioning them."

"Yes?" He was full of curiosity. "Who?"

"Dr. Ball. And Stauffer."

"Good men, pretty good men," he conceded. He wanted to know what they had asked. I said they had only had the boys repeat their story of the crime.

"That's all?"

"That was all."

Hadn't they asked anything about their life? Their homes? Their families? Their childhood? Hadn't they advanced any idea about what made the boys do it?

"No," I said, "they just asked them if they knew right from wrong."

"Goyishe kep!" Willie snapped. His use of the Yiddish expression, dumbheaded gentiles, came with a sidewise grin to me. Willie, I was to learn, came from a branch of the Weiss family that had intermarried with more recent immigrants; they retained a touch of the commoner folk. All this was to enter perhaps disproportionately into Willie's understanding of Judd and Artie.

Since he was studying them, I asked, did he have any idea what made the boys do it?

Only the beginning of a theory, Willie said. Those alienists—had they, for instance, questioned the boys about the weapon, the particular choice of weapon?

"No," I replied. "Why?"

"Just curious," Willie said. The alienists were apparently quite old-fashioned in their approach. And he moved to turn back to his work.

I stopped him with a direct attack. During that last luncheon, I asked, what had they been like?

Just as usual. Maybe a little more in high spirits, looking back at it. Talking about books—pornography and stuff.

Had he ever known about other stuff they had done? What about that famous letter of Judd's?

"What about it?" Willie grew a trifle sharp.

It just sounded, I said, as if Judd had revealed to him some crime that Artie had committed.

He grinned, as at an error that nevertheless contained a degree of acumen. "That's an interesting assumption," Willie said. "So you connect it with all that junk in today's paper about additional crimes?" He kept looking at me. "Nah, all Judd did was to hint around to me that he knew things about Artie that I didn't know." He mimicked, " 'Artie tells me secrets he doesn't tell you!' You know the way girls are with their little whisperings, and then they get all excited and dramatic and say, 'If you dare tell, I'll never talk to you again!' " Willie shook his head in admiration of his own perceptiveness. "Pure feminine psychology."

"Well, sure," I said. "Jealousy."

He laughed.

But even if they were perverts, I said, the way the crime now seemed to have been done, that had nothing to do with it.

Again that keen look came into his eyes. Did I know anything about the new psychology? Willie asked. About Sigmund Freud?

I knew the catchwords: complexes, suppressed desires.

"It's my field," Willie announced.

Did the Freud stuff help him to understand Judd and Artie? I asked.

No, no, he was far from understanding. Weiss was entirely serious with me now. He knew that I, like himself, had a special relationship to the story. "Only I've had a kind of hunch," he said. It kept sitting on his mind that there was a significance in a couple of things—two things that might turn out to contain the key.

What two things? What were they?

Willie looked at me as if I might conceivably be of help. "The implement," he said, "the implement, and then, the burial place."

"The implement?"

Yes. The weapon. The chisel wrapped around with tape.

So unused were we, in those days, to thinking in symbols that are today common to every imagination, that even under Willie's shrewd prodding the meaning of it did not occur to me. I thought of the chisel literally—a tool, then a murder weapon.

As for the burial place, I thought he meant the swamp, in its entirety. Was he perhaps hinting that other bodies might be found there? I asked him this, point-blank.

Willie must have decided, then, that I was after all not too bright. No, no, he didn't really know anything, Willie said. It was just conjecture, a hunch. Then, like an exasperated teacher, he gave me one more chance. "Who do you suppose they were really trying to kill?"

This time, I felt, as by telepathy, that I caught his meaning. "Themselves?"

He gave me the smile of reward to a dense pupil who has at last come through with one correct answer. On the first plane, yes, he agreed, self-destructiveness was clear in both of them. Look at the way Artie drove a car—he had been in any number of accidents—and look at Judd's dropping his glasses.

"Yes, of course," I said.

But self-destructiveness wasn't enough of an answer, Willie declared. Had I read the confessions? The different people they had picked to kill, at one time or another during their planning stage?

"Yes, even you were on the list," I said. "But everybody has a little list."

He brushed aside my remark. "But whom did those people represent? Whom did they really want to kill?" He stared at me. "It would make a fascinating study. Fascinating. What an opportunity! Now that they're isolated. What an opportunity for a great study!"

At that moment, I felt I knew why Willie had been the third member of their luncheon parties. Surely he fitted in, if he could now think of his friends only in terms of what a study they would make. I was reminded of Judd's remark about impaling a butterfly.

I could get no more out of him that day.

As I walked the half-empty sunny Sunday streets, the conversation lay on my mind. I groped into the new avenues he had opened. Whom had they really wanted to kill? And if they had talked of people they wanted to kill, why couldn't there have been more killings? And the chisel . . .

I called Tom. Presently he met me, driving up with his

brother Will, who was on the police force. They were in Will's
Ford.

"That chisel—" Will ruminated, after I told them of my
interview with Willie Weiss. There was something about the
chisel they hit the boy with, Will said. Like he had heard of it
before. We drove over to the Hyde Park station and Will
talked to a friend of his, Sergeant Lacey.

Come to think of it, Lacey believed he had heard of at
least one other chisel wrapped in tape picked up in the neighborhood. Some months before. Brought in by a patrolman,
given to him by one of those private watchmen around the
rich homes, who had found it on a lawn. Looked like something a footpad might have used, but it didn't check with any
crime; so as far as he knew it had been chucked away.

But of course! This was what Willie Weiss had meant.
The weapon.

We got into the Ford and went to work again, questioning
watchmen and gardeners in the neighborhood, and the chisel
began to seem almost a legendary weapon. Yes, one or another
had seen a chisel something like that, with tape on the blade,
or had heard someone speak of finding such a thing. Yet we
couldn't track anything down precisely.

When we returned to the Hyde Park station, Will's friend
Lacey told him on the quiet about a search that had just been
made in the Straus mansion, in Artie's room. In an old trunk
in the closet, under some toys, they had found a whole lot of
men's wallets and ladies' purses. No money in any of them.

*   *   *

When I got to my room there was a note under the door
to call Miss Seligman, no matter at what hour. Though it was
after ten, I called. Myra implored me to come over, to come
directly to her room, which could be entered from the hotel
corridor.

The room had a studio effect, and Myra was wearing a
Chinesey kind of dressing gown; as she took my hand, her
palm was hot and moist.

"Sid," she said, "oh, thanks for coming. I've been going
mad! There's no one I can talk to. My mother was so upset,
but of course she takes the conventional attitude; she doesn't

try to understand. Sid, they were here! I don't know if I did the right thing—I talked to them, I told them things about Artie—"

"Who?" I asked.

Two men from Horn's office had appeared. Of course she wanted to help Artie, they said to her, and she had said, of course. They had been nice men, very considerate, they had even seemed to sympathize, and they had wanted to know all about Artie, since she had known him from childhood. He had always been of exceptional mentality, hadn't he? Advanced, mature for his age? And she had said, of course, he was brilliant! And certainly not abnormal.

Now she sucked in her lower lip, in that naughty-child way she had. "Do you think I said the wrong things, Sid? Oh, I wanted to do anything I could to help him!"

I said they were probably taking depositions from everybody.

She looked guiltily at me. They had asked about the last times she had been out with Artie and she had mentioned our date at the Four Deuces with him and Judd. They had wanted to know if Judd had a girl. She had mentioned his taking out my little friend Ruth. And they had taken Ruth's name. Again Myra sucked in her lip. Her huge dark eyes burned in their dark pouches. "Oh, I'm such an idiot."

Ruth would surely have been questioned in any case, I reassured her.

Then she went to the window, open to the night over the park and the lake. Her voice hoarse, Myra told how once she and Artie had made a suicide pact—she supposed all kids did that, but people only thought of Artie as always happy-go-lucky. And now, today . . . I didn't move. After a moment she came and slipped to her knees, going limp against me. "Oh, tell me what to do," she begged. "I would do anything to help him."

"There's nothing you can do," I said. "You're not mixed up in it."

"I am, I am. Everybody who knew him is. Everybody who let him come to a thing like that."

I tried to say that it was surely a sickness, that there was nothing she could have done. "Oh, I'm worse than a whore," she cried. "Oh, Sid, I wish I were honest and decent like a whore. Do you think if I had given myself to him . . . oh, we're all such frauds—we pretend we're so emancipated. Sid, if I had, if I had, then maybe he wouldn't have got all tangled up with that awful Judd. That's what got him into it." An instant later she begged me to forgive her for her histrionics. "I feel such a failure, such a complete failure."

I believe that even at the time I saw that her obsession, her constantly putting everything in terms of sex, was only because it was the only name then given to love.

Her mother wanted her to leave town, Myra said, as had so many of the girls whose names might be linked to Artie's. But she wouldn't go; she would even testify at the trial, if it could do the least good. Then suddenly she seemed quieted.

Sunday evening, the boys were finally brought to the real jail, the heavy, square building with walls of gray stone, almost black with dirt.

Horn had got all he wanted from them; now he could let their lawyers get to them. So he turned them over to the sheriff, to be booked at last, charged with their murder.

Inside the old building with its yellowish walls the stale institutional smell engulfed them.

There was a narrow connecting bridge, between the administration building and the cells, indeed like the famous Bridge of Sighs, and Artie went first over it, striding rapidly, getting ahead of the turnkey, who snapped, "What's your hurry? You'll have plenty of time here."

*   *   *

He didn't feel out of place. The closing door, the turning lock, had familiarity. Artie looked to his cellmate with an almost mischievous glance, as though they were two kids: now the game begins. But the cellmate was a dull-witted farm lad, who didn't even seem impressed by who Artie was. After brief exchanges of what they were in for—the cellmate had done a robbery with a gun—Artie stretched on his bunk.

He had seen himself often, lying behind solid dungeon walls. After Miss Nuisance had tucked him in tight and placed his teddy bear beside him and gone out, shutting the door as the lights went off, he would turn to the bear, whispering the magic word, and it came to his lips now, the magic beginning, *"and now, Teddy. . . ."* But here the light never really went out; some greasy kind of half illumination hung over the cell floor.

And now, Teddy, they got us. But we can figure out a way to lam. We always did it and we can do it again. Like from the house in Charlevoix, climbing out of the window and swiping the car and driving like all hell—too bad there was the collision.

But the master criminal, the greatest of them all, cannot be held by locks and bars. Shall it be the special key that fits all locks, smuggled in by our moll? No, Teddy, this place is easy—you saw that guard, that screw, give me the eye, the one at the main gate. He's in our pay; he's part of the master criminal's gang. And in a few days, as soon as we're ready, we'll tip him the wink, and the gate will accidentally be left open and we'll walk right out of here.

Meanwhile we'll play the game just like we did with Miss Nuisance. We will be model little boys, model prisoners who never tell a lie. They will trust us, and we'll wander around and get the layout—the rainpipe we can slide down, things like that.

But Mumsie hasn't come. Mumsie hasn't come to say good night to poor Artie. Only Miss Nuisance. Mumsie is busy with her baby. A new baby must be taken care of by Mumsie. *All right for you!*

Is Nuisance gone? Good and safe and gone? Safe in her room? Sneak the flashlight from under the mattress. The detective book. The master criminal kidnapers. Snatch the baby right in his own house, and bring him up to the hiding place in the garret; everything works perfectly. That Italian organ grinder outside plays the signal-tune that says the ransom is ready. Only we work it with cars. A car horn. Hear that horn—*shave and a haircut, ten cents?* That means ten grand is ready.

No, we'll do it differently. We'll pretend to play cops and robbers with little brother. Yes, Mumsie, I'd love to play a game with Baby.

Shh, Teddy, here's the plot. That little stupe believes everything you tell him. You pretend you're on his side, helping him catch the master criminal, and I will be lying in wait at the top of the stairs. You bring the little bastard up, and *pow!* I've got him! It was an accident! Nobody knew the pistol was loaded. Poor baby, oh, my sweet little kid brother!

Then, punishment. They never spank you. They lock you in your room.

Revenge! Do the same to them! . . . "Now, Artie, this is your new governess, Miss Newsome, and you must be very nice to her." There she goes into her room! Turn the key on her! Listen to the prisoner pound on the door! "Oh, Artie! Arthur! You naughty—!"

Then Miss Nuisance made him sit on a chair. Mumsie didn't save him from her. Mumsie said obey Miss Newsome. All right for you, Mumsie, I'll get even with you. In some dark hallway, *pow!*

They were leading him to the scaffold and Miss Nuisance was walking behind, reading *A Tale of Two Cities* out loud to him. . . .

Turning over on his pallet, feeling something crawling under his clothing, Artie sat up. Bugs, lice.

* * *

Judd folded his trousers and his coat, placing them on the floor. He said a terse but civil good night to his cellmate, a car thief. The immense loneliness came over him. If he and Artie had been given a cell to share . . . but, no, he was angry at Artie.

He lay down with his hands under his head. And then all at once, in the quiet of the cell, Judd understood how stupid he had been in the last two days. A superman was not bound by the conventions of telling the truth! Of course Artie had a right to change the fact about who had been driving and about who had struck the blow. Artie had behaved superiorly. It was Artie who had kept the higher consistency! It was not against him, personally, that Artie had lied, but for his own self, as a god made his own truth.

A wave of relief passed through Judd. He had Artie back. Would he see Artie tomorrow? In the yard?

* * *

The next morning when they were marched into the jail yard, Judd went up to Artie at once, his hand extended. "We got into this together, let's go through with it together," he said. "I'm sorry if I did anything that might strain our friendship."

Artie blinked, then put out his hand, too, while over his face came that roguish, college-boy grin.

*   *   *

As Wilk and Ferdinand Feldscher came into the consultation cell, the boys rose, Artie with a sheepish look toward Feldscher, and Judd to address Wilk with undisguised adulation. "I am a great admirer of yours. May I say I consider you one of the greatest minds of our time? With you in the case, this will be the most interesting thing in my life!"

Well, he would try to be of help, Wilk said. But he did not see much hope; in all his experience he had never encountered such a hanging fever in the public. And the boys had done all they could to stimulate it by their wild, bragging talk. What had made them talk so much!

Raising his head to Wilk, Judd said he guessed he had wanted to show off.

"All right. Now that's finished with. Remarks like this thing about finding a friendly judge—" Wilk shook his head, eying Judd sadly. "You didn't really say that?"

Judd declared that he couldn't recall, exactly.

"Henceforth," Feldscher admonished, "no matter what is asked, by reporters or anybody, you reply, 'I must respectfully decline to answer upon advice of counsel.' Got that?"

"I must respectfully decline . . ." they parroted.

"Even if they ask you the time of day."

"I must respectfully decline . . ." they chorused. Artie was grinning.

Feldscher glanced from one to the other. "Have they questioned you about other crimes?"

Artie's face twitched.

"The papers are full of stuff. They claim you did everything from that gland atrocity to the killing of Cock Robin."

"Have you got the papers?" Artie asked eagerly. "They won't let us have them."

Feldscher shook his head. "Everybody is finding taped chisels all over Chicago." His eyes had not left Artie's face.

Artie returned his gaze unblinkingly. "I must respectfully decline to answer upon advice of counsel."

For the time being they let it stand that way.

*   *   *

All through the interview, and after returning to his cell, Judd was borne up by a sense of vindication, because a Jonathan Wilk would defend him. Then came an upwelling of grief, of regret; if only he had had such a one near him as he grew up—an older spirit, a mentor warm and near, with an arm around his shoulder, a Socrates.

He would write to Jonathan Wilk.

For the first time Judd felt his imprisonment. He needed a piece of paper to write on. It came finally, after his rattling the door, shouting, exchanging his last dollar for a ruled sheet from a copybook.

"Intelligence," he wrote, "has always been the one attribute of man that appealed to me more strongly than any other. And since you happen to possess more of it than any other man whom I have had the pleasure of meeting, this alone would cause me to bow down in abject hero worship. But, sir, I appreciate the other great qualities that bring you to undertake our case. Courage, surely.

"Is it courage for a man who after forty-six years of untiring effort has built up one of the greatest reputations for forensic ability to stake that reputation upon a seemingly impossible case? Suppose that man has defended countless murderers against overwhelming odds and has never suffered a hanging verdict. Suppose further that he is nearly seventy years old and that during an energetic life, devoted always to the weaker side, the poor and friendless, suppose this man has accumulated sufficient means for all his needs and has built a 'monument more enduring than brass.' Now this man jeopardizes a reputation of fifty years' standing and risks it upon a seemingly impossible case. It is a case which has been heralded far and wide and which has been decided by the unreasoning mob long before it reaches the courts of law! Why does he do it? He does it for the sake of his principles. Is this bravery? By God, if it isn't, then the definition of bravery ought to be revised. Nay, it is more than bravery. It is heroism."

*   *   *

And indeed it seemed that heroism would be needed. For it was Wilk's telephone now that rang incessantly with anonymous and obscene threats. A hundred and ten killers saved from the gallows? He himself would hang from a streetlamp before he could add these two to his list!

And at midnight, flaming up beneath his windows, was the burning cross.

*   *   *

When news of it came, I rushed to the Midway, to see only the charred remnants, as of a huge box kite. Fire engines were pulling away. Neighborhood people in shirtsleeves, university students, were already dispersing, in a peculiar, depressed silence.

It was the Ku Klux Klan. The first burning cross in Chicago. No, no one had seen hooded white figures. Some said a truck had stopped, a dozen men had set up the ready cross, touched matches to it, and driven off.

For Wilk? I was dazed. What had this crime to do with the K.K.K.? All I knew were the general things. K.K.K. was something to be joked about, yet vaguely menacing. All those men in their white sheets, their regalia, were subjects for Mencken's jokes in *The Smart Set*. They were symbols of stupidity. And they had seemed rather distant from Chicago. Wasn't it a Southern thing that had started after the Civil war, against Negroes? White Southerners, taking the law into their own hands, to scare the Negroes? They were in Griffith's *Birth of a Nation*. That was probably what had started the Klan going again. But it was for hicks. The nearest that it had ever come to Chicago was some town in Indiana. A burning cross had been reported there. And they would come at night and grab somebody—some minister involved in a scandal, perhaps —they would grab him and take him to a woods and whip him. And they would burn crosses as a warning, for people they didn't like. They were not only against Negroes. Catholics and Jews, too.

And Wilk. An atheist. A defender of Jews.

Then a remark of my father's came to my mind. When I had called home, on Sunday, his only remark about the case had been, "One thing is lucky in this terrible affair, Sid. It's lucky it was a Jewish boy they picked." My father, with his one yardstick. What will it do to the Jews?

It was to take me a long while to perceive the inverted, subterranean way in which there was a meaning to their all being Jewish. The burning cross, that night, failed to illuminate it for me. The immediate result of the cross-burning was a police guard set around Jonathan Wilk. Despite his protests.

* * *

Then the defense called a press conference. Wilk was sitting with his back to the windows as we filed in, but he got up at once and assumed his celebrated Lincolnesque stoop; his coat hung loosely open, and his left thumb was automatically hooked under his suspenders. He waved us in, the aging speckled skin of his hand transparent in a sunray.

"Well, boys, I see a lot of stories about a million-dollar defense," he remarked. "I wouldn't mind a million-dollar fee, but the fact is, stories like this inflame the public. Two decent families are involved. Why don't you give them a chance?"

We were handed copies of a prepared statement. The families pledged themselves in no way to make use of their wealth to influence justice. Lawyers' fees would be determined by the Bar Association. The families felt that the boys should be permanently removed from society; however, they hoped that their lives would be saved.

Did that mean an insane asylum? we asked. What would the defense be?

First, said Edgar Feldscher, the defense would try to assemble the facts.

Mike Prager snapped, "Hasn't everything already been found out?"

The outward facts, yes. But a team of the very best alienists would make a study to determine the inward facts.

"Then you *are* going to plead insanity?"

The plea, he repeated smilingly, would depend on the study. It was to be purely scientific. Indeed, the defense still held open to Mr. Horn the offer for a joint mental study.

What can they possibly be trying to pull? Mike Prager speculated, as we went down the elevator.

                    *   *   *

We took the defense offer to Horn. He laughed. "I've got my own alienists, the best in the business. Old Wilk is trying to pull a deal. First, a joint examination. Then he'll offer a guilty plea. Oh, no, you can tell old Jonathan the Great that I'm not playing. I've got an airtight hanging case and those boys are going to swing."

Had there been feelers from the defense? Was there a chance of a deal on a guilty plea before the Chief Justice?

"You know what the chances would be if I was still sitting up there!" Horn said ominously. He was reminding us that before running for state's attorney, he had himself occupied the post of Chief Justice of the Criminal Court. He was putting Judge Matthewson on notice.

                    *   *   *

The formal arraignment was to take place on the following morning, and late into the night we hovered near the Wilk apartment, still held by Horn's angry hint that there might be a plea of guilty instead of a great show trial.

Every few minutes a couple of us would go up to the door of the apartment to ask if there were any developments. Mrs. Wilk was apologetic about keeping us outside, but last-minute conferences were in progress. Edgar Feldscher had returned from Atlantic City, bringing two of his alienists. Willie Weiss was there too, hurrying in and out of various rooms, and from the doorway I managed to get his attention. He came out and walked around the block with me, talking incessantly. He was going to work with the defense! It would be a great opportunity for him to observe the methods of the top psychiatrists in the country! There was Dr. Hugh Allwin, a very advanced man who had just come from Vienna with the very latest techniques! And with him was Dr. Eli Storrs, a brilliant psychologist. "They're really going to do a job!" he said. "Nothing like this has ever been done before. Complete psychological and physiological studies, the latest gland stuff. Wilk's also got Dr. Vincenti, the best endocrine man alive!" The boys would virtually be taken apart, to see what made them tick.

But upstairs, I gathered, the insanity strategy was in question. To go before a jury was suicide. Precedent alone, straight legal precedent, presented to a judge, might be the soundest approach, for no minor in Chicago had ever been hanged on a guilty plea.

Thus it went all night long, and on the morning of the arraignment we still did not know how they would plead. I was to do the human-interest story of the arraignment: for one thing, it was taking place on Artie's nineteenth birthday.

Then, as we were leaving for court, Reese beckoned to Tom. Somebody named Al Capone, the owner of a speak-easy called the Four Deuces, had just been picked up for shooting a top gangster named Joe Howard. A new kind of cold-blooded killing. The car had simply swept past Joe Howard on Clark Street, and he had been shot full of holes.

Tom hurried to police headquarters and I went on alone to cover the arraignment of the boys. The Four Deuces, where we had all been a week ago. As I took the elevator to the courtroom I scarcely realized what a strange interweaving had taken place.

* * *

As word spread that the thrill killers would appear, there were scuttlings from all the corridors; from nowhere, the courtroom filled. Presently the lawyers for both sides arrived, and Uncle Gerald, and Judah Steiner, Sr., with his air of monumental sorrow.

The boys were brought in. I could not instantly bring myself to ask Artie about his birthday, but the sob sisters did not delay. Had he received presents from his best girls? From Myra Seligman? From Dorothea Lengel?

Artie smiled teasingly. Other questions came, for both. What was jail life like? Would they prefer hanging to life sentences? And they replied courteously, but like a vaudeville team, "We must respectfully decline to answer upon the advice of counsel," smirking as they looked over to their lawyers.

We laughed, and then for an instant they bent their heads together, and Artie came out of the huddle, grinning. "We have a statement, fellows." We all bit, readying our notepaper.

"The sun is shining," said Artie. "It is a pleasant day." So we laughed again and noted that they had recovered their friendship and their bravado.

The judge entered. It was the Chief Justice himself. In certain events, chance seems to exert itself to choose the proper persons, as if there were an ordainment to show mankind from time to time a complete symbol. So in this case Judge Matthewson had precisely the bearing for his role. He had the fullness of years, but with no suggestion of frailty of age. He looked considerate, firm, and aware of the meaning of his position.

The clerk called the case.

Horn and his staff had prepared a formidable indictment, for felonious assault, murder by strangulation, kidnaping with intent to kill—everything—as if afraid of some wizardly loophole evasion. But Wilk sat relaxed, loose, with no papers before him. When the time came, he and Ferdinand Feldscher stood, one on each side of the two boys, as they were asked, how did they plead?

"Not guilty," said Judd, as though answering a classroom question, and Artie said, swallowing his words, "Not guilty."

Horn was smiling. He would have his chance to take on the great Jonathan Wilk before a jury. The judge set the day, a few weeks ahead.

Wilk pleaded for a delay to prepare a defense. "The defense needs no more time than the prosecution!" Horn cried. He would be ready and so could they. The public demanded and was owed speedy justice.

Edgar Feldscher pointed out that complex medical and mental examinations had to be made. The Chief Justice kept gazing at the boys. "The best I can give you is an extra week," he said. "At that time we'll see if you are ready."

"If I were sitting up there," Horn muttered, "I wouldn't give them an extra day."

*   *   *

I phoned the news and hurried in to write my feature. But instead of writing about Artie's birthday I found myself impelled to write of Judd's father, sitting there in the court-room. I've come across that story, in the files:

> Judah Steiner, Sr., a man with gray hair, sat in Judge Matthewson's courtroom today for an hour. He did not move. The other men spoke, even smiled, gestured, disputed. Judah Steiner sat quite still. The corners of his thin, gray eyebrows were pinched together. His hands lay folded across his knees. Only every few minutes a sort of tremor took his legs from the knees down.
>
> When the argument began, all the others at his table pressed up to the bench. From the seats in the rear of the room came a swarm of spectators. They flowed around his chair, they hung over him, stood on the back rungs, let their breath go past his face. The man sat there.
>
> Occasionally he put his hand to his ear. He was not angry, he was not weeping. He was merely trying to understand this thing. His son had killed someone. His son. For no reason at all, and for the reason of some philosophy that he couldn't understand. He had always thought his son was brilliant. His son was brilliant. But this—there must be some explanation. He was trying to find the explanation. But nothing seemed to come.
>
> His son was standing up there quietly, calmly, easily. People were staring first at him and then at his son, noticing the same cut in the yellowing lips of the father and the firm, red lips of the boy. People were noticing the same contour of forehead, the same balance of cheek.
>
> Then they came to him with questions. What did he think? What did he have to say?
>
> He had only one answer. "Why do you come to me? I —I have done nothing."

I have done nothing. Today, the words echo ironically. But even then they set me to wondering.

I would speak to Myra, who knew the families well. I would ask her—not as a newspaperman, but for myself.

When we met that evening, she greeted me with bravado; her hand, as we went down in the elevator, was hot, pulsing.

Automatically we started to walk toward the campus, almost deserted at night in the summer, and curiously other-worldly with its high-gabled graystone shapes islanded among the square red-brick apartment buildings of the neighborhood.

Myra could tell me only of the Strauses. Her mother was a close friend. Mrs. Straus was indeed ill in Charlevoix, shattered, accusing herself, broken. "You see, she's such an intelligent woman." And it was this very intelligence that had failed. Artie's crime seemed to have controverted the very principles of progress on which Mrs. Straus's life had been founded. For she was something of a new woman, a leader. And most of all, Mrs. Straus had prided herself on her advanced knowledge of child care. This had been her greatest interest. She headed all sorts of committees for settlement work with children. And she was interested in the latest educational methods.

"Then why?" Why hadn't she known what was happening with Artie?

But how could anyone know? Anyone. The closest to him—Myra swayed, and I sat her on the stone bench in Sleepy Hollow. All those little fibs and lies as children—how was anyone to know that with him these things came to more? So much more! His brother James? But James was only a nice, agreeable young man who wanted to avoid anything troublesome in life. And the older brother, Lewis? He had already been grown up when Artie was a kid.

And what of Artie's father? I asked.

He was a man entirely occupied with his affairs. On festive occasions he would put in an appearance, at Artie's birthday parties. She sucked in her breath.

I asked, was Mr. Straus a cold person? No, Myra said, not really, and indeed the Straus household hadn't been cold at all. Mrs. Straus had given it such a warm, open atmosphere —young people were always welcomed by her, and everybody was always going in and out, on the grounds, using the tennis court. Everyone felt free at the Strauses; it was that kind of a house, with culture, good music. Of course, Mrs. Straus was quite busy—she was the leader of so many activities, for the

Symphony, and the Literature Club, and the monthly discussion group.

"I always thought," Myra confessed, "I would have liked her for my own mother; she's so much more up on things—" And Myra crumpled against me. "I was with Artie on every birthday," she sobbed. "I wrote a poem for him every year." She had written one today. She tried to recite it to me, in her gaspy, hoarse whisper.

> Oh, angry boy
> Life's a broken toy
> Which you'd destroy,
> No! angry boy—

Her voice choked. "It's doggerel," she cried desperately. "I'm making doggerel out of it all. Oh, Sid, why can't I—" I held her until she stopped trembling, and then I walked her home.

*   *   *

In my primitive way I was following the path of the psychiatrists, who began their work with family interviews. Dr. Allwin made a hasty trip to Charlevoix. Artie's father was still in a state of shock, silent, withdrawn. He would listen to the bare information of what was taking place, then absent himself.

The mother had begun somehow to encompass the blow. She was bringing herself to regard the evidence of the two mature, normal sons, and of the healthy, sunny child Billy, as proof that the other's case was indeed a sickness. Might one have known, suspected? She could sit with Dr. Allwin and attempt to recall. . . .

Of course Artie had been from infancy exceptionally willful, mischievous, and for that very reason she had felt that a strong personality like Miss Newsome was a good choice as governess. Miss Newsome had her faults, and toward the end there had been quite a struggle with the poor woman who had no other avenue of affection and had become overattached to Artie, seeking to replace his mother—but such situations frequently arose with governesses, didn't they? It was perhaps true too that since his governess was rather strict, the family had been lenient in other things, indulgent with Artie. As a compensation, yes. And it was hard to refuse him anything—he had been such a winning child. . . . She controlled herself.

Then there had been the escapades. Yes, the times he had taken things from stores, they had been quite disturbed; but the value had been small, and it had seemed a streak of mischief. He had been talked to very severely, of course, but no one thought . . . and the dreadful accident here in Charlevoix, when he had taken the car to a dance. An old woman had been in the wagon Artie had run into, and she had lingered in the hospital for several months. Artie himself had suffered a concussion. Could it be from that?

Had he changed markedly at that time?

She strengthened herself, to be unflinchingly honest. It had to be admitted that Artie had always been wild. And deceitful. Yes. She had known that he lied. So glibly, too—but how could anyone have imagined . . . ?

No, no, the doctor reassured her, it would have been virtually impossible to suspect homicidal tendencies. And he never confided in anyone?

She had always thought that possibly with James he . . . Her eyes wavered.

Perhaps, in other ways, Artie might have shown his true feelings? Sudden angers? Hatred? Jealousy within the family?

She recalled one time when his father had been going on a trip East, taking his brother James along, and Artie had wanted so badly to go to New York. He had been fifteen then, and he had screamed, even producing a tantrum quite like he used to have when he was a very little boy.

Tantrums?

Oh, very frequently. Childish tantrums, to get what he wanted. But all children did that, and she usually tried the method of letting the child scream itself out, shutting him in his room, as neither she nor his father of course believed in capital—she caught herself—in corporal punishment.

Taking a deep breath, she went on. That time, Artie had broken out with wild accusation. Nobody cared about him, he

had shouted, nobody in the family cared! He would run away.
. . . She smiled, so ruefully. Of course everybody loved him.
It had seemed so absurd. Artie's father was often impatient
with him, that was true, but Mr. Straus was not a demonstra-
tive man. And he was himself a man of such high standards
that Artie's tendency to wild escapades, the reckless driving,
the running around with cheap girls, and even that disagreeable incident in the summer, here, with Judd—all this made
him more impatient with Artie, and Artie sensed his father's
disapproval; indeed he sometimes jokingly called himself the
black sheep of the family.

She had tried, therefore—oh, she had tried to make
things always stimulating and agreeable for him around the
house. She had always invited young people for the summer,
and Mr. Straus indeed had built the gymnasium here for the
boys, particularly for Artie, and had built the boat pier on the
lake when Artie evinced an interest in boating. And in town
she had put in the tennis court so that the young people would
congregate—she had always encouraged young people to congregate, though it did seem that Artie wore out his friends
rather rapidly. For this reason, perhaps, she had tolerated too
long his unhealthy relationship with Judd Steiner. It could not
be denied. Everyone had felt there was something unhealthy,
yet they had hoped the boys would simply grow out of it as
boys do—and how could anyone have imagined that it would
come to . . . Again, she had to control herself.

She could not seem to reach further than that. Mementos, snapshots were brought out, and Dr. Allwin studied
them absorbedly: the white-clad tennis youth, the smiling boy
in the class photograph, the collegiate Artie in a roadster, his
arms around two girls—lovely girls, Mrs. Straus said, identifying them—Myra Seligman, a cousin, as bright, as nice a girl
as could be; she had always hoped, even though Myra was a
year or so older . . . And the other, a college girl, Lenore
Loeb. And then, further back, birthday parties, the children
self-consciously posed, but who could say Artie was any different from the others, in his winning stare into the camera?
Then, among the childhood pictures, one snapshot halted the

alienist: Artie in a cowboy suit, holding a toy pistol, stalking his teddy bear.

Did she remember when it was taken?

Of course she remembered it! Artie was four, yes. A Sunday afternoon—Artie was so cute, so darling that day, and Mr. Straus himself had been unusually relaxed and had taken the pictures. Why? Was there something about the picture?

No, nothing unusual, the doctor said. But yet—in the expression . . .

And he so loved his teddy bear, the mother said.

But still, the doctor mused, a kid would be grinning, or making faces, or looking toward his parents. But here, the boy was so intent, lost in his masquerade, really living the hunt. He asked, This was shortly after the governess, Miss Newsome, came into the household? Why, yes, the mother said, her brows contracted. But why?

The doctor smiled musingly. He himself didn't know, he was only feeling his way. Was this a moment that became fixed, frozen, a boy forever masquerading, forever a hunter with a pistol? "It's just that he seems so concentrated," the doctor said.

And the mother said wistfully, "Oh, yes, his games were always very real to him—you know how children are." But there was the little gasp, the fright, the uncertainty in her intelligent eyes. Did anyone really know how children are?

Could he take this picture with him? the psychiatrist asked. But of course! And he pocketed the snapshot.

*   *   *

In the Steiner house, too, there were mementos. Aunt Bertha produced them for Dr. Allwin. The elaborate Baby's Book that the mother had filled with such exalted pride—the photographs of the tiny, alert infant with his curiously brilliant black eyes. And Aunt Bertha talking all the while of the marvels of the precocious child, and how his father and mother would do anything, anything for him. She told of the incident of bird-shooting in the park, and his father getting him the only permit. And another time on vacation he had been caught fishing without a license, and a stupid sheriff had taken away Judd's rod and tackle, a very expensive outfit his father had bought for him, the best. Mr. Steiner had gone right out and bought Judd a complete new outfit. Not that the rich are especially privileged, but Mr. Steiner had always felt so proud of his son—nothing should stand in the way of a boy like that.

The alienist nodded, and meanwhile thumbed through a publication, the Mark Twain School *Annual,* bound in elaborately embossed leather. "He was the highest in his class," the aunt said, "and the youngest. Oh, that's his junior year you have there, the year before he graduated." And Dr. Allwin halted at a page of verse, one stanza devoted to each member of the junior class. The very end of it had caught his eye:

> *Now there's our Junior list*
> *And surely there's no finer.*
> *But wait! we nearly missed*
> *The mighty Judah Steiner!*

Of course, he didn't mix too much at school, she said. He was so brilliant, they were all jealous of him.

Turning the page, Dr. Allwin came upon a photograph of Artie Straus—"Most Popular Twainite, and Youngest Student Ever to Enter the University of Chicago."

*   *   *

From the brothers, there was little to be learned. Max said he had honestly tried to help the kid, but they just never had been interested in the same things. Had he ever talked to Judd on sex matters, for example? No. After that funny business with Artie that summer, he had made an attempt, but Judd was such a know-it-all, you couldn't talk to him.

With the Straus men, brother James said maybe he had covered up too much for Artie, and Uncle Gerald said there was that incident four years ago—maybe the family should have paid more attention. James told of the incident. Going through his desk, he had found a hundred-dollar Liberty Bond missing. "Artie got all excited and told some cock-and-bull story about seeing the chauffeur hanging around my room. But when Artie was out, I took a look in his desk and found the bond. When I showed it to him, he made up some

silly story about the chauffeur planting it in his desk because
he had it in for him. You know, his kind of story." James had
called him a lousy little thieving liar. And now James remembered how Artie had turned on him in bitter screaming anger,
crying, "All right! So I swiped it! So what the hell is it to you!"

What the hell is it to you! It echoed now. Was that the
kind of thing the doctor meant? "Maybe we should have done
something about things like that, taken him to a doctor;
maybe it was a sign."

But Uncle Gerald said, "You should have beat the stuff-
ings out of him, that's what that kid needed, a good beating.
Your father was just too soft with the kid."

"Well, you know Dad." Both sighed.

"Your father must have known something of his delin-
quencies, then?" the doctor asked of James.

"I guess he had an idea, but you see Dad was—well, off
by himself, never too close to us. Dad was never the kind to
get chummy or play ball with the kids or anything, and with
Artie, Dad was already an older man. Well, I'm afraid no one
in the family was as close as we should have been to Artie."

Dr. Allwin said, "People don't necessarily get close to
one another just by being born in the same family."

"It just happens between some individuals and not between others," Uncle Gerald remarked. "That's why we
sometimes have friends who are closer to us than blood relatives."

The doctor took a deep breath. Artie had apparently
never learned to give anyone his confidence, he observed. Perhaps it would be best to prepare him for the study that was to
be made. Since time was short, he should be made to understand that the doctors wished only to help him, but that they
could do so only if he were entirely frank, and held nothing
back. And as James and Uncle Gerald seemed after all to have
most influence with him, perhaps they could suggest . . .
They nodded, solemnly.

*   *   *

It was on their way to the jail that the disturbing thought
came up. Should Artie really be advised to tell the doctors
everything? Everything? The papers were still full of all those

other crimes the police were trying to put on the boys. That awful taxi-driver thing. And the drowning and the shooting. All young men, all in the last year on the South Side. So far it was clear the police had no evidence. But who knew, with Artie? What couldn't he have done, if he had done this thing! And if he now revealed, to his own doctors—James eyed Uncle Gerald, with the dreaded question.

* * *

"Well, how's it look?" Artie said to them, coming jauntily into the visitors' room.

"How are they treating you?" James asked. Uncle Gerald suddenly noticed the torn sleeve on the prison coat Artie was wearing. "What the hell are they making you wear? What happened to your clothes?"

"They got lousy," Artie said cheerily. "So the screws gave me this."

"But it's even in rags!" his uncle objected angrily.

They had wanted to give him another one that wasn't torn, Artie said, but this suited him fine. "I feel fine." And indeed he seemed quite pleased.

How did things look? Artie repeated. Any chances? And before they could answer, "Say, James—" Would James tell Dorothea Lengel to stand opposite his window at ten A.M., he'd wave to her. Babes kept sending him messages, Artie said. If it was a jury of babes, he was sure to get off!

Now seriously, Uncle Gerald said, Artie was going to have to snap out of this silly attitude. He had to work with the alienists. Everything depended on the report of the alienists.

"Oh, a battle of experts!" Artie exclaimed. "I guess you can't claim that I was temporarily insane, that's out, but how about heredity, maybe we ought to say it's in the family—how about Cousin Richard? You know, it's a fact I haven't been feeling all there for a long time—that's what had me worried —but I didn't want to bother the family."

"Don't try to put on an act, Artie," his brother advised. "Just co-operate with these doctors. They are big men. You can't fool them. Just tell them everything they want to know. All that ever happened to you."

"Everything?"

His brother met his eyes. "Even the things people never tell anybody, kid. Things you'd never tell—well, me."

"Things I did? Everything?"

That peculiar look came into Artie's eyes, conspiratorial, cunning, and yet cute.

"Artie," his uncle said, "are there—well, important things we don't know?"

"Well, do you want to know?" Was he teasing? Kidding? Now he laughed. "You believe all that crap in the papers?"

"Well, let's say this," his uncle stipulated reflectively. "If there is anything you run into that you're in doubt about, Artie, maybe you'd better ask James first whether you should tell it."

A tiny snort escaped from Artie. "Maybe it would be easier to tell the docs."

James said, "This may be your life, kid."

"The hell you care!" Artie snapped.

James gasped. Artie's voice had suddenly sounded quavering, the cry of some kid, some six-year-old kid wanting something from his big brother. James shook himself back to the present—the room, his brother, the family in deepest trouble. "We all care, kid. We want to help you."

Artie had changed back. "How's Mumsy bearing up?" he asked contritely.

"She's a little better. The doctors said for her to stay in Charlevoix. She—she sends you her love," James said. And how was the food? he asked. Were meals being sent in all right? Was there anything else Artie wanted?

Sure. They could send in a couple of broads, he said with his old grin.

*   *   *

With Judd, it was Max who explained about co-operation with the psychiatrists. As usual, Judd's response was to show he knew more than the experts. "They can't do a thing. According to the legal definition, I'm sane."

"You wouldn't think it," Max let slip, and the old hostility was there between them. "For Christ's sake, if you're not crazy, what made you do it?" Max cried. "You must have been all ginned up!"

"I'm afraid drunkenness would not be a defense," Judd remarked with cool superiority, "and although we did have a bottle in the car, I don't think we took more than a swallow. Perhaps when we were waiting in the park."

"Waiting?"

"For school to let out."

Max groaned. "Judd, kid, for crissake, why didn't you stop? All right, Artie is wild, but why didn't you call it off?"

"Back out? You want me to be a coward?" And there it stood naked between them, an accusation, a sneer with some kind of bitter laugh behind it, pointed at Max himself, as if this accusation brought Max into the crime, as if Judd were throwing it at him: You taught me, you taught your own little brother—be a man, never be a coward, never back out—that's your own goddam code!

* * *

Then for a time things became relatively quiet. Dr. Storrs and Dr. Allwin proceeded with their work. It was to prove the most extensive psychiatric study made for a court case, certainly up to that time, and I believe perhaps even to this day. While Dr. Allwin gathered family material, Storrs began the psychological tests.

The prisoners were conducted each day to a large unused cell on the ninth floor. The room seemed almost an office, with its desk and chairs, its sunlit warmth. Along one wall was a bench, and between tests Artie would stretch out, dozing, while Judd engaged Storrs in a kind of reverse quiz, usually trying to prove the worthlessness of the test he was taking.

Psychological testing had not yet been developed in the specialized ways in which it is used today. Knowledge tests, tests of mental agility, were already in wide use. But testing of emotional responses had only begun. The Rorschach, now indispensable, was not used on Judd and Artie. The thematic apperception test had only just been invented by a young psychologist at Harvard; Dr. Storrs experimented with it and found curious results.

Of the other tests, the standard intelligence forms, the results were predictable. Judd completed the Stanford-Binet

so rapidly that the scale was not high enough to rate him.
Artie's results were almost as phenomenal. The vocabulary
tests and the problem-solution tests were child's play for
them. In the memory tests, Judd explained to Storrs that he
used a system, locating each item visually in a room of his
house, so that he could recall twenty items backwards, for-
wards, or in any order whatsoever. In a word test for which
five minutes was considered a minimum, Judd completed his
paper in three minutes and fifteen seconds. Artie, too, was
rapid.

But there were a few variants from the genius attainment.

There was the silent-reading test, requiring a summary of
what had been read. Judd again proved himself superior, but
Artie, with his jumpy lapses of attention, left out salient
points; his replies were more like those of a high-school student than a college graduate.

And in a co-ordination test, in which picture cut-outs
had to be put together, Judd, who might again have been
expected to excel, suddenly became confused, scoring only 56
out of a possible 100, a score for a twelve-year-old child.

For emotional reactions, Storrs began with word association. Through an entire list, each boy reacted quickly and
with a virtual absence of emotional tone. Only the word *chisel*,
inserted between neutral words, suddenly brought Artie to a
halt. Where he had never paused more than fifteen seconds
before supplying an associated word, he now waited a full
minute before saying, "trouble."

It was then that Storrs tried the set of pictures used in the
thematic apperception experiment. For example, there was a
picture of a boy with one shoe on. Near him lay the matching
shoe, an overshoe, a slipper. What did the picture suggest?

With this simple judgment test both Artie and Judd had
difficulty. Each, in turn, couldn't quite understand what was
wanted, and each, when told simply to go ahead and describe
what was happening in the picture, produced revealing responses.

A simple response might have been that the boy would
next put on his other shoe, and then the overshoes, and go to
school. Or he might have been undressing—he would take off

his shoe, put on the slippers. And from there, the subject could go on to imagine the home situation of the boy. Would the subject produce a story of normal, everyday life? Or would he reveal in his spontaneous fantasy some troubled structure in his own life and mind?

With this and other pictures in the set, Artie and Judd produced stories hardly to be expected from young men of their age and seeming mental development. Artie at once decided that the boy might be putting on someone else's shoes, so as to leave false footprints. And on he went, in a childlike fantasy of crime. Judd ignored the little situation in the picture—the incompleted act of dressing or undressing. The boy was waiting for someone, he ventured. Something important was happening. A big decision was being made, and the boy was waiting, perhaps for his mother. It could be that there was an argument about him going on in the house. About where he should go to school . . . Then Judd looked at Storrs, cunningly, with the caught-on look of the test sophisticate.

For the first time, Storrs became noncommital. He allowed Judd to belittle the silly test but would not be drawn into a discussion. Maybe Judd was right. Maybe this type of test was as yet not well developed.

But he had an excited, eager look in his eye when he wrote down their responses to the various pictures.

*   *   *

In another week, it is Dr. Allwin who conducts the examination, aided by medical specialists for the newfangled metabolism tests and cardiograms. It is in a larger room that this work proceeds; there are windows looking out toward the lake, and the bend of the Chicago River can be seen, and old Goose Island where the first settlers came—now covered with trucks and with track after track of boxcars.

On one of these mornings, there is Judd coming in alone, finding Dr. Allwin in a white jacket, laying out a few instruments on a clean towel.

Allwin is rather chubby, pink-skinned, with deft, economical movements. He does not have anything of the penetrating cleverness of Eli Storrs, but seems rather bland, absorptive; he is extremely well-mannered, a person of fine family who gives the impression of practicing out of intellectual curiosity and perhaps a refined desire to be helpful. He greets Judd as one might greet a colleague, collaborating in pure scientific inquiry. But this morning Judd notices several hypodermic needles laid out, and turns pale.

"Anything wrong?" asks the doctor.

"What's all this for?"

"We're only going to take a few blood samples." Picking up a syringe, the doctor turns to him, but now Judd is absolutely white.

"I'm sorry, doctor," he says, "but the mere idea of blood always affects me this way. I know it is a stupid reaction, but I can't help it."

"Well, this will only take a second." Judd has an involuntary reaction of shrinking and pulling away, as the sample is taken from his ear lobe. When it is over, beads of sweat are on his forehead.

"You really have a very strong reaction, don't you?" the doctor observes.

"I've always had it." And Judd tells of an incident when he was quite young and saw a doctor examining his mother; the doctor said he would take her blood pressure. "I pictured it as blood gushing out, I suppose, in my childish imagination, and I became so sick the doctor had to take care of me instead of my mother."

Dr. Allwin makes no remark about this rather feminine reaction to the flow of blood. "How did you think of your mother?" he asks.

In his matter-of-fact, clacky voice, Judd says, "I used to picture her as the Madonna. I still do."

He feels quite easy, talking to this elderly, gentlemanly doctor, and he tells of the stained-glass window in a church, to which he was taken by the young Irish nursemaid who preceded Trudy. And how this girl said she would tell him the most wonderful story about the most wonderful woman that ever lived, a woman so pure that she was different from all other women. Then the girl told him about the Madonna.

"But your family being Jewish—they had no objection to

the girl's taking you to church?" the doctor asks with civilized curiosity.

On the religious score they were not old-fashioned, Judd says. In fact, his father declared he did not mind Judd's learning all about churches, since he was going to live in a Christian world. "I used to have the chauffeur drive me to different churches on every Sunday, and I'd go to their services. I made a whole list of the different churches and their different kinds of worship all over the South Side. I soon knew the differences between Catholic and Protestant, Methodist and Episcopal and Congregational services."

"Well, that is probably more than most Christians know," says Dr. Allwin. "That was quite an unusual preoccupation for a child."

"I kept it up as I grew," Judd says. "I classified all the religions and their different ideas of God."

"And this had an effect on you?"

"How could a kid help seeing it was all a lot of bushwa? God was three and He was one and He was a body and He was incorporeal and He was a Jewish old Moses with a beard, so as a consequence I very early detected and concluded for myself that religion was superstition."

"I see. And in this time, when you were visiting the churches, did you visit synagogues too?"

"They had a certain type of training—my father wanted me to receive the usual training for boys. You study elementary Hebrew and you are supposed to participate in a ceremony at thirteen, to take part in the services. He used to send me to Rabbi Hirsch's classes, but I got through with it all a few years ahead, and by the time I was thirteen I didn't care to take part in the ritual—it's a kind of confirmation—because I couldn't believe in any of that anymore."

"And yet you say you still cling to this image of your mother as the Madonna."

"That's an exception. Oh, even as a child I realized she didn't belong to us. And of course I later realized it was all a superstition, but I made this exception to keep this idea about my mother. And since Mother died, I prefer to see her that way."

"You mean as the beautiful lady in the church window?" The pink-faced doctor seems to be smiling with him at child-ish notions. "A heavenly being?"

"Yes." Then he continues, in that even, unemotional voice, "If not for me, she might not have died. I was responsible for her death."

"How is that?"

"It was due to my birth," Judd says. "She was never well after I was born. She became an invalid. She suffered from nephritis, due to my birth."

"I've noticed a history of nephritis in the women of her family," Dr. Allwin observes.

"I contributed to her death," Judd insists. "She was a wonderful person, a perfect person." He frequently visits her grave, he says, and adds, "I often wish I had never been born."

"You have often wished it?"

"I used to wish it for years. When I was a kid."

*   *   *

Another time, Dr. Allwin gets him to speak of those childhood years when he so often wished he had never been born. Judd explains that it was when the family lived on Michigan Avenue and he had to go to that school where there were only girls.

"You might have been proud of being the only boy among so many girls."

He hated girls, hated females. They were all so stupid, gossipy.

"And your mother?"

She was the exception, she and her sister, Aunt Bertha. But otherwise, all the females he knew were inferior, as Scho-penhauer says.

Has he never had a steady girl, a real girl?

A few times he has been attracted, but not in love. Once to a cousin. And now, just lately, he had met a girl, just in the last few weeks, a girl who made him feel different—he had even thought of running away with her, marrying her. His voice drops.

How did she make him feel different? Sexually?

No, he had not had sexual intercourse with her, though she stimulated him. But she was a nice girl and she made him feel he could understand things like marrying and having a family. . . . Judd falls silent.

"Do you want to tell me more about this girl?"

"I don't see any point to it."

He tells, all at once, of an incident with Max, when he was a little kid: Occasionally he would get Max to play with him, and once when they were playfully wrestling on the lawn, he hit his forehead on a stone and bled and cried, and Max called him a sissy. His feelings were terribly hurt, so he cried even more. Max refused to play with him after that. That was when he determined in his heart never to show Max, never to show anyone, if he felt hurt—in fact, never to let any feelings hurt him. "I discovered that emotions could hurt too much, and so I decided not to let myself be hurt that way."

Judd senses that the doctor is impressed with what he has brought out, and he feels both annoyed with himself and somewhat proud at having made a strong impression. But he is unsure and decides it is quite enough, and he becomes silent.

* * *

Another day, he finds himself talking of the few months he spent at the public school; that was when he felt even more miserable than at Miss Spencer's. The kids kept teasing him because he was such a shrimp, and a Jewboy. It was from those Irish kids at the public school that he first heard it as something dirty: Jewboy, sheenie.

"How did you feel about it?"

"That is hard to analyze at this point. Angry, I should think."

"And perhaps ashamed?"

"No—no, I would not be ashamed of being a Jew. My people were always proud of it," he adds automatically.

And he tells how those boys teased him because his nursemaid was fetching and calling for him. Then Judd tells of the strange day when Trudy wasn't there and he started home alone, and two rough kids kept after him: "Hey, sheenie! Where's your nursemaid? Some pussy! She make you play with her pussy?" Then they had hold of him, pulling him into an alley. Hey, that fat nursemaid, did he ever look under her skirt? Did he know she had a pussy there? "Yah, yah, you're her slave, she makes you do it to her. Hey, some fat pussy!" And then, "Hey, he got a pecker? Maybe he ain't even got a pecker! Hey! the sheenies they cut off a piece of the petzel, maybe they cut off too much! Hey, maybe he's a girl!" And tearing at his knickerbockers, holding him while he yelled, struck blindly. He feels their blows on his body, his face . . . kicks, blood . . . and he is running. They run after him, flinging horse manure from the street, flinging dirty words—dirty names for his nurse, for his mother—until, almost home, there comes Trudy running, waddling toward him, and his two tormentors disappear down a side street.

"This nursemaid, Trudy, she was with you for some years?"

"Until I was fourteen."

What was she like?

She didn't have a very highly developed intelligence, Judd explains. In fact, he would say she was a moron—she had gone only to a few grades in school in the old country. She didn't speak English, but was what the families called a "green girl," the kind they hired as nursemaid. He spoke German with her. But she was cunning, and she was devoted to him. Trudy would tell him his father was so rich he could have anything he wanted. Once he wanted some stamps from a cousin's collection, and she just laughed as he went and swiped them. But after that she blackmailed him, by threatening to tell on him, making him do things she wanted.

What things?

Oh, just obey her. Not tell, when she took time off. And not tell . . . about other things. He doesn't remember too well. . . . She had secrets with him, she was quite fond of him, played with him—she must have been mentally retarded. Even, he sort of remembers, sex things—maybe when she gave him his bath, how she loved her little boy, kisses all over him, and then, devouring, her big devouring mouth, and her laughing . . . Had he fearfully pulled away? Trudy's mouth, laughing and devouring and threatening, laughing, "If you're not a good little boy . . ." and laughing, as if to devour, and then he would be her little girl.

*   *   *

How is Judd's sleep? Dr. Allwin asks him. Does he fall asleep easily, or does he have some favorite fantasies, perhaps, before going to sleep? Judd becomes interested—this is a whole world of inquiry that he would not have thought of—and he talks quite freely, objectively. Yes, almost as far back as he can remember—"I used to make up these stories, before falling asleep. I was a king, sometimes, or else a slave—"

"A king or a slave? And who else would be in the fantasy?"

He tells how first it was Max in his military-school uniform. Only, at the same time, it was partly himself. "I would imagine I was in such a uniform, I was in command. And I had slaves. There was the strongest slave in the world, with wonderful muscles, like Sandow. And then, at other times, I was this slave."

"Which were you more often, the king or the slave?"

"As it went on, I was almost always the slave."

"It went on for a long time? Till the present?"

"Well, fairly recently." Sometimes, he tells, it would last for an hour. He would lie on his stomach or on his side, usually hugging the pillow. After a while it would become very pleasant, with a pleasant warm bed odor, and he would imagine this was like the body odor of a naked slave who had been exerting himself, perhaps in battle, wielding a big sword and saving the life of the king. "Then the king would be grateful and offer to give the slave his liberty, but I would refuse, because I was devoted to the king.

"There would be a great king's banquet, with many other kings arriving, and each king would boast of the cleverness and strength of his personal slave, and then there would be contests, wrestling contests, or matches of prowess with the sword, and I would always be the winner and I would be rewarded by my king.

"Then sometimes a great question would arise, and there would be two sides in the argument; the entire banquet would divide into two sides over a question of philosophy such as, Is it possible for a ruler to do wrong? There would be a champion for each side, and I would be the champion for my king's side, and I would win.

"Sometimes there would be men pitted against me in an attack on the king. They would come at me, more and more of them, until there were thousands—I suppose this was after I had seen a Douglas Fairbanks movie—and I would mow them down. But in the middle of this imaginary scene I might think to myself, This is impossible. No slave, no matter how powerful, could stand against so many attackers. So I would stop that story. But I would begin again—perhaps this time I would be on a ship, and the vessel would be captured by pirates, and we would all be sold as slaves, and in the marketplace the Grand Vizier would notice me on the slave stand, and he would observe that I was more intelligent than all the rest, so he would buy me to become tutor for the young king, and then I would be branded."

He breathes more deeply. "I would be branded on the inside calf of the right leg, a beautiful round mark of a crown—"

He breaks off.

Another time he describes the king as his camp counselor, when he was twelve. "He was like a perfect type in the Hart, Schaffner and Marx clothing ads. His name was Chesty. He was about eighteen, and I admired him very much.

"Then I would picture myself as his slave. Sometimes it would be that the king got the slave as a stray baby found in the woods in a basket, or else the king was riding past the slave market and there was a boy of ten or twelve being sold, and he was dirty and sick and half starved, and the king took pity and bought him and took him for his personal slave. Again, the slave would save the king's life and refuse freedom. The king would have the boy slave come and sit with him, and he would pet him."

"This was always your counselor, Chesty?"

"After that summer it was other fellows, sometimes a teacher, and then a few years later we went up that summer to Artie's in Charlevoix, and I began to idealize him, and from then on it was almost always Artie who was the king."

"You idealized him?"

"I would see him as an athlete, a champion, even though I knew he is not a champion. And also, I would idealize him as a brilliant student, getting all A's—"

"You knew his actual grades?"

"I knew Artie never got all A's, but I told myself he could, if he wasn't lazy. And when he told people he was Phi Beta Kappa I would corroborate it. He has an almost perfect mind, and in other ways—sociability, and the ability to make people do what he wants—I would rate him very high. In fact, I once made a chart, and I rated everyone I knew, and Artie came out highest, ninety I think."

"Did you rate yourself?"

"Yes, on that chart I got a score of sixty-two."

"Below passing?" Allwin smiles.

"It would seem so."

"What did you fail in?"

"I would say sociability mostly, and physical appearance and deeds. But I wasn't so bad as some of the others—it went down to forty or thirty for most of them—so I don't think I have a complete inferiority complex."

"I see. You were aware, through all this, that you idealized Artie?"

Judd looks directly into his eyes. "It was blind hero worship. I almost completely identified myself with him. I would watch the food he ate, the drink going down his throat, and I would be envious."

"And now?"

"Yes, even now. For a few days, I was angry with him. But now, when they take us through the corridors together sometimes, and to feel him near me, to brush against him, makes me feel I am alive." He continues to look into Dr. Allwin's eyes, not defiantly, not apologetically; Judd is entirely self-possessed, but there is between them, as a few days ago, a sense of shared pleasure in a task that is going well, even though its purpose remains obscure.

Another time, Judd recalls a reversed version of the fantasy, in which he was the king, and Artie was the slave. "We were on a sea voyage and we were shipwrecked, and came to an uncharted island. A piano was all we saved from the wreck, and I was the only one who knew how to play. By the way, I learned to play the piano in a very short time, when I was eleven years old. There were natives on the island, and I was the only one who could speak their language—I suppose this is connected with my being a linguist."

"Yes, this is a residue from reality, in your fantasy. And material can go in the other direction, too."

"You mean when things from our imagination come into our real life?"

"Yes."

Judd seems to be examining whether this has happened with himself. Then he continues his fantasy.

"The natives of the island were divided into two groups, nobles and slaves. All of my companions were made slaves, but because of my ability to play the piano I was made a noble, for the natives knew nothing of music and were enchanted. Then, as a noble, I bought Artie to be my slave. He was very ill, and I nursed him back to health. Then when he was well, I gave him the choice of three alternatives:

"First, liberty. I would free him, and the brand mark on his right calf would be eliminated."

"The slaves had been branded?"

"Yes. I would imagine this branding to be taking place, but it would not be on the island; it would be in the locker room of the Twain School, the locker room of the gym. Then we would be on the island and I would say, 'If you choose liberty, you may go, but beware, because the first noble who sees you may capture you and make you his slave.'

"Secondly," Judd goes on, "he could remain my personal slave, in every sense of the word. Thirdly, I might sell him to some other noble. But if I did, he would receive bad treatment and would beg to come back to me. He would write me secret messages, using the pet secret word of the island. He would sign himself by that word."

"And what was that?"

"Your kitty, or your pussy," Judd says quietly.

*   *   *

I have tried to feel my way into the mind of Artie, but there are areas of impenetrable density that I suppose will forever remain dark. It is curious that we all thought we knew Artie better than we knew Judd, since he was among us more, and perhaps that is why we puzzled less over him than over Judd. And another confusion resulted from our pairing them, from our feeling that they were in the crime to the same degree precisely, utterly commingled, and that since their histories and even their family patterns were so curiously paralleled, it followed that in their mechanism of behavior they had also to be twins. This tendency to confuse them was to continue all the way through the trial, with lawyers and psychiatrists again and again naming the one when they meant the other. The record is filled with these snap-ups. "Steiner—" "You mean Straus?" "Yes, yes, I mean Straus—"

Thus they were a joint personality in our minds. Yet from their revelations to the psychiatrists, different patterns could be traced.

And despite the streaks of darkness in Artie's revelations, a good deal can be made out of how these two distorted personalities conjoined, and how each functioned in their union. Artie was cunning and apt to withhold incidents in telling of his life—incidents already known about through his family. But when Dr. Allwin led him into his fantasy life, Artie, too, became easy and garrulous. Yes, he had indulged almost every night in picturizations, as he called them. There was something uncanny in the way they dovetailed with Judd's.

Judd's dominant fantasy role was that of a slave; Artie saw himself as a master. He was the chief of all criminals, commanding absolute obedience.

Even on the reverse side of their fantasies, there was an interlocking symmetry. Judd as a slave was, however, a superior being, a champion, a godlike, handsome person. Thus, while an inferior in the nominal side of his role, he was superior on the active side. He lived in comfortable quarters, and he was the mentor of kings. Conversely, Artie was superior in the nominal side of his role, he was a mastermind, a chief, yet in carrying out his picturizations he saw himself as captured and jailed, chained and in rags. He derived greatest satisfaction from imagining himself incarcerated and whipped.

And in real life their fantasy relationships were carried out with beautiful inevitability. Both now related their strange compact, made after the frat-house robbery—the compact in which Artie was the master who must be implicitly obeyed; and yet, the other side of the agreement was the sexual act in which Artie had to submit and which was carried out in the spirit of a rape, a violence, almost a punishment—but, as in his fantasy, a punishment which he passively enjoyed.

The same tendency to confuse them was found in the fact that the aberration of each seemed to stem from a nursemaid. Yet the tendencies were at opposite poles.

Judd's was the illiterate Trudy, animalistic, indulgent, teaching him to gratify every selfish desire, walking around slovenly and half naked, even taking him into her bed and initiating him as a child to perversions, as well as to normal acts.

Artie's nurse was no green girl from Germany but a young Canadian woman who gave herself the mannerisms of an aristocratic English-style governess; she read to Artie from good books such as the *Rise of the Dutch Republic;* she pushed him in his studies, tutored him, taught him the virtues—with such severity that he learned to lie and cheat in order to get around her. And while Trudy would let the boy Judd see her undressed, Miss Newsome was extremely prudish, careful not to exhibit herself. While Trudy would tell Judd that babies were brought by a stork, leering all the while so the little boy knew that the real answer was something dirty, Miss Newsome would tell Artie nothing at all, making an absolute, frightening taboo of sex questions.

Then, when he was nine, Artie's little brother Billy was born. Today we all are aware of the intense difficulty this can make for a child at about this age, though surely not everyone who has a baby brother at nine turns out to be a murderer.

But three developments came with this event in Artie's life. It was at nine, he told Dr. Allwin, that he first started pinching small articles from the counters of the Five and Ten. And it was then, too, that he began voraciously to read dime novels, hiding them from Miss Nuisance. The story of a kidnaped baby, hidden in the attic, made a lasting impression on him.

And it was then that he secured his first real information about sex.

There is the overcurious little boy, peeking, prying, trying to discover the secret of how the baby comes. Mumsie is too busy with her new baby, her adorable new baby that everyone adores, to have time to answer a boy's questions. And you never ask your father. And Mumsie and Dad are behind their shut door—you mustn't spy—and if you ask Miss Nuisance she talks about something else. Or her mouth gets shut so tight that you couldn't pry it open with a screwdriver.

Brothers won't tell you anything either. They are grown up and very busy. You never ask your father. Maybe Mumsie and Popsie are having the baby really because they want someone else, not you. Nobody wants you. Except maybe Hank, the chauffeur, who lets you hang around the garage. Miss Nuisance hates him—Hank is dirty, filthy, says Miss Nuisance. Because Hank does all kinds of things with girls. Everybody knows. Even Mumsie makes little remarks about Hank and the upstairs maids. "Hank—" and she wags a finger. "Now, Hank, you must let the new little maid alone. It isn't fair!"

Hank is working around the car, the hood is open, and the garage is filled with the smell of stuff—gas and grease and rubber; tools are all around the place, iron-smelling, and on the high workbench are parts of the car and grease rags. Every time you go near you get grease on you.

"Hand me the big hammer, Artie, will you?" The hammer has a sledge head. There is black tape wrapped around the handle for a grip, like some fellows put on baseball bats. Hank is halfway under the hood, chiseling at something, with a chisel that cuts through iron. "The bloody nut is stuck," he says. "That screw is tight as a witch's twat." That's a bad word, and then Hank laughs at a big joke he just thought of—he says he can't tell it to a kid, but then he laughs and he has to tell it anyway, a joke about a couple that got caught being lovey-dovey and the police and the fire department had to be called to pull them apart. "Pull what apart?" Artie asks. "Their faces?" And Hank roars. And that is the day Hank tells Artie about the difference between men and women. It's just like this nut and bolt, he says, just like a key and a keyhole! Women are always hiding, not letting you see, because they've got nothing to show, get it? They've got nothing there, under those skirts. Just a slit. Didn't anyone ever tell you that? Some education you got there, that Miss Nuisance, she's so holy—somebody ought to fix *her* up! Boy, it would take a chisel to crack that one open! Somebody ought to surprise her one night and do it to her, maybe she'd turn out to be human after all!

When a fellow grows up, Hank says, the pecker gets big, and sometimes it swells up, it gets as hard as a goddam hunk of steel, and Hank shakes the chisel in his hand, to show how hard it gets. Ever see a dog? Ever watch a couple of dogs? Hank laughs. Hell, do Artie's folks expect to keep the kid innocent all his life? The big brothers aren't so innocent at that—Hank knows a few places this gas buggy has been to— and he chuckles. Hank has found a few items in the back seat. Those boys are real men.

Artie has picked up the chisel Hank put down. "What's the tape on there for?" the boy asks. And Hank says, "For a grip, so the shaft won't get too slippery from the sweat of the hand." And then he breaks out into a real roar of dirty laughter. "That's a good one, but don't ever tell that to a girl!"

"What?" asks Artie, puzzled.

"That!" says Hank, taking the chisel in his fist, holding it the wrong way, the iron in his hand. "Boy, you could really knock them dead with something like this! Boy, there must be many a little man with a no-good pecker wishes he had one like this!"

And just then Miss Nuisance marches in on them. "Artie! What are you doing here?" And Artie, tense and still half puzzled, nearly jumps out of his shoes, but he recovers himself quickly, and with that frank and boyish expression of his, says, "He's showing me how to use his tools," and Hank guffaws, putting his greasy hand over his mouth as though he would explode.

*   *   *

A tool, a rod—"stiff as a rod," the frat brothers said, hard as steel, knock them over with it. Sure, he would go along. He'd show them he was a man. Hell, who said he didn't shave? He shaved! A man, a college man, good as any of them! They claimed they'd done it the first time at fifteen, at fourteen, at thirteen. He'd done it lots of times already, he said— hell, he'd done it to his governess; that's why she had to leave. Boy, what a laugh.

And in Mamie's place the fellows stood around in a circle, close. The raucous laughter . . . there was his broad all spread out and waiting, and he couldn't, he couldn't—hell, many times, when he was alone, it did—but now, "little mousey," she said, and they all roared, the bastards, the stinking sonsabitches. They doubled over, laughing at his trying— he could kill every last sonofabitch. It was their lousy liquor, hell, he'd get it so hard he'd crack their skulls with it. Laughing at him—he'd knock them dead with it!

Sonofabitch thing. Hard now in jail when you couldn't— when you wanted it, limp as a rag. With Judd that time with the two broads, that little punk Judd doing it on the other side of the car. And his own broad trying to let him off easy, wagging her finger at it—"You bad little boy, you had too much to drink, didn't you?" and, giggling, "He just wants to curl up and go to sleep."

*   *   *

With his agreeable candor, Artie told Dr. Allwin of all the early little things—about swiping money from a lemonade stand he operated with another boy, about taking his big brother's Liberty Bond, for surely the doc had already been told. Artie told of things with Judd—the Edison electric car, the bricks in windows, the time a cop shot at them, the frat house in Ann Arbor.

"Wasn't there something else, in between?"

"No—?" On the surface, there was no tension between them. But underneath, a guessing game went on. How much did the doc know from Judd, from the family?

"And wasn't there a trip to Oak Park?"

Why, yes, it had slipped his mind. Artie smiled and told

of the time he and Judd planned to hijack the cellar of Joe Stahlmeyer's house, full of Canadian stuff worth twenty dollars a bottle. Joe's folks were away in New York, so they got all set to do a real job, with black handkerchiefs, and ropes to tie anyone, and a pistol he had bought on the q.t. from a guy he knew, a punk named Casey Jellico. "No, there was nothing I did with him, doc. I guess my brothers told you all about Case—he was a bad influence on me; I guess he's in reform school now. Just a poor kid from over on 39th Street. The cops checked all that." But Casey had shown him how to buy a revolver, on South State Street, and so Artie had the revolver along and also—

He caught himself up.

"Also?" probed Dr. Allwin.

Oh, he had taken along a taped chisel, for a billy.

"Was that the first time you fixed one up?"

Yes, but the expedition had been a flop. A light came on in the house and Judd got scared, so they had gone away. All right, next came the frat robbery, getting ready the same way —black handkerchiefs, the rope, the gun, the chisel.

"Why the tape around it?"

"Well, that way it made a good handle to grip, for a billy, and solid steel inside," he ended, with a little gasp, a hiss. And it must have been such a moment as comes between people, a moment to which psychiatrists become peculiarly sensitive, when a flow of talk suddenly, even dangerously, projects itself.

How many questions stood awakened in the mind of Dr. Allwin? The discarded chisels that had been rumored found in the neighborhood, the tale of a young man living nearby, drowned, a supposed suicide . . .

In that little hiss, there was a release of more, much more than some story of playing robbers. It belonged with the suddenly unfocused, evasive look in Artie's eyes. It had escaped from some held-down element, it belonged to the small raging boy inside, the imprisoned child—to an Artie in this moment almost contacted, almost released to scream out his murderous tantrum: *I'll kill you, I'll kill you if you say I can't!*

Dr. Allwin said quietly, while closing his notebook, "And there were still other times, with a chisel?"

Artie's smiling cunning game-playing look had returned. "Am I supposed to tell you?"

"Well, that's up to you, Artie. You see, we generally seem to find out."

Artie's smile widened, while he shook his head. "You're not going to find out this stuff from the folks or Judd."

The doctor screwed on the top of his pen. "We're only here to help you, Artie."

"What if you found out something that wouldn't help me? That would hurt me?"

Perhaps they had better stop for the day, the doctor said.

*   *   *

The alienists had come to a deep cleft, and there they halted. Should they let themselves down into every crevice, or would it be best to leap over, perhaps to improvise a bridge of ropes? Storrs and Allwin must have debated long and earnestly over this dilemma, and in Wilk's apartment the discussions must have gone far into the night.

Can we judge their decision? We may say, from a purely medical viewpoint they were obliged to make every effort to explore the furthest crevice. They were engaged, we may say, as physicians, not as lawyers.

And yet, taking into account the attitudes of that day, the prejudices and the limited understanding, their hesitation can be comprehended. For whatever they learned, once learned, could not be held back. They had not been engaged to study these patients in terms of therapy but only in terms of diagnosis. They had been engaged—and the word was to be their own—in forensic medicine. In legal medicine. As experts. Did not the legal problem therefore remain a foremost factor in their work?

Their task was to study the minds of these two boys in relation to a specific crime. Would it help to know the details of other crimes? Or was it enough to know that other crimes had occurred?

We might say for them that Storrs and Allwin stood as a pair of surgeons might stand in an operating room, staring into an incision that disclosed not only a known cancer, but a number of other dreadful growths. To cut out all of them would mean sure death. Would it not be best then to close the incision quickly?

So I rationalize for them, and so they must have rationalized, if we may judge by the decision they took. Lawyers and doctors agreed: that this was for the family to determine.

*   *   *

Uncle Gerald came to Artie's cell.

With him, there was never any sense of recrimination. He was there like a father coming to help a boy. It was as though a kid got hurt and yelled, and his big brothers keep saying, "Oh, stop yelling about nothing!" And finally a kid had to pull down the whole house on himself, breaking every bone in his body, so at last they would realize, at last they would come and say, "Poor Artie! Oh, what happened to you?"

"All right," Artie said, inhaling avidly—he had run out of cigarettes and the damn screw had been holding him up a buck for a pack—"all right, there were other things."

"Judd know about them?"

"He always acted as if he had it on me. Anyway, for one of them."

Their eyes met. "Big?" his uncle said.

"Big."

"How many, Artie?"

"You could say—four."

The deeds hung between them.

"I don't want to know," Uncle Gerald said. "Don't tell me, Artie. They might get me on the stand."

"What about the docs?"

According to law, Uncle Gerald said, only this case was to be tried, no others.

"Wouldn't it make a difference if they call me nuts or not?"

His uncle reflected on that point. It could make all the difference. Yet how could one measure the effect, without knowing the actual deeds? And to know was so perilous.

"Maybe you could tell the doctors you did—a certain number of things, without saying what they were. It has to be up to you, how much you tell them."

What would the family want? Artie asked, with the sudden genuine-sounding throb that could come into his voice. He didn't wish to hurt Mumsie, the family, anymore.

In such moments, you had to believe him. Perhaps he only reached for a feeling he knew he ought to have; perhaps he truly felt it. His uncle blinked, for tears came up. Gerald Straus shook his head. "It's now a question of what might be best to help *you*, Artie."

* * *

When next he talked with Dr. Allwin, Artie kept to the line suggested by his uncle. Yes, there had been other things.

The pinkish dome inclined slightly. "These other—incidents—major outbreaks, shall we say? How many were there?"

"Four."

"Let's refer to them as *A, B, C,* and *D.*" Carefully the doctor went on to remind Artie that the press attributed certain specific crimes to him, or to him and Judd.

"That's a lot of hooey!" Artie exclaimed, but then there came over his face his peculiar sidewise smile, as though, since Dr. Allwin had made the situation easier for him, he would now make it easier for the doctor. "I never had anything to do with that monkey-gland robbery," he stated. Nor had he had anything to do with the handless stranger. But, significantly, the two unsolved student deaths were not mentioned.

* * *

Now, in the night-long meetings in Wilk's study, the entire defense position had to be re-examined. If Artie were a multiple murderer, wouldn't he be seen by any jury as demon-ridden, demented? Wouldn't his actions come clearly under the legal insanity definition of an "irresistible impulse"? And wouldn't even the simplest layman agree that he should be sent to an asylum?

And if Judd were not a participant in the other crimes, was it fair to link him completely to Artie in a joint trial? Shouldn't the two be separated? Judd had, rather, participated as one enslaved, enthralled by a madman.

Surely this possibility must have been examined, discussed, a thousand times discarded, only to be examined again by the lawyers, during the days when Storrs and Allwin were intensively at work in the Wilk dining room, writing their report.

But was separation really advantageous? To either? Would not the boys, like Siamese twins, be likely to be destroyed by the very attempt to separate them? For, as both Wilk and Ferdinand Feldscher pointed out, Horn was no fool. He could ridicule and riddle any plea that Judd was a mere accessory. Hadn't Judd taken an active part in every phase of the crime, from the inception, through the planning of each detail, to the act itself?

The public reaction to such a move would be only of heightened anger—a legal "trick." Nor could it be certain that the revelation of added horrors would cause Artie to be judged insane; rather, a jury might become even more determined to destroy so dreadful a fiend.

And there was somehow a sense that they belonged together, that they should be tried together, that the trial was a part of their deed.

Then, if Artie's mysterious additional crimes were not to be evoked, the basic question of proving insanity still remained before the defense. Plainly, would the alienists affirm that the boys were insane?

Fortunately, Dr. McNarry arrived during those days. His solid presence, Willie Weiss told me in a tone close to adulation, helped to clarify everyone's thinking. For McNarry exuded authority, without being in any way authoritative. Everything about him seemed full-packed—his clothing seemed packed with his large bulk, and his huge head, with veins standing out on the bald dome, seemed packed with knowledge.

He had been many times to Europe, he had studied Charcot's work at the Salpêtrière in Paris, he had been to Nancy, he had known Jung in Switzerland and Bleuler in Vienna and lastly, the great Freud himself; his pioneering book on psychoanalysis was therefore not the work of a quick enthusiast who had picked up the latest jargon, but of a life-long practitioner who had traveled the same paths, a physician with intensive experience in the wards, the head of one of the world's great mental hospitals.

Most excited by McNarry's arrival was Eli Storrs, for here at last was someone besides Allwin to whom he could talk his own language, someone who didn't demand "conclusions, sane or insane." He waited impatiently while McNarry had his first few interviews with the boys, so as to obtain his own, unaffected impressions; then the three doctors conferred. McNarry's material was much the same, the king-slave fantasies from Judd, the master-criminal fantasies from Artie, the childhood patterns. Eli Storrs laid out the results of his tests, eagerly watching for McNarry's reactions to the new type of study, the apperception chart.

And it was indeed over this one that McNarry paused Storrs enthusiastically offered his interpretation. In both boys there was shown a clear lack of development in the affective, or emotional, life, in the faculties of judgment. He would place them emotionally at a nine-year-old level, perhaps even at a younger stage, while intellectually they rated as mature.

At once the doctors got into an intense discussion involving McNarry's central concept of the psyche. He did not believe in separating emotion and intellect, as in two compartments. All belonged to a single biological entity that reacted as a unit.

"Well, but that unit has different aspects. Our tests obviously show us that different people react differently. . . ."

Uncle Gerald, impatient for a final diagnosis, had barged in on their conference in the dining room. He listened with a growing sense of frustration. They seemed to be having a good time, arguing about words. "Yes," McNarry at last agreed, there was a feeling-aspect, which might be called emotional in tone, and there was an intellectual aspect—

Allwin interposed, as a compromiser. The feeling-aspect was the pleasure principle of the infant. Entirely emotional. And the intellectual aspect was that which recognizes and adjusts to reality, as we grow.

Gerald Straus, with an apologetic laugh, pressed them. Would all this help to show a jury that the boys were insane?

Equally smilingly, Dr. McNarry read him a short lecture on insanity, as though for an average juryman. "People think that at one moment a man is sane, and at the next he goes insane. To a doctor, insanity means nothing but mental derangement, sickness, and just as there are all degrees of physical sickness, from a common cold to paralysis, there are all degrees of mental sickness, from a mild neurosis to a psychoneurosis to a psychosis."

Uncle Gerald nodded. "How sick can you say they are?"

"We have concluded"— the elderly Dr. Allwin took over, glancing at what they had been writing— "that each of the patients is suffering from a functional disorder. Artie's could develop into dementia praecox, a splitting of the personality, and Judd's is in the direction of paranoia."

"How far gone are they?"

"That's what we're trying to determine," Dr. McNarry said, somewhat brusquely, and Uncle Gerald subsided, listening as they resumed their discussion. McNarry had just come from talking to Judd about his philosophy. The philosophy itself he dismissed as a mere camouflage, a mumbo jumbo of hedonism, Nietzschean aphorisms, Machiavellian slogans, just a smattering of things Judd had read. (As Willie Weiss reported it to me, "a *mishmash.*")

But all these philosophies of Judd's, Eli Storrs observed, tended in one direction—paranoia. "Look how the mind seizes what it needs!" And didn't these philosophies corroborate his tests? These were the philosophies of "I want what I want." They all stemmed from the pleasure principle of the infant. Like his tests, they proved that Judd was emotionally a child.

"That's interesting," McNarry said. "You could interpret Nietzschean omnipotence the same way. It belongs to the magic phase." This was the phase in which the infant, by crying, discovered that everyone around him would do what he wanted. He had some magic power to have his wishes gratified. All those around him were his slaves. And had this phase ever ended, for Judd?

Suddenly beginning to understand, Uncle Gerald remarked, "Why, Max told me that kid didn't even lace his own shoes until he was fourteen years old. He'd have the nursemaid do it."

Dr. Storrs said, laughingly, "No wonder Judd got so

mixed up on that picture about putting on shoes!" But Uncle Gerald had become quite thoughtful. Perhaps until then the entire subject of insanity had existed in his mind only as a defense to put up. True, he had felt there was "something wrong" with the boys, but now, suddenly, through his own story about lacing the shoes, he saw the doctors' meaning. Something in him was saying, Why, it's really true! What we've been claiming is really true. All the better.

The psychiatrists had moved on to a discussion of Artie and his game of "detective." Artie had offered Allwin the explanation that he still played it only because he had to have a game he could play with his little brother Billy. In the streets of Charlevoix, they would go different ways, and at the end of fifteen minutes each would have to tell the other exactly what stores he had been seen going into, what back alleys he had ducked through—things like that. The one who produced the most shadowing-points was the winner.

But to Dr. McNarry, Artie had no longer rationalized the childish game. He had told of playing it with Judd, and even when he was alone, walking through the streets, imagining he had accomplices with him, giving them hand signals— "There's a good place to hold up, but next door in the candy store is a scout of ours, leave his place alone." Dr. McNarry added, "I believe he even built it up for me; he's cunning."

"No, he really does it!" Uncle Gerald broke in. "Why, a year ago last fall he shadowed me all the way home one night. He came up behind me when I got to my house—he had a black handkerchief tied around his face like a real holdup man —and he said, 'Stick 'em up!' Of course I knew it was Artie and I just told him to run along home." Gerald Straus gazed at them with a touch of discomfiture. For shouldn't he have seen then that there was something truly wrong? A young man of seventeen, a college man, playing games like that? Hadn't there been many, many such signs?

"That's very interesting," the alienists were saying to him; but to Uncle Gerald the whole case was now coming into focus. If he himself had never seen anything wrong about a college boy playing cops and robbers, could a jury be made to see it? It was true that just now he had comprehended. Just now, the alienists had made him see that it was a wild child inside of Artie, an ungrown child that could not yet fully understand the difference between right and wrong, that had dictated Artie's behavior. But could the alienists make an ordinary jury understand this complicated mechanism? How would such an explanation add up to a jury, except as a tricky attempt to save two pampered, evil young men?

Wasn't there some stronger way to put it before a jury?

The Feldschers, with Max and James, had come in, and now the discussion expanded, yet always kept returning to the main point: How could you make a jury see that the boys were "functionally disturbed"?

Edgar Feldscher had faith that a jury could see it, just as Uncle Gerald had finally seen how, in playing his cops-and-robbers game, Artie was confused between fantasy and reality.

"We'll have to make it stronger," Uncle Gerald insisted. Couldn't the doctors go further?

"Well, you can't claim that he has completely lost contact with reality," Dr. McNarry pointed out. "Don't forget there will be psychiatrists on the other side."

That was the real trouble. To a jury it would still be a case of alienists on one side saying black and alienists on the other side saying white. The very thought of this started McNarry off on his pet tirade. For McNarry couldn't understand how any psychiatrist could bring himself to testify for the prosecution: The entire aim of psychiatry was to unravel the causes of behavior. And if all behavior had a cause, where was guilt? How, then, could any doctor become a prosecutor? There was faultiness, to be sure—people needed to be helped, to have their behavior patterns changed—but revengeful punishment was no cure.

"At least you and Jonathan Wilk believe the same thing," Ferdinand Feldscher said. "But what jury does?"

McNarry shook his head. He had only the gloomiest view of making a jury see it, in this case. For every jury had to act as a sample of the society from which it was drawn. This was inevitable, it was the very heart of the jury system. "What you will get is the herd critique through the medium of the jury."

He reminded them of several cases in his own experience, cases in which insanity was self-evident. There was the Father Schmidt case—a priest who had cut a woman into seven parts, on the altar. Yet the jury had declared him sane, in order that he might be hung. "Juries invariably regard the insanity plea as a dodge. They discredit the experts. What they really base their verdict on is whether society has been threatened by the accused. If they feel his act to be against society, they will find him guilty; if they feel it has been against himself, as sometimes in a murder of passion, say the Thaw case, then they will tend to pity the murderer, and send him to an asylum." In this case, there would obviously be no pity.

What, then, was to be done?

What about Wilk? Uncle Gerald reminded them that, after all, Wilk was the greatest jury lawyer in the world. Surely he could make a jury see it. Even one juror would be enough.

Wilk had gone to bed with a cold; now the entire group moved into his bedroom. Between Wilk and McNarry there had been an instant communion of spirit; indeed Wilk joined fully in McNarry's pessimism. Members of a jury would have to go against their own selves, as true members of the community, in order to find pity for the accused boys. Only people who had an inner conviction against capital punishment might be helpful, and Horn would be sure to eliminate any of those. As for the partial insanity argument, you might expect a professional to follow it, but not a jury. Even a judge might find it difficult.

It was then that Edgar Feldscher revived the thought of going to a judge with a plea of guilty.

His brother said, "I've never ruled it out, in my mind. But all you've got is a plea for mercy on the grounds of their youth."

"No," said Edgar, tentatively. "Why couldn't we present the entire psychiatric evidence, as we would before a jury?"

The others looked at him as though he had forgotten his ABC's. If a judge could be convinced of insanity, he was bound by law to call a jury.

"Yes, yes, but short of insanity—"

Wilk's head had lifted. "Mitigating circumstances," he croaked hoarsely, pulling himself up to a sitting position. "A judge is duty bound to listen to mitigating facts."

"Yes, but how can you raise the question of their mental condition, in mitigation, without coming to the question of insanity? And the minute you touch on that . . ."

It was indeed the paradox, and McNarry did not hesitate to express his lifelong disgust with this curious situation in which a jury of laymen, the persons least equipped for it, were always the ones who had to decide whether a person was insane. Bring in the most learned men in the world to testify, and all their learning, all their special knowledge, could be erased by people who had no understanding of it.

Uncle Gerald had a thought. "All right, suppose a judge does at some point call a jury. We're no worse off. In fact, we're better off, because this already shows the judge doubts their sanity."

It was an impressive point. "And then, we've still got Jonathan, here, before a jury," said Ferdinand Feldscher.

"We're not doing this as a show for me," Wilk said.

Edgar Feldscher drew them back to the original idea. "We don't have to raise the insanity issue, temporary or anything. We claim they are suffering from a functional disorder, short of a psychosis. That's the exact truth, that's what we asked these men to find out. These boys are not responsible for their behavior—"

"Who is?" Wilk interjected.

"And if we are careful to keep the argument short of insanity, isn't it a mitigating condition?"

There was an instant of quietness, as they weighed it. It would be a thin line to tread—to convince the judge that they were sick, but not sick enough to be called insane. The doctors would have to avoid the very word.

"Don't worry," said McNarry. "It's not really a medical word. I never use it if I can help it."

"There's one thing I like about this plan," said Max Steiner. "It's honest to plead guilty. It's the plain truth. People will give us credit for being honest."

Wilk drawled, "It's no easier to make people believe the

plain truth than a lie. But I suppose it is always more comfortable."

Uncle Gerald was still uncertain. It was so risky to rest everything on one man instead of twelve.

"He's a good man," Wilk commented.

"He's never hung anybody," Ferdinand Feldscher said.

And so they agreed, but with one condition. "We'd better make sure how the boys feel about it."

*   *   *

Wilk wanted to see for himself how they reacted. Artie nervously agreed. They knew best. Judd had a touch of resistance. Pleading guilty. Didn't that mean merely going up to be sentenced? Then the case would never really be heard?

No, Wilk assured him; in the mitigating evidence, everything would be heard. All his ideas would be heard.

*   *   *

Thus it was that the defense made the astonishing announcement of a change of plea. In a quick, unspectacular hearing, the boys were brought into court, to declare themselves guilty. The maneuver brought a new flood of comment in the papers. Had a deal been made? What was Wilk trying to pull? Did the million-dollar defense really think they had found a "friendly judge"?

The Hearst papers were the most blistering. So even Wilk was afraid to go before a jury! In huge type, Horn vowed the boys would hang, no matter what legal tricks were pulled.

And then Mike Prager carried an "inside" story. The defense case had collapsed, he declared on "good authority," because the thousand-dollar-a-day alienists for the defense refused to declare the boys insane.

We all found ourselves crowding into Wilk's office, half of us pressed against the walls. The entire defense staff was there; Wilk looked harrowed, his voice was hoarse. He gestured to the newspapers on his desk. On top was the *American,* with its scarehead: THEY'LL HANG, HORN VOWS.

"Now, fellows," Wilk said, "if you want to know why we had to change the plea, there's the answer. You're all part of it. How can we hope to find even one unprejudiced citizen for this jury?" A judge, at least, he pointed out, might retain some professional perspective. Had not the families already declared that the boys should be removed from society? He would plead evidence in mitigation, merely that their lives might be spared.

What mitigating evidence? we all demanded.

If they had been boys from impoverished homes, Wilk pointed out, we would all agree there were mitigating conditions. But wasn't there something beyond the social condition, a lower common denominator, something that forced the boys to kill? That was what the psychiatrists were trying to find.

From the back wall we heard Mike's deliberate snigger. A dozen voices demanded, Was it true that the psychiatrists had reported there was nothing wrong with the boys? The report of Dr. Allwin and Dr. Storrs was a private one, Edgar Feldscher put in sharply. Its contents were medically confidential.

"Why?" demanded Mike. "What are you trying to hide?"

There might be some private family matters that had nothing to do with the crime, Feldscher said calmly.

Mike retorted, "There's nothing private about murder."

Wilk addressed Mike directly. "Now why do you want to go printing stuff you don't know is true?" He slapped his hand down on the newspaper. "What do you want to make up stuff like this for?"

If anything was made up, Mike taunted, then let Wilk release the facts to disprove it.

"The facts will come out in court," Wilk said, "and all of you will get them at the same time."

"I'll get them before that, if I can!" Mike snapped. "And I'll get my own facts, not the facts you want us to have. We're not whitewashing anybody."

There was a murmur, something like "Aw, play ball." But Mike marched out.

On the secretary's desk was a pile of documents, just delivered from a typing service. The secretary was in the main office with the rest of us. Mike's eye took in the doctors' names, on the top sheet. He picked up a copy of the Storrs-Allwin report and simply walked out of the office with it.

*   *   *

Mike's paper was on the street in two hours, with a full page of sensational quotes from the confidential report. Instantly, we were called to come back to Wilk's office. Even as I dodged across the Loop streets, I was skimming Mike's scoop. Under "Sex Pact" there appeared for the first time the story of their curious agreement, after the Ann Arbor robbery. There were quotations about the sex life of each, ending in dots for what was unprintable. But unequivocally the public was at last informed that they had had relations with each other.

In a special box, I found Artie's admission of additional crimes, *A, B, C, D.* What were they? the paper demanded. And on the inside page were columns and columns of quotations from their fantasies.

In Wilk's office there was an atmosphere of outrage. Edgar Feldscher handed out all the available copies of the report, with one last attempt to caution us. "This should never have got out," he said. "Not that we want to hide anything from the public, but because these studies are still incomplete. Several other alienists are to examine the boys. This report was intended for them. We hoped to establish an intelligent procedure here. We offered to give all our findings to the prosecution right from the outset; we asked to have scientists from both sides working together. Mr. Horn refused. Well, this is as far as we've got and we've yet to see any attempt at a study by the prosecution. We're standing on the simple truth that human science is not yet far enough advanced in this field to make clear and final judgments, but that enough is known to make it plain that these boys are not normal. We're not asking for any fake acquittal that would send them to mental institutions. We're pleading mitigation, mercy, because these studies show that the boys were not entirely responsible—indeed they were far from responsible—for what they were doing, in the sense that they were not in mental and moral health."

It may be that he said it as well, then, to our circle of reporters, as it was ever said in court. As we hurried out with our copies, we talked angrily of Mike and his scoop. Only Danny Mines of the *News* said, "Hell, any one of us wishes he had done it." And there was again the question never entirely resolved in the mind of the newspaperman, the fundamental question of the means and the end. In Louie's Place that night, after all our papers had caught up with him, Mike was to outshout us all, brazenly laughing at us. The report was of public interest; he had simply appropriated a copy for public use.

And it must be asked, had Mike never stolen that report, would all that we know have become known? Would even that slight mention, "He admits to four other episodes"—characterized as *A, B, C, D,* and not further examined—ever have come to public knowledge? It might be said that this admission had no effect on the eventual outcome of the trial, since the other cases were never unraveled. But as the years have accumulated, it has for me had a growing effect on my thinking about the two natures, Judd's and Artie's, involved in the Kessler crime.

All our headlines would ceaselessly demand, What were the "episodes"? Who could know, unless Artie told? Might they not have been fires, robberies, even sexual episodes with persons whose identity he would not disclose? Yet the context made it seem that Horn's guesses were close. In huge black type, the four "probable" crimes were listed. The gland robbery, the student mysteriously shot, the student mysteriously drowned, and the "ragged stranger" found dead, with his hands cut off, on a Michigan road. Could a fiend who had perpetrated these acts, and the Paulie Kessler murder too, be permitted to live?

Yet, Horn had listed these same crimes even before Artie admitted to *A, B, C, D,* and not an iota of evidence had been produced.

We all filled pages and pages with excerpts from the reports—dreams and fantasies, psychological tests, physiological examinations. Huge blown-up photographs of Judd's head and of Artie's head were hastily prepared, with phrenologists' diagrams overlaid, and arrows indicating "emotion," "intelligence," "criminal instincts," "sex glands."

The report had one stunning effect on our conception of the crime. Until then, Tom and I, like almost everyone else, had felt Judd to be the dominant power, the Svengali, the dark, sinister one; but in the office, as we digested the material, we saw that we had been wrong, everyone had been wrong. Except, I thought, Ruth.

For the alienists showed in detail how Artie had been the instigator, the leader, and Judd his "gang." Judd had been tied to him in passion.

Yet we wondered whether the homosexual admissions were exaggerated to pave the way for the plea that the boys were not normal. We read of Judd's first "relationship with a woman" at the age of fifteen, a pickup. In my meager, hushed knowledge of homosexuality, I had retained an idea that it was exclusive. Since that first pickup, the report said, Judd had experienced numerous relationships with females, "but he has noticed that his desire toward women has always been essentially an intellectual one and that he has gone merely because it was the 'thing to do.' His sex urge has been very strong. He realized this, but he felt that his mental superiority gave him the right to do as he wished sexually without the ordinary conventions of right and wrong applying to himself. . . . He denies any version of bestiality. . . ." He had been "seriously attracted" to three different girls, but was "not in love now." He had been deeply interested in one young lady quite recently. He had thought that he would one day marry and have children.

But while he spoke of these normal plans, Judd had admitted to the alienists that it was Artie who remained in his mind, even during the moments of his relationships with women. For Artie, "his affection grew out of bounds, and he felt willing to be the slave of his friend and cooperate with him in any delinquency which his friend might suggest as the price he would pay for the maintenance of his friendship. . . . The boys finally reached a very definite, formal compact. If the patient would do as Straus wanted done in carrying out Straus's fantasies, Straus would do what the patient wanted in carrying out the patient's fantasies. Their fantasies were quite dissimilar, but each required one other confederate. . . . In their compact it was agreed that Artie should have complete domination over his companion so that he might call upon him whenever he wished for explicit obedience."

The report came, then, to the crime and declared that there was for Judd "no sexual significance in pouring acid on the body, and there was no mistreatment of the body. He got no pleasure from the crime. He got no sexual reaction from the crime. . . . He makes no effort to shift the blame for the crime on his companion, although he insists he did not really desire to commit the crime. Apparently he does not try to excuse himself or to make himself less guilty in the eyes of others. Rather, he seems to be perfectly honest in his statements, and is trying to give an accurate account of the whole affair."

Yet the doctors went on to say that he was "not absolutely frank in his statements," omitting certain data, lying rather plausibly at times, but less often than Artie. "He was quite unconcerned when told that knowledge of these things was already in possession of the examiners. He was more interested, however, in trying to be sure that his account of everything agreed with his companion's."

Now we read of the times Artie and Judd had planned to kidnap their fathers, or Willie Weiss, "the Horrible Hebe," or even Artie's little brother Billy.

But as to the causes, there was no over-all explanation, not even a theory. The alienists put a good deal of stress on Judd's physical condition. "Abnormal or subnormal emotionalism is frequently found in persons with disorders of the endocrine glands. This patient is of the dyspituitarian type, with associated disorder of the endocrine glands . . . in the vagotonic or autonomic segments of the sympathetic nervous system. . . ." No one would know what was meant, but glands were at that time a sensational topic, so we included such excerpts.

Judd's case was further complicated by a peculiar detail that was to become famous in the trial. "The X-ray examination of the skull reveals a small *sella turcica,* which is the part of the skull where the pituitary gland of the brain lies. There is a marked calcification of the pineal gland, which does not normally occur in a man of his youth. The union of the bones of the skull shows osteosclerosis." This, we said, meant that his sex gland's bone cradle was hardened, while the gland pressed on to grow. Didn't the report say so? "There is usually found intellectual and sexual potency linked with involvement of the pituitary and pineal glands. . . .

"Associated with these disorders scientific research has recently shown there usually is a disorder of the increased function of the sex glands." *Oversexed!* we translated. "The whole endocrine chain of glands via their chemistry and via the sympathetic nervous system profoundly affects the intellect and the emotion; in his case the endocrine disease contributes greatly to his mental disease."

There was nothing so complex offered for Artie; only a low rate of metabolism.

While Tom rushed out the excerpts, I phoned Horn. He was in high spirits, alternating between ridicule of all that flimflam and indignant demands that the obscure parts be illuminated. *"A, B, C, D*—that's all crime means to Mr. Wilk and his friends!" Horn shouted. "Just a couple of little boys that can say *A, B, C, D,* with a murder for each!" And that gland stuff—the boys were known in jail to be in perfect health. As for all those daydreams, kings and slaves, was Wilk actually going to come into court with that nonsense? No wonder he wouldn't dare face a jury!

*   *   *

The terrible pressure of catching up with the *American* was over. We were in the downhill part of the afternoon, when reporters dawdle around the city room. Now they all gathered around us, copying out sex passages from the document. In every city room the same thing was being done, these passages to be passed around and recopied, to inspire endless ribaldry.

Going home, I took the report along. I had really only skimmed it. Sometime I would read it carefully. After supper, I passed by Wilk's apartment, and ran into Willie Weiss. He started at once on the report. Premature, hastily gotten up—but it had some fascinating leads. What did I think? The material on Judd—his tremendous conflicts: Was he a boy or a girl? Was he a Jew or a Christian? Willie had never himself realized how completely Judd was torn.

From what he said, I had completely missed the important meanings of the material. Willie was only too eager to explain them to me. We went to an ice-cream parlor on 61st Street, and Willie, with that feverish argumentative way he had, started to show me what I had missed.

Why had I paid so little attention to the family history? "Look at this —" There had been three unsuccessful pregnancies before Judd was born, and his mother had been sick throughout her pregnancy with him. Never fully recovering from this nephritis, she had lived for seventeen years. Judd had always blamed himself for her illness, even for her death, the doctors noted.

"He must have blamed his father, too," Willie added. "Here's where you get the beginning. Don't forget he's precocious. He notices, he catches on. Real early. Kids get a strange idea, when they first begin to catch on—they imagine that fathers do something terrible to mothers, they hurt them in some way, injure them. Maybe he even caught sight of them once, making love. And this child sees his mother, an invalid, and picks up only enough to understand that giving birth to him was the cause of it. That was what his father did to her. He feels his birth killed his mother, but his father killed her first. It's the classic complex, the Oedipus—"

The term was not so popular then, but passionately Willie explained to me how well the Oedipal situation fitted the case, the boy in love with his mother, hating his father.

"Breast-fed baby, wakeful, he showed early mental and nervous-system precocity. His Baby Book records his first step at three months, his first word at four months." Did I know how phenomenal that was? Willie demanded. Most babies didn't try to make a step until they were nearly a year old!

And could I imagine the excitement around such a phenomenal baby? His mother, his aunt, clucking over him, encouraging him to do more wonders—so that from the very earliest impressions, Judd was made to feel he was someone utterly extraordinary. And with this he had to keep up.

A small and sickly child, "until he was nine he had gastro-intestinal disorders, complicated by fever, headaches, vomiting." Anxiety, said Willie. He had been rather effeminate up to that age—that was the period of the girls' school. "How could this child know what he really was?" Willie demanded. "He's small, delicate like a girl: he hates girls because he knows he should be more of a boy, yet he is always thrust among girls. His mother says sending him to the girls' school will make him get along better with girls, will get him over his shyness. Poor woman, she obviously wanted him to be a girl, the whole time. His father tries to send him to public school, but his mother still insists her darling is too frail, too special, too different. The child hears them arguing about him, fighting over him. The father overrides the mother. Judd tries the public school." Of this, the report said, "He realized his superiority over the other boys in wealthy parents, in the location of his home on Michigan Avenue, in the fact that his nurse accompanied him to and from school, and that he couldn't attend the toilet in the school."

"Poor bastard, holding himself in!" was Willie's comment on this point. "Imagine this kid, feeling he is so special he can't even use the can! No wonder he got a god complex!"

We turned back to the report: "His religious fantasies have always occupied a very prominent part of his life. . . ." It went on to tell of his cataloguing all the churches, of his Madonna fixation on his mother.

This Willie seized upon. It fitted perfectly into the theory of a distorted Oedipus relationship. For what was the Madonna picture? A woman with a baby, but with the father entirely absent. Judd, the report said, had little contact with his father or brothers. "You see, by the Madonna fixation, he gets rid of his real father, whom he resents bitterly. And that leaves him free to consider himself as a magical, superior being, even magically born, the son of God.

"Remember how you puzzle about yourself when you are a kid?" Willie went on. "Remember how you wonder, Who am I really? It's typical for every child at some time to imagine he is not really the child of his own parents. And look at this—" The report spoke of Judd's innumerable sketches, all over his classroom notebooks. Of the thousands of things he drew—"a list takes twenty pages"—the first item was "Crucifixions." Over and over again he had drawn the cross. "The most interesting part of the Crucifixion for him appears to be somebody nailed to something." And there were the crosses atop which he had planted his own initials.

His mother was a Madonna, he was a Christ. And here, Willie supplied another conception that was new to me: "Remember, the church is a mother-idea, everything about the church is seductive, feminine; we even speak of the mother-church, and the synagogue is a father-religion, harder and more austere, stemming from the patriarchs."

And so Willie explained Judd's conflict over being a Jew. At the time it seemed far-fetched to me, seemed perhaps a reflection of Willie's own excessive concern with his "Jewish appearance."

"But look," Willie said, "Christ is a suffering Jew who at the same time is, to the modern world, a Christian. He is born a Jew but in reality He becomes the symbol of Christianity. Isn't this an inevitable identification for someone who is struggling with his Jewishness? Judd runs around to all the churches but hasn't quite got the nerve to renounce his father-religion, to become a *meshumed,* a convert, so he nominally rejects all religion and says he's an atheist. Wait. Look at his fixation on Artie—"

"But what's that got to do with religion? I thought it was just perversion."

Willie's eyes gleamed with the know-more excitement. "Look at Artie, a tall blond fellow who is everything Judd wanted to be in appearance, who doesn't look Jewish at all, a real collegiate *shagetz* type, and look what Judd says: 'I identified myself with him completely.' He envied the food that went into Artie's body, he wanted to be incorporated into Artie, he wanted to be Artie." Now Willie lowered his voice, producing his culminating point. "I'm sure Judd never thought of this overtly. But remember, Artie's mother is a Catholic. If Judd were Artie, he could more literally sense himself as the son of the Madonna."

I thought it was too pat. What about the alienists upstairs? I asked. What did they think of his theory?

"Oh, we discussed it. Eli Storrs thought it was interesting," he said a little flatly. Actually, Willie argued, the entire subject of Jewish self-hatred was a rather new concept. He had read the basic book, available only in German. It showed how every Jew had a wish not to be burdened with the problem of being a Jew. Then came the guilt feeling for harboring such a wish. "Haven't you ever felt it?" he challenged me.

I could not deny that his words called up something of the sort in me. "Freud himself has worked on it, in his own self-analysis. It's no mere minor factor," Willie said.

Indeed, this Jewish self-hatred was probably the biggest problem in Freud's own psyche, Willie declared. "Once as a child he saw his father step into the gutter when a *goy* ordered him off the sidewalk. It was a traumatic incident. Freud later saw that he subconsciously hated his father for being a Jew and for making him a Jew."

"All right. Then why should such a feeling make Judd kill Paulie Kessler?"

"Why? Self-destruction! They picked a boy, a Jewish boy, just at the age when Jews become Jews—thirteen, the *barmitzvah* age."

That was going too far. "They picked him at random, on the street—"

"Yes. That's what they claim," he said fanatically. "That there is no meaning, that everything is at random. Do you think that maybe, somewhere far back in their minds, it didn't ring home that Paulie Kessler was the son of a pawnbroker, the symbol of everything that is shameful in being a Jew?" He leaned back, and grinned at me.

I wanted at first to laugh. Yet his ideas echoed and echoed. Wasn't I, myself, ashamed? Didn't I sometimes feel a secret rage at my father's being a cheap Jewish cigar-maker?

I recalled Judd's continuous remarks about being Jewish. Every time the crowd had gone into a restaurant he had made some remark about Jewish food, spices, herrings. And hadn't Judd experienced a sharp disappointment in Ann Arbor when he had been almost invited into a gentile fraternity? The one he later tried to rob?

I evaded the whole question. "Boy, you must give them a lot of fun upstairs," I said.

"Yah, they call me the wild man. But don't worry. They may not put any of my ideas into the reports, they may kid around about them, but they can't push them out of their minds."

"Everything is possible," I said. "So you think that explains it? Judd hated himself for being a Jew and for being effeminate, so he went along to destroy himself, in the person of that boy they picked up. Does that explain it?"

"No," Willie said, suddenly empty and melancholy. "This was all part of it. But there is still something more, some key I haven't found."

"How do the docs explain it?" I asked.

"They don't." We read again the conclusions on Judd. "He has the symptoms that are so frequently found in persons who eventually come to believe themselves to be God. . . . His abnormal or individualistic type of thinking will become more pronounced with the passing of time. The world of fantasy will bring him so much greater satisfaction than the world of reality that he will continue to deny, more and more, the unpleasant facts of reality, to engage himself, in solace, in the realm of unreality or fantasy. The rapidity of this dementia will be enhanced because of his constitution, especially his endocrine make-up, and under ordinary circumstances one can expect that his years will be shortened because of the diseases of his heart and kidneys."

Willie shrugged. "They make all these predictions," I observed, "maybe to win sympathy, to let people feel he'll die soon in jail anyway."

Neatly the report exonerated the parents: "There is nothing in the family training, either of omission or commission, which is responsible for his present condition." Willie smiled wryly and ate his ice cream.

As to the predictions, it is perhaps unfair to recall them. I have been told that a man in jail is relieved of the pressures and anxieties of the outside world; he can relax, much as in a good mental institution, so that the deterioration the alienists expected may have been halted, in Judd, by prison life itself.

Willie had fallen silent, brooding over his only partial explanation of Judd, an explanation which he was to complete for me, in an extraordinary way, years later. I turned the pages. "What about Artie?"

"It's either obvious or a complete mystery," he said. "Maybe he's just a born maniac."

"You think it could be heredity, then, after all?"

"Why not? You know what McNarry says. Everything is inherited, and everything is acquired." His gloomy smile lit up the beauty of it. A curious thing, he pointed out. The two men in Judd's family who had become insane were classified as paranoic—Judd's tendency, with his swollen superman ideas. But Artie's relatives had suffered from a split personality, without the swelling up. Artie, too, was split: a lovable college boy, a fiend.

Still, Willie didn't believe it was entirely the fault of heredity. If these weaknesses had been detected early, perhaps the new psychiatry could have helped. But why hadn't the faults been detected? "Ah, we don't know a damn thing." He had become morose.

"One thing you did guess," I said, to restore the spark in him. "About the weapon." I told him it was his insistence about the chisel, that time in the lab, that had led us to the tales of other taped chisels, other crimes. "What was it, a hunch?" I asked, still suspecting he might know more.

Willie looked at me foggily for a moment, and then his mouth widened into his odd, almost hurt grin. "For crissake, that wasn't what I meant at all." Though he wouldn't be surprised if other such murders had been done. "Don't you see what it is? The chisel? The tool itself? What it represents?"

Nowadays we would say I must have been blocked in some way, not to have understood instantly. As he made an obscene gesture with his hand, it dawned on me. It seemed at once weird, far-fetched, and obviously true. I felt stupid, too stupid to ask the next question.

He did it for me, rhetorically. But why should Artie have had to kill people with that thing? And why only men? For Artie had been against Judd's idea to make it a girl, the report told us.

In Artie's case, too, Willie said, it was the relationship with the father that had to be studied. The very first lines about Artie said material had been obtained from his mother, brothers, uncle. "His father still keeps absolutely shut off,"

Willie observed. "Upstairs, they've been trying to get a show of support, you know, for the public. They finally got his mother to say something, but not the old man."

We read, "The grandfather, a quick, alert man, was abusive to his children and beat them severely. The patient's father has been exactly the opposite in his treatment of his children, probably as a reaction to the excessive severity of the grandfather." Willie pointed out a passage, under Artie's sex life. When Artie had caught gonorrhea, "he sought advice from his older brother and his uncle, being particularly desirous of keeping a knowledge of all this from his father, whose respect he wanted to maintain."

"Almost any kid would have done something like that," I said.

"The patient had no sex knowledge from his parents, from his brothers, from his governess. At one time, he did secure some information from the family chauffeur. . . ."

"I got mine from a dirty postcard," I said.

But then Willie found a clue. In the year Artie's little brother was born, and Artie had begun his crime fantasies, he "had some eye trouble, and his lids would tend to stick together for a period of several weeks." The next detail Willie pounced upon—the eye trouble had returned over a month ago, the time of the murder.

"I don't see—"

"You don't see! That's just it. He didn't want to see. To see that baby brother, or, years later, to see the crime he had done."

Now I recalled Willie's question in the lab: Whom did each boy mean to kill? Was it his little brother, then, for Artie? His brother, of the same age, in the same class as Paulie. And hadn't Artie even gone into the yard that day and spoken to his brother, touched him on the shoulder, while hunting the victim? And hadn't Artie and Judd actually discussed taking Billy as their victim?

But why? Merely jealousy of a kid brother?

It all went somehow into a sense of inadequacy, Willie argued, a sense as a child of not being wanted enough—or else why would the parents have another baby? And the sense of not being adequate, wasn't it connected with the fear that all children, particularly little boys, had—that they would never grow up to be real men, like their fathers?

Wasn't Artie still undeveloped, despite his great hurry to grow up? "At eighteen, his voice is still changing," the report read. "He is retarded in his masculine development." He hardly needed to shave. His sexual growth was delayed. "To cover up his relative impotence, he boasted of his marks at school; although he received only moderate grades. He convinced his friends that he was quite superior to them mentally. . . ."

Impotence? Artie, the sex braggart? But of course, that would fit. For what did we really know of his conquests? Hadn't he always let on that Myra was his mistress? And I was certain she was a virgin.

The answer to Artie was all in there, somewhere, Willie said. The weak psychic structure to begin with, perhaps inherited, and the little boy's fear he would never be big and strong like his father, like his big brothers, and then the violent jealousy over his baby brother, and then the shame at being somewhat impotent—all his angers and frustrations bringing a kind of rage of impotence that was expressed the way a kid would. "I'll show you!" With a hard tool, like a big dick with which he would knock over, kill, all those other men, the young men who made him feel insignificant—kill that rival kid brother who was so cute and beloved. And kill his own inadequate self.

The tool—wasn't it the absolute symbol, the murderous weapon feared and dreamed of by every little boy, who in his fantasies about adults sees it somehow as a dreadful, powerful, killing thing?

Willie's eyes held mine morosely, as if to remind me that I too, and he too, must have known such fantasies. Evasively, feeling uncomfortable, I asked about the other fantasies of Judd and Artie, the pages and pages in the report, the daydreams or whatever they were—

"You mean the masturbation dreams?" Willie said.

I pretended that I had myself understood them as such. "What about them?"

"They're wishes. Judd wished most of all to be Artie's slave, so he became it, and Artie wished to become a master criminal and get caught and jailed."

But even with all this inner compulsion, weren't they both persons of intelligence, exceptional intelligence? Could they not have seen where they were being driven?

"Look," he said, "in both cases, the reports show us, the emotional age and the intelligence age are out of kilter. Even the psychological tests showed they were emotionally still children. What's the emotional reaction of a kid of nine when he's mixed up, baffled? He'll strike out, blindly——"

"But it wasn't blind killing. It was a long, cunning plan," I objected.

"Won't a kid brood like that and plan? And then do something violently impulsive? They planned—and then picked up a kid impulsively."

He read again of Artie's moods, his depressions, his declaration that he had at times contemplated suicide. The moods had augmented in the last two years. When these depressed moods came over him he would feel, frantically, that he had to go out and do something—and in such moods he had gone to plan the crime with Judd. Couldn't the *A, B, C, D* crimes have been break-outs from similar fits of gloom?

"The patient has some insights into his peculiarities and says that the question has often come to him as to whether he was 'all there.' He states that during the past year he has felt different; he feels he cannot concentrate so well, that his memory is not so good, and that he cannot carry on conversations and small talk with others as formerly.

"The total lack of appropriate emotional response to situations is one of the most striking features of his present condition. This is not carried out in a consistent manner but is full of contradictions. Thus we see the patient refusing the idea of escape from jail because it might hurt his family in some way, and yet contemplating kidnaping and murdering some members of his own family without the slightest emotional reaction to it. . . . From this evidence it must be concluded that the patient is markedly different from the average individual, that he has gradually fallen off in his efficiency, contacts, and interests with the world of reality, that he has gradually projected a world of fantasy, which was satisfactory to him, over into the world of reality, and at times even confused the two. There is a definite splitting between the emotional and intellectual faculties. His crime is to be explained by his peculiar fantasies, which have grown to such an extent that they now dominate him and control his actual behavior. Although he is, in one way, in excellent contact with his surroundings, his world of fantasy is much more important and interesting to him.

"In our opinion this tendency will continue and increase so that he will become more and more wrapped up in his world of fantasy and less and less in contact with his world of reality."

And again, for the family, the report was reassuring: "There is no reason to feel that the patient's condition is of a hereditary nature or that it will be transmitted to future generations of his siblings or relatives. Neither is there any reason to feel that the family is responsible in any way for this boy's condition."

Willie was restless, playing with the long soda spoon. *Responsible.* He tasted the word.

"According to you," I said, "no one is responsible."

"I didn't say that." He threw change on the table. "I suppose you think ignorance is no excuse?" We got up.

*　　　*　　　*

I was too excited to go to bed. All we had talked about worked up in me. It was a new way of thinking, and the strain of its genesis in me was both exhausting and exhilarating. I walked in the park. It was a fine night; there had been a quick shower and everything smelled clean. Then I felt terribly lonesome. I wanted to talk to a girl—I tried to feel it would be Ruth, but I still couldn't bring her back in myself; I still felt she had gone over to Judd. I was alone, alone.

I walked alongside the lake, ignoring all the entwined couples on the grass, in cars. And as I walked, there grew in me that peculiar elation that comes to us when we are young men, eighteen, twenty—that mystical sense of infinite creative connection to the universe, that winy sense of godlike power. I had known it before, but never so painfully great. The lake, the star-powdered sky, the warm human urging and love all around me, my stimulated mind—so crowded inside with the world's evil and ugly sickness, all increased by my loneliness —this entire chaos of beauty and evil coalesced until I had an exalted, delirious feeling as of a godhead in myself. I would be able to understand everything, to comprehend the minutest working of the human soul. I would be, I would be! And this, I then knew, was what that poor, tragic Judd must have felt at times, this elation, this intoxication with his own mental powers, and this was what he had confusedly expressed in his ideas that man was even more than God, that man conceived God and hence was greater than God. Each being in his own being was God. I felt the same thing in myself, and that night I felt even larger, larger with pity.

Within it all, I knew it would pass, and I could smile at myself. But a particle would remain to me, a particle of understanding. And then, when the exaltation was gone, and I was walking tiredly home, I found myself thinking of all Willie had said. There was much in it that could have meaning, and the tool had been explained—how else could you explain it?— and I had forgotten, in the rush of all the new ideas he had conveyed, I had forgotten that other hint he had given me a few weeks ago. The place of burial.

*　　　*　　　*

On the following Monday, the trial was to begin. Scrawled letters threatened to blow up the court building if anything but a hanging verdict was the result. Editorials screamed at the waste of public funds to provide a trial for such monsters, yet gloated over our noble sense of justice that insisted on a defense opportunity, even for them. But there were also higher expectations of the trial. Some of us, perhaps imbued by Judd, expected lofty and timeless discussions, as at the trial of Socrates.

By eight o'clock the sidewalk of the County Building was lined for a solid block with citizens who hoped to glimpse the killers as they were brought from jail. There were women, mostly, and among them a very high proportion of young girls —excited flappers, their mouths flaming in their loudest lipstick, many with ill-applied spots of rouge in dollar-size patches on their cheeks, like the girls in more recent years who besieged the stage doors, waiting to waylay a favorite crooner. But there were also many middle-aged women, in clusters, avid, like the ranks that were to appear at Rudy Valentino's funeral.

And there were motherly women, too, with a strange look of anxiety in their eyes, and I noticed a sprinkling of men, some of them the usual courtroom hangers-on, and some well-dressed, hard to place.

As the hour grew, the sidewalks overflowed. A special cordon of police had been stationed in the building entrance, and a constant series of arguments was in progress, with irate citizens, with blandishing women, with people using every means of subterfuge to get through. Despite the police, the lobby was jammed, the crowd surging from one end to the other as rumors started, "They're coming!"

Upstairs, I found the hallway to the courtroom packed solid. And inside, bailiffs struggled to remove people from seats reserved for witnesses. The victors in the battle for coveted admission cards were mostly friends, wives, and daughters of politicians; pull had been assiduously used, hundreds of phone calls made. And there were the special visitors all through the trial—visiting jurists, celebrities, big lawyers passing through Chicago on their way to a vacation—all of whom wanted a glimpse of the trial of the century.

And finally, the press. Nearly half the courtroom was filled with correspondents from abroad, from national magazines, from out-of-town papers. Flanking the bench were specially installed desks for the wire services.

But there existed a higher category still. The select of the press were in the jury box. Thus we saw ourselves as the true arbiters; what we wrote was judgment.

Several in the press box were old familiars, on the case from its beginning. Mike Prager was there, sporting his belligerent sneer; Richard Lyman, of the *Tribune*, had naturally appropriated the foreman's seat; the *Tribune* had added a "fancy writer" named Arthur Kramer, who sat alongside the box, where extra chairs had been placed. Their "girl reporter," May Dawes, completed that contingent. Indeed, a dozen sob sisters were in court to cover the women's angle, competing with Peg Sweet and Rea Knowles. Rea appeared with her hair shining in a new permanent wave, to queen it over our jury box. The girl reporters were never done with describing Myra, with her large sorrowful eyes—the girl who had vowed to "stick by Artie."

Though certain mysterious "girls of prominent families" had been whisked out of town, on the verge of nervous breakdowns, there were still a few rivals to Myra, proclaiming Artie's love for them and theirs for him. And, daily, all sorts of flappers, tramps, showgirls, and even nice girls tried to get into the courtroom and into the papers by claiming they were his secret sweethearts.

Certainly Artie evoked a hysterical tenderness in women. We heard it now in the corridor, a curious feminine shrieking and gasping, as the boys were pulled through the corridor crowd; we glimpsed bare arms, hands reaching toward him, heard a few piercing girls' voices above the others—"Artie!" "Artie, honey!"—and we later described how pieces of his clothing were torn from him, for souvenirs.

Inside, the two sides had assembled. For the prosecution, there was Horn, looking ruddy, massaged, made fit for battle, low-set, a line-driver. Padua was on his left, handsome, a smiling ball-carrier. They were accompanied by Czewicki—a padded interference man, with his mountains of files and reference books—and a half-dozen others, all getting set at their table, eying their opponents, whispering, nodding among themselves.

The other team was older-looking: Wilk, in his studied shabbiness, his clothes having the same rough, worn, softened look as his face; Ferdinand Feldscher, perfectly groomed, cool, agreeable-looking, reasonable, shrewd, smooth; his brother Edgar, with his high forehead, his unlit pipe, his slightly poetic look that made one wonder what he was doing in a law court, in a murder case; and their juniors and assistants.

Then there were the representatives of the families, seated close to the rail: Artie's smooth-looking brother James, who aroused sympathy, and his Uncle Gerald, erect, alert, full of quick little movements, leaning forward to whisper to the lawyers. He was really fighting for the boy. On Judd's side, father and brother sat together; sometimes Max was to be absent, and Judah Steiner would sit alone, a monumental Job, a figure that seemed, even within the crowded courtroom, removed by some invisible wall.

Directly behind sat two small men, Charles Kessler and his brother Jonas, their faces impassive. Their lawyer, Judge Wagner, was with them.

And so the prisoners were led in. A concerted female gasp was heard. Artie exchanged a brave, almost puckish smile with his brother and uncle, while Judd cast a rather furtive glance toward his kin.

Then came the judge, in his black robe. Throughout the sweltering August Chicago heat, he was to retain in his black robe that look of being unaffected by weather as by any mere extraneous factor, of being purely a judicial being.

The case was called, and a representative of each side rose to state briefly what it would attempt to show. Horn in person declared for the State that never in all the world had so cold, vile, and excuseless a murder been committed, and that the extreme penalty was inescapable in such a case. When Ferdinand Feldscher rose for the defense, it was simply to state that their efforts would be to present evidence in mitigation, evidence which they were certain would be considered without prejudice.

Horn called his first witness, the Polish worker who had found the body.

And then, for more than two weeks, there ensued a dull parade of circumstantial witnesses, the undertaker, various policemen, handwriting experts, the diver who had found the typewriter—all in endless detail proving the crime which the defense fully conceded. But there was method to it, for by having witnesses describe the blood, the body, by having teachers describe the innocent schoolboy, and by piling up evidence of the luxury in which the murderers had been raised, Horn was indeed proving aggravation, to counterbalance any mitigating evidence the defense might offer.

The high point came when Mrs. Kessler herself was produced. We all turned sob sister that day, as the pale, tensely controlled mother, in her black dress, escorted to the stand by Horn, confirmed in monosyllables the hour at which the boy had left the house and that he had never returned, except as a corpse.

The two murderers ceased their incessant exchange of grimaces. They sat erect, their eyes fixed downward on the table. It was soon over; they had not been lynched.

During those weeks, the defense could only make effort after effort to shorten the proceedings; witnesses were rarely cross-examined, except for an occasional flash question to show the defense was in form.

Then came the coroner's physician, Dr. Kruger. Despite an air of disgust and impatience on the part of Judge Matthewson, Horn kept the doctor on the stand, describing "signs of sexual abuse." His conclusion was based on his "years of observation of such cases."

The defense objected incessantly. The coroner's verdict itself stated that no conclusion could be drawn. Surely the prosecutor was attempting deliberately to arouse prejudice!

Horn flared back. "Prejudice! Monsters are monsters!"

Finally, Wilk had the witness. This time there was no perfunctory dismissal. Had Dr. Kruger not stated that no tangible evidence existed? How then could he come to a conclusion? Oh, it was an *opinion*. Would there not be just as much basis for the opposite opinion? Then it was a *guess?* Were medical men given to swearing on guesswork?

Dr. Kruger, with each reply, seemed ready to jump out of his seat. But Wilk kept him pinned there with a barrage of medical questions. Wasn't it true that muscle tension relaxed after death? Wouldn't the sphincter muscles have normally relaxed? Particularly during all-night immersion? "Then the condition was really normal, wasn't it? You figured you would be believed, through ignorance, and because when something is bad, people are ready to believe it is even worse."

"That's my opinion and I stick to it!" the coroner's physician snapped. Wilk shrugged, and waved him from the stand.

The retinue of humdrum witnesses continued.

For Judd, the trial was the last bitter irony. Was this the great trial that was in a sense to have justified his crime by bringing momentous questions before mankind? The question of free will, the question of law and the superman, reduced to routine evidence about a fake signature on a hotel registry. And for Artie, there was no particular disappointment, only boredom; to him the outcome was interesting only as a kind of bet, a long shot on life.

*   *   *

Then came my day to testify. That morning, I scanned the courtroom rows, with the dread fear that Ruth might be there.

I had assured myself that testifying on the stand would only be like sitting in front of the typewriter. When I wrote, I gave testimony, making it as true as I knew how. That was my function as a newsman, that would be my work in my life.

Then what was it that troubled me? Was it some feeling that I would nevertheless that day be deserting my function as an objective bystander, to take the chair and participate?

As I waited in the press box, Peg Sweet gave me her tremulous, motherly smile. "Nervous?" she asked. "How does it feel?"

I smiled back, with a quip. "Are you interviewing me?"

From Artie and Judd, I was sure I received a special, measuring look, weighing how damaging I might be.

In my mind, I had attempted to formulate my replies so that I would not appear "for" or "against." I had gone over the material with Tom. Certain words of Artie's would be ugly to repeat. But we had long ago put them into print; how could we change them? *If you had to pick a kid to kill, he was just the kind of cocky little sonofabitch you'd choose.* That sentence, we both knew, was counted on by Horn as a hanging sentence.

Why had Artie had to utter those words? Then some of the new psychological probings of Willie Weiss came to me. Wasn't Artie's little brother a cocky kind of kid?

Tom came in. He was wearing a freshly pressed suit and a new-looking white summer tie. "How's the boy reporter?" he joked, and "Today's the day." I offered him the *Globe* chair, as we usually spelled each other, but Tom grinned and took a seat among the prospective witnesses.

There was a railroad employee on the stand. He introduced timetables, records, and Horn seemed to enjoy the vision of the ransom letter being carried all over the United States, attached to one train after another.

The heat was growing in the room, and the people were wiping their brows, fanning themselves; a few even gave up their precious seats and left. The two accused sank low in their chairs, showing their indifference. A Socrates trial, a dance of minds! Then, seemingly in the midst of a sentence, Horn sat down; Wilk shook his head, no questions, and I heard my name called. I started across to the stand, embarrassingly confronting the witness who still sat there stupidly, while laughter arose.

As I raised my hand in the oath, I experienced a queer intensification, an archaic fear of the absoluteness of what I would be saying; I am told that all witnesses feel this to some extent and that lawyers play upon it.

Horn advanced, smiling reassuringly, and established my identity, my employment, and that I was also a student, or rather a recent graduate, of the University of Chicago, as well as a fraternity brother of one of the accused. Then he asked my age. "And at eighteen you are a graduate of the university?" he said with a smirk. I felt foolish, even a little angry. But hadn't I been making this comparison for myself, all this time?

To graduate at eighteen was pretty unusual, wasn't it? he asked, and I found myself saying not so unusual; there were others who had graduated at my age.

"Yes." He stared at the prisoners.

Then he asked if I had been tutored by a governess to speed me through school. Wilk had risen, objecting, "No, no," in a tone that showed he was ashamed of his opponent. Without waiting for a ruling, having won his effect, Horn withdrew the question, and turned then to my work as a reporter, and the identification of the body of Paulie Kessler. "That was considered quite a scoop, wasn't it?"

Artie had picked up his head. I muttered, "Well, it was only luck."

Then, on the day we found the drugstore, wasn't it Artie who had insisted on making a search for the store? And the inevitable question arrived.

"Did you discuss Artie's personal acquaintance with the victim?"

"We did."

"Did you ask him anything about Paulie?"

"My partner, Tom Daly, asked what kind of kid Paulie was."

"And what was his reply?"

Artie and Judd were staring fixedly at me. I felt sweat break and slide under my arm. "He said, 'He was just the kind of cocky little—' and then he used a swear word 'you would pick if you were going to kidnap someone.' " They had me repeat the word to the stenographer.

Horn glanced challengingly at the defense. They did not rise. He went on, establishing that I had remembered the precise words because of the shock of the remark.

Had the remark aroused any suspicion in me? Not at the time. Then Horn led me through the account of the typewriter, without sparing me a congratulation, or failing to remark that there seemed to be different kinds of prodigies at the university.

But he was not through. "Tell me, Mr. Silver, would you mind telling the court, have you ever pictured yourself as a king, or a slave, or an ideal college hero?"

The quiet Edgar Feldscher leaped up, shouting objections. Horn beamed.

What was the purpose of the line of questioning? the judge asked. Even while they argued, there crowded through my mind my own fantasies: a football hero, a sophisticated star reporter, a great writer receiving the Pulitzer Prize. I felt myself flushing, for quickly, overwhelming these, were sexual images, harem images, and it was as though my face were an open movie screen, in front of the entire courtroom.

Horn was insisting that the alienists' reports, pages and pages filled with the boys' fantasies, had opened up this entire question. But this evidence had not yet been presented in court, Judge Matthewson remarked. If the subject arose, the witness might be recalled.

I was turned over to the defense.

I watched Jonathan Wilk, unfolding like a carpenter's rule; would he now make a fool of me? But from the first stroke of his voice I felt drawn to his side. As a witness in his hands, I now knew what it was he exerted.

There was in his bearing, on his face, in his voice, such a conviction of our mutual sorrow at this whole tragic business, at this dreadfully complex twisting of the human soul in ailment and disease, that all fear, all antagonism was dispelled.

Wilk did not have many questions to ask of me. The first was a simple one, about that awful, incriminating quotation, that Horn had boasted was a hanging rope in itself. Obviously, the utterance could not be destroyed. But Wilk proceeded to whittle it down. I was used to Artie's way of talking, wasn't I? I knew him around the fraternity house and on campus, didn't I? And was Artie in the habit of employing swear words or dirty words in his usual speech?

He was.

In fact—and with a shadow of his sad smile, Wilk turned his head toward Artie—in fact, the boy couldn't open his mouth without some filthy expression, the way some kids did to show they were grown-up, tough?

Yes, I agreed. These were habitual expressions with him.

So the swear word Artie had put in there didn't have any real significance, did it? It didn't mean anything?

No, I agreed, and found myself relieved to have this pointed out. "It was just his way of talking." For the first time, I dared let my eyes look into the courtroom, even, for half an instant, encountering Myra's eyes, her tranced white face.

Mentally I deleted "sonofabitch." The rest was still terrible, dreadfully incriminating.

Wilk seemed to have done the same thing in his mind. And now he lowered his voice to a more intimate level, and I found myself lowering mine, so that we were talking as though relaxed together somewhere in a study, discussing the unfortunate case.

Now, I had seen a great deal of Artie, and of his friend Judd, but particularly of Artie in those days before they were caught, he reminded me, and as I thought back on Artie's conduct, what had he seemed like to me?

For a moment, I could not answer. There came to me, insistently, the Four Deuces, the dead derelict, Ruth, Artie, Judd dancing with Ruth. . . . If I opened my mouth, I would talk of her—

Wilk prompted me. On the day Artie had insisted on hunting out the drugstore, and other days when he had haunted reporters and police, what had he seemed like to me?

"I would say he was obsessed," I testified. "I even remarked to my partner that Artie was obsessed with the case because he was so crazy about detective stories."

"It didn't bring suspicion upon him?"

"No; he himself had the explanation that his own kid brother might have been the victim." Willie Weiss was staring at me. Did I really believe Willie's far-fetched theory? Within myself, I felt an intensification, an acceleration of all processes, as if being a witness indeed helped me to see. It was a peculiar instant of oversensitivity; there was an exquisite shudder in it; and I even thought, Suppose someone were driven to hunt for such augmented perceptions? Suppose someone had to reach out beyond everyday actions, by hurting, by murder. . . .

"Obsessed, did you say?"

"Yes, he seemed obsessed." I left the stand, feeling somehow grateful to Jonathan Wilk for having got me to say those last things.

Tom was handled briefly, for corroboration of my testimony.

A t long last, Horn was done, and the defense was to begin. Again, the sidewalk was jammed; the halls, the elevators, were crowded; and extra bailiffs had to be called to guard the courtroom doors. It was Wilk's turn.

He rose in his piecemeal manner, and asked Dr. Mc-Narry to take the stand. Even while the doctor made his way to the chair, the opposition was clamoring at the bench. Dr. McNarry fitted his bulk into the chair, arranged his papers in his lap, and turned his face up toward the judge. He gave his name; he was sworn. Only then Judge Matthewson turned his attention to Padua, Horn, Czewicki—all three in full cry, Czewicki with an armload of books, Padua repeating as a litany, "If Your Honor please, if Your Honor please—"

"All right, what is it?"

Padua led off, with a torrent of argument about the plea of insanity, beginning with sonorous quotations from Blackstone about *compos* and *non compos,* the sane and the insane, his touchstone being the familiar axiom: the ability to tell right from wrong.

Judd had become alert; something like pleasure showed on his face—the argument was being joined at last on a question of ideas. He whispered to Edgar Feldscher, no doubt some jibe about the high school lawyer with his primitive Blackstone.

And indeed there had begun one of those basic courtroom arguments by which the law itself is gradually formed, though I understand that even today the law lags far behind our actual knowledge in psychiatry.

Padua read from the Illinois statutes, while Horn stood behind him, frowning truculently: "A person shall be considered of sound mind who is neither an idiot, nor a lunatic, nor affected with insanity, and who has arrived at the age of fourteen years, or before that age if the person knows the distinction between good and evil. . . . . An individual under the age of ten years shall not be found guilty of any crime or misdemeanor."

At the defense table, this brought grim smiles. At least a ten-year-old couldn't be hung.

It flashed through my mind that the psychiatric reports had placed the "emotional age" of the boys at nine. Wouldn't it be a clever argument for the defense to contend that the emotional, rather than the physical, age should apply?

"A lunatic or insane person without lucid intervals shall not be found guilty of any crime."

Then came the provision for temporary insanity. If at the time of committing a crime, "the person so charged was a lunatic or insane, the jury shall so find by their verdict . . ." and the person would then be kept in the state hospital until recovered.

". . . In all these cases it shall be the duty of the court," Padua read emphatically, looking up at the judge and then at his adversaries, "to impanel a jury to try the question whether the accused be . . . sane or insane."

He set down the lawbook. "Can language be more explicit, more mandatory, and more direct than the language that I have just read?"

If the defense even touched on the question of insanity, the case automatically had to go to a jury.

It was a curious moment. Wilk, the great jury lawyer, was seeking at all costs to avoid a jury. And the prosecution was trying by every trick in the lawbooks to force the case before a jury, or else to keep out the entire mass of psychiatric evidence, which was the only evidence the defense had to offer.

Now Horn took up this argument. "Insanity is a defense," he insisted "the same as an alibi. Would your honor permit the defense to enter a plea of guilty in this case and then put witnesses on the stand to show that when the crime was committed they were in California!" He could not hold down his truculence. "Have we got to a point of the law here where we can enter a plea of guilty before the court in order to avoid a jury, and then treat that plea as a plea of not guilty, and put in a defense?" His last words were roared. "Sane but insane. Guilty but not guilty!"

Very well, he had exposed the maneuver. Obstinately, he banged ahead. "Are they trying to avoid a trial on a plea of not guilty, before twelve men who would hang them? Are they trying instead to come to trial before one man they think won't hang them?"

Ferdinand Feldscher leaped up, his mouth open.

The judge made a movement, as though brushing away a fly. Horn kept on. "I insist, if Your Honor please, that we proceed without hearing any evidence tending to show that these men are insane. If not, everything you do from now on is of no effect under the law."

There was a gasp from the courtroom at his audacity. Dr. McNarry, who had been staring at Horn with a professional half-smile, now turned his gaze upon Judge Matthewson.

"From the moment you hear evidence on insanity, this becomes a mock trial!" Horn shrieked, his head wheeling to make sure the press had got his words. At last, the judge cut in. Did the state's attorney have any authorities?

Several lawyers responded simultaneously, Czewicki picking up a mass of references from the prosecution table, while, in a parallel movement, Wilk's assistant, John Geiger, rose with counter-references.

Meanwhile, as Judd and Artie listened intently, the judge leaned forward, explaining his own view. It was actually his duty to find out if the boys might be insane, in order to protect their rights—to a jury trial! "I have a right to know whether these boys are competent to plead guilty or not guilty." Suppose, he said, a defendant had come before him without a lawyer, and "the court was of the opinion from his general appearance that there was something wrong with him. How would the court determine whether he was competent to plead guilty or not guilty?"

"Before a jury!" Horn snapped.

The judge shook his head and cited a case he had tried. "The court would and could and did appoint an alienist to examine him, and when the court was told he was not insane, that he was responsible for his acts, I permitted the plea of guilty to stand and sentenced him to life imprisonment. That was only recently." The boys smiled. The judge sat back. "If this court were satisfied that these boys were insane, the court could and very likely would direct the plea of guilty to be withdrawn, and a plea of not guilty entered, and let the defendants plead insanity as a defense before a jury."

"Before a jury," Horn beamed.

This struck a New York reporter as comical, and his lone burst of laughter was heard through the courtroom. What a topsy-turvy game! If the defense alienists proved too good at their job, and convinced the judge that the boys were insane, they would fall right into Horn's hands before a jury. The trick for the defense, the New York man muttered, was to prove the boys were "not insane—jest tetched."

The judge seemed determined to give each side a point, for he went on to remark, "There are different forms of insanity. Medically——"

"Not under the law!" Horn cried.

Patiently, as one going back to fundamentals, Judge Matthewson asked Horn, "Then is there no mitigation in a murder case at all?"

"Insanity is not a mitigating thing. It exists or does not exist."

Wilk ambled to the bench, as a man puzzled. "And has the degree of responsibility nothing to do with it?"

"Degree!" Horn snapped. "Do we have a statute that says if a man is twenty per cent normal when he committed a crime, he shall get a twenty per cent term, and if he is thirty per cent normal he shall get a different punishment? And the man who is one hundred per cent normal will get the extreme penalty? Show me such a statute!"

But wasn't this the whole practice of human judgment?

"There is no such law! Insanity is a total defense, the same as self-defense, the same as an alibi."

"But if a medical condition——" Edgar Feldscher began.

Padua interrupted. "The law on the issue of an insanity defense——"

"No!" snapped Ferdinand Feldscher. "You keep saying an insanity defense when——"

"We claim——" began Wilk.

"Just let me ask one question," Padua put in.

"You are talking all the time!" Wilk snapped.

"One moment, Mr. Wilk!" Padua's voice somehow dominated, as though he were saying, I don't care how important you are! And he put his question to the judge. "If it is conceded that insanity is not a defense, have they any right to introduce any evidence of insanity?"

"No, we're not——" Feldscher shouted.

"No evidence of insanity!" Wilk echoed, while Dr. McNarry studied them all with interest.

"Then have you any right to introduce evidence as to the mental condition of these men?" Padua demanded.

"Certainly!" they cried in unison.

"Evidence intended to show that they are not responsible, or should not be held to the degree of responsibility that other people should be?"

"Certainly." Wilk demonstratively resumed his seat, as if the argument, to any logical mind, was over.

"But that is insanity called by another name!"

"You can call it green cheese if you like!" Ferdinand Feldscher sneered.

"Wait, wait! Don't get excited!" The judge leaned in.

Dr. McNarry permitted himself a chortle. Judd grinned. Artie looked worried, as if to remind us all that his life was at stake in this dispute.

Horn, with an air of enforced calm, picked up the argument. "After the defense puts on their alienists, the state in rebuttal will also put on alienists. Haven't you got a question of insanity there?"

The case seemed to hang in balance. Turning blandly toward Dr. McNarry, the judge said, "I don't know what Dr. McNarry or whatever his name is, is going to testify." He beamed upon Horn. "Nobody has said he is going to testify as to their sanity, except the State."

It was sophistry. We all had the report of the alienists in our hands. Did not the report on each boy conclude with the statement that he was mentally affected? From a legal point of view, Horn seemed right. But the real trouble was that the law itself in its definition of insanity was antiquated. Even before a jury, the argument would have come to the same thing: Was medical insanity, was being mentally affected, a consideration under legal insanity?

There in that broiling courtroom in Chicago the inadequacy of the definition was being made clear; there in those days of wrangling the law itself was being tested. If it did nothing else, if the life or death of Judd and Artie was of little significance, their case at least served to focus the world's attention on the inadequacy of our laws in the face of our new knowledge of the human personality and mind.

The argument climbed. The lawyers brought in rulings from Nebraska, precedents from Alabama, statutes from Colorado. Word of the battle had seeped down to the street, and the pressure at the door increased. As in most arguments, the issue was only a definition of a word. Insanity. The word was like a push button for a jury. The defense tried to shade it to "an affected mind."

"That is partial insanity," Padua insisted. "It is a diseased mind, and a diseased mind is necessary to unsoundness of mind in the law."

"There is no need in citing the law, because the court agrees with you," Judge Matthewson said. "If there is any mental disease, it is insanity."

There was a sudden silence. The prosecution seemed to have won. Judd, in panic, turned to Jonathan Wilk.

Wilk arose again and stepped to the bench. "Do you mean to say that the court will not consider the mental *condition* on the question of mitigation? When the mental condition does not rise to a defense?"

His question hung in the air. Mitigation, he repeated. What entered into mitigation? Didn't one consider the conditions that led to a crime? The background of the criminal, the forces that molded his character? The pressures upon him, the extent of his responsibility?

And as he spoke, the courtroom was being gradually drawn back from the definition of a word to deeper questions. What was free choice of action? What was free will? And, unsaid, one could hear Wilk's lifelong rumination, his gentle pessimism, his insistence on some form of mechanistic determinism, his claim that there was no free will. Yet even if some freedom of will did exist, "Suppose the mental condition seriously interferes with their free will and understanding, don't you think the court has a right to listen to that, in mitigation?"

Ferdinand Feldscher interjected, softly, so as not to break Wilk's spell, "Isn't it the court's duty to hear it?"

And Wilk appealed, "Could he refuse to hear it?"

It was the deeper kind of plea, for which we had waited from Wilk, the plea for compassion, yet delicately balanced, because if you carried it too far you would be saying what you really meant, that no one was responsible for any crime.

And Padua, this time lowering his voice so that, without a mocking note, it was as solemn as Wilk's, devilishly suggested, "If you had a mental condition of that kind, it would be your duty to take full advantage of it before a jury."

A grudging gasp went through the courtroom, at the young attorney's cleverness in puncturing the grand champion's spell. Padua drove home his point, speaking as though on Wilk's side, with sympathy barely spiced with irony. "It is only necessary to raise a reasonable doubt in the minds of the jury, to acquit."

Wilk was momentarily taken aback. Ferdinand Feldscher stepped in, to quote authorities again, and at times four or all six of the attorneys argued earnestly, with the judge intently taking part, as though the whole thing had become impersonal and they were all co-operatively engaged in their true work—not merely the judgment of a case, but the work of bringing further refinement to the eternal process of law. These were, indeed, the good moments of the trial, when human endeavor seemed serious.

But gradually voices rose. "We're wasting hours!"

"Wasting a few hours doesn't make any difference," said the judge. "The lives of two men are at stake here, and the issue itself is important. Two hours doesn't mean anything and a day doesn't mean anything, and a week or a month will be spent if necessary."

The morning session was over. As the boys were led out, Judd remarked to Dr. McNarry, "Well, you nearly got a word in," and Artie said, "They've got you stuck to that seat, Doc." We all recorded their wit, the hostile papers adding that at two hundred and fifty dollars a day, the doctor had no reason to complain.

* * *

When the argument was resumed, it was Edgar Feldscher who attempted to clarify the issue. "Even the most expert alienist finds it difficult to put his finger on the border line between sanity and insanity. Lots of people walk around with delusions and compulsions and go through life tending to their business, and who knows at what point they should be called mentally sick? If a man cuts his throat, isn't it possible he was already mentally sick the day before, the week before, years before, while he was apparently normally conducting his daily business?"

Though experts found it hard to define insanity, Feldscher pointed out, "Yet the law is that a jury of twelve ordinary laymen, maybe half of whom got through high school, should, on listening to testimony, be able to judge whether a man is sane or insane!"

"But that's the law!" Horn was right back at it. "An insanity issue goes before a jury."

The mild Edgar Feldscher suddenly snapped, "Let me ask, when you were a judge on this bench, didn't you, in a similar proceeding—in the Fitzgerald case—hear evidence of sanity on a plea of guilty, for attacking that poor five-year-old little girl?"

"No, I didn't——" Horn began.

Wilk cut in, a figure of wrath. "Why, every lawyer in Chicago knows you had an alienist testify that Fitzgerald was a legal moron!"

"Yes, but I didn't permit testimony of insanity!" Horn screeched. "Moral depravity is not insanity."

"An alienist testified to the mental condition of Fitzgerald," Wilk insisted.

"Testified he was a degenerate!"

"And irresponsible!" Wilk shouted in his face.

"And Fitzgerald was sentenced to be hanged!" Horn retorted triumphantly.

"You hanged him," Wilk stated, in disgust. "You hanged a diseased moron."

Judge Matthewson angrily rapped for order. For another day they debated, until Padua summed it up for the State: "Seventy per cent of all admissions to state institutions are mental diseases functional in their nature—the very language of the defense—and that is insanity. Disguise it as you will, characterize it as you may, it amounts to nothing less than legal insanity, and that is a defense before a jury."

Now Wilk ranged himself in his famous pose, his thumbs under his suspenders, his long body relaxed, fluid as he moved about, yet ready to tauten and snap just as the suspenders might stretch and snap; we were sure that Wilk at last was going to justify his presence.

He began dryly. "I understand from everything that has been said in this case, from the beginning to the end, that the state's attorney's office feels the universe will crumble unless these two boys are hanged. I must say I have never before seen the same passion and enthusiasm for a death penalty as I have seen in this case, and there have been thousands of killings before this, of much more horrible detail, where there was some motive for it. There have been thousands before and there probably will be thousands again, whether these boys are hanged or go to prison."

It was Wilk in one of his characteristic humanitarian outbursts, and Judge Matthewson permitted it, perhaps out of a sense of what was due the spectators and the world. "If I thought that hanging men would prevent any future murders, I would probably be in favor of doing it," Wilk said. "In fact, I would consent to having anybody hanged, excepting myself. . . . But I know the world will go on about the same in the future as it has in the past, and this case is like all other cases: it ought to be tried calmly and dispassionately upon the facts of the case."

Now he became the clever lawyer, turning Horn's own argument against him. "If the ability to judge between right and wrong is the only criterion of sanity, why, then we already know the boys are legally sane, so the judge can listen to anything he wants, here. Why, Mr. Horn even said my clients are as sane as he is!" What, then, was the prosecution holding things up for? "They came in here with their beloved Blackstone, hoary with time. . . ."

Horn opened his mouth, then shook his head as if to say, Let the clown have his act.

"They cited an Alabama case. Any case from Alabama, if it involves a scientific question, is ancient. A great change has come over the law in reference to insanity in the last twenty-five years. Mental science is being investigated, and it is being investigated for the benefit of humanity. In olden days they loaded a man with chains and locked him in a dungeon. We have abandoned that. We know that there are many mental conditions that come far short of the legal definition of insanity. We know that men and women may be very seriously ill mentally, and still they generally know the difference between right and wrong. They may be unable to resist the wrong and do the right, but still they are mental victims, and the courts take account of that." He turned and looked at the boys.

"We have in this state a statute which says the court, before he passes sentence on a human being, may inquire whether there are mitigating circumstances. Now what does this mean? Is there any catalogue? No, the court must tell, it is for him to decide and no one else.

"What is a mitigating circumstance? Youth itself. Simply because a child hasn't judgment. Why, we've all been young and we know the vagaries of the mind of a child. We know the dream world it is in; we know that nothing is real. These two boys are minors. The law forbids them making contracts, from marrying without their parents' consent. Why? Because they haven't judgment, which comes only with years. I can't understand lawyers who would talk of hanging boys as they would talk of a holiday—as they would talk of the races. This case has been talked out here, Your Honor, as if we had done something unusual, as if never before had there been a plea to give a human being the consideration of humanity.

"About seven years ago, a poor boy named Petnick was charged with murder and I was asked by a charitable organization to defend him. He was a grocer boy. He went to a house one day to deliver groceries and picked up a knife and killed a mother and her baby.

"I entered a plea of guilty, as in this case. I called in that case his schoolteacher to show his mental condition, and I called alienists to prove the state of that poor boy's mind. Judge Willard, a former partner of Mr. Horn here, said he would not hang that boy. And yet in this courtroom today we are told that the court may not consider such a circumstance!" He gazed reproachfully at the prosecution. "They say that's the law—you are told you can't even hear this testimony in mitigation. If that's the law, I trust this court will ignore it, as the courts do ignore it constantly!"

The words were like a bolt of sunlight. That was Wilk, so plain, so daring. "Anyway, it's as legal to sentence a man to prison as to hang him."

Horn had his mouth open. But Ferdinand Feldscher interjected, "The state's attorney virtually commands the court to hang these boys. Is it his duty to determine punishment? He has one duty—to enlighten the court as to the evidence. But it is not his place to demand a particular punishment."

Horn exploded. "In the name of the women and the children of this state," he screamed, "I ask Your Honor whether this has ceased to be a court of law! Mr. Wilk tells Your Honor to ignore the law, to burn the criminal code, and Mr. Feldscher wants to chase the state's attorney out of the courtroom!" He glared at the forgotten Dr. McNarry, the cause of the two-day argument. "You would indeed have to disregard the law, to hear this witness!"

With a brusque movement, the judge made his decision. "Under the wording of the statute I must hear evidence in mitigation and evidence in aggravation." He leaned to Horn.

"Suppose the State had wanted to show an aggravated murder——"

"Didn't they?" snapped Ferdinand Feldscher.

"They did," the judge agreed. And to Horn: "I did not shut the State off. I permitted the State to put on eighty-one witnesses, even after a plea of guilty. What for? To show an aggravated murder. Now then, the statute also says 'in mitigation.'" He spoke more slowly. "The objection of the State is overruled, and the defense may proceed."

Judd and Artie were alight, as though all had been won.

Dr. McNarry replied briskly to Wilk's questions establishing him as head of a famed Washington hospital for nervous and mental disorders, as author of numerous books, editor of leading psychiatric periodicals. His qualifications were indeed overwhelming.

During all this, I looked at the courtroom faces. Mr. Kessler and his brother sat, intent, in their accustomed places. It seemed to me that Charles Kessler was as perplexed in his mind as we all were, and that he attended the trial, not for revenge, but hoping that in some way he would come to know what was the real cause of his son's death. It was even rumored that he had been to see Judge Matthewson, to say that neither he nor his wife inevitably sought a hanging verdict, that they hoped only for justice.

Near him, Judah Steiner raised his head to gaze on Dr. McNarry, with precisely the expression of a parent facing a physician: Tell me, doctor, what is wrong with my boy? And a few rows behind, I saw Myra, her brows knitted, a pupil desperately trying to understand.

In the crowd were faces we had all come to recognize; there was the avid, overpainted woman, the one with the strident voice who literally battled her way in daily, with a press card everyone knew to be false; and there were the well-dressed women who had important connections. By the windows, where he had a good view of Judd and Artie, sat one of Horn's psychiatrists, Dr. Tierney.

What could Dr. McNarry tell? Why had the state's attorney fought for two whole days to keep out his testimony?

Taken individually, I suppose everyone in the room

would have agreed there was no excuse for the crime. And yet, it was clear that what all hoped for was to hear an excuse, an explanation. This could only be, I suppose, a reflection of some guilt that is in all of us, a fear that in the deepest unknown of ourselves there exist capacities for doing what the boys had done. And from the psychiatrists, from the sages of our time, we hope for—what? Reassurance?

Edgar Feldscher began the direct questioning, with Horn nagging at every statement, trying to make the witness say "insanity," as in some kid game in which you go down if you slip and utter the forbidden word. Yet he was at the same time trying to make the doctor admit the boys were quite normal; this two-sided attack produced a heckling effect, so that the judge had to be constantly rebuking the prosecution.

McNarry began with Artie, detailing how he learned to lie to his strict governess, and how the habit of lying evolved until "he himself says that he found it difficult to distinguish between what was true and what was not true."

Horn broke in with another objection: "If he could not distinguish between true and not true, then he could not distinguish between right and wrong, truth being right and the other being wrong. I therefore submit that we are getting now clearly into an insanity hearing and I move that a jury be impaneled."

"Motion denied," said the judge.

McNarry came to the fantasy life, telling of Artie's childhood "picturizations."

Horn tried the other tack. "This condition you have described is sometimes called building castles in the air, is it not? Is that not quite common among boys?"

"Surely," the alienist agreed. "But air castles are generally considered to be something beautiful and desirable, while these——"

"Don't most boys have daydreams about dungeons and escapes?"

Judge Matthewson said stiffly, "Let the doctor proceed without interruption; cross-examine when he gets through."

Horn wheeled, arms extended, to the courtroom, to emphasize what he was faced with.

The doctor described the shadowing in the street, the jail fantasy, and how when Artie finally got into jail he "felt as if he belonged there and was living out in reality what he used to picture to himself as a child." He told how Artie accepted the jail lice, the torn coat. He told of the curious "continuance into his present life of a practice he had as an infant, confiding in his teddy bear, 'And now, Teddy . . .'" He summarized: "Whereas fantasy life is compensatory, it also foreshadows our real conduct. We do not accomplish much of anything in the world that we have not previously dreamed of accomplishing. He thinks of himself in prison, of girls looking at him through the bars, as a master criminal. The significance is on the emotional side because it is in the emotions that the fantasy life has its roots." Artie was remaining, then, emotionally a child, a bad child seeking punishment.

His fantasy life not only lacked contact with reality in its original occurrence, but tended "in its rather bizarre and grotesque form to break through from the dream world into actual realization in real life."

To show how fantasy imposed itself and could even obliterate reality, the psychiatrist reminded us that despite Artie's general popularity everywhere, Artie had an idea of himself as unwanted and inferior. He had often thought of suicide; he had complained that no one in his family cared for him. Right now he felt he had had all there was to have from life; if he were to be executed, he would feel that he had not missed anything. This, the doctor pointed out, was another sign of Artie's disintegration, as was his complaint that in the last few years he had felt that he "wasn't all there."

The courtroom was a schoolroom, the crime itself for the moment displaced, in that we all felt something new was breaking through to us, about how we lived. Artie sat erect; he might have been listening to a discussion about some other person.

"In other words, he has grown to eighteen years of age, but he has carried his infancy with him in the shape of an undeveloped emotional attitude toward life."

Be your age, we had told Artie at the frat.

"In a well-rounded, well-integrated, well-knit personality, emotion and intelligence go hand in hand. People know, and feel about what they know, at the same level of development. Here they know, and feel about what they know, on two levels, and the two levels tend to become further and further separated until we see the marked mental disease, the malignant disease which ultimately lands patients in many of our institutions. We see a complete derangement, a complete personality split where there is no longer the possibility of bringing the two aspects of the personality into sufficient harmonious union. Artie is in a stage which is capable, if it goes further, of developing that malignant splitting."

Something of what the defense desired had now been created, for we all gazed at Artie now as at a patient in a medical clinic.

Dr. McNarry had described the progress of the disease. Would he discuss the other crimes, *A, B, C, D,* as further evidence of Artie's disintegration?

He seemed to have them in mind as he leaned forward, the light striking the veins on his huge round skull. "Now Artie's tendency was criminalistic." But he listed only the minor crimes, already well known. "To fulfill his mastermind fantasy, Artie needed a gang, and Judd was his gang. Now Judd had no fundamental criminalistic tendency."

This statement in itself startled the courtroom. There was a resentful murmur among the women.

Judd's tendencies, the doctor said, could be expressed as a constant swing between feelings of superiority and feelings of inferiority. He needed a complement, a balance, and had attached Artie as his other ego, sometimes superior, sometimes inferior, as when the king was rescued by the slave.

"Thus, in this fantasy, in either position he occupies, as king or as slave, he gets the expression of both components of his make-up, his desire for subjection on the one part and the desire for supremacy on the other, so that with their effective and emotional relationship to each other, each entire life plays into the other with almost devilish ingenuity, if I may be permitted to use the term.

"Now, in my opinion, no understanding of the Kessler homicide can be reached by a consideration of either one of these boys alone, just as we could not understand the development of any social institution solely by the study of any individual—we would have to understand how man in his social interrelations functions, in order to understand the growth of such an institution. So we can only understand this homicide by understanding the back-and-forth play of these two personalities as they were related to each other.

"It is shown in several of their joint experiences that whenever Artie tended to fall down in his role of leader, Judd always stepped into the breach and picked up the direction of the situation. In the Kessler case, it was Judd who insisted on sending the last telephone message and taking the last chance to bring the whole thing to a successful culmination, after Artie was convinced that they were fighting a losing cause and that there was no sense in subjecting themselves to any further danger. He comes in and takes the reins whenever the other boy falls down."

While Artie was a disintegrating, a decomposing, personality, saying he had had all he wanted out of life, the alienist showed us Judd as incessantly active, cataloguing churches as a child, then investigating ornithology, analyzing languages, and even now in jail projecting a book he would write to explain himself, a speech he would make from the scaffold if he were to hang. Indeed he was even planning a set of questions that he would answer from afterlife, should there prove to be any, though he did not believe any existed.

"So these two boys," Dr. McNarry concluded, in his even tone, "with their peculiar inter-digitating and complementing personalities"— he laced together the fingers of his two hands—"came into this emotional compact, with the Kessler homicide as the result." It could be described, he said, as a *folie à deux,* rare enough, since it could not result unless the precise two personalities, by perhaps one chance in millions, came together.

The doctor emphasized this, probably as reassurance to the public, to the world; but even at the time I had a doubting thought: Wouldn't the needed personalities somehow attract each other, to come together? And since then, of course, we have seen many other crimes out of such conjoinings.

Indeed, the full meaning of Dr. McNarry's diagnosis came home to me only lately at a demonstration of another such case. The demonstration, called by the same name, *Folie à Deux,* had unobtrusively been filmed. A woman and her daughter were seen, the daughter excitably telling a doctor about persecutions, of being watched, betrayed—a young woman obviously mentally ill. And the mother, rational and quiet, would suddenly chorus the daughter's accusations and suspicions—"Yes, yes, it was so, all this was true"— as though she had caught an infection of the deranged thoughts themselves. And then I realized. Had we not seen massive demonstrations in our time of entire populations so infected with some mad leader's delusions?

*   *   *

The testimony of Dr. McNarry ended with Edgar Feldscher's formal questions: "As a result of your examination and observation of the defendant Arthur Straus, have you an opinion as to his mental condition on the twenty-first day of May, 1924?"

"Yes, sir."

"What is that opinion?"

"Well, I have practically expressed it. He was the host of antisocial tendencies along the lines that I have described. He was going in the direction of a split personality, because of this inner unresolved conflict. . . . He is still a child emotionally, still talking to a teddy bear—somewhere around four or five years old. Intellectually, he passes his tests very well."

As to Judd, he, too, was "the host of a relatively infantile aspect of his personality, but he has reacted to a defense mechanism, which has produced the final picture of a markedly disordered personality make-up in the direction of developing feelings of superiority which place him very largely out of contact with an adequate appreciation of his relation to others or to society."

*   *   *

We had almost forgotten that it was a trial, a contest, until Horn came forward for the cross-examination. He began in a subdued way, as though to continue the mood of the scholarly, authoritative analysis. Getting the doctor to repeat his diagnosis, Horn strove to make him say "insanity," but smiling a small smile, the alienist declared, "Insanity is something you gentlemen know about. I don't. It is purely a legal and sociological term. It is not a medical term at all. I am a doctor, not a lawyer."

"You'd make a pretty good lawyer," Horn retorted, capturing the laughter. "But, doctor, did you say you never use the term *insanity?*"

The trap failed. "Yes, I've used it. I even used it in the title of a book, *Insanity and Crime.* As it is a book about mental disease in relation to the criminal law, I used the word in its legal sense, but I do not use it medically."

Horn did not let go easily. "Now, doctor, it is part of the defense, the desire of their lawyers, that these boys should be mentally sick and not called insane. Does that cause you to back away from a definition of insanity?"

Dr. McNarry looked properly outraged. Both Feldschers rose to object and were sustained.

Scowling, the state's attorney resorted to questioning the doctor in his own terms. "Now which is responsible for the murder, in this case, the intellectual man or the emotional man?"

"Well, you can't exactly divide man up that way. We could say that the actions originated in the drive of his instincts, and in this case were not checked as they would be in a man of normal emotional development."

Could a man with only the emotional development of a five-year-old show such consideration for others that when he got into a predicament he would ask the authorities not to divulge the name of a certain girl with whom he had been friendly? Wasn't that fairly highly developed emotion?

"If you mean the defendants," McNarry said, "Steiner was more definite. He showed the remnants of emotional feeling."

Hadn't Artie also shown feelings when he hesitated to pick a grandson of Nathan Weiss as a victim, because his father was a business partner of Weiss?

"That only shows the kind of consideration, perhaps affection and perhaps fear for his father, that a child too might have."

If Artie Straus was emotionally a child, how could he appear rational to his friends?

"That is characteristic of such persons. In Artie's case there is a warm, lovable outward nature. It required examination to bring up the boy's blind side."

Horn turned to Artie's "criminalistic tendencies," and Judd's lack of them. Did the doctor, for example, know who struck the fatal blows on Paulie Kessler's skull?

There was a moment of hesitation as Dr. McNarry glanced toward the defense table. The judge, too, seemed to be waiting for an objection. Wilk arose.

It would make no difference in the conduct of the defense if this point could be clarified, he said. The boys, by their own desire and that of their families, were being tried jointly, as they were inextricably bound in their act.

Horn repeated his question. "Do you know who struck the fatal blows?"

"Yes," said Dr. McNarry. He spoke as though the detail were of little significance. "It was Artie."

A woman's shriek sounded over the courtroom hubbub. In the press box, several of us stood up, to rush to the telephones. I noticed Myra, sudden tears on her face. Up to that moment she must still have been clinging to the idea of Judd as the devil.

Horn was asking how the doctor knew it was Artie.

"During one of our talks, there came a point where it was quite clear to me. I asked, 'It was you who struck the blows, wasn't it?' and Artie nodded; he said, 'You knew it.'"

As I pushed into the crowd at the door, I had a glimpse over my shoulder of Judd, staring at Artie with almost a reproving look. Artie looked sullen.

Then I realized that I must have known this fact for some time. I must have known it through Ruth. She had felt it, from the beginning. And since it was Artie who was criminalistic, Artie who had struck the blows, could one not say that Judd shrank to the level of an accomplice? Judd had, in a sense, been drafted, drafted by his compelling love for Artie, his king. Artie was demon-sick, and Judd, sick with a sick love. Was there less guilt in one than in the other?

The sensation had come late in the afternoon; court adjourned before I finished my call. The corridors were flooded with excited women; there seemed, indeed, to be a particularly sharp scent rising in the warm corridors from their inordinate agitation. Gabbing, denying, their eyes overbright—"I swear the whole thing is a lie. You know Artie—he loves to fib!" Surely he had fibbed to protect Judd, fibbed merely to put one over on that fancy alienist who thought he was so smart.

In that moment, I saw Myra, slipping between the clots of women, trying to escape, escape with her unhappy knowledge. I called her name. She clutched my arm, in that way she had. "Oh, Sid."

We went down in the elevator together, not talking, not wanting strangers to hear. Her fingers dug deeper into my arm.

"Sid," she gasped as we emerged, "they're putting me on the stand tomorrow."

How could that be? What of all the other psychiatrists?

"I don't know, I don't know. The lawyers just told me. Sid, I'm scared of that awful man."

I reassured her. Horn was nobody to be afraid of; it was nothing to be on the stand. She had Wilk to protect her.

* * *

I waited in the park. Myra wanted me to walk her to Wilk's apartment. The heat had not lifted, and the park was teeming. There were fleshy older people sitting on the benches, the women bulging out of their cotton dresses, the men with their ties pulled open, and on the grass were couples with kids, and just couples. Some had spread newspapers on the ground and were sitting on headlines of the trial.

All at once Myra was there with me, wispy in the twilight, her thin arms and her body taut. We stood there a moment, listening to a middle-aged woman talking to her husband. "I thought all the time it was the dark one did it, that Judd Steiner, but if it was that boy Artie, I don't understand how he could hit a kid—he looks so nice, such a nice boy. If it was him, he must be insane."

"It's the way they were brought up," the husband said. "Kids nowadays, they have everything too easy."

"I don't understand. He must be insane."

We started walking. "Perhaps we're all like that," Myra said in her low breathy voice, "the generation that refused to grow up. We're all babies emotionally."

And as we walked: "Oh, Sid, should I say he was crazy, that he always acted crazy?" When Dr. McNarry had been describing Artie on the stand, Myra said, she had suddenly seen it so clearly, she had remembered so many scenes all tumbling together, remembered a New Year's party, Artie dressing up in diapers, but that wasn't anything, was it? At every party someone did that. Or putting on a girl's hat. But the time he put on dark glasses and sat on the curb at Cottage Grove and 63rd, pretending to be a blind beggar, that was infantile—she had always said he was infantile, even to her mother, but she had thought it was just because she was a year older than Artie that she felt that way. "Oh, Sid, we think we understand so much, and we don't see anything, even in those we love. . . . Oh, the poor kid, if they do save his life, if he's sent to an asylum, and some day becomes cured, will they ever let him out?"

And, leaning against me, she expressed her terror again. What was it like on the stand? That Sunday, when Horn's men had come to see her, she hardly remembered what she had said. Could they hold her to what she had said?

As we entered Wilk's apartment, Myra was taken over at once by Geiger and Ferdinand Feldscher, who disappeared with her into a side room. There were conferences everywhere. Wilk seemed to be taking part in all of them at once, and I marveled at his energy; after the full, tense days in court, he had been going on like this, deep into every night.

In a corner of Wilk's library, several of our fraternity brothers were being prepared to go on the stand; there were even a few from Ann Arbor. In the dining room, there were members of Judd's birding class, and a few campus intellectuals with whom he had argued philosophy.

I began to understand this sudden break in strategy. Dr. McNarry's testimony had proved almost too strong; to follow him directly with other psychiatrists was to risk playing into Horn's hands, to cause the case to go to a jury. Instead, there would be an interlude, with character witnesses, friends, girls, who would restore the image of Judd and Artie as college boys, active, bright, even attractive to perfectly normal young girls. Boys who might be seen as emotionally disturbed, but not yet insane.

So Myra would go on the stand. And would Ruth follow, for Judd? Were these girls compelled in their own hearts to make a kind of wedding of it, by publicly showing that they had loved the murderers?

I kept watching the door, fearing every moment that Ruth might walk in. The tension in the apartment seemed to be mounting, surcharged with that dreadful atmosphere I was to know years later, walking into some command post at the front during some battle already engaged, with the factors unknown, and the commanders doubting exactly how much to risk, how far to try.

A hall door opened, and I could hear an entire segment of argument about whether to call the girls at all and expose them to cross-examination. Horn would stop at nothing; he would surely confront even the girls with the homosexual thing.

Suddenly a question stood clear in my mind. If Artie was the actual murderer, and Judd was involved only because of his homosexual love, what would Judd be if released from that love? Hadn't some such release been taking place, through Ruth? Hadn't he shown himself on the way to normal emotions?

As if my thoughts had summoned him, Willie Weiss stopped at my side, while darting from one group to another. And with his uncanny penetration, he asked, "Worried about your girl going on the stand?"

It didn't strike me then that with his ironic smile he could have meant Myra, since I had brought her. I needed help in the question that troubled my mind, and in some stumbling way I made it clear to him, telling him all I knew about Judd and Ruth. He perched on the edge of a telephone table, immensely intrigued.

"You mean you think Judd was about to come out of it?" he asked.

"That's what I want to know," I said. "How much could it mean?" Willie cocked his head. Interesting! He hadn't hitherto taken the thing so seriously—this business between Judd and Ruth. And just then, as Dr. McNarry passed through the hall, Willie caught his arm. "This is quite interesting," he told the alienist. And looking around: "Let's go where we can talk."

We tried the dining room, but it was in use. Mrs. Wilk, sighing, offered us the maid's room behind the kitchen, laughingly remarking that there was a conference going on even in the bathroom.

So we sat on the cot in the tiny room. There was an unshaded overhead bulb, and I felt Dr. McNarry studying me. Would he be finding out more about me than about those I talked of?

Wasn't I the reporter, he inquired, who was so much involved in the case? Unfortunately he hadn't been present during my testimony.

"I'm perhaps even more involved," I said, and told about my friend, Ruth Goldenberg.

"Your girl?"

"Well, not exactly. Not any more, I'm afraid."

"Judd's?" He identified her then as the girl Judd had not wanted to name during all the examinations, the girl Judd claimed he really felt serious about. Yes, Judd had even talked about leaving home and marrying this girl. But—McNarry touched his fingers together—it had all seemed rather a fantasy.

Willie stated the problem that was troubling me. "Sid has been wondering if this sudden attachment to a girl could be a sign that Judd was overcoming his pathology? I think it's an interesting question."

Dr. McNarry studied his fingertips. "Of course it happens. Homosexuals can behave simultaneously as heterosexuals—that seems to have been true in both these boys—but they can also go over, as we sometimes see, to normal relationships. In fact, in late adolescence that's a common pattern, isn't it? Boys who in their teens begin with a crush on older boys. That's a rather universal experience, adulation or a crush, except that it doesn't always reach the stage of an active sexual bond. But even in such cases, coming through puberty, the male attachment may weaken and a heterosexual bond take place." He gazed at me. "Judd's nineteen."

"Doctor," Willie broke in excitedly, "couldn't the crime itself—the murder—have acted as a kind of catharsis, freeing Judd from his homosexual bond?"

An appreciative smile came over the alienist's face. "But then the bond has apparently reasserted itself," Dr. McNarry said.

"Because now, in jail, he has no alternative," Willie argued. "But in the week after the crime, in fact virtually the day after, for the first time in his life he had what seems to be a true emotional reaction to a girl."

Dr. McNarry asked, "The young lady was affected by him?"

"Yes," I said, hurt by Willie's having to hear it. "I believe she intends to testify."

He looked at his hands again.

One more question pressed itself forward in me. That time with Ruth on the beach—wasn't it somehow a proof that Judd, by himself, could master his impulses? The doctor stared at me. I finally had to ask: Would it help if something like that were brought out in court?

Instantly, under his gaze, I had an intense feeling of shame at my own thought of Ruth on the stand questioned about physical intimacy.

"This is the girl Judd brought to his brother's engagement party," Willie remarked. Dr. McNarry nodded, as though he had known.

Then he sighed, not as a doctor but as one of us. "The poor wretch." He shook his head. "All in the wrong time. The poor wretch."

*   *   *

It was just as Myra was taking the stand that I saw Ruth enter the courtroom. All attention was so completely fixed on Myra that only my own sensitivity for Ruth must have made me turn my head. A bailiff was squeezing back the crowd, for with news that girls would take the stand, the mob had doubled.

Willie pulled Ruth into the room and led her to the front bench, filled with witnesses. The fellows moved together to make room for her. Ruth saw me watching her then and gave me her serious smile. She was not pale.

I felt her somehow changed, and an anguish came over me; I wiped sweat from my face, so I could furtively dry my eyes. Would Ruth say Judd had asked her to marry him? Would that somehow forever close me away, as though my girl had really given herself to another man?

The questioning of Myra had begun.

She was dressed in white, like a nurse, in a straight white linen frock, with only a few huge buttons to show it wasn't a uniform. The heat had brought glints of perspiration to her upper lip. Myra tried to keep her eyes from Artie and Judd, yet did not want to look at the crowd. She kept them fixed on Ferdinand Feldscher, who was questioning her in a soft fatherly manner.

Yes, she had known Artie since childhood; yes, they were close friends, saw each other almost daily.

And would she characterize him as a stable character?

Highly unstable, she said. He was nervous, smoked nervously, throwing away his cigarettes after a few puffs. He talked nervously, jumping from one subject to another. She had often been worried about his—his nerves. He would be talking about something serious, a book, and in the middle of a sentence he would jump to something else, a baseball game, or how he had won at bridge.

She told how he was given to lying for no reason at all, making up stories the way kids did, like his bootlegger stories, and then, often, he behaved in an infantile way, so much so that it was embarrassing, and everyone had remarked on it.

"Can you think of an example?"

"Quite recently, I had a date with another young man, and Artie dropped in just before my date arrived. When the bell rang, he put on my sash, and ran to the door. . . ."

There was giggling at the story. Horn was grinning. Of

course, Myra said, such antics could be due to high spirits, but with Artie they often became disturbing. She and her mother had discussed the question many times, wondering if there was something wrong with him.

"Would you say that he was fully developed, mature?"

"Oh, no, decidedly not. He was very childish. We hoped he would grow out of it."

"Childish? In his emotions?"

"Yes. Very much so."

The lawyer made the point over and over. Then there was a pause, while it seemed Feldscher hesitated to leave her to the cross-examiners. But there was no help for it. He backed slowly away, and Horn approached Myra; he was still grinning, but his voice was bland, almost deferential.

She was a cousin of Artie's?

A distant cousin.

She had been his playmate as a child?

One of them.

But now that they were grown, she was something more than a playmate?

After a rain of objections, he rephrased the question. Was she engaged to Artie?

"No." The courtroom seemed to expand, with an effluvial feminine exhalation.

She was aware that he had other girls?

Yes, she knew Artie had lots of girls, but she believed that she was his closest friend.

"Lady friend," Horn corrected, and there was a snicker. Myra nervously balled her handkerchief.

"Would you call yourself his sweetheart?"

She flushed and couldn't answer.

"You kissed, I presume, at times?" he demanded, hard. Despite objections, the judge directed her to answer.

"Yes," she said, her resentment helping her to regain her composure.

"And would you call these kisses from a grown sweetheart childish emotional behavior?" Over the full laughter, Horn rubbed it in. "Were they childish or mature kisses?"

The judge rebuked him. Horn resumed his suave tone,

but unmistakably he was out to kill. "As his childhood play-mate and young lady friend, you would help Artie out if you could?"

"Certainly," she said, "but not——"

And had she not sent messages to jail, saying she would stick by him?

"No!" Myra cried over the objections.

"Being a lady, you wouldn't be lying now, to help Artie out?"

"I don't lie!"

But there was a knowing murmur from the courtroom. "Oh, wouldn't she!"

Both Feldschers had rushed to the bench; Wilk was standing.

"Haven't you been lying, right here on the stand?" Horn demanded.

"No, I've been telling the truth!" She stared at him defiantly, but her voice had a fearful quaver.

"You wouldn't lie to the state's attorney? Under oath?"

"I did not!"

He glanced at some papers in his hand. "You made a statement, did you not, to a representative of the state's attorney's office, the day after Artie Straus and Judd Steiner confessed to this crime?"

"I was asked some questions by one of your men. I was very upset at the time."

"Let me read to you from the statement. Question: 'Would you say that Artie is intelligent?' Answer: 'Exceptionally.' Question: 'Mature in his ideas?' Answer: 'Oh, very mature in his ideas.' Now, do you remember giving that answer?"

"I might have said it, I don't know. I didn't know what they meant by mature—he was always bright in school, in classes. I said a lot of other things they didn't put down—" She was twisting in confusion, her lips sucked in, her handkerchief to her mouth.

"Have you been instructed by the defense as to what to say here?"

"Objection!"

"Miss Seligman, in this signed and sworn statement, you declare this man to be mature. Here on the stand you testify—" He had the court stenographer read back her testimony. The voice, toneless as such voices seem to be by rule, read back, "Question: 'Would you say he was fully developed, mature?' Answer: 'Oh, no, decidedly not. He was very childish—' "

Horn cut in, his arm outflung, finger pointing at her. "When were you lying, ten minutes ago in this courtroom, or now?"

Myra's face squeezed, contorted. She wept, and a huge windy sound of satisfaction, somehow vengeful, somehow sympathetic, swelled up from the courtroom.

"But—but—" She struggled to speak.

"Excused," Horn snapped. Ferdinand Feldscher rushed to help her as she stumbled from the stand. She shrank against him, shaking, her hysteria increasing. After a few steps she sagged, collapsing on his arm. Wilk glared at Horn with utter loathing, red spots of fury on his cheeks.

With a frantic movement, Willie Weiss was across the enclosure, on the other side of Myra, awkwardly trying to take her weight from Feldscher.

Myra's mother pushed forward, and we all rushed from our jury-box press seats as Myra was carried into the judge's chambers. But the door was closed against us. Peg Sweet kept raging against Horn, "Brute, brute! How brutal does a man have to be?" She seemed herself on the verge of hysteria; Richard Lyman solicitously quieted her.

Presently, Feldscher came out to us. Dr. Allwin had given Myra a sedative, he announced, and she was being taken home.

When I resumed my place in the press box, I saw that Ruth was no longer in the courtroom. "No more girl witnesses for the defense," Tom told me, as he left for the office to write the story. "Wilk canceled them all."

I caught Judd's eye. He looked at me steadily and I told myself that he, too, felt relieved.

And could it have helped him? Even if Ruth had been

able to make everything known—everything, even the inner, uncompleted feelings—could that have helped?

*   *   *

The hearing resumed, on a minor note. A doctor from Charlevoix testified to Artie's brain concussion, incurred in that wild automobile crash when he had been fifteen. Artie had remained unconscious for several hours.

Then came a fraternity brother from Ann Arbor, to testify that Artie had fainted at his initiation and again at a New Year's party. He had even frothed at the mouth.

Padua stepped in, asking whether the witness had ever noticed how champagne froths? And Horn shouted out, over the laughter, "They're trying to build up a phony picture of epilepsy here when anybody can see it's a plain case of a soused young punk passing out."

The whole line of questioning was abandoned. Horn strutted. The defense seemed to be reeling.

In quick succession, several of the campus intellectuals took the stand to testify about Judd's reputation for having exaggerated ideas. Jerry Fuld, an owlish Phi Beta Kappa who oddly enough was later to become a notorious Communist writer, testified that Judd believed "the end justifies the means," and that gratification of personal desires was the end to which man should aspire.

Judd had a critical, argumentative look on his face; he whispered to Wilk, who shook his head.

Then, to our surprise, the defense used Milt Lewis, despite his having produced the fatal typing notes. Milt told about the day in law class when Judd had started an argument, insisting that a superman was above the law.

"Can you fix the date?" Ferdinand Feldscher asked.

"Well, I know it was in between the crime and the apprehension, because when he confessed to the crime, we all remembered that classroom discussion."

"At the time of the discussion, did you think it was strange?"

"It was just one of his nutty ideas. He was always suggesting pretty wild ideas."

"Nutty, did you say? Meaning irresponsible?"

"Well, exaggerated. Things you couldn't take seriously."

"But you knew Judd took them seriously?"

"Yes, he seemed to take them very seriously."

"Can you recall some other such—nutty ideas?"

"He discussed nihilism with me," Milt said. "He also said he was a nihilist—"

"A nihilist, what is that?"

"A kind of anarchist who wants to destroy things."

"Even worse than an anarchist, then? Destructive?"

"Yes. He felt no restraint as far as authority was concerned, and he said he believed in destruction merely for the sake of destruction. I remember one argument when he said there was no value to life in itself; he said he wouldn't walk across the room to save my life if such a situation came up."

"Was this a part of his Nietzschean philosophy?"

Judd was whispering excitedly now; Wilk seemed to be trying to calm him.

"No, I wouldn't say it was exactly in line with Nietzsche, but some of it was pretty close."

"Would you accept the Nietzschean philosophy?"

"No," Milt said, "because the founder of that philosophy was insane a good part of his life. Nietzsche himself died in an insane asylum."

"But Judd accepted it?"

"Hook, line, and sinker," Milt said.

"So that one might feel he was not mature in his judgments?"

"Well, we thought he would get over it."

Horn's cross-examination was simple. Hadn't all the students been exposed to Nietzsche?

"The Nietzschean theory is just one small phase of the entire field of philosophy," Milt said ponderously. "It is not regarded very seriously by the professors of philosophy at the University of Chicago."

"All of you didn't take it as a license to go out and murder?" The question was withdrawn after defense objection.

Milt left the stand with the virtuous air of a man who had been fair and square to both sides.

The trial seemed to have reached a dead spot. The efforts

to create sympathy through girls, through classmates and friends, had failed. The case would have to be determined by the battle of alienists.

And a grave problem confronted the defense. It concerned the stolen Storrs-Allwin report. If neither Storrs nor Allwin were called, could the damaging items from the report be kept out of the courtroom? Crimes *A, B, C, D?* Wouldn't Horn himself produce the report?

In the morning the defense called Dr. Allwin. Edgar Feldscher led the cool, pink-domed expert through the summaries of tests, X-rays, fantasies. Not once did Horn interrupt with calls for a jury. Even when the defense produced the snapshot of four-year-old Artie in his cowboy suit, aiming his pistol at his teddy bear, Horn let it go into the record, only chortling aloud as Dr. Allwin explained the significance of Artie's "intent expression," an indication that, even at that early age, fantasy and reality were confused in the boy. Horn waited for his chance to cross-examine.

Then, holding the Storrs-Allwin report in his hand like a Bible, the prosecutor attacked. All this new method of analyzing the "chemistry of the character" was accurate, was it?

It was not nearly so exact a science as chemistry, as yet, said Dr. Allwin, but many psychological tests were backed by extensive statistical proofs, exceeding the requirements of probability.

"Couldn't the boys have cheated on some of these tests, since they are so smart, such good liars, as your report observes?"

"No," said Dr. Allwin.

"And why not?"

"Because I am smarter than they are," he said softly.

"Emotionally or intellectually?" Horn demanded with a smirk.

"Both." Because of the very abundance of the material he had received from them, consistent lying would have been most difficult, he explained. Judd, he felt, had been on the whole fairly truthful, decidedly more so than Artie. But Artie's persistent lying was part of his mental condition. He had lost the normal person's ability to distinguish between truth and fantasy.

"What is a normal person? In fact there isn't any such thing as a normal person, is there?"

"Oh, I think so."

"Well, what constitutes normality?"

"A proper balance between the intellect and emotion."

"And these boys are abnormal?"

"Yes, but in different ways."

Horn snorted. In what he understood by abnormality, they were the same, he said. In fact, to the State they were plain perverts. Wasn't that fact right there in his own report? Didn't their compact provide that Artie should consent to certain acts, in exchange for Judd's help in his criminal adventures? What were those acts?

The doctor glanced hesitantly at Judge Matthewson. The entire courtroom was leaning forward. "They were sexual acts," Dr. Allwin said.

"How often?" Horn demanded.

The real dirt was coming now. Several women pressed their way down the aisles, to get closer. Angrily, the judge ordered, "I want every woman to leave this room!"

A few left. Others began hesitantly to move toward the door, lingering there.

"Out, out! You ought to be ashamed of yourselves!"

Finally, the courtroom was partly cleared. Motioning the attorneys to come in close, the judge had the testimony continued. In a voice refined and regretful, Dr. Allwin described the acts, calling Judd the aggressor. But this was the only such relationship, apparently, that Judd had ever developed. On Artie's part, the incidents had been passive. They had occurred a few times a month.

Judd's eyes were cast down. His father's head was bent low, the eyes closed.

There lay the sickness, finally frankly exposed before us. Was it so dreadful a thing? In all the history of human behavior, of the sick and ugly and distorted and careless and sportive and mistaken things that humans did, was this so much more?

But there was something more connected with the sexual act, Horn insisted, when the open trial resumed. Wasn't it a part of the compact, that each act was linked to a crime? What, then, were the other crimes?

No, no! Ferdinand Feldscher protested. There was not even any evidence that the sex compact had been carried out, in this crime.

Forcefully, Horn read from the Storrs-Allwin report the section that had stopped us all, the section about crimes withheld. Of Artie, it said, "Without any indication, facial or otherwise, he would lie or repress certain instances." He turned savagely on the alienist. "So obviously there were gaps in Artie's story of his crimes?"

"Yes. I said that."

"What are those gaps?"

"I don't know."

"These are things that he has not told you up to this date?"

"Yes."

"And he might have been advised not to tell you these things?"

"He might have been."

As a wrestler who has at last managed to lure his opponent into his locked scissors-hold, and now may squeeze and squeeze, Horn read on: " 'His older brother does not know of these untold stories, but the patient says he will not tell him unless the family advises him to.' You wrote this?"

"Yes, that is just what I wrote."

"And that is true?"

"Yes."

"So just how important these matters are that he has been advised not to tell you, you don't know?"

"No, I don't know."

"And you don't know what effect they would have on your conclusions if you did know them?"

"I don't know," Allwin replied, unruffled, with the equanimity of a man of fine breeding and a scientist who considers his methods inviolate.

With heavy emphasis, Horn read, " 'On the other hand

there is a certain legal advantage in minimizing the broadcasting of these episodes.' When you use the term 'certain legal advantage,' you are thinking of the defense, are you not?"

The alienist acknowledged that he was.

"In other words, it is to the advantage of the defendants to have withheld certain information from you so that the conclusions you have arrived at won't be disturbed, is that true?"

"I was interested in the one crime, the Kessler crime," the doctor said.

"And don't you further state about these other crimes that Artie is 'even keeping them secret from his attorney, examiners, and relatives. Consequently no great effort should be made to bring forth details which he willfully repressed'?"

"That is my opinion." However, the doctor insisted, the essential facts about this particular case had been brought out.

And all the other psychiatrists, Horn pressed, had used this basic report in coming to their conclusions?

"Yes. They told me so."

Horn read on, arriving at the crucial mystery. " 'Though Artie denied the so-called "gland robbery" and the "ragged stranger" murder, he referred to four other episodes where the letters A, B, C, D were suggested.' That could not be very illuminating to the other doctors, to read about the letters A, B, C, D, could it?"

"Not very illuminating," the doctor admitted.

Horn read, " 'It was found forensically inadvisable to question him about these.' By 'forensically' you mean legally, don't you?"

Finally Allwin hedged. "Just a pressure of time. We were concentrating on this case and to get our report in before the doctors came from the East."

Horn shook his head. "What does 'forensic' mean?"

"From the forum."

"It means legal?"

"Yes, legal, or pulpit."

"So this might have said, 'It was found legally inadvisable to question him about these'?"

"Yes, we had so much to get out in relation to this trial that we did not go into anything else."

"Oh, no, you didn't say you didn't have time. Just get this, 'It was found forensically—' "

"Yes, that was the reason," the doctor persisted. "That is the forensic reason."

There was laughter.

Horn kept after him. "Yes, but legally it was found inadvisable—now what do you mean by that? That it would not help his case if you went into these other episodes?"

"No—to get the report through by the twenty-first if we could possibly do it."

"Why didn't you say that? That you didn't have time?"

"That is the way I felt about it," the doctor snapped.

Horn chopped the air for the kill. "You thought it would sound nicer to say it was found legally inadvisable to question him about these other crimes?"

"Episodes!" Ferdinand Feldscher broke in, to help the wilting alienist.

"Let him answer," the judge said.

"Oh, approximately."

"And you thought the court and the rest of us would understand by that sentence that you did not have time to go into these other matters?"

The sarcasm was the final jolt to the doctor. "Absolutely not," he said, testily, "and for this reason. This report was not prepared for you, it was prepared for other physicians who were coming on from the East. I had no idea this report would be submitted to the public or to you. It is a medical report."

Horn breathed a loud "Aha!" Gazing at the defense table, he remarked, "So we weren't supposed to know even this much." Then, quickly turning the pages of the report, he said, "But there is someone who knows. There is one person who knows a good deal. In your report, Artie Straus is speaking here of his associate, Judd Steiner. He says, 'I have always been afraid of him, he knew too much about me.' And you, Dr. Allwin, wrote here, 'He was somewhat afraid his associate might betray him. He had thought of pointing a revolver at his associate and shooting him.' You say Artie Straus said,

'The idea of murdering a fellow—especially alone—I don't think I could have done it. But if I could have snapped my fingers and made him pass away of a heart attack, I would have done it.' "

The boys were looking at each other with pale, self-conscious grins. Horn went on. " 'He wanted to kill his associate, because he knew too much!' What did he know?" He stared at Judd, then at Artie. If only he could have dragged them onto the stand! It was utterly clear now that the defense would never risk putting the boys in the witness chair, where they could be subject to cross-examination.

Judd stared back at Horn. It was a bold look, a look that contained inner pride. He had not betrayed, he had kept the code. Even on their worst day, the day after the confessions, when each had accused the other of the actual killing, he had not betrayed whatever it was that he knew.

That strange, brooding, perversely obstinate look of Judd's remained with me as one of the fixed moments of the trial. Could it not have occurred to Judd that if a succession of crimes proved Artie demented, their fates might have been separated? Artie's to an asylum, and his own, perhaps, for less than life in jail.

Had Judd actually taken part in the other crimes? Or had he only known of them? Artie's words in the report suggested that he had always used an accomplice. But Artie was the less believable of the two. The psychiatrists had been careful to say that Judd showed no criminalistic tendencies, careful to place the question of the four unknown crimes only in the section of the report that dealt with Artie. And Artie himself had become most excited when talking about Judd's "knowing too much," as one talks of someone who is not himself involved.

Horn blunted himself against the stone wall of the unknown, but the episodes were to remain forever a mystery, and in them, it has always seemed to me, lay the mystery of Artie, of his true mental state.

When Dr. Allwin stepped down from the stand, it was as though, for Judd, the most dangerous moment of the trial had passed. His eyes turned again to Artie, and there was a subtle smile between them, an instant of their old, intimate sharing.

As they arose to move out for a recess, they were close together, touching.

*   *   *

Those were Horn's days, and the defense seemed to recover only slight ground with a Sing Sing alienist who had specialized in juvenile delinquency. Dr. Holliday pointed out that Judd's mania for collecting things, his mania for perfection, fitted in with the "compulsive behavior" of manic patients, and that his thinking was "autistic," a new word to us then. As I understood the explanation he made, it is the belief that things really are the way we imagine they are—a kind of self-contained magical thinking, without reference to the outside realities. Both boys had this characteristic to some extent, Holliday said, for it was a splitting off from reality. The general road for both led to dementia praecox, or to use the newer term, schizophrenia. But within dementia praecox, the manic path was characterized by a blowing-up, a great exaggeration. And this was shown in Steiner's extreme mental activity, the incessant interest in giving an exposition of his ideas and of his various notions of himself. This was a blown-up, manic, or paranoid personality.

Edgar Feldscher asked him then, "Do people suffering from a paranoid personality have the ability to plan, to scheme, as in the preparation of a kidnaping or murder?"

"Yes, some paranoids exhibit the most extraordinary capacity for planning." He showed how Judd's planning even manifested itself in anticipation of his execution. He would make a great speech from the platform. He would convey his philosophy to the world; he would be "consistent" to the end.

And Artie, in contrast, was indifferent, passive. Hanging seemed hardly a real possibility to him, but something that might happen to someone else. He had said, "Well, it's too bad a fellow won't be able to read about it in the newspapers." And if he got a prison sentence, and at some time came out, Artie wanted to know if at that time he could get a complete file of the newspapers of this period. "I have examined a lot of hardened criminals in my lifetime, but——"

Horn interrupted, objecting, and Feldscher helped the doctor, by reformulation: "Did your experience in your work at Sing Sing in examining over two thousand prisoners aid you in forming any conclusions in reference to Artie Straus in his emotional responses or lack of them?"

"Yes, as I say, I have examined a number of men awaiting execution and never before have I seen just such a situation. The hardened criminal shows in every response a kind of crudity. Straus is affable, polite, and shows a habitual kind of refinement; yet he seems to be incapable of responding to this situation with an adequate emotional response. His actions can only become comprehensible when one keeps in mind that one is dealing here with a disintegrated or not completely integrated personality, a split personality, if we will."

"Or to use another term," Horn interjected rather feebly this time, "he is insane?"

The studious Holliday was followed by a gland specialist, Dr. Vincenti, an extreme enthusiast of the new science. Younger than the others, he had a quick, wide-eyed air about him, as though the whole thing were altogether too self-evident—why, the involuntary glands were the spark plugs, or better, a kind of carburetion system, turning mental energy into physical energy. Yes, he was a psychiatrist and neurologist, too—one had to study all those special branches if one were interested in the link between the body and mind. And after all, wasn't that the main thing we were interested in, the greatest field for human study? He said this with an air of happiness at the self-evident.

With the same enthusiastic air, Dr. Vincenti produced his X-ray pictures of Judd's *cella turcica,* the cradle of bone holding the pineal gland. There! Anyone could see it was already calcified! Calcified at nineteen! A *very* early age for calcification. It should still be flexible bone, growing, enabling the gland to grow. All of Judd's disorders might have resulted from this early calcification. His illnesses, his sexual maladjustment, everything!

As for Artie, his low basal metabolism was an indication of poor functioning of the endocrine glands and accounted for his periods of morbid depression, his suicidal tendencies, and his lack of sexual development.

On this medical note, the defense testimony ended. It was

a weak ending. Vincenti, with his overenthusiasm, was easy game. Disingenuously, Horn asked: The doctor was positive, was he, of his interpretation of all of this newfangled science?

Vincenti beamed. Positive.

Horn nodded and let him leave the stand. The prosecution's first rebuttal witness was a gland specialist who promptly declared that nobody knew a thing about the ductless glands. Redheaded, truculent, forthright, Horn's expert set the courtroom to howling with laughter at the high-toned pretensions of the defense experts. His ridicule of the hapless Vincenti seemed to apply to them all. Never had an expert proved he knew so much as Dr. Leahy did by explaining how little he knew.

Had he specialized in the endocrine glands? Yes, for fifteen years and more. Come to any conclusions? Exactly none. "Except for certain isolated facts, the status of our knowledge of the endocrine glands might be compared to our knowledge of Central Africa before Stanley's day. There's been some daring guesswork, but it's all a no-man's-land."

Could glandular activity have an effect on emotional growth?

"Your guess is as good as mine or any other expert's."

Even under Edgar Feldscher's learned cross-examination, Dr. Leahy was impervious. "Do you know what an emotion is?" the defense lawyer asked.

"I know some emotions."

"What is your definition of an emotion?"

"Well, I think definitions are abominable. But I mean by emotion such things as anger, fear, hate, et cetera."

And had there been no measurement of glandular secretions in connection with emotions?

"We have some measurements and knowledge of glandular effects in connection with diabetes. I've done research in that for fifteen years. But as for the effects of the ductless glands on the nervous system, I know very little and I don't think anyone knows very much."

"Have you read anything on the subject?"

"Just about everything that's come out. That's why I know that very little is known."

So much, said Horn, for Judd's famous *cella turcica*. And he proceeded to produce his other counter-alienists.

We tallied them. Against Hugh Allwin, there was the elderly Arthur Ball, a home-town authority who could stand up against the biggest man from the East. He advanced toward the witness chair with the spry manner of an elderly professor who keeps his mind young.

Yes, he had been called in, that Sunday, to examine the young gentlemen. As he used the term, he eyed them with what could only be called a kindly curiosity. Dr. Ball had found the young gentlemen in Mr. Horn's office, engaged at the moment in eating their luncheons. He recalled that Mr. Steiner had been most polite, for upon going to the cooler for a glass of water, Mr. Steiner had turned and asked whether he, the professor, would also care for a drink.

Mr. Horn had then asked the young gentlemen to tell their story, and they had done so in detail. "The other young gentleman had done most of the talking, with occasional corrections from Mr. Straus—"

"Mr. Steiner, you mean?"

"Yes. Mr. Steiner." He smiled, to accent that the confusion was natural.

"Now, doctor, from any interview which you had with Straus or Steiner, do you know anything that might throw some light on the motive for this crime?"

"I remember Mr. Straus said, 'God, I don't know why.' " Once more he was straightened out. Wasn't it Mr. Steiner who had said that? The professor looked from one to the other, fixing them in his mind. Yes, that was Steiner's remark, the short one. The tall one, Mr. Straus, had said it was for the thrill, the experience, and the money. His friend at first had said, "God, I don't know why," and then had said he thought it was because Artie wanted it done.

"Did they speak of the ransom?"

"They were going to keep the money hidden in a safe-deposit box and none of it was to be spent within a year inside of Chicago, but one of them expected to go to Mexico." He looked at them carefully. "Mr. Straus, that was." He smiled at having got it correct. "And the other, Mr. Steiner, was going

to Europe, and they thought it would be safe to spend some of
the money in those places."

Had the boys been oriented?

Perfectly oriented, well co-ordinated, completely in possession of their senses, indeed remarkably alert.

Horn opened the Storrs-Allwin report. Now, if the professor was familiar with this report—?

But the professor was not. He had not even seen it,
though he understood it was a rather elaborate report by some
distinguished members of the defense staff, who were adher-
ents of the new psychology.

Would he care to examine it?

Indeed he would, as he was always curious about new
psychology.

Smilingly, the members of the defense counsel agreed to
an adjournment, since noon was close. When court resumed,
the professor said that he had thoroughly studied the report.
Horn opened his copy, and directed attention to page 67.
Judge Matthewson, too, opened his copy, and followed each
reference.

Horn read the remarks about Judd's inattention in class-
rooms. Was the professor familiar with this type of classroom
behavior?

Alas, yes. It was hardly significant.

Were there many students who drew pictures in their
notebooks, instead of taking down notes on the lectures?

Regrettably, they were numerous.

And would he interpret it as a sign of mental disease if a
student who was deeply interested in ornithology drew pictures of all kinds of birds in his notebook?

Quite natural.

And if a student printed his initials on various pictures,
was that a sign of mental disturbance?

No, it was most common for students, and other people,
when idly drawing, to print their initials or their names.

From the evidence in the report, would he conclude that
either of the defendants indulged in fantasies to an extreme
degree?

No, they seemed no more than the fantasies that a normal boy indulges in.

Judge Matthewson was leaning forward on both elbows. Professor Ball expatiated. "Everybody has fantasies. A lawyer has fantasies about winning a big case. A golfer has fantasies about playing a good golf game, and a young man of criminalistic tendencies, like the young gentleman here, Artie, quite naturally had criminalistic fantasies. Unless one wishes to take the crime itself as proving an abnormal mind, there is nothing abnormal in the fantasies as reported."

We all noted that the judge nodded, as though he had at last heard common sense spoken.

Horn went on. Had the professor observed any lack of emotion in the subjects?

Artie had shown intense emotional reaction. After his confession, he had collapsed more than once, and he had reacted in bitter anger against his accomplice. Both had exhibited emotion—even if negative—in calling each other "Mr. Steiner" and "Mr. Straus" when they were accustomed to call each other by their diminutives. And as Judd had stated that he had systematically suppressed any show of emotion since childhood, his lesser show of emotion was self-explanatory. Yet no one could deny intense emotion in his relationship to his companion, Mr. Straus.

Smiling, Horn asked whether the professor would agree with the statement that Judd was "pathologically suggestible."

"I saw no evidence that he was at all suggestible."

And Judd's sense of inferiority in reference to his puny stature—was it so marked that it could be called pathological?

Indeed, no! The young gentleman was not, after all, a dwarf.

Finally, taking into account not only his own examination but the Storrs-Allwin report, both young men had to be pronounced unquestionably sane.

* * *

Wilk approached, conversing casually, reminding Dr. Ball of the many pleasant discussions they had had, and declaring that the defense certainly would have tried to secure his services if Horn had not been so quick in taking him away. Not, of course, that Wilk thought he was a man who would testify with equal zeal for either side; Wilk knew he was a scientist of integrity who would state his facts accurately.

Now, for example, that examination lasting a few hours, in a crowded office—with all sorts of people, reporters, messengers, detectives running in and out—had that been a good opportunity for an examination?

In some aspects, yes, the doctor said. For example, a man had to be in excellent possession of his faculties to give a detailed and accurate recital in the midst of such distraction.

Granted. But was the situation well adapted to bringing out everything connected with the mental state of an individual?

Professor Ball smiled. "Let me frankly avow, Mr. Wilk, that I would not consider it a complete mental examination, if that is what you are driving at. You might call it the beginning of one." But as far as the requirements of the case were concerned, Dr. Ball was satisfied that his conclusions were accurate.

Undoubtedly, Wilk agreed, if one limited oneself to the legal definition of insanity. But would the doctor not admit that the legal definition was inadequate by medical standards?

Well, as to that, Dr. Ball said almost merrily, it was not the question here in the court, was it?

"I'm not sure that it isn't," Wilk remarked. "I'm not sure but what that is one of the purposes, if not the main purpose, of this entire hearing. However, in regard to emotion, in dealing with a patient who is in the habit of suppressing or concealing emotion, would not a prolonged examination be necessary to determine his reactions?"

Yes, the doctor agreed. And here in the Storrs-Allwin report was the evidence of a prolonged examination. Yet he could not agree with the conclusions.

Then could he, from his own brief examination, offer evidence to the contrary? Evidence of a normal emotional life?

Dr. Ball shook his head as though admiring Wilk's argument, while remaining unconvinced by it. "Our examination did not explore their entire lives," he conceded.

Willie Weiss had hurriedly slipped Wilk a folded-open publication, and Wilk quoted from an article by Dr. Ball in a medical journal, " 'The whole past life of the patient, his diseases and accidents, his schooling, environment, and character, and the entire history of his antecedents should be examined.' "

"Yes!" Dr. Ball readily agreed. "Yes, indeed. In a case for treatment. But this is not necessary, if one seeks only to determine their legal sanity."

Wilk smiled, and gave Horn the full benefit of his next remark. "We, too, consider them legally sane. We are here to ask for mitigation on the grounds of a medical condition of mental abnormality which probably could not be observed in a rapid examination, even by so fine an observer as yourself. Did you make any notes on that occasion, Dr. Ball?"

A few. Dr. Ball brought out a folded sheet of paper; he deciphered and read aloud a scrawled word, *"Zuganglich."*

"What does that mean?"

"It is a term used in psychiatry, for 'accessible.' It is used in connection with dementia praecox. We first determine whether the patient can be reached in normal communication, or whether, as it is popularly put, he is too far gone."

"And they were not too far gone?"

"Not at all. Completely *Zuganglich."* Edgar Feldscher smiled.

Wilk asked, "You have other notes?" Yes, but the rest of his notes he had to confess he couldn't make out. Dr. Ball chuckled, joining the general laughter. One could almost have suspected that he was willing enough to have his testimony fail to hurt the young gentlemen.

Then, coming to the fantasies, hadn't the doctor written somewhere, or expounded in his classes, that dreams and fantasies were the clues to the condition of the mind?

Why, yes, the professor agreed, with a new air of interest. Sometimes insanity first manifested itself in dreams, while the patient, during waking hours, appeared quite normal. As to fantasies, or waking dreams, they were closer to reality. A dream could be composed of scenes that were impossible. But in a fantasy, the components, however far-fetched, were scenes that really could exist. Persistent fantasies wouldn't indicate a disorder unless of course they reached the delusional stage.

"That is the stage where fantasy becomes confused with fact?"

Yes, when a fantasy was accepted as reality, as actually happening, there was delusion.

And hadn't that been true in this case?

"Well, in this report, the young gentlemen are always aware that their fantasies are fantasies."

A young man, a college graduate, playing cops-and-robbers in the street, following his uncle to his door, wasn't he acting out a fantasy and making it real?

The professor smiled, as though conceding a point in a pleasant discussion. "It could appear so," he said. "But you would have to know just how far he was lost in his little game."

Wilk seemed satisfied that he had made his point about Artie. He swung now to another form of derangement. Well now, he asked, an obsession, an obsessive belief—didn't that reach up to the state of a delusion? For example, there were people who believed absolutely in religious visions and predictions, believed themselves to be saints and messiahs.

"Oh, yes," Dr. Ball agreed, "there are people who are confined to insane asylums because of such delusions."

"Some of them placed a literal meaning on passages in the Scriptures or in other religious works and became deranged on such a point?"

"Yes, you might say that."

"Now, couldn't the same thing be the result of a philosophical belief?"

"If one believed strongly enough." The doctor's lively eyes went from Wilk to Judd Steiner. But Wilk didn't ask the expected, linking question. Instead he asked whether there were states of mind, short of mental disorder or insanity, that would alert one for watching and that would even call for treatment.

Yes, yes indeed, Dr. Ball said. That was the province in which the new psychology was at work.

Wilk thanked him. Their pleasant discussion was over. Dr. Ball's real conclusions, if one thought about them seriously, were precisely those of the defense.

*   *   *

It was the second of the State's alienists who brought out, in Wilk, a kind of savage brutality that we had until then associated only with Horn. The probing, intellectual atmosphere around the defense was suddenly gone, and as so often happens, the trial became for a day a kind of slugging match in which the real issues seemed forgotten.

The witness was Dr. Stauffer, pudgy, self-assured. A familiar figure in the courts, Tom told me. "Makes his living testifying for the State." Yet his record was impressive enough; he had been head of the department of psychology at the University of Illinois; he had been chief psychiatrist of a training camp during the war; he had been in charge of the psychiatric laboratory at the State Hospital for the Insane.

Stauffer took a smacking enjoyment in his recital as Horn led him through a description of that famous Sunday examination. An old hand at testifying, he told his story with complete precision, picturing with gusto the astonishing cold-bloodedness and self-possession of the killers, and jumping ahead of the state's attorney in his conclusions about their full responsibility. There seemed scarcely any point to his lengthy recital, until Dr. Stauffer came to Artie's description of the ride with the body. "He told how they took Calumet Drive and got to a blind road near a Russian Orthodox cemetery. He related that there they stripped the body from the waist down, took off the pants, shoes, and stockings. Now, there is a little matter here I would like to speak of just before you and the attorneys, if I may, Judge, and then I can be through with that phase of it."

Again the group of lawyers huddled around the judge's bench. The doctor sanctimoniously lowered his voice. "It was because of this circumstance of undressing the boy just from the waist down." He had made that the occasion to ask a great many questions along the line of sexual perversion and homosexual practices. "I didn't want to refer to it any further here, and I simply wanted to get rid of that phase of it."

It was clear that he had got nothing out of the boys. He had raised the question of abuse, undoubtedly with Horn's approval, purely for the effect of suggestion. Wilk's face had become dark, clotted. He took his seat, with the air of a man who has gone beyond disgust.

Stauffer continued with his description of the burial, piling on the details. "Straus stated that the body was stiff and the eyes were glazed. They let the body down easily into the culvert so that it would make no splash. . . ."

He had asked Artie Straus if at any time he could have withdrawn, "and he stated that he always hated a quitter, that he had no use for a coward. To a similar question, Mr. Steiner made practically the same answer."

Categorically, the doctor testified that each defendant was sane, in excellent possession of his faculties, including the faculty of judgment. He was impressed, he said, with "the logical sequence of the entire story as it was related, the catching up of each thread when broken by discussion, or by the other party to the homicide interrupting—a logical sequence that is rare to find in its excellence of continuity and relation."

Horn asked him then whether he was familiar with the "new psychology." Certainly, said Dr. Stauffer, he was entirely familiar with it, but he did not believe in it at all. He pooh-poohed all that dream and fantasy stuff. Dreams arose out of the condition of the body during the day, and the content of the dream was of very little significance. Why, if the defense was successful here, every criminal would start studying dream books!

Through the laughter, Wilk advanced upon Dr. Stauffer, head down. He halted at some distance, as if to avoid contamination.

How long was it since Dr. Stauffer had been in the actual practice of medicine, where he might be trying to help someone?

Horn objected.

The question amended, Dr. Stauffer replied that he had not for ten years been in practice, being occupied with teaching, research, and other branches of psychiatry.

"In fact, you have been almost fully occupied testifying for the courts, is that not the case?"

Stauffer admitted that he was in considerable demand as an expert, by the State.

"And what is your usual fee?" Wilk wrung out of him that it was fifty dollars per day. "And what are you receiving in this case?" It was "the same as all the others, two hundred and fifty."

Wasn't it a fact that he had virtually gone on strike, refusing to testify unless he received this raise?

Horn was livid. Angrily, Stauffer replied, "Why shouldn't I get the same as the others?"

Just as angrily, and just as hopelessly put in the wrong, he declared that he didn't need more than two hours to make an examination. And as for the examination taking place in a crowded room, no matter! "The conditions were good. In some ways they were ideal!" he shouted.

"You heard Dr. Ball, on your own side, state that the conditions and the time limit permitted only the beginning of an examination. Do you disagree with Dr. Ball?"

Dr. Stauffer shrugged. He had every respect for Dr. Ball, but his own experience with criminals was far more extensive, so he could see through them more readily. "They talked absolutely freely, they bared their souls. Nobody from the defense had got to them as yet, to tell them what not to say!"

"Exactly!" Wilk roared. "They were without defense, without help, and for two hours you could do as you pleased with them."

"Two minutes would be enough to see through those smart alecks!" the witness snapped.

Wilk picked up a textbook. Had Dr. Stauffer studied in Germany?

Yes.

Did he recognize Dr. Bleuler as an authority on nervous disorders?

Dr. Stauffer granted that Dr. Bleuler was a man of high reputation.

Wilk read, " 'A negative finding without prolonged observation never proves a patient to be normal.' " Did Dr. Stauffer agree with that statement?

Stauffer snorted. As a matter of fact, he had observed the criminals additionally, right here in court, day after day. They were perfectly oriented. They followed every nuance of the trial as well as anyone in the room.

Wilk read another passage from Bleuler. " 'To suppose that people are well mentally because they are oriented in time, space, and presence is just as naïve as to suppose a person is well mentally because he is not a raving maniac.' "

If they were mentally sick, Dr. Stauffer retorted, then they certainly had a good time with their supposed illness, sitting there kidding and laughing.

And didn't that demonstrate their emotional deficiency? Wilk snapped. Didn't it show there was something very sick in their faculty of judgment?

"No," said Stauffer. "It shows they're heartless killers, that's all."

"Heartless killers," Wilk repeated. "But not professional killers who dishonor science by dragging smut into court, and who get paid for perjury, are they?"

Horn roared for an apology. Wilk muttered something to the judge and stalked away from the witness with a trivial wave of the hand, as though the actual content of Dr. Stauffer's testimony was obviously worthless of examination.

He had obtained his effect, annihilating Stauffer with contempt, just as he had beguiled Dr. Ball with chummy flattery.

And on the following day, Wilk produced still a third style of cross-examination, to the discomfiture of Horn's final expert witness.

For Dr. Tierney, Wilk exhibited a clear, persistent, dry method of questioning and an utter mastery of his material, so that the entire courtroom could not but relish with sheer intellectual pleasure his playing of a highly aware and resistant witness, until the lawyer got the doctor to say everything he wanted him to say.

Tierney was a local man of national stature, whom Horn had used to tally against Dr. McNarry. He had been director of the State Hospital for the Insane, he had been advisor on neuropsychiatry to the Surgeon General of the United States, and he was, like Dr. McNarry, the author of an important work on insanity and the law. A most impressive figure, dark-haired, wearing heavy horn-rimmed glasses, Dr. Tierney spoke as though each word were turned around and examined on all sides before being released from his lips.

For Horn, he confirmed that he had studied the Storrs-Allwin report and that he had studied the behavior of the defendants during all these weeks in court. Both were in full possession of their faculties, and sane.

Wilk began. "Could you tell by looking at these boys whether or not they were mentally diseased?"

"No," the doctor responded. His heavy voice went well with his dark glasses, his dark mustache. "But I could tell whether or not their appearance showed evidence of mental disease."

There was a suppressed snort from Judd at the fatuous remark.

Wilk then sought to show that Dr. Tierney had never even talked to the defendants, never asked them a single question. The doctor had seen them a day after the famous Sunday examination. They had been brought from jail to Horn's office, supposedly to pick up suitcases sent by their families.

"And did you examine these boys then? Did you question them?"

"They had already been instructed not to reply to any questions except with a formula of refusal to speak."

"In your experience with criminal cases, is it customary for the lawyers to instruct their clients not to talk?"

"Some lawyers do, some lawyers do not."

"Do you know any who do not?"

"I have examined quite a number of cases for the State," Dr. Tierney said, "in which the lawyers have not advised their clients to refuse to talk."

"What ones?"

"Well, one would be Carl Wanderer, for instance," Tierney said, recalling a notorious murderer.

"He talked, did he?"

"He did talk, yes."

"And he got hanged?"

"Yes, sir." The laughter seemed not to reach him.

"You know that nobody had a right to compel them to talk?"

"I believe that is a constitutional right, yes."

And yet, Wilk pointed out, Horn had been trying to get the boys to answer questions for Dr. Tierney.

Horn leaped into the fray. "I object. You cannot compel a man to talk, but there is no constitutional provision that you can't ask him to talk!"

Wilk turned on him. "You had no more right to bring them back into your office than you would have had to take them to the state penitentiary!"

"I didn't bring them in—the sheriff brought them in, with your permission, to get their suitcases!"

"And you tried to make use of it, tried to get them to talk some more, in violation of their constitutional rights, after you had had a picnic with them all week end, keeping them away from counsel!"

"I will confess that I violated a number of constitutional rights!" Horn shouted, the witness forgotten. "And I intend to continue that as long as I am state's attorney! When a man is charged with a crime, I am not going to ask him to hire a lawyer before I talk to him!"

Wilk turned to the whole world. "I don't think in a well-organized community a man could be elected state's attorney under the statement that when a citizen is charged with a crime, the state's attorney would violate his constitutional rights. Now, maybe Mr. Horn can get away with it, but it doesn't speak well for the community if he can."

"Well now, gentlemen, you will have plenty of time for argument after the evidence is all in. Proceed with the evidence," Judge Matthewson said.

"Excuse me, Your Honor," said Wilk. He eyed the unperturbed Tierney. His evidence, then, was to be founded entirely on his observations in this court?

That, and the written material of the other psychiatrists, Dr. Tierney said.

"Was there any testimony of fact by any of the psychiatrists that would put a psychiatrist on inquiry, as to further examination?"

"Outside of the crime itself, no." Moreover, Dr. Tierney pointed out, the boys had never aroused suspicion of mental disease prior to the crime.

"Is a split personality evidence of a mental disorder?" Wilk asked.

"Not necessarily. A person might dissociate without having a mental disorder."

"A scrubwoman who imagined she was the Queen of Sheba—would she be a case of a split personality?"

"Not necessarily. She might feel like the Queen of Sheba and be perfectly healthy mentally. To become a disorder, there would have to be a further development in a delusional state —a schizophrenia leading to a psychosis."

That was just the word he was looking for, Wilk said. Sizzy—skizzy—what was it? And as he struggled with it, everyone laughed. Ah yes, he had seen that word in the doctor's own book. "Here—maybe I've got it."

"Maybe you have, but I haven't seen any evidence of it yet."

"What other names do you use for split personality?" Wilk asked.

"Oh, they talk of delusions and they talk of hallucinations and they talk of fantasies. And schizophrenia."

"Yes. We just had it. Now, to digress a little, what is the mind?"

"The mind represents that which we commonly call *I*. It is the whole man. It is really the I-ego. It is really the sum of all one's experiences in the subjective stage, and not the objective experience."

"The sum of one's experience?" The great Jonathan seemed bewildered by these terms; he was letting us feel that this expert might be too much for him.

"Yes, one's thinking, feeling, and actions, in relation to the situations in which one is being placed and that one can recall."

"And what is emotion?"

Dr. Tierney formulated his reply quite carefully. "Emotion comes from the need of living matter to maintain itself."

"Then a person, an 'I,' a mind, is badly served by an emotional nature that does not seek to maintain itself?"

"In what way?"

"Someone who committed rash acts that could lead to death—would he be emotionally defective?"

If he was referring to suicides, Dr. Tierney said, it would again be a case where the definition of mental illness came with the act itself.

"But there are indirect forms of suicide?"

Not every rash action was evidence of a self-destructive impulse, the doctor said. Some rash actions were merely foolish. Each action would have to be judged.

Wilk nodded. He asked, wasn't a self-destructive or suicidal tendency often found in a split personality? That is, one part for, and one part against, oneself?

Yes, Dr. Tierney agreed.

"Now what was the word again? Sizzo—never mind, call it a split personality. Well, if you did find a split personality, you would examine further, wouldn't you?"

Dr. Tierney smiled. "It is all a question of degree. If you forget a word, Mr. Wilk, I shouldn't think it necessary to examine you for mental disease."

"Could a lapse of memory be considered a splitting of the personality?"

"It can be considered a splitting off of a small part of the personality, or experience. Of course, such a lapse might be considered evidence of approaching senility."

Wilk awarded him a mock bow. "Now—this schizo— what sort of persons are most liable to it?"

"Why, schizophrenic persons, naturally."

"Are you trying to evade me or make fun of me?"

"No, I'm trying to understand you," the doctor said urbanely.

"I want to know at what age it is most likely to develop into a psychosis?"

"What do you mean by *it?*"

"I mean your sizzyphasis or whatever it is. At what age does it most commonly develop into a psychosis?"

The doctor's face became stonily remote. So he had been put off guard by clowning. "I can't generalize," he said.

Ah? Wilk glanced into the doctor's own book, at the page where his finger had been all the while. "During the period of adolescence?"

"A certain frequency has been noted," the doctor admitted.

There was a stirring among the listeners. Wilk read from the book, " 'In such cases—schizophrenia in adolescence—' " and this time he had no difficulty whatsoever with the word— " 'one often finds expression in crimes of violence.' "

Horn shouted, "This has no bearing on this case, has it, doctor?"

"Wait till it's your turn to ask questions!" Wilk snapped before the judge could intervene. And as he returned to his attack, Tierney answered more slowly.

"When is this condition most often seen?" Wilk persisted.

Tierney sat silent. Wilk read, " 'This condition may most often be seen in adolescents at the time when they are emancipated from home control, and when they are leaving school. . . .' "

The doctor shrugged.

Wilk read on. " 'It may occur in persons of a high degree of intelligence. . . .' " He glanced up at Tierney. " 'At this difficult stage toward the end of puberty, the subject may develop fantasies, bordering upon autism. However, not all such cases develop a psychosis.' " He raised his eyes from the book and asked, "Would a young man of exceptional intelligence who had had a governess until the age of fifteen and was suddenly emancipated from her control, who left home at that time, leaving one school for another, a young man decidedly given to fantasies—would such a person come under this description?"

It was some years, Tierney said, since he had written this book.

"Do you intend to take this out in the next edition?" Dr. Tierney responded to the laughter with a stiffly sporting gesture of the hand, as though acknowledging blow for blow. Wilk read on. " 'The subject may go so far as to commit murder, seemingly for no motive, and he may appear devoid of remorse.' "

Artie and Judd were grinning. Ferdinand Feldscher was smiling at his brother Edgar, perhaps for finding the passage —or had it been Willie Weiss?

Now Wilk turned to Judd's condition. "Doctor, did you find any evidence in either of these subjects of a paranoid personality?"

He had noted in Judd Steiner a few superficial similarities, Dr. Tierney said. "But the main features of a paranoid personality are lacking."

"What would such features be?"

"Selfishness and a domineering character are often noted."

"Such as one might attribute to a superman?"

Dr. Tierney smiled. "That is entirely a concept. However, even this concept concerns a more developed paranoid stage."

And could Dr. Tierney recall any other features of a paranoid personality?

There was a guarded silence. "I will help you," Wilk said, looking again in the book. " 'One who is anxious to be in the forefront'?"

"Yes, but that might be considered part of selfishness. Part of an egocentric character."

"Well, let us see about egocentrics." Wilk thumbed the volume. "Doesn't it say somewhere here that an egocentric is practically the same thing as a paranoid character?"

The doctor's lips parted in a thin smile. "I don't think I will quarrel with you very much on that."

Wilk dropped his voice to a conversational tone. "Then why not say yes, and agree with me once, without so much work?"

Someone applauded. The gavel rapped. He returned to

his point. Were people with this egocentric or paranoid character usually fond of learning?

This was often a characteristic, the doctor admitted.

" 'While they learn readily, get through school and even college easily, there is really no broad grasp of the relationship of the material learned to the situations in life.' Is that right?"

Dr. Tierney hedged. Only of certain types of paranoid or egocentric personalities.

"All right, doctor." Wilk gave him an under-the-brows glance. "You still recognize this book as an authority, do you?"

Tierney nodded stonily.

"I am reading from page 157. The heading of this section is 'The Egocentric Personality.' It says: 'Individuals of this type are often endowed with a facility for learning in a parrot-like way, which enables them to acquire their lessons easily and to do well scholastically in school, many being capable of passing through college, but the quality of the learning is poor, and there is really no broad grasp of the relation of the material learned to the situation in life.' "

"That's right, as I already agreed."

But was not this the defense description of Judd, an egocentric or paranoid type of a psychopathic personality? "And I understand you to say that a psychopathic personality is not, or is not yet, in a diseased condition?"

No, not necessarily.

"But it would put a doctor on his guard to investigate?"

"If one knows one is dealing with a paranoid personality, I don't see anything further to investigate. I know a lot of paranoid personalities in ordinary society."

"If that paranoid personality has committed a crime, a murder?"

"Oh, in that case the personality should be investigated."

Time and again in the trial, it seemed to us, this point had been reached. Yet we hung on the words, as if, this once, the answer might appear.

As Wilk put the question, the scientists of the mind could read the meanings afterward—why couldn't they read them before a crime?

Because a psychopathic personality was not mentally diseased, the doctor insisted. There was as yet no proof that he would be harmful to others or to himself. He might be on the way to disease or he might be adjusted as he was. Not infrequently a psychopathic personality did develop a psychosis. One could not tell when.

"It just happens, does it?"

The number of psychopathic personalities, fortunately, was not very great, Dr. Tierney said.

"Not so great but that—since you show us they are recognizable—we could watch them with more care," Wilk said, turning and looking steadily at Judd. He had put the pieces perfectly into place; he had made the State's alienist confirm, to the precise point, the defense contention that the boy was not insane, but that he showed marked characteristics of a potential disturbance.

Wilk went back to his table. Astonished, we realized that the case was nearly over. For a month, we had come to this room as to a class. In the last weeks, we had learned a great deal about psychiatry. Only, what were the true opinions of the doctors? And even between Wilk and Horn, how much was conviction? If Horn himself were an attorney outside the services of the State, would he not be willing to defend the same boys?

*   *   *

And now indeed there came news of professional "dickering." For the sake of shortening the trial, Wilk would eliminate the remainder of his sympathy witnesses, if Horn would eliminate rebuttal witnesses.

During a recess hour, the opposing attorneys were locked together. "No deal," Horn announced as he emerged. The whole thing, he declared, had been a desperate effort by the defense to get him to drop one extremely important witness. He wouldn't do it. He was going to put on Sergeant McNamara. The defense could do as they damn pleased.

This decision of Horn's was to have a curious result, making me wonder again about the real determinants in any issue. Were the determinants ever the facts, or were they emotional factors, reactions to the lawyers in a trial, or even emotional complexities in a judge?

McNamara's material was not new to us. We had all printed various versions of his story of Judd's remark about "pleading guilty before a friendly judge."

What could Horn hope to gain by putting this into the record? Did he feel that he would be putting Judge Matthewson on the spot, so that he could not dare pronounce the predicted "friendly" sentence? Did Horn feel that his alienists had been so discredited by Wilk that only a bold maneuver could save his hanging case?

Carefully Horn led the policeman through his testimony. Had Judd become talkative with him? Had he made notes? Yes, he had written down most of the things that happened, because the case was so important. And on Sunday, May thirtieth, had Judd made any remark that struck him?

Yes, Judd had said, in discussing how he would plead, "that depends on my family—if they wish me to hang. Or else I will plead guilty before a friendly judge to get life imprisonment. There is also the insanity plea."

Judge Matthewson sat rigid, his arms, in the voluminous black sleeves, crossed tight against his chest.

McNamara told how he had been so struck by the words that he had repeated them to his wife and to some neighbors on the way to church. Also, some newspapermen had got hold of the story.

If Wilk had been bitter, contemptuous, in his cross-examination of Dr. Stauffer, he was now simply murderous. When had McNamara written down the remarks? Right after they were made? No, later on. When, exactly? That same day, the detective thought. Where was the notebook? He didn't have it with him.

He didn't? Did he think he could come into court and tell any cock-and-bull story without evidence?

The judge leaned forward. Court would be recessed. Let the notebook be produced.

An hour later, the session was resumed. McNamara produced a pocket-worn notebook, the schoolboy kind. There

were entries in pencil, some half rubbed out, most of them
having to do with petty expenses.

Wilk found the notations of the day of the cavalcade.
Where was there anything about the "friendly judge" remark?
Nothing on that day or the next.

"Then you lied," Wilk cried. "You lied under oath before
this court! You didn't write it down that day or the next—if
ever."

McNamara sputtered. It wasn't a lie. He hadn't said exactly when he wrote it down.

In a tangle of questions, Wilk had him stumbling over his
own tongue, on the point of violence or tears. McNamara
pointed out notations on a later page. "Insanity plea, or get a
life sentence from a friendly judge."

Jonathan Wilk was relentless. How could anyone know
these were Judd's words? Couldn't they be McNamara's own
conclusions? Couldn't he have put them in recently, even today? Hadn't a newspaperman invented the whole story?

McNamara shouted, "That's a lie!" Reprimanded by the
judge, he sputtered the names of the neighbors to whom he
had told the story, then, in repeating the wording, got the
quotation wrong. Finally he admitted, No, he wasn't sure of
the exact quotation.

"Or if there was a quotation at all!" Wilk snapped. But
he wasn't done with his prey. And what did the phrase
"friendly judge" mean? Even if Judd had said it, couldn't he
have meant that a jury would be unfriendly, after being stirred
up by wild campaigns to create prejudice? Was McNamara
not only a note-taker but a mind-reader?

Sweating, the policeman growled, "No, I'm not that
smart, not as smart as any million-dollar lawyers."

Wilk looked up at Judge Matthewson. There it all was.
They were bracketed together, in prejudiced minds. A million-
dollar lawyer before a judge who would be friendly to millionaires.

McNamara lurched from the stand.

Thus on this note of hatred, the testimony ended; the
case that was to explore our deepest philosophies, free will,
guilt, and compulsion, closed with charges and counter-

charges of lying, shouts of money influence, with prejudice-stirring, with words bitter and base that were yet to reach into the last moment of the trial.

Now would come the summations.

I wonder whether in all courtroom history the speaking effort of one man was ever awaited as was the speech of Jonathan Wilk for the defense of Steiner and Straus. Perhaps there was in this anticipation the sense that all the probings, all the expert testimony, had still fallen short of an explanation, and that only the ultimate effort of a great man could lift the meaning before us.

I kept wondering about Wilk in another way. For weeks he had been striving with all his might for these two boys in the crowded, dense, boiling courtroom. Yet, though Judd in particular seemed always to be trying to reach him with his gaze, Wilk did not appear to respond. It was as though Wilk defended them on principle, even, perhaps, against an inner sense of revulsion. His summation would have to be virtually an abstract plea for pure mercy, then.

And surely it would be the last great murder trial in which the tired, aging Wilk would take part; never again could such extreme circumstances arise. Pure mercy—for murder, pure, without even a concomitant sense of guilt.

So Padua pictured the killing, as he took the first turn at summation, speaking smoothly, convincingly, reciting the law from Blackstone to our own day, precedent after precedent proving that hanging and only hanging, only the extreme penalty, was called for. Mitigation? For what? For their superior intelligence? For their superior opportunities? For their superior advantages in wealth and luxury? For their waste of life, for destroying other lives as well as their own? No, as long as the death penalty existed in human law, it was mandatory in a case of this kind.

Then Ferdinand Feldscher spoke for the defense, proving by precedent after precedent that consideration of the youth and mental condition of the defendants should bring a jail sentence. A hanging would be atavistic. He, too, was persuasive, impeccable, authoritative. And he awakened a sympathy for himself; we could not forget that he was a relative. And through sympathy for him, there was sympathy for the boys.

The next day came Czewicki's turn; he unleashed an astonishing flood of oratory, his gestures choppy, like Horn's. It was a memorized speech filled with gruesome images piled one on the other; the effect was like turning the pages of an illustrated *Inferno*. His task was to deal with the psychiatric testimony, and his burden was that it should all be stricken out, that it was a virtual hoax, since the defendants were admittedly legally sane. Mad? Mad dogs were suffering from illness, but not these pervert prodigies, these vicious lust-killers.

To him, Edgar Feldscher replied, reviewing the entire relationship of psychiatry and criminal law and urging, earnestly, that the tragic case yield, for humanity, a further step in the use of the new science as an aid to justice. Of all who had spoken until then, he touched us most, for there was a deep perplexity in him, and even more than had been felt from his brother, an unashamed personal concern for the defendants. When Edgar Feldscher turned toward them in his plea that their lives were young, that one or the other, or both of them, sick as they were, might yet have much to give, his voice lost its pitch. He made a full stop, as a man not wishing to use on us the histrionic effect of a breaking voice. Edgar Feldscher ended by recalling that it had been the wish and hope of the defense that both sides should participate in the psychiatric study; it was still his wish and hope that the use of such knowledge should prevail, in place of oratory, in man's search for justice.

There remained only Wilk and Horn.

Although only one individual, Judge Matthewson, would render the verdict, the trial was not a play rehearsed behind a dropped curtain. The entire world had become a jury. Thousands of letters, telegrams, petitions, even death threats, inundated the court. Unformed emotions seemed to hang in the very air. Could Wilk move enough feeling, literally sway it, to the side of pity?

If the doors had been crowded before, the day of the great attraction brought an unimagined assault. Their shirts blotched with sweat, the linked bailiffs tried to hold back the charge, when suddenly there was a roar of pain. A bailiff's arm had been broken.

In the shock, the mob fell back; the doors were finally closed; the wounded man was helped into the judge's chamber.

For half an hour Wilk waited, until there was complete order. The judge nodded, and Wilk arose.

The courtroom had somehow a different air, for only the highest priorities retained admission. There were jurists and professors, there were several additional correspondents from abroad, there seemed altogether a careful selection of elder citizens in the room; men and women of substance had replaced the impassioned and the morbidly curious.

We think of a great speech in terms of an oration that has a rising structure and a shattering climax. All had waited in the expectancy of some such tense and mounting experience to come with Wilk's summation. And we were indeed to be moved, but not in a continuous line.

He spoke for two days, during four sessions. Though there was a structure to his plea, including a classical review of the evidence, a review of precedents, and an appeal to enlightenment, we scarcely felt the form of it. Indeed, it was in the discursive moments, when he became eloquent in his philosophy and in his humanism, that he seemed to be talking most to the point and was, of course, most himself.

In such a lengthy address there were of necessity times when his delivery was relaxed and when he seemed only to be shambling about the courtroom, in the characteristic carelessness that provided a springboard for the suddenly pointed finger, the outflung arm. But the total effect was of a piece. It was of a man talking from his heart, in an intimate and serious conversation. Much of what he said he had often said before. This was a summation not only for the boys, but for himself.

He began in a low, almost tired key, touching at once upon the question that was on everyone's mind—the avoidance of a jury.

"Your Honor, it has been almost three months since the great responsibility of this case was assumed by my associates and myself. I am willing to confess that it has been three months of great anxiety. Our anxiety has not been due to the facts that are connected with this most unfortunate affair, but to the almost unheard-of publicity it has received. Newspapers all over the country have been giving it space such as they have almost never before given to any case. Day after day the people of Chicago have been regaled with stories of all sorts, until almost every person has formed an opinion.

"And when the public is interested and demands a punishment, it thinks of only one punishment, and that is death. When the public speaks as one man, it thinks only of killing.

"In this stress and strain, we did all we could to gain the confidence of the public, who in the end really control, whether wisely or unwisely.

"It was freely published that there were millions of dollars to be spent on this case. Here was to be an effort to save the lives of two boys by the use of money in fabulous amounts, amounts such as these families never even had.

"We announced to the public that no excessive use of money would be made in this case, either for lawyers or for psychiatrists, or in any other way. We have faithfully kept that promise.

"The psychiatrists, as has been shown, are receiving a per diem, and only a per diem, which is the same as is paid by the State.

"The attorneys, at their own request, have agreed to take such an amount as the officers of the Chicago Bar Association may think proper in this case.

"There are times when poverty is fortunate. I insist, Your Honor, that had this been the case of two boys of these defendants' age, unconnected with families supposed to have great wealth, there is not a state's attorney in Illinois who would not have consented at once to a plea of guilty and a punishment in the penitentiary for life. Not one.

"We could have come into this court without evidence, without argument; and this court would have given us what every judge in the city of Chicago has given to every boy in the city of Chicago since the first capital case was tried. We would have had no contest.

"We are here with the lives of two boys imperiled, with the public aroused. For what?

"Because, unfortunately, the parents have money.

"I told Your Honor in the beginning that never before had there been a case in Chicago where on a plea of guilty a boy under twenty-one had been sentenced to death. I will raise that age and say, never has there been such a case where a human being under the age of twenty-three has been sentenced to death. And, I think I am safe in saying, that never has there been such a case in the state of Illinois.

"And yet this court is urged, aye, threatened, that he must hang two boys contrary to precedents, contrary to the acts of every judge who ever held court in this state.

"Why?

"Tell me what public necessity there is for this.

"Why need a judge be urged by every argument, moderate and immoderate, to hang two boys in the face of every precedent in Illinois and in the face of the progress of the last fifty years?

"Lawyers stand here day by day and read cases from the Dark Ages, where judges have said that if a man had a grain of sense left, and a child barely out of his cradle, he could be hanged because he knew the difference between right and wrong. Death sentences for eighteen, seventeen, sixteen, and fourteen years have been cited.

"I have heard in the last six weeks nothing but the cry for blood. I have seen a court urged almost to the point of threats to hang two boys, in the face of science, of humanity, of experience, in the face of all the better and more humane thought of the age.

"Brother Padua has not half done his job. He should read

this from Blackstone: 'Under fourteen, though an infant shall be judged to be incapable of guilt prima facie, yet if it appeared to the court and the jury that he could discern between good and evil, he may be convicted and suffer death.'

"Thus a servant-girl of thirteen has been burned for killing her mistress.

"One boy of ten, and another of nine years of age who had killed his companion, were sentenced to death; and he of ten was actually hanged.

"Why?

"He knew the difference between right and wrong. He had learned that in Sunday school.

"As if this had something to do with the year 1924, as if it had something to do with Chicago, with its boys' court and its fairly tender protection of the young.

"In as cruel a speech as he knew how to make, Mr. Padua said to this court that we plead guilty because we were afraid to do anything else.

"Your Honor, that is true.

"We have said to the public and to this court that neither the parents, nor the friends, nor the attorneys would want these boys released. They are as they are. They should be permanently isolated from society. We have said that, and we mean it. We are asking this court to save their lives, which is the least and the most that a judge can do.

"We did plead guilty before Your Honor because we were afraid to submit our case to a jury. I can tell Your Honor why.

"I have found that years and experience with life temper one's emotions and make him more understanding of his fellow man. When my friend Padua is my age, or even yours, he will reread his address to this court with horror.

"I know perfectly well that where responsibility is divided by twelve it is easy to say, 'Away with him.'

"But, Your Honor, if these boys hang, you must do it. You can never explain that the rest overpowered you. It must be by your deliberate, cool, premeditated act, without a chance to shift responsibility.

"Your Honor, I know that of four hundred and fifty persons who had been indicted for murder in Chicago in the past ten years and who had pleaded guilty, only one has been hanged. And my friend who is prosecuting this case earned the honor of that hanging while he was on the bench. But his victim was forty years old."

Wilk turned then to the prosecutor's table. "I can sum up their arguments in a minute: cruel, dastardly, premeditated, fiendish, cowardly, cold-blooded.

"Cold-blooded!" And the long arm, the long finger, pointed. "Let the State, who is so anxious to take these boys' lives, set an example in consideration, kindheartedness, and tenderness before they call my clients cold-blooded.

"Cold-blooded! Because they planned and schemed?

"Yes. But here are officers of justice, so-called, with all the power of the State, who for months have been planning and scheming and contriving, working to take these two boys' lives.

"They say this is the most cold-blooded murder the civilized world has ever known. I don't know what they include in the civilized world. I suppose Illinois. Now, Your Honor, I have been practicing law a good deal longer than I should have, anyhow for forty-five or forty-six years, and during a part of that time I have tried a good many criminal cases, always defending. It does not mean that I am better. It probably means that I am more squeamish than the other fellows. It means the way I am made. I cannot help it.

"I have never yet tried a case where the state's attorney did not say that it was the most cold-blooded, inexcusable, premeditated case that ever occurred. If it was murder, there never was such a murder. If it was robbery, there never was such a robbery.

"All of them are the worst. Why? Well, it adds to the credit of the state's attorney to be connected with a big case. That is one thing. They can say, 'Well, I tried the most cold-blooded murder case that ever was tried, and I convicted them, and they are dead. I tried the worst forgery case that ever was tried, and I won that. I never did anything that was not big.'

"Lawyers are apt to say that.

"And then there is another thing, Your Honor: of course,

I generally try cases to juries, and these adjectives always go well with juries—bloody, cold-blooded, despicable, cowardly, dastardly, cruel, heartless—the whole litany of the state's attorney's office generally goes well with a jury. The twelve jurors, being good themselves, think it is a tribute to their virtue if they follow the litany of the state's attorney.

"They say this was a cruel murder, the worst that ever happened. I say that very few murders ever occurred that were as free from cruelty as this."

He waited for the chill of these words to pass through us. Quietly, he went on: "Poor little Paulie Kessler suffered very little. There is no excuse for his killing. If to hang these two boys would bring him back to life, I would say let them go, and I believe their parents would say so, too. But

> *The moving finger writes; and, having writ,*
> *Moves on: nor all your Piety nor Wit*
> *Shall lure it back to cancel half a Line,*
> *Nor all your Tears wash out a Word of it."*

In the pause, Mike Prager remarked, "Ever hear of Wilk making a plea without Omar Khayyám?"

Wilk resumed, turning now to the State's argument. Horn had taken pains to build up the ransom as the motive. This was almost too easy to ridicule, with their huge allowances, with Artie's $3,000 bank account, with Judd's $3,000 for a trip to Europe.

"And yet they murdered a little boy against whom they had nothing in the world, to get five thousand dollars each. That is what their case rests on. It could not stand up a minute without a motive. Without it, it was the senseless act of immature and diseased children, as it was; a senseless act of children, wandering around in the dark and moved by some emotion that we still perhaps have not the knowledge or the insight into life to thoroughly understand."

He turned and gazed at the boys, interminably, it seemed, and a gloom, a heart-heaviness at existence itself could be seen coming over him, and it came over the courtroom, too. One could scarcely realize at what moment he resumed speaking, for we all felt at one with his thoughts. This was no lawyer carefully ticking off points in a courtroom. He seemed to have abolished the entire formality of the law.

"How insane they are I care not, whether medically or legally. They committed the most unprovoked, most purposeless, most causeless act that any two boys ever committed, and put themselves where the rope is dangling above their heads.

"There are not physicians enough in the world to convince any thoughtful, fair-minded man that these boys are right.

"Was their act one of deliberation, of intellect, or were they driven by some force such as Dr. McNarry and Dr. Allwin have told this court?

"Why did they kill little Paulie Kessler?

"Not for money, not for spite, not for hate. They killed him because somewhere in the infinite processes that go to the making up of the boy or the man something slipped, and those unfortunate lads sit here hated, despised, outcasts, with the community shouting for their blood.

"Are they to blame for it? It is one of those things that happened; it happened, and it calls not for hate, but for kindness, for charity, for consideration.

"Mr. Padua with the immaturity of youth and inexperience says that if we hang them there will be no more killing. This world has been one long slaughterhouse from the beginning until today, and killing goes on and on and on, and will forever. Why not read something, why not study something, why not think instead of blindly shouting for death?

"Kill them. Will that prevent other senseless boys or other vicious men or vicious women from killing? No! No more than previous hangings prevented this!

"I heard the state's attorney talk of mothers. I know that any mother might be the mother of a little Paulie Kessler who left his home and went to his school and never came back. I know that any mother might be the mother of Artie Straus, of Judd Steiner. The trouble is that if she is the mother of a Judd Steiner or of an Artie Straus, she has to ask herself the question, 'How came my children to be what they are? From what ancestry did they get this strain? How far removed was the poison that destroyed their lives? Was I the bearer of the seed that brings them to death?'

"I remember a little poem that gives the soliloquy of a boy about to be hanged, a soliloquy such as these boys might make." And he quoted Housman:

> *The night my father got me*
> *His mind was not on me;*
> *He did not plague his fancy*
> *To muse if I should be*
> *The son you see.*

The boys were looking down. Judd seemed to brush at his eyes, and two rows behind him his father sat with a strange, tranced pain, his eyes fixed on the back of his son's head.

> *The day my mother bore me*
> *She was a fool and glad,*
> *For all the pain I cost her,*
> *That she had borne the lad*
> *That borne she had.*

> *My father and my mother*
> *Out of the light they lie;*
> *The warrant would not find them,*
> *And here, 'tis only I*
> *Shall hang so high.*

> *O let not man remember*
> *The soul that God forgot,*
> *But fetch the county sheriff*
> *And noose me in a knot,*
> *And I will rot.*

> *And so the game is ended,*
> *That should not have begun.*
> *My father and my mother*

They had a likely son,
And I have none.

"No one knows what will be the fate of the child he gets or the child she bears; the fate of the child is the last thing they consider. This weary old world goes on begetting, with birth and with living and with death; and all of it is blind from the beginning to the end. I do not know what it was that made these boys do this mad act, but I do know they did not beget themselves. I know that any one of an infinite number of causes reaching back to the beginning might be working out in these boys' minds, whom you are asked to hang in malice and in hatred and injustice, because someone in the past has sinned against them.

"I am sorry for the fathers as well as the mothers, for the fathers who give their strength and their lives for educating and protecting and creating a fortune for the boys that they love; for the mothers who go down in the shadow of death for their children, who watch them with tenderness and fondness and longing, and who go down into dishonor and disgrace for the children that they love.

"All of these are helpless. We are all helpless. When you are pitying the father and the mother of poor Paulie Kessler, what about the fathers and mothers of these two unfortunate boys, and what about the unfortunate boys themselves, and what about all the fathers and all the mothers and all the boys and all the girls who tread a dangerous maze of darkness from birth to death?"

He lifted his head up from his soliloquy. "Do you think you can cure it by hanging these two? Do you think you can cure the hatreds and the maladjustments of the world by hanging them? You may here and there cure hatred with love and understanding, but you can only add fuel to the flames by cruelty and hate.

"What is my friend's idea of justice? He says to this court, 'Give them the same mercy that they gave Paulie Kessler.'

"If the state in which I live is not kinder, more humane,

more considerate, more intelligent than the mad act of these
two boys, I am sorry that I have lived so long."

So ended the first session.

The courtroom emptied slowly, the spell lingering in the
heavy, warm air.

*   *   *

In the afternoon, Wilk resumed, speaking of the clumsiness, the ineptitude of the "carefully planned" crime. "Without the slightest motive, moved by nothing except the vague
wanderings of children, they rented a machine, and about four
o'clock in the afternoon started to find somebody to kill. For
nothing.

"They went over to the Twain School. Artie's little
brother was there, on the playground. Artie went there himself in the open daylight, known by all of them, and he looked
over the little boys.

"Your Honor has been in these courts for a long time;
you have listened to murder cases before. Has any such case
ever come to the human experience of any judge, or any lawyer? Never once!"

Wilk described how they picked up their victim. ". . .
They hit him over the head with a chisel and kill him, and go
on, driving past the neighbors that they knew, in the open
highway in broad daylight. And still men say that they have a
bright intellect, and, as Dr. Stauffer puts it, can orient themselves and reason as well as he can. It is the sane act of sane
men.

"If ever any death car went over the same kind of route,
driven by sane people, I have never heard of it. The car is
driven for twenty miles. The slightest accident, a bit of curiosity, an arrest for speeding—anything would bring destruction.
They go through the park, meeting hundreds of machines, in
the sight of thousands of eyes, with this dead boy.

"And yet doctors will swear that it is a sane act. They
know better.

"You need no experts, you need no X-rays, you need no
study of the endocrines. Their conduct shows exactly what it
was, and shows that this court has before him two young men

who should be examined in a psychopathic hospital and treated kindly and with care. . . .

"We are told that they planned. Well, what does that mean? A maniac plans, an idiot plans, an animal plans; any brain that functions may plan; but their plans were the diseased plans of diseased minds. Do I need to argue it? Does anybody need more than to glance at it?

"And still, Your Honor, on account of its weirdness and its strangeness and its advertising, we are forced to fight. I sometimes wonder if I am dreaming. What do they want? Tell me, is a lifetime for the young boys spent behind prison bars— is that not enough for this mad act? And is there any reason why this great public should be regaled with a hanging?"

He walked close to the prosecution table, looking quizzically at his opponents. "My friend pictured to you the putting of this dead boy into this culvert. Well, no one can minutely describe a killing without making it shocking—but, Your Honor, I can think of a scene that makes this pale into insignificance." And gazing then at Judd and Artie, he described, in gruesome detail, the prospective hanging. "I can picture them, wakened in the gray of morning, furnished a suit of clothes by the State, led to the scaffold, their feet tied, black caps drawn over their heads, stood on a trap door, the hangman pressing the spring; I can see them fall through space— and—I can see them stopped by the rope around their necks.

"Wouldn't it be a glorious day for Chicago? Wouldn't it be a glorious triumph for the state's attorney? Wouldn't it be a glorious illustration of Christianity and kindness and charity?

"This would surely expiate placing Paulie Kessler in the culvert after he was dead. This would doubtless bring immense satisfaction to some people. It would bring a greater satisfaction because it would be done in the name of justice.

"We hear glib talk of justice. Well, it would make me smile if it did not make me sad. Who knows what it is? Does Mr. Padua know? Does Mr. Horn know? Do I know? Does Your Honor know? Is there a human machinery for finding out? Is there any man who can weigh me and say what I deserve? Can Your Honor? Let us be honest. Can Your Honor appraise yourself and say what you deserve?

"If there is such a thing as justice, it could only be administered by one who knew the inmost thoughts of the men to whom he was meting it out. It means that you must appraise every influence that moves them, the civilization in which they live, and all the society which enters into the making of the child or the man! If Your Honor can do it, you are wise, and with wisdom goes mercy."

Judd smiled at the gracefulness of it.

"It is not so much mercy either, Your Honor. I can hardly understand myself pleading to a court to visit mercy on two boys by shutting them up in prison for life. Any cry for more roots back to the hyena; it roots back to the hissing serpent; it roots back to the beasts of the jungle. It is not a part of man. It is not a part of that feeling which, let us hope, is growing; though scenes like this sometimes make me doubt that it is growing. It is not a part of that feeling of mercy and pity and understanding of each other which we believe has been slowly raising man from his low estate."

He resumed the tale of the crime. "They parked the bloody automobile in front of Judd's house. They cleaned it to some extent that night and left it standing in the street. 'Oriented,' of course, 'oriented.' They left it there for the night so that anybody might see and know. And then in a day or so we find Artie with his pockets stuffed with newspapers telling of the Kessler tragedy. We find him consulting with his friends, with the newspaper reporters; and my experience has been that the last person that a conscious criminal associates with is a reporter. He shuns them even more than he does a detective, because they are smarter and less merciful." Wilk looked at us with an appeasing smile. "But he picks up a reporter, and he tells him he has read a great many detective stories, and he knows just how this would happen.

"Talk about scheming! But they must be hanged, because everybody is talking about the case and because their people have money."

He turned then to a professional tone. "Am I asking for much in this case?" He spoke of the traditional arrangements between prosecution and defense, the usual consideration accorded a plea of guilty. "Is it customary to get anything on a plea of guilty? How about the state's attorney? Do they not give you something on a plea of guilty? How many times has Your Honor listened to the state's attorney come into this court with a man charged with robbery with a gun—which means from ten years to life—and on condition of a plea of guilty ask to have the gun charge stricken out and get him a chance to see daylight inside of three years? How many times?

"How many times has rape been changed to assault and the defendant given a year? How many times has the state's attorney himself asked for consideration for everything including murder, not only for the young but for the mature?

"What about this matter of crime and punishment, anyhow? You can trace it all down through the history of man. You can trace the burnings, the boilings, the drawings and quarterings, the hanging of people in England at the crossroads, carving them up and hanging them as examples for all to see.

"We can come down to the last century where nearly two hundred crimes were punishable by death. You can read the stories of hanging on a high hill, and the populace for miles around coming out to the scene, that everybody might be awed into goodness. Hanging for picking pockets—and more pockets were picked in the crowd that went to the hanging than had been known before.

"What happened? I have read the life of Lord Shaftesbury, a great nobleman of England, who gave his life and his labors toward modifying the penal code. I have read of the slow painful efforts through all the ages for more humanity of man to his fellow men. I know that when poaching and petty larceny were punishable by death in England, juries refused to convict. They were too humane to obey the law, and judges refused to sentence. I know that when the delusion of witchcraft was spreading over Europe many a judge so shaped his cases that no crime of witchcraft could be punished in his court. I know that these trials were stopped in America because juries would no longer convict. I know that every step in the progress of the world in reference to crime has come from the human feelings of man.

"Gradually the laws have been changed and modified,

and men look back with horror at the hangings and killings of the past. What did they find in England? That, as they got rid of these barbarous statutes, crimes decreased instead of increased. I will undertake to say, Your Honor, that you can scarcely find a single scholarly book—and I will include all the works on criminology of the past—that has not made the statement over and over again that as the penal code was made less terrible, crimes grew less frequent."

At the prosecutor's table there was quick note-making, in gleeful readiness to refute Wilk's point.

"This weird tragedy occurred on the twenty-first of May. It has been heralded, broadcast through the world. How many attempted kidnapings have come since then? How many threatening letters have been sent out by weak-minded boys and weak-minded men since then? How many times have they sought to repeat again and again this same crime because of the effect of publicity upon the mind? I can point to examples of killing and hanging in the city of Chicago which have been repeated in detail over and over again, simply from the publicity of the newspapers and the public generally.

"Let us take this case. If these two boys die on the scaffold, which I can never bring myself to imagine, every newspaper in the United States will be filled with the gruesome details. It will enter every home and every family. How many men would be colder and crueler for it? How many men would enjoy the details? And you cannot enjoy human suffering without being affected for better or for worse; those who enjoyed it would be affected for the worse.

"What influence would it have upon the infinite number of children who will devour its details as Artie Straus has enjoyed reading detective stories? Do I need to argue to Your Honor that cruelty only breeds cruelty? If there is any way to kill evil and hatred and all that goes with it, it is not through evil and hatred and cruelty; it is through charity and love and understanding.

"There is not a man who is pointed to as an example to the world who has not taught it. There is not a philosopher, there is not a religious leader, there is not a creed that has not taught it."

We looked to Judd. Would he let himself be defended by this assault on his Nietzschean creed? But he was attentive, only flushing slightly.

"This is a Christian community," Wilk went on, "so-called; at least it boasts of it. Let me ask this court, Is there any doubt about whether these boys would be safe in the hands of the Founder of the Christian religion? It would be blasphemy to say they would not. Nobody could imagine, nobody could even think of it. And yet there are men who want to hang them for a childish, purposeless act, conceived without the slightest malice in the world." A snicker was heard. Wilk rallied to it.

"Your Honor, I have become obsessed with this deep feeling of hate and anger that has swept across the land. I have been fighting it, battling with it until it has fairly driven me mad, until I sometimes wonder whether every righteous human emotion has not gone down in a raging storm.

"I am not pleading so much for these boys as I am for the infinite number of others to follow, those who perhaps cannot be as well defended as these have been, those who may go down in the storm and the tempest, without aid. It is of them that I am thinking, and for them I am begging of this court not to turn backward toward the barbarous and cruel past."

*   *   *

In the morning, with an additional detail of twenty police controlling the crowds, Wilk turned to speak of the boys themselves. "Now, Your Honor, who are these two boys? Straus, a boy robbed of his boyhood, turned into a prodigy; Steiner, with a wonderfully brilliant mind—"

Judd leaned forward, as if at last the moment of fruition had come, when a great soul would interpret him to the world. But it was to the general psychiatric argument that Wilk gave attention. The brilliant youths, from earliest childhood "crowded like hothouse plants to learn more and more and more. But it takes something besides brains to make a human being who can adjust himself to life.

"In fact, as Dr. Ball and Dr. Tierney regretfully admitted, brains are not the chief essential in human conduct. The emotions are the urge that makes us live—the urge that makes us work and play, or move along the pathways of life. They are the instinctive things. In fact, intellect is a late development in life. Long before it was evolved, the emotional life kept the organism in existence until death."

Wilk pictured the examination by the State's alienists after the boys had made their confession. "Dr. Tierney and Dr. Ball are undoubtedly able men. Dr. Tierney said this: The only thing unnatural he noted was that they showed no emotional reactions. Dr. Ball said the same. These are the State's alienists, not ours. These boys could tell this gruesome story without a change of countenance, without the slightest feelings. There were no emotional reactions to it. What was the reason? I do not know. I know what causes the emotional life. I know it comes from the nerves, the endocrine glands, the vegetative system. I know it is practically left out of some. Without it they cannot act with the rest. They cannot feel the moral shocks which safeguard others. Is Artie Straus to blame that his machine is imperfect? Who is to blame? I do not know. I have never in my life been interested so much in fixing blame as I have in relieving people from blame. I am not wise enough to fix it.

"A man can get along without his intellect, and most people do, but he cannot get along without his emotions. These boys—I do not care what their mentality: that simply makes it worse—are emotionally defective. Every single alienist on both sides in this case has said so.

"Mr. Horn worked with intelligence and rapidity. On that Sunday afternoon, before the defense had a chance to talk to the boys, Mr. Horn got in two alienists, Ball and Stauffer, and they sat around hearing these boys tell their stories, and that is all.

"Your Honor, they were not holding an examination. They were holding an inquest and nothing else. A little premature, but an inquest.

"If Mr. Horn was trampling on the edges of the Constitution, I am not going to talk about it here. He is not the first one in that office and probably will not be the last who will do it, so let that go. A great many people in this world believe that the end justifies the means. I don't know but what I do myself. And that is the reason I never want to take the side of the prosecution, because I might harm an individual. I am sure the State will live anyhow.

"But what did Dr. Ball say? He said that it was not a good opportunity for an examination. Of course there was Stauffer. 'Fine—a fine opportunity for an examination, their souls were stripped naked.' Stauffer is not an alienist. He is an orator. Well, if Stauffer's soul was naked, there wouldn't be much to show." So much for the prosecution's alienists.

But the defense alienists had indeed examined the emotional conditioning of the boys. First there was Artie's Miss Newsome. "This nurse was with him all the time, except when he stole out at night, from four to fourteen years of age. He, scheming and planning as healthy boys do, to get out from under her restraint. She, putting before him the best books, which children generally do not want; and he, when she was not looking, reading detective stories, which he devoured. We have a statute in this state, passed by the legislature last year, if I recall correctly, which forbids minors reading stories of crime. Why? Because the legislature in its wisdom felt that it would produce criminal tendencies in the boys who read them. This boy read them day after day. He never stopped. While he was passing through college at Ann Arbor he was still reading them. When he was a senior he read them, and almost nothing else. Artie was emotionally a child.

"Counsel have laughed at us for talking about childhood fantasies and hallucinations. Your Honor has been a child. And while youth has its advantages, it has its grievous troubles.

"The law knows and has recognized childhood for many a long year. What do we know about childhood? The brain of the child is the home of dreams, of castles, of visions, of illusions and delusions. I remember, when I was a child, the men seemed as tall as the trees, and the trees as tall as the mountains. I can remember very well when, as a little boy, I swam the deepest spot in the river for the first time. I swam breathlessly and landed with as much sense of glory and triumph as Julius Caesar felt when he led his army across the Rubicon. I have been back since, and I can almost step across the same place, but it seemed an ocean then. And these tall men who I thought were so wonderful, they were dead and they had left nothing behind. I had lived in a dream. I had not known the real world, which I met, to my discomfort and despair, as I grew older, and which dispelled the illusions of my youth.

"Now, to get back to Artie Straus. He was a child. These crime books became a part of his dreams and a part of his life, and as he grew up, his visions grew to hallucinations. He went out on the street and fantastically directed his companions who were not there, in their various moves to complete a perfect crime.

"We might as well be honest with ourselves, Your Honor. Before I would tie a noose around the neck of a boy, I would try to remember the surging, instinctive, persistent feelings of the child. One who honestly remembers and tries to unlock the door that he thinks is closed, and calls back the boy, can understand the boy.

"Both these boys were in the most trying period of the life of a child; both these boys were at the moment when the call of sex is new and strange; both these boys were moved by the strongest feelings and passions that have ever moved men; both these boys were at the time boys grow insane, at the time crimes are committed. Shall we charge them with full responsibility that we may have a hanging? That the dead walls of Chicago will tell the story of the shedding of their blood?

"From the age of fifteen to the age of twenty or twenty-one, the child has the burden of adolescence, of puberty and sex, thrust upon him. Girls are kept at home and carefully watched. Boys without instruction are left to work the period out for themselves. It may lead to excess. It may lead to disgrace. It may lead to perversion. Who is to blame? Who did it? Did Artie Straus do it?

"I seem to be criticizing their parents. They had parents who were good and kind and wise in their way. But I say to you seriously that the parents are more responsible than these boys. They might have done better if they had not had so much money. I do not know. Great wealth often curses those who touch it. I know there are no better citizens in Chicago than the fathers of these poor boys. I know that there are no better women than their mothers. But I am going to be honest with this court, if it is at the expense of both."

He spoke more slowly, impeded by the need to blame and yet not to blame, to show and yet not to hurt. "To believe that any boy is responsible for himself or his early training is an absurdity that no lawyer or judge should be guilty of today. Somewhere this came to this boy. If his failing came from his heredity, I don't know where or how."

The audience was staring at Judd's father. The old man raised his massive head, as if almost eager to take his share of castigation. On Artie's side, it was as though one knew at last why his father and mother had been too ill to come to court.

"I do not know what remote ancestors may have sent down the seed that corrupted Artie Straus. If there is responsibility anywhere, it is back of him, somewhere in the infinite number of his ancestors, or in his surroundings, or in both."

It was curious that when he spoke of heredity, he emphasized Artie, rather than the two. Did Wilk feel the weight of Artie's other, unnamed crimes? Did he know more of Artie's madness?

"The State made fun of Dr. McNarry, the ablest and, I believe, the best psychiatrist in America today, for speaking about this boy's mind's running back to the teddy bears he used to play with and saying, 'You know, Teddy . . .'

"Well, Your Honor, I catch myself many and many a time repeating phrases of my childhood, and I have not quite got into my second childhood yet. But suppose I could not catch myself? 'Now I have put off childish things,' said the Psalmist thirty centuries ago. Suppose we cannot put them off? It is when these dreams of boyhood, these fantasies of youth, still linger, and the growing boy is still a child—a child in emotion, a child in feeling, a child in hallucinations—that it indicates a diseased mind. There is not an act in all this horrible tragedy that is not the act of a child, the act of a child wandering in the morning of life, moved by the new feelings of a body, moved by the uncontrolled impulses which his teaching was not strong enough to take care of, moved by the dreams and hallucinations which haunt the brain of a child.

"Your Honor, *all* parents can be criticized; likewise

teachers. Science is not so much interested in criticism as in finding causes. Sometime education will be more scientific. Sometime we will try to know the boy before we educate him and as we educate him. Sometime we will try to know what will fit the individual boy, instead of putting all boys through the same course, regardless of what they are."

He looked at Artie, who stirred uncomfortably. "This boy needed more love, more directing. He needed to have his emotions awakened. He needed guiding hands along the serious road youth must travel. Had these been given him, he would not be here today."

His gaze moved to Judd. "Now, Your Honor, I want to speak about Judd." Their eyes held for an instant, until Wilk turned away. "Judd is a boy of remarkable mind—away beyond his years. He is a sort of freak in this direction, as in others—a boy without emotions."

I wondered if that could be as properly said of Judd as of Artie. There was, first, his attachment to Artie. And Dr. Vincenti had pointed out that in Judd's case there were strong remnants of emotional life. Perhaps it was rather a case of powerful suppression, diversion of feeling.

Wilk went on with his analysis: "He was an intellectual machine going without balance and without a governor, seeking to find out everything there was in life intellectually; seeking to solve every philosophy, but using his intellect only.

"Of course his family did not understand him; few men would. His mother died when he was young. He grew up in this way. He became enamored of the philosophy of Nietzsche.

"Your Honor, I have read almost everything that Nietzsche ever wrote. He was the most original philosopher of the last century—a man who probably has made a deeper imprint on philosophy than any other man within a hundred years, whether right or wrong. Nietzsche believed that sometime the superman would be born, that evolution was working toward that superman." He glanced at Judd, like teacher correcting pupil.

"He wrote one book, *Beyond Good and Evil,* which was a criticism of all moral codes as the world understands them—a treatise holding that the intelligent man is beyond good and evil, that the laws for good and the laws for evil do not apply to those who approach the superman. He wrote on the will to power. He wrote some ten or fifteen volumes on his various philosophical ideas. Judd Steiner is not the only boy who has read Nietzsche. He may be the only one who was influenced in the way he was influenced."

Today we know that more, far more were influenced, or thought they recognized in Nietzsche something of their own selves. There in 1924, in the Chicago courtroom, far from the Munich where another Nietzschean began his march in 1924, the tocsin for the era was scarcely heard.

Jonathan Wilk walked back to the defense table and picked up some notes. "I have made a few short extracts from Nietzsche. These would not affect you. They would not affect me. The question is how these works did affect the impressionable, visionary, dreamy mind of this boy.

"At seventeen, at sixteen, at eighteen, while healthy boys were playing baseball or working on the farms, or doing odd jobs, he was reading Nietzsche, obsessed of it, and here are some of the things which Nietzsche taught:

" 'Why so soft, oh my brethren? Why so soft, so unresisting and yielding? This new table, oh my brethren, I put over you: Become hard. To be obsessed by moral consideration presupposes a very low grade of intellect. We should substitute for morality the will to our own end, and consequently to the means to accomplish that.' "

His own voice hardened by the words, Wilk went on. " 'A great man, a man that nature has built up and invented in a grand style, is colder, harder, less cautious and more free from the fear of public opinion.' "

He spoke directly to Judd, as to a misunderstanding pupil. "This was a philosophical dream, containing more or less truth, that was not meant by anyone to be applied to life." Wilk went on to quote a scholarly appraisal: " 'Although no perfect superman has yet appeared in history, Nietzsche's types are to be found in all the world's great figures—Alexander, Napoleon—in the wicked heroes such as the Borgias, Wagner's Siegfried and Ibsen's Brand, and in the great cosmopolitan intellects such as Goethe and Stendhal. These were the gods of Nietzsche's idolatry. The superman-like qualities supposedly lie not in their genius, but in their freedom from scruple. They felt themselves to be above the law. So the superman will be a law unto himself. What he does will come from the will and superabundant power within him.' "

An excited gleam had come to Judd's eyes. Was Wilk defending him now? And the great accusatory question stood forth in those eyes: How was anyone to know whether the will to power led to good or to evil? To Goethe or to Borgia?

But the moment passed. Wilk seemed to shake himself out of his abstraction and slowly to load upon himself again the burden of defense. "Your Honor, this philosophy became part of his being. He lived it and practiced it. Now, he could not have believed it, excepting that it either caused a diseased mind or was the result of a diseased mind.

"Now let me call your attention hastily to just a few such cases. One of the cases is a New York case, where a man named Freeman became obsessed in a very strange way of a religious idea. He read the story of Isaac and Abraham and he felt a call that he must sacrifice his son. He arranged an altar in his parlor. He converted his wife to the idea. He took his little babe and put it on the altar and cut its throat. Why? Because he was obsessed with that idea. Was he sane? Was he normal? Was this poor fellow responsible? Not in the least. And he was acquitted because he was the victim of a delusion. Men are largely what their ideas make them.

"Here is a boy who by day and night, in season and out, was talking of the superman, owing no obligations to anyone, believing whatever gave him pleasure he should do—believing it just as another man might believe a religion.

"You remember that I asked Dr. Ball about these religious cases and he said, 'Yes, many people go to the insane asylum on account of them.' They place a literal meaning on parables. I asked Dr. Ball whether the same thing might come from a philosophical belief, and he said, 'If one believed in it strongly enough.' And we know this about Nietzsche: He was insane for fifteen years before the time of his death. His very doctrine is a species of insanity."

Judd's mouth opened. Then he sank back.

"Here is a man," Wilk continued, "a wise man—perhaps not wise, but brilliant—who made his impress upon the world. Every student of philosophy knows him. His doctrines made him a maniac. And here is a young boy in the adolescent age, harassed by everything that harasses children, who takes this philosophy and believes it literally. It is his life. Do you suppose this mad act could have been done by him in any other way?

"He did it, obsessed of an idea, perhaps to some extent influenced by what has not been developed publicly in this case—perversions that were present in the boy." Intimately, to the judge, he said, "Both are signs of insanity, both, together with this act, proving a diseased mind.

"Why should this boy's life be bound up with Friedrich Nietzsche, who died twenty-four years ago, insane, in Germany? I don't know. I only know it is.

"I know that no man who ever wrote a line that I read failed to influence me to some extent. I know that every life I touched influenced me, and I influenced it, and that it is not given to me to unravel the infinite causes and say, 'This is I, and this is you. I am responsible for so much; and you are responsible for so much!' I know that in the infinite universe everything has its place and the smallest particle is a part of all.

"I know, Your Honor, that every atom of life in all this universe is bound up together. I know that a pebble cannot be thrown into the ocean without disturbing every drop of water in the sea. I know that every life is inextricably mixed and woven with every other life. I know that every influence, conscious and unconscious, acts and reacts on every living organism, and that no one can fix the blame. I know that all life is a series of infinite chances, which sometimes result one way and sometimes another. I have not the infinite wisdom that can fathom it; neither has any other human brain. But I do know that if back of it is a power that made it, that power alone can tell, and if there is no power, then it is an infinite chance, which man cannot solve. Tell me that you can visit the wrath of fate and chance and life and eternity upon a nineteen-year-old boy! If you could, justice would be a travesty and mercy a fraud!"

Then if it was the encounter with Nietzsche's philosophy that had drawn out a capacity for evil in Judd, who was to blame for that encounter? Could the publishers of Nietzsche's works be blamed? Could the university be blamed? "Even for the sake of saving the lives of my clients, I do not want to be dishonest and tell the court something that I do not honestly think in this case. I do not believe that the universities are to blame. I do not think they should be held responsible. I do think, however, that they are too large, and that they should keep a closer watch, if possible, upon the individual.

"But you cannot destroy thought because, forsooth, some brain may be deranged by thought. It is the duty of the university, as I conceive it, to be the great storehouse of the wisdom of the ages, and to let students go there, and learn, and choose. I have no doubt but that it has meant the death of many; that we cannot help. Every changed idea in the world has had its consequences. Every new religious doctrine has created its victims. Every new philosophy has caused suffering and death. Every new machine has carved up men while it served the world. No great ideal but does good and harm, and we cannot stop because it may do harm."

He paused there; he seemed to have done with Judd's philosophy, and on Judd's face there came a blank look—was he thus meagerly explained to the world? Was this all his life was worth?

"Your Honor, there is something else in this case that is stronger still than the elements I have spoken of before. There is the element of chance. These boys, neither one of them, could possibly have committed this act except by coming together. It was not the act of one; it was the act of two. Their parents happened to meet, these boys happened to meet; some sort of chemical alchemy operated so that they cared for each other, and poor Paulie Kessler's dead body was found in the culvert as a result.

"Your Honor, I am sorry for poor Paulie Kessler, and I think anybody who knows me knows that I am not saying it simply to talk. I do not know what Paulie Kessler would have been had he grown to a man. But would it mean anything if on account of that death, these two boys were taken out and a rope tied around their necks and they died felons? No, Your Honor, the unfortunate and tragic death of Paulie Kessler should mean something. It should mean an appeal to the fathers and the mothers, an appeal to the teachers, to the religious guides, to society at large. It should mean an appeal to all of them to appraise children, to understand the emotions that control them, to understand the ideas that possess them, to teach them to avoid the pitfalls of life.

"Society, too, should assume its share of the burdens of this case, and not make two more tragedies but use this calamity as best it can to make life safer, to make childhood easier and more secure, to do something to cure the cruelty, the hatred, the chance, and the willfulness of life."

*   *   *

As he began again in the afternoon, he was once more the skilled lawyer making his points. He recalled the rarity of a hanging verdict by a judge alone, and came to the sorest point, the testimony of McNamara about a "friendly judge."

"I am sorry to have to discuss it; I am sorry to embarrass this court, but what can I do?" Was there a word or syllable on paper to prove that Judd had actually made such a statement to McNamara? Surely the judge would disregard this last attempt to capitalize on prejudice.

"I want Your Honor to know that if in your judgment you think thèse boys should hang, we will know it is your judgment. It is hard enough for a court to sit where you sit, with the eyes of the world upon you, in the fierce heat of public opinion, for and against. It is hard enough, without any lawyer making it harder. I will say no more about it, excepting that this statement was a deliberate lie, made out of whole cloth, and McNamara's entire testimony shows it."

Horn's face was solid anger. If Wilk had planned this as a taunt, he could not have devised a more effective provocation, as we were to find in the very last moments of the trial.

Then, glancing over the notes scattered on the table, Wilk walked again toward the bench, resuming his plea. "Your Honor, I must hasten along, for I will close tonight. I know I should have closed before. Still there seems so much that I would like to say.

"Crime has its causes. Scientists are studying it, criminologists are studying it; but we lawyers go on and on and on, punishing and hanging and thinking that by general terror we can stamp out crime.

"Crime has a cause as certainly as disease, and the way to rationally treat any abnormal condition is to remove the cause.

"If a doctor were called on to treat typhoid fever he would probably try to find out what kind of water the patient drank, and clean out the well so that no one else could get typhoid from the same source. But if a lawyer were called on to treat a typhoid patient he would give him thirty days in jail, and then he would think that nobody else would ever dare to drink the impure water. If the patient got well in fifteen days, he would be kept until his time was up; if the disease was worse at the end of thirty days, the patient would be released because his time was out.

"As a rule, lawyers are not scientists. They think that there is only one way to make men good, and that is to put them in such terror that they do not dare to do bad."

He pulled at his suspenders. "Still, we are making some progress. Courts give attention to some things they did not give attention to before. And there is one such thing to which we must give real thought."

And then he spoke of an aspect of the crime that few had considered. Going back over the record of hangings, he showed that a recent change had taken place. For years, no minor had been hanged in Chicago, not even on a jury conviction. Not from 1912 until 1920. "In 1920, a boy named Viani was convicted by a jury and hanged, a boy of eighteen. Why did we go back to hanging the young? It was 1920; we were used to young men, mere boys, going to their death. It was 1920, just after the war. And that time is still with us, Your Honor.

"We are anew accustomed to blood, Your Honor. It used to make us feel squeamish. But we have not only seen it shed in bucketsful, we have seen it shed in rivers, lakes, and oceans, and we have delighted in it; we have preached it, we have worked for it, we have advised it, we have taught it to the young, until the world has been drenched in blood and it has left stains upon every human heart and upon every human mind, and has almost stifled the feelings of pity and charity that have their natural home in the human breast.

"I believed in it. I don't know whether I was crazy or not. Sometimes I think perhaps I was. I approved of it; I joined in the general cry of madness and despair. I urged men to fight. I was safe because I was too old to go. For four long years the civilized world was engaged in killing men. Christian against Christian, barbarians uniting with Christians to kill Christians; anything to kill. It was taught in every school, aye, in the Sunday schools. The little children played at war. The toddling children on the street. Do you suppose that this world has even been the same since then? How long, Your Honor, will it take for the world to get back the humane emotions that were daily growing before the war?

"We read of killing one hundred thousand men in a day. We read about it and we rejoiced in it—if it was the other fellows who were killed. We were fed on flesh and drank blood. I need not tell Your Honor how many bright, honorable young men have come into this court charged with murder, some saved and some sent to their death, boys who fought in this war and learned to place a cheap value on human life."

Wilk turned toward Judd and Artie. "These boys were brought up in it. The tales of death were in their homes, their playgrounds, their schools; they were in the newspapers that they read; it was part of the common frenzy. What was a life? It was nothing. It was the least sacred thing in existence, and these boys were trained to this cruelty. One of them tells us how he was haunted by a war poster, how he dreamed of rape and of killing.

"It will take fifty years to wipe it out of the human heart, if ever. I know this—that after the Civil War in 1865, crimes of this sort increased marvelously. No one needs to inform me that crime has a cause. It has as definite a cause as any other disease. I know that growing out of the Napoleonic Wars there was an era of crime such as Europe had never seen before. I know that Europe is going through the same experience today; I know it has followed every war and I know it has influenced these boys so that life was not the same to them as it would have been if the world had not been made red with blood. I protest against the crimes and mistakes of society being visited upon them. All of us have our share in it. I have mine. I cannot tell and I shall never know how many words of mine during the war might have given birth to cruelty in the place of love and kindness and charity."

Again, he had mounted far beyond the case; the spell was upon him and upon us all as Jonathan Wilk spoke. "Your Honor knows that in this very court crimes of violence have increased, growing out of the war. Not only by those who fought, but by those who learned that blood was cheap, and human life was cheap, and if the State could take it lightly, why not the individual? There are causes, as I have said, for everything that happens in the world. War is a part of this terrible crime; education is a part of it; birth is a part of it; money is a part of it; all these conspired to compass the destruction of those two unfortunate boys.

"I do not know how much salvage there is in these two boys. I hate to say it in their presence, but what is there to look forward to? I do not know but what Your Honor would be merciful if you tied a rope around their necks and let them die; merciful to them, but not merciful to civilization, and not merciful to those who would be left behind. To spend the balance of their days in prison is mighty little to look forward to, if anything. Is it anything?

"They may have the hope that as the years roll around they may be released. I do not know. I do not know." He gazed at the defendants. "I will be honest with this court as I have tried to be from the beginning. I know that these boys are not fit to be at large. I believe they will not be until they pass through the next stage of life, at forty-five or fifty."

The words fell strangely, heavily, as if he had prophetically sentenced them. In their faces was a fleeting triumph, followed by a shudder, as each computed the years.

"Whether they will be fit by then, I cannot tell. I am sure

of this: that I will not be here to help them. So far as I am concerned, it is over.

"I would not tell this court that I do not hope that sometime, when life and age has changed their bodies, as it does, and has changed their emotions, as it does, they may once again return to life. I would be the last person on earth to close the door of hope to any human being that lives, and least of all to my clients. But what have they to look forward to? Nothing." He quoted again from Housman:

> Now hollow fires burn out to black,
>   And lights are fluttering low:
> Square your shoulders, lift your pack
>   And leave your friend and go.
> O never fear, lads, naught's to dread,
>   Look not left nor right:
> In all that endless road you tread
>   There's nothing but the night.

Something had come over Wilk's face, a complete and otherworldly beauty, as if he indeed were relieved of the shortcomings of mankind, and in that moment one might have wondered if he were not some example of the superior man, hardly in the arrogant sense, but a man one had to remember, who in the midst of his career had been broken physically to the point of death by failure and defeat and betrayal at the hands of certain of his own clients who had not admitted to him their guilt, and from those years of pain and absence from life he had come again to the fullness of his powers, a man who cast a spell of tragic nobility, of faith through his very pessimism; it was in him that might have been read the possibility in every man to become something more than himself.

He repeated: " 'In all that endless road you tread, There's nothing but the night.'

"I care not, Your Honor, whether the march begins at the gallows or when the gates of Joliet close upon them, there is nothing but the night, and that is little for any human being to expect."

He drew himself out of his spell and came to his peroration. "But there are others to be considered. Here are these two families, who had led honest lives, who will bear the name that they bear, and future generations must carry it on.

"Here is Steiner's father—and this boy was the pride of his life. He watched him, cared for him, he worked for him; the boy was brilliant and accomplished: he educated him, and he thought that fame and position awaited him, as it should have awaited. It is a hard thing for a father to see his life's hope crumble into dust.

"And Straus's son, the same. Here are the faithful uncle and brother, who have watched here day by day while Artie's father and mother are too ill to stand this terrific strain, and shall be waiting for a message which means more to them than it can mean to you or me. Shall these be taken into account in this general bereavement?

"Is there any reason, Your Honor, why their proud names and all the future generations that bear them shall have this bar sinister written across them? How many boys and girls, how many unborn children, will feel it? It is bad enough as it is, God knows. But it's not yet death on the scaffold. It's not that. And I ask Your Honor, in addition to all that I have said, to save two honorable families from a disgrace that never ends, and which could be of no avail to help any human being that lives. I have been sorry and I am sorry for the bereavement of Mr. and Mrs. Kessler, for those broken ties cannot be healed. But as compared with the families of Steiner and Straus, the Kesslers are to be envied, and everyone knows it.

"Now I must say one word more and then I will leave this with you where I should have left it long ago. None of us are unmindful of the public; the courts are not, and juries are not. I have stood here for three months as one might stand at the ocean trying to sweep back the tide. I hope the seas are subsiding and the wind is falling, and I believe they are, but I wish to make no false pretense to this court. The easy thing and the popular thing to do is to hang my clients. I know it. Men and women who do not think will applaud. The cruel will approve. It will be easy today; but in Chicago, and reaching out over the length and breadth of the land, more and more fathers and mothers, the humane, the kind and the hopeful, who are gaining an understanding and asking questions not only about these poor boys, but about their own—these will join in no acclaim at the death of my clients. These would ask that the shedding of blood be stopped.

"I know the future is with me and what I stand for here; not merely for the lives of these two unfortunate lads, but for all boys and all girls; for all of the young, and as far as possible, for all of the old. I am pleading for life, understanding, charity, kindness, and the infinite mercy that considers all."

Tears flowed freely on old Steiner's face; some said that Judd and Artie wept. We were all utterly held by some tragic sympathy in Wilk's voice, in his whole being, that transcended any effect of words.

"I am pleading that we overcome cruelty with kindness and hatred with love. Your Honor stands between the past and the future. You may hang these boys, but in doing it you will turn your face toward the past. In doing it you would make it harder for every other boy who in ignorance and darkness must grope his way through the mazes which only childhood knows. In doing it you would make it harder for unborn children. I am pleading for the future; I am pleading for a time when we can learn by reason and judgment and understanding and faith that all life is worth saving, and that mercy is the highest attribute of man."

He walked back a little, partly releasing us.

"If I should succeed in saving these boys' lives and do nothing for the progress of the law, I should feel sad indeed. If I can succeed, my greatest reward and my greatest hope will be that I have done something for the tens of thousands of other boys, for the countless unfortunates who must tread the same road in blind childhood that these poor boys have trod —that I have done something to help human understanding, to temper justice with mercy, to overcome hate with love."

The weight of attention would not depart. And he remarked, "I was reading last night of the aspiration of the old Persian poet, Omar Khayyám. It appealed to me as the highest that I can vision. I wish it was in my heart, and I wish it was in the hearts of all.

So it be written in the Book of Love,
I do not care about that Book above.
Erase my name or write it as you will,
So I be written in the Book of Love."

We did not dare speak to each other, for our words might deride sentiment. We rather made the comments professional. A great plea. His greatest. His valedictory. It could suit any case and no case at all. It was a plea for every human life.

The praise accorded Wilk, even in the papers that cried the loudest for blood, must have been the final goad to Horn, for he rushed into his hanging plea like a blinded fighter, flailing, hitting in every direction at once. It was Wilk that he attacked, as much as the murderers, for Wilk's philosophy, he argued, would condone all crime, abandon all punishment, dissolve the basic rule that protected society. At moments Horn's bitterness was so intense that it seemed that if he could—as in Artie's fantasy—point a finger and cause death, he would do so to Jonathan Wilk. There were screaming, flailing periods when his voice went ridiculously high, and even Judd and Artie smiled sardonically, and this drove him to utmost fury.

Horn began with sarcasm: "Before going into a discussion of the merits of the case, there is a matter I would like to refer to. The distinguished gentleman whose profession it is to protect murder in Cook County, and concerning whose health thieves inquire before they go to commit crime, has seen fit to abuse the state's attorney's office. We all have hearts of stone.

"We have dared to tell Your Honor that this is a cold-blooded murder. We ought not to refer to these two young men, the poor sons of multimillionaires, with any coarse language. We should have come up here and tried these kiddies with kindness and consideration!

"Your Honor ought not to shock their ears with cruel references to the laws of the state, to the penalty of death. Why, don't you know that one of them has to shave every day of the week, and that is a bad sign. The other one has to shave only twice a week, and that is a bad sign. One is short and one is tall, and it is equally a bad sign in both of them. One is overdeveloped sexually and the other not quite so good.

"My God, if one of them had a harelip, I suppose Jonathan Wilk would want me to apologize for even having them indicted!

"We are cold-blooded! We have planned, according to Mr. Wilk, for three months and we have conspired to take the lives of two little boys who were wandering in dreamland. We have been held up to the world as men who desired blood, who have no kindly instincts within our hearts."

Padua was a decent, clean-living man, he told us, and so was Czewicki; as for himself, "I believe that not even Mr. Wilk, who has known me for years, would say that Arthur Horn is a vicious, cruel, heartless monster. I am a man of family, I love my children, four of them, and I love my wife, and I believe they love me." Were he not state's attorney he would have no feeling of animosity against these two individuals. When they were in his custody he had treated them with "kindness and consideration." When he had first received Judd's name as a possible owner of the glasses he had interviewed him at a hotel, so as to keep the matter out of the newspapers. "I think the state's attorney of this county is as kindly a man as the paid humanitarian, the man who believes in doing his fellow citizens good—after he has done them good and plenty."

There was hesitant laughter.

"But as a public official selected by the people, charged with the duty of enforcing the law of my country," he shouted, "I have no right to forgive those who violate their country's laws. It is my duty to prosecute them.

"And Your Honor has no right to forgive those who trespass against the state of Illinois!

"You have a right to forgive, and I know you do forgive those who trespass against Gilbert Matthewson personally, but sitting here as Chief Justice of this great court, you have no right to forgive anybody who violates the law! You have got to deal with him as the law prescribes!

"Your Honor, in this case, with the mass of evidence

presented by the State, if a jury were sitting in that box and
they returned a verdict and they did not fix the punishment at
death, every person in this community, including Your Honor
and myself, would feel that the verdict was founded on cor-
ruption!"

The judge's face darkened, but he kept his composure.

"And I will tell you why. I have taken quite a trip during
the last four or five weeks. I thought I was going to be kept in
Chicago all summer trying this case, and that most of my time
would be spent in the Criminal Court Building. I did come up
to Your Honor's courtroom five weeks ago, but then Old Doc
Yak—what is his name? The man from Washington—Oh, Dr.
McNarry—Dr. McNarry took me by the hand and led me
into the nursery of two poor, rich young boys, and he introduced me to a teddy bear. Then he told me some bedtime
stories, and after I got through listening to them he took me
into the kindergarten and he presented to me a little Artie and
Judd.

"I was then taken by the hand by the Feldscher brothers
and taken to a psychopathic laboratory, and there I received
quite a liberal education in mental diseases, and particularly
what certain doctors did not know about them."

The defense lawyers were sitting back, smiling.

"The three wise men from the East, who came on to tell
Your Honor about these little babes, wanted to make the picture a little more perfect, and one of them was sacrilegious
enough to say this pervert, this murderer, this kidnaper,
thought that he was the Christ Child and that he thought that
his mother was the Madonna, without a syllable of evidence
any place to support the blasphemous and sacrilegious statement.

"Why, this young pervert has proclaimed since he was
eleven years of age that there is no God!" He turned to Judd.
"I wonder now whether you think there is a God or not!

"I wonder whether you think it is pure accident, with
your Nietzschean philosophy, that you dropped your glasses,
or whether it was an act of Divine Providence to visit upon
your miserable carcasses the wrath of God in the enforcement

of the laws of the state of Illinois." He waited, as though seeing the boys struck dead.

Then, turning back to the bench: "Well, if Your Honor please, after the Feldschers had completed my education in the psychopathic laboratories, then my good friend Jonathan Wilk took me on a Chautauqua trip with him, visiting social settlements such as the Hull House, to expound his peculiar philosophy of life, and we would meet with communists and anarchists, and Jonathan would regale them with his philosophy of the law, which means there ought not to be any law and there ought not to be any enforcement of the law.

"I don't know whether the fact that he had a couple of rich clients who were dangerously close to the gallows prompted that trip or not.

"If Your Honor please, when I occupied the position Your Honor graces, I had an unfortunate man come before me. He was a man of my own race, of my own faith. I don't know whether his pineal gland was calcified or ossified. I don't know whether he had clubfoot or not, and I did not inspect his mouth to find out whether he had a couple of baby teeth."

He screamed, "I don't know whether Thomas Fitzgerald developed sexually at fourteen or sixteen!

"I do know, and knew then, that under the law he had committed a dastardly crime; he had taken a little five-year-old girl, a daughter of the poor, and assaulted her and murdered her. And Mr. Wilk says that in carrying out my duty to sentence him to death I was bloodthirsty!

"The law says in extreme cases death shall be the penalty. When Mr. Wilk served in the legislature he introduced a bill to abolish capital punishment. It was defeated. If I were in the legislature I might vote either way on such a bill. I don't know. But as a judge, I have no right to set aside the law. I have no right to defeat the will of the people, as expressed by the legislature of Illinois. I have no right to be a judicial anarchist, even if Jonathan Wilk is an anarchist advocate.

"He says that hanging does not stop murder. I think he is mistaken. From the time Thomas Fitzgerald expiated his crime upon the gallows, I have not heard of any little tot in

Chicago who met a like fate to that which Janet Wilkinson met.

"He says that hanging does not stop murder. I will direct your attention to the year 1920 when we stopped a wave of lawlessness. Four judges for two months tried nothing but murder cases. In that brief period of less than sixty days, fifteen men were sentenced to death in the criminal court of Cook County.

"As a result of that, murder fell fifty-one per cent in Cook County during the year 1920.

"We had a time here when every night in the newspaper there was a column devoted to the number of automobiles stolen. We established an automobile court, and I presided in it, and after we had sent several hundred to the penal institution for stealing automobiles the Rolls-Royce became just as safe as the flivver in the streets of Chicago.

"We had a reign of terror inaugurated here for years by criminals who dominated the labor unions. They were above and beyond the law. They laughed at it and spat in its face, just the same as these two poor young sons of millionaires. Forty-one of them were convicted in the courts of Cook County. The building industry, which had been stranded for years, began to revive and take on life.

"You have heard a lot about England. Well, I never had any liking for her laws as they applied to my ancestors and people in an adjoining isle, but I have learned to have a wholesome respect for the manner in which they enforce the laws of England.

"There, murder is murder; it is not a fantasy. Justice is handed out swiftly and surely, and as a result there are fewer murders in the entire kingdom of Great Britain yearly than there are in the city of Chicago!"

He stared at the boys as a man who did his duty even if the sight of the subjects made him sick.

"Call them babes? Call them children?" Horn shrieked. "Why, from the evidence in this case they are as much entitled to mercy at the hands of Your Honor as two mad dogs are entitled.

"They are no good to themselves. The only purpose that

they use themselves for is to debase themselves. They are a disgrace to their honored families and they are a menace to this country.

"The only useful thing that remains for them now in life is to go out of this life and go out of it as quickly as possible under the law!"

There came a woman's high, hysterical wail, smothered into a sob. I looked; it wasn't Myra. She sat tense, utterly white, her lips indrawn.

"I think it is about time we get back into the criminal court, and realize we are engaged, not in experimenting, not in philosophical discussions, but we are back here trying the murder case of the age, a case the very details of which not only astonish but fill you with horror.

"Their wealth, in my judgment, has not anything to do with this, except it permits a defense here seldom given to a man in the criminal court. Take away the millions of the Steiners and Strauses, and Jonathan Wilk's tongue is as silent as the tomb of Julius Caesar.

"Take away their millions, and the wise men from the East would not be here, to tell you about fantasies and teddy bears and bold, bad boys who have their pictures taken in cowboy uniforms. Why, Marshall Field's sale in cowboy suits must have fallen off at least a hundred thousand! Why, one by one, each of their doctors discarded the silly bosh that the preceding doctor had used, and finally that grand old man of the defense, Jonathan Wilk, seeing how absolutely absurd it all was, discarded all their testimony, and substituted as a defense in this case his peculiar philosophy of life.

"All right, let's see about that philosophy.

"What are we trying here, if Your Honor please—a murder as the result of a drunken brawl, a murder committed in hot blood to avenge some injury, either real or fancied?" He went a tone higher. "A man shooting down another because he debauched his wife and destroyed his home?"

And still higher: "A murder committed by some young gamin of the streets whose father was a drunkard and his mother loose? Who was denied every opportunity, brought up in the slums, never had a decent example set before him?

"No!

"But a murder committed by two super-intellects coming from the homes of the most respected families in Chicago. They had the power of choice, and they deliberately chose to adopt the wrong philosophy, Wilk's philosophy! They chose to make their conduct correspond with it!

"These two defendants were perverts, Straus the victim and Steiner the aggressor, and they quarreled.

"They had entered into a compact—a childish compact, Dr. Allwin says! A compact so that these unnatural crimes might continue. And Dr. Allwin calls that a childish compact. If Dr. Allwin is not ashamed of himself, he ought to be. My God, I was a grown man before I knew of such depravity!"

Aghast, he shrieked, "They talk about what lawyers will do for money, but my God, for a doctor to go on the witness stand and under oath characterize an unnatural agreement between these two perverts as a childish compact! And Wilk and Feldscher say that is evidence of insanity!

"Mitigation! Mitigation!" He backed away from it. "I have heard so many big words and foreign words in this case that I sometimes thought that perhaps we were letting error creep into the record, so many strange, foreign words were being used here, and the Constitution provides that these trials must be conducted in the English language; I do not know, maybe I have got aggravation and mitigation mixed up."

Striding to his table, Horn seized his notes. "I have wondered, when I heard these doctors say that you could not make an adequate examination in less than twenty or thirty days, whether the fact that they were working for two hundred and fifty dollars a day did not enter into the matter. If they were paid by the job instead of the day, I think they could have answered all the questions here in the three or four hours that our alienists employed."

And it was not because he suspected the boys might be insane that he had called in State alienists. "I knew how much money they had for some kind of fancy insanity defense. And that is why I sent for the best alienist in the city of Chicago that very first day."

What better opportunity, in God's world, could there

have been for an examination! "These two smart alecks were boasting of their depravity before they had been advised to invent fantasies.

"Yes, as Dr. Stauffer said, their souls were bared—Dr. Stauffer, a great scientist, whom Mr. Wilk has insulted and maligned because he can't disprove his words. And every incident they told him about I put a witness on the stand to prove.

"I am not the physician that the younger Feldscher is, nor the philosopher that the senior counsel is, but I think that if I talk to a man for four hours consecutively, and he is insane, I am going to have a pretty good suspicion of it.

"And I think that if Your Honor watches a man for thirty days, day in and day out, and he is a lunatic, you are going to have a well-defined suspicion of it.

"I have sometimes thought we were dreaming here, when the learned doctors got on the stand, who had been employed to say just how crazy these two fellows were. 'Just make them crazy enough so they won't hang, and don't make them crazy enough to make it necessary to put this up to twelve men, because twelve men are not going to be fooled by your twaddle. Just make them insane enough so that it will make a mitigating circumstance that we can submit to the court!' " Knowing he had touched them there, Horn grinned at the defense table.

"Why, one of the defense alienists had talked of Judd's ornithological writings. I asked him, 'Did you read them?' 'No.' 'You were employed to examine his mind, were you not?' 'Yes.' 'What did you do?' 'I examined his urine.' "

The laughter came.

Horn picked up, now, his copy of the thick Storrs-Allwin report. "In the discharge of my duty, and in an effort to protect the people of Cook County, I have to do a lot of disagreeable things, so I decided I would read this report.

"It has gotten to be quite a famous report. I do not know but what it rivals the fame of the jokebook of Joe Miller." He held it gingerly. "If they were to be discharged today, through some technicality in the law, their present so-called mental disturbances would all disappear very rapidly. If the glasses had never been found, if the state's attorney had not fastened the crime upon these defendants, Judah Steiner, Junior would be over in Paris or some other of the gay capitals of Europe, indulging his unnatural lust with the five thousand dollars he had wrung from Charles Kessler."

He opened the report. "The doctor did not think this report would ever get into the hands of the state's attorney." He chuckled, then leafed the pages. He stopped at a page as if at random and referred to the nursemaid—the nurse, he said, who knew more about Artie Straus up until the time he was fourteen than any living person. "They tried to create the impression that she was insane and that Artie caught his insanity from her, the same as catching measles. Let us see what Dr. Allwin says about her. 'She is very reserved, quiet and strict, her memory is good. She is a woman of attractive appearance, modestly and carefully dressed.' Why didn't they produce her as a witness? Here's why: 'She denied that he ever had any fears or any disorders in his sleep'! And if anybody would know about the daydreams or the night dreams of Artie Straus, I submit this woman would know about it!"

As for Artie's addiction to detective stories. "Well, there are a whole lot of us in the same fix. I remember crawling under the bed to read Nick Carter. And when I was a student at Yale I paid more attention to Raffles than I did to real property. I think that is the experience of most normal, healthy-minded young people.

"Now, they claim that the only reason that Artie committed this slight delinquency of murdering little Paulie Kessler was because all his life he craved for thrills." Snorting, Horn read, " 'He never appeared to crave a thrill or excitement, but was rather quiet in his conduct. After Miss Newsome left, he seemed to be much the same as before, quiet, rather affectionate, extremely polite and respectful.' "

On and on he went, using the report: " 'The patient says that he will tell a lie with no compunction whatever, and that he is completely dishonest.' Then, on page sixty-six, 'He said he had failed to mention certain things because he had been advised not to mention them.' "

Horn slammed shut the report. "Here are doctors," he blazed, "who want to make Your Honor believe that their only interest is in finding out what the truth is. And yet they admit there were major episodes they did not inquire into!"

A, B, C, D! What are they? Even though the defense advised its doctors to inquire no further, the State had inquired further. The State would give the court an idea about the suppressed episodes!

The entire defense table had risen. Before he could be silenced, Horn shouted, What of the monkey-gland robbery? What of the handless stranger? What of the two dead South Side students, one pushed into the icy lake, one found in a street, shot!

And in pandemonium, the session ended.

* * *

In the afternoon, Horn turned to the motive. "Your Honor, I have shown that this psychological-thrill motive was the bunk. The motive was money. They gambled for such high stakes that even their millionaire companions could not keep up with them.

"The kidnaping was planned for ransom. Page 104, 'They decided to get a young boy they knew to be of a wealthy family.' Thrills? Excitement? Money! Page 116, 'He had no hatred for the boy. Neither he nor his associate would have done it without the money'! Money! And of his share, Artie says, 'After all, five thousand dollars is five thousand dollars'! Page 118, Your Honor, in the language of Artie Straus, 'We anticipated especially the money,' and then the doctor adds in parenthesis, 'Facial expression of interest.'

"On page 122, 'The plan of kidnaping Willie Weiss was given up because his father was so tight we might not get any money from him.'

"They thought of kidnaping their fathers. But on page 121, they decided it was not practical, that there would be no one to furnish the money.

"They wrote in the ransom letter, 'As a final word of warning, *this is strictly a commercial proposition*'! From beginning to end, Your Honor, they tell us their motive—you don't have to send East for doctors to dig for it. The motive is Money!

"Money, money, money!

"On page 124, this is Artie talking about money and his opinion of the power of money. 'He thought that on account of his millions, or his father's millions, that he was above the law.' He believed that you cannot hang a million dollars in Cook County, no matter how dastardly the crime! Well, I disagree with him. I think the law is superior to money! 'He thinks an escape could be managed by spending a few thousand dollars, by bribing the guards at the jail and by someone giving him a gun. He says this without any swagger, as though it were only a matter of careful, detailed planning, which his mind can do. He cited the escape of Tommy O'Connor, one of the most desperate criminals Chicago has ever known, who made a successful jail delivery from the same jail within the last few years.'

"What a feeling of comfort and security the mothers and fathers of this town would have, with their children going back and forth upon the streets of Chicago to school, and these two mad dogs at large! By God, every mother and father would shudder and would want to lock their children in the house until they knew that the mad dogs had been captured or killed!"

Should they be put in prison for life then, when at any later date their money might help them to escape?

And tellingly, Horn shouted, "Why, one of the books Artie Straus left in the Morrison Hotel when they registered to establish a fake identity for their murder was *The Influence of Wealth on Imperial Rome!*"

Then he read: "Page 118, 'I asked him if he would go through with his plan again if he felt certain he would not be discovered. He replied, "I believe I would if I could get the money"'!'

"And Wilk says money had nothing to do with it! Not the thrill, not the excitement. Listen again: 'I believe I would if I could get the money'!"

Artie had three thousand dollars in the bank. Was it gain from other crimes, robberies, holdups?

After Judd was to leave for Europe, Artie had "thought of other ways of continuing his career of crime." One idea was to rent a room in a bad neighborhood and hang around poolrooms and meet criminals. Another was of becoming a clever financial criminal, putting through gigantic stock swindles, like Koretz. "Money, money, money!" Horn shouted.

"Mentally sick? On page 131: 'The patient's intellectual functions are intact; he is correctly oriented, in excellent contact with his surroundings. He denies any hallucinatory experiences, and there is no evidence of their presence.'

"Finally, Mr. Wilk tells us, the cause is heredity. Some ancestor way back planted the seed there. But on page 139 their own doctors say there is nothing to show any evidence of a hereditary nature. All his evil is of his own making. 'The condition,' " Horn read, " 'is acquired within the life history of the individual and will die out when he dies.' "

As he dropped his arms, that death seemed to stand before us.

Horn took a glass of water, drinking deliberately. He turned, then, to Judd.

"No emotions, they say. He drove them all out when he was seven or eight years of age, at the same time that God passed out of his heart. Well, let's see what his companion Artie says about it. 'I had quite a time quieting down my associate.' This is during the murder, if Your Honor please. It follows right after 'he was hit over the head with the chisel.'

"On page 108: 'My associate said, "This is terrible, this is terrible." 'It took five minutes to cool him down.' Emotion or no emotion? 'I told him it was all right and talked and laughed to calm him. I joked and laughed, possibly to calm myself, too.' "

And what of Artie's lack of emotion? In reciting the crime to the doctors, " 'When he told of returning the car to the agency at four-thirty, he choked up and wiped his nose with his fingers.' Yes, he cried, over the failure of it all.

"No emotion in superman Straus? No emotion in superman Steiner? No, when they came into court they killed all emotion on advice of counsel. The desire to save their own worthless hides is the only thing that enters their thoughts. No emotion, and yet, on page 108, Judd tells the doctor that he is rather fond of small children, he could not have struck the blow because he always wants to take a crying child in his arms and comfort it! On such occasions, Your Honor, he 'notices a functioning of his lachrymal glands'!

"The report says, 'While in jail the patient has clearly been under considerable emotional tension and is rather irritable at times. The newspaper report that he is a cold-blooded scientist with no emotions and entirely unconcerned is completely wrong'! They admit it themselves! All intellect and no emotion, says Jonathan Wilk, and therefore not responsible. The report says, 'The patient ordinarily is able to make a calm, self-possessed appearance and before reporters and visitors seems perfectly self-possessed and unconcerned. On the other hand, when he does not feel the need for doing this, and when he is talking frankly with people and no longer posing, he shows a good deal of irritability and nervous tension.' "

Horn grinned at them, as though he had snatched away the mask.

"I will tell Your Honor, if you don't think they have emotions, I will tell you of another such murderer. Some of us didn't think Harvey Church had any emotions. He told his story with an air of braggadocio, and he gloated while he was telling the authorities how tough a fellow he was. But when he was told to begin his march to the gallows they carried him there in a stupor. And if it is the fate of these two perverts that they must pay the penalty of this crime on the gallows, when they realize it, you will find that they have got emotion, and you will find they have got fear, and you will find these cowardly perverts will have to be carried to the gallows."

If there could be any doubt that they deserved death, Horn reminded the court of Artie's own mother's opinion, before the murderers were known. Whoever did it, she had said, should be tarred and feathered and strung up!

"What did she mean?" Horn demanded. "She meant that a mob ought to take charge of such a beast! Yes! We have heard Mr. Wilk talk repeatedly of the hoarse cry of the angry mob. Well, there is no danger or no fear of us actually hearing the hoarse cry of the angry mob, if the extreme penalty is visited here. I am not so sure, otherwise!"

He paused, head down, like a fighter aiming for the kill. Swinging his chunky body, Horn demanded, What of the tender friendship between these two perverts? Hadn't Artie again and again contemplated killing Judd? This fact was all over the report.

"In other words, all this king-and-slave fantasy is a pure figment of the imagination of the defense. The real tie that binds in this case is that one was a criminal, the other had something on him. Straus was afraid of exposure: he contemplated murdering Steiner. And the other blackmailed him, for perversion. Straus wanted to shut the mouth of Steiner and then break with him. For that he needed something on Steiner. That is why he wanted Steiner to help him choke the life out of little Paulie Kessler."

Horn threw down the Storrs-Allwin report, as something demolished. "That is the medical defense in this case. Mr. Wilk has read you poetry. May I be permitted, if Your Honor please, to read you some prose?"

And he read, " 'The White House, Washington, D.C.' "

It was a letter denying an appeal from a death sentence. " 'I have scant sympathy with a plea of insanity advanced to save a man from the consequence of his crime, when, unless that crime had been committed, it would have been impossible to persuade any reasonable authority to place him in an asylum as insane.' " The signature was that of Theodore Roosevelt.

"Is not that the case here?" Horn demanded. "If this crime had not been committed, could any reasonable authority be persuaded to send either one of these men to an asylum as insane?

"I submit that it is safer to follow the philosophy of Theodore Roosevelt as laid down in this great state paper when he was President of the United States than it is to follow the weird and uncanny philosophy of a paid advocate of the defense whose business it is to make murder safe in Cook County."

Thus he ended his first day.

*   *   *

There remained Wilk's plea of youthfulness. Was eighteen too young to die? Fresh in the morning, Horn began: "I submit, if Your Honor please, if we can take the flower of

American manhood, take boys at eighteen years of age and send them to their death in the front-line trenches of France in defense of our laws, we have an equal right to take men nineteen years of age and take their lives for violating these laws that these boys gave up their lives to defend.

"Ah, many a boy of eighteen lies beneath the poppies of Flanders field who died defending the laws of this country.

"Mr. Wilk referred to hangings. Mr. Wilk is a student of criminology; he has written a book on it and he says the criminal age, when most crimes are committed, is between seventeen and twenty-four. If we are going to punish crime, and by punishment stop it, how can we punish if youth is a defense, when it is during those very years that crime is committed?

"The law that Your Honor is bound to enforce in this case declares that from fourteen years of age up a boy has the capacity to commit a crime and is entirely and thoroughly responsible for it."

Then, like a litany, he began reading the names and ages of men who had been hanged. It seemed to go on forever. Buff Higgins was hanged at the age of twenty-three. Henry Foster, twenty-four, Albert C. Fields, twenty-four. As the roll call went on, Artie leaned forward, intently absorbed. Harvey Van Dine, twenty-one, "the little songbird from Italy," Viana, seventeen . . .

And if but few of them had been hanged on a plea of guilty the reason was simple. Obviously, if a lawyer could not get assurance of a deal through the state's attorney, he would say, "Well then, I am going to take a chance on twelve men. They can't do any worse to me, and I'm going to give my client a run for his money."

Why hadn't it been done this time? Because the crime was so subhuman, as the defense itself had admitted, that they simply could not go before a jury.

And Horn began his ultimate portrayal of the crime, the blows on the head, the suffocation, and working himself up to hoarse, staccato shrieks: "And then what did the fiends, the perverts, do to that dead boy in the car? Did not the coroner's physician testify——"

To the banging gavel, Horn stopped. Quite calmly he

dropped that point and said, "I think, if Your Honor please, I have now covered the three defenses set forth by Mr. Wilk: the defense of mental disease, the question of motive, the defense of youthfulness. But the real defense in this case is Jonathan Wilk and his peculiar philosophy of life. When I was listening to Mr. Wilk plead for mercy for these two men who showed no mercy, it reminded me of the story of Abraham Lincoln, about a young boy of approximately their age, whose parents were wealthy, and he murdered both of them so as to inherit their money. His crime was discovered the same as this crime has been discovered, and the court asked him for any reason why the sentence of death should not be passed on him, and he promptly replied that he hoped the court would be lenient to a poor orphan.

"Mr. Wilk quoted considerable poetry to you, and I would like again to be indulged while I read a little bit of prose."

He picked up a printed sheet. It was an address, he explained, delivered to the prisoners in the county jail by a distinguished criminologist. Horn read, " 'The reason I talk to you on the question of crime, its cause and cure, is because I really do not believe the least in crime. There is no such thing as a crime, as the word is generally understood. I do not believe that there is any sort of distinction between the moral condition in and out of jail. One is just as good as the other. The people here can no more help being here than the people outside can avoid being outside. I do not believe that people are in jail because they deserve to be.' "

The courtroom was abuzz as people told each other what Horn was quoting. He read more slowly, in an unmistakable imitation of Jonathan Wilk's reflective, pleading manner: " 'I believe that progress is purely a question of pleasurable units that we get out of life. The pleasure-and-pain theory is the only correct theory of morality and the only way of judging life.' " Horn looked up. "Isn't that exactly the doctrine of Judd Steiner? And that is the doctrine expounded last Sunday in the press of Chicago by Jonathan Wilk!"

This was scarcely an exact statement. The piece had indeed appeared on the previous Sunday. It had been dug up by

Mike Prager, from a report of a sensational talk given at the county jail by Jonathan Wilk, twenty years before.

Judd was glowing at Wilk. Yet it seemed to me that Wilk withdrew into himself, that he perhaps wanted to separate himself from these long-ago words that suddenly linked him to Judd. For even in this closing moment of the trial I had the impression that Wilk could not bring himself to any warmth toward Judd or Artie; he pitied them, he was their defender in all sincerity, but they had not entered his heart.

The judge was leaning forward, staring at Horn in a quizzical manner. He seemed on the point of asking, Was it Wilk, or the defendants, that Horn wanted to hang?

There was indeed a feeling that the judge was a man who tended to Wilk's way of thought; all through the trial, Horn had made no effort to conceal that he saw the judge as a man like Wilk. And he seemed to be attacking the judge himself as he again shouted, "The real defense in this case is Jonathan Wilk's dangerous philosophy of life!

"He said to Your Honor that he was not pleading for these two young men alone. He was thinking of the ten thousand young boys that in the future would fill the chairs his clients fill, and he wants to soften the law. He wants them treated not with the severity that the law of this state prescribes, but with kindness and consideration.

"I want to tell Your Honor that it would be much better if God had not caused this crime to be disclosed, if it went unsolved, and if these men went unwhipped of justice! It would then not have done near the harm to the community as would be done if Your Honor as Chief Justice of this great court puts your official seal of approval upon the doctrines of anarchy preached by Jonathan Wilk as a defense in this case.

"Society can endure, the law can endure, and criminals may escape, but if a court such as this court should say that he believes in the doctrine of Jonathan Wilk, that you ought not to hang when the law says you should, a greater blow has been struck to our institutions than by a hundred, aye, a thousand, murders!"

The judge still eyed him with that curious, measuring look. And Horn, with a guttural growl of frustration and despair, flung in a last taunt, one that he had perhaps meant to hold back: "Mr. Wilk has preached in this case that one of the handicaps the defendants are under is that they are the sons of multimillionaires. I would not bring it up if Mr. Wilk had not brought it up. But he tried to make Your Honor believe that Sergeant McNamara lied about Judd Steiner's statement that his father's millions could find a friendly judge."

There was that peculiar atmosphere in the room, foretelling that something ineradicable was on the way, something that Horn could no longer stop himself from doing.

Horn faced the judge, eye to eye. "Did Sergeant McNamara lie?" he demanded. "I don't know whether Your Honor believes this officer of the law or not, but I want to tell you, if you have observed these two defendants sitting before you during this trial, if you have observed the conduct of their attorneys and their families with one honorable exception—and that is the old man who sits in sackcloth and ashes and who is entitled to the sympathy of everybody, old Mr. Steiner—with that one honorable exception, everybody connected with this case—" he drew breath and shrieked, his arms chopping the air—"everybody connected with this case, they all have laughed and sneered and jeered! And if the defendant, Steiner, did not say that he would plead guilty before a friendly judge, why, his actions demonstrated that he thinks he has got one!"

The words hung in the hot, static air. Horn himself had stopped, as if expecting an explosion.

Judge Matthewson arose, stared at him, then sat down. "I will disregard what you have said."

The shock of Horn's running beyond the point of recall had been so great, professionally, that those at the defense table did not even seem to enjoy their gain.

Horn finished hurriedly. "I believe that the facts and circumstances proven in this case demonstrate that a crime has been committed by these two defendants and that no other punishment except the extreme penalty of the law will fit, and I leave the case with you on behalf of the state of Illinois, and I ask Your Honor in the language of Holy Writ to 'execute justice and righteousness in the land.' "

There was a restiveness, as if no one knew quite what to do, as at the close of some formal reception when the chief guests have given no sign of leaving. Judge Matthewson seemed not to have heard Horn's final words, engaged as he had been in an effort of self-control.

"Before the State rests," he said, "the court will order stricken from the record the closing remark of the state's attorney as being a cowardly and dastardly assault upon the integrity of this court."

Horn's voice was half-choked with chagrin, rage, defeat. "It was not so intended, Your Honor."

The judge disregarded him. "It could not be used for any other purpose except to incite a mob and to try and intimidate this court. It will be stricken from the record."

"If Your Honor please, the state's attorney had no such intention."

The entire courtroom was electric, the boys sitting up with a frightened hope, a realization that something entirely extraneous was happening, perhaps a break that would save their lives.

"I merely wanted to put my personal feelings plainly before the court," Horn insisted. "It was my intention as the state's attorney——"

"The state's attorney knew that his words would be heralded all through this country and all over this world. It was not the proper thing to do."

"It was not my intention."

"This court will not be intimidated by anybody at any time or place as long as he occupies this position." The judge sat back.

After a moment he announced, "I am going to take this case under advisement, gentlemen. I have practically two thousand pages of exhibits." He would study the testimony, the Storrs-Allwin report, the confessions. "It will take some time to prepare to decide this matter and to render judgment in this case. I think I ought to have ten days or so, and I will fix the day as September ten." He arose. "There will be nothing to deter me from rendering judgment on that day, gentlemen, unless it is illness. We will continue this case now until September the tenth at nine-thirty o'clock."

* * *

During those ten days the intense and fantastic absorption with the case increased rather than abated. We were beset with rumors; there were threats to bomb the judge's home, to kill him should he fail to hang the criminals.

Nor was Judd silent. If the sentence were death, the execution, according to the Illinois law, could take place in a few months' time. His mind seemed to be churning at greater speed, to produce some proof of the importance of his life.

He released, now, the list of questions he would attempt to solve from the other side of death, should there prove to be an afterlife. These were his questions:

Is human experience carried on in any form of consciousness after death?

Is there complete omniscience?

Are the cultural experiences of the earth necessary? What of the savage mind?

Is the absence of a physical being an advantage?

Does one retain reactions registered on the mind previous to death?

Is life on earth correct in judgment, or is there a higher judgment?

What is happiness?

On the morning of the sentencing, mounted police circled the building. The crowd was immense. Precisely at nine-thirty all were in their places in the courtroom, and Judge Matthewson appeared. Among us of the press, Prager and his friends were loud with dire predictions. That was a real mob out there. If the verdict proved short of death the boys would never get out of the building alive.

I could not feel it as a lynch mob, though I was not without uneasiness. Had I not read about ordinary people suddenly turning into a murderous mob? Could this really happen with the avid-eyed girls down there, the shirt-sleeved men, the crowd that physically appeared no different from people waiting at a movie?

Since then, I see it more like a crowd waiting for the outcome of a desperately fought election. In it there was a feverish having-to-know. I've talked about it with wiser and more learned men than myself, and I realize that it was not so much the act of decision that was awaited, not so much the who-wins, but the disposition, in terms of our own selves. In each there must have been identification; in each, the hidden sense that the disposition would symbolically apply to his own darkest impulse. *If I let myself do something even as awful as this, how much would I be punished? Would I die for it?*

And so in the courtroom, after the ten-day lapse, seeing again in solemn reunion the same relatives, the lawyers, the defendants, we all rose for the entry of the judge. After the swift formalities, the boys stood before him, between Wilk and Ferdinand Feldscher, and as the judge met their eyes it was still impossible to know whether he brought them death or life. Artie was utterly pale, his cheeks twitched. Judd was impassive.

Judge Matthewson read:

"In view of the profound and unusual interest that this case has aroused not only in this community but in the entire country and even beyond its boundaries, the court feels it is his duty to state the reasons which have led him to the determination he has reached.

"It is not an uncommon thing that pleas of guilty are entered in criminal cases, but almost without exception in the past such pleas have been the result of a virtual agreement between the defendants and the state's attorney; and in the absence of special reasons to the contrary, it is the practice of the court to follow the recommendations of the state's attorney.

"In the present case the situation is a different one. A plea of guilty has been entered by the defense without a previous understanding with the prosecution, and without any advance knowledge whatever on his part." Moreover, the judge pointed out, the plea of guilty in this case did not make the task of the prosecution easier "by substituting the admission of guilt for a possibly difficult or uncertain chain of proof." For in this case the State already had ample proof of guilt, besides full confessions. "The plea of guilty, therefore, does not make a special case in favor of the defendants."

Death, then?

There were two crimes—murder and kidnaping for ransom. In both, he pointed out, it was the court's duty under the statute to examine witnesses as to aggravation and mitigation. "This duty has been fully met. The testimony introduced, both by the prosecution and the defense, has been as detailed and elaborate as though the case had been tried before a jury."

Then came the disposition of another point—was it for Horn? "The testimony has satisfied the court that the case is not one in which it would have been possible to set up successfully the defense of insanity as insanity is defined and understood by the established law of this state for the purpose of the administration of criminal justice.

"The court, however, feels impelled to dwell briefly on the mass of data produced as to the physical, mental, and moral condition of the two defendants. They have been shown in essential respects to be abnormal; had they been normal they would not have committed the crime."

The very words of Wilk!

"It is beyond the province of this court, as it is beyond the capacity of humankind in its present state of development, to predicate ultimate responsibility for human acts.

"At the same time, the court is willing to recognize that the careful analysis made of the life history of the defendants and of their present mental, emotional, and ethical condition has been of extreme interest and is a valuable contribution to criminology."

Surely, it was a decision for the defense.

"And yet the court feels strongly that similar analyses made of other persons accused of crime will probably reveal similar or different abnormalities. The value of such tests seems to lie in their applicability to crime and criminals in general.

"Since they concern the broad question of human responsibility and legal punishment and are in no wise peculiar to the individual defendants, they may be deserving of legislative but not of judicial consideration. For this reason the court is satisfied that his judgment in the present case cannot be affected thereby."

Then it was for Horn; it was over.

"The testimony in this case reveals a crime of singular atrocity. It is, in a sense, inexplicable, but is not thereby rendered less inhuman or repulsive. It was deliberately planned and prepared for during a considerable period of time. It was executed with every feature of callousness and cruelty." He raised his eyes, and spoke with another kind of pain, of the man who must touch some of the filthiest things of life. He spoke "not for the purpose of extenuating guilt, but merely with the object of dispelling a misapprehension that appears to have found lodgment in the public mind." It was on the most gruesome point of all. He was convinced "by conclusive evidence that there was no abuse offered to the body of the victim."

He returned to his paper. "But it did not need that element to make the crime abhorrent to every instinct of humanity, and the court is satisfied that neither in the act itself, nor in its motives or lack of motives, or in the antecedents of the offenders, can he find any mitigating circumstances."

Death, for certain?

The judge reviewed the possible punishments under the statutes. For murder, death, or fourteen years to life in jail. For kidnaping, death, or from five years to life imprisonment.

"Under the plea of guilty, the duty of determining the punishment devolved upon the court, and the law indicates no rule or policy for the guidance of his discretion. In reaching his decision the court would have welcomed the counsel and support of others." In some states, he pointed out, a bench of three judges served in such cases. "Nevertheless the court is willing to meet his responsibilities.

"It would have been the task of least resistance to impose the extreme penalty of the law."

Then it was life!

Already, smiles were breaking, but Judd and Artie did not dare to breathe. "In choosing imprisonment instead of death, the court is moved chiefly by the consideration of the age of the defendants, boys of eighteen and nineteen years."

Wilk's tired face glowed. For in the end, this had been his choice of emphasis, not psychiatry so much, but youth and the precedent of consideration for youth.

"The court believes it is within his province to decline to impose the sentence of death on persons who are not of full age.

"This determination appears to be in accordance with the progress of criminal law all over the world and with the dictates of enlightened humanity. More than that, it seems to be in accordance with the precedents hitherto observed in this state. The records of Illinois show only two cases of minors who were put to death by legal process, to which number the court does not feel inclined to make an addition.

"Life imprisonment, at the moment, strikes the public

imagination less forcibly than would death by hanging; but to the offenders, particularly of the type they are, the prolonged suffering of years of confinement may well be the severest form of retribution and expiation."

The entire courtroom was stirring, breathing. Perhaps Judd was already computing the years before they might be admissible for parole. But Judge Matthewson's voice took on a note of doom. "The court feels it proper to add a final word concerning the effect of the parole law upon the punishment of these defendants. In the case of such atrocious crimes, it is entirely within the discretion of the Department of Public Welfare never to admit these defendants to parole.

"To such a policy the court urges them strictly to adhere. If this course is persevered in the punishment of these defendants, it will both satisfy the ends of justice and safeguard the interests of society."

Then he read the formal sentences. Upon each, for murder, "to be confined in the penitentiary at Joliet for the term of your natural life."

In addition, for kidnaping for ransom, "to be confined in the penitentiary at Joliet for the term of ninety-nine years."

As the sentences fell like successive iron bolts, sentences of life and forever, the first surge of joy abated. But then the life-urge poured and inundated over all other feeling. Judd and Artie pounded each other, and turned to wave to those they knew in the court, and laughed with happiness, Judd quieting only for an instant as he caught his father's eye, as the old man arose, scarcely less sorrowful than before, to follow Max from the courtroom. Behind them walked Charles Kessler with his brother, their expressions inward and sorrowful, their faces as immobile as ever. It was over. Disposition had been made.

Judd was pushing toward Wilk, with his hand extended. Wilk took his hand. There seemed, momentarily, a danger of tears in Judd's eyes, but the clasp was ended by the brusque interruption of the bailiffs, who laid hands on the boys to take them out of the room as a protection for the lives that had just been given back to them.

*   *   *

During the rest of the day, the tumult over the verdict was augmented by rumors of assassination plots. Mike Prager offered bets that they would never reach the state penitentiary in Joliet alive. There was a tip that three hundred members of the Ku Klux Klan were massing in Berwyn, just west of Chicago, that they would block the road with their cars and lynch the prisoners.

It was late in the day before the convoy set out. A police cordon circled the entire block of the county jail. Perhaps this in itself served to attract crowds. There were jibes and more threats, and yet the crowd did not seem particularly menacing.

At dusk, Judd and Artie, surrounded by guards, were slipped into a large black Marmon that waited, with motor running, at the rear entrance of the jail. They were linked together by a short chain, from wrist to wrist. In their car sat four guards with pistols drawn and pump guns on their knees. A vehicle filled with police preceded their car, and two others followed. The cavalcade departed at high speed.

So nervous were the custodians that they twice came close to wreckage on the road. Once, on the outskirts of the city, a collision was avoided only by a rapid swerve that threw guards and prisoners into one heap and brought laughter from Judd and Artie. The second time, a sudden stop at a railroad crossing by the lead car forced the prisoners' car into a ditch.

But in a few hours Artie and Judd were delivered to the state prison authorities, and suddenly the entire drama was over. The walls shut in on them. For each, prison life began with solitary confinement.

*   *   *

And it was indeed so that the world seemed to envisage the remainder of their existence. As the press wires compiled reactions to the sentence, we read the *New York Times* editorial declaring that prison for them should truly mean "the oubliette," that it should be "a life extinguishment virtually as complete as death."

An Indianapolis paper declared that the judge had spoken truly when he pictured a lifetime in jail as worse punishment than execution. But could they not sometime get out?

This seemed a pervasive fear. Legal experts gave interviews showing that they might be paroled in fifty years, even in twenty years. Horn vowed that he would take action to make sure they could never emerge. The Chicago *Tribune* editorialized that despite the judge's advice against parole no one could tell what would happen. And while grudgingly accepting the sentence, the *Tribune* declared that it was more than anything a sentence against capital punishment, for if these two did not deserve to hang, then anyone hanged thereafter in the state of Illinois would be hanged unjustly.

Yet for all the rumblings, the act of disposition seemed indeed to have ended the case. Crank letters and threatening calls rapidly fell off. More temperate editorials appeared, declaring the sentence to be "civilized." The court had spoken, and the case was decided. And in a few days, we had not a line about Steiner and Straus in the paper. We ran only a Sunday article by an eminent law professor pointing out that even though the judge had attributed his decision to a consideration of youth rather than to the mitigation plea based on mental condition, the elaborate psychiatric evidence introduced into the case would prove a landmark in medical jurisprudence.

A few days after the verdict I made up my mind at last to call Ruth. Only then I learned that she had gone East, that she had transferred to Smith College.

For the next few months I stayed on the paper in Chicago. I began an affair with a girl reporter on the *News*, an "emancipated woman." Those were the beginning days of the gang wars, and I became an expert on them—always the speeding car, the fusillade, the riddled body or bodies, the interview with Chief Nolan, who said it was the Capone mob or it was the O'Donnell gang, as the case might be; then the gangster funeral, and the box-score tally, and rarely an arrest, almost never a conviction; it was just people shooting it out on the streets, it was the same as when kids did it. Bang, you're dead.

There came the question of accepting the prize for helping to capture Steiner and Straus. Ten thousand dollars was to be divided between the Pole who had found the glasses and the detective who had traced them, and several others. And Tom and I were to have a thousand dollars each.

If I refused, I would be implying that Tom was wrong in accepting. And it might seem that I was not proud of what we had done. There was not a reason in the world for refusing. Afterward, Tom and I got ritually drunk at Louie's. I said I would go to Europe and write.

I even had it in mind, when I went East, to stop at Smith College. And so I wrote to Ruth. Her reply was cordial but cool. She congratulated me on my reward "since it would help me further my writing ambitions."

I tried in a letter to explain myself, and she wrote back that the whole experience was perhaps too strong as yet for both of us, that perhaps in the future years, when I came back from Europe, we could renew our friendship.

*   *   *

The first person I looked up in Paris was Myra; she had gone abroad immediately after the trial. Myra was thinner, but more attractive than ever; her eyes were huge, her hair was sleek, and she was already the ultra-habitué of the Dôme, nodding and waving to everybody and telling me who everybody was—Hemingway and Gertrude Stein and the editor of *transition,* in which she hoped to get her poems published.

We kept on drinking Pernod, then she was showing me the real Paris. We kissed along the quays, and it must have been nearly dawn when as a matter of course we went up to my hotel room—and she was pouring out talk by then: she wanted me to take her, it was "the only way to find out." But when we tried, she became rigid, clenched, her body vibrating with her effort to break through her rigidity, and finally she said in a small voice that it was always like that—she hoped I would forgive her for trying to use me but . . .

For some time after that, we met at cafés and talked and talked. Myra was always seen with the newest young male arrivals, holding hands on the street, going off intimately with them somewhere.

After a few months in Paris, trying to write, I became restless. I would drop in at the Chicago *Globe*'s offices to look at the paper, and I began sending home little feature stories, and presently I was a fill-in man. I had some luck interviewing a few notables; soon I was working full time. I seemed always involved in a serious affair or in an important story.

I went to Italy, I went to Germany. Something of the great malaise, the gathering sickness of Europe, began to be felt, and it was as though I had already known it; the taste of it was quite familiar to me from Chicago. Everything was as though expected. So the years passed. I lost track of Myra, too.

*   *   *

Then came the troubles in Vienna, the brief abortive revolution when the socialists barricaded themselves in their model apartment houses. They were shot out in a few days. With other "experts," I predicted great upheavals. With the socialists out of the way, what could stop the paranoiac Hitler from gobbling up Austria?

I was done with the story, and lingering in the depressing aftermath of the shootings, when I got a call, one morning, in my hotel. "Herr Doctor Weiss," the clerk announced. It was Willie. He had heard I was in Vienna. Home-towners abroad were always looking up correspondents, and in a case like Willie's I was even rather excited.

I found him waiting in the lobby, gnomish as ever, his head cocked to one side as he looked at me through narrowed eyes. There was the same knowing, ironic smile on his closed lips. His cheeks were perhaps a little more taut and dry; his eyes were deeply sunken.

What was he doing in Vienna?

He seemed surprised that I asked. Where else would he be for his postgraduate work but in the home city of the Old Man?

"Let's walk," he said, explaining that he allowed himself an hour's walk every morning; the Old Man, it seemed, got his best ideas while walking.

Willie set off at a brisk gait, setting the pace for his rapid questioning. First, he pumped me dry on my opinions about the uprising; although he had been living in Vienna for two years, and obviously knew more than I, Willie contributed only a series of *aha*'s. Then, quite brusquely, as though satisfied that he had got out of me all that I knew, Willie demanded what news I had of the boys in jail. Had they succumbed to prison routine? Or was Judd, at least, finding it possible to keep up some creative, mental life?

Here I disappointed him. I was completely out of touch. I recalled only a story Tom Daly had brought to me shortly after the trial: it seemed that Artie's denial of the "gland robbery," at least, was somewhat substantiated by a tale current among the South Side police. The taxi driver had really been mutilated, it was said, by the brother of a girl he had raped.

But that still left a good deal of mystery about Artie's other crimes.

The boys should have been studied further, Willie declared. A pity they weren't being analyzed. Willie carried a walking stick—as, I learned, did Freud—and he stabbed at dead leaves as we walked, pushing them into the earth.

Had I heard of the recent death of Dr. McNarry? he asked.

I hadn't. Indeed, it took me an instant to think myself back into the trial, to place him as the head of the psychiatric defense.

What a fitting thing it would have been, Willie said, if the three families had gone through with McNarry's idea. Maybe the idea still could be revived, right now, as a memorial to McNarry, one of the first psychiatrists in America open-minded enough to accept Freud.

But what idea of McNarry's was he talking about? I asked.

Why, hadn't I known? Willie walked even faster, stabbing at leaves all the while. Just after the trial, before returning to Washington, Dr. McNarry had suggested a wonderful idea to all three families—the Kesslers, the Strauses, the Steiners. After all, they were linked in the tragedy; each had lost a son.

Dr. McNarry had proposed that the three bereaved millionaire families set up a joint fund for the study of mental diseases. "A great research center in Chicago. And he even had thought of an emblem to go over the doorway, a sculpture in bas-relief, with the profiles of the three boys." Willie cocked his head at me.

"He proposed it to all three families?" I asked.

"I think it came fairly close, at that. Paulie Kessler's father saw it. You know, that little man had a great deal to him." And Artie's mother had been most eager for the plan. "I suppose it would have relieved poor Mrs. Straus of some of her guilt feeling to have her tragedy acknowledged in that way."

But real opposition, Willie said, had come from Randolph Straus, who could not bring himself to have his son's crime thus perpetuated.

"What a pity, what a waste of great material!" Willie said. The first task would have been a depth study of the crime itself. For the true understanding of it hadn't been reached. "They should have had someone from here. After the sentence, they could really have gone into all that material that didn't come out."

What material? Was he going to tell me, even now, something of the mysterious crimes, *A, B, C, D?* Had Willie after all known something? I felt a curious reluctance to be drawn into the whole thing again, but I had to face the story. Lighting a cigarette, I asked him, "Was there really more?"

It was a different kind of material that he meant. Interpretive material. "Were you ever satisfied? Did you ever feel it was understood?"

I recalled that he himself had tried an explanation and had brought up some strange theories. There was that idea about the weapon, the chisel, and its symbolic meaning.

"That was pretty good for a beginner," Willie said, allowing himself a grin. He lighted a thin cigar.

The chisel, the tool—but something else came back to me from that long-ago discussion with Willie. Two things he had mentioned, the tool and the burial place. About the second one I had never understood. The tool had been Artie's idea. But Judd had picked the swamp.

"That's it," Willie said. "That was Judd's part. Artie, the tool. Judd, the receptacle." Was the whole act, then, a symbol? Willie must have felt my resistant bepuzzlement, for he stopped walking. He pushed his stick against a leaf, driving it into the ground. He took another approach. "Do you know about the death instinct?" All life was a struggle between the two urges, to live, to organize into more and more complex forms, and to recede back to formlessness. All life was a struggle with the deathwish, and we had seen the victory of that wish in the cases of Judd and Artie.

"Don't we always tend to fit events into the latest theory we have acquired?" I said.

"Why did Judd pick that particular place?" Willie resumed.

"The swamp? He was familiar with it. He went birding there."

"He went birding in a lot of other places. The dunes might have been more suitable, safer if he thought about it, but you see he couldn't think about it, something impelled him to go to that particular spot, instead of the dunes or the lake or anywhere." Artie, for instance, must have used other places at other times—if one accepted that there had been other crimes for Artie. Yet this time it was Judd who insisted he knew the exact spot.

"All right," I said. "Why did he pick Hegewisch?"

"It's not Hegewisch—it's the particular spot there."

"Under the tracks?" I said. "The cistern?" That had indeed always seemed peculiar to me, for it was obviously a not very safe hiding place.

"Well?" Willie demanded. "Don't you see what it represents?"

I thought of the hole, the white concrete pipe, and it represented nothing to me.

"The cistern." He was staring at me until I thought, yes, perhaps Willie was a little like Judd and Artie, possessed by his own brilliant mind. "A naked body in the cistern," he said. "It was a pretty tight fit, wasn't it, and the fluid, the body in an aqueous environment, a slow amount of fluid flowing through the cistern—"

I stared back at him, beginning to feel his meaning.

"How many times did Judd say he wished he'd never been born?"

I knew his meaning, then, and rejected it completely, almost revolted by it, even while—all the more revolting, like an obscenity—my mind kept adding the picture of the bushes screening the entrance to the pipe.

Simultaneously, a fearful feeling was sweeping up in me, a fear of unknowing in myself; perhaps it was even like the primitive man's awe before the witch doctor, a sense that there were individuals, people like Freud and even Willie, who held keys to inner knowledge, who saw meanings we could not see.

As though forgiving my slowness in apprehension, Willie became torrential. I had to picture Judd as a baby. The last baby of a mother who had become an invalid through his birth. His mother had paid such a price for having him—her life, everyone believed.

"Remember, this idea became overt with him. He told Dr. Allwin that he felt he had killed his mother because her illness stemmed from his birth. But what he actually meant, what he couldn't say, was that he felt his father had killed her, through the male demand on her."

"You got that far last time," I recalled, "including his Madonna fixation, as a way of getting rid of his father."

"Yes," Willie said, but since then, there had been some interesting ideas on the myth of virgin birth. Making the mother a goddess and a virgin—wasn't that a perfect barrier against incest wishes in the boy? Wasn't Judd particularly attached to his mother? And as he grew up, wasn't his fear of having anything to do with women a fear of using them, and therefore an incest-fear of using his mother, of hurting his mother?

"Yet he wanted to kill a woman," I objected. "It was his idea that the victim should be a girl."

"The complement of overtenderness is overviolence," Willie responded. "But there was even more to it, about wanting to kill a girl. We'll come to it."

He came to it, through all of Judd's history. Hadn't his mother wanted this last baby to be a girl? So she virtually made Judd into a girl. How many mothers persisted with their little boys in the first years, keeping their silken girlish curls, dressing them almost like girls, thinking it didn't matter—the kids couldn't really know. "So she sends him to a girls' school. The report said the old man wanted boys to be boys—let them bring pets, frogs, turtles into the house—but the mother was crazy for neatness and cleanliness. Here is where you get a couple of the characteristics that show up in Judd. All this feminine passion for order, for having things in their place. You see the conflict growing in him—is he a girl or a boy?

Until someday it would be too much to keep in; he would have to dispose of his conflict somewhere. And there was that terrific thing, when he got to public school, about not using the toilet. Holding himself in! The sissy from the girls' school! And that's just when he tells us he started teaching himself never to have any emotions, to hold it all in! Well, where is it you don't feel anything at all?"

Did he mean death? Then the other state echoed to me. We had just talked of how often Judd repeated it. *He wished he never had been born.*

We were walking again, but more slowly. "Then he goes to Twain. He's odd and sickly and always erupting all over with skin diseases, he's allergic, he can't stand the world. He's a lone kid, the crazy bird, the last one they mention in the school annual—well, hell, we all knew Judd by then. I remember him, I didn't talk to him in those years; I was older than he, but we all knew he was supposed to be queer, nasty, conceited, all that. Now, he develops his mania for languages and for birds. The languages—what's language but communication? He couldn't communicate with anybody. He had no close friends. He was looking for the key, the way to communicate, the universal language. And the birds, I haven't quite got it—flight, you know, is commonly a sex symbol—wait a minute!" Willie halted, cocked his head. "What was the first bird he was looking for?"

I must have looked stupid.

"A child, watching birds. What bird does any little child wonder about first of all? The stork. The stork story. He's skeptical. Remember, Allwin reported when the nurse first told Judd the stork story, Judd said she had a sneer on her face. So he asked his father and the father said babies were bought in stores. Little Judd was going to find out who was right. He began watching for birds, to solve the great mystery that all children feel compelled to solve. Then all this became sublimated into his bird classifications, but even in Hegewisch, he was still watching, still a child watching for the stork."

I must have looked dubious, because he said, "All right. Put that aside. We'll see. Take him from Twain. That's when he began to get these crushes, first on his brother in uniform, then on a camp counselor, and then he fixed on Artie—"

"We all had kid crushes like that," I objected. "It didn't make us all homosexual. Or did it?"

"A little bit, a little bit, all of us. But we got out of it. The trouble for Judd was, with all the girl stuff in his childhood, he still didn't know what he was. So he got into it. And his conflict must have been worse than ever. Because don't forget his nurse got him all tangled up when he was a kid, got him mixed up about sexual release, so that even if he didn't know it he wanted it the way she showed him, the first way, the oral stage, or probably he was polymorphous perverse—the exploratory stage. Then he starts with Artie. He gets a fixation on Artie, and even when he tries sex with a girl, he sees her as Artie. But he must have been struggling all the time in himself, struggling to become a male. He's in this adolescent period, the worst period, when his mother dies—the one real attachment, apparently, that he had.

"Then the scheme starts. The revenge on life. In Judd's mind, it is a scheme to kill a girl. He kept pulling for it all the time, trying to convince Artie it ought to be a girl."

"He had that mixed up with the war," I reminded Willie.

"All right. That's where he got the image. From a war poster. Man stuff. But that only added to the hatefulness of the world. And himself in it. And he was going to rid himself of all this by killing a girl. What girl?" Willie looked at me and said with finality, "The girl in himself. Judd had to kill the girl-part of himself, before he could become a man."

It was really ingenious, I told him. He had built up a really clever theory. Perhaps, I smiled, it was a good thing the alienists had not brought such an idea into court, because Horn would have had a field day with it.

"Yah?" Willie's voice became argumentative. "Now look at the act of murder. How were they going to accomplish it? They talked about it for weeks, they developed the details. There was the chisel, to knock the victim on the head—that was Artie's part, we know that. And it was Artie who used it. But then they had all these other things they planned to use. There was the ether. They were going to put the victim to sleep. Judd saw it not as killing, but the sleep of death, the sleep before life, you could say. The ether was Judd's idea, connected with the birds. But the ether wasn't all. After that, the plan was to use a cord, strangling the victim with the cord, a silken cord they wanted, not a rope, each holding onto an end for equal participation.

"Now, you're going to think this is far-fetched. But isn't this idea a birth in reverse? What were they reading at the time? Judd was full of Huysmans' *A Rebours*. Granted all that Nietzschean talk of his was a rationalization rather than a cause of his acts. But reading does suggest things. Our mind picks up what it wants. And the perversity, the inverted ideas of writers like Huysmans, the ideas like the Black Mass, the conception of doing everything backwards, by the substitution of opposites, black for white, girl for boy, death for life—the cord—you can't discard that clue entirely."

I said I would admit it as an obscure possibility; I would still go along to see where it would all lead.

"It led to the cemetery," Willie said. And, reflectively: "You know, that's a possible connection I hadn't thought of before. Judd was driving. And in his confession he says they went up a side road to a cemetery and waited there until it got dark—a couple of hours. Now, why the cemetery? Of all the dozens of side roads he might have taken? Certainly because death was in his mind, by then, and Judd must have been as though calling for his mother, the way a kid does when everything has gone wrong and he is scared. He was drawn to seek his mother; this wasn't the particular cemetery where his mother is buried—that's out west of Chicago, I think—but he had been visiting his mother's grave, he said, almost every week, and so the association was there, and he was drawn to a cemetery as to his mother; and that was where they waited, with the dead kid, until it got dark. Then they drove to the real burial place he had picked out in advance. They took this body and carried it all the way across the swamp to that particular spot, insisted on by Judd, and before they put the body into the cistern there was one more ritual, and this was Judd's too. Remember, he was so queasy he couldn't strike anyone, he couldn't touch a dead body, yet this was a thing

Judd did and not Artie: he took the can of hydrochloric acid that was intended to obliterate recognizable parts of the body —they imagined it would dissolve the flesh—" Willie glanced at me and his eyes emphasized again the birth in reverse. "Judd took this acid, and he said he poured it on the face, and he poured it on the penis." He became silent.

"They said it was with the idea that a boy might be identified—"

"Look, they knew better than that," Willie said.

"Well, it was circumcised—he could be identified as a Jew. In fact, that's how I came to identify him."

"And wasn't that part of it, for Judd?" Willie said, rather softly. "Wasn't that one of his conflicts? Didn't he have to obliterate the problem of being a Jew? To dissolve it, so that the sign would be gone, the mark in the flesh, it was even in his fantasy, the brand on the inner side of the leg, the brand that could sometime be removed."

Something in me gasped at this leap of his imagination. Yet, resist the idea as I might, wasn't it a possible connection?

"And there was more," Willie said. "Oh, the id is extremely cunning, that's one thing we've learned, it is poetic and cunning. You don't know how clever it can be, how the associations leap—I suppose because it's all open, there's nothing to block them; and how literal it can be, too. It's astounding."

And with this preparation, Willie brought out his last point, quite casually, the way an actor sometimes throws away his most important line, using reverse emphasis. "If there were no penis at all, wouldn't it be a girl that he had killed?"

I could, indeed, see how his whole argument came together. If Judd had always wanted to cease being feminine, if this had been his great conflict, if he had wanted to kill a girl symbolically in an act that was self-destruction as all murder is self-destruction, then in this final gesture with the annihilating acid—had he not been doing it? Killing the girl in himself? He had first sought to obliterate identity in the face, so that the child could be himself, and he had then sought to obliterate the male sex. The child, thus, could be representationally himself as a girl, and this child had been placed naked in a womb, returned to pre-birth. And the womb was a sewer —the way he had always thought of females, "so dirty, down there."

If he wished he had never been born—wished he had never been born as a girl kind of boy—then the gesture was complete; he had exorcised the curse on himself. He had become unborn, in the womb of the mother who was in the earth.

And then there came to me the other possibility. If he had destroyed the male element and returned the body to the womb, was it not equally understandable as a way to rectify a mistake, to say that it was as a girl that he really should have been born? There was, indeed, as Willie had said, an incredible cunning, an amazing poetic compression in this way of thinking. For here was the duality of nature symbolized—here was Judd's conflicting wish to be a boy, to be a girl—expressed in the symbol that could be fitted in either direction! In his dreadful culminative gesture, Judd had done both things, he had renounced and returned to unbirth the girl in himself, yet he had said he should have been born as a girl.

And would Judd not there, together, have had a seeming solution of both his conflicts, since a girl could not have the mark in the flesh of the Jew? It was both a death gesture, then, and a life gesture that he had made, impelled by a wish for being unborn, and a wish for rebirth.

We walked on silently.

Finally I asked of Willie, "You once thought the killing could have proven a catharsis for him. If they hadn't been caught."

Willie said, "In physical infections, the body creates poisons with which to kill the pathology and cure itself. Perhaps so does the psyche."

Another overwhelming thought came to me, changing the conception I had had until then of the crime. "Then Judd was not merely Artie's accomplice. He wasn't there only because he was in love with Artie. He had to do the murder because of some compulsion in himself. Just the way Artie did."

"That's what I think," Willie said. "Once Artie started them on it."

* * *

Automatically we had turned, to circle back. At moments, one or the other of us would speak, bringing up some neglected or confirming point, as we mused over the tragedy. Willie remarked again about the choice of spot. Wasn't it there that Judd took his class of children, perhaps literally to watch for a stork, a rare visitant in the Chicago area? And the children must have echoed for Judd his own childhood absorption in the source of the birth mystery. Thus it became inevitable that he should return the child's body there, almost as though he had delivered his soul to the original source. And what did he lose, there? His glasses, his eyes. He didn't need to see any more, in the womb or in the tomb.

For me, the depths of Willie's explanation brought on an oppressive feeling. If something like this were valid, then we were hopelessly driven, in the grasp of such dreadful forces. This was only an elaboration of Wilk's mechanistic philosophy, with the physiological determinants augmented by the mechanics of psychology and psychoanalysis.

And yet, if human minds were truly beginning to see into the mechanics, could there not come some form of control? Did this not still allow for free will?

If someone had seen what was happening in Judd, could he not have helped him? Couldn't a less dangerous form of catharsis have taken place? Hadn't he been on the verge of emergence into normal relationships with women?

Willie's mind seemed to have walked with mine. "What became of Ruth?" he asked.

Even then, her name affected me. "I don't know." I had let absence end the thing.

"Myra was here," he said.

"In Vienna?"

"She was in analysis." Suddenly there had come over his face something, a grin, a leer, so painful that I was caught in the pain. I wondered if Willie could have been in love with Myra. And only then did I fully see her in her own wretched frenetic prison, as another innocent victim of the tragic crime.

Willie continued, with an air of complete control. "I don't suppose you know you entered into her fantasies. Perhaps at a given moment you could have helped her. She's gone back to the States." He added, almost in a mutter, "I think she made a fairly good adjustment."

When we parted he met my eyes with a kind of furtive look, his mouth grinned, and he turned and strode away, his large head held firmly erect.

*   *   *

A few years later, I met Myra in New York. She was a psychiatric social worker, still overtense, the tendons of her arm taut as wires. I took her to the theater, then we went back to her interior-decorated little apartment, filled with modern art; we drank a good deal; she told me all about herself, her affairs—there had even been a brief marriage. So generous, so quick, so filled with the latest things, the newest books, the newest psychoanalytic theories, playing the newest jazz records—boogie-woogie, at the time. And always staggering with a host of illnesses and calling them psychosomatic.

She died of cancer. It was in the same year that Artie Straus was murdered, in prison, by a jealous inmate.

*   *   *

During those years, as analytic ideas became more current, I thought occasionally about Willie's hypothesis. At times I even played with elaborations. There was, for example, the fact that the burial place, the womblike cistern, was under a railway track. And as the train as a sex symbol became part of our popular vocabulary about dreams and fantasies, I saw a final detail in Judd's compulsive selection of the place—the ruthless engine of sexuality forever running over the cistern-image of the mother.

But then I would discard such ideas as intellectual play. In the thirties, in the forties, we elaborated, rather, on economic causation, and the Straus-Steiner case faded from importance.

Yet all this time, the analytical way of thinking had progressed, and today Willie's hypothesis does not seem particularly bizarre. Nor does it seem so hopeless. For even in this short span of time, a single generation, we have seen some success in the manipulation of the dark forces. Willie Weiss himself, practicing in Chicago, has gained considerable stature.

It must seem ironic to speak with an accent of hope, when during these same years we have seen an outbreak of paranoia and a Nietzschean mania connected with the death of millions. Yet today an Artie or a Judd, while still in childhood, might more likely arrive at the desk of a therapist.

Although the alienists of the twenties were careful to predict that this crime in its peculiar form could scarcely be repeated, we have had adolescents in pairs and in larger groups, and also alone, in whom the destructive urges broke through. Perhaps in coming to recognize the mechanism, we can devise controls for it. Perhaps this very pattern of disturbance increases shortly before the controls become generally available, just as the incidence in polio seemed to increase enormously shortly before the preventive vaccine was developed. And I sometimes believe that for me, in a curious way, the case itself served as a vaccine. For there was an incident, or a potential incident. It came during the war.

I never had written the books, not even the "I was there" books of the foreign correspondents, and as it happened, I never again reached the intense involvement and achievement —if achievement it may be called—of my first assignment.

When something big comes to us early in our careers we have an expectation of exceeding and exceeding ourselves; yet for some this never happens, just as, for some, no later love has the quality of first love.

I married, divorced, and during the war I was a correspondent with the Third Army. It was toward the very end of the war, in the last weeks, that the Steiner-Straus case came finally home to me.

We had crossed the Rhine; we were, in those weeks, all in a state of unrecognized battle shock, a kind of windup frenzy, and I, like some other correspondents, rode with a tank column running wild and free across Germany. For jeepmate, I had a daredevil photographer from one of the news weeklies, a man who had jumped with the paratroopers and made something of a legend of himself. He always wanted to go close, closer.

The drive from press camp to the front strung out longer each day, as the tank penetration went into high, and on those long rides, Frank and I took turns driving, and we played a kind of game. It was a game almost all men at war have played. The game was imagining a rape.

It began with tales of G.I.s, of a pair who had somehow ruled a German village for a day and had commanded the mayor to bring them two virgins. And how the townsfolk had finally conceded.

And somehow these tales evolved into a fantasy that we should find us a German girl and rape her. We had had our share of complaisant German girls and chocolate-bar girls, but this idea, this game, persisted, on the pretext that we would not truly have known war or known life until we had given ourselves this ultimate war experience.

Our game consisted in elaborating on the setup: Some day on a road just opened by the tanks, with the infantry not yet come up to occupy the area, there would appear a lone girl. . . .

We must have gone on with this game for several weeks. Every time we would spy a likely girl we would, however, find that the situation was not ideally propitious. Either the road was too busy or the girl wasn't really appetizing.

But the game held us together in a peculiar way. Only far back, in Chicago on my first job on the *Globe,* had I partnered so well. And here, as in those Chicago days with Tom Daly, it was because I felt my partner to be the real thing, the tough, complete newspaperman, the drinker who drank for love of drinking and not because the boys all drank.

As for the imaginary game of rape, I told myself it gave vent to hatred burned deep into Frank in those early Normandy days when he had had it rough with his paratroop outfit. He had seen boys picked off while they hung in their caught silk in the trees, and he needed a revengeful release on the krauts.

Then one day we found the ideal situation. It came as we were drawing near the Elbe. Our own troops had halted at an agreed-upon line, but we correspondents would drive a few kilometers into unoccupied territory, scouting for the meeting with the Russian troops that would symbolize the end of the war.

That day, Frank and I went a little farther forward than the others had gone. It was a nice open road, and Germans could be seen working in the fields here and there, as though there had never been a war.

As we rounded a bend, we saw a felled tree across the road. We pulled up. And there was a fräulein. She was walking along a field, carrying a lunch basket. She was everything we had specified in our game: young, perhaps seventeen, and very pretty.

Frank shouted, "Halt!" and she halted. "Come here!" She approached. We both got out of the jeep. Only a shallow ditch was between us and the girl. All around, the area was deserted. Moreover, we were beyond the final line; our army would never come here to receive complaints.

"Where are you going?" Frank demanded in pidgin German. She said she was fetching lunch to her father, in the field.

"Have you seen any Russians?"

"No," she said, trying to keep her air of calm.

Frank looked at me. "This is it," he said. And he ordered the girl, "Lie down."

She stared at us.

"Lie down!" he commanded, and pulled out his revolver. Though correspondents were not supposed to be armed, most of us carried pistols.

"Nein—nein—" the girl began to stutter.

I felt parched. All these weeks we had been building ourselves to this. Surely we had meant it. Surely I had meant it too.

And at the same time I felt terrified of Frank. He'd do it and then shoot her. I had shared it all the way, goaded him on; I had wanted it, too. And if I stopped him I was a quitter, a coward.

I laughed, a forced laugh. "Can it, Frank. The hell with her," I said.

He gave me a wild look, as though he would slam me one. The whole thing could just as well have gone the other way. "It isn't worth it," I said. "The war's over."

He seemed to sway a little. Then he stuck back his revolver. He laughed. The girl gasped, turned and ran. We climbed into the jeep.

*   *   *

After the war I was living in New York, working on the foreign desk of a news service. One evening at a respectable kind of party of United Nations people and such, I met Ruth. She was there with her husband, an economist. She was sitting across the room from me, and for a moment we weren't sure we recognized each other.

I got up and went to a refreshment table, and presently she stood beside me. "Yes, it's me," she said.

She looked nice. That was always the word, a nice girl, a nice woman. It was twenty-five years since I had seen her.

We filled in about our lives. Ruth had two kids in high school.

We didn't speak of Judd. When the party broke up and we were both at the door in a little crowd, there was a moment of hesitation between us. Looking at her, I was thinking, *It could have been.* It all could have been. And it could all come back. And I thought, it could even have been, for Judd.

So I said, as she was about to invite me, "I suppose you're in the phone book. I'll give you a ring sometime."

And I tended my job and married again, and we live in Norwalk.

I'm fifty this year. So is Judd Steiner.

*   *   *

So it happened that one day the news came through that Judd was going to have a parole hearing. And somebody around the place, an old-time newsman like myself, said, "Say, weren't you . . ."

Later, I recalled Jonathan Wilk saying something about there being no thought of a chance for freedom for those two, "not until they are forty-five or fifty, when they have come into another phase of life."

My editors put through this assignment for me to go and

interview Judd in prison, for after all, perhaps better than anyone else still alive, they said, I knew the story. What I wrote about him, they said, might have a good deal to do with whether or not he would be released.